A GREAT RAGE seared me.

Throwing off caution, I reached into the bottom of my mind for the darkest of my Misfit Talents to stun the Herder.

But before I could summon it, an arrow hurtled through the air to bed itself in the center of his sunken chest. He sucked in an agonized breath and clawed at the wooden stave, trying vainly to withdraw it. Then his eyes clouded and he collapsed, blood bubbling obscenely from his lips.

I disengaged my probe with a scream, almost dragged to my own doom by his swift spiral into death. Panting, I stared down at him in astonishment and, for a moment, silence reigned in the village clearing.

"The Herders will kill us all for this," a woman wailed, shattering the stillness.

ALSO BY
ISOBELLE CARMODY

✦

THE OBERNEWTYN CHRONICLES

Obernewtyn
The Farseekers
Ashling
The Keeping Place
Wavesong
The Stone Key
The Sending
The Red Queen

✦

THE GATEWAY TRILOGY

Night Gate
Winter Door

✦

LITTLE FUR

The Legend Begins
A Fox Called Sorrow
A Mystery of Wolves
Riddle of Green

ISOBELLE CARMODY

THE REBELLION

THE OBERNEWTYN CHRONICLES

Includes two complete novels

ASHLING • THE KEEPING PLACE

BLUEFIRE

Ashling copyright © 1995 by Isobelle Carmody
The Keeping Place copyright © 1999 by Isobelle Carmody
Cover art copyright © 2007 by Penguin Group Australia
Map copyright © 2008 by Penguin Group Australia

All rights reserved. Published in the United States by Bluefire, an imprint of Random House Children's Books, a division of Random House, Inc., New York. The works in this collection were originally published separately by Penguin Books Australia Ltd, Camberwell, in 1995 and 1999. Published here by arrangement with Penguin Group Australia, a division of Pearson Australia Group Pty Ltd.

Bluefire and the B colophon are registered trademarks of Random House, Inc.

Visit us on the Web! randomhouse.com/teens/strangelands

Educators and librarians, for a variety of teaching tools, visit us at randomhouse.com/teachers

Library of Congress Cataloging-in-Publication Data is available upon request.
ISBN 978-0-307-93218-1 (tr. pbk.) — ISBN 978-0-307-97583-6 (ebook)

Printed in the United States of America
10 9 8 7 6 5 4 3 2 1
First Bluefire Edition 2011

✦ CONTENTS ✦

✦ Character List ✦

Alad: Beastspeaking guildmaster

Angina: Empath guilden and enhancer; twin brother of Miky

Aras: young Farseeker guilder

Ariel: sadistic enemy of Obernewtyn, previously allied with the Herder Faction

Atthis: Elder of the Agyllians, or Guanette birds; blind futureteller

Avra: leader of the Beastguild; mountain mare; bondmate to Gahltha

Bodera: ailing rebel leader in Sutrium; father of Dardelan

Brocade: rebel leader in Sawlney

Bruna: Sadorian; daughter of Jakoby

Brydda Llewellyn (aka the Black Dog): rebel leader allied with Bodera and Dardelan

Cameo: true-dreaming Misfit, killed by Ariel and his allies

Cassell: rebel leader in Halfmoon Bay

Ceirwan: Farseeker guilden

Daffyd: former Druid armsman; farseeker; unguilded ally of Obernewtyn

Dameon: blind Empath guildmaster

Dardelan: rebel leader; son of Bodera

Dell: Futuretell ward

Domick: former Coercer ward and bondmate of Kella; living in Sutrium

Dragon: powerful Empath guilder with coercive Talent; projects illusions; in a coma

Druid (Henry Druid): renegade Herder Faction priest and enemy of the Council; leader of a secret community that was destroyed in a firestorm

Elspeth Gordie (aka Innle, the Seeker): Farseeker guild-mistress; powerful farseeker, beastspeaker, and coercer, with limited futuretelling and psychokinetic Talent

Enoch: a coachman; ally of Obernewtyn

Faraf: pony ridden by Elspeth in the Sadorian Battlegames

Fian: Teknoguild ward

Freya: beast empath; enhancer with a powerful effect on others' Talents

Gahltha: Beast guilden; bondmate to Avra; a formidable black horse sworn to protect Elspeth

Garth: Teknoguildmaster

Gevan: Coercer guildmaster

Gilaine: daughter of the Druid; beloved of Daffyd

Grufyyd: bondmate to Katlyn; father of Brydda

Gwynedd: rebel Norselander; second to Tardis

Hannay: Coercer guilder

Idris: young rebel formerly of Aborium; trusted companion to Brydda

Iriny: halfbreed gypsy; half sister of Swallow

Jacob Obernewtyn: Beforetimer; wealthy patron of Hannah Seraphim

Jakoby: Sadorian tribal leader; mother of Bruna

Javo: Obernewtyn's head cook

Jes: Elspeth's older brother; Talented Misfit killed by soldier-guards

Jik: former Herder novice and Empath guilder with farseeking Talent; died in a firestorm

Kasanda: deceased spiritual leader of the Sadorians; left signs for the Seeker to help in her quest

Katlyn: herb lorist living at Obernewtyn; bondmate to Grufyyd; mother of Brydda

Kella: Healer guilden with slight empath Talent; former bondmate to Domick

Lina: young, troublemaking beastspeaker

Louis Larkin: unTalented highlander; inhabitant of Obernewtyn; honorary Beastspeaking guilder

Lukas Seraphim: first Master of Obernewtyn, which he built on Beforetime ruins; Rushton's grandfather; deceased

Madellin: ailing rebel leader in Port Oran

Maire: gypsy healer; grandmother of Swallow and Iriny

Malik: rebel leader in Guanette

Marisa Seraphim: second wife of Lukas Seraphim; researcher who knew location of Beforetime weaponmachines; deceased

Maruman (aka Yelloweyes): one-eyed cat prone to fits of futuretelling; Elspeth's oldest friend

Maryon: Futuretell guildmistress

Matthew: Farseeker ward

Merret: Coercer guilder with beastspeaking Talent

Miky: Empath guilden; twin sister of Angina; gifted musician

Miryum: Coercer guilden

Pavo: former Teknoguild ward; died of rotting sickness

Powyrs: rebel sea captain

Radek: rebel leader in Morganna

Reuvan: rebel seaman from Aborium; Brydda's right-hand man

Roland: Healer guildmaster

Rosamunde: one-time lover of Jes; unTalented inhabitant of Obernewtyn

Rushton: Master of Obernewtyn; latent Talent

Salamander: secretive, ruthless leader of the slave trade

Sallah: rebel mare; companion to Brydda

Selmar: Talented Misfit and one-time ally of Rushton; killed by Ariel

Swallow: Twentyfamilies gypsy and heir to D'rektaship

Tardis: rebel leader in Murmroth

Yavok: rebel leader in Aborium

Zarak: Farseeker guilder; previously a Beastspeaking guilder

Zidon: horse ridden by Malik in the Sadorian Battlegames

ASHLING

for Helen Stannard-Williams,
for the most enduring love of all:
friendship

and

for Scott
Do you now fly the spirit trails
you sought in life?

PART I

◆

THE DAYS OF RAIN

✦ 1 ✦

AT FIRST SIGHT, the gypsy woman appeared to be embracing the stake. Her languid pose and mocking smile made it seem impossible that she was about to be burned. Blood dripped steadily out of slits that ran from elbow to wrist, yet she showed neither pain nor fear.

The gray-gowned Herder before her lifted his palms to the sky as he chanted the purification prayer. He was old, bald, and toothless, but his eyes glowed like live coals as he made the warding-off signs.

"Beware, demon," he hissed. "You have found an easy vessel in this foul gypsy's body. Yet I will drive you out."

Shockingly, the woman laughed aloud.

"You know I am not possessed, Herder. Say the truth and be done with it. Tell them that you burn me because I tried to heal a baby when your own worthless treatments had done more ill than good."

The villagers, standing in a cluster about the stake, rustled like leaves in a windblown tree, but no one spoke in the woman's defense, and none met her eyes.

"You used herb lore," the Herder said. "It was such dabbling in forbidden arts that brought Lud's wrath upon the Beforetimers for their conceit. The Herder Faction heals with humility, trusting to Lud's guidance instead of sinful pride. The plagues were Lud's warning that the Landfolk tread the same dangerous and prideful path when they close their ears to the Faction, for Herders are the voices of Lud." He blinked and seemed to rein in his religious fervor. "The woman who allowed you to defile her child will also be burned for heresy."

A woman screamed and fainted, but no one moved to her aid.

"You are a fool," the gypsy's voice rang out. "You will not be allowed to burn her when the Council can have her sweating her life out in one of their stinking farms."

"I am a Herder. Lud and the Faction rule me, not the Council," the priest snapped. There was a sullen mutter from the crowd, but the Herder glared them to silence. "She invoked the black arts. Council lore grants me the right to burn her and any who treat with her."

"What black arts?" the gypsy demanded contemptuously.

The Herder turned back to her. "You told the woman her child would die, and one day later it did. You cursed it and thereby revealed the demon within."

"I treated the babe but saw quickly by its symptoms that it was too late to save it," the woman said. "It could not tolerate the potions you fed it. I told the parents it would die so that they might say their farewells and not waste the child's final hours."

"Do not waste your *own* final moments with lies," the Herder jeered, pushing a gloating smile into the woman's face.

Her hand snaked out suddenly as if to grab him, and the priest wrenched back with a strangled cry. She gave a throaty laugh of triumph. "What are you afraid of, old goat? Do you think my gypsy skin might be catching?"

"Beg, demon! Proclaim your guilt, and the cleansing will

4

be swift," he screamed, almost hysterical with fury.

She laughed again, a humorless bark. "Cease your ranting, old man. Kill me so that I don't have to see your ugly face anymore."

Even from the back of the crowd, I could see the Herder mottle with outrage. Then his lips folded into a vindictive smile. "Evil must not be permitted to think itself triumphant," he said silkily, and then turned to speak a word to his acolyte, eyes glittering with malice.

The boy proffered a selection of long-handled metal tools.

"Th' bastard's goin' to brand her before he burns her," Matthew hissed into my ear, his highland accent thickened with anger.

"Am I blind?" I snapped. The amount of blood pooled about the woman's feet told me she would likely not live long enough to feel the flames of purification, let alone to be rescued. Despite her boldness, her face had grown as white as smoke.

"We mun do somethin'," Matthew whispered urgently. He gestured to our gypsy disguise, as if it made some point of its own.

"Be silent and let me think." I sent the thought directly to his mind.

The sensible thing to do would be to accept that it was too late to save her and withdraw before anyone noticed us. I looked at the gypsy again. Her chin lifted in defiance as the Herder approached with the brands.

I cursed under my breath and slid down from Zade's back, mentally asking the horse to stand quietly until I called. I told Matthew to turn the carriage around and go back to the main road, not trusting his instinct for drama.

"What will you do?" he asked eagerly.

"I'll think of something," I said shortly. "Wait for me out of sight."

As soon as he was gone, I pushed my way through the crowd, at the same time extending a delicate mental probe. Fortunately, the Herder was not mind-sensitive, so he was not aware of my intrusion.

"Where is her wagon?" I demanded aloud.

The Herder swung to face me, his eyes narrowing into slits at the sight of my gypsy attire. "By what right do you question a voice of Lud?" he snarled.

"By right of blood," I said.

It was Council lore that blood kin might speak in defense of their own. In the past, this had not stopped Herders doing what they wished and later making excuses to the Council for excessive zeal. But with the growing rift between Faction and Council, the priests' power had waned, and they were less wont to openly flout Council lore. In any case, it was only a stalling tactic, since I had no proof of kinship to the gypsy.

"Her wagon has been burned, as have all her Luddamned utensils and potions," the Herder said grudgingly, but his memory showed him riffling through the wagon and removing various pieces before the thing was flamed. My probe slid sideways into a memory in which he tortured the gypsy's bondmate to death, and I shuddered inwardly.

"You have proof that you are related?" he demanded.

"All gypsies are brothers and sisters," I answered, not wanting to be caught openly in a lie.

"Do not taint my ears with the practices of your foul breed," he hissed. "I asked for proof of kinship—you have shown me none, therefore be silent."

I saw his mind form a plan to report me to the soldier-guards for sedition, thereby ridding himself of me in case I

6

was related by blood. He turned back to the gypsy and snorted in annoyance to find her hanging limply from her bindings.

Alarmed, I reached out a probe, but her body still pulsed with life. She had only fainted.

The Herder cast down the brand and reached for a torch to fire the woodpile at the foot of the stake. A great rage seared me. Throwing off caution, I reached into the bottom of my mind for the darkest of my Misfit Talents.

But before I could stun him, an arrow hurtled through the air to bed itself in the center of the Herder's chest. He sucked in an agonized breath and clawed at the wooden stave, trying vainly to withdraw it. Then his eyes clouded and he collapsed, blood bubbling obscenely from his lips.

I disengaged my probe with a scream, almost dragged to my own doom by his swift spiral into death. Panting, I stared down at him in astonishment, and for a moment, silence reigned in the village clearing.

"The Herders will kill us all for this," a woman wailed, shattering the stillness, her eyes searching the trees for the archer.

"Not if we kill these gypsies and throw the bodies in the White Valley. We can say we saw nothing of what happened," a man began, but before he could continue, another arrow whistled through the air, piercing his neck.

He crumpled to the ground with a rattling gurgle.

That was enough for the rest. It was one thing to watch someone else die, and quite another to risk your own life.

People scattered in all directions, crying out in terror.

I did not know who had loosed the arrows, and there was no time to find out. Situated on the border of the highlands and lowlands, Guanette was visited regularly by off-duty

7

soldierguards seeking amusement. At any minute, several might be drawn by the screams to investigate.

I rushed forward to the stake. Fortunately, the cuts on the gypsy's arms were shallow, since the aim of bloodpurging was to exact a full confession, not to kill. Still, the cuts were enough to drain her blood slowly. I ripped at the hem of my skirts and bound the torn strips around her arms, automatically setting up a barrier to repel the chaotic wave of unconscious thought that flowed from the gypsy as our flesh met. Then I cut through her bonds with shaking fingers, staggering as she fell heavily into my arms. A thick pot-metal band around her upper arm grazed my cheek.

All at once, my hair was wrenched savagely from behind, and I was pulled over backward, dragging the unconscious gypsy on top of me. For a second, I lay still, winded; then the acolyte launched himself at me, renewing his attack, raining blows on my head, his eyes alight with fanatical rage.

"Demon gypsy! Holocaust scum! Halfbreed!" he screamed in a reedy voice. "They've killed my master! Soldierguards!"

Fighting free of the gypsy's dead weight, I shoved the boy hard, toppling him to the ground. He glared up at me, a handprint of the gypsy's blood on his chest.

"You will die for this," he hissed. "Lud has granted my masters great power to kill their enemies. One day we will destroy all of your kind, even the stinking Twentyfamilies."

I turned from him in disgust and hauled the woman to her feet. This was no easy task, for she was tall and full-bodied, and her arms and upper body were slicked with blood. By the time I had her upright, Zade had responded to my mental summons. From the corner of my eye, I saw the acolyte's eyes bulge in astonishment as the horse knelt to receive the woman's body.

I groaned aloud as two soldierguards burst through the trees, wielding short-swords.

One dropped like a stone, pierced by another deadly arrow from my mysterious helper. The other soldierguard gave the dead man a sick look and flung himself behind a cart, scanning the treetops fearfully.

"Quickly, climb/get on my back," Zade sent, rising to stand upright. "Gahltha will be angered if you are harmed in my care."

Obediently, I vaulted onto him and wound my fingers in his mane, clamping my knees around the unconscious gypsy.

"Go!" I shouted, and he leapt forward.

Using coercion inwardly, I locked my muscles in place to ensure stability. Then I turned my head, sending an outward coercive bolt at the acolyte to erase all that he had seen. The block slammed into the boy's stunned mind, but not swiftly enough to prevent him from throwing the bloodpurge knife.

It pinwheeled toward me with uncanny accuracy: blade, hilt, blade . . .

There was no time to summon the mental energy to deflect it, but instinctively, I threw my head backward.

A split second later, the knife hammered into my temple.

I'm dead, I thought, and the world exploded into painful pieces, sending me into the abyss.

✦ 2 ✦

I WAS STANDING on a high plateau at the beginning of a path that led down into the terrible seared deadness of the Blacklands. It was night and darkly quiet. The distant noise of liquid dripping slowly into liquid was the sound of seconds dissolving and falling away into the sea of time.

Far across the Blacklands, I saw a flash of dull, yellowish light. I blinked, and suddenly I was down in the valley; the bleary gleam I had seen from afar shone from the gaping maw of a tunnel cut into a rocky outcrop.

Entering, I walked until I reached the source of the light: two great carved doors set deep in a granite arch in the tunnel wall. Incredibly, though made of stone, the doors were ablaze. Opposite them, illuminated by the glow, was a small grotto. I felt a surge of terror, for within it, dead and stuffed, was the Agyllian Elder, Atthis.

Then a voice spoke inside my mind—Atthis's voice from the past.

"Long ago . . . I dreamed one would be born among the funaga, a Seeker to cross the black wastes in search of the deathmachines, one who possessed the power to destroy them. . . . You are that Seeker. . . ."

The voice had grown steadily softer until it faded altogether.

"Atthis?" I whispered, but the bird in the grotto was as

10

cold and silent as the rock, her clouded eyes gleaming with reflected flame.

I turned to face the doors again, for there was something about them that tugged at me. Before I could understand why, they swung open. Standing in their fiery embrace was a radiantly beautiful boy with gleaming yellow hair.

"Ariel . . . ," I whispered disbelievingly.

He gave a prim, cruel little smile. "Of course it is I. Did you really think we were done with each other?" His voice was as I remembered: high-pitched and taunting. "You cannot hide from me. But my revenge will wait, because there is a thing you must do for me."

"I won't do anything for you," I hissed.

"Do as you wish and you shall still do my bidding," he said with an angelic smile. "And when you have served my purpose, I will kill you. Until then, let me give you a gift of pain to remember me by."

I backed away from him, but before he could do anything, Maruman leapt from the darkness into the tunnel. The old cat was huge—the size of a wild wolf—and he positioned himself between Ariel and me, tail twitching back and forth. Tattered ears flat to the skull, he gave a yowling cry. The sound lifted the hair on my neck.

Ariel's eyes widened with terror. He made a warding-off shape with his fingers, and all at once, as if by moon-fair conjury, it was not Ariel on the threshold of the burning doors but another blond boy—Jik.

The sight of the empath filled me with sorrow, and I barely noticed that Maruman had vanished.

"Promise," Jik murmured, the word barely audible against the crack of flame.

"Jik—" I began.

11

"Promise!" His voice drove into my mind, his eyes bright with dread.

Before I could summon the wit to answer, he lifted a hand to me. Instantly, fire licked at his sleeve and leapt into his hair.

At last I found my voice.

I screamed, but the noise that came from my mouth was a slow, rumbling growl that shook the world.

I opened my eyes and squinted in the dim light, my heart pounding sluggishly. The stone walls and tapestry hangings told me I was in the Healer hall at Obernewtyn.

I frowned. I had dreamed a long, oddly chaotic dream. And before that? The effort of trying to remember made my head throb.

Thunder rumbled ominously, and I looked out the window. Storm clouds darkened the horizon, and distant flashes of lightning threw the edges of the high mountains into sharp relief. Closer, in the gardens, the treetops whirled in a dervish dance in the rising wind.

As if my waking had been a cue, it began to rain heavily. I started as someone moved to the window, blocking my view.

"So the Days of Rain begin," Rushton murmured.

The sadness in his voice startled me, for the Master of Obernewtyn rarely displayed emotion. I felt immediately uncomfortable at his presence.

"It is just as well this season is brief, for, in truth, it casts a shadow on my spirits." Dameon's voice rose out of the darkness. The blind empath spoke with the slightly stilted formality of the highborn, for so he had been before being charged Misfit. Why were the leaders of Obernewtyn at my bedside?

"They feared for you, ElspethInnle," Maruman's voice whispered into my mind.

The old cat was curled by my head in his usual position. "You were in my dream!" I beastspoke to him. "But you were much bigger."

"Things are not always what they seem on the dream-trails," he sent composedly.

"I wish it were summerdays all th' time." Matthew's voice came from a chair alongside the window. "I wish it were summerdays all th' time."

"Softly," Rushton murmured. "You will waken her."

"I'm awake," I rasped. My mouth felt dry and furry.

Rushton turned on his heel to face the bed, and I could not see his face at all. After a momentary stillness, he crossed to a table, poured water into a mug, and brought it to me. I was careful not to let our hands touch as I took it from him. Lifting my head slightly, I drank a mouthful, then froze at a sudden vision of a knife spinning through the air toward me.

"What happened in Guanette?" he asked.

I reached up to touch my temple. There was a slight lump on my head but no broken skin. Odd. I explained the sequence of events in Guanette after Matthew's departure, assuming he had told the rest. "The Herder's acolyte threw a knife at me just as I mounted Zade," I said at last. "The hilt must have hit me."

I had thought the blade struck me. I even seemed to recall the feel of it cutting into me. Or had that been part of the dream?

"Who would've thought that weedy acolyte had such a throw in him," Matthew marveled with what seemed to me tasteless relish. "It's just lucky ye'd locked yer muscles in place. Zade brought ye to th' wagon absolutely frantic. I near died meself when I saw ye covered in blood. I thought ye were mortal wounded and raced back to Obernewtyn. It were only when I got ye here that I realized it were th' gypsy's blood on ye, fer ye'd nowt a scrape."

Something in his description bothered me, but I could not pinpoint it. I sat up, wincing as a bolt of pain struck my temples. Instinctively, I set a suppressing barrier, a kind of mental net, to capture any hurt. It was a useful measure that enabled me to put off enduring pain. It was dangerous, however, to let too much pain build up.

The Healer guildmaster entered the chamber. "Is the gypsy all right?" I asked him.

"It is difficult to tell," Roland answered gravely. "Because she lost so much blood, she is weak, but the problem is more that her body appears resistant to healing."

I frowned. "How long have I been asleep?"

"Only a night. But you slept like the dead, if you will forgive the expression," the Healer guildmaster added dryly. "Obviously, the blow concussed you, for there is only a slight abrasion at your temple. But you always did heal fast." He let a little pointed silence form, reminding me that he still believed there was more to the healing of my scarred legs the previous year than I had told.

"Fortunately, it was not a serious wound," he went on, "since your mind will not allow healing access. But I suppose you know that well enough."

I hadn't known. Since a healer's talents required access to the unconscious levels of the mind, it must be some sort of instinctive reflex.

Roland shrugged. "Speaking of healing, you should be resting now." He looked around at the others.

14

"I'm goin'," Matthew said, rising. He looked down at me. "I'll tell Alad yer awake. Gahltha is madder 'n hell that he was nowt with ye. He's convinced ye'd nowt have been hurt if he were."

"I hope he hasn't blamed Zade for what happened," I worried as the Farseeker ward departed.

Dameon came to the bedside, and as he bent to touch my hand, I kept a tight hold on my emotional shield, wary of the Empath guildmaster's phenomenal Talent.

"I am glad you are safe, Elspeth," he said in his soft tones.

I nodded, forgetting he could not see, but he did not wait for an answer, gliding from the room with the slow grace that was a sign of caution but that sometimes appeared to be an uncanny instinct guiding him in compensation for his blindness.

Roland glared at Rushton.

"A moment," the Master of Obernewtyn said.

The Healer guildmaster shook his head in exasperation and moved away.

"You seem to go out of your way to try to get yourself killed," Rushton admonished gently, pulling a chair to sit by the bed.

From this angle, a lantern on the far wall cast enough light to show me the craggy plains of his face, but it was not possible to make out his expression. Nevertheless, there was an intimacy in the moment that filled me with discomfort.

Maruman snorted derisively and curled back to sleep, for human emotions irritated his senses.

"I had no choice," I told Rushton awkwardly, wishing Roland had not left us alone.

Rushton's feelings for me had been distorted during a partial mindbond we had undergone during the battle for

Obernewtyn. Once, injured and delirious, he had called me his love. To my relief, he had not spoken of it since. Rushton had Misfit Talent, but it was latent, and I reasoned that his feelings for me were the same. Nearly suffocated already by his solicitude, I had no desire to face the restrictions that would surely arise from waking his overt affections. Besides, there was no room in my life for such things so long as I secretly awaited a summons from Atthis.

"You know, you talked in your sleep," Rushton said.

My heart beat faster at the thought of what I might have said. "I dreamed. It made no sense."

"You called out Ariel's name."

I heard again the dream—Ariel's promise to kill me—and felt chilled.

"He can't hurt us while he is locked up in the Herder cloisters as an acolyte," Rushton said.

If *he is in a cloister,* I thought. That was what we had heard, but I could not believe that Ariel would have tied himself to an organization weakened by its estrangement from the Council. Ariel had always sought power, and a Herder acolyte would be little more than a lowly servitor for his masters.

"You said Jik's name, too," Rushton went on.

I felt abruptly depressed. "I dream of Jik often. I wonder what it means."

"Too much death is all it means," Rushton said sharply. "That is the way of the world, and you have to accept it. What happened to Jik was not your fault, Elspeth. No one could stop a firestorm. You should not judge yourself so harshly."

"I don't," I snapped. "My dreams judge me."

"Well, what are dreams but tricks of the mind?"

"Are they?" I asked coolly. I was less convinced of that.

Sometimes dreams were gateways through which messages might come. Beasts called them *ashlings:* dreams that called.

Thunder rumbled again, and Rushton glanced back over his shoulder at the slanting gush of rain, just as a distant flash of lightning illuminated the clouds.

I took advantage of his inattention to turn the conversation to less personal matters. "Did Matthew make sure he wasn't followed when he brought me back here from Guanette?"

Rushton turned back from the window. "The only person he saw leave was an older gypsy who rode hell for leather toward the lowlands. He is almost certainly the one who shot the arrows. I don't know whether he had any interest in you, but fortunately, he did not try to track the wagon. Just the same, I will ask Gevan to have his coercers keep their eyes open so they can turn him aside if he does appear."

"I'm surprised the other soldierguard didn't come after me."

"I expect the gypsy put an end to him and to the acolyte. The villagers are probably still arguing about who should report the whole thing. It wouldn't surprise me if they had not even removed the corpses."

"The queerest thing was how frightened the villagers were of the Herder. I thought the Faction had lost influence, but you would not have thought so to see them cowering."

"I must send word to the safe house in Sutrium and ask Domick to investigate the relationship between the Herders and the Council. At his last report, they were still at odds, and I will be happier if that is still so," Rushton murmured.

To my relief, he rose, his thoughts absorbed by these larger concerns. "I was thinking of sending someone down to make contact with the safe house anyway. Domick's reports have been scant of late, and he has sent no word yet about how our offer of alliance was received by the rebels. I will speak of it at the next guildmerge if I have no word from them by then."

Briefly, his eyes returned to me. "We will have to decide, too, what to do with your gypsy when she wakes."

"*If* she wakes," Roland said, coming over determinedly. Rushton nodded and allowed himself to be ushered out.

I lay back, weary and curiously depressed. Rushton had been right about one thing—there had been too much death. Grieving had drained the heart and soul out of me, and sometimes I felt as if all that was left of me was a pale, shadowy wraith. And now the gypsy might die, too. Well, I had known that even as I strove to save her.

I looked out to the mountains, which were almost lost in the blackness of the stormy evening, and wished for the thousandth time that Atthis would call and that I might begin to live and act, instead of waiting.

✦ 3 ✦

LANTERN LIGHT GLIMMERED on patches of wet, black stone, dulling the pallid glow that emanated from a thick phosphorescent crust on the rock wall.

Fian reached out and prodded gently at one of the scabbed mounds, and a cloud of glowing insects rose, exposing uneven patches of bare rock as they flitted away into the echoing darkness.

"Do ye know these little beggars eat th' holocaust poisons but are nowt poisonous themselves?" he murmured.

I was startled at that but did not comment. There was no reason to be silent, yet the thought of the mountain of stone pressing down on top of the subterranean cave network seemed to compact the darkness and thicken it, leaving no room for words.

I looked back, searching in vain for a glimpse of daylight, but even the rock shelf we were walking along vanished into the shadows a few steps behind. The teknoguilders had laboriously cut the ledge out of the cave walls, it was designed to run from the White Valley entrance, shaped by the flow of the upper Suggredoon River, around the cavern walls just above the level of the subterranean lake. In spite of the constant flow of water from the Suggredoon, the lake remained at the same level, because a steep channel offered an outlet through the other side of the mountain to the lowlands.

The only other way to move about the caverns was by raft, poling between buildings and along the straight, narrow waterways that, leagues below, had been streets. Clusters of the strange, glowing insects that were the cave's sole inhabitants lit segments of the stone walls and crumbling buildings, reflecting them in pale disconnected shimmers on the dark water, but the majority of the dead city and the caves that contained it were sunk in eternal night.

As ever, I could not help wondering how the city had survived the shifts in the earth that had buried it under a mountain. How had the enormous dwellings, hundreds of floors high, not been crushed in the geological upheavals of the Great White? Was it yet another impossible feat of technology of the Beforetimers that kept the city intact?

Or had fate saved the ancient city for some purpose of its own?

I shivered.

"This way," Garth panted, an undercurrent of excitement in his tone. He moved along the path and around the perimeter of the ancient city with an energy and agility that belied the Teknoguildmaster's bulk.

Behind him came the Teknoguild ward, Fian, with Rushton and myself at the rear. We were moving in single file, because the ledge path was too narrow to walk two abreast. I stared at Rushton's back, wondering what had possessed him to permit an expedition of guildleaders into the least accessible water caves. Ordinarily, he was violently opposed to our taking part in anything dangerous, considering us too valuable to be risked. Garth must have presented a compelling case.

It would have been nice if either of them had thought to tell me what we were going to see, I thought with a flicker of irritation. I glared up at the broad space between Rushton's shoulders. As if he felt my gaze, he glanced back, but I let my eyes fall quickly.

"Damn!" he muttered as he stumbled in the darkness. "How much farther is this?"

"Nowt far," Fian assured us, holding his lantern higher. His eyes, gleaming with amusement, met mine fleetingly over Rushton's bowed head. In spite of my mood, I found myself smiling in response. There was something irrepressible about the highlander. His eyes sparked with intelligence and a wry humor that stopped him from being as painfully earnest as so many of his guild in the pursuit of knowledge. And he was one of the few at Obernewtyn who had not treated me with stultified awe since my return from the high mountains last wintertime, which had been deemed miraculous by some, since I'd been assumed dead.

We came to a place where only a brief, murky stretch of water separated the ledge from a sloping island of rubble formed by the collapse of one of the towering Beforetime monoliths. Dark water lapped sluggishly on the makeshift landfall. Garth leapt across the intervening space with a grunt, and on the other side made his way to the foot of an intact building. The light from the lanterns reached no farther than the row of square windows on the second level; black shadows obscured the floors above. At this end of the caverns, the ground sloped up so that most of the towering building was above the water line.

"This is it," Garth wheezed, flapping his hand in a flourish at the construction. "All five hundred floors. Oh, you needn't worry," he added, seeing my look of horror. "It's quite stable, because a good deal of it is buried in the rock above and behind, including what would have been the front door. The astonishing thing is that we discovered this at all, especially with so much of the city underwater or tainted. Of course, the very fact that so many buildings are still standing is incredible in the first place. We are becoming convinced that this city was one of the last built before the holocaust. The degree of technology here is far superior to that of other ruin sites and may well explain how this city survived when so many others did not. But there are certain strange facets to the architecture. . . ."

"Garth, get on with it," Rushton said brusquely.

Garth gave Rushton an offended look and turned to enter the building through a hole that had been cut in one of the immense walls. I glanced up, and the row of empty windows seemed to look down like eyes.

"It took an age to knock th' hole in the wall," Fian said, coming through after us with the second lantern. "Them Beforetimers built solid."

"And we had to be careful. Our main fear was that we might destroy something irreplaceable," Garth explained.

The building was cast along the lines of all Beforetime constructions, walls and floors bare, squared and uniform with no ornamentation. The Beforetimers were admittedly inspired at construction, but they lacked imagination.

Garth led us along the hall and up three featureless gray flights of stairs. Stepping out of the stairwell onto a small landing, the Teknoguildmaster lifted his lantern to reveal that the wall facing us had words carved into it: "Reichler Clinic Reception."

I stopped dead.

My mind rushed back to the moment when I had found the book called *Powers of the Mind* in a Beforetime library. Standing in the darkness of another ruined city, I had read enough to understand that there had been Talented Misfits before the holocaust. The book had spoken of tests performed at the Beforetimers' Reichler Clinic that proved conclusively that human beings of their era possessed Talents not unlike our own, though these had been largely latent. The clinic had claimed that, in time, more and more people would be born with such powers, though it would take a great catalyst to awaken the conscious mind to latent abilities on a grand scale. We had taken this as proof that we were not mutated freaks, as the Herder Faction and Council claimed, but a natural progression in human evolution. And what greater catalyst could have occurred than the Great White?

However, the teknoguilders had regarded the book with skepticism after their initial euphoria, fearing it might merely be one of the fictions the Beforetimers had produced in such number. But the discovery of the actual Reichler Clinic must resolve all doubt.

"Worth a bit of a walk through the dark, eh?" Garth sounded pleased by our reactions. He poked at my arm. "I thought since you discovered the book and argued so strongly that it was true, you should see this, my dear," he added.

"Strange to think of Beforetimers comin' here to be tested to see if they was Misfits," Fian said dreamily.

I felt a strange chill at the thought that, a thousand years before, a girl like me might have come to the clinic, wondering if she was a freak because she could use her mind to speak to animals or to other people.

Garth led the way through a door, and we found ourselves in a large room with metal benches. Windows along one wall opened to the darkness of the caves, while along another wall was a line of boxlike metal structures that were unmistakably

Beforetime machines. These were smaller than the ones in the Teknoguild cave network in the mountains to the north.

"We know the Reichler Clinic was a paranormal research center," Garth said in a lecturing tone of voice. "*Paranormal* was a Beforetime word for 'Talented' or 'Misfit.' As Fian said, people would come here to be tested. We had no expectation of finding the clinic, and once it was found, it never occurred to me that we would find much in the way of information, because damp has destroyed all but the most impervious materials in the city. And even they will not resist decay forever."

"Garth . . . ," Rushton began.

"Patience," Garth said, as if Rushton were an importunate novice. "As I was about to say, I did not expect to find anything here, but I was wrong. It appears that the people who ran the Reichler Clinic were forward-thinking, and they sealed much of their information in a slippery, waterproof, transparent material they called *plast*." He bent down with a grunt and opened a cupboard, lifting out a sheaf of what first appeared to be pieces of paper. On closer examination, they proved to be made of some sort of pliable material. There were words on the sheets, but I could make nothing of them.

"The plast-covered paper is absolutely impervious to water, although it is not resistant to heat. As you see, a good deal of the matter contained on the sheets is in one of the peculiar linguistic codes the Beforetimers were so fond of using. Hiding their information in this way always seemed to me a paranoid and pointless business, but as it transpired, they had cause to be careful and secretive. My guild is beginning to fathom many of the codes, and these sheets are in one that the Beforetimers called *Jerman*. Fian has specialized in this code, and he was able to translate enough to come up with some very odd intelligence—not about the Reichler Clinic but about another Beforetime organization." He nodded regally at Fian, who took up the narrative.

"I believe th' code was used to store information that th' folk who ran th' Reichler Clinic wanted to keep secret," the highlander said. "I've only just begun decodin' th' plasts, but it's clear from what I've read so far that they wanted to conceal th' fact that some of th' Misfits they tested were not latent."

"Conceal it from whom?" I wondered, and Fian nodded.

"That's what got to me, too. Why would they want to hide what was basically proof of th' things they wrote in that book ye found? Th' answer was in th' plast sheets. Th' Reichler Clinic were bein' investigated by a powerful organization called *Govamen*, which was connected to huge weapon-tradin' houses that made a profit out of sellin' weapon-machines. Govamen was supposed to be stoppin' wars an' finding other ways to resolve conflict between Beforetime factions, but in reality it reaped coin from th' very people who wanted th' wars to go on—namely th' weaponmakers. Of course, th' connection between Govamen an' th' weapon-tradin' houses was illicit. Th' Reichler Clinic folk learned of it by chance when they was tryin' to find out why they were bein' investigated."

"You mean this organization conspired to promote war for profit?" Rushton demanded.

"I would not go that far," Garth said. "However, it does seem to offer an explanation as to why the Beforetimers had so many wars. It is a thing that has always troubled me about them."

"I still don't understand what this had to do with the Reichler Clinic hiding things," I said. "It wasn't forbidden to be a Misfit then, was it?"

"No. But th' Reichler Clinic people learned that th' part of Govamen investigatin' them was devoted to research an' development of paranormal abilities as weapons," Fian said. "This was th' symbol of th' research cell from Govamen."

He stopped to point to a tiny picture atop one of the plasts. It showed three minuscule birds flying in an endless spiral around a word I could not interpret.

"Look closely," Garth invited.

I did, and my eyes widened at the realization that the birds pictured were Agyllians—Guanette birds, as Landfolk called them.

"Fascinating, eh?" he demanded.

"Yes," I agreed faintly, thinking he had no idea *how* fascinating.

The Land resonated with myths about the huge red birds, which were believed to be virtually extinct. But I knew that they dwelt in nests on high citadels of stone in the tallest mountains to the north, because they had once brought me there to save my life in the hope that I would one day destroy the Beforetimers' remaining weaponmachines. I wondered if it could possibly be a coincidence that their image adorned material produced by the mysterious organization called Govamen, with its sinister connections to the weaponmakers.

"Th' section in Govamen that used this as their mark"— Fian tapped the design—"had apparently gone a lot further in its paranormal research than simply testin' th' minds of volunteers. It had actually tried to alter th' brains of animals

26

to produce artificial Talents. Seems they had some spectacular initial results that came to nowt. From what I have translated, th' Reichler Clinic people feared Govamen's interest in th' clinic meant they had th' idea of usin' th' people that they had tested as latent Talents. An' by usin' I mean kidnappin' an' experimentin' on, against their will."

I felt sick. That meant Misfits had been no safer in the Beforetime than we were now. Perhaps it would always be so.

"This is all very interesting," Rushton interrupted. "But you could have told it to us safely and simply back at Obernewtyn. I presume there is some reason you have dragged us into this miserable place?"

Garth sighed. "All right. I could have told you what I am about to show you, too, but it is so momentous I felt you would wish to see it. Perhaps I was wrong."

The stocky teknoguilder moved to the other end of the room, and as the light from the lantern he carried reached the far wall, I could see a mural had been carved there, depicting a mountain scene in perfect relief and intricate detail. It was a magnificent work, and it seemed vaguely familiar.

"It's Obernewtyn," Rushton said in a stunned voice. "Or at least, it is where Obernewtyn is sited. The same spot. The trees are different, but you can tell by the positioning of the mountains. But why on earth would its image be carved here?"

"I think ye'll find th' answer to that when ye read th' inscription on th' wee plaque," Fian said, pointing to a small metal square with raised lettering on the wall beside the mural.

Rushton leaned closer, and I heard him suck in a startled breath of air.

"What is it?" I demanded.

He gave me an unseeing look, and I slipped past him to see for myself. The words read "Presented to the Founder of the Reichler Clinic, Hannah Seraphim, by her devoted admirer, Jacob Obernewtyn."

"Seraphim," I whispered, staring at Rushton. "That's your family name. And Obernewtyn . . . What can it mean?"

He opened his mouth to speak, but abruptly the dazed look of amazement faded into a frown. "Listen," he said, tilting his head.

Then we all heard it. Someone was calling out.

"It's Matthew." I recognized the farseeker's voice. "He can't farseek underground."

I crossed to a window and peered out. From above, the watery caverns looked even more eerie. I spotted the ward by his lantern light bobbing along the ledge path and shouted to him that I would come down. My voice echoed weirdly, reverberating between water and rock.

"I told him to do a routine scan of the villages for new Misfits," I explained to the others. "Maybe he's found someone."

"Be careful," Rushton cautioned.

I nodded impatiently and hurried back downstairs, wondering why after so many Misfit rescues he felt the need to warn me to take care.

Matthew looked so relieved when I joined him on the ledge that I realized he had something more than a wild Misfit Talent to report.

"What is it?" I demanded, panting slightly.

"Ceirwan farsought me," the farseeker said. "He says ye mun all come back at once. Maryon's had a futuretellin' vision about th' gypsy woman we rescued—an' it sounds like trouble."

28

We rushed back to Obernewtyn, only to discover that Maryon had fallen into a second futuretelling trance from which she had yet to emerge. The Futuretell guilden had been unable to tell us anything more about her guildmistress's futuretelling, other than that it concerned the gypsy I had rescued and the future of Obernewtyn.

We could do nothing but go on with other matters until Maryon awoke. The whole affair completely overtook the excitement of finding the Reichler Clinic, and as we made our way to the kitchens for a late nightmeal, Rushton asked me not to speak of the finding until the Teknoguild had prepared a presentation.

"It seems strange to think of your being related to the very people who were interested in Misfit powers in the Beforetime," I murmured. "Do you suppose Jacob Obernewtyn built this place?"

Rushton shook his head. "My grandfather, Lukas Seraphim, built Obernewtyn as it is now, but Louis Larkin once told me that it had been built on the ruins of an older building. It's my guess this Jacob built the original house that stood here."

"I wonder why Hannah Seraphim started the Reichler Clinic in the first place." The discovery meant Rushton could trace the line of his descent back to the Beforetime—he must surely be the only person alive who could do that.

But Rushton only gave me a look. "It is a long time past, and her world is dead. The teknoguilders' discovery of the Reichler Clinic is useful only in that it confirms absolutely that there were Misfits like us in the Beforetime. We have the present to deal with, and that is quite enough without wasting time on historical puzzles. I am far more concerned to find out what a nameless gypsy could possibly have to do with Obernewtyn."

I did not sleep that night for wondering what had been so important it had necessitated our immediate return.

The following morning, Matthew came to my chamber before firstmeal to inform me that Maryon had awakened. Rushton had called the guildleaders to his chamber.

I was careful not to wake Maruman as I dressed, and on leaving had to resist an urge to gather the bedraggled cat into my lap and stroke the rough fur and misshapen head of my first and dearest friend. Every time Maruman disappeared, I worried, knowing he wandered far from Obernewtyn in the throes of his occasional strange fey fits. On his previous disappearance, he had been gone for almost a full cycle of the moon. When he had returned, his already damaged right eye had been so severely infected that Roland had no alternative but to remove it.

If he suffered for the lack of it, he made no complaints.

I hurried then to Rushton's chamber. His face was stony as he opened the door and stepped back to let me enter.

The other guildleaders were seated about the small room, their faces grave. My eyes flew to the Futuretell guildmistress standing in a shadowed corner. Her dark eyes glinted enigmatically across the room at me, and my heart began to beat unevenly.

"What has happened?"

"All in good time," Rushton said tightly, gesturing to an empty seat. I flushed, for he did not normally speak so sharply to me.

He opened his mouth, then shook his head as if thinking better of whatever he would have said. Instead, he turned to the Healer guildmaster. "You'd better begin, Roland," he growled, flinging himself in a chair.

"Elspeth, as you know, the gypsy you rescued is resisting healing," Roland said. "We cannot work against her body to force her to heal, and it is impossible to enter her mind, because she has a natural mental barrier."

"Are you saying she is dying?" I asked.

"Right now, we are keeping her stable. However, if this goes on for much longer, she will die."

"Maryon?" I said, turning to the tall woman in the shadows. "What did you see in your futuretelling? What has the gypsy to do with Obernewtyn?"

Rushton rose and began to pace about the room.

The futureteller made a graceful gesture with her long fingers. "I saw many things. A journey over th' great water; a gray stone fortress wi' a Guanette bird flying o'er it." Maryon spoke these words in a high oratory tone, but now she dropped into a more normal voice, and its very flatness gave her words greater power. "I saw yon gypsy woman mun be returned safe to her people within a sevenday fer th' sake of Obernewtyn."

"Seven days!" I cried. Futuretellers often came up with obscure deeds they said must be performed for this reason or that, or for no reason at all that they would divulge. But this was the most dramatic I could remember in some time.

"Futuretellin' is nowt an exact study," Maryon said. "There is much to see that defies understandin'. But I did see that th' gypsy's people may be found in Sutrium."

"Sutrium!" That was almost worse than not knowing. Sutrium was the largest town in the Land—and the most dangerous, being the base of the main Councilcourt.

Belatedly, I realized no one else had reacted to the mention of it—they already knew this. I wondered why Rushton had not waited for me before telling what was to be told. It was not as if I had delayed coming or had been difficult to find.

"Given that they are gypsies, I dinna know how long her people will bide there," Maryon was saying. She shrugged. "All I can tell ye is that they are there now." She broke off suddenly and there was an awkward silence.

"Are we voting on whom to send with the gypsy?" I asked at last.

"There will be no voting on this matter. *You* will take her," Rushton said tersely.

I was genuinely astonished. Rushton had managed to convince the guildmerge to ban guildleaders from trips to the lowlands, because there was too much risk. Now he commanded me as if I was a novice to make a journey to the most oppressive city in the Land, with an unconscious gypsy fugitive!

"I will impose a sleepseal on her," the Healer guildmaster said in such a way that let me understand this had been discussed, too. "It will slow down her heartbeat and her dying. Kella can remove the seal in Sutrium, just before you hand her over."

"Why am *I* to take her?" I asked slowly.

Rushton's green eyes stared into mine for a moment; then he turned to Maryon. "Tell her."

The futureteller drew herself up to her considerable height. "Fer Obernewtyn's sake, Elspeth, th' gypsy mun be returned to her people. This was the futuretellin' fer which I sent to recall ye from the city under Tor. But yesterday, when I fell into a second an' deeper trance, I learned another thing: *You* mun be th' one to take her back. Nowt fer Obernewtyn's sake but fer yer own."

"Mine?" I echoed.

Maryon went on, her face grave. "On th' journey, you—an' only you—will have th' chance to learn what the word *swallow* means. If ye fail, I have foreseen . . . that ye'll die afore th' next Days of Rain."

✦ 4 ✦

ON THE SIDE of the road were patches of scrub and a few of the immense white-trunked ur trees that characterized lowland terrain. Matthew had not seen many of them before, but the trees had grown in great profusion around my childhood home in Rangorn.

I thought fleetingly of picking berries in their shade with my mother. Then I sighed and shook myself.

Rushton, Dameon, and Ceirwan had seen us off at first light, the gravity of the expedition diverted at the last minute by a hysterical tantrum of the young empath-coercer Dragon, whom we had rescued on a previous expedition. She had suddenly realized she would not be going with us, and it had taken all of Dameon's empathy to prevent her from flinging herself after us as the gypsy wagon pulled away in the gray mountain dawn.

My last sight of Rushton had been of him frowning after me, arms folded across his chest.

Thunder rumbled now, and I looked up at the lowering sky, wondering if we would reach Sutrium before the storm broke. We had not long passed Glenelg Mor, its sodden earth invisible beneath a veil of mist.

I sent a brief command for Matthew to take up the reins, rather than letting them hang down loosely. "It will look odd if someone comes along and sees no one is steering the wagon."

"Gypsy horses are trained to stay on the road while their owners sleep. Besides, who in their right minds would be out so late with a storm brewin'?" Matthew grumbled, but he did as I bade.

A few minutes later, a horse galloped around a bend behind us. I gave Matthew a pointed look, though in truth he was right about seldom meeting anyone on the road. He did not notice, because he was all agog at the sight of the exotic-looking gold-skinned rider—wrapped in a purple cloak and bent low over the horse's neck—who thundered past and out of sight around a bend in the road ahead.

"That were one of them Sador tribesfolk," Matthew said excitedly. "I'm goin' to visit Sador someday." His eyes glowed at the thought.

The road to the remote region had only just been opened up in the last year, as the Blacklands taint along the eastern shore of the Land faded, allowing a slender, and some said dangerous, passage along the coast.

The Council had always maintained the Land was all that remained unpoisoned of the world, while the Herders preached it was all Lud had seen fit to spare of the corrupt Beforetime. Seafarers had long known this to be a lie, but they had a rigid code of silence imposed by the Council. Even so, word had leaked out, initially as gossip and rumor. But with Sador suddenly accessible and known to all, it seemed more likely than ever that there was a world beyond the Blacklands.

Looking before us to where the Sadorian rider had disappeared, I remembered Gahltha, who was scouting ahead for danger. I asked Matthew how long the horse had been absent.

"Nowt long. He won't go too far with you here."

I ignored the questions implicit in his tone. There was no way of explaining Gahltha's transformation from a vicious human-hating fury into my devoted guardian without relating the whole fantastic story of my deliverance from death by the Agyllians. It was Atthis who had called the black horse to carry me down from the high mountains, and whatever the ancient bird had said to keep him waiting through the long months of my convalescence had altered Gahltha completely. Gahltha now believed utterly that I was to rescue beasts from their long slavery to humans. No surprise that he and Maruman both had insisted on accompanying me to the lowlands.

I sighed, sick of living my life at the directive of the vague whims of fate and futuretellers.

At the conclusion of our impromptu meeting the day before, Rushton had suggested I say nothing of Maryon's predictions concerning myself to the general population of Obernewtyn. I had been only too glad to agree. Success would simply add to the myth surrounding me, and if I failed, it would not matter what had been predicted. Matthew had been told that the purpose of the journey was to return the gypsy to her people, which was true enough, and that while in Sutrium we would inspect the safe house and inquire as to whether Brydda Llewellyn's rebels would accept us as allies. Rushton still had no answer since his visit to Sutrium, and he feared missing an opportunity to ally ourselves with those who could very well be the next rulers of the Land.

If only they would accept us.

I glanced back over my shoulder to where the gypsy lay on one of the wooden pallet beds, Maruman curled fast asleep at her feet. I judged her to be about forty years of age. Her features were too strong for beauty, but she was handsome and her hair was as black as my own. One sleeve had ridden up to reveal the potmetal bracelet she wore above her elbow.

Her stubborn resistance to healing had begun to take its toll. Despite Roland's sleepseal, there was an unhealthy pallor to her skin.

"She's nowt dead yet," Matthew said defiantly.

I frowned at him. "Let's hope she lives until we get to Sutrium and that we have no trouble getting her through the gates."

"We have papers," Matthew said.

"Yes. False ones. But, Ludwilling, the soldierguards will not have a description of her yet—or of me."

The farseeker paled. As usual, he had given no thought to the realities of the situation in his dreams of heroic deeds.

"I wonder where th' gypsy who shot them arrows in Guanette rode to in such a rush. I dinna see him very well through the trees, but he were tall and well-muscled. He had gray hair in a gypsy plait, an' he were wearin' a blue shirt," Matthew said dreamily. Beyond his sloppy shielding, I caught a glimpse of a vision in which a tall gypsy hero thanked us regally for the return of his companion.

"There's no possibility of us chasing after this gypsy and just handing the woman over as if it were a public play," I said sharply.

Matthew flushed and his shield slammed into place. "Ye said ye'd give her to her people, an he mun be one of them."

"And so I will, but discreetly." *If she lives,* I thought. *And if I can find them.*

Matthew let out a formless exclamation of surprise, dragging me back from my worries. We had reached the top of a long rise, and Sutrium lay before us in the blighted light of the gathering storm.

It had grown much bigger than I remembered, spreading farther west until it joined up with settlements along the side of the Suggredoon River and stretching east and north into straggling outlying districts and farmlands. Beyond the city lay the great sea.

In some ways, Sutrium was not unlike the coastal town of Aborium. We had journeyed there on the very expedition that had led to the rescue of the empath-coercer Dragon. Whether it was my imagination or the knowledge that Sutrium was the home of the main Councilcourt, it seemed a dark and menacing place.

Unlike Aborium, there were no watchtowers. It was too big for such things to be of any use. But in any case, there was no need, since there were three huge soldierguard camps on the city outskirts. One lay slightly inland on the banks of the Suggredoon; another closer to the sea, near the ferry port; and the third to the east, among the farmlands.

How would the very first Councilmen, who had sworn not to follow in the steps of the Beforetimers, view the sprawling city? I wondered. Surely all their fears that humans might tread the same doomed path of progress would be realized at the sight of it. In my mind's eye, I saw for a moment the shadowy, half-drowned city beneath Tor.

Thunder sounded again, and as if it were some heavenly signal, Gahltha emerged like a shadow from a thick copse of Ara trees a little way down the slope. He waited, a dark shape against the pale speckled trunks and tremulous clouds of foliage, until Jaygar brought us close.

"The way to the funaga-li barud is not watched by danger," the black equine sent in his stringent mental voice.

"Funaga" was the closest rendering of the beast thought symbol for human. The form used by Gahltha was subtly derogatory, for though the old acid bitterness had vanished from his nature, there were still traces of it when he considered humans outside of Obernewtyn.

"It would be wise for ElspethInnle to ride this equine," Gahltha sent. "Only the funaga walk without shackles/ burdens in this place."

"Wait a moment," I sent, and climbed into the back of the cart to change my skirt for trousers. Coming out again, I stood up on the wagon's bench seat, and the black horse came alongside, allowing me to transfer smoothly to his bare back. Sensing his approval at the ease of my mounting, I felt smug. Gahltha had taught me to ride as gypsies did. And there had been many times during his painful lessons that I had felt certain they were simply a sadistic way to murder me. Yet I had survived, and there were few now at Obernewtyn who could match my skill. In fairness, that was because few rode as frequently. None among us rode a horse except at its invitation, since all thinking beasts were regarded as equal to human-folk. I would as soon ask Matthew to carry me as ask one of the equines. Horses took part in expeditions at their own choosing, masquerading as beasts of burden. They never carried humans otherwise, except at great need.

Gahltha was the exception.

After bringing me from the high mountains, he had insisted on going back into them often; whether out of nostalgia or to remind himself of his promises, I never knew. Each time he went, he asked that I ride on his back. At first I had refused, disliking the way it increased the mystique my activities had already woven about me, but his determination had worn me down. And like him, I had come to love the headlong gallops over the whispering grasses, flattened to his back and feeling as if the two of us were, in those moments, a single wild spirit.

This had the unexpected result of causing the proud Obernewtyn equines to question whether carrying humans must always be a sign of slavery. More than one of the beasts had suggested that a time might come when it would be useful to have Misfits who rode well. The matter was still under discussion among their kind.

"We must be nearin' th' outer gate," Matthew sent as we reached the first shingled dwellings at the outer edge of the sprawling city. He got into the back to cover the woman's face, and I concentrated on summoning the mental focus I would need to coerce the soldierguards at the city gates if there was any difficulty.

I reached out to take Gahltha's reins in my fingers as Matthew returned to his seat. My hands and body, like his, were stained a light gypsy tan. Brydda Llewellyn's mother, Katlyn, who had come to live at Obernewtyn, was a skilled herb lorist, and to aid our most common disguise, she had perfected a dye that simulated gypsy skin tone and that would not wash off easily. Despite prevailing prejudices, it was far safer to move about the Land as homeless gypsies than to pretend to be normal Landfolk, for they rarely traveled.

I concentrated on the disguise, enhancing it slightly with coercion so that people would see a boy in the gypsy clothes—just in case news of the incident at Guanette had spread to Sutrium.

With a mental apology to Gahltha, I pulled the reins tight. They did not drag at his mouth, being a modified bridle that only looked as if it would control and direct a horse. The old bit and bridle were anathema to human and beast alike at Obernewtyn, but even so, I wondered if it would not have been wiser to use it on expeditions that would take us into the heart of Council territory, where spies would be watching for any deviations.

Well, it was too late now.

To my relief, there was a crowd at the gate; traders and farmers and the odd green-clad jack returning after a day's work trading outside the city. The number of people lined up to show papers would mean a longish wait but less individual attention.

Approaching the end of the line, we fell in quietly behind the rest, ignoring cheeky signals from a cluster of children. Such a reception was so common for gypsies that we would have stood out if we had reacted to it.

For the most part, the people about us were grim-faced and sour-looking, and many bore the ugly marks of plague survivors. There was no chatter or end-of-day banter, only a brooding silence. People did not look into one another's eyes, and the few words spoken were punctuated with wary, sliding glances.

It was a timely reminder that Sutrium was a dangerous city, filled with a treachery that must not be underestimated. The main thing was to get past the gate without any sort of fuss that would draw attention to us.

I looked up at the dark clouds, willing the storm to break. The soldierguards would scarcely glance at us if it was pouring rain on their heads.

Jaygar's mental voice speared into my mind without warning. "I will kill/trample funaga-li!"

As if suddenly mad, the horse began to push his way through people in front of us, dragging in his wake the wagon containing the unconscious gypsy, Maruman, and a helpless Matthew.

✦ 5 ✦

I SENT OUT a coercive mental bolt, forcing Jaygar to a halt. Then I looked around frantically, trying to see what had provoked the normally placid equine to such a dangerous outburst.

I did not need to look far.

My own fury swelled at the sight of a small mare ahead of us trembling under the weight of a load of wood. But what made my blood boil and what had surely incensed Jaygar, was the sight of a fat youth sitting on top of the load, unconcernedly eating a bun.

Even as I watched, the mare staggered sideways under the weight of her burden, and the lout cursed her unsteadiness, whacking her with casual cruelty over the head.

"Release me!" Jaygar raged. "You have no right."

I did not loosen my mental hold. "I have the right to restrain any beast/funaga who endangers the rest," I sent, quoting from the expedition charter Rushton had made us draw up over long guildmerge sessions. Jaygar knew as well as I did that Avra had approved it on behalf of the Beastguild. "Now will you obey/calm?"

The horse snorted angrily. "You would risk us/all for an unknown funaga but not for this beast?"

"Risk comes from acting in thoughtless haste," I gritted. "I will help the beast my own way. Now, will you obey, or must I waste more time in arguing with you?"

Chastened, Jaygar agreed, and I asked Gahltha to come up beside the mare. To my astonishment, he refused.

"I will not let you endanger yourself," he sent. "This equine is one alone, and your life's purpose will save/help many more than one life."

"She is your kind," I sent. "Surely you don't set my life above hers?"

"Protect Innle before/above all," Gahltha sent.

"Is that what Atthis told you?" I fumed. "Well, I am not Atthis's servant/slave. I won't spend my whole life waiting to perform a single deed, Gahltha. Not for you, nor for Atthis. I will do what I can now, because tomorrow might never come. Now take me up beside the mare, or I will get down and walk!"

After a long moment, Gahltha moved forward, but there was an offended stiffness in his bearing. I wished I had the empathy to show him what I felt. So often words said only half of what you wanted to say, even words sent directly from mind to mind. But empathy was the one power I lacked utterly.

As we drew level with the mare, I made myself calm down. I did not want to show an interest that would be remembered later. From the corner of my eye, I noted the exhausted sag of her head and the scars on her knees and fetlocks from previous falls. Taking a deep breath to quiet my outrage, I reached out a probe to examine the bindings on her load. When I detected a weakness, I began to work at it with my mind, backward and forward.

This was exhausting, because the probe had to be densely focused to produce even the slightest physical force, but anger gave me additional determination, and in a short time, the tie snapped with an audible twang.

The lout on top of the load gave a bellow as he and the wood crashed to the ground.

A second after, a streak of lightning split the sky. People looked up fearfully, ever mindful that this might be a firestorm. But it began to rain, and it was not the burning rain of a firestorm.

The lout got to his feet, red-faced with embarrassment, and flayed the mare viciously. She was so exhausted that she barely flinched under the onslaught.

"Get out of my way," I said insolently, pushing Gahltha forward to distract him. I blinked to clear the rain from my lashes.

"Halfbreed trash!" he yelled. "Don't tell me what to do."

"Then do something of your own will," I rejoined promptly. "Show us you can move your fat bum as fast as you flap your lips."

He stepped forward, lifting his stick to strike me, but Gahltha snorted and reared, pawing the air. The youth cried out in fright and cowered back.

Thunder cracked again and lightning slashed above, shedding an eerie light on the motley crowd as the rain gathered force. The storm created a mental static that interfered with my Talent. I concentrated hard and prayed it would not get any worse.

"What's going on back here?" demanded the gate soldier-guard, striding back along the line.

"The stupid horse lost its load," the lout blustered. "Then that gypsy tried to set his horse on me. Savage brute of a thing."

"T'was the lightning affrighted him," I said, lowering my voice.

"He overloaded the mare and the ropes broke," a woman said, spurred by a coercive prompt. I did not want the soldierguard to focus his attention too specifically on me.

"Look at the poor thing," another woman shouted after a mental prod. Then she blinked and looked startled with herself.

"It's a wonder it didn't keel over in the very path," someone else growled of his own accord.

"And what if it did?" the lout demanded truculently. "It's my property. I'll kill it right now if I feel like it." I felt Jaygar's anger like the sun on my back.

"Do that and you'll be fined," the soldierguard snapped.

"Fined?" he squawked. "I've a right to do what I want to my own horse."

"I don't give a damn what you do to the beast, just so long as its corpse don't clutter up the way. Now get this mess out of the road. Load it to one side and be quick about it."

Muttering and cursing, the lout dragged on the mare's bridle to shift her onto the grass verge and began to move the wood. She stared out unseeingly, her eyes like dusty pebbles.

"Greetings, littlesistermind," I sent.

She blinked and turned her dull gaze to me.

"This funaga is cruel to you," I continued.

"All your kind are so. Your blood is curdled with cruelty." Her mental voice was infused with a dreamy kind of hopelessness. She didn't seem surprised to have a human talking to her. Perhaps she thought she was hallucinating.

"Not all funaga are this way," I sent, but the mare was silent with disbelief or lethargy. I sighed, thinking this was not the moment to convert her. "If you hate this funaga, why not run free?"

"Funaga are everywhere. The wind spawns them. If not

this one, another would own me," she sent without bitterness. "When I take the longsleep, I will run free."

Beastspeaking was often difficult to understand, because sometimes animals used words differently than we did. Equines called *sleep* the "shortsleep" and *death* the "longsleep," believing the two states to be related.

I shook the wetness from my face and licked my lips. The rain tasted sweet and cold.

"If there were a barud for freerunning in thiswaking, would you dare to run? Could you escape?"

"There is no such place," the mare sent flatly.

"Littlesistermind, I tell you such a place does exist, and if you go there, you may run free and nevermore wear the cold-metal in your lips."

"A barud with no funaga? That is as likely as skyfire without its roar." The flash of cynicism told me not all of the spirit had been beaten out of her.

"There are funaga," I admitted. "But these have the power to speak with beastminds, as I do. And none of them thinks of owning or breaking or hurting. They think of equines as brother/sisterminds."

She showed her disbelief again. I asked Gahltha and Jaygar to speak to her mind and convince her. Only when the black horse came close and showed her the false bit did she believe, and then she listened carefully as he described a route that would bring her to Obernewtyn.

The lout glared at me. "Get that black demon away from my horse, halfbreed."

I shrugged and drew Gahltha away at once, resigned to the knowledge that he would remember me when the mare disappeared. I sent to her, warning her to be careful she was not followed when she escaped from her human masters.

"Run safe, littlesistermind, and perhaps we will meet again in thiswaking."

"I am called Faraf," the mare sent. "And I swear this will be so: nevermore shall I curse the funaga as one, for I know now that some burn with the heartfire."

My eyes pricked with sudden startled tears, for the mare had paid me a great compliment. Beastlegend told of a heart that burns eternally with the souls of all beasts who die or are yet to be born. This shared heart symbolizes the harmony between beasts, no matter what their physical form or how they prey on one another.

Beasts excluded humans from this cycle of harmony, believing they have no true soul. This offered an explanation for humankind's terror of death and their desire to dominate.

In implying that I shared the heartfire of beasts, the little mare was naming me her equal and the bearer of a true soul.

I felt my spirits lift, for the rescue of the gypsy and the exchange with the mare reminded me that no matter what Atthis or Maryon or Gahltha thought, I was the mistress of my own life.

We had drawn almost level with the gate now. In front of us, the soldierguards were checking the soggy papers of a jack.

"Ye'll be lucky to find buyers for that lot," one of the soldierguards told the green-clad trader. "No one's got much coin these days, an' them that has coin wants exotics from Sador or lavish trinkets from the Twentyfamilies. Even with the Herders sayin' it's all Lud-curst." I was surprised at the accent, for most soldierguards came from lowlander stock. I also wondered what sort of trader a Twentyfamilies was. I did not know what the word meant, but I was sure I had heard it before, and recently.

"We're away next," Matthew sent.

I saw that he was nervous. "Remember, don't be apologetic or humble. It isn't the gypsy way, and it will seem odd."

The Farseeker ward had been on plenty of expeditions, but this was his first visit to the lowlands. It was one thing to fool a highland villager and another entirely to lie barefaced to hardened soldierguards.

"There may nowt be humble gypsies, but there's plenty of silent, surly ones," he said. "I'll be one of them, an' you can do th' talkin', same as ye did when we was caught by Henry Druid that time."

Henry Druid was a rebel Herder who had disappeared after being driven from the Faction for refusing to destroy his collection of Beforetime books. On a previous expedition, we had stumbled onto his secret camp, but it had since been destroyed by a firestorm, the Druid and his people killed or scattered.

"My talking didn't stop them taking us prisoners," I pointed out. Gahltha twitched, as if reproaching my inattention. The soldierguards had finished with the jack and were waving him through the gates. I noticed a man staring at Gahltha and realized the rain had washed away the dirt I had rubbed into his coat. Even at his most unkempt, the black horse had always been magnificent to look at. More than once, there had been trouble on expeditions because someone had coveted him. I had gotten into the habit of daubing his coat with filth as a safeguard.

I sent a swift message to him as the soldierguard gestured for us to come forward. Gahltha's smooth gait became an uneven, lopsided lurch, his head drooped low, and I was amused to hear him wheezing loudly as if his wind were gone.

My amusement faded as the soldierguard reached up for my papers, for the other with the highland accent had turned to the wagon and bade Matthew pull the curtains open. We had decided to pretend there were only two of us, just in case the Guanette incident had been reported and they were looking for an injured gypsy. If either moved to examine the rig, I would have to coerce them.

My heart leapt into my throat as the highland soldierguard climbed onto the running board and peered inside the cabin.

"Nothing to trade?" the other soldierguard asked me.

"Some beads and braiding," I said, trying to pay attention.

The soldierguard sneered. "No market for low-quality halfbreed work."

I shrugged, riveted to the wagon. One step farther and the other soldierguard could not help but see the gypsy. But there was a loud hiss and the man fell back in fright.

"What's that? Some sort of fangcat?" he demanded of Matthew.

"It . . . it's injured," the farseeker stammered.

"Looks like it needs knockin' on th' head," the highlander growled, drawing out a short-sword.

"Perhaps, but it is said Lud curses them who hurt cats," Matthew said in a desperately sinister voice.

He had gauged it well. The soldierguard was a highlander and fortunately was as superstitious as the best of them. He backed away hastily, letting his sword drop.

At that moment, the light rain became a drenching torrent, and with a curse, the soldierguard examining my papers thrust them unceremoniously into my hand and reminded me that gypsies had to report to the Councilcourt for an extension of permit if we stayed more than a sevenday.

"We won't be here more," I said, hoping that was true.

"You did well," I told Matthew when we had been passed through the gate. "Maruman says to thank you for preventing the man from knocking him on the head."

"Thank Lud for Maruman," he said fervently. "Another step an' that soldierguard would've seen th' gypsy."

In a few minutes, we had reached the outer rim of the labyrinth of narrow streets that was the city center of Sutrium. Dwellings here were built right up against one another, often with no more than a single dividing wall to separate them, and had steeply thatched roofs that hung in shaggy fringes over doors and windows. Most were several floors high, which meant the streets weaving through them were shadowy and cold, seldom touched by the sun's rays. But there were gaps, too, where nothing stood. I saw several before their significance struck me: They marked where dwellings had been burned. In some places a whole row of houses had been burned, while in others a single house had been razed and those on either side left untouched.

"'Tis ice-cold out." Matthew shivered. "Feels like wintertime rather than the Days of Rain."

"Better to be cold here," I said, turning my attention back to the road. "Stops us getting comfortable and careless."

"I dinna think there's much danger of that," Matthew said. "Besides, I was nowt thinkin' of myself." He jerked his head toward the wagon's cabin.

"Look there," I interrupted, pointing to a striped awning. "Just as Domick described it."

"Were we supposed to turn left or right now?"

"West toward the Suggredoon. That would make it right." *I hope,* I thought.

Responding to my mental directive, Jaygar veered away from the main road down the next right-turning side street. It

50

proved to be a narrow lane lined with workshops and frowsy, dilapidated apartments. Even in the rain it stank of urine and refuse.

Without warning, a window opened and a bucket of swill was hurled across the stones.

A little farther on, a man opened a door and stared out at us. He bore the scarring of a plague survivor.

The plague had erupted the previous year in Aborium or Morganna, spreading rapidly to Sutrium and all the other populous coastal cities and killing one in three who contracted it.

In the aftermath of the disease, there had been almost no one to work the farms, and this had resulted in terrible shortages that had seen hundreds starve. The shortages continued, as many of the farms still lay abandoned and unproductive.

Uneasily, I realized that meant there was little to sell in cities other than information. The sooner we located the safe house and got off the street the better.

We came around the corner and groaned at the sight of the sea, a seething gray mass in the rain. "We should have turned left back there," I said. I was surprised when my senses detected powerful static from the direction of the water. There had to be something nearby tainted with holocaust poisons, I thought.

Gahltha turned around so that I could direct Jaygar in maneuvering the cumbersome wagon from behind. I opened my mouth to speak to Matthew and almost bit my tongue off when Gahltha suddenly leapt forward and galloped at a breakneck pace back along the lane. I managed to keep my seat thanks to our mountain rides, but I almost flew straight over his head onto the cobbles when he came to an abrupt halt and swung sideways, facing into a short dead-end street.

"What the hell are you doing?" I demanded. Then I faltered, feeling the panicky shift in my mind that could mean only one thing.

Someone was tampering with my thoughts!

The alien probe sensed my awareness and fled from my mind. As an immediate consequence, I could see what I had been prevented from seeing sooner.

Crouched in the middle of the alley was Dragon, dripping wet and staring up at me with defiance and fear.

✦ 6 ✦

"WHAT DO YE mean ye followed us?" Matthew shouted.

Dragon backed away from his fury into the corner of the wagon, bumping the bedshelves. The blankets fell from the gypsy's face; I was startled anew by her pallor.

"Have ye any idea how worried they'll be at Obernewtyn when they find ye missin'?" Matthew raged aloud, for Dragon's formidable and instinctive mindshield made farseeking her nearly impossible.

"Keep your voice down," I snapped.

We had climbed inside the wagon. It got us out of the rain, but it was hardly the safest place for a screaming argument.

"Did ye hear—" Matthew began wildly.

"I would have to be deaf not to," I interrupted in a cold, quiet voice. "Whatever Dragon did or didn't do is not going to matter a damn if someone calls the soldierguards on us for causing a disturbance."

The empath-coercer gave me a mutinous look. "Dragon come, too," she said.

Even dirty and wet, her glorious mop of red curls dangling in rattails, she was still incredibly lovely in the wagon's lantern light. I prayed we were not the only ones she coerced out of seeing her. Once seen, Dragon would not be easily forgotten.

What puzzled me was how she had followed us. We had

made good time to make it to Sutrium in a day, so she could not have kept up on foot. She must have been in the wagon the entire time.

"Won't go back," she added mulishly, as if she feared she had not been clear enough.

Since there was no question of simply sending her back, I might have reassured her, but she must not be allowed to think she had won.

"This is a bad thing you have done, Dragon," I said sternly. "I am very angry. Dameon will be terribly worried about you."

Dragon adored the gentle Empath guildmaster who had taken her under his wing. With a stricken look, she burst into noisy tears and choked out that she had left a message with Louis Larkin to say she had gone to visit some of her animal friends. That mollified me slightly, for no one would worry overmuch to begin with. At least she had not gone away completely heedless of the trouble it would cause. Everyone would assume she was sulking over our departure for a little while, and since she had fended for herself alone for most of her life, no one would think of finding her and forcing her back to Obernewtyn too soon. But we would have to send a message back as soon as possible.

Dragon was staring at me with a woebegone expression. I put my arms around her thin shoulders with a sigh, knowing there was no use in trying to treat her as if she were any other disobedient novice. Despite her beauty and incredible illusion-making Talent, only the thinnest veneer of ordinary human behavior lay over the wild, half-starved waif I had coaxed from the Beforetime ruins outside Aborium.

And the truth was, had I not been so preoccupied with my own thoughts, I would have felt her clumsy coercive manipulations and sent her back long before we had reached Sutrium.

"Surely yer nowt goin' to let her gan away wi' this?" Matthew demanded.

"No, I'm going to turn her over to the soldierguards to teach her a lesson," I said sarcastically, wondering at the extent of his reaction. Did he think I would blame him for her presence simply because she'd grown attached to him? "What's done is done. Now let's move."

Dragon promptly turned her head and stuck her tongue out at him.

"Enough," I said firmly. "Lud knows how many tales will be told tomorrow about a gypsy wagon lurking in a side street. I think we have done enough to get ourselves noticed. Now let's find the safe house. Get the wagon turned around, Matthew."

The farseeker obeyed begrudgingly. Dragon's eyes were huge with apprehension when I turned to face her. "Not go back," she begged.

"I won't send you back," I promised. "We're going to the safe house now to see Kella. You remember Kella?" Dragon's eyes warmed and she nodded eagerly. "Good. Now you must be very quiet or else the soldierguards will stop us. Can you do that?"

This time she nodded solemnly. "Quieter than Maruman stalking a squeaker," she vowed.

Hearing his name, the cat stretched luxuriously and peered down at us, his good eye glowing in the darkness.

"Maruman, will you keep her/mornir quiet?" I sent. *Mornir* was the name the animals at Obernewtyn had given Dragon. It meant "brightmane."

The old cat assented and began to wash himself industriously. I looked at the gypsy. Her breathing was labored, her eyes sunk into their sockets. If she did not get help soon, she would die in spite of Roland's sleepseal.

Well, I could do no more than I was doing.

Cautioning Dragon again to stay quiet, I climbed out of the wagon, pulling the curtain to the cabin shut behind me. The lane ahead was empty, and it was still raining hard, but it was too much to hope we had not been noticed. I remounted Gahltha, and we retraced our steps as swiftly as we could, but it was full dark before we reached the small trading market that Domick had described as the nearest landmark to the safe house. In the daylight on a good day, it would doubtless be a pleasant spot to linger, but tonight it was a wet and windy pool of darkness and completely deserted.

We crossed the square to a street leading off, abutted by a trader office on one side and a huge wagon-repair shed on the other. A sign glistening wetly in the wagon light told us the entrance to the repair yard was from the side street.

The gates were standing ajar, creaking slightly in the wind, when we came to them. Beyond, the place was sunk in darkness. The shapes of half-dismantled wagons were standing about in the open, and the shed was nothing more than a square of shadow.

"Are ye sure this is it?" Matthew sent. "It dinna look as if anyone is here."

"They wouldn't advertise their presence," I replied, though in fact it did look deserted. Jaygar pulled the wagon into the yard.

"There's a light in there," Matthew sent. I looked where he was pointing, and sure enough there was a dim glow from one of the shed's windows, hidden from the street.

"I'll go," I sent, and slid off Gahltha.

Inside, the shed smelled of damp metal and sawdust, but at least it was dry. The light was coming from a small room set in a far corner of the enormous structure. Through a doorway, I could see a youth sitting at a table, the light from a lantern glancing off his cheeks.

He jumped to his feet when he spotted me. "What do you want, halfbreed?"

"I . . . I have a wheel rim that needs some attention," I stalled, startled by his aggressive tone.

"You'll have to go somewhere else. We don't fix halfbreed wagons," he said.

Before I could think how to respond, a door opened beside him and Kella stepped out. Seeing me, the healer's mouth fell open.

"Elspeth! By all the heavens! How did you get here?" Without waiting for an answer, she rushed across and flung her arms around me.

I stiffened instinctively. Misunderstanding, the healer let her arms fall to her sides and stepped away awkwardly. "I'm sorry," she said.

"No, I'm sorry," I said. "I'd forgotten how it feels to be treated like an ordinary human being."

She looked bewildered. "What do you mean?"

I laughed dismissively. "I don't mean anything, except that I am glad to see you." I looked pointedly at the strange youth.

"This is Balder," Kella said lightly. "He is one of Brydda's people, lent to us as a watchman. Balder, this is a friend of mine and of Brydda's."

The boy nodded politely, but his eyes were cold.

I drew Kella out into the great shed on the pretext of seeing the wagon. "Why is he here?"

"I told you, he is guarding the safe house. It's all right,"

Kella said. "He doesn't know anything except that we are friends of Brydda's and that I am a healer. Brydda always sends someone when Domick goes out of the city on errands for the Councilcourt."

There were a dozen questions I wanted to ask her, but now was not the time. "We'll talk about this later. Matthew and Dragon are in the wagon—"

"Dragon!"

"There is also a woman who needs healing," I said.

Kella stiffened. "Take me to her," she commanded, imperious in her healer role.

Dragon was sitting wide-eyed in the corner of the wagon with Maruman, who had solved the problem of keeping her put by sitting on her lap. With barely a glance at them, Kella climbed into the cabin and pulled the blankets back from the pallet bed. Her eyes widened at the sight of the unconscious gypsy, but she composed herself swiftly and laid her fingers lightly on the woman's neck. A moment later, she shook her head.

"It's impossible to treat her here. Let me send Balder away, and then you can bring her in."

She left, and a few minutes later, the rebel came out of the shed wrapped up in a dark oiled coat. When I was sure he had gone, I jumped down into the rainy dark and between us, Matthew and I carried the gypsy inside.

"On th' floor?" the farseeker asked as we reached the smaller room within the shed.

"Through here," Kella directed, opening the door she had come through earlier. Beyond was a rickety set of steps going up into the darkness. Seeing the expression on my face, she gave a faint smile. "Things are rarely what they seem. You, of all people, should know that."

At the top of the steps was a dark landing and a door with blistered whitewash. Kella opened it with a flourish, and bright light and warmth flowed out.

"The safe house," she said proudly. "You can't tell from below, but the whole top of the shed is another floor. No light shows outside, because all the windows face the sky or else are blacked out with heavy cloth."

She stepped into a short hall and opened a door. "This is our healing chamber. Bring her in."

The room was long and narrow, with a row of straw mattresses made up as beds. The healer drew back the blankets on the nearest of these, and we lay the gypsy on it.

"I'll unharness Jaygar and take the bridle off Gahltha," Matthew said, turning to the door.

"Bring Maruman and Dragon up, too," I requested, crossing to the door and closing it behind him. When I returned, Kella was kneeling by the mattress, holding the gypsy's hand.

"These are not fresh wounds," she said, a question in her tone.

In as few words as I could manage, I explained my rescue of the gypsy, Roland's diagnosis, and the sleepseal he had imposed.

"I don't understand why you brought her here," Kella said, beginning to unravel the stained bandages. "If Roland couldn't help her, I doubt I can do better. I daren't take the seal off yet, but at least I can bathe her wounds and change the bandages." She moved to a small cooling cupboard, took out a stone jug of whitish fluid, and returned to bathe the gypsy's arms.

"Maryon said her own people will be able to treat her," I said. "That's one of the reasons we're here."

"Gypsies know a great deal about healing," Kella agreed.

59

She rebandaged the woman's arms deftly and pulled the blankets up. "That is all I can do for now," she said, rinsing her hands in a bowl. "At least it will stop any infection from setting in. You will have to move swiftly if you are to return her alive to her people, though. Even with a sleepseal to slow everything down, an injury drains life energies, and she does not have much left to lose."

We went back into the hall, and she indicated another door. "That is one of the sleeping chambers, and there is another closer to the kitchen." She opened the door alongside. "The bathing room. There are three bathing barrels, and we even have water piped in. Fire heats the water while it's still in the pipes, and then it comes out of tubes to the barrels once you remove the stoppers. Unfortunately, it takes ages to heat. I'll light it if you like?"

I shook my head and gestured for her to go on.

Despite its considerable size, the kitchen was cozy and welcoming. It had been whitewashed so that even without windows, it seemed light. The air was warm and redolent with the odor of hundreds of tiny bunches of drying herbs hung in neat rows along all the walls. There were shelves of foodstuffs and in the center of the room, on a woven rug, a thick scrub-wood table and some stools. A fire blazed in a narrow hearth. As I crossed at once to warm myself, Kella filled a kettle and bent to hang it on a hook suspended over the flames.

"It's like a breath straight from Obernewtyn to see you here," she said with sudden fervency. "I miss you all so much. I dream of the fields and mountains, and then I wake and am still here."

The depth of longing in her eyes made me feel ashamed. In spite of Maryon's doom-filled predictions, I had been glad to get away from my cloistered existence at Obernewtyn, while poor Kella lived in constant danger to keep it safe.

"Sutrium is awful," she went on. "I never imagined people could be dragged so low. Even before Rushton took over, there were times for laughter at Obernewtyn. Here no one laughs, and if they do, people stare at them as if they have gone mad. And it is a hundred times worse since the plague. I pity these people their gray lives."

"Don't pity them too much," I said dryly. "Those same pitiable souls would stand by and watch us burn without lifting a finger."

"It's true enough. We're nowt but freaks to them," Matthew said, coming through the door carrying Maruman. The cat leapt to the ground and began prowling about the room, smelling it. Kella knew better than to react to his presence and pretended not to notice him. Instead, she beamed at the ward.

"Lud, but you've grown now that I see you properly, Matthew. Has Brydda's mother been using herb lore on you instead of her garden?"

Matthew laughed. "Seems to me it's yerself who's shrinkin'!"

I thought his jest curiously apt, but Kella only slapped playfully at his arm and urged him to dry himself in front of the fire. Then, catching sight of Dragon hovering in the hall behind him with her shoulders hunched miserably, the healer gave an exclamation and held out her arms. Dragon rushed at her, and it was some minutes before she could pry herself loose from the girl's impassioned embrace.

"What a grub you are, love," Kella laughed. "It's a miracle you manage to stay dirty in so much rain. Will you let me wash your face?"

Dragon froze, her blue eyes livid with fear. "No bath."

"No bath," the healer assured her, knowing as well as anyone Dragon's inexplicable terror of water. "Just a bit of a damp cloth."

Kella ushered her from the kitchen, and Matthew scowled after them.

"What do you want done about her, Matthew?" I snapped. He was as bad as Dragon, I thought, with less excuse for it.

There was an awkward pause. "They've done a good job here," Matthew said at last. "There is even a special yard where th' horses can graze without bein' seen."

I drew off my soaked boots and poured some of the boiling fement into two mugs, handing him one as a peace offering. "They've had quite a bit of help from Brydda Llewellyn by the sound of it."

"Of course," Matthew said easily; then he gave me a sharp look. "And why not? Surely ye dinna worry he'd betray us?"

I shook my head. Brydda's father, Grufyyd, and his mother, the herb lorist Katlyn, had come to live at Obernewtyn after the Council learned their son was the notorious rebel the Black Dog, so betrayal on Brydda's part was completely out of the question. "It's not Brydda. It's the others. That rebel boy who was downstairs, for instance. Did you see the way he looked at us? If he feels that way about gypsies, how is he going to react when he discovers we're Misfits? There's no point in us pretending we're all allies until it has been agreed to officially by the rebels. We don't really know where we stand with them."

"Is that really why we're here? Did Maryon's prediction have something to do with the rebels?" Matthew demanded.

I was glad when Kella's return prevented my answering. "I've put her into bed," Kella said. "The poor little mite was asleep before her head brushed the pillow. But why on earth did you bring her here?"

I explained, and the healer shook her head in wonder. "She must be very attached to follow you all this way, Elspeth."

Matthew rose, pulled on his coat in one ferocious motion, and went out the door, saying he was going to unpack the wagon.

Kella stared after him in astonishment. "Whatever is the matter with him?"

I laughed and, even to my own ears, it sounded bitter. "I am beginning to suspect it wasn't me Dragon followed but Matthew. I think he volunteered for this expedition specifically to get away from her."

"Oh, poor Dragon," Kella said compassionately. "I remember she followed him everywhere when I was last at Obernewtyn, but I thought it was just a fleeting infatuation."

"More's the pity it wasn't," I said, suddenly emptied of ill humor. I stood up. "I am going to wash and put on some dry things."

"There are clothes in a trunk in the bathing room," Kella said. A lantern was lit in the bathhouse from Dragon's wash, and as I peeled off my soaking clothes, I caught sight of myself in a mirror hanging on the wall: a long, lean girl with irritated moss-green eyes and thick, black hair falling past her waist. I glared at myself and realized abruptly that I felt less pity for Dragon's love than exasperation at the inconvenience of it.

What a terrible business loving was. It was a troublesome and tiresome emotion destined more often to enrage the recipient than to please them. Rushton's love for me, if that was what it could be called, had him determined to shut me up like a bird in a gilded cage, while Dragon's love for Matthew had driven him out of his home. What right had people to love you when you had not wanted it or asked for it?

Of course, in Dragon's case, the only wonder was that no one had foreseen the outcome of throwing together a volatile girl, who had spent most of her life in wretched loneliness, with a boy of Matthew's easy charm. Yet Dragon had ultimately saved Obernewtyn with his help. Her heartache and his irritation must be considered a small price to pay for that.

It seemed there was always a price to pay for loving.

I had a sudden vivid memory of a time when, taken in by Dragon's illusions, I had thought Obernewtyn destroyed. From my hiding place, I had spotted Rushton. He had been haggard, grim-faced with burning eyes, and I had imagined he was despairing over the loss of Obernewtyn. Only later had I understood that his sorrow arose from his belief that I was dead.

I shook my head and turned to rummage for dry clothing, not liking the tenor of my thoughts nor the way Rushton's face haunted me.

I fled to the kitchen, bringing the lamp with me, and pulled up a stool to join Matthew and Kella in front of the fire. Maruman came over and leapt onto my lap. His mind was closed, and I did not try to force entry to it.

"How long before Domick comes home?" I asked Kella, wincing as the cat's claws penetrated cloth and flesh. "Are you expecting him tonight?"

The healer nodded, the smile fading from her lips.

I guessed she was wondering if our arrival would put Domick in danger, and for the first time, I was aware of the strain in her face. There were lines around her eyes, and her hands fidgeted constantly in swift, nervous gestures. I had been surprised at the strength of the longing in her voice as she talked of Obernewtyn, but now I truly thought of what her life in the safe house must be like. Every day she watched her bondmate leave, knowing he went to work under the very noses of the Councilmen. If discovered, he would be killed.

It seemed far easier to take action than to sit and wait. People like Kella had the worst of it—the waiting and wondering and being helpless. In asking when Domick would return, I had surely voiced a question she never dared permit herself to ask.

Hearing the stair door creak and heavy footsteps in the hall, I felt an echo of the profound relief I saw on Kella's face.

But when the kitchen door opened, I did not recognize the dark-clad man who stepped inside.

✦ 7 ✦

It wasn't until Kella crossed the room to embrace the man that I realized it was Domick.

The last time I had seen the coercer was at Obernewtyn just around the time he and Kella had established the safe house. Then, Domick had been on the edge of manhood, brown as a gypsy, with shoulder-length dark hair and bold, serious eyes. There was no sign of that youth in the man who now stood before me.

His skin was milk pale, and his long hair had been cropped very short. But most of all, it was his expression that made him a stranger—or the lack of expression. His face was a gaunt mask, the eyes two hooded slits. If he felt any surprise at seeing us in the safe house, it was not evident.

As a coercer, Domick had possessed that guild's characteristic aggression, but his love for Kella had seemed to temper his intensity. I could not begin to imagine what had happened to turn him into this hard-faced man.

"Has something gone wrong at Obernewtyn?" he asked in a voice as even and emotionless as his expression.

"That is a harsh greeting for old friends," Kella scolded him gaily, and I saw that she had not mentioned his transformation because she did not perceive it. It seemed that love was truly blind.

Domick exerted himself to produce a semblance of liveliness. "Kella is right. Forgive my abruptness. It has been a bad night, but it is good to see you both." He smiled, but his eyes remained remote, and again I found myself wishing for empathy—this time to tell me what seethed under the stoniness of his face.

The coercer removed his oiled cloak, and I saw the tension in his movements as he crossed to hang it on a peg beside the fire. Sitting down, he reminded me of a spring coiling tight for a hard recoil. Maruman watched him, then hissed and sprang from my lap to prowl about the room.

"You have chosen a bad time to visit," Domick said, glancing up to indicate the rain thundering down on the roof.

"Needs must," I said.

He gave me a swift look. "Need?"

For the second time that night, I told the story of the rescue of the gypsy, and of our decision to return her to her people when Roland could not heal her.

"It was a risky thing for you to have gone in alone to face the Herder," Domick reproved. "Those villagers might have killed you at once."

"Not with th' gypsy shootin' arrows at them from th' trees," Matthew said gleefully. "Besides, we could hardly leave her to burn, now, could we?"

An odd expression flitted over the coercer's face. "Sometimes you have to endure a lesser evil in dealing with a greater one."

Kella stared fixedly into the fire, as if disengaging herself from the conversation, but Matthew was openly indignant.

"Ye mean we should have left her? I doubt she'd call that a lesser evil!"

Domick shrugged. "If you had been caught, it would not have helped her, and it may well have done great, even

67

irreparable, damage to our cause. Which, then, would be the greater evil? To let an unknown woman die, or to intervene and see your friends perish for it?"

"We got her free, didn't we? An' we weren't caught," Matthew returned stubbornly. "If we thought like you, we'd nowt even have tried. *There's* evil fer ye. Nowt even tryin' to fix somethin' that's wrong."

"You are naive," Domick said dismissively. "If the woman is as sick as you say, there is every likelihood she will die despite your help."

Matthew flushed. "Maybe I am naive, but rather that than bein' someone with ice fer blood an' a clever tongue an' shifty brain instead of a heart!"

They stared at one another for a moment; then Domick relaxed back into his seat. "And is that the reason you have come to Sutrium, Elspeth? To take an irrelevant gypsy back to her people?"

I suppressed a surge of anger at his callousness and the temptation to tell him what Maryon had futuretold about this "irrelevant" gypsy. But with the woman so near death, there was enough urgency without piling the burden of a portentous vision on their heads.

"I would also like to see Brydda Llewellyn," I said mildly. "Maybe he could suggest some safe way to locate her people."

"I am not sure there is any way that is safe," Domick said. "Is she a halfbreed? I suppose she must be," he answered himself.

"I think so. Yes," I added more positively, remembering the Herder had called her that. "Does it make a difference?"

Both Kella and the coercer nodded.

"A Twentyfamilies gypsy would not break the Council lore forbidding healing," Domick explained.

"Twentyfamilies?" I echoed, surprised to hear the odd word again. "What does that mean?"

"It is what pureblood gypsies call themselves," the coercer said. "It was not a name any but traders of expensive trinkets knew until the Herders started bandying it about. They hate gypsies and Twentyfamilies most of all, because it was they who negotiated the safe passage agreement with the Council that exempts gypsies from Herder lore. Herders preach that gypsies ought to be made to settle. They claim the plague was spread by their wanderings."

"The Herder in Guanette said the plagues were a punishment from Lud because of people ignoring the Faction," I said.

Domick shrugged. "Same thing. There is a lot of talk to that effect encouraged by the Herders, but it will not give them power to force the Council to make the Twentyfamilies settle. The halfbreeds are not so lucky, for the safe passage agreement no longer includes them, yet nor are they allowed to settle. They are persecuted by Landfolk and Herders alike, as you know. But it is worse since the plague."

I began to see that returning the gypsy before Maryon's futuretold deadline would be even harder than I had anticipated. Hitherto, I had imagined I understood something of gypsy society, but in truth, what I knew arose solely from memories of a single friendly troupe that had come through Rangorn every few seasons when I was a child. I did not even know if they had been pureblood or halfbreed.

"You talk about Twentyfamilies gypsies and halfbreeds as if they were two separate races," I said.

"That is very nearly what they are," he answered. "The division between them has its origins in the days when gypsies first came to the Land. Some say they walked here; others say they came by sea. Either way, they didn't want to be ruled by Council or Herder lore, so they came to an agreement with the Council to remain as visitors, never settling or farming the Land, never owning any of it."

"I know all of that," I said, faintly impatient.

"I suppose you know, too, how they got the Council to agree to let them remain as visitors?" Domick snapped.

Abashed, I shook my head. "I'm sorry. Tell it your own way."

He went on. "In exchange for safe passage status as visitors, the gypsies offered a yearly tithe: a percentage of the craftwares their people produced. Their works were rare and beautiful, and for a time everyone seemed to benefit from the arrangement.

"In those early days, some gypsies mated with Landfolk, so halfbreeds were born. Initially, there was free trade of knowledge and blood between full and halfblood gypsies. But that ended with the Great Divide," Domick said. "Purebloods do not now teach their skills to halfbreeds; therefore, halfbreed wares are pale echoes of their work, based on half-recollected formulae and recipes. Invariably inferior, they bring scant coin, whereas the purebloods make more than enough to live well from what remains of their work after the tithe."

"Why dinna Twentyfamilies gypsies teach th' halfbreeds th' craftskills?" Matthew demanded indignantly. "A halfbreed mun have at least one pureblood in their line of descent. Dinna this tie mean anything to them?"

"It was a matter of survival for the purebloods," Domick

said. "On the whole, halfbreeds weren't as scrupulous about obeying Council lore as the Twentyfamilies. That caused a lot of strife. Finally, the Twentyfamilies leader had no choice but to announce the Great Divide, cutting halfbreeds off absolutely from purebloods. The Council accepted the division, because it allowed them to control the troublemaking halfbreeds without breaking contract with the Twentyfamilies. And the purebloods had to maintain the exclusivity of their work, because it was their only leverage with the Council.

"And that keeps them safe even from the Herders," the coercer added. "The Faction wants gypsy traveling stopped, because they want all in the Land under their power. Of course, the Council has a vested interest in keeping things as they are, because if they make the purebloods settle, the bribe tithe will cease."

"Naturally, greed would decide th' day," said Matthew with a flash of cynicism.

"The halfbreeds should be so lucky as to have something the Council wanted. It is hard on them. It would not be so bad if they were permitted to settle and become ordinary Landfolk; but in spite of the division, people regard gypsies as gypsies. They resent the wealth and inviolability of the Twentyfamilies gypsies, and they take it out on the halfbreeds."

"There have been a number of incidents just recently in which halfbreeds have been beaten or attacked," Kella said, her eyes worried. "Your disguises are now dangerous, because you are obviously not Twentyfamilies and as halfbreeds, you are fair game."

Why had Domick not warned us of this in his reports? Before I could ask, Matthew spoke. "Why can't we say we're Twentyfamilies? Fer that matter, why dinna th' halfbreeds say it? There's enough color variation for that not to matter."

"Twentyfamilies gypsies would know you were an impostor regardless of skin color," Domick said.

"How could they know?" Matthew persisted.

The coercer shrugged. "They just do. You might farseek them and find out how, if it mattered enough. Yet, what point would there be in it? Your gypsy can only be a halfbreed. To reach her people, you must be one of them."

That was true enough.

"And even among the halfbreeds, you will have trouble getting information, because gypsy or not, you will be unknown to them," Domick said. "Given the climate, they are understandably wary of strangers. If, by chance, they discover you are not a gypsy, they will probably kill you, thinking you are a Herder spy."

I frowned into the fire.

"And that is another thing you must consider," Domick went on inexorably. "I have heard no report of the affair in Guanette at the Councilcourt, but just because it has not reached the Council does not mean the Faction is ignorant of it. If they do know, they are certain to have spies watching the gypsy greens with descriptions of you in their pockets."

"I will keep the gypsy woman out of sight and go about as a boy," I said firmly, stamping ruthlessly on a little flutter of fear in my stomach.

"Best to abandon the gypsy disguise altogether, but of course the tan would give you away," the coercer said.

"I can brew something that will fade it faster," Kella offered.

I nodded. "It would not be a bad idea to have such a mixture on hand. However, given what you have said, I doubt any gypsy would speak to me unless I was obviously one of them, so I will have to remain as I am for the present. Maybe I can coerce them into thinking they know me."

Changing the subject, I told Domick how Dragon had come to Sutrium and asked if he could send word back to Obernewtyn that she was safe.

"It will take a sevenday at least," he warned. "My reports go through Enoch, and he daren't let himself be seen going up to the mountains, since they're supposed to be deserted and Obernewtyn a tainted ruin."

I nodded. "Rushton had worried at the lack of news from you. It's good to know you were just being cautious."

Domick glowered. "I am always cautious. And we have had to be even more so lately. At the height of the plague, Enoch would have been stoned if he traveled openly enough to cause people to fear he carried the disease from place to place."

"The plague seems to affect so many things," I mused.

"How was it at Obernewtyn during the plague?" Kella asked, and I realized how little she must hear of home and everyday events in Rushton's businesslike missives. It would not occur to him that his spies might need to hear the small details of life in the mountains.

"It was not so bad in the highlands," I said, "though Rushton insisted we stay in the mountains for some time. How did you manage?"

Kella's expression was suddenly haunted. "It's so dirty here that people went down with the disease in the hundreds. So many died that there were not enough left to bury the dead. The corpses bloated and stank, and the disease spread and spread. And all to the Herder Faction's benefit," she added in sudden anger.

I was surprised. "You don't believe Lud sent it on their behalf?"

"That's not what I meant," she said. "I am sure it was nothing more than a disease born of filth and ignorance. But the Herders were quick to warp it to their purpose. They claimed only those hated by Lud would die." There was a terrible bitterness in her voice. "Are babies and old dodderers evil? Does Lud hate children and sick people? For they were the first to fall."

"The strange thing is that so few of the Herders died," Domick said pensively. "It seemed to prove their claim that Lud was protecting them. They did not care at all when plague killed off the sickly and the weak, but when it began to eat up the strong, they were less delighted. After all, if everyone was killed, who would be left to be preached at?"

Kella laughed. "They really started to worry when the crops were ready and there was no one to harvest them. What would they eat? Would they have to till and labor for food with their own white hands? The Councilmen were panic-stricken, of course, and right from the beginning, the majority of them had barricaded themselves in their homes with supplies. But still many of them died as well."

She fell silent.

"What happened in th' end?" Matthew asked, as if looking for a happy ending to a bedtime tale.

Domick answered him. "It went on and on, until half the city was dead or dying, and finally the Herders told the Council to lock up the houses of the dead and burn them with the corpses inside."

Kella gave a sob. "Yes. That was their solution. They told the Council to employ the purifying flames of Lud. So the soldierguards went out, burning any house where there had been plague and quite a few where there was nothing, whether there were people inside or not. Dozens were burned alive."

I swallowed back horror as Domick moved to take Kella in his arms, his expression more masklike than ever.

"I did what I could," Kella whispered into his shoulder. "But there were so many. . . ."

The coercer met my eyes over her bowed head, and for a moment there was a flare of some emotion in his eyes, but it was gone too quickly for me to interpret it.

"It was difficult," he said in a cool voice. "Brydda was bringing those of his people who had contracted the plague here. Most arrived too late to be helped. Other times there were so many needing healing that Kella had to choose which lives to save and whom to let die. She almost killed herself trying to heal them all. She would not rest or eat."

"How could I rest with people dying every minute I slept? How could I eat in the midst of all that death?" she whispered.

Domick rose and led the weeping girl out, leaving me and Matthew to stare at one another.

"I dinna know it had been so bad," the farseeker said in a subdued tone.

I said nothing, for though horrified by Kella's story, I was concerned that people had been brought so haphazardly to the safe house. Yet the thought gave me hope, for surely the rebels would not use it and Kella's healing skills so freely if they did not mean to ally themselves with us.

Maruman appeared from behind a cupboard and climbed into my lap again, making himself comfortable before the fire. I was fascinated to feel his mind curling around mine in much the same fashion as his body shaped itself to my lap.

"Maruman/yelloweyes guards ElspethInnle," he sent, as if I had posed a question.

Domick returned.

"I have coerced Kella to sleep," he said in a somber voice. His eyes met mine. "She is exhausted in body and spirit. You cannot know what it was like for her. She nearly went mad when she learned of the burnings. You must take her with you when you go. She cannot bear it."

"It doesn't seem to bother you," I said.

"I am not Kella," he responded flatly. "I am a realist. There was plague, and the burnings ended it. Therefore, the method worked."

"It was a brutal solution," I snapped. I did not like the coldness in his voice when he spoke of Kella, nor his apparent acceptance of the Herder Faction's murderous solutions.

"Brutal?" he said. "Perhaps. But this is a brutal world. Yet it did not endear the Faction to the Council, for all its success. Too many Councilmen died and too few Herders."

Diverted, I frowned. "Then there is still conflict between the Faction and the Council?"

Domick nodded. "There is a feeling among Councilmen that the Herders have too much hysterical power over the masses, that they are fanatical and dangerously extreme. Of course, since the plague, they command the power of life and death—or so the ignorant are led to believe—so there is no question of the Council doing anything immediately to limit their power. But, I daresay, they will find a way to curb them in the end."

"Do you think the Council would ever disband them altogether?"

He shook his head decisively. "I doubt they will do more than pull a few teeth. The Faction serves a purpose, and the

Councilmen know it. They have just recently sent a pack of Herders to soften up the Sadorian tribespeople. Why bark yourself when you can have a dog do it?"

And if the dog turns on its master? I wondered.

Domick stood up abruptly and reached for his cloak. "Come."

My bones ached and I was still cold, but I stood, lifting Maruman from my knee. The old cat gave me a haughty look and stalked away. I pulled on my sodden boots and took the cloak the coercer handed me.

"We will be back before midnight," he told Matthew.

The farseeker nodded and leaned forward, lifting both hands to the fire. I felt a stab of envy.

"Where are we going?" I asked, clumping down the dark stairs.

Domick's eyes glimmered in the darkness as we stepped out into the windy night, and his words were an echo out of the distant past: "You wanted to talk to Brydda Llewellyn, didn't you?"

✦ 8 ✦

THE STREETS WERE all but deserted as we passed through them like two shadows. Houses were everywhere sunk in darkness, but here and there were more of the blackened gaps I had noticed that afternoon. I shuddered, now understanding them in the light of Kella's story.

A woman peered out of a window at us, and I wondered whether I should have insisted we take the horses. Gahltha would be angry that I had gone without him, but Domick had argued that we would draw more eyes on horseback than on foot. Because of a rising trade in stolen horses, few rode at night.

Even so, Gahltha had ways of defending himself that would discourage any thief.

With a shock, I realized I had grown so accustomed to the black horse's presence that I felt curiously vulnerable without him.

A curtain twitched as we passed another window and a memory surfaced. "Is there still a curfew in Sutrium?"

Domick lifted his head as if to dispel a dream, and I wondered what he had been thinking about. "There is a curfew, but it does not come into effect until midnight," he said. "It is not strictly enforced, because there are worse things than soldierguards to contend with. Only fools asking to be robbed or murdered wander the streets after dark."

"Marvelous," I said sourly.

"Since the plagues and the loss of crops, there is no work and little food," the coercer went on, as if I had not spoken. "There are a legion of poor in the city. Some beg for their needs, and others take what they want. Hard times make for hard folk."

Involuntarily, I smiled, recognizing in the phrase Brydda's love of neat sayings. "One of the Black Dog's homilies?"

Domick gave me a startled look, then said defensively, "He has a way of putting things that makes them memorable. It is a fine and useful quality in a leader."

There was not the slightest flicker of humor in his voice. He had always been serious, seldom speaking more than was necessary or laughing aloud, but now it seemed he had built a deep wall of reserve around himself. I wanted to ask why, but his manner did not invite intimacy.

"Do you see much of Brydda?" I asked instead.

The coercer gave me a wary look as we passed under one of the few lit street lanterns, and it struck me forcibly that something was very wrong.

"I see him," he said noncommittally.

"How is he, then?"

Domick was silent so long, I thought he meant to ignore the question, but at last he spoke.

"Superficially, he is the same as ever: brave as a lion, swift to laughter, loyal, proud, and silver-tongued. But to my mind, his policy of elusiveness is affecting his mind."

"You mean he is going mad?" I asked, startled.

Domick gave me a pale echo of a genuine smile, which fleetingly stripped the years away from his face. "I mean, it is affecting his way of thinking. He is the kind who needs to trust. He is happiest with loyal comrades constantly about him. He remains close to Idris and Reuvan, who you'll remember came with him from Aborium. Yet even those friendships are strained. For the sake of security, the Black Dog has chosen a lonely path."

He fell silent and I considered what he had said. No one knew better than I how loneliness tainted a person's thinking. Solitude could become an addiction, a canker of the soul, ever hungered for as much as it was loathed. All the years I had spent in the orphan home system after my parents were killed, I had kept myself apart—even from my brother Jes. With informants about, friendship was dangerous in the best of cases, and I had extra reason to fear, being a Misfit. This had made it hard for me to trust or to relate to people, even when it was safe to do so. And, in spite of all the years of longing for friends, now that I had them, part of me yearned to be by myself again.

But Brydda had not learned the orphan's lesson. I could well imagine the effect enforced solitude would have on him. It saddened me to think of the laughter dimmed in the merry giant.

"And you?" I asked impulsively. "Do you think of your path as a lonely one?"

Domick gave me a strange look but made no response.

We fell silent as we passed an open veranda where an old woman swept her porch. She watched us go by, as if poised to run inside and bar the door. I felt her eyes following us through the rain until we passed out of sight.

We came into a street running right alongside the shore. A boardwalk was built level with the cobbled street, but beneath it the ground dropped away to a narrow, rocky beach. Rain fell into the water with a hissing susurrus. Again, I was conscious of a strong mental static, which indicated the water was tainted in some manner. I did not recall this from my previous visits to Sutrium. Perhaps there had been a recent firestorm?

The sea was so dark that it seemed as if we traveled along the rim of an abyss. This would be a good place for an attack, but I resisted the urge to look over my shoulder.

Thoughts of one fear begot another, for without thinking, I asked, "Have you heard anything of Ariel lately?"

The name evoked in the coercer the same heavy silence it caused anyone who had been at Obernewtyn before Rushton became its master.

"He went to Herder Isle just before the plague struck," he said at length. "It seems that he remains in the Herders' good graces, though I do not know why. They were as angry with him as the Council when the soldierguards he sent to Obernewtyn found nothing. I would have expected them to cast him off as the Council did."

"You know, it has always bothered me that Ariel was so certain Obernewtyn had not been destroyed by firestorm that he sent the soldierguards to catch us in the lie," I mused.

"His Talent must have given him the knowledge," Domick said.

I gaped at the coercer, astonished. Why had it never occurred to me that Ariel was a Talented Misfit?

Domick went on, unaware of my reaction to his words. "Kella thinks he has empathy because of the way he generated fear, but I think he is a latent coercer—it would explain his skill at manipulating his way into power. I doubt he's a futureteller, for he's been caught off guard too often; a true dream would have been enough to tell him that Obernewtyn still stood."

True dreams were common among Misfits and often contained fleeting flashes of the future.

My mind circled back to my own question: Why had I never thought of Ariel being Talented? I had known he was a Misfit, but above finding him morally corrupt and sadistic, I had never considered what it was that had *made* him a Misfit. Why?

The answer came swiftly.

Because I did not want it to be so.

I wanted to believe that all Talented Misfits strove for right and justice. The thought of someone so wicked having a Talent, being part of our community . . . It left a bitterness in my mouth.

The rain began to fall more heavily. The coercer looked up with a muffled curse and lengthened his stride. I drew up the hood of my cloak to stop water dripping down my neck and hastened to keep up, my thoughts running ahead of me.

Ariel as a coercer—even as a weak and unaware coercer—was a fearsome notion.

In the early days at Obernewtyn, there had been much concern over the morality of coercion and even talk about trying to convert it to healing or some other use. But in its aggressive form, it had proven too necessary to our survival.

Instead, there had been a move away from separatism. These days, guilds aimed to train novices to use all their powers, though Misfits still generally chose to specialize in one specific Talent as part of the process of becoming guilded. There had been some resistance to crossguilding, until it was realized that development of a lesser Talent often enhanced the primary ability. For instance, as a farseeker with coercion, I could coerce from a distance, instead of needing to be close to a subject, as a typical coercer must. And the combination of beastspeaking, farseeking, and coercing meant I could coerce animals without being close to them physically.

Domick plucked at my arm and pointed across the street to a dingy inn whose signboard proclaimed its incongruous name: The Good Egg. "That is where we will make contact with Brydda."

"The last time I went into an inn looking for Brydda Llewellyn, I was nearly arrested," I said, following him reluctantly across the street.

"We will not ask for him openly," Domick said. "It is just a matter of ordering a certain obscure brew, which will not be in stock, in a particular quantity. Then the Black Dog will be signaled and will send someone for us as soon as he is able."

There was no time for more talk, as the door swung open and a group of drunken revelers stumbled out into the night. Domick grasped my elbow, steering me past them and into the inn.

Though cavernous, it was poorly lit—as all such places were, for the people who came to drown in their cups seldom wanted to be seen doing it. The inn was surprisingly crowded for a city supposedly full of the poor, but perhaps there was always enough coin for oblivion. The room reeked of cheap, sour fement and old sweat, but I was grateful for the warmth created by the throng.

I took my cloak off with some trepidation, having no alternative but to let myself be seen as a girl because of the clothes I had put on in the safe-house bathing room. The garments were not necessarily that of a gypsy, but my tan skin marked me, so I made the room see me as a full-grown gypsy woman rather than as a girl.

I could have completely coerced one or two people into seeing me any way I chose, but not a whole roomful. Coercing a large number of people was more of a general influencing, or accentuating what existed already in their minds. It was a surprisingly effective trick even when those with natural mindshields were about, because a group of people tended to operate as a single—and not very intelligent—mind. Still, I had to work within reasonable limitations.

Domick apparently had his own feint in mind. To my surprise, he suddenly reached out and drew me into the circle of his arms.

+ 9 +

"Ho, Mika!" someone cried.

Domick turned, digging his fingers into my shoulder.

"Join us," said a lean man with close-set, crafty eyes that moved over me like prying fingers. "Who is your companion, my friend?"

"Her name is Elaria," Domick said in an arrogant voice that startled me almost as much as his putting an arm around me. He slid into a seat, pushing me before him, and I found myself crushed up next to an old man with a grizzled face and faded blue eyes.

"Elaria, I am Kerry," the lean man opposite introduced himself with a leering smile. He stabbed a blunt finger at the old man beside me. "That is Col, and by me here is Oria."

Col merely grunted, but the blond woman, Oria, gave me a friendly nod, which filled me with suspicion. Since when were people remotely civil to a gypsy?

As if accommodating my doubts, a thick-necked youth farther down the trestle scowled at me. "Halfbreeds are thieves an' plaguebirds," he said loudly in a highland accent.

"You are a fool, boy, blighted with stupidity—which is a greater affliction than plague, since one cannot even hope for recovery from it." Domick's eyes were contemptuous. "Would I walk about with a carrier of the cursed plague?"

Oria and Kerry roared with more laughter than the

witticism deserved. As the blond woman moved her head, I saw that her face was disfigured on one side by the savage spore of the disease.

"Ruga, you've been put in your place fair enough." Kerry leaned across the table toward me, and I fought the urge to slap him away. "She's comely enough," he approved. "But my taste don't run to gypsy flesh. Specially not one with a face as sober and sour as a judge."

"No doubt she finds you a sour eyeful, too," laughed the woman.

"Well, like I was sayin'," said the young highlander somewhat huffily from farther down the trestle, "I'm thinkin' of joining th' soldierguards. I'd just as soon step on a few necks as have mine stood on."

The oldster beside me gave a sneering laugh. "Join up and you'll just as likely find yourself warring with the tribesfolk in distant Sador. And I've heard they roast over their temple fires and eat those they take prisoner."

"There will be no war against Sador," Kerry said swiftly, his eyes flickering to Domick's face and then quickly away.

"The Council has sent Herders on a mission to make peace with the Sadorians," Domick said.

"Peace?" echoed the bleary-eyed Col. "The Council don't want peace, 'cepting maybe a big piece of Sador. And who knows what them Herders are after?"

An awkward silence ensued; then Kerry said with forced joviality, "Best keep your words for other company, old man. There's some here who might not take kind to your speculation."

"You have no need to worry about me," Domick said. "Fools blow air out of their mouths as often as their bums, and either way it causes a stink and comes to nothing."

I looked around at the people at the table and, seeing their expressions, understood suddenly why Kerry and the woman had behaved so oddly, fawning on Domick and being civil to his gypsy companion.

They were afraid of him.

Abruptly, Domick rose and left the table, saying he wanted to order a drink. I tried not to look disconcerted at being left alone there, but I sensed the others at the table studying me covertly. Unnerved, I shaped a general coercive probe suggesting that I was defective. Given the general prejudice against gypsies, it was not difficult to plant a negative thought, and as the idea took root, they relaxed.

Only the plague-scarred Oria continued her scrutiny. I entered her mind and discovered she believed me to be a spy left by Domick to garner information. It was clear this disturbed her, but I did not trouble to delve deeper to learn why. I merely grafted into her thoughts a memory of having seen me before with different men at different inns and of having observed enough of my behavior to judge me defective.

Her disquiet faded, and she dismissed me from her mind. Turning to the old man, her brow creased with exasperation. "You are a fool with a mouth big enough to lose yourself in, Col. Don't you know who that was?"

He shrugged. "Some official or other. What do I care who he is? I've seen him here before."

"And that makes him safe?" she hissed. "He works for the Councilcourt."

"He sweeps the floor an' runs messages," said the highlander, Ruga, from down the table. "I heard him say so once."

Oria sneered at him openly. "Of course he would say that."

The old man frowned. "Well, what does he do, then? Is he a spy?"

I felt myself start, but no one noticed. The blonde leaned

across the table and lowered her voice. "You heard what happened to Jomas?"

Col merely nodded, so I was forced to read the memory evoked by the woman's question directly from his thoughts.

A man called Jomas had spoken out against a Councilman, claiming the official had charged his father with sedition in order to obtain his farm. Jomas had been arrested and charged with sedition the very next night and was tortured so savagely that he had never walked again.

"So what? Everyone knows they torture seditioners," Col said.

Oria looked around before speaking. "Neither Jomas nor his father were seditioners and well you know it. But the point of the story is that Mika was here when Jomas was mouthing off about that Councilman."

Col snorted. "And for that you'd have me fear him? This place is full of folk who'd sell their mother for the price of a mug. Anyone could have reported Jomas's mouthings."

"I went to see Jomas when he recovered," Oria said fiercely. "He told me he was there when they tortured him."

"He?" the oldster echoed, confused.

"He," Oria repeated. "Mika." She lowered her voice. "He is a torturer."

I was so shocked that my probe faltered in its hold on the group.

"We should not talk of such matters," Kerry said, his tone suddenly anxious. "People who talk too much have a way of disappearing into the interrogation rooms beneath the Councilcourt."

"Sometimes elsewhere," Oria added darkly as I regained control.

I could barely follow the turn in conversation as someone else asked if there were truly prospects for war in Sador.

"That's not why they're recruitin'," retorted Ruga. "They want more soldierguards because of them rebels with Henry Druid gettin' too big for their boots."

"Henry Druid is dead," Oria interrupted. "He died in a firestorm in the highlands. The rebels they're after now are those led by Brydda Llewellyn."

"Not Brydda. Bodera," Kerry said.

"What does it matter who leads them?" sneered Col, glaring into his mug. "I hope there *is* a war, whether it is with them demonish-looking Sadorians or the rebels, and they all kill one another."

The table fell silent again as Domick reappeared bearing a small jug.

"I don't know how you drink that mucky syrup," Oria said brightly. "But if you ordered it more often, old Filo would keep some for you instead of your having to wait while he sends out."

The coercer made no comment. He drank with every evidence of enjoyment, then set the mug down and looked around the table.

"You should be careful of loose talk," he said casually. There was something in his voice that brought everyone in the immediate vicinity to silence.

"There are those who are not what they seem," he went on in a sinister tone. My heart began to thump. *Now* what was he doing?

"Take that man." He pointed to a drunkard at the nearest table, staring about owlishly. "He seems no more than a sot. But is he really? Perhaps he is something more than he seems.

Perhaps he has drunk less than he makes out and flaps his ears for seditious talk."

Oria laughed uneasily. "You jest."

Domick smiled and sipped at his golden mead.

Suddenly the oldster beside me slammed his fist down. "I'll not pretend! I am no seditioner to sit here cowering. You think we don't know what you are?"

The room fell silent, and all attention was on Domick, waiting to see what he would do.

"And what am I?" he asked in a soft, dangerous voice.

"I've a right to speak," Col blustered, the silence penetrating at last.

Domick sipped the last of his drink; then he dabbed fastidiously at the edges of his mouth with a handkerchief. "You should use your tongue for less dangerous talk, old man," he said at last. "Fortunately for you, I sweep, I write letters, and sometimes I deliver them. That is all I do. Anyone who would say otherwise . . . should think twice."

He rose, pulling me up with him. I kept my head down, trying to look moronish and insignificant. Domick nodded languidly to Kerry and Oria. "Perhaps, when next I come, the company will be better."

Kerry smiled stiffly and bade us walk safe.

Outside, I pulled on my cloak with suppressed fury. "Are you crazy? There is not a person in there who will forget your face or mine after that little display. And how is it so many people know you work for the Council? Is this some brilliant new strategy based on telling your business to every stranger you meet?"

Domick was looking out into the night, his face empty of expression. "A Council employee is often investigated in the interests of security. If I had no life to investigate, I would be instantly suspect. I must have a background to fit my role, and those people are part of it."

"You might have warned me," I snapped. "What if I hadn't been able to improvise?"

"Guildmistress of the farseekers, veteran of hundreds of daring and brilliant rescues unable to improvise?" he demanded dryly. "Yet I would have warned you, had I expected them to be there."

"Perhaps they deliberately came tonight to avoid you," I snapped.

He shrugged. "That is likely true. They have no love for me. Why are you so angry? I would have warned you if I could, but once inside, it was too late."

I opened my mouth to deny anger, then realized he was right. My temper had risen from fear.

"That was unnecessarily dangerous," I said, forcing myself to be calm. "You deliberately frightened them. Why?"

Domick's eyes were like the holes of the Blacklands as he stepped out into the night. "The people back there are not bad folk. They are just poor and ignorant. They speak too freely of matters better left unsaid. I am trying to teach them to keep their mouths shut."

"And what if there had been trouble in there? What would Mika have done? Would his job protect him if someone decided to take offense to his bullying?"

"You don't seem to grasp what it means to be employed by the Council," Domick said softly. "There is little it would not protect me against."

I snorted in disbelief. "Only those high up in Council employ warrant that sort of protection. Not a sweeper of floors."

"You think that after so many seasons of faithful service

the Council would not reward a loyal worker?" Domick asked quietly.

A chill crept along my veins. "You mean . . ."

He laughed hollowly. "Let us say that it has been some time since I have swept a floor in the Councilcourt, Elspeth."

I licked my lips. "The people back there believe that you are a torturer. Why didn't you coerce them against believing such a rumor? It can't help you to spy. What possible advantage could it give you to let them think it?"

"The protection and power wrought by fear," Domick said. "But even if the rumor had served no purpose, I cannot stop it. I could not coerce everyone to disbelieve a rumor that is so universal."

"This . . . this rumor that you are a torturer . . . how did such a thing begin?"

He did not answer, and my heart began to beat unevenly. "Domick, what is it you do at the Council now?"

"I am not a torturer," he said at last in a grim voice. Then his eyes went over my shoulder. I turned to see a hooded figure standing in the rain.

"Look, there is our man," Domick said. "Brydda has sent him to collect us."

+ 10 +

IDRIS BOWED, HIS round face lit by the sunny smile that I remembered from my last journey to the coast. "It is good to see you again, Elspeth."

The young rebel had appeared outside The Good Egg wrapped up in a cloak and gestured for us to follow. It was not until we reached a small dark hovel, a few streets away from the inn, that he had drawn back the hood of his coat to greet us.

"What is this place?" I asked as the blond rebel turned to the door of the hovel. It seemed to be nothing more than an abandoned husk and was surely far too small to be useful as a safe house.

"It is just a house," Idris said, forcing the sagging door open and ushering us before him. Inside the front hall, it was dark, and we stood in silence as he found and lit a lantern. The hall was empty, its walls scored black from fire. Idris removed his cloak and carefully hung it on a wall peg. Following suit, I remembered that he had always been meticulous and slightly plodding.

He brought us through empty, musty rooms to the back of the place, saying, "There are any number of houses standing vacant since the plagues." He pointed to an outbuilding's door, under which a slice of light showed. "They have proven very useful to us as temporary residences."

"Don't people wonder at seeing lamps in abandoned houses?"

Idris shrugged. "No doubt, but it does not matter. We rarely spend more than a few days in any one. This is the last night we will spend here." He pushed open the door.

The room behind it was a complete contrast to the great, warm homelike place Brydda had used as a headquarters in Aborium. It was bare but for a number of rough stools and chairs drawn around a little fire, a table piled with scrolls and maps, and a small supply of firewood stacked up on the floor. It was clearly hastily assembled, and no attempt had been made to render it comfortable. The room was dimly lit by a single guttering candle stuck in a mug on the table and by the warmer glow of the fire. Black cloth had been tacked over the only window, but as soon as we entered, Idris extinguished the brighter lantern he carried, the gesture belying his unconcern about being seen.

"Where is Brydda?" I asked.

In answer, the large-backed chair directly before the fire swiveled to reveal the big rebel holding a knife.

"Little sad eyes," he said in his rumbling voice.

Watching him sheath the knife and rise, I thought the old nickname suited him better than it had ever suited me. The rebel leader seemed more hugely bearlike than ever, his hair falling almost to his shoulders in a great shaggy pelt of midnight curls. Yet there was a tinge of silver amidst the darker hair at his temples and in his beard, and fine lines about his eyes that I did not remember. The unsheathed knife told its own story. This life was taking its toll on him, as Domick had said. Brydda was like a lamp, with the flame burning dangerously low.

He gathered me into the affectionate ursine hug I remembered so well. That at least was unchanged, and my heart swelled with a gladness that startled me and made me feel absurdly like bursting into tears.

I watched as he greeted Domick with warmth and was interested to see that, for a moment, even the coercer lost some of his icy reserve.

"Let me give you both something to eat." Brydda gestured to the fire where a battered pot hung. "It is only a broth, I am afraid. These days we do not have the time or leisure to feast." The note of regret in his voice was palpable.

"I will do it," Idris said, pushing Brydda's hand aside and lifting the pot from the hook. He opened the lid and a delicious odor wafted out. My stomach, ever ready to herald its state, growled loudly.

Brydda burst out laughing.

"I have not eaten for ages," I defended myself. "I do not feel so hungry when I am traveling, and we have just arrived."

"I am the opposite," Brydda said ruefully. He accepted a mug of soup from Idris and handed it to me. "I eat as though for ten men! Ah well, we are what we eat; that is evident. And how was the road?"

His eyes sharpened at this. He had switched effortlessly from friend to seditioner chief seeking information. I drank and thought a moment before answering. "It was emptier than usual. More soldierguards and fewer ordinary travelers. Toll gates were heavily guarded. I would say the Council is tightening up on travel, trying to keep a record of who is going where and why." I glanced at him from under my lashes. "Perhaps trying to prevent rebel groups from liaising with one another. And from what I heard at the inn tonight, your people are, at least in part, the reason for an increase in soldierguard recruitment."

Brydda nodded approvingly. "'Little sad eyes' I called you, but perhaps 'sharp eyes' it should have been. A good summation. And what do you think all these clues suggest?"

"That you have stepped up your activities and have been careless enough to let the Council know it," I said promptly. "Or maybe you meant the Council to know it, for some reason. Or . . ." I hesitated to voice the third and obvious possibility.

"Or we have a traitor in our midst telling the Council they had best get ready for a fight," Brydda finished bluntly.

"And had they?" I asked quickly. "Are your people planning to move openly against the Council?"

Brydda made a vague gesture. "I suspect the increase in recruitment is less for fear of us than the Council's way of dealing with the number of people without work since the plague. So many who would have found work on farms have come to the city. The Council would have been wiser to restore the farms. But they are also making sure there are plenty of soldierguards if it comes to war over Sador—they covet the spice groves there." Here his eyes sought Domick's, and the coercer nodded confirmation.

I frowned at this further evidence of close interaction between the rebels and the safe house.

"The crime rate in the cities has tripled since the plagues," Domick said. "And the Council reasons that employing more soldierguards will reduce the number of people out of work and will control those who have chosen robbery as a way of filling their bellies."

The rebel chief drank some soup. "Not a bad stratagem,

but of course one wonders where the coin is coming from to pay them." He paused, seeming lost in thought for a moment.

"Then the increase in soldierguards has nothing to do with seditioners?" I persisted.

Brydda gave me a swift look. "I did not say that. It is true the Council have begun to regard us more seriously as a threat, and that may be another reason for their increase in recruitment. In part, this is unavoidable. We have heightened our profile among the people, for we will need them behind us when . . ." He stopped.

I turned to stare at the rebel chief squarely.

"Are you planning to attack the Council, Brydda?" I asked flatly.

"Of course. You knew that all along."

I felt my temper rise. "Do not play word games with me."

I heard Idris and Domick gasp aloud but did not take my eyes from Brydda's.

"You mistrust me?" he asked sorrowfully.

"Never," I said. "But I think you mistrust us. Or you think of us as fools to be put off. Don't underestimate us, Brydda. We can read the signs as well as anyone, and rumor says the rebels prepare for rebellion."

There was a charged silence; then Brydda sighed heavily. "Will you believe me if I tell you that no date is named as yet for rebellion?" he asked.

I hesitated, then nodded. "If you say it, I will believe it."

"Good, for I do say it." The rebel leaned forward to throw some wood on the fire; then he looked at me again. "Rushton sent you to ask about the alliance, didn't he? That is why you are here?"

"One of the reasons," I admitted, ignoring Domick's

involuntary movement at my side. "He wonders why you delay in responding to our offer of alliance."

Brydda gave me a penetrating look, then sighed. "Perhaps I *have* underestimated you. There is a problem with the alliance, and that is why I have evaded Domick's queries. I had hoped to be able to present Rushton with a united acceptance of your offer, but . . ."

My heart did an unpleasant dance. "You won't accept us, then?" My tone was colder than I had intended, but it was too late to retract it. And in light of his words, perhaps it did not matter.

The big rebel leaned closer. "Elspeth, you talk as if it is *my* decision. It is not."

"You are their leader."

To my surprise, he shook his head.

"When first you knew me, I was the leader of a small rebel group in Aborium devoted to bedeviling the Herders," he said. "But I was compromised. Just after we met, as you know, I left the Aborium group to be run by my second, a stolid, reliable fellow named Yavok. I took no one with me but Reuvan and Idris."

Brydda was silent a moment, his eyes distant as he looked into the past.

"While in Aborium, I had come to know the leader of the Sutrium group, an old fox named Bodera, whom I learned to admire. I had told him my dream of uniting all the rebel groups, and when he heard I was to leave Aborium, he invited me to work toward that end with him in an organized effort to overthrow the Council. The most difficult thing is that each rebel group operates almost in isolation. Fortunately, Bodera was one of the first rebel leaders, and he knew all the others. They respect him tremendously, so he was exactly the right person to serve as a focus. It was only because Bodera asked it that the other rebels listened to my ideas."

"Then he is the leader of the rebels?" I asked.

Brydda sighed. "No single person is the leader. That is what I am trying to tell you. But Bodera has great influence on the men who lead the various groups, and because of this, he was able to get the rebels to accept me as a sort of roving over-seer whose task is to bring everyone together long enough to fight the Council. But it has been an uphill battle. And when Bodera dies, it is very possible the whole thing will fall apart."

"Is he so old, then?" I asked, fascinated by this glimpse into rebel affairs.

"Old, yes, but it is not age that kills him. He has a peculiar slow form of the rotting sickness contracted when he was a boy on Councilfarms. In those days, they sent children with their parents if they were charged with sedition, rather than sending them off to orphan homes."

From my own experiences in the orphan home system, I knew children mined whitestick, a poisonous residue of the Great White. In its raw state, the substance had to touch the skin in order to transmit its poisons, and we had been given gloves to collect it. Sometimes I still woke at night sweating because I had dreamed of touching it by accident, as so many orphans did.

Once collected, whitestick was sent to the Councilfarms where it was treated to strip away the poisons so that it could be used in medicines and as a power source. The transfor-mation of whitestick was dangerous, because during the process, it emitted the poisons that, over time, caused the dreaded rotting sickness. This was why a long Councilfarm sentence was, in effect, a delayed death sentence.

Brydda blinked, searching for the tail of his narrative. "I have convinced Bodera of the need for an alliance with your people. But the leaders of the two largest rebel groups reject you."

"Do they give reasons?"

Brydda ran a huge hand through tousled curls. "You come to the heart of my reluctance to present you with the matter. Of the two who oppose you utterly, the first is Tardis, who runs the rebel organization in Murmroth. He has taken over recently from his father, who was a stiff-necked bigot. Tardis responded to the proposal of an alliance between rebel and Talented Misfit forces with predictable repugnance. He wrote that, Talent or no, Misfits are not true humans and he will not make an alliance with mutants. The one bright note is that, unlike his father, Tardis does not favor wholesale extermination of your people. His note said that we do not make contracts with cows or horses, and neither do we kill them for being less than human." He smiled wryly. "I am afraid Tardis regards your ability to communicate with animals as further proof of your inhumanity."

"And the other rebel leader?" I asked quietly.

"Malik. He is based in Guanette and runs most of the rebel groups in the upper lowlands and around the Gelfort Range." Brydda's voice held a flatness that told me he disliked this man. "He is more violent than Tardis in his rejection of Misfits. He thinks you are freaks and should be eradicated like poisonweed in a kitchen garden.

"There are others who oppose you, too, but they might be argued around. If not, they are less important. Tardis and Malik are the keys. Without them, there will be no rebellion."

Brydda tugged at his beard, a familiar signal of his inner disturbance.

"Then there is to be no alliance?" I strove to sound undeterred.

Brydda sat forward in his seat in sudden agitation. "Do not think that! It is the very reason I have hesitated to tell Domick what has been happening. There is always hope."

"What hope?" I demanded. "That boy you had guarding the safe house reacted like I was poison because he thought I was a *gypsy*. How is he going to react when he knows I am a Misfit? We can't make your people accept us."

With a wave of bitterness, I wondered what hope there was for Misfits to ever live normal lives if even our own allies thought of us as freaks. If we did trick them into standing beside us in battle, what would it ultimately achieve? Not the acceptance we dreamed of. And how long would it take before loathing tolerance became hatred and, once again, persecution?

"There is hope in gaining Bodera's support of you," Brydda insisted. "And there is always the possibility that we can change the minds of the other rebels. One of the main problems is that the rebels still think all Misfits are shambling mental defectives. Second," he said swiftly, forestalling my outrage, "your youth has convinced them that there would be no military gain in an alliance with you."

"And in the face of this, you can say that there is hope?" I asked incredulously.

"I believe so," Brydda reiterated firmly. "The first thing is to make my comrades think of you as human beings."

"A simple matter."

Brydda ignored that. "I think you should meet with them."

"Rushton already did that, and it was obviously no use."

He patted my arm. "I meant you specifically, Elspeth. Rushton was introduced to them as your leader, but the rebels think of him as your keeper, as if you were a troupe of trained bears. I think they need to meet a real Talented Misfit."

"To what end?" I snapped. "Would you parade a freak before them to confirm their prejudices?"

The rebel shook his head. "I would have them meet and speak with a lovely young woman gifted with remarkable abilities. Not a mutated monster. I have not dared explain Misfit abilities in much detail, because they would only increase your monstrosity in the rebels' eyes. But if they could meet you and accept you, then we could show them what you can do. After that, your age will not matter, I warrant."

I sighed. He was right. It was worth a try, only because the alternative was too bleak to contemplate. "When would such a meeting take place?"

Brydda's eyes sparkled. "There is to be a meeting of the rebel leaders soon. The day is not yet set, but it would be within a sevenday."

I felt a sick thrill of nervousness. "Where?"

"It must be held outside Sutrium," the rebel said promptly. He looked over his shoulder at Idris, who, though silent, had stood close to Brydda throughout our conversation.

The boy nodded, and Brydda reached out to ruffle his hair. In the wordlessness of this exchange, I saw the depth of the friendship between the pair.

"It is my strict policy to keep the locations of rebel meetings secret until the last minute so they cannot be revealed to anyone." The big man shifted forward in his eagerness. "Think of it, Elspeth—all you need to do is convince one or two rebel leaders to regard you as human. At the worst, it will be a positive beginning."

I thought it more likely such a meeting would simply confirm the rebels' prejudices. People had a way of seeing what they wanted to. And in spite of all Brydda's precautions and countermeasures, the big man had said there was a possibility of a traitor being in the rebels' midst. Which meant a definite risk.

On the other hand, if by some slim chance he was right and I did manage to change the rebels' attitude toward us, the risk would be a small price to pay.

"I will send word to Obernewtyn to see if the guildmerge will condone this meeting."

Brydda frowned. "I am not sure there will be enough time to send for approval. It is a great pity you have no birds here."

Idris smiled at my expression of bewilderment. "We have learned that if some birds are raised in a certain place, they will return to that place unerringly, no matter how far away they are released. Each of the rebel groups now raises birds, and we exchange them so that we always have the means to send messages swiftly. These are carried in tiny cylinders fastened to a bird's leg. It was done this way in the Beforetime."

Brydda slapped his leg. "But wait! You would not need a homing bird, Elspeth. You could simply beastspeak your message to a bird and ask it to fly to Obernewtyn."

· Before I could respond, the door burst open behind us.

Brydda whirled, drawing his knife in one smooth-flowing movement and landing in a crouch. Idris had just as swiftly taken a sword from his belt.

It was only the seaman, Reuvan, whom I had met before in Aborium. His handsome face was red from exertion, and he was so intent upon delivering his message that he did not notice me or Domick. "There is a drunk in an inn who claims Salamander is in Sutrium," he panted.

Idris was at the edge of my vision, and I was startled to see his pleasant features twist in a spasm of hatred.

Brydda slid his knife home and turned to us. "I am sorry

to cut short our supper, but I must go at once. I will come to you soon at the safe house, and we will talk again. But think on what I have said, Elspeth. The only hope of an alliance rests with your being able to alter the way rebels see Misfits. A meeting may be the only means of achieving that."

A moment later, we were outside in the dark, alone.

"Who is Salamander?" I asked Domick.

"It is the name of the man who runs the slave trade," Domick said. His tone was stiff. "Why didn't you tell me you were here to find out about the alliance? Doesn't Rushton trust me now? Has he sent you to check up on me?"

I shook my head helplessly.

✦ 11 ✦

I WOKE NEAR dawn to the muted sound of rain falling. The air felt clammy, and I wondered what had disturbed me.

I let my thoughts drift and had the fleeting impression of an unfamiliar mind touching mine as lightly as the shadow of an intruder might fall on a sleeping form. I then realized Maruman's mind was curled up around mine and gently extricated myself. I wondered if I'd simply mistaken Maruman's presence for something else.

The door opened and Kella peered in, holding a lantern high.

"What's wrong?" I asked, sitting up.

Maruman stirred on my pillow and opened his golden eye. I had the odd impression that he had been awake all along.

"It's the gypsy," the healer said softly so as not to disturb Dragon. "She woke me screaming."

I jumped out of bed and pulled a thick shawl around my shoulders.

We ran along the corridor and into the healing chamber. As I approached the gypsy's bed, I saw that her eyes were open but unfocused, just as Maruman's were when he was in the midst of his mad dreams. One eye was blue and the other a mottled brown. Kneeling by the mattress, I forced myself to be calm as her queer gaze swiveled to me.

"Can she see me?" I asked.

The healer shook her head. "She's broken the sleepseal but isn't really awake. She's having some sort of nightmare, but her system won't be able to take the strain for long."

"She's going to die?"

"If this goes on, yes. I need to get into her mind to relieve some of the pressure, but as a healer, I can't work against her will, and her mind is refusing me access." Kella's eyes narrowed. "*You* could get into her mind through her subconscious."

I looked down at the gypsy and felt a ripple of unease at her steady regard. "And do what?"

"Wake her," Kella said. "I'll do the rest."

I licked my lips. They felt dry and rough.

The subconscious could not be shielded, so if I did as Kella wanted, the deepest thoughts and desires that formed the basis of the gypsy's character would be laid bare to me in all their seething disorder. We had agreed unanimously in guild-merge that we could establish no system of dealing with the unTalented until they regarded us as equals. As long as they saw us as freaks, we could not afford to have any scruples about using our coercive abilities to plunder their minds and use what we found there against them. It was war, Rushton had said, and we must win before making terms.

Yet this gypsy was not my enemy, and the thought of entering her undermind filled me with revulsion. My reaction was emotional and instinctive. When I had first been sent to Obernewtyn, Ariel and his masters had invaded my mind using a coercive machine. My only defense had been to enter into a partial mindbond with Rushton and use his latent abilities to strengthen me and shield my mind from their torture. Such a bond had meant a kind of mental nakedness, the thought of which even now made me tremble. Rushton had not abused the mindbond by blending entirely as bondmates might, but the affair had left us uncomfortable, intimate strangers, and me with an abiding dislike of mindbonds.

"Elspeth," the healer murmured, drawing me out of my thoughts. "I know this is hard for you, but healers enter unconscious minds all the time and do not regard it as a violation. It's simply a matter of not absorbing while you are in there—of separating yourself mentally."

I ground my teeth together. She was making a good point. To enter for healing purposes was hardly a brutal invasion. And in doing so, I would be saving Obernewtyn—and myself, if the gypsy could help with Maryon's second prediction.

Steeling myself, I leaned closer to the gypsy.

"Do you hear me?" I asked aloud, still reluctant to begin. She made no response, either by word or gesture, to indicate she heard what I was saying. I sighed. "All right. I'll deep-probe her and bring her out if I can."

I closed my eyes and extended a probe delicately toward the gypsy. My mind butted gently against her shield, then slid down the outside of it, seeking the point at which it would dissolve in the maelstrom of the subconscious.

I was astonished to find the shielding continued right down into the subconscious. I quested against it. It was definitely the sort of shield unTalented minds produced naturally, but it had been somehow displaced from the upper levels of the gypsy's mind. It was scarred and buckled, and I began pushing coercively, testing until I found a weak place where I could enter.

Almost immediately, I came upon a wall of forgetting. Again, this was not usually found at a subconscious level.

The wall was eroded and had fused in places with the mindshield. This suggested the original forgetting established by the mind had begun to give way, allowing whatever had been repressed by it to rise to the conscious level. From what I could see, the gypsy's mind had reacted instinctively to protect itself, collapsing its shield on top of the memory in an effort to bury it. Obviously, this had worked for a time, though it had left her unconscious. Now the memory had begun to erode the fused barrier made up of wall and shield, causing the fit that had so alarmed Kella.

Curious, I pressed myself lightly against the fused barrier, wondering at its strength. It was paper-thin, and before I could stop myself, I had slipped through into . . .

. . . a small room. I/we are alone. My/our hands and legs bound tightly. I/we cringe at the sound of Caldeko's screams. What are they doing to you, my love?

The Herder and the boy are bringing me/us to him now. Showing him to me/us. The thing that was once Caldeko is barely recognizable as human. The mindless keening that rises from it fills me/us with horror/fear.

Caldeko opens his eyes. His soul reaches out of them to me/us, begging for release.

The Herder smiles coldly. "Tell me about the Twenty-families."

(How does he know?) I/we shake my/our head but I/we are afraid. (Block)

He waves his hand at the boy, who has a brand.

Caldeko's shrieks fill my mind. Split me open.

I/we scream and struggle to reach him.

"Tell me his given name," the Herder says.

I/we dare not speak. Must not. But Caldeko is my/our soul's joy! I must answer.

Caldeko is suddenly silent.

"Fool," the Herder snarls at the boy, "you have killed him. If she will not speak to save her bondmate pain, she will never speak to save herself. Well, we will make her an example. . . .

Caldeko/beloved is gone in terrible agony because I/we would not speak.

The pain of the tearing/the guilt/the grief is unbearable. I/we push it down into the darkness, because I/we cannot exist with it burning at me.

I/we make a wall of forgetting to bind it.

Peace.

Now I am at the stake. My arms are cut and bound. I am to die. I do not fear. I go to join my beloved. But, oh, the thought of Caldeko gives the memory/the monster life, and it rises to savage me. (I betrayed/I failed)

I panic and reach. Again I have it trapped, but the new barrier is flimsy. It will not last long. No matter. Soon the flames will come, and it will be ended.

But they do not come. I live. There is only one escape. Now I must go down and down into the deepest darkness. But something opposes . . . me. . . . Everything . . . slows . . . down. . . . I . . . am . . . weak. . . . But . . . I . . . fight them and now, now it is easier. Soon it will be over.

The spiral begins. I go down. I want to go to escape the memories (I failed to speak/I betrayed/he died/I killed him).

I fall. I dive.

I hear the song. Death sings my name.

I felt myself pulled down, dragged with the gypsy woman in her search for death. I fought against her, struggling frantically to disentangle our minds. We were too deep. I sensed the humming magnetism of the mindstream, which offered the oblivion she sought.

Desperate, I drew on the dark strength of the violent power at the depth of my mind to tear us free from the pull of the mindstream.

I wrenched us away into . . .

. . . a pale shining room. She/we are looking at a man with skin as black and polished as an old tree root. He wears odd clothing. His eyes are frightened. He takes her/us by the shoulders and shakes her/us hard.

"We have no choice, Emma," he whispers. "We have to escape. Their actions have already set it all in motion."

"But if what Cassandra foresaw is to happen, we will give them what they seek," she/we say.

"She said one of our number will give in. One will reveal what we have kept hidden. But it need not be you or me. We can escape."

Emma/we opens her/our mouth. "But where can we go? There will be radiation sickness when it comes—better to die at once."

"There are places that won't be hit so badly, where humanity will go on. We will join them. But Cassandra said we must make sure no one ever knows about us or what we can do."

"Oh God, why? Tell me why this has to happen?" Emma/we cry hysterically.

The man squeezes her/our arm awkwardly, as if he is not used to such gestures. "I don't know. Come with the rest of us. We're going to the Reichler Clinic first. Hannah and Jacob believe the mountains will be safe. . . .

. . . The mindstream tugged, dragging me/us free, pulling me/us down. . . .

A familiar voice called to me, harsh and intrusive.

"ElspethInnle! Remember your promise. You must live to come when the oldOne calls!"

It was Maruman.

"How are you here?" I asked dreamily, drifting downward, mesmerized by the shimmering siren call of the mindstream.

"You must not go down any more. Stop!" he sent urgently. I felt a searing pain on my hand, and I suddenly realized that I was on the verge of sharing the gypsy's suicide.

I fought to free myself, but again Maruman spoke. "Bring the funaga. Bring her, for she is needed."

I reached back and dragged the gypsy up with me. She screamed in fury and fought me. I drew again on the murderous power hidden in my mind for the strength to reject the mindstream. I gripped her tighter still. I could not hold her so close and remain separate. Our minds merged again. . . .

Something is holding/pulling. I am caught/something makes me live/stay/suffer.

Let me go. Let me die. I cannot bear it.

WHO ARE YOU?

I screamed and opened my eyes.

"Elspeth!" Kella was shaking me, white to the lips.

"What?" I felt dazed, confused, shattered. My mind churned with grief and guilt. Disjointed, impossible memories seethed in me. And my hand! Blood welled from three savage slashes across my palm.

"What happened?" the healer demanded. "One minute you were sitting there calmly, and the next you started to convulse. I thought . . ." She sank down on the edge of the gypsy's bed. "Lud, but you scared me!"

"I scared myself," I said shakily, pushing the heaviness of my unbraided hair from my face. I felt hot and cold at the same time, and my hands were trembling uncontrollably. I dabbed at the blood.

"Maruman scratched you," Kella said. "He climbed onto your lap when you were in the gypsy's mind, and when you started to shudder and groan, he scratched you. He must have been frightened. I . . . I slapped him, and he ran out."

"He saved my life," I murmured. "I had gone too deep, but he brought me out of it."

"Oh no," Kella said, aghast. "And I slapped him!"

There was a small moan from the bed, and I turned to look at the gypsy. Her eyes were open still, but tears now coursed down her cheeks. Her expression was aware, anguished. "What have I done?" she whispered hoarsely.

"It doesn't matter," I said wearily. "Everything will be okay now."

The gypsy buried her face in her hands. "Doesn't matter? You don't know. You can't imagine . . ."

Her eyes glazed over, and her eyelids shut. I looked up to see Kella frowning in concentration. "I've put her back to sleep. It's just a light sleepseal—not like the one Roland put on her whole body. She is out of immediate danger but still terribly weak. I have closed her wounds and hastened the healing, and her body is responding. What on earth happened?"

I took a deep shuddering breath and looked down at the gypsy. There seemed no connection between the tempestuous, desperate will I had encountered inside her mind and this passive form.

"She had locked a memory behind a wall of forgetting, but it was leaking all over the place. She was trying to die so as to escape it. Roland's seal slowed her down, but she broke through. I was testing the wall, but I had neglected to erect a separating shield around myself. Our minds merged."

Kella's eyes widened. "And?"

"I relived the memory she was trying to escape. The Herder we rescued her from had tortured and killed her bondmate in front of her to make her tell him the name of some Twentyfamilies gypsy. She refused to speak. When her bondmate died, she was convinced she had betrayed him."

I felt a surge of sorrow for the loss of a man I had never known, a residue of the accidental joining. "She thinks if she had talked, he would have lived." I shook my head sadly. "But the man was on the verge of death before they brought her in. I don't think he even knew what was happening."

The healer was ashen. "Monsters," she whispered. "They are monsters to be capable of such barbarism." Kella bent to draw the covers up around the gypsy. Abruptly, I remembered the odd sideways shunt that had hurled me into the depths of the gypsy's mind and into one of the racial memories that Maryon said arose occasionally from the mindstream like bubbles. The memory was already blurred at the edges like a dream, and even as I groped for detail, it dissolved.

But I did remember one thing. There had been something in the dream about the Reichler Clinic.

I shook my head. The foray into the gypsy's mind had drained me, and my wits drifted with weariness. The previous day and night seemed to have been going on for years.

Kella washed the scratches Maruman had inflicted,

worrying all the while about her treatment of him.

"He will understand," I said. We went into the kitchen, and I took a poker and stirred to life the embers of the previous night's fire.

"Domick told me you met with Brydda last night," Kella said, hanging up a jug of mead to warm.

I nodded. Domick had spoken little on the journey back to the safe house, furious at the lack of faith Rushton had demonstrated in sending me to speak with Brydda directly. And though Brydda had accepted the blame for the lack of news, I still felt uneasy with Domick since seeing how much he had changed.

"Greetings, ElspethInnle." Maruman was sitting under the table, his yellow eye glinting. "I am glad you did not take the longsleep."

"You saved me."

"Of course," he sent complacently. "Maruman guards the dreamtrails."

"Elspeth?" Kella prompted, unaware of my exchange with the cat.

"I'm sorry. What did you say?"

"I said surely there is no hurry to return the gypsy to her people, now that she has wakened. You will be able to wait until she recovers completely."

I sighed. "It is more complicated than that. I did not want to worry you, but Maryon has futuretold that we must return the gypsy to her people in a matter of days. Otherwise, Obernewtyn may be in great peril."

She was aghast. "But that is impossible!"

"I meant to ask Brydda about the best way to do it, but I didn't get the chance. I'll find a way."

"That's not what I meant," said Kella. "You cannot move

114

her. Her system has undergone a terrible shock, and she was already weak. She needs to be allowed to rest. . . ."

"There is no time," I snapped.

"Then she has even less time, for you will kill her if you move her in the next couple of days." There was a deep crease between the healer's eyebrows. "Does she have no rights of her own, Elspeth? Is Obernewtyn more important than her life?"

I bit my lip in sudden shame. I had not thought of the gypsy at all, only of myself and Obernewtyn. I felt sick. "You are right," I said. "I will not move her until you say it is safe. But, Lud, pray it is soon."

Kella's face softened. "I did not mean to criticize you. After all, it is not for yourself but for Obernewtyn that you fear." I flushed but held my tongue. "In any case, you cannot return her until you find her people. That is your task, and mine is to heal her. I'll do my very best to have her well enough to be shifted before the days are up," she vowed, squeezing my hand.

Just then, Dragon came in, and I was glad of the distraction. Her face and hands were unusually clean and her hair roughly braided. Her beauty struck me anew, and from Kella's expression, she felt the same.

"Hungry," Dragon said.

My stomach chimed in agreement. Kella laughed and rose to carve some slices of bread and cheese. My mouth watered as she toasted them; then for a time there was silence as we ate. Kella did not join us but fed crumbs of cheese to Maruman as an apology. He sent to me that he felt no ill will for the slap she had administered, but he accepted her offerings with feline fastidiousness, seeing she needed the reassurance.

"Good," Dragon announced at last, patting her distended stomach. Then she gave me an anxious look. "Dragon stay?"

"I suppose you must, but you're an awful nuisance," I sighed.

"Nuisance," she echoed with an identical sigh.

I stifled a grin and put my arm around her. "Dragon, I'm going to let you stay, but only if you promise to do exactly as you are told."

"Promise," she agreed after some thought. "Promise and stay."

"Is Domick still asleep?" I asked Kella.

At once the strained look returned to her eyes. "He went early to the Councilcourt."

I nodded and looked into the fire, reflecting on his behavior at The Good Egg. Kella would be a great deal more worried if she understood more about what Domick did when he was not with her.

I wondered how the healer, with her horror of torture, would respond to the knowledge that people thought her bondmate a Council torturer. My own wild fear, that the rumors had been true, now seemed absurd in light of what I'd seen in the gypsy's memory. No Misfit could stoop to that, not even a coercer.

Then Ariel's lovely, vicious face floated into my mind, giving lie to that certainty. But I thrust it away. Domick was no Ariel.

Only then did it occur to me that Domick had still not told me what he did now at the Councilcourt.

✦ 12 ✦

"Do you understand me/ElspethInnle, who stands before you?" I sent, framing the thought carefully.

The bird tilted its head and eyed me, but I could sense no thought from it other than an instinct to eat and a subliminal memory of flight that filled me with restlessness.

"Well? Are you buying the creature or communing with it?" the stallholder demanded.

Resignedly, I handed him a coin, and he passed over the cage. "You must be starting up a breeding pen with all them birds you keep buying. Store them in your wagon, do you, boy?"

I took the cage and turned away, ignoring him.

"You found one?" Kella whispered eagerly, coming over from another stall.

I shook my head. "I can't get any sense out of it."

The healer stared at me. "Oh, Elspeth! Are we going to free this one like all the others?"

"What else?" I asked in a disgruntled voice.

Brydda's suggestion of using a bird as a messenger had seemed a marvelous one. It was always easier to communicate with tamed or partly tame animals, so I had decided to search the numerous markets for a captive bird that would agree to carry a message to Obernewtyn. This search would also give me the opportunity to randomly probe a large number of people for information about gypsies.

I found an astonishing amount of Herder-induced superstition and wild surmise but very little real information. Landfolk despised all gypsies but hated and envied the Twenty-families with a passion that surprised me.

Kella had accompanied me to the market to replenish her supply of herbs, leaving a disgruntled Matthew to watch Dragon and the gypsy, but she had lingered, drawn into my search for a messenger bird. In many ways, she was of more use here than I, for I had quickly discovered that the birds available in the market were not sentient in the way that Maruman or Gahltha were; they used a mode of communication closer to empathy than farseeking. I was able to receive only the vaguest images from their minds. Kella was able to use her slight secondary empathic ability to muster some response from them, but it hadn't been enough to convey what we needed.

Those few who were able to comprehend farsought speech seemed to have no grasp of time and had very short attention spans.

However, having felt, even dimly, a bird's longing for freedom, I had not been able to leave it caged. So far, I had purchased fifteen of the wretched creatures and set them free, running our store of coin dangerously low.

Kella made a strangled noise, and I thought it a sign of frustration.

Then I realized she was trying not to laugh.

I sighed, wondering why I was still trying, when it had been perfectly obvious for some time that the idea was doomed. After trying so many, I was beginning to believe that the Agyllians had the only avian minds capable of full communication with humans.

"I'm sorry for laughing," she said contritely.

"It's good to hear laughter," I said. "It helps me to forget Maryon's deadline and that I must make some reply to Brydda, when he comes, as to whether I will meet with the other rebel leaders. Since these birds will not lend themselves as messengers to carry word to Obernewtyn, I will have to make the decision myself."

"Domick will have sent a message off this morning," Kella said.

"Nevertheless, it will take too long to arrive to give me any direction. I will be back at Obernewtyn by the time it gets there."

And perhaps I will return only to die before the next Days of Rain. The thought crept insidiously into my mind.

I wished I'd had the chance to tell Brydda about the gypsy and ask his advice. Lud only knew how long it would take him to call on the safe house. I racked my brain for some sensible way to find the gypsy's people, but nothing came to me other than finding out where they set their wagons up in the city and going among them. The other obvious alternative was to have Kella waken the gypsy again so I could ask her. But I was reluctant to do that. I still felt a twinge of shame at the selfishness of my attitude toward the gypsy. Let her waken when she would.

Maneuvering the cage through the market throng, I noticed a ragged gypsy lad trying to sell something to a stallholder; a halfbreed, as evidenced by his poverty, the lad was clearly receiving short shrift from the trader and departed finally with a doleful expression.

If I could coerce some general information out of this gypsy about his people, I would be able to face any number of them without quaking in my boots for fear that I was about to give myself away as an impostor. It was odd how blithely I had gone about pretending to be a gypsy, when I thought I knew all that needed knowing about them. Now, awareness of my ignorance terrified me. Swiftly, I shaped a light probe and sent it after the lad.

The probe slid away from his mind, blocked by a natural shield.

"Damn," I muttered, withdrawing.

The Teknoguildmaster, Garth, had a theory that normal people were developing unconscious shields that keep us from reading them. Even back in my days in the orphan homes, I had known there were unTalented people with natural mindshields that kept me out or mind sensitivity that warned them if they were being read.

I did not like the idea that such natural defenses were developing in response to and alongside our own abilities. Not just because it would make our work more difficult, but because it would put paid to the theory that Talented Misfits were simply the next step in human evolution. It would mean instead that we were simply *one* strand in human evolution and the unTalents another. That practically brought us back to the Herder theory that Misfits were mutant deviations from "true" humanity.

"The poor thing," Kella murmured, her eyes following the gypsy lad. "They are not allowed to farm or settle, and no one wants to buy from them. No wonder they take to thievery. What else are they supposed to do?"

I thought again of our gypsy and of the whole question of half and pureblood. She was a halfbreed, but she had let her bondmate suffer torture rather than speak the name of a Twenty-families gypsy. Yet Domick had told me with absolute conviction that Twentyfamilies were estranged from halfbreeds.

I scowled. For a moment, I forgot my guilt and indulged anger instead. I had saved the gypsy from the Herder flame only to see her attempt suicide—and draw me with her! Even if I had broken free and let her go, her death would have meant my own if the futuretelling was true. It angered me that my life should hinge on a woman who valued her life not at all.

"Does it have to be a bird?" Kella asked.

I blinked at her, having lost the thread of the conversation.

"Does it have to be a bird you use as a messenger?" she reiterated.

"Any other animal would move too slowly and would be as vulnerable on the ground as a human messenger," I said. "I might just as well send Matthew."

"Gypsy pig!" a man hissed as I brushed past him.

I ignored him, but Kella paled. Belatedly, it occurred to me that I was endangering the healer by being with her. There was a definite antagonism in the eyes of anyone who looked at me. The Herders' slur campaign against gypsies had been more than effective.

The sooner we got back to the safe house, the better.

Gahltha whinnied softly as we approached the public holding yard, and in spite of my tensions, I smiled at the sight of him. I had asked Dragon to dirty him, and the empath had surpassed herself. His coat was so matted and filthy that it was impossible to tell his color, and he smelled truly disgusting. For once, there had been no need to worry about leaving him alone since he looked and smelled far too disreputable to be worth stealing.

"Is the bird/sahric useful/capable?" Gahltha inquired politely. *Sahric* meant "those who sing." I noted the coolness in his mental voice and realized he had not forgiven me for going to The Good Egg without him the previous night. I had promised not to do it again, knowing he felt his guardianship to be a sacred trust from Atthis, but clearly he still felt slighted.

"I'm afraid this bird/sahric is no more capable of hearing me than any of the others," I sent, looking glumly at the cage.

I mounted him and then offered my spare hand to Kella. She wrinkled her nose in distaste and volunteered to walk.

Suddenly, her eyes shifted to something beyond me, her smile vanishing.

"What is it?" I resisted the urge to swing around and look for myself.

"That gypsy who was watching us before. He's on the other side of the holding yard on a horse. I'm sure he is following us."

I forced myself to be calm and think. Mistakes were made when people panicked.

"Are you sure it is the same gypsy?" I asked at last. Kella was easily agitated and much given to morose reflections. When she had first claimed a gypsy was watching us, I had dismissed it as overactive imagination. Gypsies were too much on both our minds.

"I was sure before and am surer now. He is looking directly at us," the healer said forcefully. She looked near to fainting.

"Perhaps I should beastspeak his horse and ask it to tip him on his head," I said. As I had hoped, her fear evaporated into concern at my flippancy.

"Be serious, Elspeth. He has obviously followed us

through the market, and he might now follow us to the safe house."

"He probably follows us because he finds you attractive," I said robustly.

She colored. "But I . . . I . . ."

"Oh, never mind. I won't tell Domick you have been flirting with gypsies. Or perhaps I will, since he neglects you disgracefully."

Her color deepened and then fled. "Oh, Elspeth, he's coming around this way! I'm sure he's trying to see your face."

My heart bumped against my breast, but I kept my voice calm for the healer's sake. She sounded on the verge of hysteria. "This is what we are going to do," I said. "You are going to go back into the market and pretend to shop. If the gypsy follows you, I will ask his horse to drop him on his head. If he follows me, Gahltha and I will lead him out of the city and give him a run for his troubles. Either way, stay at the market a little while and then make your way carefully back to the safe house."

Kella nodded, eyes wide and frightened.

I handed the birdcage down to her. "Take this."

She took it and moved off as I had bid. I waved, turning my head slightly and scanning the area with peripheral vision.

Sure enough, he was there—the same tall, rangy gypsy in costly blue silk that Kella had pointed out earlier. I was puzzled. What reason could he have for his interest in us, other than the slight curiosity value of a halfbreed gypsy boy walking with a Landgirl? He did not fit the description of the gypsy Matthew had seen leaving Guanette. And that would have been odd in any case, since in Guanette he would have seen a girl when now I was disguised as a boy.

From the corner of my eye, I studied him. His dark hair was bound back in a plait, and the band of fabric about his brow was stained to match his shirt. Kella had said the elaborate and expensive garments marked him as Twenty-families, but this did not seem conclusive evidence to me. After all, a halfbreed gypsy might be vain enough to spend his coin on such things.

I pretended to adjust my trousers, watching to see if he followed the healer. Sitting astride his gray horse, he stared intently after her. But as she walked off, his eyes moved toward me.

I pretended to spur Gahltha. "Head out of the city."

The black horse wheeled, and after a moment, I looked back as if I had remembered something to say to Kella. Seeing her gone, I shrugged and turned forward casually, but my heart was beating wildly. "He's right behind us," I sent.

"The gray equine ridden by this funaga who follows is named Sendari," Gahltha sent suddenly. "He/Sendari tells that he has not been owned/ridden long by this funaga. He says this one's hands and feet are skilled and gentle."

I frowned. His ownership of many horses seemed to confirm Kella's surmise that our pursuer was Twentyfamilies, but it still did not tell me why he was following me.

"Does Sendari know why this funaga follows?" I asked, just in case he did.

Gahltha paused, then reported the answer to my question. "He/Sendari tells that this funaga has ridden about much in these days soonest past, but he has arrived nowhere. He has spent much time standing/idle."

Watching, I thought uneasily. *Looking for us?*

I decided to probe the gypsy and sent my mind questing, but to my frustration, I encountered yet another mental shield. Cursing, I withdrew, thinking it an odd coincidence that all three gypsy minds I had tried to enter possessed natural mindshields. Garth's theory that more unTalents were developing mindshields was beginning to look as if it might be true.

I was indecisive. There was no subtle way to find out the gypsy's motives. His natural shield would prevent my coercing him except at a subconscious level, and there would be no gain in that. I could ask him outright what he was doing, but I would have no way of coercing the memory of our meeting from him.

"Let's lose him," I sent to Gahltha. Obedient, he broke into a fast canter along a road leading toward the farmlands east of the city.

I could hear the clatter of hooves behind me, but Gahltha did not increase his pace, saying it would confuse Sendari's rider if we behaved as if we were being followed. He was right, for the gypsy made no attempt to overtake us but rode at a distance.

Only when we reached the edge of the outlying farmlands surrounding Sutrium did Gahltha break into a full gallop, and I flattened myself to reduce wind resistance, thrilling to the race.

"He/Sendari follows," he sent.

"Can you outrun him?"

"There is no need," the black horse sent, with a faint echo of his old haughtiness. "Only the funaga race one another for no reason. Equines race for mate or lifesaving. Sendari knows that you are Innle. He will do what is needed."

I was discomforted by the thought that the gray horse would let us get away because he believed I was a figure from beastlegend. I had tried endless times to convince Gahltha I was not their heroic savior. It was enough that the Agyllians had incorporated me into their dreams and futuretellings without finding the animals were trying to do the same thing.

We rode swiftly along the dirt road; then, without warning, Gahltha turned sharply, cutting across a long, sloping grass plain. I clung tightly in case he stumbled on the rough tussocky ground, leaving it to him to decide how to proceed.

Looking ahead, I saw that he was making for a thick copse farther up the slope. He slowed only fractionally as we entered the trees, and in moments, we thundered out the other side of the stand onto open ground.

A rush of exaltation filled me as the ground blurred beneath us, and I gave a wild cry as we crested the hill.

Glancing back over my shoulder, I saw that the gray had fallen into a limping walk, just short of the copse. Even as I watched, his rider dismounted.

"He/Sendari has pretended lameness," Gahltha reported, coming to a halt, too.

I saw the rider kneel to examine the leg and was impressed. Most men would have lashed their mount half to death rather than lose a quarry.

As if he sensed my thoughts, the gypsy stood and looked up to where I sat on Gahltha. I could not see his expression, but as we turned to ride away, I had a mad urge and held up my hand to wave in a cheeky salute.

The city center lay visible on the other side of the hill, and we went straight overland, jumping farm fences and hedges at a full gallop and making for a main road snaking through the hills and trees. We came out wider than I realized, for when we reached the road, we were in full view of a gate—from outside the city. There was no possibility of withdrawing without looking suspicious, for the soldierguards manning the gate were gazing at us.

My heartbeat quickened as we approached for the second time in a few days. Fortunately, it was not the same gate I had entered before.

"Papers, boy," a burly soldierguard demanded. It was an expedition rule that each of us carry papers on us at all times when we traveled away from Obernewtyn, so that was no trouble. I dug in my pocket and proffered them without a word, concentrating on reinforcing the coercive suggestion that I was a boy.

The other soldierguard stared at me narrowly, but it was not until his eyes dropped to Gahltha that I became concerned. He sauntered over and rubbed at the dried filth on the horse's coat.

"Got some white, does he, under all that muck?" he asked.

It was such a strange query that I probed his thoughts.

He was comparing Gahltha to a description that he had been given of Zade. Fortunately, Zade was smaller and had white markings on his forehead and back legs.

"All black," I said. Digging further in the soldierguard's mind, I found a description of a gypsy girl that was clearly me, and, to my horror, there was also one of Matthew and the wagon.

Word of our rescue of the gypsy in Guanette had finally reached the Council.

"Been in the highlands recentlike?" the soldierguard asked, moving around and casually taking a hold of Gahltha's rein. I told myself firmly that there was no reason to fear—Gahltha did not fit the description he had been given, and I was nothing like Matthew. Even so, my heart pounded.

"I came from Murmroth way just yesterday, and just now

from Kinraide by Rangorn," I said in a bored voice, coercing the soldierguard who eyed my papers into seeing yesterday's date on the entry stamp and a watermark from the Suggredoon ferry. I wrinkled my nose and gestured at Gahltha. "Mud keeps away the flying biters, but it smells none too good."

The two men exchanged a glance, and the one with the papers nodded. The larger soldierguard's thoughts told me he had decided that neither Gahltha nor I fitted the descriptions they had been given.

He shrugged, releasing the reins. "All right, then, boy. Get on."

I rode off, trembling with reaction, and not just because news of the incident in Guanette had reached Sutrium at last.

While in the soldierguard's mind, I had learned that the Council intended to institute a gate search for the missing gypsy and her two rescuers the very next day. Each gate would have a copy of the original Normalcy Register—which recorded each child at birth after Herder inspection—against which to check the authenticity of travelers' papers.

This told me that either they thought we were heading for Sutrium with the gypsy woman and hoped to trap us as we entered the city . . . or, worse, they knew we were here already and meant to stop us getting out.

✦ 13 ✦

IT WAS JUST on dusk as we rode into the market square along-side the safe house. I had taken a circuitous route from the city gate.

I asked Gahltha to stop and took a long careful look around the market. He moved restlessly under me, sending that his flesh itched and stank abominably and asking why we had to go so slowly.

"I have to make sure we weren't followed," I sent firmly.

He trotted into the lane leading to the wagon-repair yard without comment. I slid off his back and removed the false bit and bridle, lighting a lantern. "I'll wash/brush you down," I sent.

We walked together to the high gate leading to the grassy courtyard. At the far end of the yard was a shed where hay and oats were kept. Jaygar was a shadow grazing in the deeper darkness alongside it, and he lifted his head to greet us.

I hung the lantern from a nail and stepped into the shed to find a brush.

"Clean Gal-ta?"

I started at the voice rising from the shadowy interior of the feed shed.

"Dragon?" I called softly.

The empath-coercer emerged carrying the curry brush.

She looked even dirtier than usual, her face woebegone and tearstained.

"What are you doing here?" I asked her.

She held up the brush. "Dragon dirty Gal-ta. Dragon clean Gal-ta. Dragon waiting and waiting."

"Does Kella know where you are?"

"Kella sad," Dragon said earnestly. "Cryingcryingcrying here." She pointed to her slight breasts. "Water here." She touched one of her eyes. "Not see. Not hear Dragon."

I frowned. The empath's ability to perceive emotions was improving dramatically if she could sense inner tears. "And Matthew? Where is he?"

Dragon scowled. "Matthew say, 'Dragon go away.' Dragon go. Not need Matthew. Dragon wait here with Jaygar. Dragon loves Jaygar!"

I sent an inquiry to the roan.

"Mornir has been here since sundeath," he confirmed. "Water came from her eyes."

Dragon's tears did not surprise me. Matthew had been unremittingly cold to her since our arrival at the safe house. He was being childish, but it was a personal matter between them, and I did not wish to intervene. Better if he and Dragon resolved their own difficulties.

Poor Kella's tears were somewhat more worrisome, for her emotions were already stretched taut.

"See if you can do as good a job at cleaning Gahltha as you did in dirtying him," I told Dragon absently. "Come inside when you have finished."

She nodded and set to work with the brush, seeming glad of something to do. I was sorry for her boredom and loneliness, but perhaps she would learn from it that disobedience did not always produce what was desired.

Domick, Kella, and Matthew were in the kitchen. The Farseeker ward spotted me first.

"Thank Lud," he cried fervently, jumping to his feet. "We've been worried sick. I tried to farseek ye, but there is so much static about. Maybe it's just from all these minds crammed together, but it feels like trying to see over Blacklands or tainted ground."

"Kella said a gypsy followed you at the market," Domick interrupted. There was no sign of the previous night's anger over what he perceived as Rushton's mistrust.

I told them what had happened.

"Perhaps this gypsy simply mistook Elspeth for someone he knew," Domick said dismissively. "In any case, you lost him, and I have more important news. The Council is about to institute stringent new measures for checking papers in an attempt to catch two renegade halfbreed gypsies who set another gypsy free in Guanette, killing a Herder and two soldierguards in the process."

There was a tinge of righteousness in his tone.

"You realize this will make it more difficult for you to leave Sutrium. And as soon as you begin asking questions of gypsies, the Council or Herder Faction will hear of it, because information is as good as coin. Someone will talk, and then the gates will be nets, waiting to catch you. And the soldierguards within the city will look for you as well. There will be random street searches, and if you are wandering about . . ."

"I have no intention of wandering about," I said crisply. "Nor will I be asking indiscreet questions. If I had to, I could simply have Kella wake the gypsy woman, and she could tell me whom to contact."

To my surprise, Kella nodded easily. "If you want, I can break it now. It's only a light seal, and it will not harm her to talk."

"I do not like the idea," Domick protested. "Why not simply put her in the street before waking her? She can make her own way to her people."

Kella gave Domick a fierce look. "What if she is recognized before she has time to find them? And how will she make her way anywhere in her condition?"

"Her welfare is not our concern," he answered coldly. His eyes shifted to me again. "I don't understand why you are so determined to deliver her personally. Or why you have risked so much for her. She could report us."

"And what will she have to report?" Kella asked. "A wild story about being saved by gypsies who live inside a building in the city? In any case, she is hardly likely to march off to the Council to tell her story, is she? And since we will not be dumping her in a street, she is unlikely to be caught by them and forced to speak." She stopped abruptly, staring at her bondmate. The tension between them was fraught with unspoken angers.

"As for letting her creep away herself," I said gently, "it would be a waste. I want to find out more about the gypsies, and this will give me the perfect opportunity. Or so Maryon advised," I added.

"Maryon did?" Domick echoed, his belligerence lessening. "You did not say that the Futuretell guildmistress had spoken of this."

"Didn't I?" I asked offhandedly. I stood up and looked pointedly at Kella. "Shall we go and wake her, then, and see what she has to say?"

The healer laid a gentle hand on the gypsy's forehead.

The woman stirred almost at once and opened her eyes. I was startled anew at their queer coloring. She gave me a

132

deeply suspicious look, her heavy brows drawing together over the bridge of her nose.

"Who are you?" she rasped hoarsely. "Where am I?"

"You are in a safe house," Kella said soothingly, giving her water to moisten her throat. "You have been very ill."

The woman's head turned sideways, and she frowned up at Kella for a long moment before her odd eyes shifted back to me.

"I do not know you."

"I am a friend," I said, relieved that she had no memory of her previous brief wakening.

Her chin lifted. "I would not forget the face of a friend. Yet your voice sounds . . . familiar." She sounded as if this were more cause for suspicion than comfort. "What is this place?"

"As she said, it is a safe house."

"Whose safe house? This Landgirl's? Or yours? A gypsy girl dressed up as a boy."

"I am no more gypsy than I am a boy," I said bluntly. "I dye my skin and dress like this so as to travel unnoticed about the Land. I was traveling through Guanette when I came upon you. I stole you from a Herder who was about to roast you, and he was killed. Now the soldierguards are hunting me and you both. Your friend in the trees shot that Herder, not I, but the Council believes I did it."

Her eyes were suddenly wary. "My friend?"

"The gray-haired man who helped me get you out of Guanette," I said, bending the truth slightly.

Her eyes widened with alarm. "He helped you?"

I nodded, still narrowly skirting a direct lie. "If you tell us how to contact him, we will send him word that you are here."

Her eyes narrowed. "Where is here?"

"We are in Sutrium."

Her eyes darkened with mistrust. "You brought me all the way to Sutrium? Past the city gate and the soldierguards?"

"I hid you in our wagon."

She nodded as if such trickery were commonplace, and perhaps it was among her kind. "Why did you bring me here?"

"Why not?" I could not tell her Maryon had commanded me to bring her to Sutrium.

"Why did you help me in Guanette?"

"Perhaps because we may be of some use to each other and might even become friends."

She closed her eyes. "I have no friends."

"Then a stranger did you an unbelievable service if that gray-haired man was not a friend," I snapped.

Her eyes opened, glinting. "As you have done? If he was a friend, why would he ride off and leave me with strangers?"

I felt my cheeks redden and realized I had underestimated her intelligence. "We became separated. He rode toward Sutrium," I said less aggressively. "Look, all I want to know is how to bring you to him."

Her eyes were abruptly cool. "I do not recall asking for aid. Then or now."

"You were in no condition to ask for help then. Nevertheless, I gave it and thought you would be pleased," I added, unable to prevent irritation from seeping into my tone.

"You interfered of your own free will," she snarled. "I was not afraid to die."

"No," I agreed shortly. "You were afraid to live."

There was a flare of pain in her eyes then. "I am not afraid of anything," she said, but there was a frayed edge to her tone. I guessed she was remembering snatches of her attempt to die and wondering at her dreams, for so would she judge my communications with her subconscious mind.

Her eyes went from me to Kella and back again. "What do you want of me?"

"No more than to return you to your people." That was almost true. I tried to get into her mind again, now that she was conscious, but the block remained firm. Any further pressure and she would feel me.

"Why?" she demanded flatly. "I am no Twentyfamilies with a fat purse to reward you."

I decided to take refuge in indignation.

"You are a fugitive wanted by the soldierguards and the Herder Faction, and they are no friends of mine. I helped you and I expected no more than a little gratitude. Well, that is too high a price for your life, it seems. Instead you insult me and accuse me of sinister motives. Well, if you want to die, that is your business, but I have vowed to return you to your people, and that is what I will do. With or without your help."

There was a prickly silence.

"Help me to dress and show me a door and you will not need to trouble yourself," she said stonily.

Again she had outmaneuvered me. "No."

She nodded, as if she had anticipated the answer. "If you will not let me go, then I am your prisoner."

I thought quickly. "In your weakened state, you are bound to be picked up by the soldierguards and questioned. You would speak of us and this place. I cannot risk it."

"Who are you?" she said again, her expression openly baffled. Then she seemed to think of something and glared at me anew. "You needn't think I will tell you anything. . . ." She stopped.

"Anything about your Twentyfamilies friend?" I asked without thought. Instantly, her face changed, and my heart sank.

Angry at my own mishandling of the matter, I said bitterly, "I don't suppose you know what *swallow* means either?"

Her eyes widened in shock, the pupils swelling to devour the color. "Where . . . where did you hear that?"

My mind raced. "You said it in your sleep," I lied.

"It must have been gibberish," the gypsy said, closing her eyes again, her voice indifferent. "I do not know what it means, and I am afraid I can tell you nothing about my blood kin since I remember nothing more about myself than that I am a gypsy. If that gray-haired man you saw was a friend, I do not remember him either. Or even my name."

She was lying, but there was nothing I could do to make her speak.

"Well, perhaps in time you will remember," I said icily. "Just as I might recall why I bothered to save your life!"

I made a sign to Kella to put her back to sleep.

"Wretched, ungrateful woman," I snapped as we left the chamber.

Kella shrugged. "You can't really blame her, the way things are for halfbreeds. For all she knows, this whole thing could be an elaborate trap. You must admit it would look odd."

Which is the closest she would come to telling me I had been clumsy. I sighed and my temper faded.

"Will you try talking to her again?" Kella asked, stopping outside the kitchen door.

"I think not. If she will not be forced to speak by the torture of her bondmate, there is no way she will tell her story to a pair of strangers with no good reason for helping her," I said.

136

"Damn the woman for being so difficult. I will have to find her people the hard way."

"The hard way?"

I nodded. "I will have to go among the gypsies and probe at random people in the hope of finding some clue as to where she might safely be taken. It *must* be time for luck to work for me rather than against me. Where do gypsies camp when they stay in the city?"

Kella gave me a quick, comprehending look. "They are permitted to camp on any green, but most go to the largest green over near the Suggredoon."

"Both half and pureblood gypsies?"

She nodded, clearly troubled. "Gypsies don't think in terms of physical boundaries, so in spite of the Great Divide, Twenty-families camp alongside halfbreed wagons. But that does not happen often. Twentyfamilies gypsies come to Sutrium only in the Days of Rain, when they are to tender the yearly tithe. Other-wise they avoid cities." She hesitated. "If you go there, you might encounter the Twentyfamilies man who followed us. Perhaps you could wait a few days until they have gone."

"I dare not wait," I interrupted. "I will have to risk it."

Domick and Dragon were seated at the kitchen trestle when we entered, but Matthew had gone. No doubt he had de-parted when Dragon came in. I shook my head.

"What happened?" Domick asked.

"She will tell me nothing. I will have to go among the gyp-sies after all and see what I can winkle out."

"You must be careful," Domick said worriedly, and for a moment, he seemed like his old self. "I spoke to you of Fac-tion and Council spies, but remember, the gypsies themselves are dangerous to cross. They may value the woman, but your knowing about her makes you a risk. The best way to protect her and themselves would be to kill you. Thinking you are a gypsy might stay their hand, but if they guess for a moment you are not what you pretend to be . . ."

"I will be careful," I promised.

"Have you decided whether to meet with the rebels?" Domick asked as I ladled a mug of fement from a freshly boiled and fragrant pot.

"I have," I said. "I am going to do it. Rushton wants to know where we stand with the rebels, and this meeting will give us an answer one way or the other. As soon as it is over, we will go at once to Obernewtyn."

Domick nodded soberly. "That is best. But be careful tomorrow, for all our sakes." He rose and reached for his cloak.

"You are going out again?" I asked, surprised.

"I have to go back to the Councilcourt. There is some sort of delegation from Sador arriving tonight."

"Sador," I murmured. There had been a lot of talk about the distant province of late. A year ago, only the few seamen who plied that part of the coast had even known of it.

He nodded. "They are coming by ship. I expect they will request the removal of the Faction mission from their domain. They have been sending delegations to that effect from the first sevenday the Herders dwelt among them." He pulled on his cloak. "The Herders were sent not long after the road was opened. They are interfering in the Sadorian religion, and the Sadorians don't like it. The Earthtemple in Sador regulates how much spice is harvested, and it will allow only a small yield. It is my guess the Herders have been sent by the Council to erode the power of the Earthtemple and take it for themselves. Then they will increase the spice yield."

The coercer then departed with a perfunctory farewell that

obviously distressed Kella. I felt for her, and spoke to give her time to compose herself.

"I should alter my appearance again. I dare not go out as a girl since the soldierguards have my description. I would need to have a coercive cloak the whole time, and that's a risk. Since that Twentyfamilies gypsy saw me as a boy, I will have to think of something else. Perhaps I could remain a boy but cut off my hair. . . ."

"No!" Kella looked horrified. "It is so long and beautiful. Like black silk."

Glad to have distracted her, I was nonetheless embarrassed by her words. "I don't care about hair."

"But gypsies do," she said insistently. "They do not cut their hair—men or women."

That was true enough. I had forgotten for the moment.

"Cut?" Dragon said. She was holding a knife in her hand and looking so hopeful that both Kella and I burst into laughter.

Dragon hooted along happily.

"What's so funny?" Matthew asked lightly, coming in with his hair wet from a bath.

Dragon's laughter died, and her eyes followed the ward as he moved across the kitchen and peered into the pot.

"I hope that is not for us," he quipped, sniffing at the herbal preparation.

He could not have helped being aware of the empath-coercer's obsessive regard, but he made out that he had not noticed her.

"What about something to drink?" Kella asked Matthew. He sat down and nodded.

"And will you sit and be waited on?" I snapped, disliking

the lazy way he expected the healer to bring him his mug. He flushed and rose to help her, and I found myself thinking of him as he had been when first I came to Obernewtyn, with his thinness and his limp and his quick dark gaze. A child then, and not yet a man now, for all he looked like one.

"Dragon will drink," Dragon said, looking up at him with pathetic eagerness.

The farseeker scowled, but he filled a mug with the steaming liquid and handed it to her ungraciously. Dragon took it and drank with the solemn air of a Herder acolyte performing a sacred rite.

Matthew turned pointedly away, and I felt my temper stir. He might not relish Dragon's adoration, but there was no need for him to be so unkind. He had used all of his charm to make her obedient when he was developing her powers so that she could defend Obernewtyn, but now he was refusing to deal with what he had set in motion.

I forced my anger back, knowing Dragon would detect it if I was not more careful.

Matthew went to refill the empty pot from a stone jug on a bench, and Dragon trailed across the kitchen in his wake, drawn as if by some force she could not control. The farseeker did not notice her standing at his elbow, and when he turned back, he cannoned hard into her, sending both the full pot of fement and Dragon's mug smashing to the floorboards.

"Fer Lud's sake, ye idiot!" he exploded. "If ye'd drunk th' stuff instead of gollerin' at me like a fool, this wouldn't have happened!"

Dragon's face was white as paper. She turned and ran from the room without a word.

Matthew was left standing amidst the debris of broken

mugs and steaming fement, looking from one to the other of us. "Ye dinna understand!"

"I understand that was unnecessary," I said coldly.

He paled and ran his fingers distractedly through his hair. "Ah, Luddamn it. Yer right. I'll go an' apologize."

"Why?" Kella demanded fiercely. "She should not be surprised. More fool her for expecting anything more of you."

"Kella, I'm sorry . . . ," Matthew began, but the healer tossed her head, her blue eyes flashing.

"Don't tell me!" she said stonily. "I'm not the one you should be talking to. You don't deserve her love, Matthew. She's worth ten of you, but you're too stupid to see it."

"She's a savage," Matthew flared, stung by the disgust in her voice.

Kella laughed contemptuously. "You don't have the slightest idea who or what Dragon is, even after all these months you've spent with her. She's a lot of things, but she's no savage. Eating with fingers and having dirty clothes doesn't make a person a savage. Cruelty and thoughtlessness do. That makes *you* the only savage here."

I was amazed to hear the gentle healer speak with such passion. Matthew glared at her, then turned on his heel and stalked out. A moment later, the stair door slammed.

I felt as though a firestorm had roared its destructive way through the room.

Kella let out a great sobbing breath and sank into a chair. I crossed to sit by her and lay a tentative hand on her arm. "Dragon will be all right. It wasn't as bad as all that. . . ."

The healer shook her head. "It's not Dragon, Elspeth. Matthew was wrong, but I should not have spoken to him like that. It . . . it is Domick. You saw how he was tonight. I've tried and tried not to see, but I can't lie to myself anymore. He no longer cares for me. Sometimes I think he hates me." She looked at me with tormented eyes. "He's changed. That is why you did not tell him what Maryon said, isn't it? I know it. Of course, I know. Oh, Elspeth, I just want to go home to Obernewtyn."

She began to weep in earnest.

I stared at her helplessly. After a long minute, I crossed to the sky window and stared up. Rain fell lightly but steadily on the glass.

"Perhaps it is time for all of us to go home," I said softly to the night.

✦ 14 ✦

I sank into the hot, soapy water with a sigh.

My backside and legs ached from hours of riding about Sutrium, and I was chilled to the bone by the constant icy drizzle that had fallen.

It had been altogether a miserable and fruitless morning. I had gone to the biggest green and then to as many other greens as I could find. At each, I had tried to farseek gypsies at random—but every single one I had tried had been mentally shielded! The Twentyfamilies gypsies were even more tightly blocked than the halfbreeds. I had been forced to assume that all gypsies possessed natural mindshields, though of varying strengths.

As I had done with the gypsy woman, I could have entered any of the gypsies at a subconscious level, but there was simply no point. I would not find what I needed in their underminds.

In desperation, for by now there was no other course, I had tried talking to some gypsies clustered around a well, thinking to draw them gradually to talk of the woman who had escaped the Herder fires; but Domick had been right—they were impossibly suspicious of strangers, including gypsies who were unknown to them. I had not needed empathic Talent to be immediately aware of their hostility.

I might have kept on but for the patches of static arising

from the buildings. This had puzzled me until it came to me that the Council might be using stone from Oldtime ruins to build within the city. The amount of residual poison was not high enough to cause the rotting sickness, but having to circumvent it stole my energy. The other problem was the mysterious, stronger static given off by the sea and the Suggredoon. There were several smaller greens close enough to these to make farseeking difficult, if not impossible.

I had returned to the safe house exhausted, disheartened, and convinced the only hope of success now lay in letting the gypsy go and following her. I was not sure that would qualify as returning her to her people, or even if it would enable me to learn the meaning of the word *swallow*, but what else could I do?

Kella had interrupted my depressive account to suggest a bath. "You can't think properly when you are all tied up in knots, cold and tense and miserable."

I had been too tired to argue, though when peeling off my garments, I had wondered how I could possibly relax.

But I sank deeper in the hot water and felt some of the stiffness melt from my bones. I closed my eyes with a sigh.

My mind drifted a little, and I found myself wondering if snow had fallen in the highest valleys yet. Gahltha and I had loved to ride through the light snowfalls, scattering the powdery whiteness high.

My thoughts moved down to the valley where Obernewtyn lay, as if I rode there on Gahltha's back. I visualized the farms and orchards visible from the foothills of the higher mountains. The last crops would be readying themselves for harvest, and Alad's beastspeakers would soon be working hard.

Unbidden, the image of Rushton came to me with a queer ache.

I blinked and the image faded, leaving me to ponder what it was about Rushton that made me feel suffocated and tense whenever I was with him, and yet think of him so often when we were apart. A queer contrariness, yet it had always been that way between us. When we had met, he had been pretending to be a farm overseer at Obernewtyn, hiding his true identity from Ariel and his masters. My first sight was of him carrying a squealing, struggling piglet.

The memory made me smile, though at the time, I had feared he could somehow sense my powers and would report me. I had been no more content at his attentions than the pig! But he had not reported me, and in time we had become allies. Yet, in truth, we had never been friends.

I thought of Dragon trailing helplessly after Matthew and shuddered. Starkly, I heard the words Rushton had rasped to me once in delirium: "Elspeth, love." I had tried to rob those words of their meaning and to tell myself his emotions were latent or distorted—that he did not truly feel love but some lesser thing because of our mindbond.

But it was not true. None of it.

He loved me and I knew it. Had always known it. And I?

I became aware that my hands were trembling violently where they rested on the rim of the bathing barrel. I thrust them under the water and wrenched my mind forcibly away from Rushton.

I thought of guildmerge, and my emotions calmed.

There was something infinitely reassuring about the thought of the huge circular room lined with books where guildmerge was held. It was the heart of Obernewtyn. The memory of it was so real that I could almost smell the smoke from the fire and hear the crack of mountain pine above the hum of conversation. I seemed to feel Avra's breath tickling the hair at my neck, for the mountain mare always stood at my side during guildmerge. Sometimes she would reach down and touch her nose to Maruman, who invariably slept on my lap when not away on his travels. Other times she would nudge Alad, signaling her desire to communicate or to reproach him for failing to interpret her clearly enough.

Life at Obernewtyn revolved around the guildmerge and what it stood for: community and purpose. In contrast, Sutrium was dark and chaotic, devoid of hope or purpose. All at once, I felt a longing to be home at Obernewtyn that was as savage and powerful as a hot knife in my belly. The strength of it took my breath away.

Then the irony of it struck me just as forcibly, for I had been only too ready to leave for Sutrium. Ever had it been my way to long for Obernewtyn when I was severed from it and yet to hate it when I was there.

I blinked in surprise, seeing this was exactly how I felt about Rushton.

How strange.

But perhaps not. I loved Obernewtyn and the feeling it gave me of being part of something larger than myself, but often I felt absorbed and devoured by it as well. In many ways, I had used my secret quest to raise a barrier between Obernewtyn and my lone self. My fear of Rushton—if that was the right word for it—was the fear that giving myself to him would cause me to lose myself, that in some queer way I would be absorbed and no longer myself.

Shivering—and only partly from the chilled water—I

climbed from the barrel and toweled myself vigorously. Better to worry about what to do with the gypsy than to think of Rushton. That was a far more immediate problem.

Dressing hurriedly, I went to the kitchen. A fire had been lit, and Matthew was repairing a tear in his breeches.

Before I could speak, Kella rushed in behind me. "Dragon," she cried breathlessly. "She's gone."

Matthew jumped to his feet. "Gone? What do ye mean, gone?"

"Just what I said," Kella answered. "She refused to answer the door to her chamber this morning. I thought she needed time, so I left her. But just now I noticed that the door was open, and she wasn't in there!"

"Well, for Lud's sake," Matthew said impatiently. "She'll be downstairs with—"

Kella gave him a look of such searing fury that he flinched. "Stop telling me and let me tell you! I've checked everywhere. The horse yard, the healing hall, the bathing room, the repair shed. She's gone, I tell you."

Her eyes accused Matthew, and he paled. "It's my fault. I meant to apologize for shoutin' at her when she came out," he whispered.

"You should have gone in to her," Kella blazed. "That's the usual way to go about an apology. Or did you expect her to beg for that as well?"

"Kella . . ."

The healer swung to face me. "We have to find her!"

"Do you have any idea where she might have gone?" I asked them.

"To Obernewtyn!" Kella said at once, voicing her own longings.

"She . . . she might have gone to th' market," Matthew said hesitantly. "I . . . she's been pesterin' me since we got here to take her."

He flushed crimson under the healer's scathing look. "What are ye lookin' at me like I murdered her for?" he shouted, his highland accent thickened with anger. "I'm nowt responsible fer her. She shouldn'a be here in th' first place."

"Well, maybe you'll be lucky and she'll be killed. That would teach her obedience, wouldn't it?" hissed Kella.

Matthew whitened to the lips.

"That's enough," I said, shocked at the cruelty of her words. "The thing is to find her, not to decide whose fault it is that she's gone. Matthew, you go out and look for her on foot. I'll farseek her, and if I can't find her, I'll go out on Gahltha. Leave a channel open for me. I'll reach out to you," I said, knowing he might not be able to farseek me in the fog of static that was Sutrium.

He ducked his head and hurried out as I turned to the healer. "Have another good look around the safe house. See if she has taken anything from the chamber with her."

She nodded and ran out.

I sat down on a chair and composed my thoughts, blocking out all apprehension and shaping a probe to Dragon's mind-set. If she was near, and not on badly tainted ground, the probe would locate her.

It took less than a minute.

She was wandering through the stalls in the central trade market of the adjoining district. I fixed her position in my mind and then farsought Matthew.

"I will go there straightaway," he sent, his mind leaking emotional surges of relief and anger.

Kella came in. "She has taken nothing with her."

"She is in a market in the next district. Matthew has gone there on foot. I'll go over with Gahltha and bring her back."

"Thank Lud," Kella murmured.

I hurried along the hall and down the stairs, farseeking to Gahltha as I went. Fortunately, I was clad in boyish clothes, so there was no need for me to waste time in changing. Only the gypsy who had followed me would know me in that guise, and if I had outwitted him once, I could do it again.

Gahltha was waiting, snorting with impatience at my slowness.

"You have forgotten the coldmetal painmaker," he chided as I vaulted onto his back.

With a curse I dismounted, found a bridle in the wagon, and buckled it on him with an apology.

"Do not sorrow for forgetting the fetter, ElspethInnle. Would that all the funaga would forget. Where is the little mornir?"

I sent Gahltha an explanation as I remounted, and as soon as we were clear of the little square, he broke into a brisk trot. It had stopped raining, but the drains ran swiftly, filled to overflowing after a day and night of rain. In seconds, the chilly breeze had leached all the bath's warmth from my bones.

I resisted the urge to ask Gahltha to go faster, knowing it would attract too much attention. I could have used a coercive cloak to stop anyone noticing us, but the more obtrusive the behavior, the more energy required to hide it. The effort of cloaking a wild gallop over any distance would virtually drain my immediate energy, and I had the sudden, uneasy premonition that I was going to need my powers very soon.

I chafed at the delay, my mind filled with visions of Dragon wandering through the market with her unforgettable face and hair. If anything alarmed her, she would resort instinctively to her phenomenal power, calling up the dragonish illusions for which she had been named.

I breathed a sigh of relief as the market came into view at the street's end, but drawing nearer, I felt a stab of dismay. This was a far larger market than the one beside the safe house. If anything happened here, hundreds would witness it. The feeling of danger increased as Gahltha brought me to the perimeter of the crowds.

The empath-coercer could not have chosen a more perilous time to come to the market; late afternoons were traditionally the busiest part of the day. Hoping for a bargain, men and women shopped as late as possible, for it was well known that traders believed that a day without a sale offended Lud and that they would be punished by another poor day to follow.

I never ceased to be amazed by their paltry image of a Lud who would care for the sale of a bit of fish or a stretch of cloth.

The horse-holding yard was filled to capacity, which meant I would have to tie Gahltha to the less secure bars along the outer edge of the corral. Gritting my teeth at the delay, I led him into a side lane and scooped some mud from the bottom of a drain. I had almost finished smearing it over him when I heard footsteps.

I knelt and pretended to examine his fetlock. Peering covertly behind, I nearly fainted at the sight of a troop of soldierguards marching along the lane.

There was nothing to be done but to concentrate fiercely and produce a general coercive cloak that would stop them noticing me.

"Seems as if we ought to have more to do than play nursemaid to some Herders," grumbled one of the soldierguards at the front of the column.

"Council wants to keep them happy because of them financin' th' Sador business," another muttered.

The Herders were financing the invasion of Sador? Could it be so? Where would they come by such coin?

"More like they don't dare move against them, for fear they'll get Lud to send another plague."

"It was nothing more than coincidence that they predicted pestilence and the plague came," snapped another soldierguard. "Council'll put them in their place before long, and that'll be an end to our nursemaiding them."

"Will it? Herders have coin aplenty, so I've heard, and they ain't averse to greasin' soldierguard palms. I ain't fussy as to where coin comes from, long as I get some."

"Shut up and get a move on," called a lean, surly-looking captain at the back of the column.

Their voices faded as they passed out of the lane, and I leaned against Gahltha's noisome flank, weak-kneed with relief.

Gathering my wits, I farsought Matthew to warn him that soldierguards were in the market and possibly Herders as well. As my probe touched him, a panicky burst of images and words surged painfully into my unprepared mind.

I blocked the chaos and requested the use of his eyes. Instantly, Matthew made himself passive so that I could literally see through his eyes. It was a difficult maneuver but one we had perfected.

He was standing in the midst of a crowd of people facing one of the market speaking stones, onto which people climbed to advertise wares or make announcements. Standing

151

atop it was a Herder, his red armband marking him as one of the more important priests in the Faction hierarchy. Two brownband Herders stood on either side of the speaking stone like guards.

But none of this explained Matthew's panic.

"Look!" His voice rose in my mind. His head turned, and I saw Dragon. Standing out in the open between the crowd and the speaking stone, her blue eyes ablaze with fury, the flame-haired empath-coercer was standing protectively in front of two small children. She resembled some avenging goddess out of a Beforetime story, the sun burnishing her red-gold curls and her face glowing with unearthly loveliness.

Her mouth moved, and only then did I realize that she was shouting at the Herder priests!

✦ 15 ✦

Sᴵᴄᴋ ᴀᴛ ᴛʜᴇ magnitude of the disaster unfolding, I flung myself onto Gahltha's back, bidding him to carry me to the other side of the square. Passing through the center of a trade market on horseback was forbidden, but I used my coercive power recklessly, forcing people not to notice us and clearing a path.

I saw that the group of soldierguards had taken the easier and longer route around the perimeter of the market, and I prayed for something to delay them.

"What in Lud's name has happened?" I demanded of Matthew.

Rather than explaining, he sent a vision of a woman and the two children being manhandled by the Herders. The woman had shouted something at the redband priest and had been struck to the ground. One of the brownband Herders had grabbed at the little boy, who had screamed in terror and clung to his sister.

Dragon had flown from the crowd of watchers like a spitting fangcat defending its young, and the beleaguered Herder had retreated with alarm.

"I arrived just as it began," Matthew sent. "The priests were collecting boys to be taken and trained as acolytes on Herder Isle, and the mother refused to let them take her son." There was a pause before he continued. "The senior Herder has just told the brownbands to take both children. I'm afraid Dragon will . . . uh-oh!" Matthew sent frantically.

By now, I was close enough to hear the empath-coercer's childish voice, and I craned my neck in order to see her over the heads of the crowd. She had her arms around the two cringing children and was glaring at the approaching Herders purposefully.

"Don't," she cried in a warning voice that froze my blood. "Don't dare!"

Then she dropped into a fighting crouch she must have learned from watching the coercers train and bared her teeth at the priests.

They fell back again in astonishment, and there was a murmur of amazement from the crowd.

I could not repress a groan. Dragon would vision. I was amazed she had not done so already. I had to stop her from unleashing her incredible powers in front of so many witnesses.

"Lud preserve us," Matthew sent despairingly along the probelink between us. "Th' soldierguards are here!"

I turned. Sure enough, the troops had reached the speaking stone. Their captain was looking around, taking in the fracas at a glance.

"What is going on?" he demanded, marching up to the senior Herder. But before the Herder could answer, the captain's eyes fell on Dragon. He gaped, thunderstruck.

For a moment, I thought I saw recognition in that look, but then I realized that was impossible. Dragon had led a solitary, feral existence before coming to Obernewtyn, and she'd not left our sight since. Still, something in that look filled me with fear, and I directed a savage coercive bolt at Dragon, augmenting it with the destructive power at the depth of my mind—a power I had once used to kill but had since been able to keep in check, swearing never again to take a life. Still, I had no time to fashion a subtle arrow of it, and my probe clubbed through her shield, obliterating it and knocking her instantly unconscious.

She slumped to the ground, and the two children screamed in fright.

Their mother leapt to her feet and pulled them away from Dragon, just as the soldierguard captain stepped toward her.

Without hesitation, I stamped coercively on his will. The rough nerve control I imposed would fade swiftly, so I had little time. I sent a swift instruction to Matthew and another to Gahltha.

Immediately, the black horse reared up with an ear-shattering scream. People on all sides scattered wildly to escape the flailing hooves.

"Someone has fed my horse prickleberries!" I cried, pretending to have no control.

Gahltha rolled his eyes and bucked, lashing out with razor-sharp hooves, and the three priests dived away from the speaking stone with cries of terror, apparently convinced he was on the verge of the hysterical rage caused by ingesting the poisonous weed.

"Captain?" One of the rank-and-file soldierguards tapped his superior, and the captain stirred, for this was enough to break the trance I had imposed. He looked around; then his eyes widened in fury, and he cracked his fist into the other man's face. "Fool!" he raged. "The red-haired girl. Where is she?"

Time had run out.

"Go!" I sent, and Gahltha bolted out of the square and down a feeder lane.

155

"A gypsy youth took her!" someone cried out.

I cursed, for I had hoped no one would notice Matthew scoop up the unconscious Dragon in all the fuss.

He sent that they had taken refuge in a burned-out house. I took the location from him. They were still close to the market.

"Are you sure it's safe?"

"Safer than on the street," Matthew sent fervently. "Besides, they'll never think I'd hide so close."

I hoped he was right. "Is Dragon all right?"

"She's unconscious," Matthew said. "How in Lud's name did you—?"

"You stay put, and I'll bring Gahltha," I interrupted.

I used the last of my reserve to drop a complete coercive cloak over Gahltha and myself, wishing I had time to rest. My diversionary tactics had obliterated my coercive suggestion that I was a boy. Even thickheaded soldierguards would work out that Matthew and I were the same gypsies wanted for the murders and sedition in Guanette.

By morning, the streets would be crawling with squads combing the city for us as the gate search surged inward.

The clouds cleared from the sky, and the sun shone properly for the first time in days. Everything in the sodden city steamed as we made our way in a wide arc around the market where Dragon had confronted the Herders, and into the next district.

Coming around a blind corner, I found my way blocked by yet another of the small markets dotted throughout the city.

My first instinct was to circle it. I had had enough of markets. But it was not long until dusk, and I did not want to waste any more time. Dismounting, I took Gahltha's rein, leading him behind me.

Brushing along the aisles, my eye was caught by a table laden with swatches of colorful cloth. I stared, for I had never seen cloth dyed so brightly before.

"Sador dyes," I heard a stallholder tell a customer.

One of the pieces on the stall table was deep green, with a sheen as soft and yielding as the coat of a newborn pup. I ran a thumb over it, fascinated by the alien texture.

"Get yer dirty paws off it, ye halfbreed slattern."

I dropped the material in shock, feeling as if I had wakened from a drugged sleep. What in Lud's name had I been thinking of to stand about admiring a piece of cloth with half the city out looking for me? But I knew what was wrong: I was almost dazed with fatigue. It always happened when I used the strange power at the depth of my mind.

Now that the wretched trader had identified me as a girl, I could not make myself into a boy in his eyes, but I could stop anyone else from seeing me.

I began to back away, weaving a general coercive net, but the burly stallholder lumbered from behind his stand with unexpected speed and pushed me hard, sending me stumbling back against Gahltha's warm flank. Anger filled me, as hot and unreasoning as fire.

I choked it back, realizing too late that I had let my coercive cloak fall again. Since it worked by heightening and enhancing disinterest and inattention, there was no way I could reinstitute it with so many people goggling at me. Especially not with my energy so depleted.

"If you won't let a customer feel the cloth she might buy, I'll move on," I said pacifically, and backed away.

"Since when did halfbreeds buy when they could steal?" sneered another man, blocking the way from behind.

His skinny companion leered and stepped in my path when I tried to sidle by them. "And since when was a gypsy civil and honest at the same time?" he asked in a sinuous, high-pitched voice. "If you ask me, this one speaks too soft to be trusted. And why does a girl wear trousers, except for ease to run when she has stolen something?" He looked around at the gathering little crowd, seeking their support.

Several nodded, and I began to feel truly uneasy.

I let Gahltha's rein slip from my fingers.

"Shall I/Gahltha bolt/rear, ElspethInnle?"

"No!" Using the black horse as a diversion yet again would be as good as posting a sign saying the gypsies wanted for the market fracas were still close by. I dared not risk it with Matthew and Dragon in hiding so near.

"Find Matthew and Dragon and take them back to the safe house," I sent, giving Gahltha a mental map of their location.

"Gahltha must protect Innle," he protested.

"No! There are people here with knives and arrows, and they would think nothing of killing an equine. Obey me," I commanded. "I can take care of myself in this."

Reluctantly, Gahltha withdrew. Fortunately, no one noticed he was riderless and apparently ownerless, because all attention was riveted on me. "I think we ought to give her a good whipping just to teach her what we think of gypsy thieves," said the thin man who had stopped me from leaving. He unlaced a long whip from his belt with a practiced flick of his fingers.

Two louts cheered and offered to lay on the first stripes to show how it was done, and other people crowded nearer. I looked around and my skin broke into gooseflesh, for I had no alternative but to let myself be manhandled and whipped.

I clenched my teeth and steeled myself, invoking a coercive suggestion that the thin man should use the whip lightly. At the same time, I cursed and struggled as anyone would when the two louts grabbed me and ripped the gypsy shirt, baring my back.

"Now we'll see ye dance." The thin man laughed and flicked the whip. It whistled viciously through the air, and I screamed when it struck, though I felt nothing, for I had erected a mental barrier to postpone the pain.

I would experience the sting later, when there was no need to keep my wits about me.

The whip struck again.

"A weak blow," cried the cloth trader, and he strode out to commandeer the whip. I reached out a coercive probe to soften his blows, too, but, to my horror, he was naturally shielded.

I could not reach his mind without his knowing it—and maybe not at all in my weakened state.

"I'll show you how she dances to my music," he promised, and swung his arm as hard as he could.

The whip hissed, tearing into my skin. I felt no pain, but I screamed, writhing inwardly at the thought of the agony I would have to endure when the barrier was dissolved.

He struck again and again, with no sign of stopping. Perhaps this was the death I had been promised. Maybe Maryon had misjudged the number of days or misread her vision. Maybe my time was already up.

"Dance, gypsy! Give us a show!" cried the trader as he lifted his arm again. His lips and eyes shone with lascivious pleasure. "I thought gypsies loved to dance."

"That is so," said a caressing masculine voice, and

suddenly I was free, falling forward and grazing my knees on the cobbles.

Clutching my shredded clothing, I turned to see the dark-haired gypsy who had ridden after me the day before. This time he was on foot, and the two louts who had held me were sitting at his feet with dazed looks.

The trader gave a roar of anger and rushed forward. With lightning swiftness, the gypsy stepped aside and plucked him up by the scruff of the neck. The oaf must have weighed as much as Gahltha, yet the gypsy held him dangling in midair as if it were no effort at all.

"You have made a mistake, Littleman," he was saying to the dangling trader in a lecturing voice. "A gypsy dances as an expression of pleasure in movement or song, or for a lover. Not for moronish illbreds who would not know beauty nor grace if it bit them on the bum."

I was astounded that a lone gypsy would speak that way to Landfolk. Yet no one made a move to intervene. In fact, people began to edge away.

The stallholder was by now purple in the face and in imminent danger of suffocating, his jerkin screwed tight around his neck.

"What is that you say, Littleman?" the gypsy asked with exaggerated politeness.

"Erk!" the man squeaked, clawing at his collar.

I stifled an incredulous giggle as the gypsy put his ear to the trader's mouth. "Your pardon? You say you want to apologize to this girl? Do I hear you aright?"

The trader shook his head, then changed his mind and tried to nod.

"What was that?" The gypsy hauled him closer, drawing the cloth around the trader's neck even tighter.

"Ahhk," he gasped, batting his arms as if he were a bird about to fly away.

"You'd best put him down before you kill him," I said. The trader's eyes were rolling about in an alarming way, and his lips were blue.

The gypsy ignored me. "Ahh! Now I understand. You wish to apologize by gifting a piece of cloth to her."

"Ug," the trader said dully.

"A fine gesture," the gypsy said, opening his hand and letting the man fall in a gasping heap at his elegantly black-booted feet. "Now, what cloth was it that you wanted?"

I stared up into his bold, laughing eyes. "Uh. I don't think . . ."

"The green?" he said. "A good choice. It will suit you." He took up the cloth I had touched and held it up to my face. His knuckles brushed my cheek, and I flinched.

"You startle like an unbroken pony," he murmured.

The blood rushed to my cheeks, and he laughed, turning back to the trader, who had risen unsteadily to his feet. "The green it is. Now wrap it up, Littleman, and I will consider amends made and say nothing to the Councilmen."

The trader took the cloth in trembling fingers, rolled it up, and slid it into a paper sleeve. The gypsy took it and threw a few coins on the ground.

I was stunned at his audacity and thought the Twenty-families' tithe to the Council must be magnificent indeed to let him get away with such high-handedness.

Suddenly he reached forward, grasped my arm in a powerful grip, and propelled me behind the stall and down a side street. A few paces down the street, he thrust me into a shadowy doorway and pressed himself against me; I panicked and struggled.

161

"For Lud's sake and mine, girl, be still," he said in a hard urgent voice.

"Let me go!" I cried.

"Shut up," he hissed.

"Shut up, yourself!" I flared, temper overcoming fear. He pulled me against his chest and closed a hard hand over my mouth. "Shhh," he said quietly and distinctly into my ear.

Then I heard the sound of running feet on the cobbles and I froze.

"I tell you it was the girl from the other market. The one on the black horse that caused all that fuss," panted a man nearby. "The captain said there is a big reward for her or one of them other two who was with her."

Their footsteps receded. When the gypsy released me, I spun away from him angrily and rubbed my lips where his fingers had mashed them against my teeth.

"It would be polite for you to give your name to your rescuer," he said.

I glared at him. "I didn't need rescuing!"

"No? Then you wanted to be whipped? I apologize for intervening, but there are gentler pleasures." The wicked expression in his dark eyes made me step back involuntarily.

"I suppose you caused all that trouble over at the other market a little while ago as part of your quest to be whipped. It must have disappointed you to have escaped so easily. What have you done with your horse, though?"

My heart jumped. "I don't know about any other market or a horse."

"No?" He smiled. "Then I must have been mistaken in thinking you rode a black horse from the city just yesterday dressed as you are now, to appear as a boy."

I flushed. "All right. I ride a black horse and wear boyish

162

trousers. So what? Why did you follow me yesterday? And why did you help me just now?"

"So I *did* help you, then?" he asked mockingly.

I scowled and gathered my will to give him a coercive mental jolt, hard enough to penetrate his mindshield, but, without warning, he stepped forward and kissed me full on the mouth.

Wit and breath fled at his audacity.

Releasing me, he spoke. "If I had known it was so easy to silence you, I would have done that sooner."

I scowled, mortified and furious that I had not pushed him away. Did he think because he was Twentyfamilies he could kiss anyone and they would like it? Childishly, I rubbed my hand across my mouth.

"Revulsion rendered me silent," I snapped. "Why did you do that?"

Heavy eyelids drooped secretively over his eyes. "Because I wanted to," he said.

I did not know what to say to the simplicity of such an answer.

His mouth shifted into a lazy, curving smile. "But what I want even more is to know this: Why are you pretending to be a gypsy?"

PART II

✦

THE TWENTYFAMILIES

✦ 16 ✦

"WHAT ARE YOU talking about?" I demanded scornfully, gathering myself to run if he tried to catch hold of me again. "Of course I am a gypsy."

"Your back is bleeding," he said mildly. "You need treatment, and there is a gypsy rig nearby where you can clean up. I will take you there, if you wish. . . ."

I bit my lip, mistrusting his apparent indifference. Yet I dared not cross the city on foot in bloody disarray. Aside from that, here was the opportunity to learn why the man had followed me the previous day. Moreover, this might be my last chance to locate the gypsy woman's blood kin before Maryon's deadline.

"Very well," I said.

His lips twitched into a faintly ironic smile.

As we walked, I took good care to stay out of the reach of his long arms and a little behind him. I was shivering, but not from the cold. The pain from the whipping was locked behind the suppressing barrier I had set up, but there was no way to block the shock of it from myself.

True to his word, he led me to a rig set on a tiny green not far from the market. Alongside it, four horses grazed. One of them was Sendari, whom the gypsy had ridden the previous day. To my discomfort, he recognized me as we approached the rig and trotted over to push his soft muzzle against my hand. I could

167

not reach his mind to ask him to withdraw, so I stroked him and pretended not to see the startled look the gypsy gave us. In some situations, it was safer to say nothing rather than to try explaining the inexplicable.

The rig itself was magnificent. Every panel of wood was intricately carved in an elaborate scene. It made our own poor wagon seem fit only for firewood. The carvings were unusual and reminded me vaguely of the stonework mural in the Reichler Clinic under Tor. Then again, they were also like the carvings that had once graced Obernewtyn's huge entrance doors.

"It is very beautiful," I said sincerely.

He nodded. "This is the skill of my family. It is a very ancient art." He caressed a ridge in the dark, smooth wood.

"This is *your* rig?" I asked, wishing that I could simply read his mind for the information I needed.

"Maire!" he called suddenly.

An extraordinarily ugly crone poked her head through the brocaded curtain. Her skin was much darker than the man's, and her snow-white hair hung to her waist in stark contrast, but she had the same black penetrating eyes. Squinting against the dusk light, she regarded him with disfavor. "What do you want?"

"This girl was whipped by some louts in the market. Her back needs treatment. Can you heal her?"

The old woman sniffed and raked me from crown to toe with her sharp eyes. "Can I? Yes. But should I? Will I?" She took up a battered box of woven reed, climbed from the wagon, and hobbled over to the smoldering remains of a fire. She was tiny and wore a bed dress of deeply embroidered silken material the color of the summerday sky. Setting the box on a log, she flicked a derisive glance at the man. "I suppose you rescued her. Your father would be delighted to hear what a hero has sprung from his loins."

When he made no response, she glared back at me. "Well? Are you going to show me your wounds, or do you want a body servant to strip you? I daresay your rescuer would oblige."

I felt myself redden but turned and shrugged to part the ripped shirt. She gave an exclamation that told me the wounds were as savage as I had feared. It also made me realize the weakness I was feeling might not just be due to over-using my Misfit powers.

"Am I a bird to fly up?" the old woman shrilled. "Kneel down, for Lud's sake!"

I did as she asked, thinking how much she reminded me of Louis Larkin, kindness hidden behind a shield of irascible carping. Tutting and muttering to herself, Maire bathed the flesh, then gently peeled away the cloth stuck to the wounds. Rummaging in her box again, she withdrew a bottle, and a moment later, the unmistakable odor of herbal preparations filled the air. The old crone was an herb lorist. I jumped at the feel of cold ointment on my bare skin. She slathered it on with a liberal hand, then stuck a dressing over my whole back.

"'Tis done," she said, slamming the box shut.

I thanked her and pulled my shirt about me as best I could.

She watched me with an odd expression on her aged face. "You are a tough one, girl. Not a flinch for all the nerves exposed and hurt. No Twentyfamilies would have done as well, for all their infernal pride."

I saw, too late, that I should have pretended discomfort when she was working on the open wounds, but the suppressing had prevented me feeling anything, and I had been too preoccupied to think of it.

I made myself shrug. "Halfbreeds are tougher than milky purebloods."

She snorted. "Except that you are neither."

I felt the blood drain from my cheeks.

"I am a gypsy halfbreed," I said faintly.

She cackled ironically. "So you say and so those rags you wear would have it, but it is not true. There is nothing in your face from Twentyfamilies stock. Not darkness of eye, not thickness of lips, nor any other physical characteristic that belongs to my people."

"I am a halfblood. I throw to my mother," I declared, watching the man from the corner of my eye. His expression had not changed, though the old woman's question exactly echoed his own accusation.

"Why were you whipped?" Maire asked.

"I touched some material, and the trader selling it objected."

I wondered why she did not reiterate her accusation. The gypsy man had changed the subject in exactly the same way, rather than demanding proof or arguing the point. It struck me that these gypsies were shifty folk who sidled about things rather than coming on them bluntly. I began to wonder if it had been such a good idea to come after all.

"Gypsies are not popular in these times," the man said in a neutral voice. "What is your name?"

"Elaria," I said. I felt as if there were undercurrents here concerning me, which I could not read.

The man shook his head. "That is not your true name."

Fear skittered along my backbone. How did he know that?

"Do Twentyfamilies know everything, then?" I sneered, drawing indignation from a little surge of anger. I did not like to be called a liar, even when it was true.

"Has no one told you that Twentyfamilies gypsies have the gift of truth?" he asked.

I licked my lips. "Truth?"

"Twentyfamilies know when a lie is being told."

My heart began to pound, for suddenly I remembered Domick's warning about making sure the gypsies did not guess I was an impostor.

Then I scowled, for how should he know if I spoke true or not? He was no Misfit coercer to read my mind—I would have sensed the intrusion if he was. He was guessing, or somehow I had given myself away.

The gypsy laughed suddenly. "You've spunk enough, for all your face reads like a book. Well, if you don't believe in gypsy powers, then let us say I know you lie because you lack the signs by which our kind know one another."

"What signs?"

His smile broadened. "That question marks you a liar even more than the absence of the signs."

"What signs?" I demanded, putting my hands on my hips.

In answer, he rolled up one sleeve.

I stared at the elaborate painting on the inside of his wrist and up his arm. Three birds were depicted flying in a spiral of black and green, shot through with red.

My mouth fell open with astonishment—it was the exact design Garth had shown me on the plast documents from the Reichler Clinic!

The arm painting was executed in greater detail, but there was no doubt that it was the same. But what on earth could it mean? How in Lud's name had a *gypsy* come to wear it? And could it possibly be coincidence that I, who had seen the design under Tor, should see it again so soon?

Both gypsies were looking at me so oddly that my heart

skipped a beat. I searched my memory for the thread of the conversation. "I . . . What if I were to say I have no arm picture because it was washed off?"

The gypsy lifted his arm and spat on the painting; then he scrubbed hard at it. This had no effect and told me that the paint was indelible.

"All right." I shrugged, thrusting the monumental puzzle of the arm painting to the back of my mind. "So, I don't have one. What of it? Not all gypsies have them."

At least, the gypsy in the safe house did not bear any such markings.

"You did not let me finish before you rushed to tell me how your 'arm picture' washed off. This is a mark worn only by those of the Twentyfamilies and entitles us to pass through the gates of any city unsearched and untouched. No 'mongrel halfbreed' would wear it." There was a note of bitter self-mockery in his tone as if these words were someone else's, and this robbed them of offense.

He lifted the same sleeve higher to show me a metal band around his upper arm. "This is what I meant to show you. All gypsies, full and halfbreed, wear these; yet, when I held you in the lane, I felt nothing. It tells anyone who might wish to know, whether you are bonded or promised or no."

I flushed, remembering the gypsy woman's metal band.

"And what of this?" He showed me a woven band on his thumb. "All gypsies wear these, too; weaved into the ring are signs telling the line of their descent. We bear these and other such things about us so that we may exchange knowledge about one another without the Landfolk hearing it. Do you still claim to be a gypsy?"

"Believe what you will," I told him stubbornly. "That is what my father told my mother, and he left in such a hurry, he did not have time to teach my mother the finer points of gypsy culture. Her family threw her out when it was learned she carried a halfbreed child, and so she brought me up alone in Rangorn. Then she died," I snarled, so carried away by the part I had imagined for myself that I felt bitter for the sake of my poor mother.

"The Twentyfamilies left without leaving his name, I take it," Maire asked, her eyes inscrutable.

I felt I had misspoken, but it was too late to change my story. "So my mother said."

She nodded and gathered up her box. "I will give you a shirt to wear in place of that." She hobbled back to the wagon.

"Well," said the gypsy man, "that is quite a story."

I did not know what to make of this, so I said nothing.

"Do you know that a girl fitting your description rescued a gypsy halfbreed from the Herder flames in the highlands?" he asked casually.

"That is nothing to do with me," I said.

"No?" He squatted down to poke at the fire, and the flames lit his face.

Only then did I register that the sun had fallen below the city skyline. The gypsy's sleek dark hair and hollowed cheeks gave him a devilish look as he fed the fire until it blazed high, sending showers of sparks into the sky. I stood awkwardly watching him and wishing the old woman would hurry up with the shirt. The sooner I got away, the better. But still I felt weak—my mind was taking longer than usual to recover.

"They say there is a rich reward for the wanted girl."

My heart began to bump.

"It is my guess that the girl who caused the ruckus in the market today and this Guanette gypsy are one and the same. What do you think?"

I shrugged, not trusting my voice to remain steady.

"Tell me, was it you or the boy you were traveling with who stuck a knife in the Herder in Guanette?" he asked casually.

"*We* didn't kill anybody. . . ."

I stopped, aghast that I had fallen into such a simple trap. I took a step backward, but at the same moment, the old woman appeared out of the dark and thrust a shirt into my hands.

"This is the girl from Guanette?" she asked the man.

He nodded and said lightly, "She rode a black horse then, though not the magnificent creature she outrode me on yesterday. The lad with her traveled in a false gypsy wagon."

The old woman turned to me, and I did not know whether to run or stay before the anguished intensity of her expression.

"Is she alive?" she whispered. "The woman you cut from the stake?"

I opened my mouth to say I didn't know what she was talking about, but the glint of tears in her old eyes stopped the lie.

"She lives," I said softly.

"Praise be." She grasped my hand.

"You . . . you know her?" I asked.

The crone nodded, mopping her eyes with the end of her bed dress. "Her name is Iriny, and she is . . . is very dear to me. I had feared her dead. Where is she? Is she in the city with your companion?"

Instantly, I regretted the impulse of pity that had made me tell the truth without thinking it through first. I could hardly lead them to the safe house. Yet this was the solution to my problem of what to do with the gypsy woman, for clearly these people knew who she was and cared for her.

"She is in Sutrium," I conceded, trying to decide how best to proceed. "She is very weak."

"Dying?" the man asked abruptly.

"Not now. But she almost did. She seemed to want to die."

"Ahh," the old woman moaned, rocking herself back and forth. "My poor girl." She fixed me with a sudden fierce stare. "Where is she? I must see her."

"She is in good and healing hands."

"You will take me to her now," the man said, advancing with a threatening air.

"No!" Maire said. She looked back to me with frank entreaty.

"I will bring her to you," I promised, ignoring the man and his threats.

"When?" he demanded.

"As soon as it is safe to bring her across the city," I told him coldly. "The soldierguards are looking for me—and her. Tomorrow it will be worse because of the business in the market today."

"That is so," he said darkly, his eyes troubled. "Yet we Twentyfamilies are to leave Sutrium in three days."

I blinked in wonder at him, for the Twentyfamilies' departure from Sutrium coincided exactly with the end of the sevenday deadline. Was this, then, the reason for the deadline Maryon had set?

The gypsy took my silence for a question. "On the reckoning of our history, we began our journey to the Land on that very day eons past. It is our custom to always leave Sutrium in the final hours of that day in remembrance and as a sign of good faith to the Council. You see, it was also on that day that we made the agreement of safe passage. We regard it as an auspicious day for journeys."

"Yet I will remain until Iriny comes," Maire said in a voice that brooked no argument.

He nodded. "And so shall I, if there is need. But the sooner we can get her out of the city the better, and it will be a simpler matter to get her out in a group than as a lone Twentyfamilies wagon leaving later than it should." He gave me a sharp look. "I will organize a rumor to say that you and your companion have left the city with Iriny. It will not take long for the soldierguards to run after the scent and leave the city free. When this happens, bring her swiftly and safely to us, and I will reward you in good coin."

"I'm not interested in your coin," I snapped indignantly. "I did not save her life for coin, and I wouldn't bring her to you if I thought you meant her harm, no matter what you offered."

He looked genuinely taken aback, and indeed, I was surprised at the extent of my anger.

"He is a fool as all men are," Maire said dismissively. "Put on the shirt."

I did as she bid, turning my back to strip off the ripped shirt and don the other. When I was finished, she looked at me, then went to the wagon and brought back a bundle of clothing.

"What are these?" I asked as she put them into my arms.

"They are Twentyfamilies skirts and gewgaws. Wear them when you return, and no one will trouble you. But make sure it is night when you come. A dark night, if you can. And speak to no one, unless you cannot avoid it; especially avoid Twentyfamilies gypsies." The old woman gave me an imperious little push. "Go now," she said. "Walk safe and bring her with you when you come again to us."

A thought occurred to me like a burst of lightning on a dark night. "I don't want coin as a reward, but there is something I would ask. . . ."

"Of course," the gypsy said, his eyes flashing with triumphant cynicism.

"I want you to tell me all about Twentyfamilies gypsies and halfbreeds," I said. "I want you to tell me how you came to the Land and everything you can remember about where you came from before that. And I want you to paint that mark you wear on my arm and tell me what it means and how you came to use it."

The man looked at me in blank astonishment. "Only Twentyfamilies bear that mark. . . ."

Maire prodded his arm. "She knows that, fool. Can't you see she means to pass herself off as one?"

The man's eyes widened in disbelief. Then he gave me a narrow stare. "You would play a dangerous game, girl. Do you know that Twentyfamilies are by lore permitted to kill impostors?"

"How should anyone know me for an impostor with such marks and these clothes?"

He smiled. "I would know."

I ignored that. "There is another thing. I also want to know about 'swallow.'"

His brows shot up. "Who told you of Swallow? Did Iriny speak his name in her delirium?"

So Swallow was a person. I had not expected that. I ignored the question, because answering it would reveal the extent of my ignorance. Instead, I gave them both a challenging look. "Do you agree with my conditions?"

177

After a long tense moment, the man gave an unsmiling nod.

The old woman touched my hand. "Bring her safe to us and you shall have what you want. Better still, you shall meet Swallow if you wish it."

The man made a negating gesture, then shrugged. "So be it. But do not bring Iriny here when you come."

"Where, then?"

He frowned in thought. "Sometimes the best way to hide a leaf is in a forest. Do you know the main gypsy green?"

I nodded.

"Bring her there, then. That is where we will wait for you."

I nodded and walked away down a lane without a backward glance. As soon as I was out of their sight, I threw a full coercive cloak about me and sent a farsense probe to detect anyone who followed.

Only then did I dare to relax and allow myself to feel relieved at having all but completed my appointed task.

With some effort, for I was not yet much recovered, I farsought Matthew using an attuned probe. It located him at the safe house, and I felt a surge of relief. Perhaps the streak of bad luck that had dogged us since leaving Obernewtyn was over.

· 17 ·

I ARRIVED BACK at the safe house to see the rebel Reuvan mounting a tan mare. I was taken aback to recognize the horse as one that had come to Obernewtyn for refuge the previous wintertime.

"Greetings, ElspethInnle," the mare sent, her dark-flecked eyes solemn.

"Greetings, Halda," I responded, concealing my surprise.

Ever since Brydda's beloved mount, Sallah, had chosen to remain with him after he set her free, animals would occasionally come to Obernewtyn claiming that Sallah had sent them and asking for Avra, mistress of the Beastguild. Most would remain only a short time, supposedly to be trained to live in the wild, before going out into the vast mountain wilderness.

Alad, the Beastspeaking guildmaster, was convinced that some were trained in a different sort of survival and sent back to Sallah. He believed she was the leader of a lowland arm of the Beastguild and a sort of animal network of spies, organizing their own rescues or sabotages.

I had thought this unlikely, but seeing Halda made me wonder, for she had been one of the equines who supposedly had gone into the wild.

Reuvan had not noticed my approach, so I coughed to get

his attention. When he turned, the flesh was bloodless beneath his tan.

"What is it?" I demanded, wondering if there was ever to be a moment in Sutrium unmarred by disaster.

"Idris is missing," he answered in a hoarse voice. "Brydda sent me to see if he had come here."

"Was he sent here?"

The seaman shook his head and took up the rein. "I must go. There are other places he might have gone if he was injured. Brydda asked me to try them all."

"Can I help?" I asked.

Reuvan appeared not to hear me. He lifted his hand in a distracted farewell gesture and urged Halda on.

I hurried upstairs and into the kitchen.

"Where have you been?" Kella cried, jumping to her feet.

Matthew rose, too, his face pale and set. "Idris . . ."

I nodded wearily. "I know. I've just spoken to Reuvan. Did he ask you to farseek Idris?"

"It would ha' done no good fer him to ask me to farseek anyone here. Too many minds an' too much holocaust tainting."

"But he would not realize that," I said impatiently. "I suppose he was too distracted. I'll try."

I shaped a probe to Idris's mind-set, but since I had never farsought him before, I did not know his exact mind signature, which meant it was not a strongly defined probe. Forced to compete with the miasmic static rising from the sea and the river, and from various areas of the city, I had no great hopes of locating him.

I opened my eyes and shook my head. "I didn't find him, but I'm still weak from the business this afternoon." In fact, though I did not say it, I felt as if all my energy were being siphoned away through some secret channel. I forced myself to concentrate.

"Did Reuvan say how Idris disappeared?"

"Apparently, he dinna come back two nights ago from some errand he had been sent on," Matthew said.

This puzzled me. Reuvan had seemed dreadfully upset considering Idris had been missing so short a time.

"Greetings, ElspethInnle," Maruman sent.

The old cat was curled on a blanket beside the hearth. I went to kneel beside him and warmed my hands at the fire. "I am tired," I sent.

He turned one flaring yellow eye to me, and for a fleeting moment, there was a mindless emptiness in it. Then his gaze sharpened. "You are tired because your body heals its hurts. This is a place/barud where there is much hurting. No matter. Soon we will leave."

I stared at him. "What?"

"Soon we/you will go far away. Very far . . ." His eye was cloudy again. I felt a surge of alarm at the thought that the old cat was on the verge of another fit of madness. Yet he had recently returned from a period of wandering madness, and the attacks did not usually happen in such quick succession. Perhaps he was simply tired. Lud knew that could make you a little mad.

"I/Maruman am weary," the cat sent as if to confirm my thoughts. "The H'rayka searches in the dreamtrails of Elspeth-Innle, and I have fought many battles to guard the way."

Abruptly, I was wide awake.

"Maruman, who/what is H'rayka?"

"H'rayka is the one who brings destruction," the cat sent.

I felt a rush of pure terror. Atthis had told me that if I did not find the weaponmachines and disable them, another human, whose fate path twinned my own, would locate and activate them, raining a new doom on the world. She had called this person "the Destroyer."

And now Maruman said a Destroyer was searching my dreams.

I had never considered that the Destroyer might be someone I would have to confront. I had seen our search for the weaponmachines as a sort of parallel race. Surely Atthis would have warned me if this person was hunting me.

Another possibility occurred to me. What if Maruman was trying to tell me that the Destroyer had begun searching not for me but for the weaponmachines? This seemed far more likely.

Suddenly I was more angry than scared. If the Destroyer *was* searching for the weaponmachines, why was I wasting time in Sutrium?

Why hadn't Atthis called me?

"The oldOne called," Maruman answered my despairing thought. "You do her bidding here in barud-li."

I stared at him. "I do the bidding of Maryon/tallone."

"Maryon/tallone hears the ashling of the oldOne/speaks the oldOne's words to Innle."

I struggled to stay calm. "Are you . . . are you saying Atthis sent a dream to Maryon to make me come to Sutrium?"

"A path forms itself like snow in the high valley of the barud," Maruman sent dreamily. "First there is this piece of coldwhite and that piece, and they are alone and nothing. But soon they join and cover the earth."

The obliqueness of his answer exasperated me, for past experience told me this was his way of indicating that he was sick of a subject. Any further questions would be met with increasingly obscure answers.

The old cat gave me a sly look, then curled to sleep.

I tried reading his subconscious thoughts but could not penetrate the drifting mists of distortion.

I sat back on my heels and stared into the fire.

Could it be true that Atthis has sent Maryon's visions? If so, then the need to return the gypsy to her people must be somehow connected to my secret quest to find and destroy the weaponmachines. Or perhaps the return of the gypsy had been nothing more than an excuse to get me to Sutrium. Yet the deadline Maryon had given fitted with the Twenty-families' departure, and I had learned, at least in part, what *Swallow* meant.

But why even bother to send messages through the futureteller instead of speaking to my mind directly? I had sworn to heed Atthis's direction, so it could not be through fear that I would refuse to obey.

Yet there was a precedent. The first time Atthis summoned me had been through Maruman's mind. In any case, if Maruman spoke the truth, I had no more cause to fret at leaving Obernewtyn or fear I would somehow miss a summons.

It struck me suddenly that rather than spending my time worrying about my destined quest, I should simply live and trust in the fates to bring me where I was needed.

I stared into the flames with a feeling of having perceived a tremendous truth.

For a moment, in spite of weariness and concern over Idris and the rebel alliance, I felt a sense of clarity and purpose such as I had not experienced since standing on the high peaks of the Agyllian Ken. It seemed that simply by existing, I fulfilled the purpose of my life.

"There is blood on your shirt," Kella said, sounding startled.

"Some louts in the market whipped me," I said.

"Let me see," she commanded.

I flapped my hand for her to leave me be. "It has already been cleaned and treated—by a gypsy herb lorist."

In a tired way, I enjoyed the amazement on their faces. I let them speculate a moment before telling them what had happened—leaving out the gypsy's kiss. It shamed me to think of it. Nor did I complicate matters by telling them about the triple Guanette bird design or the mysterious Swallow.

But what I did tell them was enough to have them all agog.

"When will ye take her to them?" Matthew asked.

"When Kella says it is safe for her to travel. After that business with Dragon in the market, all the eyes in every rat hole and cranny of the city will be peeled for gypsies, so even if she was able to move now, I'd wait a day or so. Unfortunately, neither of us will be able to move about too easily, Matthew, and certainly not together."

"Iriny," Kella said. "Strange to give her a name after so long. She is sleeping naturally now, and her wounds have begun to knit nicely."

I nodded and looked around. "Where is Dragon?"

"Sleeping still," Kella said. "It's not surprising. You must have had to hit her hard to knock her out right through her shield. I didn't even know that was possible."

The stair door slammed and Domick came in. Kella recounted the day's events to him, but the coercer seemed more concerned about Idris than anything else.

"When did Reuvan say he was seen last?" he demanded.

"Last night. Or mayhap yestermorn," Matthew said.

"He has only been missing a day and a half," I pointed out as the coercer began to pace back and forth. "Surely this is a little soon for everyone to be panicking."

"Did ye try farseekin' him?" Domick demanded.

"I did, but I could not find him. It was an unfocused probe, though, and there's a lot of static in the city; he could be in a blank spot. Or he might just be sleeping. You know it is much harder to find a sleeping mind even with an attuned probe."

"He might also be dead," Domick murmured.

I glared at him. "Do you take pleasure in being so miserable and hopeless?"

His hard eyes met mine. "In suggesting Idris is dead, I offer hope. If he is not, he may very well wish he were."

"Wh-what?" Kella gasped faintly.

"None of you seems to have grasped what Idris's disappearance may mean," Domick said. "If someone has him and questions him, he will be made to tell all he knows. . . ."

"The safe house," Kella whispered, lifting a hand to her lips. "He knows where it is and all about us."

"He knows everything about Brydda and the rebels, too," Domick reminded us brusquely.

I groaned, seeing more than that. "Lud save us. He knows about Obernewtyn!"

"He'd nivver give us away," Matthew said stoutly.

Domick turned a bleak look on the Farseeker ward, and suddenly they seemed decades apart in age.

"You don't have any idea, do you? Faced with a skilled torturer, you or I, even Rushton, would tell all. And Idris is a boy. Make no mistakes—if those who have him want information, he will tell them everything he knows."

✦ 18 ✦

After a heated discussion, we decided not to abandon the safe house immediately but to wait until first light in the hope that Idris would be found. At the coercer's urging, we spent the night packing Kella's precious store of herbs and her healing implements into woven boxes.

When we were almost finished, Kella went to wake Dragon so that she could apply the skin dye. After the incident at the market, we dared not let her remain undisguised.

Domick took out a city map, which showed the location of the nearest green.

"I wish you would reconsider," he said.

"I wish you would stop suggesting it," I snapped.

The coercer wanted us to go directly to Obernewtyn to alert Rushton and evacuate the valley. I had argued against doing anything so drastic before we had clarified exactly what the rebels knew of Idris's disappearance. After all, Reuvan had not suggested there was any danger to us or to the safe house.

Kella pointed out that he might have been too distraught to think of warning us. "He seemed almost dazed when he left the safe house."

I was sure that Brydda would have sent someone to warn us if there was any need and had said so, arguing that we could lose ourselves quickly and easily in the morning bustle of traders moving into their places at the markets. If we stole away in the night, someone was certain to report it. We had agreed to go to the nearest green, where we would wait and watch. If there was no raid on the safe house, we would return to it after a while; if there was a raid or any suspicious activity at all, Matthew would ride at once to warn Obernewtyn, and the rest of us would follow in the rig.

"You must go back to Obernewtyn, too, if the safe house is lost to us," Domick told Kella as she rinsed dye from her fingers.

"What about you?"

"I will stay at an inn as Mika."

"I will stay with you," she said stubbornly.

"Mika has no bondmate, and I don't want you connected with him in case something goes wrong and he has to disappear."

Kella blinked hard at his peremptory tone, then turned away to pull the last of her dried herbs down from the wall racks. His words reminded me of something else.

"Domick, didn't your last report mention people just vanishing without a trace in Sutrium?"

The coercer nodded.

"Maybe, whatever happened to those other people is what happened to Idris. And since those disappearances have nothing to do with the Council, then surely we need not fear—"

"We don't know that the Council has anything to do with them," Domick interrupted.

"But your report—"

"Contained conjecture as well as facts. I simply said that I had heard nothing to make me think the Council was behind the disappearances. But I don't hear everything that goes on, and sometimes the very fact that I have not means only that people have been warned to hold their tongues." He shrugged. "There are so many factions within the Council and the soldierguard ranks, all with their own plots, and if I have learned one thing in the time I have spent here, it is that sooner or later, everything is linked to everything else."

There was something profound in his words, which struck a note of response in me, but it was swamped by a wrenching weariness.

"You remember when we went to see Brydda the first night you got here?" Domick went on. "Reuvan came in and spoke of Salamander."

I nodded. "You said he has something to do with the slave trade."

"He is its leader. Salamander buys the people who disappear, and the increase in disappearances corresponds with an increase in the demand for slaves."

"Buying them from whom?"

"The rumor is that the disappearances are the work of an organization that specializes in kidnapping or removing people for a price. I think it is likely that Salamander set it up to ensure his supply. No one in the slave trade knows what he looks like, because he is fanatical about keeping his face and identity secret. He delegates like a king to a whole herd of people and rarely appears in person. When he does, there is almost no prior warning. It has long been rumored that he is a Councilman or some other high official. No doubt he is well aware that the mystery surrounding his identity creates an atmosphere of terror and suspicion and keeps his people silent and obedient."

"I dinna know th' slave trade had a leader," Matthew said.

"It did not—until Salamander came on the scene. Once, it was only the odd ship that stole people from the Land and sold them to lands over the seas, which were supposed not to exist. Then a ship with a flag showing a flaming salamander began to attack and sink any vessel known to trade in slaves. Invariably, one crewmember would be kept alive, tortured, then cast ashore to tell the story of a ship with Beforetime weapons that spat fire. In no time, the trade virtually ceased, for no one wanted to make themselves a target for such a nemesis. It had seemed for a while that someone wanted to end the practice completely, but instead he was only ensuring he would have no competition."

I had a sudden vision of the hatred that had flared so unexpectedly in Idris's mild eyes when Reuvan had said Salamander was in Sutrium.

"Idris's family was taken by slavers, weren't they?"

"His father and his sisters," Kella said. Her shoulders were hunched forward, and there were dark shadows under her eyes. Whenever she looked at her bondmate, there was pain in her eyes.

Domick was oblivious. "If Idris has been taken by the slavers, he will be tortured for information that could be used, before he is sold. Blackmail is another of Salamander's specialties, and you can be sure he knows the value of a seditioner with inside knowledge of the rebel organization. He would sell it dearly to the Council. Perhaps he would even sell Idris himself. So we are back where we started."

It was a grim prospect, for Idris and for Obernewtyn, and we fell into a weary, staring sort of silence contemplating it. This was broken when Domick slammed a hand on the arm of his chair.

"Look at us sitting here and yawping into the fire like a herd of defectives! Don't you see that it doesn't matter who has Idris? If I am right, someone may be on their way here now! How will we escape with Dragon, and the gypsy unable to walk?"

He was right. I stood up and flung the dregs of the fement onto the fire. It gave a vicious hiss and belched a sullen cloud of smoke.

"All right," I said shortly. "Let's get everything down to the wagon."

Kella continued the last bit of packing while Domick and I transferred the boxes downstairs. Matthew took them from us and packed them into the cramped interior of the gypsy rig, sweating freely in spite of the chill air.

"If Idris is made to talk, won't he mention this room you keep?" I asked.

Domick shook his head and motioned for Matthew to take the other end of the box he carried. "He knows nothing about it."

"But he knows about you."

"He knows about Domick," the coercer corrected. "Not about the Council worker Mika. Even a physical description of me will fit a number of others. And if he does tell them of a spy in the Councilcourt, I will know they are seeking me long before they realize which one I am and will vanish."

He had it all worked out, and no doubt he was correct, but part of me wondered if this new Domick was not pleased for an excuse to hurry us all out of Sutrium.

"But why risk it at all?" Matthew demanded, shoving a box in place against the others.

The coercer's voice was curt with dismissal. "Because my position is too valuable to abandon lightly. Apart from that, if Idris is brought to the Councilcourt, I might be able to wipe his mind so he would be unable to speak of the rebels or of us."

The ease with which he proposed to erase the boy's mind

shocked me. I stared at him for a moment, half tempted to loose a farseeking probe in case any surface thoughts drifted free of the coercer's mindshield. It would not be ethical to probe him, but if he was careless, I might learn what had so altered him. What stopped me asking him outright was the fear that whatever was wrong arose from his relationship with Kella. And no matter how it hurt her and chilled me to see him this way, the changes did not seem to be affecting his work for Obernewtyn and therefore were none of my business.

The sleepless night and the long day that had preceded it were taking their toll, and I thought longingly of my bed upstairs. It was hard and lumpy, and bits of straw poked into me in the night, but I could think of nothing more wonderful at that moment than to sink into it and pull the covers over my head while there were still a few hours of night left. Sometimes I longed fiercely to have only myself to worry about.

"After what happened with Dragon yesterday, all the gypsy greens will be under observation. It would be safer for you to go straight back to Obernewtyn," Domick went on relentlessly as we made our way back up to the kitchen.

I lost my temper. "Do you suggest we take the gypsy back with us to Obernewtyn? And if the greens are watched, then the gates will be watched, too, which means the risk of being identified as we leave will be doubled."

"Returning her to her people is surely less important than keeping Obernewtyn safe," Domick persisted. "As for the gates, you can coerce yourself past them, because you know who to coerce. In the city, you will have no idea who watches with hostile eyes, and if you are recognized, you will still have to pass the gates to escape."

I shook my head in exasperation and brushed past him to

enter the kitchen again. Domick went on and on like water dripping on stone. Everything he said made sense—*if* Idris had been taken by someone who would ask about us.

"The gypsy cannot be taken on the trip back to the mountains just yet," Kella said, having heard my words. "After a couple days of rest and quiet—"

"I am sure she would prefer a little discomfort to being captured along with us and burned at the stake!" Domick interrupted coldly. He looked around the bare kitchen. "Surely everything must now be packed, Kella, or must you also bring such necessities as the bathing barrels?"

The healer's shoulders slumped as Domick turned on his heel and stalked out, and I wondered how long her love for the coercer could survive his insensitivity.

"He is rough in saying it but right," I said gently to her after a moment. "It will do the gypsy no good to be healthy if the soldierguards get hold of her. There are times when we must endure what comes and take our luck. Go and prepare her to be carried down to the wagon."

"A trip into the mountains might kill her."

"We are not taking her back to Obernewtyn. I will return her to her people. She must be back with them before we leave."

Kella's eyes widened; then she nodded soberly, remembering Maryon's deadline. Or Atthis's. It was possible I had already done enough to save myself and Obernewtyn in finding the gypsy's people and learning that Swallow was a person, but there was no way of telling.

Therefore, the gypsy must be taken to Maire. The trouble was that Kella and Matthew would have to come as well.

I was still trying to decide if it would be best to have them wait somewhere for me when Domick departed, saying he was expected at the Councilcourt.

Dragon trailed into the kitchen. In spite of the muddy dyes Kella had used to disguise her hair and skin, and a wan, woeful expression, she was lovelier than ever. She put her hand to her forehead and rubbed at it fretfully.

"Are you all right?" I asked.

She blinked at me, her blue eyes pink-rimmed. "Head hurts."

Small wonder after the ruthless jolt I had given her, I thought ruefully, drawing her to warm herself by the fire. It was not much of a reward for her courage in defending the woman and her children, yet what else could I have done?

Kella entered, frowning. "The sleepseal on the gypsy will hold only a little while longer. Seals are progressively less effective when applied in succession, and her mind is fighting it. It will hold for a few hours. No more."

"It will do. I'll get Matthew to help me bring her down in a minute." I nodded at Dragon. "Is she all right? She says her head hurts."

Kella examined the girl, looking intently into her eyes and touching her temple lightly. Rummaging in a basket, she made a soothing herbal mixture, and we both watched as Dragon drank it.

"She'll be fine once the herbs begin to work," the healer said softly. She glanced around the kitchen at the bare walls and sighed. "I suppose we might just as well go at once. I have sometimes longed for something that would send me back to Obernewtyn, yet now I am sad. I cannot imagine this place without me."

"Nor can I," said a gruff, familiar voice.

We both whirled to see Brydda Llewellyn standing in the kitchen doorway.

"Brydda!" Kella cried gladly, and flung herself into the rebel chief's arms. The big man hugged her, then gently put her away from him. His voice was grave.

"The soldierguards are searching the city for a gypsy girl and boy who freed a woman from a burning in Guanette. They are picking gypsies up all over the city and questioning them. The descriptions they are giving fit you and Matthew too well to be anyone else. They also tally with reports dozens of people gave after an incident in a city market where two gypsies and a red-haired Landgirl attacked Herder priests about their business."

I felt sick. Not only had they connected the market incident to the one in Guanette, but also Dragon's description was now being bandied about.

"Brydda—" I began, but he cut me off as if he had not heard me.

"I thought it must be you, so I came to . . . to warn you." There was an odd twitchiness in his manner.

"Has Idris come back yet?" I asked with sudden foreboding.

He shook his head.

"Then we must leave here at once in case the soldierguards come," I said firmly, and tried to propel him back toward the stairs. It was like trying to push a mountain sideways.

"The soldierguards won't be coming," he said.

Matthew came into the hallway behind us, but his welcoming smile faltered as he took in the strangeness of the older man.

"Something is wrong, but let him tell it how he will," I sent, forestalling his questions.

Dragon was staring up at the giant rebel in wonderment. Clearly, Kella's medicine had done its job. He stirred under her gaze and frowned down at her. "So it was you in the market, Dragon. What a little beauty you are. . . ."

"Bir-da," she said shyly.

The rebel's eyes lost their feverish look as he dropped to one knee to make himself her height, but she would not be coaxed nearer.

"Brydda, if the Council has Idris, they will force him to tell them about this place. . . ." I spoke more in an attempt to draw the rebel back to normality than in expectation of an answer.

"Idris will not talk," Brydda interrupted.

I bit my lip. After Domick's chilling assertion that a skilled torturer could make anyone talk, I did not understand Brydda's conviction that Idris would not be made to speak. Especially since a friend had once before been tortured to betray him.

Unless his suppressed Talent had told him something.

I was trying to decide how best to frame a query when the big rebel rose with catlike grace and moved past us to the dying fire. Kella and Matthew exchanged worried glances as he lowered himself onto a chair.

Dragon sidled gradually nearer until she came to lean against his knees and stare into his face. He did not appear to be aware of her at all.

"I am so tired . . . ," he said, rubbing his fingers in his eyes.

"Brydda, how can you know the soldierguards won't come here?" I asked, coming to stand by the fire, too.

The rebel did not answer, but, fascinatingly, Dragon's face twisted with the emotions she was receiving from the big man. Her ability to receive emotions had been slower to develop than her power to transmit them, but physical contact enhanced all Talent. Brydda had no idea of what was happening, because the empath-coercer's face was turned slightly away from him. It was disturbing and oddly grotesque to read the movement of a grown man's thought in Dragon's mobile young face.

First there was grief and guilt, then anger and frustration, and at last a sort of wretched despair.

"It does not matter how I know, only that I do," he answered at last, his face impassive.

"Do you know who has Idris?" I asked, keeping one eye on Dragon.

Her face again mirrored the rebel's inner turmoil, and I felt a deepening disquiet. Who could have taken Idris for Brydda to react so strongly?

The big man was staring into the red embers of the half-extinguished fire, still redolent with fement. "Idris was investigating something for me when he disappeared," he murmured at last. "He asked me to use him. But I should never have done it."

A terrible weary despair dragged at Dragon's youthful features forming a grotesque mask.

"You have heard of the disappearances in Sutrium?" Brydda asked.

"Yes. Do you think that is what happened to him, then?"

He gave a croaking laugh. "My curiosity is what happened to Idris. My infernal hunger for knowledge. I found the man Reuvan had told us about—a sot at an inn, boasting about knowing Salamander. I bought the fellow a drink, and it took me no longer than that to know he had lied. The slavemaster would never trust his face to such a ninnyhammer. I needled him a bit just for the sake of it, and he wound up telling me that his master knew Salamander. I had a feeling there was some truth in this, so I decided to have him watched. He shut up after a bit, as if he realized he had said too much. I did not want to frighten him off, so I played the gull for him. I got roaring drunk and let him rob me before I was thrown outside."

The rebel's eyes had grown as cold as sharpened icicles. "Idris volunteered to keep an eye on him while I organized a roster of watchers. The sot was lodging at the inn, and Idris had only to watch him and note the name of anyone who spoke with him while I was gone. I did not expect anything significant to happen."

He gave me a bitter look. "'Stay put and watch,' I said. But the sot went out about an hour after we left, and Idris followed. I was so busy gloating over having finally caught hold of Salamander's elusive tail that I took no account of the fact that Idris's passion to have the slave trade destroyed was far greater than mine. . . ."

"Do you think this man realized Idris was following and took him prisoner?"

"He was a drunk, and for all his smallness, Idris was strong and tough."

He fell silent.

"Then . . . what?" I asked.

Brydda did not answer. His face was as still as a carved image. Kella pinched me and pointed to Dragon. The flame-haired girl was staring out blindly, tears coursing down her cheeks.

A heavy dread settled in my stomach as I realized that Brydda had been speaking of Idris in the past tense.

Kella had reached the same awful conclusion. "Idris is dead, isn't he?" she whispered.

The big rebel jerked convulsively at her words. "Dead? Yes," he said flatly.

Dragon's face twisted, revealing the emotions the big man would not express, and she began to tremble. I signaled Kella to get her away from him.

"Are you sure?" I whispered.

The rebel turned dry eyes, hectic with self-hate and grief, on me. "I am sure. His body was found this morning washed up on the banks of the Suggredoon."

Dragon let out an anguished howl, voicing the jagged spike of Kella's shock.

"We'll find whoever did it," Matthew vowed through gritted teeth.

I gave him a pointed look. The last thing we needed was high drama at such a moment. He rose and went out, muttering that he had to unpack the wagon. Kella went, too, taking Dragon out of the range of Brydda's searing anguish.

"Salamander killed him," he said when we were alone. "I have sworn I will crush the man and his foul trade once and for all, in the boy's name."

I bit my lip, but I knew I must say the unspeakable. "Brydda. Idris might . . . still . . . have been made to speak, before . . ."

The rebel shook his head emphatically. "His body did not show signs of torture. And he would never . . . never betray me willingly or easily." The last words were voiced in a savage rasp, and I blinked my own sudden tears away.

Brydda went on after he had regained control of himself. "No doubt the slavemaster killed Idris because the boy saw his face; killed him as a routine precaution, thinking him no more than a curious lad who had seen more than was good for him. If he had suspected Idris was a spy, Salamander would have had him tortured. That he didn't tells me Idris was killed as thoughtlessly as if he were a fly or an ant in the wrong place at the wrong time."

"How can you be so certain it was Salamander who did it?"

Brydda's face was grim with certainty. "A tiny lizard shape was carved into his forehead—Salamander's murderous trademark."

I felt a sick wave of horror. "I'm so sorry," I whispered, knowing there was no way to console the rebel for the loss of a boy he had loved like a son.

Brydda took a deep shuddering breath and seemed incredibly to compose himself to a bleak serenity. "I will not grieve while Idris's killer breathes. Salamander will pay for the boy's life with his own blood."

I shuddered inwardly at the mad, cold fire in his eyes, dismayed by the notion that one death could compensate for another. But I understood the guilt-driven anger that motivated him.

The rebel chief turned burning eyes on me. "That is the other reason I came tonight. You can help me to trap him."

I blinked, startled. "Salamander?"

He nodded grimly. "You can use your powers to lead me to him."

"When?" I asked warily.

"Now," the rebel said.

✦ 19 ✦

"*Now?*" I ECHOED, incredulous.

Brydda inclined his head and rose slowly, as if his bones were stiff and pained him. Yet the ember glow from the dying fire rendered him mysteriously younger. "Come, I will explain as we go."

"I won't go without knowing what I'm getting myself into! You are my friend, but I have a responsibility to Obernewtyn."

He stared at me for a long moment, then sat back down, grief and fury extinguished with visible effort. "Listen well, then, for there is not much time. There was information on Idris's body about a meeting. . . ."

"Surely, Salamander would have found any message Idris carried? It must be some kind of trap."

The rebel shook his head emphatically. "It was not a message to any eyes but mine. Idris and I have a special code in case . . ." The momentary eagerness in his face faded to a grim recollection of his loss. "The message said that a Councilfarm overseer named Evan Bollange had approached the sot soon after I left the inn, offering five able-bodied Councilfarm workers whose deaths had been staged. The poor wretches had been smuggled into the city, drugged, and hidden under the boards of a manure cart. A time and place were named

200

for a meeting between Bollange and the sot's master, a slaver in Salamander's employ, to discuss terms.

"The sot left the inn, and Idris followed. That's all I can say with certainty, for he wrote no more in his message. But it seems to me that the sot went to inform his master of the meeting date with Bollange. Salamander was either meeting with the slaver at the time or simply watching him, and Idris got too close. And he was not the only one.

"The sot was a minion, chosen precisely because he would boast—for an organization that is *too* secret will have no clients. Like all such, he was disposable. He was found yesterday with his throat cut. Such culling is not uncommon among Salamander's people. The sot had served his purpose for a time, but the slavemaster could not risk leaving so obvious a trail."

Brydda's eyes were hard and suddenly purposeful. "Yet, in his arrogance, he made a mistake. He let us find Idris's body, never knowing there was a message on it, telling the time and place of the rendezvous between Bollange and the slaver. They are to meet before dawn this day, in an inn on the other side of the city. If you will help me, we must leave at once."

"You are going to spy on the meeting?"

"I have no intention of spying," Brydda said, his eyes aglitter. "I intend to intercept Bollange and take his place."

"You would pass yourself off as a Councilfarm overseer?"

He shook his head. "There is every likelihood that the sot described Bollange to his master; therefore, I will be his brother, Arkold Bollange."

"You must be mad! The slaver will never believe such a far-fetched story!"

"I do not need to convince him for long," Brydda said calmly. "I doubt he would tell me anything even if he *did* believe me. But I only need to get close, because you will come with me as my assistant and read his mind. He must know enough about Salamander to reach him at need."

I gaped at his audacity. "And what if the slaver decides to just kill the overseer's unlikely brother and his gypsy assistant?"

"That is a risk," Brydda agreed, sounding as if he were admitting that it might rain. "But I doubt he will do that, even if he is extremely suspicious, because we offer something Salamander wants—slaves." He stood up suddenly. "Will you help me?"

I sighed, then stood.

"Rushton will be furious. He will like this no more than that I have decided to take your advice and meet with your rebel leaders."

Brydda's eyes widened. "Good on both accounts! Opportunities must be seized upon when they arise. We need leaders, truly, but sometimes decisions need to be made on the battlefield, in the heat of the moment. Without those capable of making such decisions, any force might founder. Rushton would appreciate the need and your ability to rise to it and make a decision without consultation."

"I wonder," I murmured dryly, pulling on my boots. I went to my chamber, donned a hooded cloak, and plaited my hair.

When we came down into the wagon-repair shed, Gahltha stirred, sending a stern reminder of my promise not to go out without him.

"He insists I ride him," I told Brydda. "If there is trouble, he is a savage fighter. Jaygar has been trained to fight as well, and he offers to bear you."

Brydda shrugged. "I had thought to walk, but if we take

the horses, we can get away fast if something goes awry." He signaled his thanks to Jaygar.

I was silent, impressed that the rebel did not simply accept Jaygar's offer as his rightful due. He genuinely regarded the horses as equals. Though he rode Sallah often, and in fact had stolen her from a Herder cloister, he never took her for granted. Sometimes I was convinced he had so easily accepted my Misfit powers solely because, through me, he had been able to devise a finger-signal language that enabled him to communicate with horses. He had been delighted when the Beastspeaking guildmaster, Alad, had asked to learn the language so it could be taught gradually to all at Obernewtyn who were not beastspeakers and to the beasts themselves.

As we rode out into the early morning, I wondered if Alad was right about Sallah being the lowland beast-leader and, if so, whether Brydda had any idea of it. It would not surprise me at all to find he had allied himself with the equines over his own kind.

The streets were all but deserted at this hour, and we did not see any soldierguards; nonetheless, I was unable to rid myself of the feeling that we were being watched. Certainly we made a strange enough couple, a gypsy boy on a magnificent, if dirty, black stallion and an enormous dark-haired man wrapped in an oil cloak and mounted on a stocky roan.

"I scent no funaga," Gahltha assured me.

I relaxed fractionally, reporting this to Brydda.

"Nor should there be," he said quietly. "I am taking us through parts of the city that are virtually deserted except during trading hours."

Brydda ceased his scrutiny of the streets to look at me for a moment. "As soon as we return, I will send birds off, to let the group leaders know about the meeting with you. It will take a few days for them to reply, though they have birds as well, because they will confer and scheme before responding."

"Is it wise to let the rebels know in advance that I am to come?" I asked.

"We must ensure that as many rebel leaders as possible come to hear you speak. Otherwise, the report they hear will depend upon the bias of the teller. And even if they were favorably inclined toward you, it is easier to dismiss second-hand reports as exaggeration. I will phrase my message so that every rebel leader feels they will miss out on something vital unless they attend. The rest will be up to you."

There was no sign of Brydda's earlier shattered disorientation; the big man was shielding himself from the pain of Idris's loss by concentrating on plans and schemes.

I said nothing, knowing he would have to deal with his pain eventually and that no words would ease it. I remembered how deep the hurt of Jik's death had cut into me. Words had not helped then—and sometimes I had longed for silence as much as forgetfulness. Time had abated the immediate wrenching sorrow I had felt at the boy's death, yet even now the thought of it sometimes made a dull ache in my chest, like a long-healed scar echoing its birth.

Suddenly Brydda signaled Jaygar to stop.

"Idris's message said Bollange had been told to seek out the street of five inns," the rebel said, looking about. "We are almost there, so we will wait here to intercept him."

"Do you know what he looks like?"

He shook his head. "I am confident he will come this way, and there will be few enough people about at this time. But you will know for sure when he comes," he added, touching his head to indicate that he meant me to use my farseeking powers.

It seemed a vague sort of plan. But then, Brydda had an

uncanny intuition—he called it a "knack"—so I held my tongue and let him lead the way into a narrow lane between two high buildings. We dismounted, and the horses moved deeper into the lane to wait.

"What am I to do when I have him?"

"You must turn him back," Brydda said softly. "Can you do that so that he will not know what has happened?"

I sighed. "I will try, but his mind might be—"

"Someone/funaga comes," Gahltha sent urgently.

I froze, and at once we heard a quick, light step. It was a woman carrying a basket, and a few minutes later two boys ran by. Then, on the third sound of footsteps, I sent my mind flying out and breathed a sigh of incredulous relief to find the wiry little man coming down the street was indeed the very person we were waiting for. Best of all, his mind was wide open to me.

Gently, I riffled through his memories before coercing him into forgetting why he had come out. In the gap left by what was erased, I took an older memory of a rousing night's drinking from his memories and reestablished it as the memory of the previous night. I pinched a nerve and gave him a headache to match, then sent him around the next corner and back to his lodgings bewildered and disorientated.

"It's done," I said aloud. "He has forgotten everything about this meeting and believes he has been out carousing. I have made him forget about the slaves, too. He now thinks they really did die in an accident. You will have to free them, though."

"You know their location?"

"Of course."

"Good," Brydda said grimly. He cast a look at the sky. "We had better go on. The instructions said the overseer must stop at the public trough and drink, to identify himself."

We left the horses to wait and made our way onto the street of five inns. There was a dirty-looking trough about halfway along, and Brydda stopped at it and cupped his hands to scoop some of the brackish water to his mouth. I let my mind loose, but I could detect no watcher. It made my skin creep to think that Salamander might be somewhere about us, watching from a window or a pool of shadow.

A ragged boy stepped out of a doorway, and I gasped in startled fright. His lips were blue, and he was shivering violently. His eyes slid to me uneasily, then back to Brydda. "There was to be one man walking alone."

"It is none of your affair," Brydda growled. "What are the words you have been told to say to me?"

The boy seemed reassured by Brydda's roughness. "You are to go to the last inn on this street and ask for the man in the best room."

He turned and darted away down a lane.

"He was frightened," I murmured, but Brydda had begun to walk again.

The last inn proved to be a cheap roominghouse with a den attached for casual drinking. I grimaced, for the frowsy Good Egg had been positively luxurious in comparison. A rank smell assailed us at the door, rising from piles of stinking refuse to one side.

I gagged at the stench as Brydda knocked, wondering what had possessed me to agree to such a mad scheme. My powers would do us no good at the moment, because I could feel that the wretched place was constructed of rock lightly tainted with Beforetime poisons. Fortunately, this would not matter once we were inside the walls—as long as they did not lie between the slaver and ourselves.

"I/Gahltha am here. I will kick the wall down if you do not return," the black horse sent stoutly. I felt slightly less afraid, knowing the fierce equine meant exactly what he said.

A man with yellow-stained teeth opened the inn door a crack and squinted out at us. Brydda drew a little scrolled note from his pocket and handed it through the opening. "Give this to the man in your best room."

The innkeeper grunted in derision, but he took the note in his grimy fingers before slamming the door shut. "What was in it?" I asked.

"A note from my brother, Evan, introducing me as his proxy. And now we can do no more than wait and keep our sword hands free."

We waited in silence, and I spent the time adopting various creative ways of breathing in an effort to filter out the foul stench of the place.

The door opened again, and the man indicated that we were to enter. Brydda gave me an encouraging pinch as I preceded him. If possible, the smell inside was worse, and it was all I could do not to vomit. The rebel seemed completely impervious to it. I gulped and was glad I had an empty stomach.

The innkeeper brought us to a room with a brown door and held out a dirty paw. Brydda dropped a coin into it, then knocked, and the innkeeper scuttled away as if he did not want to be there when the occupant appeared.

This made me very nervous.

The door opened a slit.

"Enter," a papery voice rasped, and a shiver ran up my spine at the sound of it.

At first, I thought the chamber completely unlit, but it was simply that Brydda's bulk had blocked the light of a cheap lantern, which was shaded to throw its light toward us, leaving the rest of the room in darkness. The windows, if there were any, had been blacked out.

The only thing I could see clearly was the pitted surface of a wooden table and two enormous scarred hands with thick, powerful wrists resting on it. Between the hands was a curved dagger, carved with odd symbols, and the little scrolled note Brydda had sent in.

The atmosphere of threat in the room was almost palpable, and my heart began to gallop as Brydda stepped forward. "I am Arkold Bollange, sirrah. . . ."

"You do not resemble your brother," the man said, his skepticism patently obvious.

"Different fathers, sirrah," Brydda said, and it was all I could do not to goggle at him in astonishment. In the blink of an eye, without the benefit of even changing his shirt, the rebel had transformed himself into a self-important fool whose pompous facade barely concealed the sniveling coward lurking beneath.

I did my best to shape myself into the sort of cringing nitwit that I imagined such a man would choose as a servant. At the same time, I loosed a probe. It moved sluggishly because of the taint in the walls and floor. The first thing it told me was that the man seated behind the table was not alone. There were three others standing against the wall behind him.

I bent my mind upon one of them and learned that he and the man next to him were hired killers. The third was known to them only as the slaver's assistant. The two hirelings carried knives, unsheathed, and had instructions to kill instantly after a certain combination of words.

I tried the slaver's assistant, but his mind was shielded.

"Why did not your brother come himself as was arranged?" the slaver was asking Brydda.

"As he wrote in that note, sirrah, Evan feared he was being followed and sent me in his place. I am here only as an emissary to discuss, ah, price."

"Who is this gypsy?" The slaver's voice cracked out like a whip, and I jumped.

The two men with knives tensed, and so did I. "My servant," Brydda blustered. "You could not expect a man of my stature to go about in an area like this without even a body servant? I can't very well use my own people. You need not worry about him, though. He is defective except for a peculiar strength with his hands and feet that make him a useful guard in spite of his small stature."

Again the silence, and I prepared myself to coerce the two with knives if the slave supplier gave the signal to kill.

"Very well," he said at last in his sibilant voice. "But I do not want him brought again. I do not like gypsies, full or half-bloods. They are trouble and are carriers of disease."

"Of . . . of course, sirrah," Brydda babbled.

The slave supplier became businesslike as he spoke of the price he would pay for each slave and how this would increase with the number of slaves offered. The men in the shadows relaxed.

"How will I reach you if there is a problem before collection?" Brydda asked.

"There will be no problem," the slaver said with chilling finality.

"Of course not," Brydda babbled idiotically. "I understand perfectly."

The slave supplier stood, and even his hands were swallowed up by the shadows. A moment later, a bag of coins fell onto the table.

"This is an advance on the payment for the five. You will

get the remainder when I get the slaves and make certain they are sound-limbed and not defectives."

"I assure you . . . ," Brydda blustered.

I swiftly summoned a coercive probe, realizing I had been so busy listening to the interchange that I had forgotten what I was there for. Sending the probe to the slave supplier, I was flabbergasted to find my way barred by another farseeking probe. Wrapped delicately around the slaver's mind, the alien probe had taken on the shape and feel of the host mind and in some places was indistinguishable from it.

Unwilling to disturb the probe until I knew its purpose, I cast about until I found its source. It was the man in the shadows whose mind I had been unable to read. The slaver's assistant was a Talented Misfit!

I hovered uncertainly, my mind reeling with shock. I had promised Brydda to get what information I could about Salamander, which meant getting past the othermind.

I clenched my teeth and readied myself to attack.

"Collection of the slaves will take place in two days," the slave supplier was saying. "Here is a map. The shed where you are to bring the slaves is marked on it. When you hear a knock thus . . ." He rapped in a sequence. The movement brought him into the light for a fleeting second, and I glimpsed bad skin, dark-brown eyes, and a vicious slash of a mouth before he moved back into the shadows. "Then you will open the door. Do you understand?"

I braced myself for a battle and let an aggressive coercerprobe fly toward the slaver's assistant. To my complete astonishment, I met no resistance. The othermind opened to me—and I recognized it!

✦ 20 ✦

WHEN WE CAME outside, the sky arching above was a deep, icy blue, and there were few stars, for the sun was near to rising. We could only have been inside the inn a short while. I felt as if we had been in there for years.

Gahltha whinnied a welcome, and I stroked his neck in mute affection, realizing unexpectedly that whatever the enigmatic stallion felt for me, I loved him.

"What did you find?" Brydda asked as we mounted.

"Another mindprobe," I said. "Wrapped around the slaver's mind."

Brydda turned to stare at me. "Are you saying there was a Misfit among those who skulked in the shadows of that room? Protecting him?"

"Not just a Misfit. A Talent. And not protecting, though that is what I thought at first. *He* was trying to get into the slaver's mind, too. I traced the mindprobe back to its owner. Do you remember Daffyd, who brought Dragon to Obernewtyn when I was ill?"

"The Druid's armsman? The probe was his?"

I nodded; then we both fell quiet, for we had come to a lane where people were bustling about in preparation for the day's trading. In one tiny market square, a fire had been lit in a metal barrel, and cloaked men and women stooped over it, warming their fingers. They were busy and preoccupied with their own affairs, which made it easy to weave a coercive net that would make it difficult for anyone to keep their eyes on us. I wondered at the absence of soldierguards, given the events of the previous day.

I thought of my first meeting with Daffyd—a chance encounter, if such meetings were ever really chance. I had been waiting in the Councilcourt to undergo the Misfit trial that would see me sentenced to Obernewtyn. Daffyd and another man had been waiting to see about a trade permit for the high country. I could not recall what words had passed between us that day as we sat there, but somehow, Daffyd had given me the courage to hope.

I had never forgotten his brightness in that dark moment.

We had met a second time after I had been taken captive by the fanatical ex-Herder, Henry Druid. Daffyd had been one of his armsmen. It had been at the Druid's secret encampment in the White Valley that Daffyd and several others had been simultaneously awakened to their Misfit Talents and emotionally enslaved by a powerful Misfit baby, Lidgebaby; it was there that he had fallen in love with Gilaine—daughter of the Druid and despised by her father for her muteness.

I had shown them how to free themselves from Lidgebaby's powerful overmind in return for their help in escaping. When a firestorm razed the Druid camp to the ground, Daffyd alone had escaped.

Discovering the loss of his friends, he had been heartbroken, but he remained with us in the mountains for some time. He had left us during the last summerdays, after Maryon had dreamed of his friends. He had been convinced they had survived and was determined to find them. Maryon had told me the dream had been vague and the faces unclear, but Daffyd had not cared.

We had not seen nor heard from him since. Until now.

"Elspeth?" Brydda murmured with faint exasperation, and I realized we had entered an empty street.

"I'm sorry, I was thinking about Daffyd. Yes, it was his probe. I am sure that his working for the slaver has something to do with his friends from the Druid camp, though there was little time for him to explain. I farsent him the location of the safe house, and he said he would come when he could."

"It is a pity we did not know that he worked for the slaver all along. It would have spared you reading his mind. I doubt that was a pleasant experience."

I licked my lips. "Brydda, I didn't farseek the slaver. I couldn't. His mind is sensitive, and he would have felt me at once. Daffyd stopped me just in time. He has spent months trying and still has not managed it."

"If he has been working for the slaver for so long, he must have some notion of where Salamander is," Brydda said.

"I think not, since he is trying to get into his mind for that very reason: to find Salamander. That much he did tell me."

The rebel said nothing.

"I'm sorry, Brydda."

"I know you are not to blame, Elspeth," he said heavily. "But if Daffyd does not come by tomorrow night with the knowledge of Salamander's whereabouts, we will have lost the chance to stop him."

"But surely we can follow the slaver until he meets with—"

"You don't understand. Two nights hence, when I do not take the five slaves to the abandoned warehouse as agreed, Salamander will guess something is wrong. Knowing his reputation, there will be a short and savage bloodletting during which anyone with any connection to him will be slain. That slaver we met tonight will be one of the first to go if he knows

213

what Salamander looks like or how to reach him. And perhaps Daffyd, too, though his ignorance might protect him. So you see, there will be no one to follow back to the source."

"Daffyd will come," I said, crossing my fingers.

The air was damp with the promise of more rain, and dark clouds obscured the waxing moon as we came in sight of the safe house. In the gaps between clouds, the sparse morning stars were winking out one by one.

We rode into the yard, dismounting to the squeak of leather and the jingle of metal buckles on the harness. When the horses were released into the grassy holding yard, Brydda bade them thanks with his finger signs, saying aloud to me that he would not come up. "Reuvan expects me back by sunrise, and it is moments away. Where are the drugged Councilfarm workers being kept?"

I told him the cellar's location that I had taken from the overseer's thoughts.

"I will return tomorrow night," the big man said as he strode away. "Let us hope Daffyd has come by then with some news for us."

Instinctively, I glanced up, seeking the pitted face of the moon. Maruman had always attributed his darkest foresight to it, and I had come to see it as a bad omen, too. As if summoned by my thoughts, the moon suddenly sailed clear of the clouds.

I felt a mindless rush of fright at the sight of it glaring down on me like the eye of some unearthly hunter. But even as I laughed at my melodramatic imagination, I felt oddly unsettled, and it took me a long time to sleep.

I woke just before midday.

Gray daylight streamed in through the sky windows of the

sleeping chamber, but there was no warmth in it. I stretched under the covers, then sat up reluctantly, reaching for my robe. Ariel's face came into my mind, and I froze in the act of climbing out of bed, remembering that I had dreamed of him.

We had been in the stone tunnel again.

The stone tunnel was a recurrent image from my dreams, and once I had asked Maryon what it could mean. She had replied that it was either a place where I would one day go, or it represented me or some aspect of me.

I belted the robe, letting the dream flow back into my mind. This time, instead of pursuing me with a knife or some other horror, Ariel had been walking beside me, his hand nestled in mine, small but very cold. He had smiled up at me as we came to the part of the tunnel where the doors of Obernewtyn flamed.

With the strange logic of dreams, it had seemed perfectly reasonable to me that the doors, which I had commanded be burned, should exist here.

"Why did you burn them?" the dream Ariel had asked in his piping, eager voice. His eyes had seemed to bore into mine with hypnotic intensity.

"Because there was a map carved into the design," I had answered. "I did not want anyone to find it."

This was the truth. Everyone at Obernewtyn believed the doors had been burned to free the inlaid gold in the design so that we could make guildleaders' armbands from it. But my true object had been to destroy the hidden map carved into the doors, which showed the location of the very Beforetime weaponmachines that I now knew I would one day seek.

Louis Larkin had once told me that he remembered, as a boy, Marisa Seraphim's purchase of the great doors. She was long dead now, but there was a painting of her at Obernewtyn.

She had been very beautiful, but everything in the picture spoke of her brilliance and will and nothing of her heart. Her diaries had revealed a woman as clever and ruthless as a teknoguilder without soul.

In the dream, Ariel's face had possessed that same brilliant, soulless quality as he moved forward to peer at the doors.

Drawing on my slippers, I wondered what it meant that Ariel had asked such questions in my dreams. I had the powerful feeling that he had asked something more, but I could not recall what or if I had answered. The questions had ended when I had heard Gahltha's cool mental voice calling my name. He had emerged from the shadows behind me in the tunnel, dark and even more magnificent than in life.

"Ride on me," his mind spoke to mine.

I had responded instinctively, vaulting onto his back. We had ridden a road that led eerily up into the clouds and the sky, leaving Ariel and the dreamcave far below. We had ridden impossibly high, until Gahltha sent to me that he was unable to go farther. Before I could say it did not matter, he bucked violently, sending me flying up like a stone from a catapult.

I had screamed in fear, but all at once, an Agyllian flew beneath me. I clutched convulsively at the warm feathers and thin bones.

I had thought the bird was Atthis, except the Elder was blind and would have been too small to bear me. This bird was enormous, but pure white rather than red like the Agyllians.

"Things bear their spirit shapes on the dreamtrails," a voice had whispered, but so faintly I could not tell whose it was. The bird bore me silently ever up and out, through a

216

swirling rainbow of color and light that ended only when I awoke.

It had been a peculiar dream. Not an ashling, for all its vividness; perhaps no more than the distorted summation of a long day of turmoil. Even so, it was hard to throw off.

I took refuge in practicalities. A swift farseeking scan told me Matthew and Kella were busy shifting the last boxes from the rig back into the safe house. There was no sign yet of Daffyd. Or, for that matter, of Maruman.

I gathered up my clothing, careful not to wake Dragon, who was still sound asleep. I crept from the room and padded along the hallway to the bathing chamber to splash my face and neck before dressing.

My eyes looked out of the mirror at me, bloodshot but alert. That was when I realized with horror that I had done nothing about the mental barrier I had set up to catch the pain of the whipping in the market. I knew better than anyone the danger of allowing too much pain to build up, for when freed, it had an accumulative impact—the pain from a simple leg cramp, left for too long, could become a crippling agony.

My heart thumped with apprehension as I began carefully to dismantle the barrier. I went very slowly, so as not to flood my senses with too much of the stockpiled pain at once. It was always difficult to regulate the flow.

To my surprise, nothing at all leaked out of the minute gap I had made. Puzzled, I removed the barrier completely, but there was not even a slight ache waiting to be endured.

My expression in the mirror was blank with astonishment. Stored pain could not be released without experiencing it, so what had happened? Had Maire's herbal ointment somehow absorbed or counteracted the pain? Or had I dismantled the barrier and endured the pain in my sleep? A suppressing

217

barrier *could* split open of its own accord, but it was hard to imagine sleeping through it.

On the other hand, it might explain the queerness of my dreams and the sluggishness that had filled me on waking.

Well, I had no complaint if that had been the case. Relieved to have been let off so lightly, I decided not to push my luck and disturb Maire's bandages. Instead, I simply put on a clean shirt and went to the kitchen. Over a late firstmeal, I told Matthew and Kella what had happened in the meeting with the slaver.

Not unexpectedly, Kella disapproved. As a healer, she did not accept the notion of revenge. But to my surprise, Matthew also chided me.

"Ye know Rushton would nowt approve. An' ye should at least have let me know where ye was goin'."

This caution was so unlike the farseeker that I stared at him.

His eyes fell away from mine, but I caught a swiftly shielded memory of Dragon with her arms about the two children in the market. This Dragon was not the dirty urchin Matthew usually saw when he looked at the empath-coercer. She was older, and her eyes shone with courage. In its own way, it was no more a true picture of her than the old one had been, but at least it was no longer derogatory.

Matthew had always peopled the world with villains and heroes, and his head was stuffed full of wild scenes of courage and drama. The fleeting and idealized memory of Dragon defending the children suggested her mad-headed bravery had forced a change in his attitude toward her. Clearly, he was finding that confusing enough to distort his other cherished attitudes.

Domick arrived during midmeal. He was unsurprised to

hear about my encounter with Daffyd, saying only that he had expected the armsman to turn up sooner or later. He had come to tell me that the search for the renegade gypsies had been shifted to Rangorn. "There is a rumor that you were sighted up that way, and three troops of soldierguards have been dispatched to search the area." That explained the absence of soldierguards on the street that morning.

I was impressed. The gypsy who had rescued me from the whipping might be arrogant and conceited, but he had said he would get the soldierguards out of the city, and he had done it.

Even so, I could not help being puzzled by the scale of the search, and I said so.

"Th' Council mun have some reason fer orderin' such a sizable search," Matthew agreed.

The coercer shrugged. "If they even ordered it. The soldierguards may have done it on their own. They have the power, and given that some of their men were killed in Guanette, they might want revenge."

"But rank-and-file soldierguards are a mercenary lot," I said. "They fight for coin, not for justice or loyalty to their fellows. I cannot see it troubling them that a soldierguard or two died. They would simply give thanks to Lud that it had not been them."

"Well, then it may be the Herders' doing," Domick said impatiently. "The fact that gypsies killed one of their people would enrage them, and they might be putting pressure on the Council to strengthen the search."

Especially if they believed a Twentyfamilies gypsy was involved, I thought. If they could prove that, it might destroy the accord.

"I want you to find out for sure whose doing it is," I said

firmly. "And where the coin is coming from to recruit all of these soldierguards. I heard a soldierguard say the Faction is going to fund a war against Sador. If the Herders are splashing bribe coin about, we must know from whence it comes."

Domick snorted scornfully. "How would the Faction have coin to finance wars? What coin they have is extorted from their congregations. It would not be enough to bribe one soldierguard, let alone a captain. You make too much of this and worry where there is no need. The search is concentrated on Rangorn, as I told you, so what does it matter? They will not find you there."

There was an arrogance to Domick's surmising that dismayed me. Yet he might be right that I was overreacting. After all, how much did they know that would hurt us? Only that there were a few audacious youths who had flouted Herder authority on two occasions—unlikely, but not impossible. I still was not completely convinced that this was the reason why a larger than usual number of soldierguards might be sent out. But since there had been no obvious use of Misfit powers on any of the three occasions, it must be seen as a mystery relating to gypsies, not Talented Misfits.

After the meal, the coercer returned to the Councilcourt, and Matthew accepted Kella's offer to learn how to bake bread.

I decided to spend the afternoon trimming the horses' hooves and reshoeing them. This was done whenever we came to the city, for it was the only time horses were forced to walk on stones and cobbles. In the mountains, they had no need of metal shoes.

The afternoon shadows were long, striping the yard, when I hammered the last nail into the last shoe and stretched the taut muscles in my back. I took a comb and began to smooth

Jaygar's tangled mane, worrying at how this life had changed Domick.

I would let Rushton make the final decision whether to bring Domick in. Regardless of his usefulness as a spy, my own instinct said we ought to bring him back to Obernewtyn. Surely, with Domick's inside knowledge, someone else might be insinuated in his place. And it would be wise to have someone else trained, just in case something ever went wrong.

For a second, I had a remarkably vivid vision of the coercer lying slumped in a Councilcourt cell, his hair long and matted, his body covered in sores and filth. I thrust the revolting image from me and made the warding-off sign, for I believed, as Maryon did, that things could be made to happen by thinking of them too much.

I finished the roan's mane, acknowledged his thanks, and turned to Gahltha, my thoughts circling back to Maruman and the hazy look that had been in his eye when I'd last seen him. It had been more than a full day, and I had been unable to find him with a finely attuned farseek probe. I knew the cat's mind as well as my own, but if he had fallen into one of his mad states, his mind would change its shape, rendering him invisible to a probe that was specifically shaped to his sane mind.

Was he wandering, mindless, in Sutrium? I wondered if I should have restrained him for his own good. Since I loved him, hadn't I the right to stop him from harming himself?

With something of a shock, it occurred to me that this was the sort of thinking that had made Gahltha try to stop me from helping the little mare Faraf. And that had once caused Rushton to forbid me to go on dangerous expeditions.

I would never exchange freedom for safety, I thought, regardless of the danger. I had the right to risk my life as I chose.

"Truly, danger is part of freedom/freerunning," Gahltha sent unexpectedly. "It is easy to forget this when it is not us/me."

"It's easy to have one rule for others and another for myself, but there's no honor in such double standards," I sent mildly.

"Honor?" Gahltha snorted. "That is a little word for a great thing. Funaga have freerunning thoughts. But instead of admiring/joying in them, you would cage them with words. Some things will not be so tamed."

I smiled a little, thinking how Maryon and her futuretellers, or Dameon in his most reflective mood, delighted in such complex ethical and moral discussions as this. They never tried to come up with a final answer. For them, the reason for such a mental journey was in the wordy road traveled.

But it was not enough for me to admire words and ideas as beautiful abstractions. I had to see how they could be applied. And I knew only too well that what worked in words was often very different when you tried applying it to a real situation. In essence, freedom of choice sounded a fine and noble thing. But in reality?

Putting away hammer and brushes and heading back upstairs into the safe house, I admitted wryly that it was difficult to be philosophical about Maruman and his right to freedom when I only knew I loved him and wanted to protect him.

The kitchen was filled with the exquisite fragrance of freshly baked bread, and Kella and Matthew were so engrossed in examining the results of their afternoon's work that they did not notice my entry.

"That first one was like a lump of stone," Matthew

laughed. "I will take it back to Obernewtyn and offer it to Gevan as a new kind of weapon."

I had crossed quietly to the fire when I caught a movement at the door. I turned to watch Dragon glide into the kitchen, hollow-eyed underneath her murky skin-stain. Her eyes swept the room, coming to rest inevitably on Matthew, but there was no vestige of the adoration that had hitherto marked her regard for him. She stared at the Farseeker ward as if he were a window opened on a barren landscape whose existence she had not before noticed.

Something in her bleak regard chilled me to the bone.

Matthew sensed her eyes, but the moment he looked up, she looked away. Kella gave an exclamation and hurried over to her.

"How do you feel, love? Does your head still hurt?" She rubbed her floury hands on her apron to clean them, then curled an arm around the empath-coercer's shoulders, drawing her close.

"Hurts," Dragon echoed dully, standing passively in the healer's embrace.

Kella's brow creased in thought, and she shifted to her bench and riffled through a disordered pile of herb parcels to mix another herbal infusion. Once Dragon had swallowed the last drop, the healer tried to get her to eat something, but the girl showed no interest. She said listlessly that she would rather go back to sleep, and the healer led her out.

Frowning, Matthew lay a damp cloth over two more loaves he had just kneaded. Only then did he notice me standing by the fire.

He flushed, and I wondered at his thoughts.

Kella came back and, noticing me, offered to slice some

bread for supper. I nodded and moved to help her. "What will Brydda do if Daffyd doesn't come tonight?" she asked.

"He will come," I said firmly, refusing to give voice to my fears. "In the meantime, after we have eaten, I am taking our gypsy home."

✦ 21 ✦

Daffyd had not come by the time I was ready to leave, and resolutely I dismissed him from my mind.

"I am taking you to your people, Iriny," I told the gypsy.

She started at hearing her name, but her strange two-colored eyes were defiant and shuttered. "Do as you will," was all she would say.

I explained that we had given her a sleep drug so that she would not be able to tell where she had been kept, nor how long the journey had taken to the gypsy camp.

"I don't care if you give me poison," she said, and there was a flash of pain that told me her mind was on her bond-mate. Her eyes closed as Kella imposed another sleepseal.

It was strange, watching her fall into a deeper sleep. The gypsy had been with us for almost three sevendays, yet we knew as little of her now as when she had come among us. There had been no true exchange. Now we would never know, for there was scant likelihood of our ever meeting again.

Matthew and Kella carried her between them down to the cart and installed her safely inside while I changed into the elaborate Twentyfamilies attire Maire had given me. The loose, wide-necked shirt was designed to slide off one shoulder, but it exposed the bandages on my back. The other shirt she had given me was stained with blood, so after a moment's debate, I unwound the bandages gingerly, reasoning that since there had been no pain, the wounds must be a good way to healing.

To my surprise, they had healed completely. I was unable to feel any scabbing. I would have to ask Maire about the ingredients she used in her miraculous ointment; Roland would give much to have such a recipe.

Buckling a thick belt with its dagger pouch about my waist and sliding a knife into it, I came down to the rig to find Kella packing blankets around the unconscious gypsy.

Matthew was in front of the wagon, holding out the leather harnessing so that Gahltha could back into it. The horse's skin twitched with loathing as the farseeker buckled the straps that bound him to the false gypsy rig.

"Well!" Kella said, her eyes widening as she noticed the elaborate gypsy clothing.

I laughed self-consciously and flipped the full Twenty-families skirt to reveal a multitude of red and green petticoats. "Elaria has never been so well dressed."

"If only Rushton could see you like that," she giggled; then she flushed at my astonished look and began to fuss with the blankets.

"Let us go," Gahltha sent tersely. "I/Gahltha do not like the feel of this funaga bond."

We departed, and though the moon had risen early, it was low on the horizon, and, as on the previous night, ragged drifts of dark cloud made the evening a matter of shifting ambiguities and anonymous shadow. I set about erecting a formidable coercive enhancement of the rig to make it seem more fitting as a transport for a Twentyfamilies gypsy. The last thing I wanted was to be stopped because the rig did not match the rest of me.

As it happened, this was hardly necessary, for there

appeared to be no soldierguards about, and the few people hurrying along, huddled deep in their coats and cloaks, paid no attention to me. It was a freezing evening, and I shivered in the light gypsy attire. I had not worn a cloak, because I wanted the Twentyfamilies clothing to be completely visible. I dragged a blanket around my shoulders from the back.

With little to do but sit and shiver, my thoughts wheeled back to Kella's words and their meaning. The healer had long been aware that something lay between Rushton and myself, perhaps because of her empath abilities.

What *would* Rushton make of the gaudy Twentyfamilies clothes? He had told me once that gypsy clothes made me look like another person: wilder and more reckless. In truth, I did feel bolder in gypsy clothes, but the Twentyfamilies attire made me feel different again; more than Elspeth Gordie and more than Elaria the halfbreed.

In my mind's eye, I saw Rushton standing in the misty mountain dawn, watching me ride away, his expression brooding. A waiting look, yes, but also a questioning look. And what sort of answer would Elaria of the Twentyfamilies give to that unspoken query, dressed as I was?

"Funaga play too many games/hide much," Gahltha sent. "Beasts have not so many faces for truth-hiding. Why not say what is true, be what is true? Why hiding/pretending/untruthtelling?"

"I don't know," I sent soberly. "Perhaps because the truth is sometimes frightening."

"Truth is fair/light/bright. Lies are darkness/fear/ignorance."

"Sometimes it is hard to know what the truth is. And sometimes truth is pain. Easier to hide the truth and make a secret of it than to face it."

"Truespoken," Gahltha sent.

We came out from a narrow street, and I was glad to see before us the dark wilderness that was the largest of the city greens at night. Fires bloomed like orange flowers in the darkness, illuminating the side of a great shaggy tree and the edge of a wagon. The faces of the gypsies were pale blobs clustered about each separate campfire, hemmed about by ragged shadow, the spaces in between fires pitch dark. The green had seemed smaller when I had come there in the daylight, and more ordered.

As Gahltha picked his way down the uneven rows of gypsy wagons, parked in clusters with a little cooking fire at the center, the night was filled with spicy food smells and strains of music—singing and the languid strum of gitas, sprinkled with frequent bursts of laughter. At one campfire, I saw a girl and a boy dancing closely, spinning away and back to one another in graceful accord.

"Gypsies dance for a lover. . . ." The gypsy's words came to me like a caress. I thought of his kiss and flushed, thrusting the memory from me.

A warmth and a camaraderie filled the night around me. I squinted as we wove about, trying to distinguish the elaborately carven wooden rig that belonged to Maire. We passed several Twentyfamilies rigs, but none resembled hers.

After a time, I began to despair, for aside from the difficulties of seeing in the dark, the wagon rows were crooked and folded hither and thither about on themselves. This meant several times we found ourselves going the same way we had passed already.

"Gahltha/I can farseek Sendari?" Gahltha offered.

At the same moment, an older Twentyfamilies gypsy stepped from the darkness and called out to ask my name. I chose my words very carefully. "I . . . I call myself Elaria." This was true enough.

He came nearer, and I had the same sensation as I had with Maire, that he was looking not at me but somehow around me. Suddenly I was very glad of the darkness.

"I am seeking Maire, the healer," I said, tensing in case the name provoked a reaction.

The man nodded mildly. "Well, she is here, but that is all I can tell you. Usually, she sets her wagon over yonder."

I nodded my thanks. Even so, we needed directions from Sendari to find the wagon, which was parked under a tree that seemed to wrap its branches around the rig protectively. A fire had been lit, and thick cuts of wood were set on end around it as rough stools.

The gypsy man who had rescued me from the whipping was seated at the fire. Beside him sat a plump, dark-haired gypsy girl and opposite were two gypsy men. The three were clearly Twentyfamilies—richly clad and with a certain haughtiness in their bearing. I wondered if one of them was Swallow.

Hearing Gahltha whinny to the other horses as we drew closer, the gypsy man looked up casually; then his eyes widened. He jumped to his feet, dismissing his companions with an imperious flick of his fingers. The two men went at once, giving me impassive looks, but the girl glared, first at the man, then at me, before flouncing off into the darkness.

"You look better in these than in the boyish trousers you wore last," he said when we were alone.

If I had been Maruman, hackles would have risen on my neck. "I have brought Iriny," I said tartly, climbing down. "She is in the back of the wagon."

I moved to open the curtain and show him, but he caught

my arm to stay me and looked about before letting me go. "Have a care. We do not want anyone seeing her."

"You could have said so without mauling me." I rubbed my arm, though in fact he had not held me tightly. I merely wanted to make the point that I did not want him grabbing at me.

He smiled, flashing white teeth, but before I could think of something cutting to say to wipe the leer from his mouth, he had crossed to Maire's wagon and hammered on the carved panel.

"Maire!"

The old gypsy emerged in a pale nightdress and woolly shawl, her white hair hanging long and loose like skeins of cloud about her neck and shoulders. Her expression sharpened when she caught sight of me. "You have brought her?" she asked eagerly, climbing down with sudden agility.

I nodded, and to my astonishment, she flung her arms around me and pressed me to her withered bosom. "Lud keep you, girl!"

After another long look around, she and the man carefully lifted the unconscious woman from the cart, laying her gently on the ground by the fire. Maire knelt by her and opened her eyelids with a gnarled finger.

Finally, she looked up at me. "Is she drugged?"

"No," I said. "She is sleeping. Our healer said she would wake tomorrow."

Maire looked impressed. "She is so accurate at diagnosing?"

I shrugged, and let her make what she would of that as an answer. To my relief, she bent and continued to examine Iriny, paying special attention to the scarred inner forearms.

"These are healing well," she said approvingly.

I was gratified for Kella's sake. "I daresay they'll heal faster with your miraculous potions."

"Is she all right, then?" the man demanded, interrupting our courtesies in an impatient voice.

"Haven't I just said so, you idiot?" Maire snapped with a sudden return to her old manner. "Are you going to stand there huffing like a fool or get her into the wagon before she dies of cold?"

Obediently, he bent to lift Iriny gently in his arms, staring down at her with a tender expression far removed from his earlier supercilious haughtiness. He climbed into Maire's rig, and the old healer followed.

The dark grass and the flickering flames of the campfire bent beneath a cold wind that plucked hair from my plait and flapped the elaborate skirts about my knees. Suddenly I felt very alone.

"Not/never alone," Gahltha sent from the darkness with all the intensity of a vow.

The gypsy man climbed from the wagon, a glint in his eyes that I did not trust. "I suppose you want your reward now?"

"Since you will leave tomorrow, yes," I said. "First, I want to know who Swallow is. Maire said I could meet him."

"And so you have," the gypsy said. "Swallow is one of *my* names."

I tried to hide my surprise. "One of your names? What does that mean?"

"Nothing more than I said. 'Swallow' is one name, just as 'Elaria' is one name. But there might be others a person would wear in different circumstances."

I scowled. "What does 'Swallow' signify, then?"

"Swallow is the man you see before you."

"Then you will not keep your bargain?"

He crossed his arms over his chest. "You asked to meet Swallow. Here is Swallow."

I wanted to shout at him for playing words against me, but I was too busy wondering why knowing who he was could save my life. Regardless, I had surely fulfilled Maryon's quest.

I put my hands on my hips. "There was another part to this bargain, *Swallow*. You promised to paint onto my arm one of those pictures you have on yours. Unless you have found reason to renege on that promise now."

Instead of becoming angry at my implication that he was a cheat, his smile merely broadened. "Gypsies always keep their promises. But perhaps we should discuss it first. . . ."

"There's nothing to discuss," I snapped.

He gave me an amused look and shrugged. "Very well."

His tone was so meek that I was instantly suspicious. "Sit down and I will prepare what is needed," he murmured.

I sat, watching warily as he went over and reached into a trunk set on the side of Maire's rig. He came back with a woven box somewhat smaller than the healer's box of potions and sat opposite me. Opening it, he withdrew a series of sharp spikes and some little glass bulbs of color.

"Where are the brushes?" I demanded.

"Brushes?" The gypsy gave me an innocent look, but the flames reflected in his eyes danced.

"The . . . the brushes you use to paint the design on. And what are those?" I pointed to the sharp little skewers laid out neatly alongside the box.

"They are needles; I use them to apply the design," the gypsy said, attaching a spike deftly to the top of a bulb of color. "The picture is created by a series of tiny stabs, which allows the color to seep beneath the skin and set. First I prick out an outline of the design, and then I fill in the color. Usually the process is carried out over many days, but since you want the whole thing at once, it will take the entire night."

I felt foolish and angry. "You did not tell me—"

His eyebrows lifted. "No? It must be because you did not want to be told anything. Traditionally, the designs are marked onto Twentyfamilies gypsies when we are swaddled babes and too small to be afraid."

I bridled. "I'm not afraid. What are you doing?"

"Putting them away," he said calmly.

I took a deep, shaky breath and did not speak until I was certain my voice would be steady. "Not before you keep your promise." I pulled up the sleeve on my shirt and held out my arm.

He stared at me, for once apparently bereft of witticisms.

"Well?" I snapped, angry because I was beginning to feel sick with apprehension. "If it is going to take all night, you had better get started."

"You want me to use these on you?" He held up one of the sharp spikes.

I nodded, not trusting to the firmness of my voice.

His eyes glimmered, and slowly he again took out the bottles and needles.

I swallowed a great lump of terror and looked away from the needles into flames that seemed to shudder with fear.

"In the Beforetime, it was called a *tattoo*," Swallow said. There was no mockery in his voice or his eyes now, but I would not have cared if he had sneered openly at me.

My arm felt as if it were on fire. Some obscure pride had made me endure the pain rather than sealing it away behind a mental net. The individual pricks had not been so terrible, but now my arm felt as if it had been savaged by a hive of virulent bees. Only the strange, long story he had told me as he worked had helped me bear it. Contrary to common gossip, Swallow said the gypsies had come from the sea, led by one who had vanished when they reached the Land. And though the story had taken hours to tell, I sensed there was much left unsaid.

Swallow passed his arm across his forehead, wiping away beads of sweat. For a moment, our eyes met; then he bent over his design again. I tensed involuntarily, expecting another endless series of needles, but he released me almost at once.

"It is done. Of course, you won't see the full effect until the scabs form and fall away."

Then he gave me such a queer, searching look that I felt uncomfortable. I glanced down for the first time, and a wave of nausea struck me at the sight of the raw and swollen welts.

What have I done? I thought in dismay.

"Maire!" Swallow called, dropping the needles into a pot of water suspended above the fire. I took a deep, steadying breath. The stars had faded. It was the second night in a row I had been awake to see the dawn.

He moved to the wagon again and rapped on its side. "Maire! Wake up. It is done."

The gypsy healer had called us a pair of fools before stumping off to her bed. "It offends her sense of fitness," Swallow had said, his eyes gleaming with mischief.

Maire emerged from the wagon, dressed in day clothes and wearing a full apron. She ignored my arm and looked critically into my face. After a moment, she shook her head.

"It is madness. Well, let me see."

I held my arm out obediently, hoping she would apply some more of her miraculous salve, but instead she only mixed me a foul potion to drink.

Swallow laughed at my expression. "The cure is worse than the ill when Maire is displeased."

She gave him a scathing look and bent to examine the tattoo. "It is a good job, though I would as soon not add to his conceit by saying so."

Swallow grinned, then his eyes turned back to me and narrowed into the same discomfortingly searching gaze. He rose. "And now to complete the process, an honorary toast offered by the D'rekta. I am not he, but I will do, as the heir apparent."

Maire gave him an astonished look as he crossed to the wagon and climbed inside. After a moment, she took a bottle from her basket and sprinkled a sweet-scented powder onto the tattoo; then she bandaged it carefully and instructed me to leave it untouched for some days.

"What is a D'rekta?" I asked when she was done.

Maire gave me a haughty stare, and for a minute her resemblance to Swallow was startling. "The leader of the Twentyfamilies. Each D'rekta is the eldest blood descendant of the first, who led our people from the lost lands. The present D'rekta is Swallow's father, but there is little love and much duty between them. . . ."

Swallow returned carrying a small box—not a woven container this time, but a box made from wood and carved in the same wondrously intricate style as the wagon itself.

"The making of the Twentyfamilies mark is generally toasted by the D'rekta," he said. He opened the box and removed a jeweled goblet from its velvety recess. It was the most exquisite thing I had ever seen, all streaked with iridescent green and purple and globs of shimmering gold. If this was a sample of Twentyfamilies tithe ware, I did not wonder that the Council would keep their pact.

He took out a small corked vial made of the same dazzling material, unstoppered it, poured a measure of the liquid it contained into the goblet, and raised it to me. "I am for you, as you are for me."

He drank, and I heard Maire's indrawn breath when he refilled the glass and offered it to me.

"No!" Maire said in an outraged voice. "You make mockery of the ancient promises."

He looked at her, his face deadly serious. "There is no mockery in what I do, Maire."

The old woman glared. "Have you gone mad? She is not Twentyfamilies. Nor is she even a gypsy despite all her talk. Indeed, we know nothing of her other than that she saved Iriny. For that I thank her, but she is no part of our destiny."

Swallow took the healer's withered hand with a tenderness that made a nonsense of their bickering. "Trust me, Maire. She may not be a gypsy, but she is part of the ancient promises."

Her face sagged with shock. "But how can this be . . . ?"

"What is all this?" I demanded, but they ignored me, seeming to commune or to pit their wills in some silent way.

The old woman broke away first. "So," she said in a subdued tone.

Again Swallow offered the goblet to me. "Drink."

I shook my head. "Not until I know what I am drinking and what it means. I won't be bound by something I don't understand."

The gypsy's dark eyes bored into mine, but I met his look,

236

and at last he set the goblet down. "The toast I offered is an oath of fealty to the ancient Twentyfamilies promises, by those whose fate is bound up in them. As is yours."

"I know nothing of these promises. And, as you have said, I am no gypsy. What could they possibly have to do with me?"

"I will tell you," he said with a queer fierceness. "This night I have done a thing"—he gestured at my arm tattoo—"that, were it known to my father, would see me hunted to death by my own kind. Anyone seeing it on you and discovering you were an impostor will know a Twentyfamilies made it, for no other has the secret. That will end the truce between the Council and my people. If you are captured and tortured, you will speak of it and of me and Maire, and again our lives would be worth nothing. Nor the lives of my people, for we will be forced to settle and become part of this Land."

I shook my head impatiently. "If giving me this was such a terrible thing, why didn't you just refuse?"

"It was the reward you named for returning Iriny."

"Even so, you might have refused."

"It was a promise," he said sternly.

I shook my head. "I don't understand. Your people are supposed not to break Council lore or have anything to do with those who do. What is Iriny to you that you would risk so much for her?"

"She is my half sister," he answered flatly. "Before my father bonded with my mother, and before he was D'rekta, he loved a halfbreed gypsy. She who bore Iriny. It mattered not with whom he bonded, since he had an older sister who was to inherit the D'rektaship. But when she broke her neck in a fall, my father was forced by duty to set Iriny's mother aside and choose a Twentyfamilies woman so that he could have a pureblood child. He chose a Twentyfamilies cousin to Iriny's mother, and I am their son."

Again there was a flash of that deep bitterness in his eyes. "'Swallow' is not my formal name but a pet name I was given as a child by Iriny."

I blinked, suddenly convinced that Swallow was the Twentyfamilies gypsy the Herder in Guanette had wanted Iriny to name. I resisted the urge to warn him, for how would I explain knowing it? Let Iriny tell him when she woke.

"My daughter bonded with the D'rekta, but there was no love between them," Maire said.

I stared from one of them to the other. "He is your grand-son, then?"

Maire wrinkled her nose, seeming to recover her equilib-rium.

Swallow gave a hard-edged laugh. "There is too much di-vision among our people. When I am D'rekta, I will dissolve the Great Divide. The answer to the halfbreed problem is not to sunder ourselves from them but to make them understand why we must remain separate from Landfolk. When I am D'rekta, any gypsy who swears fealty to the ancient promises will be one of us, whether they be purebloods or no. But until that time, I must appear dutiful and seem to believe in tradi-tion. It is only as Swallow that I am free to help Iriny and, through her, the halfbreeds."

"Swallow is the name you take on when you are among the halfbreeds!"

He nodded. "I help them as best I can. Unfortunately, my sister does not confine her good works to halfbreeds, hence her plight in Guanette. Landfolk are not overgrateful to those who aid them. I warned her, but Iriny does not care about her safety."

"You do?" retorted Maire. "And do not speak ill of Iriny. She is an angel."

"She was almost a dead angel," Swallow said.

"How did you know we had her? Iriny, I mean," I asked curiously.

Swallow's dark eyes glimmered with amusement. "The day you rescued her in Guanette, I was the archer in the trees."

My mouth fell open. "You! But Matthew said your hair was white. At least . . ."

He grinned. "A little flour ages a man dreadfully. I heard Iriny and Caldeko had been taken, and I came to help them as Swallow. I was too late for Caldeko, but I was determined to save Iriny, even at the cost of my identity or my very life— for, regardless of the Great Divide, she is blood kin and I love her. I was in the trees waiting for the chance to arrow that Herder when you walked out of nowhere claiming to be her sister."

I felt myself flush. "It was all I could think of. . . ."

"Do not mistake me. When you spirited Iriny from Guanette, you saved me having to reveal myself. That was the first debt I owed. Then you healed her and brought her here. Even the Twentyfamilies sacred mark did not seem too great a price for all of that."

Swallow's eyes shifted to where Gahltha stood in the wagon traces.

"That day in Guanette, I saw a horse come to you, though you made no sign, nor did you call to it that I could hear. It knelt at your side as if to pay you homage and received

Iriny's body gently. And when you mounted and were struck by the knife, it traveled from the village without letting you or Iriny fall. That seemed surpassing strange and an omen of some force to me.

"I rode directly to Sutrium, for I had to be present at the Council tithe, and my absence would be cause for dangerous questions. I thought you would follow and let it be known about the greens that you had Iriny.

"When no one came, I began to wonder if you were a gypsy after all. In retrospect, there were discrepancies—the things you had said to the Herder and your behavior—but I could not begin to imagine who would choose to mask herself as one of the most despised creatures in all the Land, for so the unlucky halfbreeds style themselves."

I kept my expression still and polite.

"The only answer I could come up with was one who had a greater secret to hide," Swallow said.

✦ 22 ✦

"I GUESSED THAT you and your friends were seditioners or escapees from a Councilfarm," Swallow went on. "I do not ask you to tell me if I am right. Yet, when next we meet, there will be no lies between us."

"Next time . . . ?"

He held up a hand. "Let that rest for a moment." He lowered his hand and hesitated, as if trying to frame what he would say in words. "You asked why I include you in the ancient promises. Know that there are those among my people with the sight—an ancient power passed down from the first D'rekta—which sometimes allows those who possess it to see what will happen before it comes to pass."

Futuretelling? His eyes caught my involuntary movement, and he stopped, but I said nothing.

"This is a strange power and perhaps a fearsome thing. My people do not invoke it lightly, for if it were known, those possessing it would be burned. One of my people with such power told of Iriny's capture. When I returned from Guanette, the same seer told me that Iriny would be brought safe to Sutrium by those who held her, but he could not tell if she would return safely to us. So I waited and set those I trusted to watch for you and your wagon. They saw nothing.

"Then, one night, a voice spoke in my dreams, such as the

241

first D'rekta heard, telling me that if I were to find Iriny, I must go at a certain moment to a certain market."

From the edge of my sight, I saw Maire gape at him and understood this was as much news to her as to me.

He looked at her. "You know I am no seer, Maire, and so it seemed madness to obey a dream voice. Yet there was such power in it that it was not in me to disobey. When I came where the voice had bidden me, I saw you, Elaria, dressed as a boy, with a Landgirl, buying birds. I meant to speak with you when I rode after you, but you outrode me."

The gypsy's face was pale and tense, his eyes looking inward, dark with wonder.

"The voice spoke again into my dreams that night, sending me to another market, lest all promises be broken. That is exactly the words I dreamed: 'lest all promises be broken.' What could it mean but the ancient Twentyfamilies promises? I obeyed and so came to find you being whipped. 'Save her,' the dream voice had told me. 'She is everything to you.'"

We stared at one another. I thought my expression must mirror his, pale and shocked. Two people, I thought, sent out by seers to find each other. There was a terrifying symmetry in it.

"I obeyed the voice because . . . such voices of power speak for higher reasons than to save the life of one man or a girl—even if horses do bend knee to her or become lame in her aid." I felt myself flush.

He nodded gravely, as if my silence was an answer to something. "I obeyed, too, because it ill behooved me to disobey; I, who must someday carry the weight of the ancient promises of the Twentyfamilies, for they are also matters of high destiny."

I wanted to laugh to bring us down from such heights, but

his expression was deadly serious and forbade such cowardly evasion. And a voice inside asked me who I was, of all people, to sneer at his talk of destiny and high things. Was not my own life ruled by the very incomprehensible mystic forces he was striving to name?

"Last night, as I held your arm and made the tattoo, I knew that the time of the ancient promises foretold by the first D'rekta draws near." He looked to Maire.

The healer paled. "Can it be so?"

"I saw a vision," he said. "I saw this girl speak the words of the ancient promises in the place where first they were made."

"No," I whispered, backing away. *Not again*, I thought incredulously, fearfully. Not another mysterious fatebinding. First the Agyllians had bound me to their quests, and then the beastkindred claimed me for their legends. And now the gypsies wished to chain me with their ancient promises?

Surely it could only be Atthis's doing? Why had she seen fit to let Swallow believe I was connected to these ancient promises? So that she could use him, just as she used Gahltha and Maruman's belief in beastlegends to make them watch over me?

"Do not fear this," Swallow said. "I will stand by your side when that day comes. I feel the weight of that meeting across my soul and across the fatepath of the Twentyfamilies like a great, heavy shadow."

Something burned in the gypsy's face that frightened me, for it told that he truly believed his words, and believing a thing so passionately must bring it to pass.

"This is madness," I said, but even to my own ears the words lacked conviction.

"Do not fear it," Swallow said. "I will consult the seer again, and perhaps when next we meet, I will know better what is to come. And we will meet again—sooner than you think—and I will stand at your side in battle."

He glanced around. Here and there, people had begun to emerge from their wagons to stir their cooking fires, for the sun had risen, not bright and red as on the day before but wanly, veiled in gray cloud. I saw this as from a great distance.

"The green begins to stir though it is early, for this day we of the Twentyfamilies go from Sutrium. You should leave now, before full light. People are more inquisitive under the sun's honest glare." He took up the little jeweled cup and offered it. "Will you drink before we part?"

My skin rose into gooseflesh. Learn what *Swallow* means, Maryon had charged me. Or Atthis. Well, I had done that, and perhaps this toast was part of it. I felt powerless to resist the fey forces that seemed to drive this man as much as they drove me.

I shivered and reached out to take the cup, drinking a little sip of the bittersweet elixir. He took it from my cold fingers, leaning near. "Have courage, girl. Never did I dream that I would live in such a time and, even less, that I would be part of the ancient promises, yet so it must be. There is great honor in such a fate."

There was a wild joy in his eyes that frightened me as much as anything he had said. An exalted recklessness.

"Come," Maire said briskly. "Before you go, let me look at the whip marks to see how they are healing."

She had stood apart from us during the matter of the drinks, as if she did not want to hear what passed between us. I was relieved at her words, for they brought me back to earth and freed me from the searing radiance of Swallow's face.

I rose to face the old woman, composing myself. "The scars are healed already, thanks to your salve."

Maire snorted, so I turned and lifted my shirt to show her. There was a long curious silence, and I craned my neck to see the tiny woman. My heart bumped against my rib cage at the look on her face.

"What . . . what is it?"

She let my shirt fall, her expression bland. "Nothing. You are right. The whip marks have healed."

I searched her face, but there was nothing of the amazement I had seen a moment before. I had imagined it, perhaps. After all, why would the mere sight of my back healed by her own potions give rise to such a look?

"I . . . I'd better go," I said to her. "I hope Iriny recovers completely." I turned to Swallow, forcing myself to meet his eyes, their black longing. "I do not think we will meet again, but I thank you for this." I touched my arm gingerly. "I swear that I will be careful and sparing in my use of it, and that no harm will come to you because of it. Goodbye."

He bowed. "I will say only this: ride safe, for whether you believe it or no, we will meet again."

Gahltha made no comment as I climbed into the wagon, though he had been privy to much of what had taken place. I had felt the light touch of his mind several times through the night.

Well, why would he object? I thought somewhat bitterly. He, too, believed I was part of higher matters and relished his own role in them. Too bad that I had no choice.

As we passed from the green, I glanced back through the forest of wagons to Maire's elaborate rig. Neither she nor Swallow were to be seen, and even as I watched, the last ragged flame from the fire, into which I had stared for so many hours, flickered and died in the rising wind.

Threading through the streets back to the safe house, I was
certain that the voice that had summoned Swallow to my aid
belonged to the Agyllian elder, Atthis. But did the birds always act in such secretive ways? Why not come to my mind
and warn me? I thought of the tattoo I have been given and
wondered if the Agyllians had any knowledge about the design since it featured them.

Only when Gahltha came to a halt did I start awake and realize we were back at the safe house. I was so fatigued that I
had actually fallen asleep sitting up.

In fact, I still felt tired; this puzzled me. I always seemed to
be tired lately, as if there was some hidden but constant drain
on my energies.

Gahltha almost ran the wagon headlong into Matthew,
who was coming out the gate at a breakneck pace mounted
on Jaygar. I braked the wagon, and the rig slewed to a halt.

"Where have ye been?" Matthew cried, his accent thicker
than usual. "I were about to go out lookin' fer ye."

I stared at him wearily, too tired to be bothered with his
histrionics. "I have been with the gypsies. You knew that."

I brought the wagon properly into the yard and climbed
down to release Gahltha from the harness. He did not trot
away but turned to nuzzle at me.

"Elspeth, it's Dragon . . ." Matthew slid clumsily down
from Jaygar's back.

"What is it?" I asked. "Has she run off again?"

"She . . . she were complainin' that her head hurt earlier. . . ." Matthew passed a shaking hand over his eyes as if to
erase a nightmare.

Suddenly I was wide awake. "Tell me."

He opened his mouth, but before he could speak, tears spilled down his cheeks.

I swung around and ran into the shed and upstairs to the safe house.

"Dragon!" I yelled, slamming open the door. "Dragon, where are you?"

Kella emerged from the healing hall, her face grave and sorrowful. "Inside," she said.

Dragon lay on the mattress nearest the door. The gypsy had occupied the same bed, and it was as if one pale corpse had been exchanged for another. The empath-coercer's red-gold hair lay like frozen flames over the pillow.

"What happened to her?" I whispered.

Kella shook her head. "I don't know exactly. She and Matthew were arguing. I heard a thump; then Matthew burst out of the kitchen yelling that Dragon had fainted."

"She fainted?" I cried. "Is that all? You scared the living daylights out of me! Matthew met me at the gate as if someone had been killed."

"Elspeth, you don't understand," Kella said. "This is no ordinary sleep. Dragon has fallen into a coma. I can't reach her!"

✦ 23 ✦

"How LONG HAS she been like this?" I demanded.

"Not more than half an hour," Kella said. "It happened after firstmeal."

I felt sick. "A coma. I don't understand. How could it just happen like that for no reason?"

From the corner of my eye, I noticed Kella open her mouth and then close it again.

"What is it?"

The healer bit her lip. "It's possible that you . . . damaged the blocked part of her mind when you forced your way past her mindshield to—"

"Are you saying I caused the coma?"

"You go too far and too fast," Kella said, the softness of her tone a protest at my stridency. I resisted an urge to shout at her that it did not matter how loudly I talked—Dragon would not hear it. Kella pulled the covers around the empath-coercer's neck and gestured for me to follow as she left the room.

In the kitchen, the scent of food cooking only served to heighten my feeling of unreality. A fire blazed on the hearth, but it was some moments before my mind registered that Brydda was sitting in a chair before it.

He rose to greet me.

"I had gone out to the market to get some milk and then

bumped into Brydda downstairs," Kella explained. "We were coming up together when we heard them arguing. When we came into the kitchen, Dragon was lying on the ground."

"I struck too hard," I said.

The healer sighed. "There is no certainty of that. Damage to a blocked memory is not uncommon. Sometimes an eruption occurs spontaneously, and once disturbed, the memory inside will develop and shift until the block is shattered. Often that is the best thing, but Dragon's memory block is very deep-seated. The chances of her mind being able to deal with a flood of unresolved memories is slim. The whole healthy mind would typically be sucked into a sort of mental whirlpool revolving around whatever has been repressed. Eventually, all normal thought would be absorbed, and there would be nothing left in her mind but that single matter replaying itself again and again."

My skin prickled with horror as the meaning of her words sank in. "You mean she will be defective when she wakens?"

Kella held up her hands. "I said that *would* have happened, but Dragon's mind retreated, which is the best thing that could have happened under the circumstances."

"You call a coma the best outcome?"

"Everything is relative," the healer said firmly. "At some level, Dragon obviously sensed the block was damaged and likely to break open, and she willed herself inside it. This means that, right now, she is caught up in a loop of blocked memories: reliving over and over what she has repressed as she tries to resolve whatever caused her to block it out in the first place."

"Then she'll come out of it when she has sorted herself out?" Brydda asked, struggling with unfamiliar concepts.

Kella shook her head helplessly. "That is what we must

249

hope. But there is no predicting how long it will take. It could take a year or a day or a minute."

I stared into the healer's face, seeing only my own culpability. With a flash of despair, I thought of Jik and Cameo and wondered if it would always be my fate to lead those around me to destruction.

"Elspeth, you blame yourself too much," Kella chided.

I glared at her. "Too much? How much should I blame myself, then? And who will take the rest of the blame? Dragon?"

"Perhaps," the healer said quietly. "It may be that this is indeed her own doing."

"It is *my* fault she's in a coma," Matthew said, hearing the last as he entered the kitchen.

Kella gave him a weary look. "I wish the pair of you would stop fighting over who is to blame and listen when I say the coma might be a natural development."

"Natural?" he murmured.

She nodded vigorously. "Exactly. This would have happened sooner or later, because Dragon never intended to forget her past. She didn't push her unwanted memory into her subconscious, the way the gypsy woman tried to do. Instead, she encysted it in her *conscious* mind—forgotten, yet not forgotten. She stored it as if whatever she has suppressed contained both something unbearable and something precious."

I tried to decide if her words offered hope or absolution, but my weariness had returned with redoubled force. I felt numbed.

"I have to get some sleep," I mumbled, but did not move.

"I am sorry for what has happened to Dragon. Truly I am," Brydda said, shifting forward to look into my face. "But life rarely permits us time to regroup or to mourn. I have come here because I need your help, and sad as this is, it does not change my need."

"Again?" I asked bleakly. "I could not help you last time. And I have been out all night. . . ."

The rebel shook his head. "I do not need you until tonight. You can sleep until then."

"What then?"

Brydda's expression hardened. "Daffyd has not come, and I am supposed to take the slaves to the warehouse for the slaver's people tonight. I mean to deliver them as agreed so that I can track them back to Salamander. Eventually, they will have to come to him. I cannot have them followed, because Salamander will certainly have someone watching. He would be a fool if he did not. But you could use your mind to track the slaves safely."

"I could," I said. "If they are not shielded and if they are not taken over tainted ground or water. And if a thousand other things that could go wrong don't."

Brydda looked taken aback at my fierceness.

I tried to explain. "It is difficult enough to farseek a Talented and a known mind in a city streaked with impenetrable tainted areas and among all these other mind patterns, let alone someone who is both unTalented and unknown."

Matthew sat forward, a flare of eagerness driving away the despairing guilt of moments before. "Th' slave you use as a marker need not be unknown or unTalented."

I stared at him, uncomprehending.

"I could take th' place of one of th' slaves," Matthew said. I only stared at him.

"Ye'd have no trouble keepin' a probe on me. Ye could do it from here."

"No," I said. "The blind spots . . . I could lose contact with you—"

"Nowt fer long, if ye follow physically as well," Matthew interrupted. "Farther back than anyone would bother with but close enough to feel where I am, even if ye can't farseek me. I'd have my mind open to ye all th' time."

"It's out of the question," I said.

"Very well," Brydda said firmly, stopping Matthew's protest before it was uttered. "But you will trace the slaves?"

"If I lose them, they will be condemned to live as slaves."

The rebel's face hardened. "As they would have done had I not intercepted them. Perhaps they would think it fair odds, since I am trying to stop this foul trade altogether."

"The end justifies the means?" I asked cynically. "Have you given them a choice?"

The rebel frowned. "As far as they know, they are still captives held by slavers. They are resigned to their fates. This is the real world, Elspeth, and I am doing the best I can. I will not lose this chance," he said harshly.

I sighed. "I will track them. But I'll have to come to the warehouse so that I can get a fix on one of their minds."

Brydda rose and took a scrap of paper from his pocket. "Here is a map showing where it is. The slaver said he would send his people to pick up the slaves before dawn, so I suggest you arrive well before that. I will be waiting for you."

"He also told you to get rid of me, so it will be better if I do not come inside."

Brydda frowned. "I doubt he will come in person, but perhaps you are right. We should not take the chance. You will have to get into position somewhere outside. Will that be close enough?"

I nodded and committed the route and warehouse location to memory before handing the paper back.

"You should assume you are being watched as soon as you get into the area."

"Am I nowt to come, then?" Matthew asked, caught between pleading and demanding.

Brydda looked at me.

"You had better come with me," I decided. "When we arrive, you will go inside the warehouse with Brydda and pretend to be his assistant. With different clothes and in the darkness, you can pass yourself as a seaman's lad. The skin stain has faded enough. With you inside, I can use your eyes to see what is going on there and communicate with Brydda even as I track the slaves."

The rebel nodded. "When you let us know where they have been taken, we will ride after them." He frowned. "No. On second thought, Salamander may have Matthew and me watched for some time after the slaves are taken to ensure we don't try to follow. I will have some rebels stationed nearby. Can you ride to them and tell them where the slaves are taken?"

I nodded, feeling incapable of more. Brydda stood and squeezed my shoulder. "Get some sleep," he murmured.

"Ye should have let me do it," Matthew said sullenly after Brydda had gone. "There would have been no risk."

"There is risk in everything," I said, thinking of Dragon. I stood up.

"Wait!" Kella protested. "You haven't told us what happened with the gypsies. . . ."

Kella and Matthew both stared at me expectantly. I yawned and rubbed at my eyes. "I'm too tired to go into it all now, but I took her back." I looked at Kella. "The gypsy healer said you were a good healer."

She flushed with pleasure.

I stumbled down the hall and into my bedchamber, falling

into the bedding fully clothed. Dimly, I wondered if it was possible that something was wrong with me. I felt incredibly fatigued, and this was not the first time. I had felt the same unnatural tiredness after the whipping. Perhaps this time it was because of the tattoo. Every time I was injured, my mind and body seemed to withdraw.

I flung my hand out, seeking the comfort of Maruman's rough, warm fur, but the place where he slept by my head was cold and empty. With an ache, I wondered where he was and if he was safe.

"Sleep the shortsleep. . . ." I heard Gahltha's voice in my mind. "I/Gahltha will guard the dreamtrails in place of Maruman/yelloweyes."

And sleep claimed me again.

✦ 24 ✦

THUNDER GROWLED IN the distance, and it began to rain.

I felt a prickle of unease, for a storm could play havoc with farseeking powers, and it would make retaining a link with one of the slaves that much more difficult.

Incredibly, I had slept all day, waking only when Matthew had roused me after dusk. But I was much refreshed; the numbing exhaustion was gone.

We had decided to ride together on Gahltha, for one horse would be far easier to cloak than two. As usual, Matthew's emotions impeded his ability to shield. This, combined with our close physical proximity, meant that I was shortly awash in his remorse over Dragon's coma.

Strengthening my shield to block his emanations, I felt a touch of anger that he would wallow in his guilt after having treated Dragon so shabbily.

"You should dismount here," I said. We were still several streets over from the warehouse, but I wanted to take no chances. "You had better get your mind fixed on what is ahead of us, rather than on what cannot be helped."

I ignored the farseeker's sudden rigidity and the belated, mortified strengthening of his mental shield as he dismounted.

"You go on to the warehouse," I said, "and after a bit, I will follow. When I'm in place, I will farseek you to find out where Brydda's people are waiting."

Matthew nodded; then he shuddered violently.

"What is it?"

"I dinna know. I felt as if someone walked over me grave. Maybe ye should come inside, too. Anyone might spot ye in th' street."

Touched by his concern, my irritation at him faded.

"I will make sure no one sees me," I promised. "I have to stay out here so I can trail the slaves without being seen."

Matthew still hesitated.

"Go on," I urged, giving him a push. He turned to go. On impulse, I called, "Be careful."

"You be careful, too," he called in a low voice, and loped off.

I let a small farseeking probe drift with him. When he had gotten inside the warehouse, I signaled Gahltha, who turned into a lane a short way along the street. I dismounted, and he moved swiftly into the shadows at the end of the lane. It was a dead-end alley with no doors opening out into it, which meant no one could come up behind me. On one side, the sloping roof of an adjoining building had sagged into a dip at the center and thereby cast a deeper pool of shadow. This was where Gahltha positioned himself.

I stayed farther up the lane and leaned against the corner in the shadows. From this position I would be all but invisible even without coercion, and I could see both ways along the street leading to the warehouse. I set loose a general farsensing net, which would alert me to any movement in the streets, then shaped a probe to Matthew's mind signature and sent it flying in the direction of the warehouse.

As soon as he felt me, the farseeker opened his mind to permit me access to the synapses and nerves that would enable me to see through his eyes. I occupied these only passively for the moment, taking in the cavernous warehouse as Matthew looked around slowly for my benefit. The view was wavering and indistinct as if I were peering through a stream of water, but the image would sharpen if I took active use of his sight.

Dimly, I watched Brydda approach. The big man's face looked slightly less battered than usual, and it took me a moment to realize Matthew's hero worship of the older man was coloring his view. If I took over his sight, I would see Brydda clearly. Or rather, I would see him as I usually did. Intrigued with this thought, I wondered how much my own view was shaped by my emotions.

They spoke for some minutes, but I could not hear what they were saying; then they came down to the end of the warehouse.

"He is taking me to see the slaves," Matthew sent.

The five men stood passively in a little group, and I was puzzled by their stillness until Matthew sent to me worriedly that they had been drugged by Brydda to prevent their being questioned by whoever came for them, which could give the whole thing away.

I suppressed a surge of consternation at this news. I had not thought to warn Brydda that drugs would bar me from the slaves' minds.

Matthew and Brydda spoke again at some length. Through the farseeker's eyes, I saw the rebel's look of surprise. Then he shrugged and nodded.

"What is he saying?" I asked Matthew curiously.

"He is saying the drug will take about three hours to wear off."

"I will have to—"

I broke off at the touch of Gahltha's soft muzzle against my shoulder. At the same time, I became aware of the warning tug of my farsensing net. I had been so engrossed in what was going on inside the warehouse that I had not felt a thing.

"Funagas come," Gahltha sent succinctly before moving back into the inky shadows at the end of the alley.

My senses told me there were two people walking swiftly along the street toward the warehouse, talking in low, intent voices. I poked my head out a fraction. They were some distance away, but I could see in the light of the single street lantern that they were both men; one was small and slender, while the other was at least twice his companion's size.

I shaped a probe and tried to enter the larger man. He was a Misfit but not Talented. His mind was buckled and distorted—hopelessly defective. I could pick up nothing more than a miasmic desire to cause pain, and I could not enter.

Shuddering, I withdrew and entered the smaller man's mind. It was something of a relief that he was neither defective nor naturally shielded. It was a moment's work to learn that he had been hired by Salamander, but there was no memory that would show me what the slavemaster looked like. He had simply been approached in an inn by a beautiful dark-haired woman bearing a note with Salamander's mark. It offered a relatively large amount of coin for what seemed to him a minor job. He had hired the defective because of his strength and brutish appetites, and because it never hurt to have a bit of muscle on one's side.

His thoughts showed that he admired Salamander's ruthless efficiency as much as he feared him. Apparently, the slavemaster had a reputation of being generous to those who performed their given tasks well and utterly vicious to those who failed.

He did not expect to fail, though.

His instructions were simple. Just before midnight, he was

to go to the warehouse where he would find a man named Bollange waiting with five men. Though it had not been said, he understood that these men were to be sold as slaves. The woman had given him a bag of coin, which he was to give to Bollange once an examination of the slaves had proven them sound of limb. He was to bind and gag the slaves, then bring them outside where a wagon would collect them.

His final instruction was to kill anyone who tried to follow or stop the wagon.

I mouthed a curse at the realization that here was another dead end. He did not know who would come to collect the slaves, nor where they were to be taken. Withdrawing, I sent out a roving probe.

Several streets distant, I found what I was looking for—a man sitting in a closed wagon, waiting.

I was relieved, knowing there would be no need to track the slaves now. I could simply read their destination from the wagon driver's mind.

Unfortunately, when I tried to enter him, a strange buzzing vibration distorted his thoughts so that I could not negotiate them. I then tried to enter at his subconscious level; though this was also slightly distorted, I gained entry and rose up to his conscious mind. His thoughts at this level were chaotic, and only by chance did I encounter the driver's thought that he enjoyed the slightly hallucinogenic quality of the Sadorian spiceweed he was chewing. It had been gifted him by the same dark-haired emissary from Salamander. That explained the queerness of his mind.

Unable to gain a hold, my probe slithered loose before I could learn the slaves' destination. When I tried to reenter, his mind barred me even at the subconscious level. This suggested that the spiceweed produced a certain sensitivity to mental intrusion.

Glumly, I withdrew; if I could not gain a hold on the driver's mind when he was stationary, I had no hope of keeping track of him once he began to move.

The only solution now was to track the wagon physically, using my coercive powers to hide myself and Gahltha from any watchers. There would be no time to inform Brydda's waiting rebels.

To my consternation, the two men stopped right in front of the lane where I was concealed. I drew back slightly into the shadows. At first I thought they had spotted me, but I soon realized they had simply stopped to confer.

A slight coercive enhancement of my hearing enabled me to make out their words.

"I want you to stay out here and keep watch," said the smaller of the pair. "I'll go inside and see Bollange. If anyone comes along, kill them."

"Kill," the hulk echoed.

"Exactly. Now, when I come out with the slaves, you stay where you are. Understand? Stay and watch for a while. That way we'll see if this fellow has traitoring on his mind. If he has, we'll get a bonus for putting him out of the picture. You got that into your skull, Lill? You stay and watch until I come back for you."

"Lill watch?"

The second man nodded. "Yeah. And if anyone so much as pokes their nose out the door, you know what to do."

"Stay?"

"No, stupid! You kill. Get it? If anyone comes out, kill them."

"Wait. Watch. Kill." The brute repeated the words lugubriously.

260

"Right. Now go and hide. That alley looks like a good spot."

He pointed straight toward the lane where I was hidden!

Frantically, I tried to coerce the shambling giant against the idea, forgetting that he was defective and therefore impenetrable. By the time I thought of coercing the second man to change his instructions, he had already gone striding off toward the warehouse, his mind on other matters.

There was nothing I could do but remain utterly still as Lill bore down on me. I dared not even shift back to where Gahltha was.

For a minute, we were literally face to face, and I thought my heart would batter its way right through my chest. Fortunately, he barely glanced down the dark end of the lane, turning instead to face the street and the warehouse. "Stay. Watch. Kill," he muttered to himself.

Behind him in the shadows, a bare handspan away, I could feel sweat crawl down my back. Trying to stay calm, I shaped a probe and sent it to Matthew to warn him that I was trapped in an alley by a man whom I could not coerce and dared not confront physically—especially since any confrontation would alert Salamander that his network had been contaminated, setting off the very bloodbath we were at pains to avoid. I told him swiftly about the second man approaching the warehouse and about the carriage driver.

Dimly, I registered the sound of knocking at the warehouse door.

"Tell Brydda not to send the slaves, because I have no way of tracking them. Have him quibble about the coin," I sent urgently, knowing Matthew would have to speak to Brydda before the hired thug was inside the warehouse.

I slid along my probe and into Matthew's waiting mind.

261

The interior of the shed swam dimly into focus. I was startled to find that Matthew seemed to be standing behind the Councilfarm workers. Was he trying to keep himself out of sight?

"What is happening? Did you tell Brydda?"

"Everything is fine," Matthew sent with admirable calmness, and my panic subsided slightly. "Are you all right out there?"

"I am as long as I don't move a muscle or make a sound."

"Lucky ye've no need to move with a farseekin' probe."

My heart began to thump again. Could he have possibly misunderstood me? "Matthew, I told you I can't farseek the carriage driver any more than I can farseek the slaves."

"You can now," the farseeker sent. "I've taken th' place of one of th' slaves. Ye need nowt blame Brydda—I told him ye'd changed yer mind. As things transpire, it's lucky I did."

I could not deny that entirely, but I was filled with a terrible foreboding.

"Matthew, if something goes wrong . . ."

"Nothin' will go wrong. Ye'll trace me, an' when ye can move, ye'll lead Brydda to me an' th' others."

I bit my lip. It sounded simple, but life seldom went according to plan. On the other hand, we had no choice now. The slaver's hired thug was inside the warehouse, and Matthew was committed to his course of action. It was not the time to tell him that sacrificing himself was no way of atoning for his treatment of Dragon.

The slaver's man was now examining the slaves, feeling their limbs and making them walk about to ensure they were not lame. Matthew's eyes did not look at him directly, and this annoyed me until I realized he was deliberately letting his gaze wander as if he was drugged like the others.

I had a single clear glimpse of the squat fellow and his

mouthful of blackened teeth as he peered right into Matthew's face. As his lips moved, I wished I could hear through Matthew's ears as well, but we had not yet found a way to achieve that.

"What is happening?" I asked Matthew.

"He's claimin' we're all defectives. Brydda is arguin' that we are drugged," Matthew sent. "Now th' slaver is sayin' he has no instruction to say we're meant to be drugged."

There was a pause.

"Brydda's makin' th' fellow think he's a coward. He said he was nowt takin' any chances on us tryin' to run away or fight him. It looks as if he's bought it. Yes, he's givin' Brydda the bag of coin."

Abruptly, I withdrew from the farseeker's mind, conscious of a warning tug on my senses. At once, I became aware of the clatter of carriage wheels on the cobbled street.

The carriage driver had come for his passengers.

In front of me, Lill flattened himself to the wall as the wagon rattled past the lane opening. It was a closed rig without windows; once Matthew was inside, there would be no using his eyes to orientate myself.

I crossed my fingers hard that nothing would go wrong.

I returned to Matthew's mind and found he had now been bound and gagged along with the other four. "The man has told Brydda to stay inside the warehouse until daylight. If he comes out before that, Salamander will have him killed."

My heart sank at the thought of being forced to stay perfectly still in the lane all night.

"Now he's bringing us outside. . . ."

Through the farseeker's eyes, I saw the wagon and the surly carriage driver. He said nothing as he climbed down and unbarred the back of the carriage. The slaver's hired man loaded in the five, including Matthew, and slammed the door shut, plunging the interior of the wagon into darkness.

I left a probe with Matthew and withdrew to my own mind to watch the carriage trundle past again.

The hired thug strode off down the street, and Lill shifted forward stealthily to watch the warehouse. I waited with my ears peeled for any sound in the street.

"Wait," the brute muttered in a disgruntled tone after some time, and he relaxed slightly. Only then did I relax, too, realizing Brydda must know not to come out. There was nothing more to do but wait until the other man came back for Lill.

My probe was still securely locked into Matthew's mind, and I tested it for the thousandth time.

"Dinna hold on so tight," he protested with a mental wriggle.

Apologizing, I loosened my grip.

"I think we're stoppin'," the farseeker sent suddenly. "Perhaps—"

The carriage door was flung open, and I could see nothing as he was blinded by the brightness of a lamp. Matthew blinked rapidly, trying to restore our vision.

As his eyes adjusted, I saw the face of the man holding the lamp. A feeling of terror assailed me, for it was the very same soldierguard captain who had seemed to recognize Dragon in the market!

"Who's there?"

The surly grunt dragged me instantly back to my own body as the hulking Lill turned to peer into the shadowy lane. I realized with dawning horror that I had gasped aloud!

He dropped a great paw to his belt and withdrew a long-bladed knife, squinting to see more clearly as he took a careful step forward.

One more step and he would literally fall over me, but his eyes were on the end of the lane. He had no idea how close I was. I was paralyzed with terror.

"Move/shift," Gahltha sent sharply. A split second later, he gave a shrill whinny and charged the thug.

The man issued a bellow of fright and stumbled backward, dropping the knife as the black horse leapt at him and over into the street. He turned his head to watch Gahltha gallop away into the night, and as he did so, I sprinted lightly to the sagging roof above the alley and hauled myself up. The sound of hooves on the cobblestones drowned out any noise I had made, and I lay completely still.

There was a long silence as the thug got to his feet and retrieved his knife. He turned and came down the lane, brandishing it purposefully. Fortunately, it did not occur to him to look up, and when he found no one, he shrugged in bafflement, muttering to himself about abandoned horses as he returned to his position at the head of the lane.

I lay for some moments shivering before I realized that I had lost contact with Matthew.

I remembered the soldierguard captain with renewed shock and sent out an attuned probe to find Matthew, wondering what on earth a soldierguard was doing with slavers.

The probe would not connect.

With burgeoning fear, I tried again and again, concentrating fiercely on Matthew's mental signature.

It would not locate.

On the verge of panic, I swept the entire area surrounding the place where I had last had contact with the farseeker.

Nothing.

✦ 25 ✦

THE GIANT, LILL, abandoned his post several hours short of daylight after a sudden downpour. Drenched to the skin, I hurried into the warehouse to tell Brydda what had happened. The cloudburst had ended by the time we came out, and Gahltha emerged from his own hiding place to carry us to where Brydda's people were still waiting for me in an abandoned house. The rebel leader gave them instructions to scour the area where I had lost contact with Matthew.

I went back and forth in the area, riding Gahltha farther than a carriage could have traveled in any direction. I farsought Matthew until the heavens opened up again, the season showing its claws. I stopped only when torrential rain fell so heavily that it obscured the surrounding streets like a gauze curtain, and the storm rendered me all but mindbound.

There was nothing to do but return to the safe house and break the news about Matthew. Brydda and Reuvan had come with me, leaving their people to continue searching.

We huddled over a fire lit hastily by Kella. The noise of rain on the tin roof was thunderous, and water ran in a gurgling torrent along the roof guttering.

"Maybe you couldn't farseek Matthew because he is asleep," Kella offered timidly.

I coughed and pulled a blanket closer about me. "I was inside his mind when he saw that soldierguard captain, Kella.

266

Matthew recognized him just as I did. There would be no way he could just drop off to sleep after that. Not in such a short time. I was out of touch for a couple of minutes at most."

"I meant he might have been *put* to sleep," the healer persisted. "If he was drugged or knocked unconscious . . ."

"I would not be able to communicate with him, but if I was close, I would have felt his presence when Gahltha and I combed the area."

"Maybe you made a mistake about where they were when you lost touch."

I shook my head.

"All right," Brydda said. "Then maybe more time passed than you reckoned. The Suggredoon is not far from where you lost them. If they put him on a boat while you were out of contact, you could not have reached him, because, as you said, the water has been tainted."

Reuvan disagreed. "A boat could not have come up to the river wharf, because it would have been low tide and there is a barrier of exposed mudflats."

I said nothing, numbed by so much catastrophe. My throat ached with despair. I looked down at my hands clasped together in my lap, feeling a strong urge to weep.

Matthew's image floated before my eyes, alternating eerily with the thin limping boy I had first met and the young man he had become.

"It is as if he was just snuffed out of existence," I murmured, then was aghast at what I had said.

The slavers had killed Idris. Why not Matthew as well? I blinked away a horrid vision of the farseeker's body washed up on the tide.

"What if the soldierguard captain recognized Matthew from the market? He would know straightaway something was wrong. Maybe he suspected a trap and just . . . just . . ." I could not speak my worst fear.

I found I was weeping after all.

Brydda clasped me in his big arms. "If this soldierguard had known the lad, killing him outright would be the last thing he would do. Salamander would want to question him, wouldn't he?"

My eyes widened as an incredible thought occurred to me. "Brydda . . . what if the soldierguard *was* Salamander!"

I broke off in a savage fit of coughing that scratched my throat and made Kella eye me sternly. But she was distracted by Domick's arrival. As the coercer divested himself of his sodden cloak, Brydda told him what had been happening.

Domick maintained his calm. "I think you are right in guessing he is not far from where you lost contact with him. Salamander would not risk the wagon being stopped and searched by soldierguards, even with some of them in his employ. He would have instructed his people to get the slaves somewhere safe until he was ready to take them by boat."

Brydda nodded. "Domick is right. Salamander does nothing in haste, and he never exposes himself or trusts anyone. He would have the slaves taken somewhere so he can watch and make sure it is not a trap. That's the way he works. Slave ships depart from Morganna, so Matthew and the others will have to be taken over the Suggredoon. That means they must travel by the ferry or by a hired riverboat. Since we cannot find where they have been hidden, we will set a watch on the Suggredoon."

"It might be wise to watch all the city gates," Reuvan said. "They might be taken inland first and across the river at the Ford of Rangorn. Salamander will have to figure out the least dangerous way to get five drugged and bound men out of

Sutrium. That rules out the ferry, since the slaves would have to walk on board if they were to journey that way. Drugged slaves would be obvious at once."

"Not necessarily," Domick said. "With some drugs, the five slaves would simply obey instructions to walk onto a ferry or out of Sutrium and be rounded up outside by their masters later."

Reuvan and Brydda looked thoughtful.

"I have never heard of such drugs," I said.

"They are brought in from Sador," Brydda said. "They are a by-product of the spice groves."

"I have not had the chance to make a report about them to Rushton yet," Domick said. "They enable you to function normally in every way except that you are utterly docile and suggestible. It is much simpler to deal with obedient puppets than with unconscious bodies or men and women who have been drugged into a shambling idiocy. This soldierguard captain would certainly know of them well enough, since the Council have them using it on prisoners."

"But it doesn't make sense that he would drug them," Kella objected. "You said the other four slaves were already drugged and that Matthew was pretending. Why would the soldierguard bother doing it again?"

"How would this soldierguard know they had been drugged?" Reuvan demanded. "You said there was no conversation between the man Salamander had hired and the carriage driver when the slaves were transferred from the warehouse to the wagon. And there would be no way of telling, with the slaves gagged and bound, who was drugged."

"A drug would not stop me from sensing Matthew," I insisted.

"Would you have even recognized him?" Domick asked. "If Matthew was given such a drug, even if your probe touched his mind, it would read it as the mind of a stranger."

"All right," Brydda said, sitting forward in his seat. "Now we are getting somewhere. If we assume the carriage driver was instructed to take them to a certain place and then this soldierguard, who might or might not be Salamander, met him and administered a Sadorian drug, what then?"

"They were moved indoors?" Kella suggested.

Brydda nodded his head slowly. "Salamander has done everything in a roundabout way. That is part of the secret of his success. The obvious thing would be to have the carriage brought to its destination, but maybe they are kept here for some time, drugged as a further safeguard. But no matter where they are or how they got there, the slaves will have to be moved from the city to Morganna. I think we ought to concentrate on that and forget trying to find them in the city."

I felt hope stir in me. "But if Matthew is drugged, as soon as it wears off, I'll be able to farseek him."

Domick sighed heavily. "I am sorry to be a doomcrow, but whoever has them might not let the drug wear off. And even if they give it a break, which they would be wise to do if they do not want to damage their slaves, then you would need to be farseeking at the right moment to reach Matthew. Even you cannot farseek indefinitely."

"It will not hurt to try. How soon before a single dose of this Sadorian drug wears off?" Brydda asked him.

"Several hours, more or less," the coercer said after some thought. "It might have worn off already. The drugs react differently with each person. Weight and how much has been eaten and drunk need to be taken into account for even an approximation. But the other thing we have to consider is that the soldierguard may have got a good look at Matthew—his dark skin would stand out in the daylight—and if he did not recognize him before, he might have done so now."

Brydda thumped the table in excitement. "But don't you see, that will work for us! If this soldierguard recognized him from the market, he would definitely let the drug wear off so that he can be questioned."

For the first time, Domick looked convinced. "You are right. They would be fools not to interrogate him." A darkness flickered in his eyes.

"How frequently can you farseek in a day?" Brydda demanded, looking at me.

"If I was fresh, every hour or so." I turned to Kella. "Can you drain the fatigue from me?"

The healer stood up and put her hands on her hips. "Are you mad?"

"I am not planning to scan the whole of Sutrium," I snapped. "I will be using an attuned probe, and it will only take a few minutes to send it out. Either it will find Matthew or it won't. It may be our only chance to save him."

Kella's ire faded. "I can only drain your fatigue the once. You have not eaten all night, and it would be better if you slept a little. Later—"

"Later may be too late," I interrupted her grimly.

The healer sighed and held out her hand. I gave her mine and relaxed completely as her Talent hummed through my body. Gradually, the night's tensions drained from me into the healer, and with them the chilly stiffness from all the hours of waiting motionless on the roof and the queer lightheadedness I had begun to feel.

When I opened my eyes, I felt as if I had just woken from a sound night's slumber. Kella's eyes were closed as she dissipated the fatigue poisons she had drained from me.

I closed my own eyes again and concentrated on shaping a probe tuned to Matthew's mental signature. Sending it out, I kept my fingers crossed, but before long it was obvious I would not locate him that way.

On impulse, I sent out a farsense searcher probe. Starting at the place where I had lost touch with Matthew, I let my mind fly out in ever-widening circles, dipping fleetingly into every mind I encountered just in case I happened upon a mind or group of minds that were oddly distorted. If that happened, Brydda could check to see if it was Matthew and the four slaves.

I moved gracefully in a spiraling mental dance, because awkwardness would waste energy. I kept fanning out until I felt my little store of energy fading; then I withdrew into my own mind and opened my eyes.

The others were all staring at me hopefully. I shook my head, not trusting the steadiness of my voice. Brydda began to pluck agitatedly and absently at the beard hairs beneath his jutting chin as I described the many tainted areas in Sutrium.

"That is only your first try," Reuvan said. "It is quite likely this drug has not even had a chance to wear off yet. And we can search the areas you can't farseek in."

"That is true," Domick said, getting to his feet and pulling on his coat. "I must go back to the Councilcourt," he added, in answer to our questioning glances.

"But you've been there all night," Kella protested. "And you have eaten nothing."

He glanced about and took up one of the loaves Matthew

and Kella had baked together. "This will do. I have no time for more."

The healer stared at the loaf as if she wanted to cry.

"Is something happening at the Councilcourt?" Brydda asked. "Surely you do not always work such long hours."

Domick shrugged on his sodden cloak. "The Council is shifting us about at random to see who moves easily and who resists. It is a thing they do occasionally. A security measure. In fact, I have been thinking I might stay at an inn for the next few nights, just in case I am under investigation. That is what I came to tell you."

He did not look at Kella when he spoke, and her expression told me this was the first she had heard of it.

Reuvan rose, saying he must leave, too. Kella stood up swiftly, saying she would walk them both out. Her face was pale and set.

✦ 26 ✦

"He is so cold," I said to Brydda when we were alone.

The rebel gave me a stern look. "Do not blame Domick for being good at what you and your people have asked him to do, Elspeth."

I shook my head. "Does being good at spying mean he has to be so cold and remote? So hard?"

"Of course it does," Brydda said sharply. "Spying requires a person to turn themselves inside out in their efforts to pretend to be what they are not. In a sense, Domick has had to become the enemy, and that means he must work against the very things he believes in most passionately. He must do and witness things that are abhorrent to him, and yet pretend to approve. And he is in constant peril. Of course it has changed him. How could it not? If he had not hardened, what he does would have destroyed him."

Chilled, I thought of Domick's knowledge of torture methods and his certainty that anyone exposed to them would talk, and I remembered the rumor of his presence in the torture chamber. "Sometimes you have to endure a lesser evil in dealing with a greater one," he had said.

Oh, Domick, I thought. He had said he was not a torturer. But of course he must have seen terrible things—torture and death and executions, experimentation with new drugs. He was spying in the Councilcourt, for Lud's sake. What sort of naive idiot had I been to think he would simply sweep floors and gather up the odd secret?

Brydda rose and threw a knot of wood on the fire. "I have received replies from almost all the rebels as to whether or no they will attend your meeting."

I nodded without enthusiasm. A meeting with the rebel leaders was just one more possible disaster in the making.

Brydda gave me a level look. "You are going to meet with them still, I trust?"

I nodded again. "I'll go, but I just don't see that it will change anything."

"Not if you go with that attitude," he said shortly. "It will be held in Rangorn. I will not tell the others the location until the day of the meeting. Less chance of a leaking mouth."

I was startled out of my dejection. "But Rangorn is thick with soldierguards scouring the place for me!"

"Exactly why it will be the safest place to hold a meeting. By the time we get there, they will have given up searching and left." He smiled disarmingly. "There are plenty of good reasons for choosing Rangorn, but in truth, I have an urge to see the trees I climbed as a boy."

"What am I supposed to do at this meeting?"

"Answer their questions as best you can and remember that the aim is to make them see you as a Talented human rather than a Misfit," Brydda said. "When the question of your abilities arises, I would speak of farseeking as the power to communicate over long distances with others who possess the same power. Say nothing of mind reading or coercing unTalents. You might explain beastspeaking since that is unlikely to frighten them, and they have already heard mention of it. And empathy since it is fairly harmless. But I would not mention futuretelling at all. Also don't let yourself be pressured into demonstrations."

"You want me to impress them without scaring them."

"In a sense," Brydda agreed with all seriousness. "The main thing is that you establish yourself as normal and human in their eyes. And I think it would be best for now to let the rebels believe you are truly gypsies. If they knew the truth, they would want to know the whereabouts of your stronghold. It would not occur to them to ask about a gypsy stronghold because of the safe-passage agreement."

"But you'll be there, won't you?" I asked, puzzled at the advance instructions.

"Of course," Brydda said. "But if I appear too much on your side, they will feel threatened. It would cause them to see me as a rival, and ultimately that would endanger the rebellion. Certainly, it would not serve you. That is why I chose to have the meeting in Rangorn—it is neutral territory, because no rebel leader controls it."

I frowned. "Why would your rebels need neutral territory when they are allies?"

"An ally is not a friend. At best, these are reluctant allies. You must remember that these rebel chiefs are working toward smashing the established order."

"Yes?" I said blankly.

"Well, think about it. What happens when the current power structure of Herder Faction, Council, and soldier-guards is obliterated? Who will run things?"

"You mean they're worried about which of them will be in charge when it's all over?" I asked incredulously.

"It is something that must be considered," Brydda said.

"This is not a fairy tale where everyone lives happily ever after. Following the rebellion, there will be chaos and, in the midst of it, a struggle to decide who will have power over whom in the Land. Many of those who rule the various rebel groups are prepared for that and are determined to come out on top. For that reason, there is great rivalry between the most powerful groups. Indeed, some of the leaders hate one another more than they hate the Council or the soldierguards!"

"But that is stupid," I said.

He smiled sadly. "Stupid, yes, but it seems it is the nature of humankind to want control over one another. Why do you think I prefer the company of horses? Of course, in some ways, the rivalry is my fault. Before I brought them all together with the notion of revolution, there was no competition, because no one imagined it would be possible to get rid of the Council. No one thought further than simple survival. Now, of course, they think of afterward. . . ."

"Is that what the man you have joined wants? The Sutrium leader?"

"Bodera? No. There would be no point. And his son, Dardelan, is too young to be regarded by the rest as any sort of competition. That is what gives Bodera his neutrality and his best advantage." Brydda fixed me with a hard look. "It is because of this that I have been able to set the rebellion in motion. As to this meeting with you, make no mistake, they come more to keep an eye on one another than to give you a hearing. But they will hear you."

With a faint chill of apprehension, I wondered if the future of Talented Misfits lay only in changing one set of oppressors for another. What if someone like Tardis or Malik came out on top?

As if he had read my thoughts, Brydda said, "I have not heard yet from Malik. Bodera predicts he will send his refusal at the last moment to be difficult."

"Your Bodera sounds like a wise man," I said. "I would like to meet him."

The big rebel smiled with affection. "Truly he is worth meeting, but the rotting sickness has distorted his features dreadfully, and he dislikes being looked at. You will meet his son, Dardelan, though, and he is very like his father. He will attend the meeting in Bodera's stead."

"To remind the other rebels that he, and not you, is his father's chosen successor?"

Brydda nodded. "The rebel leaders are a suspicious lot, and it will not hurt to reassure them."

"Who else will come?"

"Tardis will send an emissary. That is not good, but it is better than nothing at all. There are few responses from the upper lowlands seditioner groups, because Malik has a strong following in the region and he has yet to respond. They will vote as he does, and only after he does.

"Malik sees Tardis as his most serious rival, because the Murmroth group is the largest next to his own. The west-coast bloc has the numbers to rival them, but they have been unable to amalgamate. The bloc is made up of rebel groups from Port Oran, Halfmoon Bay, and Morganna, each with its own leader. The trouble is that none of the three wants to step down. They have promised to send representation, but if one comes, I daresay all will come. None will want the others to gain an advantage.

"Naturally, the other major groups encourage the dis-cord, for they have a vested interest in keeping the situation as it is, though for the sake of the rebellion it would be best if one leader took control of the bloc."

On one level, I listened with fascination to the internal machinery of the rebel network, but on another I was conscious that Brydda was talking as much to take my mind away from thinking of Matthew as anything else. "Elii of Kinraide is a strong leader, but his numbers are small . . . ," Brydda was saying.

I stared at him, wondering if this could possibly be the same Elii who had guided me and other orphans from the Kinraide orphan home to harvest whitestick. Then again, Elii was not an uncommon name.

" . . . as well as Bram and Jakoby of Sador."

"Sadorians!" I was startled out of my lethargic drift. "I don't understand. What do the Sadorians care about our struggles? The Council has no jurisdiction over them."

"Not yet it doesn't," Brydda said darkly.

Abruptly, all the gossip I had heard of the distant region coalesced in my mind. "They support the rebellion because they don't want to be absorbed by the Land and ruled by the Council!"

"Exactly. It is inevitable that this will happen if the Council's might is not curtailed, and the Sadorians are too intelligent not to see it. I approached them, but—"

"You went to Sador?" I interrupted.

The rebel nodded, smiling reminiscently. "It is a strange place—nothing at all like the Land. There they worship the earth, and human life is seen as short and unimportant. Ever since the road opened to Sador, the Sadorians have had to endure Faction missionaries. Interestingly, like the gypsies, Sadorians are nomadic.

"Bram and Jakoby are simply two of the wisest of the tribal leaders. There is little strife among the tribes mainly, or so it seems to me, because they do not own the desert they call Sador. They shift about constantly, so there are no boundary disputes or territorial struggles. And when there are disputes, I believe they have devised some sort of ritual to mediate."

"How did you get them into the rebel alliance?"

"I simply pointed out to them that overthrowing the Council would ensure their autonomy." He shrugged. "But I think they had already worked that out. They are a very practical people."

"I wonder what they will make of me?"

Brydda's expression was unexpectedly wry. "I doubt they will come. I have asked them more out of courtesy than anything else. At present, we are allies only in principle—not in practice. But we will see."

For a moment, his eyes were distant and distracted. Then he sighed and suggested I try farseeking Matthew again.

The probe returned without locating him.

Three times before midmeal, and then three more times in the afternoon that long, gray day, I farsought Matthew, each time to no avail. Rain fell intermittently, and Reuvan came with progressive reports as the rebels scoured the tainted areas I had named. They found no trace of Matthew or the others. Brydda remained with me, talking when I was not trying to farseek. By dark, I felt exhausted and strangely hot.

Drawing up a mental probe for the eighth time, I shaped it to fit Matthew's mind with difficulty. When I sent it out, the probe felt heavy and unwieldy. It did not surprise me that such an uninspired search did not find him.

Opening my eyes, I seemed to see the flames on the hearth

through a gray haze, and even shaking my head required a tremendous effort of will. I felt dizzy, and it seemed that I must be too close to the fire, but I had no energy to pull myself away.

"Elspeth?" Brydda said from a long way off.

The room began to sway and dim, and there was the sound of voices, but it was too hard to understand what they were saying. I closed my eyes, and it seemed the flames were inside my skin. For a terrifying moment, I thought I was burning at the stake.

"Damn you! Where is it?" cried a disembodied voice.

"Elspeth!"

I dragged my eyes open and looked up to see Brydda's bearded face hovering above me. The world rocked. It took a moment for me to understand that the rebel was carrying me down the hall in his massive arms.

"Must . . . keep trying . . . ," I said, struggling feebly, though I could not for the life of me recall what was so urgent.

"Sleep," Brydda said with gentle insistence. "Sleep . . ."

I dreamed again of the dark tunnel. This time I was being pursued. Something huge and savage was pounding along the tunnel after me, closing the gap between us with impossible speed.

"Be gone!" Gahltha sent, leaping out of the darkness behind me. I whirled as he reared in the tunnel, blocking the way. But in the dream, there was something different about him. Before I could understand what it was, I found myself again on the threshold of the flaming doors. Incredibly, the Teknoguildmaster was beside me.

"It's amazing, isn't it," Garth demanded, "what can be

concealed when it is right in the open?" He looked at me. "Of course, you realize what it means?"

I shook my head.

"It means that you are really a gypsy."

His words seemed to come from a long way off.

"The gypsies keep the signs," someone whispered.

I knew the voice and tried to sit up. "Atthis! Why don't you speak to me?"

Hands pushed at me, and I fought against them.

"Atthis?"

"Sleep," said a familiar voice. "Sleep and heal."

"Who?" I croaked.

"Sleep . . ."

I woke, groggy and lethargic. Staggering to the bathing room, I plunged myself entirely into a barrel of icy water. The cold took my breath away, and I washed swiftly, aching and gasping before getting out and rubbing myself hard enough to make my skin tingle.

In the kitchen, Kella was nursing a cup of spiced milk. There were dark shadows under her eyes when she looked up, but an amazement in her expression startled me.

"What is it?" I asked.

"You . . . you're all right?" she stammered.

I stared at her, bemused. "Of course I am. Why shouldn't I be?"

"Last night you had a terrible fever. You were delirious and pouring with perspiration. After everything that has happened, I was afraid . . ." She shook her head: "I can't believe you look so well!"

"It must have appeared worse than it was—or I'm tougher than I look," I said. "Where is Brydda now?"

282

"He left before first light." The healer frowned and answered my unvoiced question. "None of his people has found any trace of Matthew."

Depression fell over me like a blanket. "And Dragon?" I stared into the fire as I spoke and tried to keep my voice even.

"No change," Kella said quietly.

She poured some milk and sat it near my hand, but I pushed it away. She shoved it firmly back. To my surprise, the warm, creamy liquid tasted delicious.

"Have you seen Maruman?" I said.

"No. I suppose he has gone exploring. You know how he is. Almost as bad as a teknoguilder."

"I hope you're right. I'm going to try again for Matthew." I closed my eyes and shaped a probe, letting it fly with a prayer. I cast it far, right to the edge of the Suggredoon and the sea rim, but there was no response.

I opened my eyes and saw my own despair writ large on the healer's face.

"What are we going to do?" she asked in a frightened voice. "Brydda says you must leave Sutrium in a few days to meet with the rebels. Will you go if Matthew has not been found?"

"I have agreed to this meeting, and I have no choice but to go. We'll find him." I looked at the healer levelly. "Kella, there is something else. I want you to come with me when I go back to Obernewtyn."

"What about Domick?"

"We need him here for the time being," I said.

"Why shouldn't I stay with him?" Kella's voice was defensive, truculent.

"Your face is becoming too well known to people who dwell hereabouts. This is a good safe house, and we don't

283

want to endanger it by overusing it. Domick can keep an eye on it, but he will be staying at an inn for the time being."

I gave her a quick look and saw that she was unconvinced. "Aside from that, I need you to look after Dragon."

The protestations died on her lips. Sipping at my warm milk, I watched the healer over the rim of the cup.

"It need not be forever," I said softly when the silence had gone on for too long.

"Everything is going wrong," Kella announced in sudden despair.

Hearing her voice my own thoughts had an unexpected effect—I felt a sudden surge of stubborn optimism.

"No," I said.

The healer looked startled at my sudden belligerence.

"We have to have hope. It is the least we can do. Matthew is missing, but wherever he is, he will trust that we have not given up on him. He will believe that we are searching, and he will be doing his best to find a way to reach us. We Misfits are hard to kill."

Kella smiled, a quick genuine twitch of her lips. "You are proof of that."

I smiled back. "We have all proven it."

Hope ignited in her eyes, and I was surprised to feel my own heart lift fractionally.

"You really think everything will be all right?"

She sounded suddenly very young. I smothered a resurgence of doubt. "Of course. You'll see. It's only hopeless when we've given up hope."

"And Domick?" she asked after a minute.

I looked at her quickly; the animation had died from her face.

"You know something is wrong with him and so do I," she

said. "I have tried to get him to talk to me, but bit by bit he has withdrawn. Now we are like strangers. If I leave now . . ." Her eyes shone with tears, but pride kept her from shedding them.

"Whatever is the matter with him has something to do with his spying," I said, considering my words carefully. "It is something he needs to work out on his own, or I am sure he would have told you what was wrong. But he still loves you."

"Then I should not leave," Kella said quickly.

"That is exactly what you should do!"

I hesitated, then decided she needed some hard words to stiffen her backbone. "Why do you suppose he has been spending so much time away from the safe house if not to be alone—to get away from you? Perhaps he feels smothered by your worrying about him so much."

I did not believe this. But Kella needed to come home, and Domick wanted her to go. Perhaps her presence was a strain he could not bear on top of everything else. Kella looked stricken, and I wondered if I had misread her, but after a moment, her face settled into determined lines. "Maybe you're right," she said at last. She was silent for a time, her brow furrowed in thought. "All right, I will come back to Obernewtyn. Domick will know where to find me when he wants me."

"Good girl," I said, heartened by her courage. I wondered if I would have had as much in similar circumstances. "Now all we need to do to complete the day is find Matthew."

"*I know where he is,*" came a familiar farseeking voice.

✦ 27 ✦

I JUMPED TO my feet, knocking the chair to the ground. Kella gaped at me in amazement. "What is it?"

"Daffyd is in the yard below!" I cried aloud to her. "He's just farsent that he knows where Matthew is!"

Her eyes widened in joy, and we hurried downstairs.

I stopped dead at the sight of the ex-Druid armsman as Kella let him into the repair shed. He was wearing an oiled cloak that glistened with rain.

At the inn, Daffyd had been concealed by the darkness, and before that, I had not seen him for an age. Like Domick and Brydda, I saw now that time and whatever straits he had undergone had altered him. He had lost none of his tan, which suggested he still lived an outdoor life, but there was a new intensity and a depth of pain in his dark-brown eyes that made me wonder what he had been doing since he left us. He was taller than I remembered and thinner, the skin on his bones so scant that he looked frail. But when he embraced me, I felt his indomitable will in the sinewy strength of his arms and was reassured.

"I am sorry I did not come sooner, but they are very watchful," he said. "Even now I dare not be gone too long, or they will become suspicious."

"You said you know where Matthew is," I said eagerly.

Daffyd gave me an assessing look. "I do, but before I tell

you where he is, you must make me a promise."

I stared at him, bemused. "What?"

"I have spent much time working my way painstakingly into the slaver's organization, waiting for a time when Salamander would expose himself. That time is near, and I can't let you do anything that would stop him appearing."

"Is Matthew with Salamander?"

"The slaver you and Brydda met, Ayle, has Matthew and the other slaves, but Salamander will come for them. If you free them, you must do it at the last minute. You don't have any idea how fanatically suspicious Salamander is. If he gets the slightest notion that something is wrong, there will be a lot of dead people and dead ends, believe me, Matthew and I are likely to be among the cold ones."

"I'll be guided by you," I said quickly. "We will not act until you give the word."

"Do you speak for Brydda as well?"

I paused. "I can't speak for him," I said at last. "But he has also been searching for Salamander, because the slavemaster killed Idris. He won't want to frighten him away any more than you do."

"Salamander kills like other people breathe. I suppose Brydda wants revenge."

"He wants to smash the slave trade," Kella said.

"That is a fine desire," Daffyd said. "But this is a trade that brings a river of coin into the hands of slavers. Killing Salamander will not end it altogether. But I wish him luck. My quest is somewhat more personal." There was something unbending in his face now.

"You are still looking for Gilaine and the others?" I temporized.

"Always," he said, the terse word a vow.

"Then Salamander has them?"

"Not now. But he had them, and he is my sole link to them." He frowned, seeming to weigh things in his mind. Finally, he spoke again. "Matthew is being held with a whole lot of other slaves in a warehouse on the banks of the Suggredoon."

"One of the river wharfs?" Kella asked eagerly.

Daffyd nodded, but his eyes did not leave mine.

"Then we were right. He means to use the Suggredoon to get them out of Sutrium," the healer said.

"Matthew is drugged, then?" I asked.

"He was, though he did not appear to be," Daffyd said. "I near died when I spotted him among the others. When I could touch him, I tried to farseek him to find out what he was up to. That was when I discovered that he had been drugged.

"I managed to get the job of redosing the slaves, and I let Matthew's dribble onto the ground and kept my fingers crossed that he would not give me away before his mind was clear. Eventually, we were able to exchange stories. I promised to come and find you, but it took all night to think of an excuse that would not cause suspicion." He glanced outside where it had begun to rain again.

"I don't understand," I broke in. "I farsought Matthew all day yesterday. If he was free of the drugs, how is it that I couldn't locate him? Is he on tainted ground?"

Daffyd shook his head. "The place where he and the other slaves are being held is built to extend over the Suggredoon. I think there is something tainted in the water, because sometimes the fish glow at night or they are grotesquely deformed."

I opened my mouth and huffed a sigh of relief. That explained everything. Probably whatever was tainting the river had also affected the sea along the shore. And from Daffyd's description of Matthew, it looked as if Domick had been right about the slave suppliers using Sadorian drugs. The only mystery was why the soldierguard had stopped the wagon partway to administer the drug dose.

"How does the soldierguard captain fit into the whole thing?"

Daffyd gave me a blank stare. "What soldierguard captain?"

I did not want to divert Daffyd when we had so little time, so I shrugged dismissively. "How did Gilaine and Lidgebaby end up in Salamander's hands?"

Daffyd's eyes gleamed with obsessive fire. "Well you might ask, for it is a strange and dark story. And long. Too long for these few moments. Suffice it to say that they were sold to him as slaves. I have infiltrated the slave trade specifically to reach Salamander so that I can learn where they were sold and to whom."

He looked around again, as if he feared someone might have followed him. Taking me by the arm, he drew me deeper into the shed and out of sight of the yard gate.

"There is to be a change in the way things are done. A streamlining, Ayle called it. Moving forward, all slaves are to be brought to a single spot in Sutrium—this will be regularly changed. The slaves are to be picked up by boat and taken over the seas to be sold."

"Straight to sea from Sutrium? No more routing them through Morganna?" I asked, my mouth dry.

"Ayle said nothing of that, but I would guess this slave boat will stop at Morganna as well. He is to manage the sorting house in Sutrium, and I suppose there will be another sorting house and another Ayle in Morganna—maybe one in every coastal town." Daffyd's eyes narrowed. "What I know for sure is that Salamander will come in person, and that means I have the chance I've been waiting for."

"Chance?" Kella murmured, voicing the question shaping in my own mind.

The armsman flicked a look at her. "I mean to farseek Salamander to learn where he has taken Gilaine and Lidgebaby. If that does not work, I will force him to recall by cruder means. If he has truly forgotten, he will pay for his amnesia with his life."

"Hard to believe that Salamander would come to pick the slaves up himself," I said. "It seems so out of character for him to expose himself like that."

Daffyd shrugged. "He is setting a new aspect of the slave trade in place, and he does not trust any other to do it properly. In any case, while he is aboard the ship, he will be in no danger. I daresay he will not come ashore longer than it takes to load the slaves, and it is likely he will be masked. But a mask will not keep me from his mind. And I will have some time; it will take more than a little while to board so many slaves."

"So many slaves?" I was puzzled.

Daffyd laughed bitterly. "I told you, Ayle's warehouse is to be the new sorting house. Every day, more slaves are brought in to await Salamander's ship. There are more than one hundred already waiting for collection."

"One hundred!" I echoed, astounded.

"It is nothing to what will be coming, according to Ayle. These are early days."

"How long before this ship comes to take the slaves?" I asked with sudden foreboding.

"Ayle said tomorrow."

"Tomorrow!"

Daffyd nodded grimly. "Remember, you must not act until the last moment."

I nodded back, thinking this *was* the last moment. We would be lucky to get anything set up in such a short time. "Does Matthew have any ideas how we might get him free?"

Daffyd gave a rare, crooked half smile. "I think Matthew thought you and Brydda would come up with those minor details."

I shook my head in exasperation.

Daffyd looked again from the repair-shed door into the driving rain. "I must go back now. Is there anything you want me to tell Matthew?"

"Tell him to be ready," I said decisively.

"I will." He pulled up the hood on his cloak and turned to face me, his eyes shadowed. "Remember your promise."

He strode away without waiting for a response and was lost behind the curtain of rain even before he had reached the gates to the repair yard.

I turned back to look at Kella.

"He is so full of hatred," she said. "I have only slight empath Talent, and yet it burned me."

"He loves Gilaine, and he is emotionally linked with Lidgebaby. And his brother was in the camp, too. I wonder how they got into Salamander's hands in the first place. And how they escaped the firestorm that destroyed the Druid camp."

"What are you going to tell Brydda?"

"Yes, what?" Brydda asked, stepping out of the shadows behind us.

We both whirled to face the rebel.

"It seems I do not have to decide that question," I said coolly, not liking that he had deliberately hidden himself and listened to words that had not been intended for his ears.

"Perhaps it is lucky for us both that you do not," Brydda said with equal coolness. He shook his head, and the harshness melted from his expression. "I did not mean to overhear. I did not recognize Daffyd and so I hid. Only when you spoke did I realize who he was, and by then it was clear he would not welcome my presence."

"What will you do, then?" I asked.

"What would you have me do?"

"You heard what Daffyd said. He wants to find out where Salamander took Gilaine and the others. I would ask, as he did, that we do not get in his way."

The rebel's eyes were somber. "Perhaps I have given you some cause to doubt me, but I tell you now, on my life, you can trust me. Daffyd wants Salamander alive so he can milk him for information, and I want him dead. Both our wishes can be met."

"What did you have in mind?"

Brydda gave a feral smile. "Rescuing Matthew and taking Salamander captive so that we can question him to our heart's content. And when he has no more to tell us, then I will deal with him."

I shuddered and wondered if there was ever any other way of dealing with hatred and violence.

"Well?" Brydda prompted. "Shall we see how a sly Salamander deals with the Black Dog's teeth?"

I looked at the rebel steadily. "If I don't agree?"

He frowned. "You gave your word. I was not meant to hear what I heard, and we are friends. Therefore, by virtue of that friendship, I will abide by your decision."

I felt ashamed of my doubts. "You are a better friend than I am," I said. "I will say yes, but I must let Daffyd know that this has become a rebel operation."

"Let us go there tonight. I will need to have a look at this warehouse and the river wharfs in order to formulate a plan, and we will find a way to communicate it to Daffyd."

I nodded. "Come by at dusk, then. Did you come for anything in particular?" I added as the big man turned to go.

He slapped his head. "Of course. All of this drove it from my mind. I came to tell you that Malik has agreed to meet you but that he refuses to come unless the location of the meeting is changed."

"But you said they did not know where—"

"They don't. But he proposes his own location. He says the meeting should occur on truly neutral territory and has named Bodera's home in Sutrium."

"Oh Lud," I said uncertainly.

"Malik sent his letter directly to Bodera, which suggests that, in spite of all my efforts, he has begun to see me as a rival."

"What did Bodera say?"

Brydda scowled. "Unfortunately, he thought it was a good idea. He is proud to think that his home is neutral territory."

"Then what is the problem? If he is not troubled . . ."

The big rebel ran an agitated hand over his unruly thatch. "It is dangerous to have these sort of meetings in a permanent place that we use. And, apart from that, the location of the meeting will be known in advance of the day, which increases the chance of treachery."

"How much danger will there be?"

He shrugged. "Not so much as all that, I suppose, since none of the leaders would risk giving away a secret meeting at which they themselves might be taken prisoner or slain. The other thing, of course, is that the rebels do want the rebellion to occur, and a raid at Bodera's house would immediately put an end to it." Brydda shook his head. "I don't know. Maybe I am worrying over nothing, but I think it sets a bad precedent. And I don't like putting Bodera in danger."

"I suppose I must accept the risk if you and the others do. When will the meeting take place?"

"Within the sevenday," Brydda said. "And the sooner it is over, the better I'll feel."

✦ 28 ✦

I SPENT MOST of the day sitting by Dragon's bed, holding her hand.

I had brought her out of a different kind of solitude to Obernewtyn, and now she was lost to us again, locked behind the fortress of her own mind.

In the late afternoon, the rain clouds parted to reveal a watery sun. I donned fur-lined boots and a thick cloak just the same, determined not to freeze as I had the last time I kept a midnight vigil outside a warehouse.

I went down to ask if Gahltha wanted a blanket.

"I/Gahltha am not cold," he sent.

"Maruman/yelloweyes has been gone longlong days," I sent, wondering as always why the beasts called a one-eyed cat "yelloweyes." Although, I did it just as unthinkingly. Perhaps because, like Dameon, the old cat often saw better than those of us with two eyes.

Gahltha gave me a level look. "He does what he/yelloweyes must."

I frowned into his dark eyes. "Do you/Gahltha know where he/Maruman is?"

"The voices of his chaos/madness call him when they will, and he/Maruman must hear them. The strain of guardianship caused the voices to call."

I frowned, confused. "Guardianship?"

"Of the dreamtrails. I/Gahltha know that it is not easy. Yet I have sworn to Maruman/yelloweyes that I would take his place. I did not know how until he/yelloweyes showed me. The dreamtrails are strange/dangerous. On them are beasts like none that walk the earth and shapes that hide/conceal other shapes, yet one grows better at it."

I wondered if I was understanding him correctly. In my mind's eye, I saw the black horse leap into the tunnel of my dreams, urging me to run while he fought off whatever it was that followed me. Maruman's H'rayka? A dark unease filled me at the thought that somehow those nightmares were real.

"Are you/Gahltha saying that Maruman/yelloweyes asked you to look after me . . . my mind or my dreams, and then went away in his madness/mindchaos?"

"Did I not say so?"

Was it possible I was being somehow stalked in my dreams? Impossible as it seemed, I shivered, for if the H'rayka was my mirror image, wouldn't he possess the same powers as me?

"Sallah comes," Jaygar sent.

I turned to see Brydda ride into the yard on the white mare Sallah. The golden afternoon sunlight gave her a dazzling regality. I was surprised Brydda did not try to hide her beauty as I did Gahltha's. But perhaps his size was enough to dissuade thieves.

"Greeting and hail, ElspethInnle," Sallah sent formally.

"Greetings," I returned, embarrassed at the thought that the white horse might have communicated to Brydda her belief that I was the incarnation of a savior figure in beastlegend.

"Beastsecrets are not for the funaga," Sallah sent with clear reproof.

"Am I not funaga?"

"You are Innle," Sallah sent.

"Are you ready?" Brydda asked.

I nodded, and Gahltha came forward so that I could mount him. Wordlessly, we rode out into the yard where Kella waited by the gate to say goodbye.

"Be careful," Jaygar sent after us.

"Always," Gahltha returned.

It was chilly already, and I was glad of my cloak. Gladder still that the rain had stopped. With luck, it would remain clear until we were safely back at the repair shed.

"We had better dismount," Brydda said when we neared the river piers. "I have a few rebels in a house close by. They have been watching the place all day. We can leave the horses there and go the rest of the way on foot."

I gave him a quick look, disturbed that he had already set his people in place.

"Just in case of trouble," he promised, sensing my disquiet. "I wanted to have some idea of the movement of traffic about these river piers. I had no particular knowledge of them."

The house turned out to be yet another of the city's burned-out hovels. I was glad to find that only three rebels awaited us in the yard behind it. Reuvan was one of them. Beside him was a tall, lanky fellow I had not seen before, with woolly brown hair and a beard to match. The third was the blond woman with the plague-scarred face whom I had met at The Good Egg. I searched my memory for her name—Oria. Fortunately, she was engrossed in the examination of a map and had not seen me arrive. For Domick's sake, I swiftly erased my face from her memory. When Brydda introduced us, she gave me a searching look, but there was no recognition in it.

"What have you found out?" Brydda asked her briskly.

She flicked her fingers at the bearded man, who had a steady, seasoned look about him, and drew us into a room whose windows had been blackened. He lit a small lantern and unrolled the piece of paper Oria had been studying.

"Here is the sea," he rasped, stabbing a brown-stained finger at the paper. "There are four pier warehouses that traders lease privately from the Herder Faction. They are spread apart a little so that carts can draw up between them. As you see, there are the same number of piers. Each warehouse has its own, and here, opposite, there are sheds for storage—one for each warehouse. They are quite often leased out separately. A rough road runs between them."

"The Faction owns the pier sheds, too?" I asked.

Oria nodded. "They bought them recently from the Council, and the wharfs. They use the river to travel straight from their cloister on the edge of the Suggredoon to Morganna and Aborium and then to Herder Isle. The Council controls all of the main sea wharfs and warehouses, as well as the ferry that checks the riverboats, but they leave the river to the Herders now. Of course, other boats use the wharfs to ship wares in or out, and they pay the Herders for it. Small vessels mostly. The Herder ships are the largest that use the wharfs."

I nodded but felt chilled at the thought of being on property controlled by the fanatical Faction.

"The pier manifest says there are only two ships due in tomorrow. One of them must be the slave ship," the bearded rebel put in. "Unless it comes in unscheduled."

"Is the pier empty now? Can we get any closer?" Brydda asked.

Reuvan shook his head. "A Faction boat docked about an hour back, and there are at least a dozen burlymen and seamen roving about. We'll have to wait until they're done, but it should not be too long—they are loading straightaway."

Oria touched Brydda's arm, and there was a clear look of devotion in her eyes, though her voice was brisk and businesslike. "The other thing is that troops of soldierguards have spent the day running some sort of training exercise on the banks of the river right by the warehouse that juts out over the water. Their camp is not far from here. Once it is dark, they will certainly be leaving, too."

"I wonder if the soldierguards are making Ayle nervous," I murmured.

"No doubt he is thanking his lucky stars that the exercise was run today rather than tomorrow," Brydda said with sharp humor. "Imagine them trying to shift a hundred slaves under the noses of the soldierguards."

"A hundred," Oria murmured. "It is hard to believe how brazen this is."

"Since we have to wait anyway, I might try to reach Daffyd," I said, sitting on an upturned box to make myself comfortable.

"I doubt he will be out in the open with so much going on," Brydda said. He looked at Reuvan. "Do you have any food? I have not eaten all day and . . ."

His voice faded as I closed my eyes and shaped an attuned probe to Daffyd's mind signature. The mental static was very strong this close to the water, which meant I had to concentrate fiercely to keep my mindprobe intact. Given Brydda's warning, I was shocked when the probe not only reached its target but elicited a strong reaction from Daffyd—as if I had thrust a brand into his mind.

The intensity of his response was blistering.

"I have prayed and prayed you would reach me," he sent frantically. "Elspeth, it was a ruse! They're loading the slaves aboard a ship right now! They're going to leave as soon as it's done!"

✦ 29 ✦

"WE DARE NOT go any closer," Reuvan whispered from our hiding spot behind a pile of crates. "The soldierguards are still there, marching back and forth like a lot of fools. I can't imagine what they are doing, but they will have to go when it gets dark. We should wait until then to get nearer."

"This is madness," Brydda said softly. "Burlymen and soldierguards all milling about while the slavers openly load an illicit cargo of drugged slaves."

"Daffyd didn't sound as if he was making a mistake," I said softly. "He sounded panic-stricken and deadly serious."

"Keep your voices down," Oria warned. "Sound carries far and easily by the water."

"We have to get closer," Brydda said, frustrated. "Ask Daffyd if he can—"

I shook my head. "I can't reach him. He must have gone back into the warehouse, and the static from the tainted water is like a stone wall."

"Luddamn it!" the rebel chief hissed.

"I don't understand," said the brown-bearded rebel. "The only ship on the manifest for tonight is *The Calor Lady*, and like I said, that is a Herder ship."

"That is the least strange thing about this whole affair. Herder ships are for hire at the right price, like any other,"

Brydda said. He looked at me. "Can you hide us somehow? We need to get closer."

I glanced instinctively at Oria and the other rebel. Their faces showed slight curiosity but nothing more, and I wondered how much Brydda had told them of me.

"I can cloak two of us," I said.

"Wait here," Brydda instructed the others.

"Just a minute," I said quickly. "I can feel Daffyd again."

I closed my eyes, and the general probe I had left in case the farseeker emerged sharpened into an attuned probe. Like Matthew, his farseeking power was too weak to combat the static from the Suggredoon on its own, but I could make up the difference.

"You'd better do something now if you are going to, Elspeth," he sent urgently. "Matthew is in the last lot, and they are going to load them shortly. Once he is on the ship, you will have no hope of helping him unless you brought an army."

"What about Salamander?" I sent. "Have you managed to farseek him?"

"No!" Daffyd's mental voice was savage with disappointment and rage. "He has not come ashore, and I cannot reach him over the damn water!"

"Ask him about the soldierguards and the Herders," Brydda hissed into my ear.

I shook my head angrily, for he had distracted me, and it was difficult enough to focus in the static.

"Daffyd?" I sent. "Why are they boarding them on a Herder ship?"

There was no answer.

"He's gone, but he said they're going to load Matthew any minute."

"What about Salamander?"

"He hasn't left the ship."

Brydda scowled. "The man has the instincts of a fangcat. It is almost as if he knew we were waiting for him." He took a deep, steadying breath. "Well, let's get nearer."

He led the way, and I concentrated on cloaking us coercively as we emerged from behind the crates and made our way through a narrow lane toward the water. I could smell the faintly brackish scent of the Suggredoon and hear its rush before I saw it. The static from the tainting was incredibly strong, and I wondered what had caused it. Certainly the upper reaches of the river, which fed the lake beneath Tor, were clean.

The row of sheds came into view, and through the gaps between them, I could see they were separated from the river by a stone walkway. Right on the bank were the warehouses, facing away from the river. The warehouse jutting out over the water was farthest away from us and set back a little from the rest. People were moving about in front of it, and even from this distance, I could see the huge front door stood ajar.

Tied up alongside it was a ship, its three masts and a small part of its bow visible behind the bulk of the warehouse. Judging from the movement of people about it, the gangplank lay on the warehouse side of the ship.

Brydda pressed my arm and pointed past the warehouse to an open field, where fifty or so soldierguards in full regalia were marching in formation. They were paying no mind whatsoever to the ship.

The whole scene was bathed in the ever-deepening pinkish gold light of the predusk. In less than an hour, the sun would set.

"It can be no coincidence that the soldierguards are here," Brydda whispered.

"Do you think they were hired by the slavers?"

"Not this many," Brydda said. "Too much risk of someone talking." He gave me a searing look. "Of course, a soldierguard captain might have some hidden reason for ordering his troops to perform their exercises here."

I bit my lip and wondered again about the soldierguard captain.

"Can you get us any closer?" the rebel prompted.

I shook my head decisively. "There are burlymen loading a wagon from that shed just up there. You can't see them from here, but I felt them with my probe. Too many to coerce into blindness."

Brydda and I stared at one another, and with dawning horror, I saw resignation shape itself in his eyes.

"We have to help Matthew," I cried.

"Shh," he said sternly. "I know how you feel, but it is impossible to attack openly. If he is to be rescued, it can only be by stealth and wit. Between the seamen, the slaver's hirelings, the burlymen . . . Even with your powers, there are only five of us, six counting Daffyd, and Matthew makes seven—if he is in any state to fight."

"There are nine—if you count the equines as two more," Gahltha sent sternly, and I turned to see that the black horse had followed us.

"I/Gahltha hid myself," he sent imperturbably. "Sallah watches over the other funaga."

"Hell!" Brydda started in fright when he noticed the horse. "What in the name of . . . ?"

I shook my head impatiently, knowing two horses would not tilt the balance in our favor in an open battle. Then I spotted Daffyd coming from the warehouse with a small group of shuffling slaves. He led them along the pier and then vanished between the building and the ship.

"Elspeth!" Daffyd sent as soon as he felt my probe. "I'm taking this group to the ship, and Matthew is in the next lot. It doesn't matter if you cause a fuss, because Salamander is out of my reach anyway. Help Matthew . . ."

His voice faded, and the contact dissolved. I guessed he had stepped onto the gangplank and out over the water.

I sent a swift command to Gahltha and pulled myself up on his back. At once he started forward, evading Brydda's grasp.

"Elspeth!" the rebel hissed, not daring to come out in the open after us.

"Stay still and no one will see you," I said over my shoulder as I urged Gahltha forward.

"Elspeth, there is nothing you can do!" he said. "For Lud's sake, come back."

Gahltha's hooves clattered on the pier boards, drowning out Brydda's frantic whisperings.

"Go along the pier/ride slowly," I sent to the equine. Then I turned my mind to the warehouse. "Matthew!" I sent. "Matthew!"

But, of course, there was no answer.

Closer to the warehouse, I could see *The Calor Lady* properly. It was an elegant vessel with slender lines and its name stamped in red on the bow. Underneath was the distinctive Herder insignia. Given what Brydda had said, it had probably been hired for the occasion to encourage people to mind their own business. Though I could not see why, since they were brazenly loading slaves in public with soldierguards paying no mind to them at all.

The vessel rested low in the water, underlining Daffyd's warning that most of the slaves had already been boarded. No doubt the armsman had contrived as best he could to put

Matthew's boarding off to the last moment. If this was imminent, it meant the ship's departure also loomed, as well it must if they meant to catch the out tide, cross the sandbars at the river mouth, and reach open sea by nightfall.

I came level with the burlymen I had sensed. They had been loading bales of wool onto a wagon from a shed opposite the first of the four warehouses. But they had ceased their labors to watch the loading of the slaves. I felt dizzy with confusion. They were watching as if it was nothing out of the ordinary. There had to be more going on than officials turning a blind eye.

"Good riddance, I say," said one of the two.

His thickset companion nodded, and I could not stop myself staring at them. Since when had slavery gained such general approval?

"Reckon the Herders should have rounded 'em up a long time ago. Waste of space they are," the first man said.

His silent companion nodded again.

"Can't see them succeedin' in healin' this lot, though, no matter that they say Lud'll help 'em. Even if they do have skilled healers on Herder Isle. Once a defective always a defective, I say."

I struggled to keep my face expressionless, but suddenly I understood what was going on. No one knew these people were slaves! Those watching thought that Herders were taking a load of defectives to their Isle for treatment. That was why the soldierguards were doing nothing and why the whole thing could be done in broad daylight without fear. And the new Sadorian drugs meant none of the slaves behaved as if they were drugged.

My heartbeat quickened as the two burlymen turned to stare at me.

"Gypsy slut. Ought to round *them* up, too," said one.

This time the other was prevailed upon to grunt his assent. I felt sick. I had been so concerned about Matthew that I had forgotten to maintain my coercive enhancement of my boyish apparel. At any minute, I was sure to be recognized by the soldierguards. I inserted a sharp coercive command to the burlymen to get back to their work, and they reacted as if galvanized. They would remember me later, but in the face of everything else, this seemed a minor problem.

Then I coerced an image of myself as a sun-browned seaman's lad. It took a steady surge of power to hold the image, and this, along with trying to combat the sea static, was proving a frightening drain on my mental energies. Soon I would have no reserve of power.

Yet what else could I do?

I sent to Gahltha to slow down as we came level with the warehouse from which the slaves were being led. At the same moment, a man brought a small knot of people outside, and I slowed to let them go before me, glad of a reason to delay.

"Elspeth!" Matthew sent.

I stiffened, for if the farseeker could reach me, it meant he was among those who had just been brought out.

"Matthew!" I sent gladly, urging Gahltha up beside them.

"Ride on past fer Obernewtyn's sake!" he sent urgently.

Startled by the intensity of his command, I obeyed.

As I passed around the little clutch of people, I glanced down at them casually. The farseeker was less than a handspan from me, his expression carefully blank.

"Go slowly/be lame," I sent, and Gahltha began to affect an exaggerated limp.

After a few steps, I pulled him up and slid off his back, pretending to examine a hoof. With a careful eye, I measured the distance between myself and the little group of slaves. Matthew was only three or four steps away.

"It's no good," the farseeker sent suddenly. "This time I've got myself in a fix ye can't get me out of."

"What are you saying?" Fear made my mental voice strident. I pretended to pick a rock from Gahltha's hoof.

The man who had brought out Matthew and the others went back to close the doors, leaving the slaves standing alone. Matthew turned his head to look at me.

"Elspeth, ye know ye mun let 'em take me," he sent. "Ye can't fight them all yerself."

"Brydda is with me, and Sallah, and there are three rebels besides."

"Against dozens of soldierguards and burlymen, not to mention the ship's seamen?"

"Then I'll create a diversion, and you can run for it. I'll pick you up, and we'll ride clear on Gahltha."

"How? I'm shackled to these other slaves, ankle to ankle an' wrist to wrist. There's no time to do anythin' about that. Right now, these slavers think I'm nothin', an' I'd as soon keep it that way."

"Then I'll make a fuss to stop them boarding. I'll pretend to recognize one of the others. I'll say you're not defectives— that's what everyone watching thinks. Better to be taken to the Councilcourt by the soldierguards than spirited away to Lud knows where on a slave ship. And maybe then Domick . . ."

"Listen to me," Matthew sent. "Th' soldierguards are mixed up in this somehow. I dinna think they would take us to th' Councilcourt if you made a fuss. I think they'd just bundle us aboard, an' then you an' Brydda would be caught too."

"Matthew, they'll take you away!"

"I know," he sent calmly. "An' ye'll let 'em, because we both know that this time we're outnumbered. Look, I'm nowt afraid. Wherever this ship goes an' whatever happens, there'll be other ships. An' I'll be comin' back on one of them. I swear it. Tell Daffyd I'll keep a lookout for his Gilaine."

"Get a shift on, lad," said a surly voice right behind me.

I froze, recognizing it as the voice of the slaver Ayle. I did not dare turn around. I knew I could not coerce him, because he was mind-sensitive. I tangled clumsy fingers in Gahltha's mane and, without turning, hauled myself onto his back.

"Go," I sent, and the black equine moved forward.

Daffyd appeared right in front of me. He paled at the sight of me, but my whole mind was too tightly focused on maintaining contact with Matthew to let me communicate with him.

"What's wrong with you?" I heard Ayle demand of Daffyd. I held my breath for his answer, slowing Gahltha.

"Seasick . . . ," Daffyd muttered, passing me.

Ayle bellowed with laughter. "Well, here's the last lot. You can kiss the ground when yer done." There was a little pause; then the slaver's voice reached out to me. "You hear me, boy? Get a move on. You've no business here."

"Go!" Matthew sent.

I heard Ayle's purposeful tread behind me.

"Please!"

With a heart as heavy as a stone anvil, I signaled Gahltha, and he moved forward. After a few steps, I glanced back and saw Ayle retracing his steps, shaking his head and muttering about half-wit gypsies. At the same time, I saw Daffyd take up the leading chain of the last little group of shackled slaves and move toward the gangplank of *The Calor Lady*.

"I love ye, Elspeth," Matthew sent fiercely, meeting my eyes. "I'm sorry about Dragon an' all . . ."

His mental voice faded as he reached the gangplank and walked out over the water.

Every instinct in my body rebelled against riding away, yet I knew Matthew was right. There was nothing I could do to help him.

Almost at once, the gangplank was withdrawn. The seaman standing ashore threw off the ship's mooring knots and leapt aboard. *The Calor Lady* drifted from the shore, borne by the swift-flowing tide that would take it to the sea, its sails snapping and fluttering as they were unfurled slightly to turn the ship.

Matthew was no longer visible. He had been taken below like the other slaves, but I could not take my eyes off the receding vessel. I was stricken by the feeling that I had failed the Farseeker ward and would never see him again.

I watched as a tall youth with white-blond hair and a great flapping black cloak came out on deck and leaned against the rail, staring back at the shore.

He was extraordinarily beautiful, long boned and slender, probably younger than me by a few years, with skin so pale it seemed to gleam in the fading sunset. My eyes lingered as I mused on how uncommon that sort of fairness is in men.

As I watched, he ran his fingers through his hair.

My mouth fell open in shock, and I stared at the blond youth with incredulity, remembering where I had seen that languid hand drawn through fair hair before.

The mannerism was Ariel's.

I had only ever thought of Ariel as a young boy, but I had not set eyes on him for years. Of course, he would be grown near to manhood now. I told myself it was impossible, that

310

this was another blond youth. Ariel had traveled to Herder Isle to become a priest.

But this is a Herder ship! I remembered with utter dread.

My eyes hurt with the effort of trying to see more clearly, but the light was fading to a golden dimness, and the distance had grown too great. I could see no more than the white blob of the youth's face turned toward the river's mouth. But even as I watched, I saw his head turn until it seemed that he was looking straight at me.

PART III

✦

THE SADORIAN BATTLEGAMES

✦ 30 ✦

I CONCENTRATED ON walking, putting one foot in front of the other and keeping up with Brydda. It required all my energy. Listening to his words was more than I could manage.

It was early morning and the dismal start of a chilly and miserable day. Five days had passed since Matthew had been lost to us. The streets were blurred with a light drizzle of the sort that penetrates as damply and effectively as heavy rain.

We were making our way across the city for the long-planned meeting with the rebels at Bodera's home. Since leaving the safe house, the rebel had offered a monologue of advice and warnings, but somehow I could not make myself care about the meeting enough to hear what he was saying. Matthew's loss meant much more to me than any political alliance.

"Malik arrived with Brocade of Sawlney and with letters of authority that allow him to represent and vote on behalf of the Saithwold and Darthnor groups. And Tardis has sent a man called Gwynedd," Brydda was saying.

I nodded absently. Matthew's face seemed to float before my eyes, borne on a tide of grief and regret. My mind circled back for the hundredth time to our abortive rescue attempt. Not once had I imagined we would fail. It was useless to wish now that I had thought it out more carefully and had been less certain of outwitting the ruthless, clever Salamander.

Since then, I had thought of a dozen perfectly good ways to get the Farseeker ward from his captors that had not occurred to me at the time, and somehow that made it all the worse.

"Elii of Kinraide has come, too, but the real surprise is that Cassell has come on behalf of the entire western bloc. You will recall I told you of the three rebel groups that have been unable to choose a single leader?" Brydda's eyes sought mine.

Did I remember? Yes, I nodded.

Reassured, Brydda brought his brown eyes back to the way ahead. "Well, then, his presence alone may mean that Cassell has gained control of the group and that it has at last been welded into a unit—in any event, it will give Malik cause for concern."

I pulled my cloak tighter to stop water dripping from the saturated tendrils of hair down my neck and glanced up at the heavy gray sky. Matthew had always disliked the Days of Rain, saying they drowned a man's spirit and dragged at his soul.

Ariel's face came to me then, his lips tilted in a mocking smile. I imagined him exactly as he had been when I met him: sweet-mouthed, with soft white skin and a golden nimbus of fair hair floating like a halo around his head. He had been as beautiful as an angel, but the radiant exterior had concealed a heart that was rotten and black to the core. And then his image changed, aging and altering until the face that mocked me was that of the dazzling blond youth on the deck of *The Calor Lady*.

I was tormented by endless imagined scenarios in which Ariel came face to face with Matthew, whom he had known when they were both orphans in the old days at Obernewtyn. What would happen when Matthew, who had wanted to kill Ariel for torturing little Cameo to death, learned he was on the same ship as his most hated foe?

I could only pray that with so many slaves, Matthew's face would be lost in a sea of others; in spite of the farseeker's courage and strength, he was no match for Ariel's vicious subtleties.

"The biggest surprise, of course, is that Jakoby has come. . . ."

The odd name slipped through my haze of despair. "Jakoby?" I said aloud. "Isn't that one of the Sadorian tribe leaders?"

The rebel nodded approvingly. "Jakoby came by ship. From what I can make out, the Sadorians had no intention of attending this meeting until one of their Temple guardians had some sort of significant dream, and so they decided at the last minute to send someone. There was not time enough for a land journey, so it was a ship or nothing."

"Because of a dream?" I asked warily.

"Some matter of smoke shapes and feathers burning." Brydda dismissed this with a flick of his fingers. "The sort of ritual whose outcome can be read to mean anything—I expect the Temple guardians wanted to get our measure, so they came up with a guiding dream."

I swallowed, my mouth dry at the thought of such dreams.

"Anyway, Jakoby has come. Other than that, Dardelan of Sutrium will stand in for his father as I told you. . . ."

My mind began to drift again. Jakoby had come by sea, and Matthew had been stolen away by the waves.

Brydda stopped suddenly, swinging around to look into my face. I met his searching gaze with composure, but then, without the slightest warning, my eyes filled with tears. Fortunately, the street we were walking along was empty, for, within seconds, I was sobbing my heart out into the rebel's chest.

"Elspeth, girl," Brydda said, patting my back with awkward gentleness and drawing me into a doorway. "I am truly sorry about Matthew, and I know his loss is a mortal blow to you," he said.

"You don't understand. It's all my fault," I choked. "First Dragon and now this. And last time I came to the lowlands, it was Jik. I'm not fit to lead an expedition. Everyone I care about dies or is hurt terribly."

Brydda put me from him and looked into my face with stern sadness. "I know how it is to feel responsible for the death of a friend," he said. "But we are their leaders as well as their friends, and leadership often means putting people we care deeply for into danger."

"But that's wrong," I said in a hoarse voice.

"Which is more wrong? That a leader risks those he cares for or that he cares nothing for whom he risks? And those who follow us are their own people; they make a choice to follow us, and we must honor it. As we love them, we must accept that their tragedies come from their choices—not ours, else we are no more than moon-fair puppeteers, and they, sawdust dolls."

Involuntarily, I shivered, but Brydda seemed as oblivious to the cold as he was to the rain.

"Matthew chose to join Rushton's cause," he continued. "You do him no honor to grieve and put on funeral weeds. He has powers that will stand him in good stead wherever he goes." He gave me a slight shake. "Now dry your eyes, Elspeth, and take hold of your will. Let Daffyd discover what he can. Until then, put what has happened from you. There is work to be done, and this meeting is important to all of us. Prepare yourself for it."

"How?" I asked miserably.

"The same way we all do at such times," Brydda said harshly, the calmness suddenly drawn aside from his eyes as if it were a veil, revealing raw pain. "Do you think I have forgotten Idris already? Of course I have not. I fear some part of me will always be grieving for him. But I cannot let grief get in the way of a cause that both Idris and I believed in. So I act. I pretend. And some of the time I am able to forget that it is a pretense, and for that little period, I forget my pain."

"Act?" I echoed blankly.

He shook me again. "Pretend, Elspeth. Pretend that you are clever, wise, brave, calm, courageous—in the same way that you pretend to be Elaria the gypsy."

A man and a woman came out of a nearby door with a child between them. The parents ignored us, but the little girl looked deeply into my eyes, seeming to search for something.

"We are almost there," Brydda said when they were out of earshot. "They are expecting you to be a fumbling half-wit, and I have made no attempt to question their misconceptions. Their surprise will give you an advantage. For Obernewtyn's sake, you must show your best and most impressive face, as well as your most human one. This is not the time to be cold and withdrawn. You must give them something to warm to. Once we are in there, I cannot be seen to instruct or direct you—especially since Malik already suspects that you are my pawn."

I took a deep shuddering breath; then I drew on an expression of determined calmness and turned it to the big man.

"Hmmph." Brydda's lips twitched in a faint smile. "Well, that is not so good, but it will do to be going on with." The rebel turned a corner into a lane that was too narrow for me to walk alongside him, and I fell behind. At once, the false smile fell from my lips and eyes. If he wanted acting, then acting he would have—but I would not pretend to myself.

As we walked, I tried to recall Brydda's warnings about subjects to be avoided and what I must and must not say, his advice on how to behave if this or that happened. My mind seemed to whirl with a tempest of words that would not connect.

"We are here," Brydda said suddenly. His tone was light, but his eyes betrayed tension. He flung his hand to indicate a tall cream wall in which was set a heavily carved wooden door. He paused, his hand poised over the gate latch, to look at me. "Are you all right?"

I nodded resolutely, though in truth I felt like sitting on the footpath and howling.

Brydda merely nodded and pushed the gate open. Beyond it was a little lush wilderness in miniature, open to the sky. It reminded me with painful insistence of a leafy glade where, during breaks from the summertime harvest on the farms, Matthew, Cameo, Dameon, and I had often gone to sit before Rushton took over Obernewtyn. Matthew and I used to lie flat on our backs, searching the clouds for images of the future, of our hopes and our dreams. My eyes misted, but I blinked savagely as a thin boy a few years older than me came through the trees to meet us. Either he had been waiting, or the door had given him some silent warning of our approach. He had a long serious face, flyaway gingerish hair, and sad blue eyes that were unchanged by his smile.

"Welcome, my friend," he said in a warm, unexpectedly deep voice, clasping the rebel's hand. Then he bowed formally to me.

"You are Dardelan?" I guessed.

He nodded. "I suppose it is not hard to guess. Brydda probably told you that I am by far the youngest rebel you will meet today. A fact that Malik has seen fit to mention in at least a dozen ways since his arrival," he added ruefully to the big rebel.

"I am Elspeth Gordie," I said, holding my hand out to him.

He shook it solemnly, then led the way along a little winding path to the terrace of a graceful-looking residence.

"This is a wonderful idea," I said, waving my hand behind us as we passed into an overheated hallway. "Much better than building up against the street. Far more private."

"The Beforetimers used to have many such walled gardens—one to each residence, or so my father says," Dardelan murmured, ushering us inside. "They were very keen on privacy. I must apologize for the heating. I know it is too hot, but my father's illness makes him very susceptible to chills."

"It is nice to be warm," I said politely, though in fact I felt stifled by the hot, closed atmosphere of the house. "Brydda told me of your father's illness," I said on impulse, thinking of the teknoguilder Pavo. "I had a friend die of it. I am sorry."

Dardelan nodded acknowledgment, and his eyes held a measure of speculation that indicated I was not what he had expected. He led us through the house via a dark hall into a huge sunken room. It was windowless, being at the center of the dwelling, as near as I could make out. Two lanterns cast a murky light over the room's occupants.

A subdued hum of conversation fell into silence as they became aware of us, and I felt myself suddenly to be the cynosure of all eyes. I bore the visual dissection in dignified silence, blinking and waiting for my eyes to adjust to the dimness.

After a long pause, a handsome older man, with smooth gray hair and eyes the same shade, rose and stepped forward into the lantern light. "So, the Misfit," he said in a sneering voice. There was an arrogance in the way he eyed me from head to toe. I waited for him to introduce himself, but when he did not, taking into account his deliberate discourtesy and arrogant bearing, I guessed he was Malik.

I lifted my eyebrows and stepped farther into the room. "I will move closer to the light so that you may get a better view, should you wish to count my teeth and toes."

An astounded silence met my words; then an elderly man gave a startled bark of laughter.

But Malik was too experienced a player to let this pinprick upset him. "You are even younger than the stripling," he said disparagingly, as if my words had been callow rather than clever. And, in addition, he had managed to turn the words into a sideways jab at Dardelan.

"To be young is not necessarily to be weak," Brydda said pleasantly. "Whereas to be old . . . but you know what it is to be old, don't you, Malik. It renders the mind resistant to anything new." As he spoke, he moved to stand near Dardelan, symbolically allying himself with the youth rather than with me. I was, I realized suddenly, truly alone.

Malik gave Brydda a stiff smile. "I am older, true, but I am proud of my years, for age brings caution and experience and wisdom, and these things are well in one who would command. But perhaps that is why you surround yourself with children and freaks, Brydda. With such an obedient and malleable following, you would have no need of age or its virtues."

Dardelan colored slightly but wisely he held his tongue.

"I am no leader," Brydda said mildly.

Malik snorted, and it must have been obvious to the others in the room that he regarded Brydda as a rival. His eyes came swiftly back to me. "Does it speak, we wonder?" he inquired brightly. "Or has your parrot exhausted its meager repertoire, Brydda? Perhaps you should have toiled harder to gift your little pet more words to play with."

I had to bite my tongue to keep from showing anger before I spoke. "I speak when I have something to say, not to admire the sound of my voice," I said flatly.

The rebel's eyes glittered with malice, but his smile did not falter.

"Malik, this is Elspeth Gordie," Dardelan said. "It is impolite for us to speak to a guest without using her name."

"She is no guest of mine, boy," Malik snapped. "I have higher standards. She is a gypsy halfbreed and a Misfit to boot."

The man who had laughed earlier leaned forward in his seat, and I realized that prematurely gray hair made him appear older than he was. His face was unlined, and I guessed his age to lie between Brydda's and Malik's. He was far less robust in appearance than either of them, yet there was a craftiness in his eyes that suggested the muscle he used to reign was one of brain rather than brawn.

"There is not much to you but skin and bones, child," he murmured. "Are they all like you, these warriors Brydda says you would bring to strengthen us?"

I saw then the part I was meant to play at this gathering. I was to be a pawn for these men to score against one another. Anger drove away my dreary sadness. I would be no one's pawn. I made myself smile.

"Do you measure your followers by their mass, sirrah?" I asked sweetly. "We Talented Misfits measure ourselves by our deeds, and surely you of all people would concede that size does not always indicate courage or cunning or even strength." I let my eyes fall momentarily to his own slender frame.

It was difficult to tell in the half-light, but I thought his pale cheeks flushed slightly. "I am Cassell," he said at last. "And talk is cheap."

"That may be so of rebel talk, sirrah," I rejoined promptly. "But my words bear my honor; therefore, they are valuable indeed."

This time his brows raised. "Well, you can talk a good fight."

I sensed I had won a slight victory but did not press the point. A movement on the other side of the room caught my eye. When the man who had made it rose, it was all I could do not to gape. It was the Elii I had known as a girl at the Kinraide orphan home. The orphanage guardians there had always predicted that Elii would die of the rotting sickness as his father had, for he had led orphans questing for whitestick. But he showed no sign of ill health. Nor did he show by word or gesture that he remembered me.

For that I was grateful, since he had not known me as a gypsy but as an orphan. And perhaps the simple answer to that was that I had changed, too.

He shook my hand and looked into my face, and I remembered that he had always been prone to judge by instinct rather than by the words people offered. The man alongside him had a stern, ascetic face and disdainful eyes, and wore his yellow hair in two flaxen plaits. Dardelan introduced him as Tardis's representative, Gwynedd.

Dardelan moved me past the silent Murmrothian to a hugely obese man named Brocade, who did not trouble himself to rise. He might have been brother to the Teknoguildmaster, except that where much of Garth's bulk was muscle, Brocade was like a plump, overstuffed powder puff. He was dressed in as much lace and silk as any maiden would wear on her bonding day. From Brydda's lecture, I remembered this man was a staunch ally of Malik's and resisted the temptation to ask Cassell if this was the sort of size he liked behind him.

Brocade had a haughty, self-important air as his eyes swept over me disparagingly. "The creature is very badly dressed considering the importance of this meeting," he said in an affected tone. "Are all your Misfits the same color as you? I am not fond of that darkish skin color, for as a rule, such belongs to people of inferior mentality."

I was too dumbfounded by this absurdity to respond.

A drawling and unusually accented female voice arose from the darkest corner of the room. "This is a very interesting observation, Brocade. I must be sure to mention it to Bram and the tribes when next we speak."

I turned with the rest to see a woman unfold herself from a couch as gracefully as a cat. Standing, she was at least a head taller than any man in the room and possessed of considerable exotic beauty. Her skin was a striking yellow-gold, and her tawny eyes were slanted up at the outer edges. Her hair was as straight and black as combed silk and cut perfectly level at her jaw and across her brow. The hair and eyes and graceful movements made her appear almost catlike, and the impression deepened as she displayed an amused, feline smile.

Yet the look she bent on Brocade was anything but amused, and he swallowed convulsively, numerous chins wobbling in alarm as her fingers slipped casually to the hilt of an ornate knife in her belt.

"I did not mean to insult your people," he bleated. "Your color is not the same as this creature's."

"What has color to do with anything?" Jakoby asked, for I knew it must be her. She wore voluminous trousers, a long tunic belted at the hip, and flat sandals.

Her fingers caressed the hilt of her knife absently, and Brocade followed the movement with bulging eyes. "I meant no offense," he said.

"None taken," Jakoby said pleasantly. "Provided you retract your statement. But if you wish to stand by it, then I must demand a bout to see whether your pale skin really reflects greater wit than other colors."

"A . . . bout? You can't mean I should wrestle you? A woman?"

Her brows arched. "Is my gender also cause to think me inferior?"

"No! I—I—I retract!" Brocade stammered, mopping his damp brow with a scrap of silk.

Jakoby gave a throaty laugh of derision; then she turned to me and held out her long hand. I put mine into it, expecting her to shake it, but instead she seemed to weigh it in hers thoughtfully as she stared into my eyes. Then she turned my hand over and examined the palm minutely. After a long moment, she closed my hand into a fist but kept it in her own hard grip, looking again into my eyes.

"A good hand, girl. One that must grasp many threads of destiny. A hand whose owner is at once open and true, and yet who is the keeper of terrible secrets and a seeker of them."

Before I could wrench my hand away, Jakoby released it and turned to face the rest of the room.

"I vote for an alliance with this girl's people," she announced.

THERE WAS A moment of astonished silence before Malik leapt to his feet with a snarl of fury.

"I do not know how things are done in Sador, madam, but here we talk before deciding such issues as whether to ally ourselves with the likes of this creature."

"You talk. I have decided," Jakoby pronounced imperiously.

If the moment had not been so fraught, the look of baffled and impotent fury on Malik's face would have been comical.

"Jakoby, we honor you and know that your ways are different," Brydda interposed smoothly. "Were we in your land, we would abide by your customs. But this is our land, and here decisions among allies are made by a majority decision through a vote, taken from all participants after everyone has had their say."

The Sadorian grunted and flung herself into a seat with feline grace. "Very well. Talk," she said in an openly bored tone.

Malik looked perfectly furious, and the other rebels were clearly discomforted by her contempt. I tried to imagine this domineering gold-skinned woman at a guildmerge, where everything was decided by consensus, and failed utterly.

"Lady," Dardelan said, "you are a chief in your land. This, my father told me, is the Sadorian way, to choose the best and brightest by means of ritual challenges and then to allow them to lead without interference. But this is not Sador, nor is it

Sadorians whom you will battle. The Council, the soldier-guards, and the Herder Faction are Landfolk, and perhaps in this light you may concede that there will be times when we will know better how to deal with them. Maybe you will learn something useful from observing our ways, just as we will learn from you. Isn't that the advantage of an alliance?"

Jakoby made no response to this speech, but she had lost her bored expression.

"On behalf of the western bloc, I would like to say—" Cassell began, but Malik cut him off by snorting rudely.

"'On behalf,' Cassell? Do you have signatures over letters from Radek and Madellin explaining their absence and entitling you to represent them?" Malik demanded.

"We have come to an understanding—" Cassell began, but Malik interrupted him again with a loud laugh.

"An understanding—a very vague and useful term, is it not?"

Cassell flushed with anger, but he was not quick enough to compose a cutting rejoinder.

I glanced at the Sadorian, wondering how she felt about their petty bickering. It was no great advertisement for Land ways.

Elii rose to speak. "I want to know what these Misfits can do," he said in his gruff accent. "I thought that was what we were here for."

"That is what I was trying to say earlier when I was interrupted," Cassell interposed with a dark look at Malik.

"I am not concerned with her tricks," Malik said flatly.

"I would like to hear what Elspeth has to offer," Dardelan said diffidently.

Brocade laughed coarsely. "No doubt you would, but we speak of war, boy, not bedsports."

Dardelan flushed bright red, and I felt the blood from my own cheeks.

"If you would conduct a war the way you conduct this meeting, then I think it *best* if you stick to bedsports," I snapped.

Brydda's eyes warned me to be careful; a display of temper would undo any favorable impression I had managed to make.

"I suppose Misfits know better than human beings how to run a meeting," Malik sneered.

Anger surged through me. Malik's continued attempts to label me and his implication that we were neither normal nor human would not stop until I had answered him decisively. Yet I would remain calm and dignified if it killed me, I vowed.

The effort of keeping my temper leached all emotion from my voice, and when I spoke, it sounded curiously toneless. "We do not consider ourselves abnormal but only possessed of certain additional abilities. We lack nothing that any other human being has in the Land, excepting perhaps a place in the order of things. It is the Council who names us Misfit, along with dreamers and defectives. I do not know whether we conduct meetings better, but do I know that our aim when we meet is not to use words as sly daggers but to exchange information." Sensing I had their undivided attention for the moment, I shifted to address the room rather than Malik.

"I came here today to offer you the opportunity to find out how my people can help you win your rebellion against the Council. Yet I am treated with as little courtesy as if I were your enemy. You insult me and sneer, and from this, I might judge that you wish me to depart."

Malik's eyes sparkled with triumph, and anticipation of his disappointment enabled me to infuse a sweetness I did not feel into my words. "Yet, in case not all who are in this room share Malik's opinions and attitudes, I will speak my piece in spite of all his efforts to stop me." I hurried on before the furious rebel could cut in. "I have told you that we have additional abilities, and that is so. There are among us those who can communicate mind to mind over some distance. These we call *farseekers*. In a rebellion, with one such at your side, you could constantly exchange information and intelligence among yourselves and seek advice without leaving battle posts."

I sensed I was speaking well, for all but Brocade and Malik had lost their skeptical looks and were listening intently— even the stern, silent Gwynedd.

"Others among us have the ability to empathise—that is, to receive or transmit feelings. Such an ability at your command would enable you to strike fear or doubt into a soldier-guard captain at the crucial moment in a battle, or even to send love and friendship into the hearts of attacking forces to confuse and distract them."

Malik laughed, but no one paid any attention to him. I felt a wild thrill. I had them!

"Some of us can communicate with beasts, which would enable us to project instructions and conflicting commands to enemy horses, thereby defusing a mounted charge."

"That fingertalk of Brydda's," Malik sneered.

I shook my head, refusing to let him shake my confidence or control. "Brydda's success at his fingerspeaking is admirable, but communicating with beasts, for those who have the Talent, is generally done via the mind as with farseeking. Were I nearby or even some distance away, I could reach out a voice from my mind to the horse on which a soldierguard is mounted and, provided my request was polite and reasonable—"

"Polite!" Cassell sounded startled and amused.

I looked at him gravely. "I find courtesy serves in any situation. Don't you?"

He looked faintly abashed.

"Of course," Malik jeered, drowning out whatever answer Cassell might have made. "We could all take a lesson from this and curtsy to our dogs and goats before breakfast."

Brocade guffawed loudly. "I think I can conduct my forces without advice from my horse."

I resisted the urge to suggest his horse could probably do a better job of it and went on to point out that, apart from our additional abilities, there were others among our number who had trained themselves as warriors and who were prepared to stand beside the rebels and fight.

"Are there other abilities?" Jakoby asked.

I glanced at her but did not let her catch my eyes. "Some of us have herb lore and are healers," I said, keeping my fingers crossed that she would not persist. "All of our abilities we would place at your disposal if we were allied, in the hope that by defeating our common enemies, the Land will become a place where we can all live in peace, without persecution or slavery."

"A pretty speech," Malik sneered. "But the heart of the matter is that you wish to trade your dubious and unproven additional abilities for acceptance among normal humans." He turned his burning eyes to the others. "We oppose the Council because of its misuse of power, not for its attempt to clean the human race of holocaust poisons and mutations. If we were to accept aid from these Misfits, we would have to give up trying to cleanse our race of deformity and mutation. Such a move would say that, hereafter, we will permit any freak or defective obscenity not only to live, but also to exist alongside us, to share our Land, our food, our crops; to bond with our sons and daughters."

There was a charged silence, and I felt frozen by the hostility in the faces that turned to me.

"She is a Misfit, and I see no monster," Dardelan said softly. "Is she the kind you mean when you speak of freaks and mutants, Malik?"

The boy had formidable subtlety, and I wondered what the father must be like, to have such a son.

"She is not visibly deformed," Malik conceded with ill grace. "But what of those she represents? No doubt they have sent her precisely because she was the most comely among them. After all, they would not send a monster, would they?"

"There are none among us whom you would see in a crowd and know as Misfits," I said. "None of us is physically deformed."

I stopped, for this speech soured my mouth. I could not compromise what I believed, not even to win these people.

I looked directly into Malik's eyes. "But were such a one to come among us, grossly deformed or not, we would not turn them away excepting that they were deformed of spirit or soul."

From the corner of my eye, I saw the Sadorian shift involuntarily as if the words held some goad, but when I looked, her face was impassive.

"See!" Malik declared. "She has said that she and her kind would accept grossly deformed mutants, as long as they possess these Talents. And with such a philosophy, how many generations before we would be reduced to a herd of howling beasts? Rather the Council should continue to prevail than that. The thought of allowing mutants to exist alongside normal, decent Landfolk is an obscenity to me and one I could never condone.

"But," he went on quickly, striding to the center of the room, "if your own values and decency are not enough to let you see what the ultimate outcome of this alliance must be, then think on this: These Misfits are little more than children, despite all the abilities they claim. Is that not so?"

He shot me a look of icy interrogation.

"The majority of us are young, that's true, but—"

"There you are. Condemned out of her own mouth," Malik cried. "Are we to act as wet nurses to monstrous children in the very midst of battle? Is it not a burden rather than an asset that we would gain in shackling ourselves to her people?"

"Youth means nothing," Elii said sharply. "I was a youth when I set up my rebel group. It's guts and brains that count, not age—and this girl sounds to me as if she has enough of both. I've no love for mutants, but she is no freak. And if her people can do what she says they can, then they would give us an advantage the Council and the soldierguards could never counteract."

There was a moment in which I thought Elii had actually won them over for me.

"Your brain is surely addled from whitestick," Malik snarled. "Oh yes, by all means, invite these freaks to fight alongside you, Elii. And while you are at it, employ the cripples and the scum that clog the lanes of every city street and would as soon cut our throats as guard our backs. But in the remote chance that you would win with such a force, remember that you will not easily set them aside when war is done.

"I will seek out instead the best and worthiest to fight behind me, and though my force be less in number, it will prevail, for it will be made up of true humans, not distorted copies and ghastly shadow creatures. Every one of my force shall know what they are and be proud of it."

"Your instinct for drama never ceases to enliven our meetings," Brydda said, as if the whole of Malik's impassioned

333

diatribe had been nothing more than a puppet show for the rebels' amusement. "However, it might be as well to point out that this meeting is not to decide the future of the human race but merely to ascertain if this girl's people can aid us when we rise against the Council."

His dry businesslike tones diminished the effect of Malik's wild rhetoric, but the gray-eyed rebel was not done yet.

He stepped up to Brydda, his eyes narrowed. "I am not a fool," he hissed. "You want these Misfits to join us, and you connive with soft words and wiles to this end for some secret purpose of your own that eludes my reasoning." He swung to face the others. "Ask yourselves that, too, my comrades. Why does Brydda Llewellyn support an alliance with them? Is it that he seeks control of the rebel forces with their help?"

"My father also favors an alliance," Dardelan said coldly. "Do you also claim Bodera has secret purposes?"

Malik gave him a startled look, as if a duck had suddenly defended itself against a vicious dog.

"Do we need them?" Cassell asked, and the others turned to stare at the older man. "I ask if we need these Misfits, regardless of how useful they will be. Can we win without them? It seems to me that is a question we ought to be addressing."

"There are more soldierguards than there are of our people," Brydda said. "The simple answer is that we need everyone we can get."

"No!" Brocade shrieked. "I say we dare not take them among us, no matter how great is our need. Misfits are despised by Lud. If we accept them, it is the same as rejecting Lud, and we will be punished with another plague or some worse thing than that. Lud will visit disaster on us, and perhaps because of their eldritch aid, we will lose when we would have won."

I cast a look around the room and saw that all the rebels, even Elii, were looking thoughtful. I had underestimated fat Brocade badly.

I swallowed, and found my mouth dry with fear and tension and too many empty words. In that moment, I glanced at Malik. His eyes looked straight into mine, filled with naked loathing. His eyelids fell like shutters over the expression, but the hatred was burned irrevocably into my mind. In that instant, I understood that there would be no winning Malik's vote and no compromise. Not ever.

"Cassell was right in asking if we need them. I say we do not! This is a war we will wage, and to win it, we need only good armor and weapons and the warriors to use them—strong, committed adults. But most of all, we need strong centralized leadership."

The others were all nodding approval, the question of alliance shunted neatly aside.

"I say we strike soon, before the new intake of soldierguards is fully trained," Malik went on forcefully, and I realized he was on the verge of taking over the meeting and perhaps the rebellion. With his smooth, handsome face and eyes that glowed with confidence, he looked the picture of a leader of men. I knew then, as if by futuretell vision, that if Malik assumed the mantle of leadership now, Misfits would be doomed after the rebellion. He and his people would hunt us down and destroy us.

The rebels had begun to argue and discuss the merits and disadvantages of different seasons to mount a successful rebellion. I glanced at Brydda, but his face was blank and unhelpful. Well, he had warned me that I could not expect his aid—especially not when Malik had practically accused him of using us to seize leadership.

I noticed that alone of all those in the room, the Sadorian

woman was watching me from her shadowy corner, her yellow eyes glinting. This reminded me vividly of Maruman and, oddly, gave me the courage to do what I did next.

"The question of alliance has not yet been voted upon," I said loudly and firmly.

Malik gave me an irritated look. "Children should be at play, not meddling in the affairs of their elders and betters."

"Then let us speak plainly as children are wont to do," I said, still loudly. "You, Malik, wish to set yourself up as the leader of the rebellion and of all these others sitting here, because you think you are better than them and because you desire the power that would accrue to such a position after the battles are over."

Malik flushed, then whitened, to hear me name his ambitions so nakedly and shorn of all softening or justification. Even Brydda looked aghast. It seemed that in the world of men and battles, only the truth was too shocking to be mentioned aloud.

But Malik was caught, because, without looking like a fool or a liar, he could not deny what I had said, when every person in the room knew it must be true.

"Each person has their expertise," he said at last through clenched teeth. "Mine is to lead."

For a moment, the capricious balance of power was tilted in my favor. I looked into Gwynedd's blue eyes. "What of Tardis? Does he also not possess the ability to lead? What of"—I stretched my memory—"what of Yavok, and indeed of any one of you in this room? Are you not all leaders of your groups because you possess exactly that same expertise to lead as Malik? And, in that case, why should he be set above you?"

"*One* must rule in wartime," Malik snapped. "In the end, a single person must be put above the rest. A rebellion must have a commander to whom all intelligence is sent. Once the battle begins, only one person can direct its course, can have the power to say go or stay, fight or retreat. A horse cannot have two heads or ten, and if it must have one, then give it the one who knows the trail best. I am a warrior. I know tactics, and I know the feel of battle."

"Malik is right. Sooner or later, we must choose one to lead us in battle, and that is his strength," Elii said.

It was well said, but I had a final card to play in this game of words, and Elii had brought me neatly to it.

"Why choose at all when, with my people by your side, each of you may lead your own forces and confer whenever you need? With farseekers to link you, there is no need for one warlord! Why not go on as you have begun—each ruling your own people and conferring through mine when there is need? And then, when the war is won, choose one among you whose gift is peacetime rule, if you decide it is necessary."

"It makes sense," said Elii. "If each of us conducts our own share of the war, then what need have we of a leader in the aftermath of the rebellion? Could we not continue to rule our own provinces?"

"Bodera sent Brydda here to convince us with his silver tongue to join together, because divided we were nothing more than thorns in the Council's side. With great eloquence, he spoke of the need for us to be welded into a single unit with a single aim. Remember those words? And now he would have us splinter into tiny groups. Do you not wonder why? Could it be that divided we will be easier for him and his mutants to conquer?" Malik demanded.

Brydda stood up, his face showing anger for the first time. "I did not know Misfits like Elspeth existed when this began. But since they do, it seems to be wise to look at what they can

337

offer us. But the decision is not mine to make, whatever Malik implies. It is yours, and I am nothing more than Bodera's and Dardelan's man."

"All I am offering is the means for you to retain independence," I said.

"I, for one, know my master would prefer to retain control of our people," said Gwynedd in a thin, sardonic voice. "It would surprise me if any rebel leader would say they wished someone to rule over them."

"Without having to decide who is going to run things, we might better concentrate on winning our battle," Dardelan put in.

"So speaks the wisdom of the ages," Malik sneered.

"I speak for my father," the young man said quietly.

"Again, I offer an alliance with my people," I said. "We will allow ourselves to be dispersed among you—"

"No!" Malik snapped, banging his hand on the table. "Who is this girl to offer alliance to us? Is she the ruler of her people? I think not. Why does not her master come among us, or is he so grossly distorted that he cannot be seen?"

"Some of us have met him," Cassell said mildly. "He is not a Misfit at all."

"Well, what sort of man is he who chooses to rule freaks? And I ask you again, how do we know that these mutated brats can do what she claims? I want more than children who can whisper to one another across the land, in exchange for accepting this girl and her freakish kin as comrades. I want warriors who can fight."

Jakoby rose, and so great was her natural presence, we all looked up at her. "You wish to see if she and hers can match your people in battle, Malik? Is that it? And if they could, what then? Would you accept them as allies and equals?"

"I would accept a cow if it could prove itself my equal," he snapped.

The others laughed, and though I kept my face still and calm, I seethed inwardly.

"Then there is a way to solve this matter," Jakoby spoke above the laughter. "In Sador, we have the Battlegames. It is a series of ritual contests that run between dawn and dusk on a single day. I offer you this as a way of solving this deadlock. By it, you will learn if this girl and her people can turn their talents to winning war." She turned her glowing golden eyes on me. "And your people will have the chance to prove yourselves and gain the alliance you seek. If you fail, then it is as well that this alliance does not come to pass."

"You said contests. Who would be contesting with whom?" I asked, my mind reeling at this new possibility.

Jakoby shrugged. "An equal number of yours and those who would test you. His people." Her eyes flicked to Malik.

"Where would these Battlegames be held? And when?" I asked.

"I do not see the point of playing games," Brocade interpolated.

I did not take my eyes from the Sadorian woman.

"A trial of honor is fitting at such an impasse," she said calmly, glancing at Brocade. "As to when and where, I offer Sador on behalf of my people. And whatever the conclusion of the Battlegames, the occasion may well be used to decide our own final strategy in dealing with the Council and its soldierguards."

That rendered all of them silent and thoughtful.

After a long minute, Malik nodded, his eyes glittering with triumph. Perhaps he was seeing that, as a victor of this mock battle, he would naturally assume leadership of the rebels. I had probably played right into his hands.

"Then it is agreed that your two peoples shall meet at the Battlegames and that the fate of the alliance between you shall rest upon the outcome?" Jakoby asked.

"Done," Malik said savagely.

I stared at him helplessly, wanting to ask for time to think, yet knowing I must not hesitate. If I refused the contest now, Malik would win by default. Yet to agree without consulting the others went against everything that guildmerge stood for.

I thought of Malik's eyes, filled with open hatred, and knew there would be no other way to get him to agree to an alliance. And so, truly, there was no choice after all.

"All right," I said softly.

There was a momentary hiatus, then a babble of talk.

"I do not think fighting among ourselves is . . . ," Dardelan began.

"My master would agree that this is fair, I think . . . ," Gwynedd said.

"It solves one thing, certainly," Cassell said musingly. "The need for us to meet together to plan the rebellion has been pressing for some time. Can it be organized for all of the rebel leaders to come to Sador?" Here he looked to Brydda.

Jaw clenched ominously, the big rebel nodded. "I will send birds out, and the groups who have their own will send replies by the morrow as to whether they will journey to Sador or be guided by those who will go and, in the latter case, whether they will assign their vote to another or go with the majority on decisions."

"How long would such a journey take?" Cassell asked. "I do not like the idea of being away from the Land for too many days."

"Isn't Sador very far and the road to it dangerously close to the Blacklands?" Brocade asked.

"By road it is far, but by sea it is two or three days only," Jakoby said.

"By sea!" Dardelan murmured, his eyes wide.

"We should think about this," Brydda cautioned.

"I have thought it through, and it seems to me that this is a good idea," Elii said decisively. "I have no love for sea travel, but it is a journey of two days that we talk of. If these Misfits beat Malik at this contest, it is worth whatever the bother afterward to let them stand with us. If they fail, then it does not matter. More importantly, to my mind, we will be able to organize the rebellion once and for all."

The others nodded at this blunt pronouncement with varying degrees of enthusiasm.

"Well, then, it seems we are to journey to Sador together—let us hope the ship does not sink, or the rebellion will be scuttled before it begins. At least this mock battle should be amusing," Cassell said, as if I had volunteered to bring a troop of clowns or tumblers to perform for them.

"What is to keep Sador from treachery when we are all in their hands?" Brocade asked querulously.

Jakoby gave him a look of scathing violence. "Were you not a barbarian, I would cut your tongue out for that insult," she hissed. "Sadorians do not betray allies."

Brocade stared up at her like a stunned rabbit.

"You do not have any honor," she said, leaning toward him like a snake readying to strike. "Yet you understand fear too well, for I think you are old friends." She stared into his eyes, and he grew so pale I wondered that he had not fainted.

At last she withdrew a fraction.

"You have no reason to fear, for since we of the plains desire none of your squalid little Land, there would be no point in our hostaging or slaying those of you who would choose to come." Her eyes flicked contemptuously around the room, finally coming to settle with less fury on Brydda. Then she frowned, seeming to have some unexpected thought.

"It comes to me that I am at fault in this," she said at last. Her voice was calmer now, but colder than the sound of the Brildane howling in the icy wastes of the highest mountains. "I should not have expected you to recognize honor. As a token of faith that you will understand, I will leave my own daughter in this city, and I shall not come for her until you are returned from Sador. Is this acceptable?"

Dardelan stepped forward and bowed to the Sadorian chief. "Lady, I need no proof of your goodwill. But I offer my father's house where your daughter may stay in fitting comfort. She will be guarded as carefully as if she were my own sister," he said earnestly.

I blinked back sudden tears; this was the sort of romantic gesture Matthew would have made under the circumstances.

The cold light in Jakoby's eyes softened. "I think you will find a daughter of Sador does not need much protecting."

Dardelan bowed. "I will speak with my father, and preparations will be made at once."

"So it begins," Gwynedd said, and there was a curious finality in his voice.

"I am ready," Malik said; then he laid his head back and laughed wolfishly.

Brydda closed his eyes and sank into a chair.

◆ 32 ◆

WALKING BACK TO the safe house very late that night, the difficulties of what had been agreed to preyed on my mind.

Madness, Brydda had called it, and he was right. But I did not see what else I could have done. He had wanted me to impress the rebels with my normality, but right from the start, it had been only too clear that most of them could not and never would see us as normal.

And whether Brydda admitted it or not, Malik had been on the verge of taking control of the rebellion. If that had happened, we would then have had to start regarding them as deadly enemies.

I had to make guildmerge see that the Battlegames could not possibly alienate the rebels from us further. Nothing would be lost.

I sighed.

Not quite nothing. We must lose our innocence, for to agree to the contest meant literally casting aside all of our dreams of peaceful coexistence and gradual friendship. It meant accepting that we would only ever be tolerated, and even that must be fought for. Well, they would have to face that unpleasant truth sooner or later. It was only too clear to me now that we had been naive to think we could win the rebels by offering our help. We had wanted to believe that opposing the same enemies made us allies, but that was not so.

I tried to anticipate how guildmerge would respond to my suggestion that we use the Battlegames to teach the rebels to respect us—even to fear us—so that they would think twice before turning on us, no matter what happened in the rebellion. What other choice had we but to play by their rules?

Rushton would understand that—his whole life had been one of compromise to obtain his birthright. But I could imagine how Roland and Maryon would take it.

Under their leadership, the Healer and Futureteller guilds had opposed the Coercer's Talent contests when the idea was first mooted in guildmerge, claiming that competition promoted aggression. They had been narrowly outvoted, and the contests had since become an important event during our mountain moon fair.

There had been unexpected benefits. Mindmelds had increased in coordination, and individual skills had been honed and strengthened with the competitions as a goad. In addition, the stress of competition occasionally revealed unsuspected secondary and even tertiary abilities.

Though there was rather more at stake than a crown of flowers, the Battlegames was still a contest.

Of course, Roland would point out that what had begun as competition between guilders had swiftly metamorphosed into stylized displays of skill, with both competitors playing to the audience rather than trying to outdo each other; it was as much a team effort as anything else.

I would answer that it might be so with the Battlegames.

But that would expose the main weakness of my argument: I did not know what the Battlegames entailed, any more than Malik or Brydda did. Jakoby had refused to elaborate, saying only that they were not for the fainthearted and would test our ability in battle decisively. She would give no hint about what qualities and abilities might be needed. All we knew was that each side should muster a team of ten and must reach Sador within five days, for Jakoby had explained that Battlegames were held only on full-moon days during the Days of Rain.

I had come to Sutrium galvanized by an impossible deadline, and now I would leave the same way. Life seemed to resound in echoes and oblique reflections.

I could still hear Malik's malicious laughter ringing in my ears, as jagged as pieces of broken glass falling through the night. He had laughed, I thought, because he imagined I had played right into his hands in agreeing to the contest. That might have been expected from Malik, but it had shocked me a little to think that Brydda felt the same.

"How can your people win against Malik and his warriors?" he had demanded just before our parting. "He is the best strategist among us. He will win these Battlegames, no matter what they involve. It was madness for you to agree, for in doing so, you have made an alliance with Misfits conditional on a win. I don't know what possessed you."

"You said there could be no rebellion without Malik," I had pointed out. "I tell you, he would never have agreed to an alliance any other way than this. Now, at least Malik has committed himself to accepting us if we beat him, and Gwynedd seems to think Tardis will agree, too."

Brydda had only shaken his head and insisted I tell Rushton that the whole matter could be dismissed as a mistake if he would send a message quickly, saying I had overstepped my authority. He had even promised to send Reuvan to the safe house with a bird that might be loosed from Obernewtyn with this message.

Out of honor, I would have to convey Brydda's words and the doubts that fueled them. I wondered if Rushton would take the rebel's advice or mine.

Coming through the repair-yard gate, absorbed by my thoughts, I was utterly unprepared to see the object of them leaning against the side of a small gypsy wagon.

I stopped dead, a fist of reaction clenching in my gut. Rushton's arms were folded across his chest, and he was clearly deep in thought, a closed, brooding look on his face.

Though I had not spoken nor made a sound, he must have sensed he was no longer alone. He turned his head toward me. His green eyes seemed to reach across the yard with all the force of a jet of flame.

"Elspeth."

Just that: He spoke my name flatly, almost coldly. He straightened and walked across the yard, and I felt the blood rise in my cheeks. I made myself walk to meet him, to show I was not disconcerted, only to find that this brought us too close for my comfort. Before I could prevent myself, I stepped back.

Rushton's face sharpened to a kind of ironic enjoyment at my awkwardness. He stopped and made a little bow, as if something had been agreed to between us.

"I have been waiting for you. Kella said you had gone to meet with the rebels."

I nodded, my thoughts chaotic, but on the heels of my reaction to Rushton's presence was a rising fear. "How . . . why are you here? What has happened?" I demanded.

"Nothing. Not yet, at least. We are here because Maryon sent us."

I was about to ask who else had come when it struck me,

with some force, that there was only one explanation for this expedition. Maryon had foreseen the journey to Sador.

Could it be that need would be answered so gracefully after all the misfortune that had haunted our time on the coast?

Rushton nodded. "So it's true, then. She said you would understand."

"Understand?"

"Maryon futuretold us coming here, but she did not know why. She said you would."

And again that awful, swirling, helpless feeling of being a leaf borne on some impossibly strong tide. Maryon had known that I would know. It was too much.

"You just came without knowing why, because . . ."

"Because Maryon said it was vital for Obernewtyn. Yes." Rushton nodded, a faint challenge in his green eyes. "It would be a little late to be deciding now that we would not live our lives by the whimsical wisdoms of futuretellers, don't you think?"

"But that was . . ."

"Dangerous, foolhardy, rash? Of course." He spread his fingers into a gesture of acceptance. Then his expression hardened, and the mockery in it died. "Why are we here, Elspeth?"

I took a deep breath. "I think because of something that happened at my meeting with the rebels."

"Do you think you might manage to be a little less cryptic?"

"You were right when you said they regard us as freaks. The meeting did not change that, in spite of Brydda's hopes. That was why Brydda had not contacted us—he was trying to make them change their mind," I said. "The two main rebel leaders in particular wanted nothing to do with us. . . ."

I told him everything then, about Brydda's intention in bringing me to the meeting, about Malik and Tardis and the power struggle between them, and finally about the Battlegames.

It was impossible to know if he was angry. He was too good at keeping his thoughts and emotions hidden.

At last he sighed. "We had better go and tell the others to prepare themselves for a sea journey."

Maryon had named the members of the expedition herself, Rushton told me. My heart sank when I saw whom she had sent. No wonder Rushton had sighed when I told him of the Battlegames.

The young Empath guilden, twins Miky and Angina, were sitting across from each other at the table sorting herbs. Receptive Miky intercepted my astonishment and swung around, her face creased in a welcoming smile tinged with mischief. "I bet we are the last people you imagined seeing here."

"That is saying it mildly," I said.

The stocky Coercer guilden, Miryum, was seated by the hearth with a pile of toasting forks on her knees. She had been rubbing the points over a whetstone as we entered, but hearing Miky, she threw them down and strode across the room to thump me on the back with painful enthusiasm.

"It is good to see you, Guildmistress. This is a queer business, is it not?"

I was distracted from answering by the sight of an unfamiliar plain-faced girl with yellow hair.

"Greetings, Guildmistress Elspeth," she said. "I am Freya. I believe you left Obernewtyn a sevenday or so before I arrived." She gave me a sweet smile that lit serene gray eyes, and I realized I had been wrong. She was not plain at all.

"Greetings," I said faintly.

The enormous, soft-spoken coercer Hannay was helping Kella to slice cheese and bread. "Greetings, Guildmistress," he rumbled, and went on slicing.

Beside him was the Teknoguild ward, Fian. "Kella told us about Matthew. I am sorry," he said gently, and his highland accent hurt because it reminded me vividly of the farseeker.

"And Dragon," Miky murmured, her face falling. "Poor little Dragon. If only Maryon would have let the others come and get her."

I stared at the empath. "What do you mean, if Maryon had let the others come?"

"She foresaw Dragon following you," Rushton said briskly. "We wanted to come after you to get her—you had only been gone a few hours. But Maryon said you needed to have her with you, that it was necessary." His eyes met my growing fury with bleak resignation. I remembered the words he had just said to me, about living by the whims of futuretellers.

I shook my head, anger making my eyes burn and my head hurt. Did we have no will to exert? No choice? I remembered, with a kind of sickness, that it was Maryon's futuretelling that had sent Jik with me to the lowlands and to his death. "Did she dream of Dragon falling into a coma as well, when she stopped you bringing her back?" I snarled.

"Maryon foresaw Dragon following you, Elspeth," Rushton said wearily. "But Dragon chose to come after you of her own will. And you cannot have it both ways. If Maryon was right in predicting that Dragon would follow, then it must be that she was also right when she predicted the necessity of it happening."

I wanted to scream at him. If Maryon saw me walking off a cliff, would he not try to prevent my death? Might there not be moments when a futuretelling was shown as a *warning*? Would so much have been altered had Maryon defied her vision? What difference would it make if Dragon had not come to Sutrium, other than that she might not now be comatose?

A great deal, I realized with a queer chill. I might just as well ask how many ripples a single fallen leaf would cause in a stream and how far they might spread.

"Dragon's not dead. She's just asleep," Angina said softly, his empath Talent swirling out to enfold me in hope and compassion.

I sat down. "I know . . . I know. I'm sorry."

There was a moment of silence, and then the others began to talk, filling the void with words to give me time to recover myself.

"It was awful on the road, Elspeth," Miky murmured presently. "We were searched at the gate, and when they started to check our papers against a birth register, I near died."

"Miryum and Hannay had to coerce us through," Angina said eagerly, taking up his sister's lead, his face a masculine echo of hers. "Even so, we were lucky, because the second gate guard had a natural shield. A good thing he wasn't the one checking."

"I can't believe we're really here in Sutrium!" Miky said. "When Rushton came to firstmeal an' told us that Maryon had futuretold another expedition to follow you here, we never guessed for a minute we'd be on it."

Angina took up the story without missing a beat. "We

350

thought there would be a guildmerge and a voting, but Rushton said Maryon already knew who was to come."

Why these Misfits, Maryon? I wondered with sudden suspicion. *What are you up to now?*

"She said it was vital for Obernewtyn," Miky went on.

Doesn't she always? I thought bitterly. Hannay's inclusion made sense, as much because of his deep patience as for his utter reliability. And Miryum's coercive powers were formidable. But why choose Miky, who had great empathic Talent but no secondary ability and no physical strength; and Rushton, who could not reach his powers; or this Freya, who, no matter what her Talent, was a newcomer to Obernewtyn?

"She would nowt say more'n that," Fian spoke with all the disgruntlement of a thwarted teknoguilder, interrupting the dual flow of the twins' story.

"She didn't know any more than that," Miky said quickly.

"But Elspeth knows," Angina chimed.

The others looked at me expectantly, but I realized I did not know why they had come. Not them in particular. And there were only seven of them.

Then all at once, it occurred to me there might be more of them. There must be.

"Who else came?" I asked with a shimmer of uneasy premonition.

Rushton gave me a queer, lopsided smile, anticipating my reaction.

"One other. Dameon."

I stared at him incredulously. Maryon had sent Dameon, the gentle and blind Empath guildmaster, to do battle with Malik and the rebels for the future of Obernewtyn!

✦ 33 ✦

DAMEON WAS SITTING by Dragon's bed, holding her hand. She was oblivious of his presence, though some foolish bit of me had hoped he might have reached her. But, no, she was locked in a sleep that must be close to the equines' longsleep, suspended in some netherworld between life and death.

I could have wept for the sadness in his face and the bowed shape of his shoulders. I felt a rush of love at the sight of him that was nearly painful.

Of course, he sensed the surge of emotions. I saw it in his sudden stillness.

"Elspeth," he murmured in his gentle voice.

Only then did he turn his face to me, his white-blind eyes gleaming in the light of a single candle guttering low in a wall sconce behind me.

"I could bear everything, if only she would wake," I murmured, coming to stand beside him.

He rose to meet me, letting go of Dragon's fingers to take mine.

"She will wake," he said. His words were a promise, but how could he know? He was no futureteller.

"Oh, Dameon," I sighed.

"There was a Beforetime story in one of the books you brought back from the underground library, which told the tale of a sleeping princess," he said, drawing me to sit by him.

"A story," I said flatly.

He smiled, and the compassion in his expression was like a slap, for what right did I have to expect him to comfort me? Was Dragon not his charge, as a member of his guild? Had he not known Matthew longer?

"The story tells of a beautiful princess who may or may not have had red hair and who, cursed, pricked her hand on a poisoned needle," Dameon went on. "She fell into an enchanted sleep from which none could wake her."

I looked down at Dragon and shivered.

"She slept long, until a prince came who was her truest love, and the enchantment between them allowed him to break the spell."

"How?" I breathed, drawn into the story in spite of myself. "What did he do to wake her?"

"He woke her"—Dameon took Dragon's pale hand again and lifted it to his lips—"with a kiss."

I thought of Matthew—the only love Dragon had ever known, and an unwilling one at that. Would that love ever return to kiss her awake?

"It is a . . . lovely story," I said huskily.

Dameon nodded. "It is. Miky and Angina have made it into a song, and they will sing it to you."

"Dameon . . ."

He shook his head and gathered me into his long arms. "I know."

He patted my back as if I were a very young child or a frightened animal, his empathic Talent wrapping me in a warm blanket of affection and reassurance. I was dimly surprised to find he had erected an empathic barrier between us. He must have sensed I would not want my emotions bared to him.

"Matthew has been taken," he said gently. "But no slaver or shackle will hold him for long. He will return, just as he swore he would. As full of gossip and wild stories as ever."

Listening to his soft accent, I felt for the first time that it might truly be so.

"Well, this is touching," Rushton said from the door. "When you have finished the tender reconciliations, perhaps you will spare us a moment."

Sitting in the kitchen with the rain pattering against night-dark windows, Rushton told me for the first time what Maryon had futuretold.

"She said she saw eight of us journeying to Sutrium and your face, Elspeth, at the end of the journey. There was more—something about thirteen going over water." He hesitated, and I sensed there was something here he kept back. "She said it had something to do with Obernewtyn and figuring out what to do next." He frowned, as if this was not exactly right. "Something about finding the right road to tread."

He made a gesture indicating that I was to go on from there, and so I did, telling the group all that I'd told Rushton.

"I do not understand why this Jakoby woman would make such an offer," Miryum said suspiciously when I had finished. "What does she get out of helping us?"

"She wouldn't see it as helping us or the rebels," I said. "There was a problem, and she simply offered a Sadorian solution. Sadorians are . . . are not like Landfolk, and I don't think you can judge them by our values. But honor is very important to them, so I don't think they would cheat or lie."

"Are you so sure this woman's offer of the Battlegames is what Maryon's futuretelling concerned?" Dameon asked softly. "She said nothing about battles."

354

"It would be too much of a coincidence for it not to mean Sador," Hannay said. "Where else would we go on a journey over water? Across the Suggredoon? Maryon said Elspeth would know, and she knows about the trip to Sador and the Battlegames."

"Could it have meant something about rescuing the Farseeker ward?" Freya asked. "He has been taken over water, after all."

"Where would we search for him, and how?" Rushton asked. He shook his head regretfully. "I wish we were going to find Matthew, but my instincts say the journey foreseen by Maryon is the one offered by this Jakoby. It fits too neatly. Why else would so many of us come, if not to take part in these Battlegames and win the alliance we need?"

"But there are not enough anyway," Miky said. "Maryon said thirteen of us would go over the water."

"It is possible this battle will not happen. Perhaps we must go to Sador for some other reason that has yet to be revealed," Dameon said slowly. "Maybe we will have the chance of proving to this Malik and the other rebels that we are human."

I hesitated, then shook my head, not wanting to give anyone false hope.

"There is no point in us going into this imagining we can all be friends afterward. We will never be accepted by the rebels. But the Battlegames are at least an opportunity for a temporary alliance. And they will also provide us with a chance to show the Maliks of the Land that we can defend ourselves from them!"

"A show of strength," Miryum said approvingly.

"If you like. Or maybe just revealing ourselves for what we are."

"And what are we?" Dameon asked, his voice threaded with sadness. "Warriors? Misfits? That is part of our trouble. We do not know what we are, and so we are constantly reacting to things, rather than taking the initiative."

"Maryon said we would find the road to tread on this journey over water," Rushton said pensively. "We have to see what happens."

"There is another thing you should know," I said, remembering. "After the contest, the rebels plan to meet and to decide once and for all when and how the rebellion will be staged."

Rushton's eyes flared with an unholy green fire. "Well, that puts it in a very different light. By winning, we would have gained the right to take part in their councils."

"And of course we will win," Miryum said. "Whatever the nature of these games, I do not think we need be frightened of ten unTalents. Hannay, Elspeth, and I could deal with them between us."

It was late the following day before we stood on the deck of a ship bound for Sador.

Contrary to Maryon's futuretelling of thirteen, there were only eleven of us, counting Dragon. We could not leave without her, and Kella had assured us that the journey would not hurt her. Domick had embarked on a Council errand to Morganna, and he wouldn't be back for a day. And we were forced to leave the horses behind in Sutrium—much as Gahltha disapproved—for fear that the travel and the climate would do them harm.

No amount of searching had located Maruman. I couldn't help worrying, though I knew the old cat could fend for himself. He had made his own way to Obernewtyn before; he could do it again.

Reuvan, calling to drop off a homing bird at Brydda's instruction, had learned we meant to travel to Sador at once. Advising that we leave it to him to organize a ship, he arranged passage to Sador's Templeport with a seafaring friend and longtime rebel supporter.

Powyrs turned out to be a jolly, bold, brown-faced man with twinkling eyes and a habit of winking that startled us somewhat until we were accustomed to it. He had no qualms about carrying gypsies. I had the feeling he would not have given a damn if we told him we were Misfits.

I was standing on the deck of Powyrs's sturdy little ship, *The Cutter*, waiting for the Council inspectors to give final clearance to sail, when Kella pinched my arm to get my attention. Leaning close, she whispered into my ear in an absurdly furtive way that Reuvan was coming. I was not surprised that he had come to see us off, but I was startled to see that Dardelan was with him, as was a long-limbed, exotic girl with yellow, almond-shaped eyes and a satiric smile. She could only be Jakoby's daughter. If anything, she was more beautiful than her mother.

"You are the first to leave, but the rest of us will not be far behind," Reuvan said as they approached us. "Malik and his cronies are traveling tomorrow, and I will travel with Jakoby and the rest on the Sadorian ship, the *Zephyr*, on the next day."

"Am I to be presented, or shall I stand like a nameless dolt?" the dark Sadorian girl asked haughtily.

Dardelan flushed and apologized. "This is Jakoby's daughter, Bruna; Bruna, this is Elspeth."

"I am pleased to know you," I said.

"Ah. I-am-pleased-to-know-you," Bruna said, exactly mimicking my intonation.

Unnerved a little by this and by her frank scrutiny, I busied myself introducing the others. When Dardelan and Rushton shook hands, they exchanged a measuring look and seemed satisfied by what they saw.

"You will like my land, of course," Bruna said haughtily. "Your people are welcome there, for like the tribes, they have no need to mark the ground where they have been, like a rutting beast marking its territory. Unlike these Landfolk." Her eyes ran over our halfbreed gypsy attire approvingly, but she gave poor Dardelan a look of amused contempt.

"In Sador, there is room to run with the wind and ride the kamuli," she went on, seeming to address all of us now. Wearing little, despite the gray, chilly weather, she was as oblivious to the cold as she was to the stares of passersby. No wonder Jakoby had looked amused when she said Sadorian women needed scant looking after.

The girl waved an imperious finger under Dardelan's nose. "And now you will guide me to the place of many trees. The forest. These I do not see in my own desert, and there might be some beauty in them worthy of a song."

"Of . . . of course," Dardelan stammered, and she bore him away.

"A pup watching over a bear," Reuvan said.

"A bear cub," I corrected, thinking that for all her imperiousness, Bruna lacked her mother's subtlety and dangerous grace.

It began to rain lightly as the inspectors arrived and set about searching the ship from top to bottom, seeking any Landgoods that were being exported without tax being paid to the Council. When Powyrs suggested we go inside, I was glad enough to do so. The fishy smell of the ship's oiled deck and the movement of it running up and down the swelling waves were making me feel distinctly queasy.

"I will want to cast off as soon as this is over to catch the out tides. Go into the main salon," Powyrs said. He looked at Reuvan. "I will come there and warn you before we are to depart."

As we trooped along the deck, I could not help but think of Matthew being led onto *The Calor Lady*'s gangplank in chains. Had he felt this strange, unsettling nausea? Was he somewhere out over the ocean being rained on, too?

I glanced back and noticed an old beggar in filthy brown robes come up to Powyrs and speak with him. At first the seaman shook his head decisively, but then he stopped and seemed to be listening intently. I was curious enough to farseek, but the queer static from whatever had tainted the sea about Sutrium's shores prevented this.

"Come on," Miky said, tugging at me.

The salon turned out to be spacious and light, despite dark wood paneling and floor-to-ceiling bookshelves. This was due to three enormous box windows along the outside wall, crisscrossed by wide-spaced metal grilles. Cushioned seats were built into the windows, and a table, chairs, and various other pieces of furniture were fixed to the floor. The salon adjoined the galley, and Kella's eyes lit up as she surveyed its miniature neatness.

Rushton dropped into a window seat and gestured to Reuvan, Miryum, and Hannay to sit beside him. They talked in low, serious voices while Angina and his twin began to tune their instruments. Kella came out of the galley and stood at a window. Her eyes looked out to the sea, but I was sure she saw nothing but the face of her bondmate.

Powyrs had taken Dameon below to a cabin with Dragon. I moved to the door with the thought of going to sit with him, but Powyrs returned, blocking my way.

"Casting off!" he warned in a stentorian bellow. "All who will not sail should get ashore."

Reuvan rose. "I'd better move. A seaman is ruled by the tides, and if catching the tide means an unwilling passenger or two, then so be it."

The ship lurched suddenly, and all of us pitched sideways save Reuvan, who was accustomed to walking on a shifting deck.

He smiled somewhat wistfully. "You must learn to dance with the sea—not tread on her toes."

We went out on deck to bid him farewell. The rain had ceased, and the clouds had parted to reveal the sun sinking toward the horizon.

As the ropes were cast away by Powyrs's crew and the shore began to slip away, a curious but definite feeling of loss assailed me, a feeling that I had somehow cast off from my life and was sailing toward a new one.

From the look of those gathered along the edge of the deck, I was not alone in this feeling. The others gazed back to the shore, their faces reflecting their unease. This was the first time any of us had left the Land. There were numerous disaster stories Landfolk told about the perils of the seas, and suddenly the wildest tales seemed to gain substance.

The sun sank into the sea, becoming increasingly large and orange as it did so, staining the gray-edged clouds that framed it a livid pink. I was intrigued to feel the taint in the water fading. That meant whatever had caused it was confined to the shore area. Perhaps some Beforetime container had broken under the sea, spilling its poisons.

"That's that, then," Kella said huskily when the sun finally vanished and Sutrium fell into a purple haze that merged with the horizon. "I feel as if I'm leaving a part of myself here."

I forbore pointing out the obvious.

"To Sador," Miky sighed dreamily on the other side of me.

"I feel sick," Miryum said, and I was startled to see that she looked bright green about the face and lips.

"I do not feel so well myself," I murmured.

· 34 ·

KELLA SET ABOUT adjusting our senses to the movement of *The Cutter*, but some of us responded better to her treatment than others.

The empaths were only mildly affected by the motion of the waves and were quickly eased. I was less fortunate.

Because of the instinctive blocking ability I appeared to have developed as a response to intrusion, I had to hold my mind open to the healer. This was not easy, and when she was done, the wooden decks continued to pitch, rendering me queasy and disoriented.

Disappointed, I asked Powyrs if there was not some seaman's remedy that would settle my stomach.

He looked at me intently for a moment, then shook his head. "Your illness is not physical. It is a matter of the will. You resist the ocean as if it were an opponent. But you cannot defeat the sea—it is too great and too uncaring. You can only surrender to its power. While you fight, you will suffer."

I laughed and said he talked as if the sea were alive. He only shrugged. "Laugh, but it is true. All things that exist live, though maybe they do not measure life as we do."

I thought this absurd. The fish in the sea lived, but not the sea itself. It was just water. But seafolk were as notoriously superstitious as highlanders, and I liked Powyrs too much to make fun of his beliefs.

The coercers suffered worst of us. That was not unexpected, for coercers were always disturbed by anything that altered their balance or perceptions. Roland believed this had something to do with the nature of coercing and how the deep probe was shaped to serve their Talent. The more powerful the coercer, the more severe the response. Accordingly, Hannay was nauseous but Miryum violently ill. All Kella could do was render her unconscious with a sleepseal.

Like me, Hannay resigned himself to an uncomfortable few days.

That first night, my stomach churned at the thought of food, and I sat a little apart as many of the others ate a mushroom stew and regaled Kella with news from Obernewtyn.

Turning to a window, I looked through the reflection of the room and its ghostly occupants to the dark sea beyond.

I shook my head at the sudden melancholy that assailed me. Perhaps it was that I had grown accustomed, these last two sevendays, to strife and activity and urgency. Sea travel was not like travel on land where there were always things to be done, if only to break camp and set up bedding at night. We journeyed, and yet we went nowhere.

I sighed, wishing it was not my nature to see life as if it were the reflection in a window. I could never just accept it. I had to be squinting my eyes and looking to see what was underneath it, tormenting myself with doubts and questions. And it was worse when I had nothing to distract me.

The moon penetrated the clouds for a moment, lighting up a small cluster of rock spikes. Powyrs had said these were good shoals because you could see them. But there were many more such shoals hiding just below the surface that could tear the bottom from a boat if the seamen were not vigilant. The ocean's teeth, he had named them, winking.

I was like a wary seafarer, never trusting the smooth, glimmering surface of life for fear of the hidden teeth. Perhaps that was why I could not settle as the others had and enjoy the enforced idleness. Even when there was no need, I watched for the teeth.

I scowled at my own face in the glass, telling myself again that I should be content. After all, Maryon's dream had solved my immediate problems.

I bit my lip, understanding that this was what lay at the root of my strange discontent. I had left Obernewtyn driven by Maryon's dreams. But once away, I had done as I chose. I made decisions and acted on them and felt as if I owned my life. Now Maryon and her dreams had reached out to wrest control from me again. I was not the wary seaman after all. I was a ship, floating on the tides and eddies of capricious fate just as *The Cutter* was driven by the sea. But at least the ship had a captain. Who was the captain of my voyage? Atthis? Maryon? Certainly not me.

I thought of the futureteller. How did Maryon feel to know that she had only to speak of her dreams to be obeyed? It was true power. But Maryon did not control her dreams, so, in a sense, the power was not hers. The dreams controlled her, pulling this way and that, demanding to be told or acted upon. Was the self-knowledge she and all her fellow futuretellers sought worth this slavery to their dreams?

The salon door banged open, and I turned to see Rushton enter.

Of us all, Rushton had adapted most easily to the movement of the ship. From almost his first steps on deck, he had mastered the graceful rolling walk affected by Powyrs and his crew. His cheeks were red, his hair wildly tangled, and his eyes bright as they swept the room. He was clearly finding his first sea journey exhilarating.

"I am ravenous," he said.

The door behind him burst open again to reveal the old beggar who had been speaking to Powyrs at the bottom of the gangplank just before we departed.

"You can't come in here . . . ," Hannay began firmly.

The beggar threw off the hood of his brown robe to reveal a familiar tanned face in the candlelight.

"Daffyd!" I murmured. There were cries as the others recognized him, too.

He ignored them, his eyes sweeping the room to settle on me. I gasped, for only when he faced me properly could I see that his left eye socket was swollen to twice its size, his lip split, and his cheek marked with bloody striations.

"What in Lud's name has happened to you?"

"I escaped from Ayle," he said hoarsely.

"Sit down, man," Rushton said, steering him to a window seat beside me.

"He found you out?" I asked.

"Ayle found nothing out. Salamander told him I was a spy."

I was confused. "He can't have returned already?" My heart rose. "Unless the slaves have only been taken to Morganna or Aborium . . ."

Daffyd shook his head. "Salamander told Ayle, the day he came to take the slaves, that I was to be locked up until he got back." He shuddered. "Lud knows how he learned I was a spy or what he planned to do to me when he returned. As soon as I got a chance, I broke out and fought my way free. I headed straight for the city gates, but Ayle was quicker. I spotted his people just in time. I would never have made it, and I knew if they were watching one gate, they would be watching them all."

"You went to the safe house?"

He nodded. "It was all locked up. I had no choice but to try sending out an attuned probe to you. It near killed me to hold it together when it got near the sea, but it locked on to your mind a split second before the static got the better of me. That was long enough for me to learn that you were sailing at dusk for Sador. I told your captain that I was a friend. I hope you do not object to another traveling companion."

"We are glad to have you," Rushton said, but he spoke as if his mind was elsewhere.

"That's twelve of us," Miky breathed beside me.

"Elspeth believes she saw Ariel on board the Herder ship that took Matthew away," Rushton said. "Did you see him?"

Though I would not have thought it possible, Daffyd paled further.

"It seems unlikely, since there is no connection between Ariel and this Salamander . . . ," Rushton said.

Daffyd stood up abruptly and stared down at him. "You are wrong." His face was clenched in misery, and he began to pace. "I said at the safe house that there was not enough time to tell my story. Now I wish I had taken the time."

"It would be a simple matter if lives were lived by hindsight," Rushton said. "There is much we would not begin if we could see how it would end."

Daffyd would not be consoled. "Matthew was my friend, and I ought to have done something. If Ariel was aboard . . ."

"From what Elspeth said, there was nothing you could have done," Rushton said firmly. He pulled Daffyd back down and motioned to Kella to wash his wounds. When the healer was settled and bathing the gashes, Rushton asked Daffyd what connection there was between Salamander and Ariel.

"I will tell you," Daffyd said, "but I must start at the beginning. After leaving Obernewtyn with Kella and Domick last summerdays, I traveled to the White Valley and the site of the Druid encampment. My plan was to see if I could find any clue as to what direction the survivors might have taken." His eyes were distant, as if he truly gazed into the past and saw the events he described unscrolling before his eyes.

"I left the valley without any sign to give me hope and tracked all through and around the Gelfort Range. I found some few scattered camping places, but there was never any way of knowing whose they had been. I went about small settlements in the highlands and in the upper lowlands, talking and asking questions. I sometimes pretended to be a Councilman and at other times a Herder agent.

"Then one night at a dingy inn in a tiny settlement, I came face to face with one of the Druid armsmen from the camp."

Daffyd's face reflected the elation he must have felt at this first breakthrough in his long search. But the smile faded at once. "He told me that shortly before the firestorm destroyed the camp—mere days—Ariel came to see the Druid."

I seemed to see that pale, impossibly fair face turning to me on the deck of *The Calor Lady*.

"As you know," Daffyd went on, "Ariel was working as an agent for the Herder Faction back then, and for the Council, while at the same time styling himself a secret friend to Henry Druid. On this last visit, he told the Druid that the Council had learned the location of his secret camp and that soldierguards were being dispatched to clean it out. He advised the Druid to prepare his people for battle, insisting that they would be able to defend the fortified camp, and he suggested sending the young, the frail, and the elderly out of harm's way up into the foothills of the Gelfort Range. Ariel claimed he dared not remain to help drive off the soldierguards, since it would betray his identity and put an end to his usefulness as a spy. But he offered to lead those who would not fight to a safe place in the hills until it was over."

Daffyd's face twisted in a spasm of uncontrollable rage. "The Druid thanked him for his friendship and loyalty and did as he suggested. When Ariel had gone, Henry Druid decided to send out a small advance party to give warning of the soldierguards' approach. The three scouts rode out a bare hour before the firestorm razed the camp to the ground—the man who told this story to me was, of course, one of the three. They saw the storm and returned when it was over to find nothing remained of their camp. They looked for Ariel and those who had been led away, but there was no trace of them. Nor, in the days that followed, did any soldierguard force materialize."

It took a moment to understand what this must mean. "Ariel lied!" I said incredulously.

Daffyd nodded, his eyes bleak. "What other answer could there be? I suppose he true-dreamed the firestorm and saw it as a natural and anonymous way to end a potentially embarrassing and no longer necessary connection with an outlawed priest. The visit was simply to ensure that the Druid and his armsmen were in the camp when it burned." His voice was choked with rage and despair.

I saw that Rushton had grown pale. At first I thought he was experiencing the same shock as I, at this suggestion that Ariel had powers like ours. But then I remembered that, long ago, the Druid had befriended Rushton and treated him as a son. He had not seemed terribly affected when the firestorm destroyed the camp, but there was a difference between being killed in a firestorm from nature's random arsenal and being lured into a deadly trap. Ariel had even found a way to use nature for his perverted ends.

"What of the people he led out?" Kella murmured.

I could guess what was to be told next—the answer was threaded through all that had happened.

"When the three surviving armsmen could not find them, they split up. Two went to the west coast. The third man remained, and it was he who I met. For a time, we traveled together, but we found no trace of the others. He began to fear that taking them from the camp had simply been Ariel's means of getting out before the firestorm struck, a ruse, and that he had killed them after. But I could not accept they were dead. So we parted, too. Gilbert went to join the other two armsmen, and I—"

"Gilbert?" I said, remembering vividly the red-haired armsman who had befriended me when I was captive in the Druid camp.

First Daffyd, then Elii, and now Gilbert. Who else would I meet out of the past, circling back to merge their lifepaths with mine? Did it mean anything or nothing?

Daffyd frowned. "You remember him? Strange that you should recall one face out of all the Druid's men. He spoke of you but thought you were dead. Of course, I did not enlighten him."

I nodded. The last time I had seen Gilbert had been on the banks of the upper Suggredoon, a look of helpless anguish on his face as my raft was swept away by flood-swollen waters into the depths of Tor.

The armsman went on. "Well, we parted as I said. I came

to Sutrium, and it was there that I met another from the Druid camp, a woman. She was calling herself by another name and tried at first to pretend I was mistaken, but eventually she admitted the truth. She told me she had been a slave fleetingly but had escaped being transported and sold with the help of a seaman who had fallen in love with her. He threw her clothes overboard and pretended she had drowned herself, but he warned her never to speak of it, for if the truth was known, they would both be killed.

"I asked how she had been taken by the slavers in the first place. 'Taken'? she mocked me. 'I was *given* to the slavers. Betrayed and sold with no chance to run or fight. My bondmate saved me, but he could not save all of us. The others have gone over the waves, wherever slaves are taken.'"

Kella gasped aloud. "Oh Lud. Ariel sold those he had taken from the camp to the slavers!"

Daffyd nodded. "I was a fool not to have seen it sooner. The woman told me they saw the camp burn and could do nothing. There had been men and women, hired thugs, waiting in the hills to bind them and lead them away. Ariel had sold them to Salamander."

Daffyd ran his hands through his hair. "You know, the thing that gnaws at me is that I had been only a little distance from their camp the day they were taken out of the mountains by the slavers. If only I had been able to farseek Gilaine as soon as the storm ended."

There was such anguish in his voice. The static thrown up by the firestorm would have prevented his farseeking, but that he had not gone looking for them at once was my fault. I had been injured terribly, and we had just found Jik's charred body. I had begged Daffyd to take Dragon to

Obernewtyn before the pass to the mountains was closed by snow.

"I felt . . . helpless. Hopeless," he went on in a barely audible voice. "It had been months since they had been sold, and they were long gone on the slave ships. For the first time, I felt they were truly lost to me. I wanted revenge on Ariel. You cannot imagine how badly. But he had gone by then to Herder Isle.

"So I turned my mind to the slave trade with the idea that perhaps I could inveigle myself a job and learn where they had been taken. It is madness of a kind to be so persistent, yet somehow I felt that if they lived, I must find them."

Daffyd's eyes burned with near-fanatical hatred; the search for Gilaine, Jow, and Lidgebaby defined his existence now. Truly, he was not so far from madness.

"I suppose this woman from the camp did not actually see Salamander?" Hannay asked.

Daffyd laughed harshly. "No. No one has ever seen Salamander's face—except perhaps Ariel. It was only after the sale of the Druid's people that Salamander moved in properly on the slave trade, killing anyone who stood against him, terrorizing the rest, and streamlining the operation into one smooth, efficient monopoly. I thought Ariel's connection with him was a passing thing, but if he was aboard the ship with him, perhaps there is more to it."

"I wonder what Ariel got out of the bargain. Coin?" Rushton murmured. "He would not aid the slaver for nothing."

Daffyd's expression hardened. "Perhaps. They are as like to one another as two buds from the same plant. Both are secretive. Both love pain and desire power."

The desperation returned to his face.

I laid a hand on his arm. "What will you do now?"

"Survive," he said harshly. "If Salamander wants me dead, I will live to spite him. He will have the city scoured for me when he returns, and it pleases me to think that he will be thwarted. We will have our day of reckoning. And when I am done with the slavemaster, I will find Ariel."

✦ 35 ✦

It did not take much persuasion for Daffyd to let himself be shown to a bed. He was clearly exhausted far beyond his endurance.

I felt too nauseous to sleep and decided to go out on deck. Perhaps some fresh air would make me feel better.

The wind had risen, and it fluttered my clothing and snapped the sailcloth. The sea was higher, too, and slapped against the wooden hull in a broken rhythm. I shivered and pulled my cloak about me, trying to imagine what it would be like to do as Powyrs suggested and give myself to the sea.

"Wet, doubtless," a voice clove into my thoughts.

I started violently, for draped languidly on a mast strut right in front of me, licking one paw, was Maruman!

"How in Lud's name did you manage to get aboard?" I demanded. "And where have you been?"

For once, my questions did not rouse his ire. He stretched with slow and infuriating feline grace and jumped lightly to the deck to rub against my leg.

"There you are!" Powyrs bellowed, and swooped over to scoop him up.

I froze, but instead of scratching the seaman, the bedraggled feline lay quiescently in his arms, an alarming mixture of complacence and thwarted mischief in his single gleaming eye.

"I wondered where he had been hiding," Powyrs said, pretending severity. He looked at me and winked hugely. "The fools I have working for me think he is a bad omen, but he is too smart for them to catch and throw over the edge as they would like. He torments them, the naughty thing. Darting out and scaring them. Twice he has made seamen fall overboard." He beamed at Maruman with paternal pride, and I could barely stop myself laughing aloud.

I stood up and reached out to pat him. Powyrs's muscles tightened as mine had done moments before, but he relaxed as the cat allowed himself to be petted.

"Well, you are honored. Usually he will suffer no one to touch him but me," he said, sounding astonished.

"He is magnificent," I said, repressing a grin at how utterly Maruman had beguiled the burly seaman.

"Of course," Maruman sent haughtily.

"He can be savage," Powyrs warned. "You'd best leave him be, except when I'm holding him. He's used to me. Reminds me of the sea, he does. My father said to me when he advised me against being a seaman; 'The sea is a wild beast that eats the lives of those who would try to tame it.'"

"You didn't listen, then?" I smiled.

He shrugged. "I never liked tame things, even as a boy." He glanced over and noticed one of his seamen mending a sail. Snorting in derision, he set Maruman down gently before stomping over to instruct the seaman on his deficiencies.

"Well, I see how you managed to get yourself aboard," I sent, grinning at him.

Maruman made no response. He leapt up onto a box beside me, and I felt a surge of pure happiness as he climbed onto my arm and clawed his way up to my shoulders to drape himself about my neck. I breathed deeply, taking in the slightly fishy smell of his coarse fur, as if it were the scent of fresh flowers. Oddly, I no longer felt sick.

I yawned and decided I would go to bed. For the first time in many days, I felt content.

"I am glad to see/carry/smell you," I sent, repressing my usual instinct to cuddle him close and tell him I loved him.

"I am glad also," Maruman sent with rare sweetness.

The tiny cabin I had chosen contained only a bed and was no more than a closet. Its virtues were that it was situated on the main deck, which meant there was no need to grope my way down ladders in the darkness, and I would have some privacy. In a short time, I was leaning down to let Maruman jump onto the narrow bed, which was fixed to the wall under a small round window looking out to sea. The moon slid out of its envelope of cloud, and the old cat sniffed suspiciously at the pillow where its silvery light fell. Then he turned to me, his eye filled with moonlight.

I froze in the act of taking off my sandals.

"The oldOne sent ashling to Maruman/yelloweyes. Say come. Maruman coming. Say: tell Innle. Maruman tells," he sent.

"Tell me what?" My heart pounded.

"Maruman flew the dreamtrails with the oldOnes. Saw Innle on blackdeathroad. Going to the endmost means end of barud. Obernewtyn finished and all gone for Innle."

I stared at him. Atthis had sometimes called my quest a black road. Maruman seemed to be saying that if I completed my quest, Obernewtyn would not be there anymore. But what did that mean? That it would be abandoned? Destroyed? And why would Atthis want him to tell me this now?

I took my sandals off and climbed into the bed, shifting

Maruman to make room for myself. Maybe I was misunder-standing him. After all, beastspeaking obeyed no rules. Com-munications were entirely idiosyncratic, dependent on how much Talent a beast possessed, their mood at the time of com-munication, their relationship to the human with whom they communed, and, sometimes, even on what was to be told. Beasts interchangeably used their own odd dialect, human words, and imagepictures enhanced by empathised emo-tions. And Maruman was harder than most because of the distortions of his mind.

Maybe Maruman had not meant that Obernewtyn would fall but that it would be lost to me. The Agyllians had warned me that my quest would lead me away from my friends. But I had always assumed that, when that quest was over, my life would be my own. It disheartened me to think this might not be so.

I remembered Ariel saying in my dream, "Do what you wish, and you do my bidding." Was that my mind's way of warning me that free will was an illusion and that my life would never be mine to command?

"It would be a little late now to decide that we would not live our lives by the whimsical wisdoms of futuretellers, don't you think?" Rushton had asked the previous day.

And it was too late. My sworn quest was the central and defining truth of my life now. Just as Daffyd's long search for Gilaine shaped him, so my quest shaped me. If there was a black road, then I was on it already and had been all the days of my life. And I would walk it to the end—no matter where it led me. Even if it meant I could not go back to Obernewtyn.

Then it came to me. Perhaps Atthis had sent Maruman to test my resolve.

"Rest/sleep," Maruman sent insistently. "All things seem

dark under the whiteface." He curled against my chest, and we slept.

I dreamed I was on land, walking through country as Ludforsaken and desolate as the drear vista of the Blacklands I had once seen from the top of the high mountains. The road beneath me was black, and I saw that its darkness had climbed into my limbs, staining them a sickly purplish yellow—the livid shades of advanced rotting sickness that told me the road was poisoning me.

I wondered then if Maruman had meant that I would not be able to return to Obernewtyn because I would be dead.

I woke to unexpected stillness.

It felt as if the ship were not moving at all, and I wondered if at last my senses had realigned to shipboard life. There was a weight against my arm, and I opened my eyes to find Maruman sprawled alongside me, his head resting on my elbow. I eased myself out from under him and turned on my side to watch him sleep. Poor, dear muddled Maruman filling me up with his garbled thoughts and gloomy predictions. In the daylight, such cryptic nonsense did not seem so terrible.

I leaned forward and kissed him very softly, knowing he would be furious if he caught me.

Kella poked her head in the door.

"Oh good, you're awake, Elspeth. Come and see this."

I put a hasty finger to my lips and pointed to Maruman. The healer's eyes widened at the sight of the cat asleep in the rumpled bedclothes, and she backed out of the room. I climbed from the bed, ran my fingers through my hair, and laced on my sandals.

Kella was waiting for me outside. "How in Lud's name did he get here?" she demanded.

"He must have had a true dream. He got aboard even before we did and settled himself to wait. He's got old Powyrs twisted round his paw."

Kella's eyes shone. "I'm so glad he's all right. Oh, Elspeth, maybe it's true what Powyrs says about them being good luck."

"'Them'?" I asked, baffled. "Cats?"

She shook her head and beckoned, and I followed her to the edge of *The Cutter*. "Look out there," she said, pointing.

I looked and was startled to see that the ocean was utterly still, stretching away like a mirror on all sides of us. Now I understood why my nausea had abated. Not a breath of air stirred the sagging canvas sails or rippled the glassy sea. We were so completely becalmed that a reflection of the ship and my face stared back with perfect clarity from the water. There was no sign of the coast, but Powyrs had explained to us the previous night that he would have to set a course directly away from land to begin with, in order to avoid the shoal beds clustered thickly in the sea between the Land and the Sadorian plains.

And then I saw three sleek, satiny, silver-gray fish, as big as grown men, propelling themselves high into the air, somersaulting, and plunging back into the water.

I gaped, astounded at their strength and agility.

"They have been known to save the lives of humans who fall from the deck," Kella murmured.

"Good luck is right," I said. "Good luck for the drowning seaman."

I watched the strange fish leap out of the water as if they were moon-fair acrobats. They must be incredibly strong to lift themselves out of the sea like that, I thought. I had never tried to communicate with fish before, but some instinct told me these might be capable of beastspeaking. The sea was utterly clear of tainting, and I could have tried, yet I found I did not want to. These lovely creatures were oblivious to the humans watching them, and I was content to have it so. Humans had caused so much sorrow for the beastworld; let these remain untouched.

"Ah, ship fish. They are nowt truly fish, you know," Fian said, coming to stand beside me.

I jumped, for I had not heard him approach.

"Of course they are," Kella said.

"They are warm-blooded, an' they suckle their babes on milk after bearin' them whole as humans do. An' they need air." He held up a thick book with a mottled green cover. "This book tells all about them. Ship fish are much like humans."

"Are they descended from the merpeople?" Kella asked. She had become fascinated with accounts in Beforetime books of a race of humans with gills and fishtails who had dwelt under the sea.

Fian frowned. "I dinna know. This books says nowt of them, other than that ship fish were sometimes mistaken for them. It does say that Beforetimers had boats that would go under water."

"Where the merpeople lived?"

Fian frowned at the healer. "I told ye, it doesn't say. Perhaps this was written after they became extinct. Apparently, there were ruined cities under th' sea. . . ." He looked down at the tome in his hand. "Powyrs has even more books in a trunk in his room, an' he has told me I may look through them."

"So many books," the healer murmured.

"And all about th' sea," Fian said. "Enough for a lifetime's study, and I have only a few days." He cast a final long look at the ship fish and turned to hurry back into the salon.

Kella shook her head. "Teknoguilders," she said with faint disparagement. "How can he think of books when there is this to see?"

But a little later she grew tired of the ship-fish antics and went in.

I decided to climb up to the small upper deck, for it would give me a better view. It was piled with boxes, and I sat on top of one, dangling my legs and looking out at the sea. I had never known such stillness. It seemed to accentuate the vastness of the world and, in contrast, my own insignificance, but it was not an unpleasant feeling. In the face of this endless sea, I was no more than one of the ship fish, jumping in my bit of the ocean, making my little waves. There was a queer peace to be found in the thought, and I tried to draw the immense calmness into my heart to erase fear and anger and sadness.

My concentration was shattered by a muffled explosion of laughter.

"It tickles," I heard a female voice giggle. I recognized Freya's melodic voice and smiled, wondering whom she was with.

A moment later, I saw Rushton stroll to the rail, and my amusement evaporated.

Even as I watched, Freya stepped up beside him and shook her head, the springing golden curls catching and diffusing the morning sunlight into a pale halo.

Rushton appeared to be doing most of the speaking. Then he grasped Freya's hands in his and stared into her face intently as if waiting for some response. Freya's head was sunk as if in thought.

At last she nodded.

Rushton's face suffused with joy. He flung his arms around her and hugged her tightly.

A terrible, savage pain clawed into my chest.

"You don't know how much this means to me," I heard Rushton saying as they moved toward the steep little stairs leading down to the main deck, obscured now by the sail. "I don't want to tell anyone just yet. Let it remain our secret for now. . . ."

Their voices faded, and the pain in my chest intensified, spreading through my body like some exotic plague germ. The image of Rushton holding Freya in his arms seemed to have seared itself onto the inside of my eyelids so that I could see it even when my eyes were squeezed shut. I pulled my knees up to my chest and held them tightly, making myself into a ball.

"Rushton," I whispered.

And who is she? I thought bitterly. *Where did she come from, to steal him while my back was turned?*

I clenched my teeth, resisting sour envy. While my back was turned? No, Freya had taken nothing that belonged to me. What could it possibly matter that he had turned to her? There was no room for anything in my life but my quest to destroy the weaponmachines.

Perhaps that was what Maruman had been trying to say the previous night—that there would be nothing for me at Obernewtyn when my quest was over. Maybe this was the price I must pay—not just Obernewtyn, but Rushton's love.

I took a deep, shaky breath and made myself look into the gray calmness of the sea all around me. The ship fish had departed.

I had not wanted Rushton's affections or encouraged them. So why did it hurt so much to learn that they were lost to me?

It does not matter, I thought fiercely. *My feet are already on the black road. It is too late to choose another, and this one I must walk alone.*

✦ 36 ✦

WE WERE BECALMED for two days, but by early afternoon of the third day, *The Cutter* was making up lost time, running before a stiff wind.

We were sitting in the salon, and Fian was describing the discovery of the Reichler Clinic to Daffyd.

Maruman stirred restively on my knee but did not waken. The others had taken his appearance with some equanimity, since they had only the day before learned of his loss. But I felt it was nearly miraculous to have him with me. It was Angina who pointed out that Maruman made us the thirteen that Maryon had predicted.

"Hard to believe you just stumbled on it," Daffyd was saying.

"In a city so big? No, it was more than chance. I believe we were *meant* to find it."

"After all, Hannah Seraphim was Rushton's ancestor," Kella added, her eyes shining. "Some things are meant to be."

And some are not, I thought, and was unable to stop my eyes from going to the table at the far end of the chamber where Rushton was talking with Hannay.

Why was it so hard not to look at him all of a sudden? Before this journey, I had done anything I could to avoid his gaze and his attention. I had refused his every overture, convinced that the force that sometimes crackled between us arose from him, that my own feelings were no more than re-actions to it.

But in this new life of pain, the knowledge that Rushton no longer loved me seemed to have released a tempest of conflicting emotions all my own. I could not believe he had endured what I now felt—this hard, painful burning in the chest, this ache in the belly and throat. How could this be love?

If it was, it was as bad as ever I had imagined it must be. I should think myself fortunate that Rushton had turned from me before what simmered between us had burst into flame.

I focused my eyes on Fian, wondering how soon I could reasonably retreat to my chamber again. Then his words caught my attention.

"It wasn't until we had read a lot of the plasts that we realized what we had found wasn't the Reichler Clinic after all," he said.

"But we saw the name carved on the wall," I protested.

He nodded. "We misinterpreted it. What we found was exactly what the sign said—a *reception center* for th' Reichler Clinic. Nowt th' place itself. Th' real Reichler Clinic was where Garth always thought it mun be—in th' mountains."

"At Obernewtyn?" Kella asked breathlessly.

The teknoguilder shook his head. "Obernewtyn, or th' building that stood there before *our* Obernewtyn, was likely th' main residence for the Misfits. Th' actual Reichler Clinic labs were almost certainly sited where the cave of the Zebkrahn now stands. We have long known some Before-time building once stood there, but we little dreamed which building or that it—"

"Labs? For experimentation on the Misfits?" I interrupted with real horror.

"I dinna think the experiments run by the Reichler Clinic would have been harmful or dangerous," Fian said. "Better to call them tests, as the plasts do. Hannah Seraphim would nowt have stood fer anything wrong. Fact is, we're pretty certain she was what th' Beforetimers called telepathic. In short, a Talented Misfit."

I was surprised, though it was the obvious answer to why she had opened the clinic in the first place.

"This were kept a secret, along wi' th' names of those who came to be tested. Ye might say th' Reichler Clinic we saw under Tor were a front fer an operation very like ours, or, I should say, it became so after Govamen began to stalk Talents."

"I still don't understand what they did with them," Angina grumbled.

"There are indications, as Garth explained last guildmerge, that—"

"I know, they were trying to use them somehow for warmaking. But how?" Angina asked.

"As to that . . . ," Fian began with some heat, but he stopped again and shook his head fractionally. "Well. We will know more of that when we unearth th' clinic."

"Unearth it?" I asked sharply. "Then the clinic was buried by the holocaust like the city under Tor?"

"No," Fian said. "And nor was the city under Tor. Both were *originally* built under the earth."

He let us clamor for a moment before going on with a rather smug expression. "Th' upheavals are to blame for th' flood waters, but no more."

"But why?" I asked. "Why would anyone want to build a city under the ground?"

"Because of the whiteface." Maruman's sleepy thought

385

drifted into my mind. I looked down at him, startled. When he snored, I decided he must have been sending in his sleep.

"I suspect the Reichler Clinic was built under th' earth so that it would be hidden. But we will know more once we have got into th' lower levels of th' caves."

I thought of the tattoo on my arm, still hidden from the others in its bandage. Perhaps the Teknoguild had learned something more of what it meant. I would ask Fian about it when I had a moment alone with him.

Freya came into the salon, and I felt a wave of despair. Was this how it was to be? Every time I had begun to build a wall of calmness, it was to be shattered by the smallest thing? I half expected her to sit with Rushton, but she crossed to the galley and set about making up a tray of food.

On impulse, I touched Angina's arm. "What is Freya's story? How did she come to Obernewtyn?"

"She ought to tell you herself," he said, and before I could stop him, he called out to her. I forced myself to smile as she approached, wishing passionately that I had kept my mouth shut.

She was very small and dainty and, like Rushton, had adapted gracefully to the ship's movements. I felt myself to be as long and gangling as a string bean beside her.

"I have wished for the chance to speak with you, Guild-mistress," Freya said. "Rushton spoke of you on our journey here, and truly, your life has been one of danger and marvels. My own story is nothing to yours."

My heart bumped against my chest in a sort of frightened leap, and all my hard-won composure vanished at the thought that Rushton might have confided that he had once loved me.

"Tell her," Angina prompted Freya.

She flushed prettily. "Rushton rescued me."

Of course.

"I had come to Darthnor with my father. He is . . . was . . . a horse trader." A fleeting unhappiness showed in her eyes. "Along with his horses, there came a day that he offered his daughter for sale. . . ." She swallowed as if her throat hurt. "Rushton offered to buy me and the horses as a lot. He seemed a great man when he rode up on his white horse and threw a fortune in coin at my father's feet."

What sort of life had she led to be flattered that a man offered to buy her as a lot with horses? If Rushton had done that to me, I would have just as likely picked the coin up and thrown it back at him! Though probably he had meant it to be a gesture of contempt for Freya's father.

"I did not know until later that Alad was with Rushton and that the horses had told him I was . . . a Misfit," she went on. "But he said he would have bid whether I was Talented or not, for people should not be sold any more than beasts. He told me about Obernewtyn, though not where it was, and offered to bring me there, where I could stay and commune all I wished with horses, or I might have a bag of coin and go where I willed."

Her lashes tilted secretively, and I saw that she had not needed much convincing to choose Obernewtyn. I felt a rush of savage jealousy and was astonished. Was this violent, pointless rage part of love, too?

"You are a beastspeaker, then?" I asked, and was horrified to hear how cold I sounded.

"Not exactly," Freya laughed, obviously taking my sharpness for a joke. "I am an empath, I suppose, but am not able to receive anything much."

Thank Lud for that!

"She may not be much good at receiving emotions," Angina said cheerfully, "but she has a unique variation of projective empathy."

"Unique," I echoed.

Angina gave me a frankly puzzled stare.

"Dameon calls her an enhancer," he said. "She can enhance another's Talent. Her ability seems to be closest to what I do when I amplify Miky's projected emotions. Only Freya can do it to whomever she chooses or switch it off altogether."

Freya's remarkably expressive eyes darkened. "I cannot reach everyone. Never my father. There was a wall in him—a natural mindshield, Dameon called it. And since I saw no one but him, I scarcely knew I had a Talent before I came here. I lived in terror of my father, for he was violent and angry much of the time. He kept me with him only because I could calm even the most uncontrollable horses."

"The interesting thing is that her empathic Talent works with animals as well," Angina said eagerly.

"Sometimes it made people furious when they sold a wild horse for a few coins, only to see me riding it a little later," Freya went on. "Several times we had to leave moon fairs quickly because someone claimed I had used the black arts on their horse. My father feared he would be called up by the Herders to explain.

"In Guanette, we had to leave before my father had completed his bargains. That is what made him drink and decide to sell me in Darthnor. I wonder, now that he is sober, if he thinks the price for me was fair," she added sadly.

The clear hurt in her face robbed me of bitterness. I could imagine how little joy there had been in her life. My head ached with the effort of trying to bring order to the whirl of my emotions.

"All that's over now," Fian said. "Freya's in great demand with the novices, because whenever she's around, they're all smarter and quicker than usual."

"Unfortunately, my ability to enhance is only an illusory sort of boosting," she said diffidently. "It lets me show them what they could do, and so they strive harder."

"Which means they learn better and faster," Miky said, wandering over to join us.

"I am still learning myself," she disclaimed, flushing. "Speaking of which, Dameon is waiting to give me a lesson as soon as he has eaten." She smiled at me again, her eyes revealing, of all things—the most painful to me just then—shy admiration. "Rushton told me you are a beastspeaker and might easily have led that guild instead of Alad, if you had wanted it. I wish I could speak to the horses the way you do, rather than simply feeling at them, but I am learning to use signals with them."

She turned to retrieve the tray of food and went out of the salon with it.

"She's nice, isn't she?" Miky asked.

"Yes," I said bleakly.

I looked over at Rushton and found him watching me. I dropped my eyes quickly, feeling dizzy and heart-sore.

A little later, he crossed the salon to look out the window where I was seated. Flustered by his nearness, I looked out, too, and watched a lone seabird spiraling on the winds.

"I think I could love this life," Rushton said softly. "It is very peaceful."

Something in me trembled in fury. How easily he used the word *love*. I wanted to ask if his love for the sea would be more enduring than his love for me, but I bit my tongue and swallowed the salty taste of blood.

"We are very different," I said icily.

His hands tightened where they rested on the sill. They were brown and strong, and the thought came to me of how they would feel against my skin. Ruthlessly, I pushed the vision away, mortified at my lack of control.

To my relief, Powyrs came in to convey a request from his men that the twins play them a few songs. They had played a great deal to while away the anxious hours as we waited for the wind.

The empaths obliged and collected their instruments. Powyrs made to follow them out, but Rushton stopped him to ask about Templeport.

Powyrs glanced wistfully at the door as the strains of music drifted in, but, obligingly, he set down his jug.

"It is the only real settlement in all of Sador. The tribes are nomadic and move constantly about the desert, living in tents. They believe they should not leave any sign of their passing. The only permanent construction in all of Sador is their Earthtemple, and that is in Templeport. They regard the port itself as a necessary evil, because it is the only place along the Sador coast where boats can put in. All the rest is murderous high cliffs."

"What else is there besides a temple?" Rushton asked curiously.

Powyrs shrugged. "There are lots of people from the Land, and maybe from other places, but they are not allowed to build huts or houses. They have to set up tents, like Sadorians. Being nomadic is part of their religion, and it is terribly important to them."

"What *is* their religion?" asked Fian, abandoning his books to listen.

"It is not easy to tell such a thing simply. Central to it is their love of the land. By that, I mean the earth itself. To a Sadorian, nothing is more important. All life rises from it and returns to it. They think humans are no more important than any other creature. They don't believe in Lud at all. They think the land is infused with an earth goddess. They don't have priests, but some Sadorians are sent from birth to be Temple guardians. It is a great honor. Everything in Sador occurs under the guidance of the Temple and its guardians."

"It sounds very different to Herder lore," Daffyd murmured.

"Truly," Powyrs said. "Where a Herder believes humans are made by Lud to rule over the world, the Sadorians believe they are important only as part of the harmonious whole. The Herders claim everybody has to think their way or Lud will send the Great White again. In Sador, belief is a matter of personal choice." He leaned forward, his blue eyes twinkling sardonically. "Funny thing is, Sadorians are a lot more devout by choice than Landfolk bound by Herder lore."

"I gather you don't like the Herders," Rushton said.

Powyrs winked angrily, a peculiar combination. "What's to like? I admire the Sadorians, though I don't go for putting land before people. Now if it was the sea . . ."

"How can these Sadorians live off a desert?" Hannay wondered.

"Most of their needs come from the spice groves inland at the foot of the mountains. Sadorians weave cloth from a fiber they get from the trees' bark, and they get sugar and medicines from its leaves and sap, and a potent fement from its berries. Most importantly, they get spice from its flowers, and they trade that for everything else the trees cannot offer."

"What about water?" Fian asked.

"There are natural springs all around the perimeter of the

desert that water the groves, and in the desert there are isis pools. The Sadorians call them the tears of the goddess."

"What of the slave trade?" Rushton asked. "Do the Sadorians involve themselves in it?"

Powyrs chuckled. "Oh yes. The Sadorians involve themselves, all right. They send slavers and anyone proven to have dealt with them out into the desert without water. If the slavers make it to the other side, they are freed."

"Do many survive?" Kella asked.

The seaman grinned wolfishly. "One that I've heard of, and he was stark raving mad. The Temple looks after him, though, just as it does anyone who is sick or aged or who can't keep up the pace of the kar-avans."

"Kar-avans?" Kella echoed.

"They are what a group of Sadorians on the move call themselves. And Sadorians are always on the move."

The ship listed slightly, wiping the smile from his face. "Got to watch these fools who call themselves seamen or they'll run my *Cutter* up on a shoal," he muttered, hurrying outside.

"I have to get a look at that Temple," Fian said with all the fanatical determination of a teknoguilder on the trail of new information. "Garth will kill me if I don't."

"And I'll kill you if you start any fuss," Rushton said with perfect seriousness. "We're not here to tread on Sadorian toes. There's every likelihood that this Temple will be out of bounds to Landfolk."

Fian subsided, looking chastened; then, at Rushton's request, he and Kella went to retrieve the twins, Dameon, and Freya.

When we had all gathered, Rushton squared his shoulders in the way he did when conducting guildmerge. "Tomorrow we will reach Sador," he said. "I have no doubt we can win these Battlegames, but this is the first time we will pit ourselves against unTalents who know what we can do, and this will season us and allow us to see how we function under stress. I want you all to store up impressions about the battle, thoughts and suggestions that can be shared during guild-merge when we return to Obernewtyn.

"One warning. Under no circumstances are you to use your Talents on anyone in Sador, except during the games. No farseeking or coercing, no empathising. Although these rebels will be our opponents in the Battlegames, we hope to fight beside them in the future as allies. We must be able to offer a code they will trust and assure them they will not be violated by our abilities."

He glanced once about the salon to emphasize this point. The others nodded, but I thought of Malik's cold laughter and doubted any code Rushton could promise would impress him. Everything would hinge on winning.

"Daffyd has agreed to fight with us," Rushton went on. "Dragon cannot take part, and we should assume that Dameon will be unable to participate as well. That makes us ten if we include Daffyd and myself. And though I have no usable Talent to offer, I have battle skills, and there may be need for these."

His green eyes shifted to me, but I looked away quickly, afraid of what he might see in my face.

"I do not feel that I will disadvantage us," he added pointedly, and I realized he thought my refusal to meet his eyes indicated my disapproval of his inclusion.

At the end of his speech, Rushton asked me coldly to see him in his chamber after the nightmeal.

✦ 37 ✦

I DID NOT GO.

In time, I would be able to face Rushton calmly, but not yet. I could not trust myself. What if somehow I betrayed my feelings? Perhaps I already had by speaking so stiffly to Freya. My thoughts ran wild. What if Rushton wanted to see me alone so that he could apologize for not loving me any longer? What if he tried to explain his attachment to Freya?

These were stupid thoughts, and it was the fear of making a fool of myself that made me cast about desperately after the nightmeal for some plausible excuse not to go to Rushton's chamber. I found myself plucking nervously at the bandage covering the tattoo Swallow had given me, and this produced an idea.

I would go and see Fian about the Govamen mark. He was ensconced in Powyrs's chamber, and I doubted anyone would think of looking for me there. The tattoo was reason enough to have forgotten Rushton's summons. I would tell Rushton of the tattoo—and I imagined the apologetic and slightly flippant smile I would wear as I said it—and explain how it had come about. I would casually mention that the gypsy had kissed me. Just as if people were always kissing me, so that I hardly even bothered about it.

Let him dare try to pity me then!

Having worked myself into a fury, I marched off to

Powyrs's cabin, taking good care to let no one see me enter.

"Elspeth," Fian said, sounding surprised. He had to flatten himself against the wall to get the door to the tiny chamber open, but there was hardly enough room even when it was closed. He waved me to the only seat that would fit and propped himself on the corner of the rickety wooden table piled high with books.

"I'm glad ye've come. Ye know there are actually some Beforetime maps amongst these papers? I am tryin' to . . ." He stopped. "Lud, I do blather on. It is a Teknoguild failing, I know, to imagine th' world revolves around us. Did ye want somethin' in particular?"

I bit my lip, suddenly unsure of how much I wanted to tell.

"I did," I said slowly. "Do you remember the mark on the Govamen plasts we saw beneath Tor?"

Fian wagged his head impatiently. "Yes, yes. Three Guanette birds goin' round one another?"

"Was there anyone else who might have used the same mark other than Govamen?"

"Unlikely," Fian said. "It appears on every single piece of research an' plast from Govamen, an' I think it was especially devised fer them. In fact, th' plasts appear to have been stolen from Govamen—we think the Reichler Clinic had a spy working there. It would have to be one of th' scientists—that's what th' Beforetimers called teknoguilders."

"You think this scientist wanted to help Misfits stay hidden?" I asked curiously.

"Or help them to escape, if Govamen had them already. Why do ye ask about th' mark anyway?"

I took a deep breath. "Do you have any idea what gypsies were before the holocaust? Where they come from?"

"There were people called gypsies in the Beforetime, but

they were swallowed up into other races long afore the Great White. Our gypsies are just people who took on some of their philosophies—there's no true connection." Fian's puzzled expression deepened. "What is this all about, Elspeth?"

I went on to explain much of what Swallow had told me.

"Amazin'," Fian said after some time. "You must write this down for our records. I had no idea gypsy society was so complex. But what has any of it to do with th' Govamen mark?"

"The purebloods wear it on their inner forearms."

"That is odd. Why would a gypsy wear th' mark of a long-dead Beforetime organization?"

"Exactly what I am wondering," I said. "And how do you explain that the gypsies regard it as a sacred mark?"

"Perhaps their mark only *looked* like th' Govamen symbol," Fian suggested.

I rolled up my sleeve to reveal the grubby bandage around my arm and gestured for Fian to pass over a jug of water sitting on a tray.

He stared as I dipped my arm in it and let the water penetrate. "A Twentyfamilies gypsy gave the mark to me," I said. "You will see if it is exact or merely alike."

Fian listened, horrified, to my description of the tattoo procedure.

"Let's keep our fingers crossed it is healed properly," I said, carefully separating the sodden bandages. When I lifted the last layer away, we both stared.

"Is this a joke?" Fian demanded crossly.

I was mute with astonishment, for other than the crisscross reddening left by the bandage, my skin was utterly without mark or discoloration.

The tattoo had vanished!

Leaving Fian's tiny room, I dismissed his suggestion that I had been tricked into thinking I had been given the tattoo. If Swallow had intended to rook me, why would he have told me so much about himself? Besides, I had seen the needles and felt them pierce my skin.

But I could hardly blame the teknoguilder for his doubts. Unfortunately, only Swallow could answer what had happened.

I sighed and decided to relieve Miky, who was sitting with Dragon. Maruman was sleeping curled up at the foot of the mattress, but he woke as I entered.

When the Empath guilden had gone off yawning to her bed, I sat on the floor and took Dragon's small, limp hand in mine. Maruman rose, stretched, and came to curl himself into my lap. We made no attempt to communicate, and I was grateful for his silent companionship. It had been a long, confusing, painful day, and I just wanted to lay my head on the bed and be still.

I put my cheek against Dragon's hand and stared out the small circular window at the sky. Almost at once I slept.

I dreamed of walking along a black road. Rushton was behind me, calling. "Wait. I will come with you."

I walked faster, thinking of him holding Freya. "Elspeth . . ."

But his voice faded. I was crying, but I walked faster still.

I fell then into a deeper dream: a chaotic tumult of images that made no sense.

There was a chair, red and bulging with carvings of grotesque faces. One moment the faces appeared to convulse with mirth, and the next, they seemed to shriek with agony.

I saw a tall, beautiful woman smile.

"All the women in my family have it," she said in a soft, musical voice.

Then the same woman was slumped in the carved chair. Her hair was red like Dragon's, and her breast, too, for she had been stabbed there, and the knife still protruded from the gaping wound. Bending over her was a bald man with a pale, greasy face and a bloody hand. "Who will ever know it was my hand that struck the killing blow?" he whispered with feral glee.

The vision changed, and I was aboard a ship going over the waves. Then I was in the sea, and the water about me was tinged with the red-haired woman's blood, for she was beside me in the water. I tried to keep her afloat, but the waves were violent and kept tearing us apart.

"My daughter," she rasped. "You are . . . you must . . ."

"Templeport ho!" a voice called, and I woke with a start to a blazing hot day, my head aching abominably.

I got up stiffly, disentangling myself from Dragon. I rubbed at my stiff back, ignoring Maruman's grumbles at being disturbed.

The others were outside already when I got there, all pressed up against the side of the ship and staring out through the goldshot salt haze at Sador. I was astounded to see how high the sun was. I had slept near through to midday! The air outside was dry and hot, and breathing seemed to burn the inside of my nostrils.

The soaring sea cliffs lay before us, running as far as I could see in both directions. They were sheer and utterly inaccessible. But right ahead of us, the cliff was cracked as if split by a giant axe, and sand from the desert beyond had trickled out to form a spit, pointing out into the dark sea like a white finger. This, Powyrs said, was Templeport.

As we came closer to the tip of the peninsula, we could see a cluster of tents fluttering white like scattered blossoms, but there were no buildings and no greenery at all. Little wonder. The spit would be barren, saturated as it was with salt from the sea, and the pitiless heat would scorch anything that tried to grow. The shore wavered and danced through shimmering waves of heat, appearing as insubstantial as an illusion.

"How can anyone live here?" Miky said. This had been directed at Angina, but her twin was busy murmuring softly into Dameon's ear, describing the scene.

I kept a tight shield around my mind, for Dameon always seemed to sense my darkest moods. The image of Freya and Rushton was still fresh in my mind, and I had no wish to confide my feelings to the empath, for all that I loved him dearly. Some pains were not to be shared.

"It is too hot," Miryum grumbled, her voice slurred by her long sleep.

"You'd best get used to it," Hannay said. "The ship will be cool compared to the land."

"Hmm," Miryum grunted. "Well, at least the ground will stand still under my feet."

"There is the Earthtemple," Powyrs said, pointing.

I scanned the spit for a building but could see nothing.

"Oh Lud," Daffyd murmured suddenly. "There. In the cliff. No wonder it is called an Earthtemple."

The Temple was part of the cliff and visible only because the cliff exterior was carved from top to bottom. Closer, I could make out windows in the carving. From the number of them, the Temple must be enormous.

I felt someone at my side.

It was Rushton, and his eyes were accusing. "I asked you to come and see me last night."

"I . . . I had to see Fian," I stammered. "He . . ."

Rushton's eyes blazed with such fury, I faltered. He turned on his heel without a word and went to stand with Freya and Hannay.

"What in Lud's name are those?" Angina exclaimed once we had disembarked.

He was pointing at a group of great, shaggy, dun-colored beasts with four legs and a lump of flesh pouting up from their backs.

"They are kamuli," Powyrs said, looking over his shoulder with a grin. "The Sadorians use them rather than horses, and they are not mutants, however much they might look it. They existed in the Beforetime and were called 'desert ships' because they traverse the sands effortlessly with their soft, splayed hooves."

"Sadorians do not use horses, then?" Freya asked curiously.

"Inland they do," the seaman said. "Where the spice groves are, the ground is hard and there is thick forestation that makes horses more suitable as transport."

I noticed Kella watching me and made an effort to look interested.

"Act," Brydda had once advised me. "Pretend that you are clever, wise, brave, calm, courageous." Pretend, and some of the time you can forget it is pretense.

It was incredibly noisy on the spit. Everyone seemed to shout at the top of their voice—a great deal of bartering took place literally from ship decks—and there was a tremendous

400

bustle as people carried boxes and bundles to and from the ships. Yet the scene was, for all its loudness, curiously color-less. The savage blaze of the sun seemed to bleach everything to a blinding bone-whiteness that made my head pound and my eyes water. More than anything else, I longed to sit in a bit of shade and drink a cold mug of water.

Unfortunately, the only shade available was that cast by the towering Sadorian cliffs, looming on both sides of the sloping pass that led up to the desert, and that was a goodly step away.

Powyrs pointed out a spot farther up the spit where it widened at the base of the cliffs. "About halfway to the cliffs, there is a place where visitors set up their tents. Can you see them? Nearby are stalls where you can purchase food, and at the very base of the cliffs there is a freshwater spring. The water will cost you nothing, but you will have to change your coins for barter tokens at the Earthtemple if you want to buy food."

Watching us go, the plump seaman gave Maruman, who was draped around my neck, a long look of bewildered wist-fulness that spoke of the strength of his attachment. I had co-erced all memory of their brief association from his mind, but clearly the impression had been deep and some residue re-mained.

✦ 38 ✦

RUSHTON, HANNAY, AND Miryum cleared the rough shale and, with the twins' aid, set about erecting the tents we had bought in Sutrium at Jakoby's suggestion. Daffyd and Freya were charged with getting water, and Fian and I were to exchange our small store of coin for Temple barter tokens. Dameon elected to walk with us, and since the spring was on the way to the Temple, we went that far together.

I was relieved to find that Freya's presence no longer disturbed me nearly as much as Rushton's. Not that we did much talking. The heat beating down on our heads and thrown back as a reflection from the dazzling white sand was terrific. By the time we reached the cliffs, we were all gasping for breath.

We threw ourselves down at the edge of the icy spring and drank deeply before retreating into the dense shade cast by the cliffs.

"Incredible," croaked Daffyd in a low voice.

"Where does such heat come from?" Freya asked weakly, fanning her face with her skirts.

"Ugh," Fian groaned. "I've just realized we'll have to climb up th' rest of th' spit to change th' coins. Powyrs told me th' Temple entrance can only be got to from th' top of the cliffs."

I would have groaned, too, if I had been able to spare the

energy. The first impression of coolness in the shade had begun to abate, and already I was hot again. We sat a good while before I could bring myself to move.

Standing up reluctantly, I noticed two halfbreed gypsies among the throng of Sadorians. They stood out as much as we must in this land of tall, gold-skinned people in their flowing robes. Powyrs had said gypsies were treated well here. That being so, I had no doubt more would avail themselves of the coast road when the poisons had receded a little farther.

"Uh-oh," Fian murmured.

He had risen, too, and was gazing back down the spit. I turned to see what had caught his attention. A number of gray-clad Landsmen stood talking, yellow cloaks fluttering at their shoulders—senior-ranking soldierguards.

I had known there were soldierguards in Sador, yet still it was a shock to see them. Even more so were the two Herders with them, clad in white robes and arrogance. I was astounded to see a number of Sadorians clustered about the priests. Could these possibly be converts?

Even as I watched, the taller Herder lifted his pale face to the Earthtemple, his lip curling in scorn. Letting my eyes follow the same direction, I was startled to discover that what I had thought randomly carved patterns on the cliff were, in fact, a multitudinous swirl of faces.

"You'd better get on," Daffyd advised.

"Perhaps you should not go," Freya told Dameon when I offered him my arm. The Empath guildmaster smiled unerringly down at her. "I am not ill. I am only blind."

She flushed.

"I am going to have another drink before we start," Fian announced.

Daffyd caught his arm. "Don't be a fool. You will be sick if you fill your belly with water, then walk in this heat. Drink when you return."

It was a steep walk up to the top of the cliffs, but Fian found breath enough to describe what he was seeing to Dameon. I was glad of his monologue, for it freed me of the need to speak and kept the Empath guildmaster's attention from me. Before long, though, we were all trudging along in silence again.

"The sun is like a hammer on my head," Fian panted when we stopped to rest halfway. "It did not look so far from the camp. At this rate, it will be dusk before we are back."

My own head was pounding, yet the heat in the desert running back from the cliffs must be a thousand times worse. Still the Sadorians spent their lives sailing the sea of sand on their desert ships. Strange how differently humans could live and still be human.

The Earthtemple had two facades.

The grandest was the one it presented to the sea and to the spitroad. We had been sitting literally with our backs against the base of it when we were by the spring. The road from the spit had risen gradually to the height of the clifftop, where a small rocky path had peeled off to the left, running down into a deep fissure. A man had told us this would bring us to the entrance of the Earthtemple.

After making our way carefully and with some relief down the shaded path running along a deep sloping cleft, we discovered the second facade of the Temple. It was neither gilded nor carved, and there were no windows. A single, rough-hewn portal served as the doorway, while a great, plain slab of stone, set upon a smaller pivoting stone, served as its door.

Its simplicity seemed far more in keeping with the Sadorians' philosophy as expounded by Powyrs than the ornate, carved facade of faces it presented to the sea.

The stone door was currently tilted to allow a slender opening on either side, and beyond, the darkness was so complete that it was impossible to say what lay within.

There were at least thirty people lined up outside in five separate queues. One line seemed to consist of very elderly people, worried-looking adults with sickly children or babes, and others with rough bandages or hacking coughs.

A young man with wild eyes, held tightly between two plump, distressed-looking women, lashed about babbling and shuddering. Clearly, he was undergoing some sort of seizure.

This, then, must be the line for supplicants seeking healing.

The line next to it had more animals than people, therefore, this must be where beasts were brought to be examined for disease before they could be sold. The animals were all small, so the larger beasts, such as horses, must be dealt with at some other point.

In the third line, there were Sadorians carrying sacks. An acrid odor suggested they were the spice gatherers Powyrs had mentioned, bringing in their tribe's quota to exchange for barter tokens.

At first I wondered why the queues were not advancing; then I noticed a number of barefooted men and women clad in hooded linen tunics moving along the lines.

"The Temple guardians," Fian murmured. "Looks as if all of the ministerin' is done outside." He sounded disappointed.

I waved him back and moved closer to listen to an exchange between one of the hooded guardians and a Sadorian woman of middle years.

"What do you seek of the earth?" the Temple guardian asked. His voice and shape proclaimed him a man, but I could not see his face. As with the other Temple guardians, this was concealed by the drooping hood.

The woman launched into a detailed litany of physical ills to which he listened with great patience. When she could find nothing more to complain about, he rummaged in a small pouch bag tied at his waist and removed a twig. Pressing it into her hand, he bade her in a gentle voice to soak it in boiled water, then drink the fluid.

Fian poked me in the ribs, his eyes bright with suppressed laughter. "It's no more than a wee bit of relaxin' herb he's given her. A sop."

I nodded absently, wondering what the fourth line was for. Its people did not look sick, nor did they lead beasts or carry spice.

A smaller guardian approached a man in this line. "What do you seek of the earth?" asked a girl, her voice muffled slightly by the hood.

"Wisdom, Guardian. My son desires to bond, but he has yet to make his first spice gather." He seemed undaunted by the fact that the voice could not belong to a girl much older than his son.

"Is the girl he would take worthy in your eyes?" she asked.

"Yes, it is only his youth that troubles me," the man answered. "In truth, it may be that *he* is not worthy of *her*."

The diminutive guardian nodded sagely. "Say to the father of the girl that he must set the boy a quest to determine his worthiness. If he fails, then he must wait another season. If he succeeds, then he shall have her."

The father nodded and went away.

"That's no more'n a bit of common sense. Th' man's a fool

nowt to have thought of it fer hisself," Fian muttered.

"Perhaps he had thought of it but needed reassurance," Dameon murmured.

Another Temple guardian came out of the shadowy doorway with two clinking bags slung about her waist. She passed briskly along the farthest line, exchanging coin for tokens.

"Wait here," I said, and took my place at the end of the line. When the guardian reached me, she asked, from the depths of her hood, "What do you seek of the earth?"

"I . . . We have come to pay our respects to the earth goddess and to get some barter tokens," I said politely.

She nodded and counted the coin I offered into one bag at her waist before giving me a handful of small, pale metal discs from another. She lifted her hand to my forehead and made a sign, but the words were drowned out by a scream.

I turned swiftly to find the frenzied youth had broken free of the women and was rushing toward me.

I thought he meant to attack me and flung up my hands, but to my astonishment, he threw himself at my feet. "Do you bring the Moonwatcher?" he whispered fiercely.

The two women had hurried forward and pulled him away from me, apologizing profusely. "When these fits come on him, it is as if he is possessed by demons," one said.

The Temple guardian who had been attending to me waved the women and the now-silent boy back to their place in the line, then turned to me.

"Who are you?" she asked in a strangely tense voice.

My heart began to gallop. "I . . . I am a visitor from the Land."

"Whom do you visit?"

I did not know what to answer, so I told the truth. "Jakoby has invited me. She is—"

"I know of Jakoby," the woman said shortly, and now her tone was indifferent. She lifted her hand and made the same mark on my forehead. "May you nurture the earth and find harmony."

She moved to the man behind me, and I returned to Dameon and Fian, feeling somewhat bewildered.

"What happened?" Fian demanded.

"I'm damned if I know," I said.

As Fian had predicted, the day was indeed drawing to a close by the time we returned to the spit. The shadows were lengthening, and people were lighting cooking fires and lamps. Already the moon had risen, and it hung like a great coppery disc, low on the skyline—a full moon.

As we reached the trade area, Fian suggested we get some food to take back to the camp. The atmosphere surrounding the selling tents was as familiar as the rest of Sador was strange. In the mill and jostle, there was a similarity to markets in Sutrium and Kinraide and Morganna, which reassured me in some deep way. Well, that was not so surprising. After all, people had to eat and drink and trade and speak.

All about us, men and women were involved in the mundane business of haggling with traders. Here, at least, there were almost as many Landfolk as Sadorians.

"Got any silver to sell?" demanded a squint-eyed jack. Dameon smiled in the direction of the voice and shook his head. The man recoiled as if his blindness might be contagious.

"Need flints or salt?" a woman in the tent alongside him asked.

"Maybe later," I said.

She spat on the ground in disgust. "Filthy gypsies."

"Like a girl, pretty boy?" whispered a woman with lustrous painted eyes, peering at Fian from the shadowy interior of another tent.

He shuddered and backed away with comical haste into one of the odorous desert ships sitting with its legs folded queerly beneath its body. The creature snorted fiercely and eyed him with pouting ire.

"Greetings," I sent, wondering if its mind would accept me. It regarded me for a long moment, but either could not or would not understand.

"You want to buy this fine animal?" a Sadorian trader asked, appearing from nowhere at the beast's side.

"I don't think he likes the color of my eyes," I said, and walked on, leaving him to stare after me.

"How can they live in this heat?" Fian panted as we reached our camp at last. "It's practically dusk. Doesn't it ever cool down?"

"I suspect the night will be cold," Dameon said.

Fian snorted as if coolness here was something no sane person would believe in. "They are surely mad to live in such a place."

"Perhaps so," said a familiar voice.

I whirled to find myself staring at a tall woman, clad in a flowing cloak of beaten animal hides atop a thin shift of some golden material that matched her eyes and bared the full, dark muscular length of her legs and arms. Her hair was woven into tight, metal-beaded braids, which clinked whenever she moved.

"Jakoby," I said.

Rushton approached us and bowed. "I am pleased to greet you. Elspeth has told us much about you. We feared you might have been becalmed, as we were."

"The winds were good to us." Jakoby smiled enigmatically,

her face illuminated fitfully by the fire that had been kindled in the angled embrace of the tents. The others stared at the Sadorian woman in wonder. She looked about at them, taking time to examine each of the faces carefully.

"Your chosen warriors are young indeed," she said at last. "But age does not always signify, as the Landman Elii said. Will you come now? The two of you," Jakoby asked.

I faltered under Rushton's green glare.

"We will be glad to accompany you," he told Jakoby tersely. "Where do we go?"

"To meet Bram, who is to judge the Battlegames, and the Temple's overguardian, who shall preside."

"Are all of the rebels here?" Rushton asked.

"Not all, but all who will come. More, I think, than Brydda expected."

We were turning to leave when I heard Miryum's voice ring out angrily and the sound of a blow.

Hurrying around behind one of the tents, we discovered the stolid Coercer guilden standing over a Sadorian man, who sat in the dust, his nose running with blood.

"What happened?" Rushton demanded.

"Him," Miryum said fiercely, glaring at the man as he got to his feet.

"What did he do?" I asked.

Miryum looked over to me. "He . . . this fellow was making fun of me," she muttered wrathfully.

"This is not so," the man said carefully. He bowed low to her and then to Jakoby. "I am sorry if I have given offense. I spoke ravek. I did not mean to insult her. Do you wish me to kill myself?"

Miryum gaped.

"Well?" Jakoby asked her mildly. "Do you want him to kill himself for insulting you?"

"But surely you can't mean he would . . . would . . ." The coercer looked more disturbed than I had ever seen her. "Of course he mustn't . . . kill himself. Not for a joke."

"Very well, you may leave," Jakoby told the man indifferently.

"It was not a joke I made," the man said gravely. He bowed to Miryum and then again to Jakoby before backing away.

"What on earth did he say to you?" I asked.

Miryum reddened. "I will not say."

Jakoby walked slowly, adapting her long stride courteously to our pace.

"What is a ravek?" I asked her.

Her teeth flashed in the darkness of her face. "It is an endearment between those who are heartfasted. It means 'you who have my heart beneath your foot.' The man your friend struck offered to make her his ravek. That is a formal proposal of bonding in Sador."

In spite of everything, I smiled. Obviously, Miryum had caught some of his meaning but hadn't known how to take a compliment.

Jakoby stopped before a large tent.

She lifted the tent flap, and the muted sounds of laughter and the clink of plates and knives spilled out into the dusk. She gestured for us to enter.

Inside, a fire burned in a ground hearth lined in stone. Three trestle tables were set around it in a U-shape and piled high with all manner of food and drink. Seated at the tables were both familiar and unfamiliar faces.

At the central table on a raised dais was a wizened Sadorian man with skin the shade of old bronze and hair as white and tight-coiled as the fleece of wild mountain goats. He wore a cloak of what appeared to be animal pelts sewn together about his skinny shoulders, as Jakoby did.

It was not difficult to guess that this was Bram.

I ran my eyes swiftly around the rest of those seated.

Plump Brocade was at one end, seated beside Tardis's yellow-haired emissary, Gwynedd. Brocade was wearing a jewel-encrusted vest stretched tight across his wide belly. A little farther along sat a tall, fair, proud-looking woman. She wore no jewelry, and her hair hung white and unbraided and perfectly straight about her shoulders like a snowy veil. She sat with Brydda and Dardelan.

Also next to Brydda was a stooped man who smiled faintly in greeting when our eyes met. I guessed this was Yavok, who had taken over for him in Aborium. Brydda had called him trustworthy.

On the other side of Bram, among a great number of strangers, were white-haired Cassell and Elii. It seemed Brydda's recruiting journey had borne fruit. But I had no doubt they were here first for a war council, rather than to see whether we were fit allies.

Last of all was Malik.

When our eyes met, his lips curved into a sneering smile that made me instantly conscious of my sweaty, dust-smeared face and clothes.

"It is the Misfit and its master," he told the dark-eyed man on his right, just loudly enough for us to hear.

I felt Rushton tense with anger beside me.

"As you see, this master is but a stripling himself," Malik went on scornfully, not bothering to pretend to be speaking in

412

an aside. Rushton's silence had made him bold, for he took it as weakness.

Jakoby said nothing, and I sensed she was waiting to see how Rushton would deal with this.

The Master of Obernewtyn merely settled a long, impassive stare on the rebel, whose smirk faltered, then faded altogether.

"What are you looking at, boy?" he growled.

"I am not sure," Rushton said. "It might be a man, but then it might be a kind of performing ape. It is hard to tell in the firelight."

Malik stared at him incredulously. Then he rose with a curse, pulling out a knife.

"Enough," Jakoby said imperiously. "The Battlegames do not commence until the morrow, and it is unseemly to sour our feasting with such behavior before then. All things in their right time."

Malik resumed his seat, though he was pale with fury, and Jakoby ushered us up to Bram. I was surprised to see one of the hooded Temple guardians in the seat beside him. The hood gave no sign of its wearer's sex, but I thought it must be a wizened old creature, for it was very small. No doubt the overguardian Jakoby had mentioned.

"Bram, this is Elspeth Gordie of whom I have spoken," Jakoby said. "And Rushton Seraphim, who styles himself the leader of these Misfit gypsies."

"Seraphim," Bram echoed. "An old name, I think."

Rushton bowed. "I do not know if your name is old or not. I have heard only a little about the Sadorian people, but it has made me curious to know more, and I am pleased at this chance to speak with you."

Bram chuckled fruitily. "Yet I think this is not an occasion

413

for speeches. I hope you do not think to win the Battlegames with words alone."

"We are prepared to meet whatever challenge is offered," Rushton responded smoothly.

"Good." Bram's dark eyes shimmered in the firelight. "I have heard from those among my people who watched for your arrival that your force contains warriors who are even younger than you. And though you may count yourself a man, you are too young to be seasoned properly to battle. Have you hope of winning against such men as Malik, whose prowess is legendary?"

"I would not have come otherwise."

The old man cackled. "No? But sometimes battles must be faced whether or not there is a hope of winning them. This is a truth known to men and women of honor."

"No battle is lost until it is lost. Men and women of courage know this."

Bram nodded in appreciation. "True enough! You speak well, lad. I regret that you are not yet a sworn ally and therefore have no place at this table. Yet, if your people acquit themselves well and survive the testing tomorrow, we might yet sup together and have this speech you desire."

"Survive?" Rushton echoed carefully. "Surely there is no question of not surviving since this is only a contest."

The overguardian stirred.

"These are the Battlegames, lad, where matters large and small may be decided without massive bloodshed," said Bram. "It is war in miniature. If death was not possible, there would be no true testing. Of course, death is not the aim, nor is injury inevitable."

There was a silence, broken by Malik's cutting laughter.

"Look. The boy is nearly unmanned with fear at the thought that death might wait for him."

"The morrow will bring what it brings," Rushton said softly. He turned his eyes back to Bram. "If it is permitted, I would like to know something more of the Battlegames."

Bram's smile died, and for a moment, he looked like a weary old man. "Are you in such a hurry for war, lad? You were more handsome when you spoke of talking and learning." He sighed weightily. "Malik asked the same question, and I told him what I now tell you. The Battlegames designed by my people are many, but the earth goddess will decide which of these may be played." He drew himself up and summoned a formal and ceremonious air. "Once, among the tribes who were much sundered during the time that followed what you Landfolk call the holocaust, there were wars occasioning great bloodshed among our people, and harm was done to the earth. Then came one among us who heard the voice of the earth goddess. She commanded us to build the Earthtemple, that others might come there and learn to hear the voice of the land as well. And so it came to pass. Through her disciples, the earth goddess forbade war forever. But still there were disputes, great and small, which needed mediation. Hence were the Battlegames devised, both to decide issues and to expiate the violent urges that are the plague of humanity.

"Each of the games is designed to test some specific quality in a competitor—courage or wit or charm or honesty or fitness. In your case, the games will test fitness for battle. But the earth goddess alone knows which of the many games will be selected, for they will be chosen at random using a tool we call *dice*. Some games are short and others long, so there is no way of telling how many will take place at a single contest. The games commence at sunrise and end at sunset, for these are moments of power."

"Are all ten of a team to play each game?" Rushton asked. I guessed he was thinking of Dameon.

Bram shook his head. "Not necessarily. The number of participants for each game will again be randomly selected by a further throw of the dice, but it is up to the two leaders to choose who will fill the places. For each Battlegame completed, there will be a spoken assessment, and then when the day ends, the winner shall be named."

Bram reached for a piece of bread. This appeared to mark the end of the discussion. All along the trestles, men and women reached for goblets or turned to whisper to one another.

"There is just one thing more," Rushton said.

"And that is?" Bram inquired through a mouthful of bread.

"I want you to understand that we intend to use all of our powers in these Battlegames, but outside this contest, we would never use those abilities on allies."

Bram chewed and swallowed. "You should return to your camp now. Eat well and rest. You will be brought to the field of battle before dawn."

Jakoby escorted us outside. "If you can, forget about the Battlegames tonight. Worrying and wondering about what will come will not avail you. Rest well."

She turned and went back into the tent, leaving Rushton and me alone in the dark.

✦ 39 ✦

"We'd better get back," Rushton said. "The others will be waiting to hear what happened."

I shivered, though it was not cold, and followed him back across the spit.

"I am . . . sorry," I said at last, with stiff formality. "I did not know there would be danger. Jakoby didn't tell me that when she offered the Battlegames."

"You think she meant to deceive you?" He did not look at me when he spoke.

I shook my head. "I do not think it would have occurred to her that it would matter there was danger."

"Then there is no blame to be laid."

Rushton's voice was remote, and I knew he was still angry with me. I had never felt further from him. I had the urge to say something that would restore even the old uneasy comradeship between us, but his silence daunted me.

We walked without speaking the rest of the way back to the camp.

Angina saw us approach as he stirred the cooking fire, and he alerted the others with a cry. In moments, they were clustered around us. In swift, unemotive words, Rushton told them what had happened.

"The Battlegames are more than a contest, then," Miryum

said dourly, but without fear. "Is it possible that one or more of us may die?"

"Possible," Rushton said calmly. "But certainly not inevitable. We will know more when we know which games are to be played."

"I do not like the sound of this Malik," Hannay said.

"He is a hard, strong man," Rushton said. "A bitter man and a tough fighter by all accounts. I do not relish the thought of being his opponent, but if we fare well tomorrow, that strength will be at our side when we fight the Council. Wars make for strange bedfellows. We need the rebels, and it seems this is the only way to win them."

"I wonder if such a victory as this will truly win us anything worth having," Dameon said as Kella handed him a mug of mulled fement.

"It will win us the aid we need against the Council," Rushton snapped. "We cannot afford the indulgence of philosophizing about what constitutes victory. Save that for when the fighting is over."

He took a long deep breath, then shook his head. "I am sorry. I did not mean to snap, my friend. I am . . . tired." He sat down on the ground, facing the fire, and invited us all to do the same. "Let us not talk about the morrow anymore. It will come all too soon. We will nourish our bodies with food and rest, and our souls with a song."

Miky's face lit up and she went to get her gita. Freya brought us plates of stew, then settled herself beside Rushton. Watching the smile that she gave him, I found I had no appetite.

I longed to comfort Rushton, but what could I truly offer him? Even if he had loved me still, I could not say that I would never leave him, because I would. I could not speak of undying love, because I was not certain this bitter, painful emotion his embrace with Freya had roused in me was love.

A great sadness filled me as I stared into the red heart of the flames and listened to the lovely, haunting song the Empath guilden had made from the Oldtime story of the sleeping princess wakened by a kiss. As it rippled out into the night, I could not help but think again of Dragon, locked in her secret, internal battle with her past, trapped in a fortress of her own mind's making.

Powyrs had agreed that the comatose empath might remain aboard the ship, for he was to bring us back to the Land when the Battlegames were over. He thought we were to perform at a bonding of one of the tribal chiefs. Little as we had liked leaving Dragon, she was safer on *The Cutter* than with us.

"In this long sleep, in this fortress of dreams, I live a shadow life and in it dream of one who will come . . . ," Miky sang softly, and Angina took up the harmony in his deeper voice, at the same time elaborating the melody with tiny bells and empathising it delicately with his Talent.

I rose quietly and slipped away from the fire to crawl into one of the tents. Removing only my sandals, I stretched out fully clothed.

"Greetings, ElspethInnle," Maruman sent, and I looked up to see him enter the tent. I made a place for him beside me. The red glow of the fire through the tent opening made his fur appear bloody and discolored. He slept at once, but my mind was too active to let me sleep. On impulse, I shaped a probe and let it soar away from the spit and over the dunes like a nightbird.

I did not try to direct its flight but let the music take me where it would.

Here and there, I encountered the silvery shimmer of other minds—small nocturnal creatures foraging. Once, I was drawn to a brighter shimmer and held for a moment by a deep mind that was clearly intelligent and just as clearly non-human.

I flew until my mind was calm.

At long last I returned to my body. The fire outside had died, and the music had stopped. I fell asleep.

It seemed only a moment later when someone shook my shoulder.

"Elspeth, wake up," Miky said. "The Sadorians have come to take us to the Battlegames."

I opened my eyes, unable to believe it was morning already. Maruman had vanished, but a warmth by my head said he had not been gone long.

"They said to hurry," Miky urged. "We have to be there before the sun comes up, or the whole thing will be called off."

I sat up, pulled on boots instead of sandals, and crawled out of the tent. It was still dark, and the air was cool and pleasant. The moon had set, but a few stars still pricked the darkness. Wordlessly, Kella pressed some of the bread and cheese I had purchased the previous day into my hands as Rushton announced to the two Sadorians that we were ready.

We were conducted quietly through the sleeping camp to the road where a host of shaggy kamuli and several other long-legged Sadorians waited. As we mounted the seated beasts and settled ourselves in the wooden contraptions that served as saddles, I farsought Maruman with an attuned probe. He was prowling about the cliffs in search of eggs.

"If there is any trouble, go aboard *The Cutter* with Dragon and Powyrs," I sent. He did not deign to respond, but I knew he had heard me.

When we were all mounted, one Sadorian perched precariously behind each of us, they made a clicking noise with their tongues and the kamuli rose with a great drunken lurching. They walked with a slow, rolling lope that reminded me horribly of the pitching movement of *The Cutter*. No wonder they were called ships of the desert.

"Oh no," Fian moaned as the kamuli made their ponderous way up the spit slope toward the cliffs. "We're headed out into th' desert."

"It was the obvious place," Hannay said mildly. "We'd better start praying to Lud for a cloudy day, or the sun will fry us."

"The rebels will find it just as hard as us," Angina pointed out cheerfully.

We had traveled for about an hour into the trackless desert, and the sky was empty of stars when the Sadorians pulled their beasts to a halt. I looked around, but there was nothing on all sides but featureless dunes. Were these Battlegames to take place here in the middle of nowhere where there was no shelter and no water? If so, where were the rebels and the Sadorians? I looked up at the sky again. In the east, there was a lightness that heralded the dawn.

One of the Sadorians rode up to Rushton and said something I couldn't hear. Then he pointed.

I could see nothing but sand dunes.

"He said the place where the games will be held is there," Ruston said loudly, sounding puzzled.

The Sadorians clicked their tongues and the kamuli continued.

"I can smell flowers," Kella said, and a moment later, we found ourselves riding along a long, narrow crack in the

421

ground. Past its edges, we could see that it opened up into a great cave under the earth. It was too dim to see much, but I could smell greenery and flowers, and at the very bottom of the hidden chasm, I could see the glimmer of water.

"This mun be one of their isis pools," Fian said in sudden excitement.

"So this is where their goddess weeps her tears," Kella said dreamily. "No wonder they can spend so much time out here."

"You'd never find it if you didn't know exactly how to get to it," Daffyd murmured.

Miky described the valley to Dameon as the Sadorians turned the kamuli onto a narrow track that wended its way downward. Powyrs had said there were a number of isis pools in the desert, and I had imagined wells. I wondered if they were all like this. Clearly, the wave of earth and rock almost covering the chasm protected it from the sun but let in enough light to allow growth. The combination of heat and water produced humidity that generated a luxuriant growth of plant life. The air became increasingly moist as we descended.

By the time we reached the bottom, sunrise was only moments away. From a distance, Jakoby emerged from what I had taken as a mass of greenery but now saw were row upon row of Sadorian men and women.

We dismounted, and she brought us to Bram, who sat cross-legged on a raised dais under a gigantic drooping tree with coiling, pale green leaves and long, creamy pods. The overguardian of the Temple sat at his feet. The rebels stood in a cluster to one side, and the ranks of Sadorians were arrayed behind them.

Malik and his chosen nine stood ramrod straight in two disciplined lines facing Bram. Jakoby indicated that we were to take our place alongside them. The rebel I stood beside was almost twice my height, his muscular arms scarred. I knew those looking at us must see the contest between us as absurdly unequal.

Jakoby took her place at Bram's side and looked expectantly at the sky. She stood that way until we saw the sun rise through the crack where the sky was visible, casting pink and orange rays that stained the few straggles of cloud. I realized they had been literally waiting for sunrise to begin the Battlegames.

"Are you prepared?" Jakoby asked, and I jumped at the loudness of her voice in the still dawn.

"I am," Malik intoned.

"We are," Rushton said.

Jakoby looked to Bram, who inclined his head, then clapped her hands. The little hooded overguardian rose and offered the dice—two small cubes with a different number of markings on each face. Bram leaned forward with a grunt to take them up and mumbled a few inaudible words before flinging them high.

All eyes turned up to watch the two gleaming cubes whirl in the air, and then down to see what number of marks they offered to the sky.

"Six," Bram said. "The Pit, then."

Wordlessly, the overguardian gathered the dice and passed them back to Bram. He threw them again, and this time they fell showing four marks between them.

"Each leader will choose four from among his number to contend in the first Battlegame," Jakoby announced in a ringing voice.

"Choose," Bram said.

There was a momentary hiatus; then Rushton took a half

step forward. "Is it permitted for me to speak?"

The old Sadorian lifted straggling white brows at him. "I told you last night this is not a battle that can be won with words."

"I only wanted to ask how you expect us to choose well without knowing more about this Pit."

"I will answer your question with another. How do warriors face lack of knowledge in a battle?"

Rushton bowed and returned to face us, beckoning us to gather close.

"You must choose for diversity," Miryum advised him.

"Maybe we can take some sort of clue from the name," Dameon suggested.

"The Pit," Angina murmured.

"I suppose it will be in the ground. Another of these rifts. Therefore, climbing may be needed, or lifting." Rushton swept his eyes over us. "Hannay is strongest physically."

"Powyrs told me th' Sadorians sometimes use pits to catch fangcats," Fian said. "There may be beasts, therefore."

Rushton nodded. "Freya," he said at last. He did not look at me and, hurt, I did not suggest myself.

"Maybe th' pit is worked by some mechanics," Fian continued.

Rushton frowned for a long moment. "Yes. You, then, Fian. And Miryum, because she is a powerful coercer as well as strong physically."

Neither he nor Miryum looked at me, although they both knew I also possessed coercive abilities. But neither of them knew how strong I was, because I had always tried to downplay my powers.

Sweat beaded Rushton's lip as the four Misfits were led away with Malik's rebels. I guessed it had been hard for him not to name himself. I felt a surge of admiration for the strength of his will. Malik had not named himself either, but it seemed to cost him nothing.

"They are permitted to choose a single implement each from the armament," Jakoby explained. She pointed as she spoke, and we watched as the eight contestants vanished into a small gray tent billowing in the freshening dawn breeze that swirled through the gap in the earth and stirred the heavy air.

"How can they choose without knowing what they need?" Angina asked Rushton indignantly. "This is madness."

"Perhaps not," Miky disagreed with her twin. "After all, Malik is in the same position, as you said."

It was growing steadily hotter, and I shuddered to think of what the surface temperature must be. Looking up, I saw that the roof of the cavern was moss covered and wondered how often there were rockfalls.

The eight returned. The rebels had chosen between them a double-edged sword, a huge axe, a long knife with a frill of jagged spikes about its tip, and a net. The Misfits had taken a coil of rope, a wide flat shield, a tapered stave of wood, and a knife.

Bram clapped his hands again, and we were led toward another pit—almost a miniature copy of the rift we were standing in and, like the larger chasm, invisible until you were almost upon it.

When we were standing on the edge, I saw that a cage had been set into the rift, neatly dividing it. Inside the cage were two bears. The larger was lumbering slowly back and forth, while the smaller sat in a corner of the cage, its paws clasped around the bars.

"Let the first Battlegame commence," Jakoby's voice rang out.

The Sadorian servitors immediately lowered the Misfits

425

into one end of the pit by rope and the rebels into the other.

"I do not like the look of this," Miky murmured uneasily.

"Shh," Angina hissed. "Watch."

The servitors shifted to other ropes, and the cage was hoisted up, removing all dividers. The bears seemed more bewildered than angry at this turn of events. They appeared not to have noticed the people at either end of the chasm.

For a long moment, no one moved; then the smaller bear noticed the Misfits. It stood up and lumbered toward them, growling slightly.

Without hesitation, Freya stepped forward in front of the others, her face serene.

"She is empathising it," Miky murmured, her face absorbed.

Without warning, two of the servitors at the sides of the pit lifted long, thin pipes to their lips and blew.

Both bears started violently as the darts found their mark. The larger gave a tremendous roar of fury and reared up onto its hind legs, clutching at its back.

Both Misfits and rebels in the pit froze.

I could tell from the dawning despair on Freya's face that she had lost touch with the bear. That she could not regain a hold suggested that the darts had been drugged.

The larger bear turned to stare at Freya, its eyes red with fury. With a low growl, it advanced on her. The smaller bear seemed confused, staring from its companion to the girl and back.

Hannay and Fian stepped forward to stand on either side of Freya, lifting stick and shield to fend off the beast. Freya did not move. Her eyes were fixed on the smaller bear.

"She is sending calmness and compassion," Dameon murmured.

The smaller bear stared back at her, plucking fretfully at

the dart lodged in its fur, and even the larger beast seemed to hesitate.

It shook its head slightly.

"She's getting to them," Miky whispered.

On the other side of the pit, there was a sudden and unprovoked movement. The rebel with the sword ran forward and drove the blade deeply into the smaller bear's side.

I watched in impotent horror as the bear fell without a cry and lay utterly still.

Freya shrieked horribly and fell into a faint, for her mind had been linked empathically to the bear's. If Freya had been a farseeker or a coercer, she would be dead.

I reached out my mind, seeking the bear's life force, but there was nothing. Thoughts swirled out from the larger beast, revealing that the smaller bear had been its cub.

I felt Kella trembling violently at my elbow.

The female bear approached her cub's body and prodded at it. Then she put back her head and howled with such anguish that it rent my heart in two. While she was thus distracted, the four rebels moved forward in a solid phalanx.

I poised my mind to drive them back, then realized I must not interfere for fear of a forfeit.

I looked to the Misfits in the pit. Hannay had dragged the unconscious Freya to one side, and Miryum had slipped past the grief-stricken bear, raising her knife to the rebels. She was trying to keep them away from the bear!

The creature looked up from its cub's corpse, focusing on the coercer's back. It rose slowly, eyes blood-red, and growled with chilling hatred.

Fian ran around to its side, waving his shield to draw the bear's attention from Miryum. I wondered in horror what he was trying to do.

All at once, it snarled and shambled toward Fian, raising massive paws to strike. Even from a distance, I could see the wicked sharpness of its talons. Fian leapt out of the way as the bear swiped at him, and Miryum jumped to one side, leaving three rebels face to face with the enraged creature.

It growled again, and the rebels hastily backed away. Miryum and Fian stood perfectly still, faces set and grim.

I looked back to where Hannay was trying to revive Freya and saw the fourth rebel creeping behind him with a knife. My mind flew back to a dark cavern and the Zebkrahn machine, and Madam Vega with her knife poised above Rushton's throat.

I felt the inimical force in the depths of my mind coalesce, and knew that I could not sit back and watch Hannay die simply to win a contest.

Before I could act, Freya opened her eyes. Something in her expression must have warned the big coercer, because Hannay reacted instantly, spinning and using the force of the turn to drive his elbow savagely into the rebel's groin.

"Oh no!" Kella whispered beside me, and my eyes flew to where the rebel with the bloody sword and the other with the ax had driven the bear back toward Miryum. The third joined them, grinning triumphantly.

But his smile faltered, and a moment later, he flung down his net and began to execute a frenzied dance, slapping bare arms and legs as if they were on fire. His two companions gaped at him incredulously. Then a second rebel abandoned his sword and seemed to be trying to throttle himself. The she bear appeared baffled and had ceased her growls.

"Miryum is coercing them," Miky murmured.

The remaining rebel, realizing that whatever ailed his companions arose from the stolid coercer, slammed his fist into her temple. She fell to the ground, leaving Fian standing alone.

Again, the rebels began to harry the bear back toward him. Abruptly, the rebel with the axe stopped and clawed at his eyes.

Hannay was coercing now, but he had nowhere near Miryum's strength. The rebel with the knife ran at him, and he was forced to release the other man's mind to defend himself.

"Lud, if only they had nowt struck Miryum down. A little more time and she could have held 'em all in thrall!" Daffyd muttered.

All at once, the bear seemed to go mad. It howled and clutched at its head, raking the air with its razor claws.

"The drug must have progressive effects," Kella murmured.

The servitors at the pit worked another set of ropes, and a hidden passage appeared in the side of the rift wall. The three rebels ran for it, and the bear snarled, charging after them, but the gap was too narrow. Thwarted, it turned.

Freya, whey-pale, worked frantically to revive Miryum. Hannay and Fian positioned themselves in front of them, shield and stave raised.

The fourth rebel, now recovered from Hannay's blows, climbed stiffly to his feet. Seeing no one was watching him, he caught up his knife and rushed at Hannay, his face a mask of hatred. The motion caught the eyes of the crazed bear, and it turned and charged.

Freya staggered out to set herself in the bear's path. The beast stopped, and its wild eyes focused their madness on her.

"No!" I whispered.

Step by step, Freya approached the bear, drawing gradually within reach of the lethal claws and killing embrace. The bear made a crooning sound.

"She has it," Miky whispered.

Indeed the bear seemed mesmerized. Then it groaned, clutched at its back, and keeled over.

"No!" Freya screamed, flinging herself beside the creature. It did not move, and she looked up out of the pit with a face that streamed with tears. "You bastards! It is dead."

"Poisoned," Kella breathed.

"The first game is ended," Jakoby announced.

✦ 40 ✦

"Interesting," Bram said.

We had returned to the side of the isis pool. In the light flooding through the crack, the water was as blue as a summerdays sky. Miryum had been laid on the grass beside Bram's dais, and Kella was tending her. Jakoby had warned us that if the coercer failed to resume her position before the third game commenced, she would be disqualified, reducing our number to nine. That would not happen, because, if necessary, Kella could heal her quickly. But this would drain her energy, so we had decided to wait to the last minute and hope the coercer would revive naturally.

Jakoby had not mentioned Freya's cry, and the blond girl stood beside me, pale but defiant. Malik's mocking smile said all too clearly that we had fared badly in the first Battlegame. But the day was young, I thought, gritting my teeth.

"Interesting to note what each group saw as the object of the Battlegame," Bram said. "The rebels sought to slay the bears and, if possible, to have the bears slay their opponents. Failing that, to get away alive. Would you concur?"

Jakoby nodded.

"In attempting to attain these objectives, the rebels were swift, aggressive, and sure. They worked well together when it was useful, never hesitating to cut their losses at need."

Jakoby nodded again.

"The Misfits' behavior, on the other hand, appeared primarily defensive to my eye. They sought to protect both themselves and the bears. Since the female was trying to kill them, this was a confused and somewhat sentimental strategy to adopt. The Misfits' mental powers are clearly considerable, but they didn't use them in any decisive way in this instance. If they can control the bears, why not have them attack the rebels? Why not have the rebels turn on one another?"

Bram closed his eyes and seemed to sink into a small trance after this speech. After a moment, he roused himself and announced that the second game would begin.

The dice were thrown again, and this time their number indicated a Battlegame Jakoby called "the Wall." A second casting gave two players to each team.

Rushton chose Angina, because he was agile and we thought the wall might have to be scaled, and Hannay again, because he was strong and a coercer, in case the wall had to be shifted or broken down.

We had not lost heart despite the first battle, for we were confident that we would perform better now that we had some idea of what the games might entail. The most important thing we had learned was that we must define our objectives when they were not specifically named.

When Angina and Hannay were taken off with the two rebels, Rushton frowned after them. "I hope we do better than in the first game."

Miky gave him a swift, startled look. "You can't mean you think they should have killed that bear."

"Of course not," he said. "I do not see what else they could have done. However"—he looked at me—"do you think Malik instructed his men to kill us if they got the chance? Or were their attacks in the pit instinctive?"

I let him see the answer in my eyes, and his frown deepened.

Angina and Hannay returned, now clad in loincloths, and they seemed to be arguing furiously. None of the four contestants bore any weapons. They were ushered past Bram's dais and over to the bottom of the rift wall, where Sadorian servitors bound Angina's wrists and ankles. One of the rebels was similarly bound.

"What on earth can they be expected to do tied up like that?" Miky said worriedly.

The servitors now turned their attention to Hannay and the second rebel, buckling each of them into stout leather jerkins and swathing their bare limbs in what appeared to be bandages. Boots reaching to the knee were strapped on their legs, and long heavy gauntlets were pulled over their hands.

"The climber must scale the rift wall to the summit," Jakoby said.

Miky frowned. "But how can Angina climb with his arms like that?"

"A strong cord will attach the climber to the burden," Jakoby went on.

We listened, aghast, as she explained that one in each doublet was to drag the other with him as a helpless bundle. The arms, legs, and hands of the climbers were bound in cloth to protect them from the cliffs, which were impregnated with streaks of holocaust poison. The burden had no such protection and must rely entirely on the skill of the climber.

"But . . . coercers are no good off solid ground," Miky reminded us, ashen cheeked.

"They had to let Hannay climb. Angina could never lift him," Rushton snapped.

Miky looked sick.

433

"At least it's not Miryum. Hannay won't be as badly affected as she would," Kella said stoutly. She did not say what she must have been thinking—what we were all thinking— that Miky's twin's life was in the hands of a man who could not bear heights.

The bout would be over, Jakoby announced, when both pairs reached the desert above.

"Climb," Bram shouted.

We watched with bated breath as the game began.

To begin with, the rebels were at an obvious disadvantage, because they were both of equal height and weight. This gave the climber an arduous task. But Hannay climbed with agonizing slowness. Soon, the rebels were some distance above.

Then, all at once, Hannay began to climb swiftly, his hands and feet sure. Gradually, he closed the gap between himself and the rebel pair.

"Angina's helping him not to be afraid," Miky said with a flare of pride.

Now the pairs were level. But the climber in the rebel team had reached a small ledge that allowed him to stand and free his hands. He began to take chunks of rock and hurl them at Hannay.

"He's trying to dislodge them!" Daffyd cried.

The big coercer paid no attention and had soon risen above the rebel climber. The rebel turned his attention to Angina and went on hurling stones and abuse.

Suddenly Hannay stopped climbing.

We stared, straining our eyes to figure out what had happened.

"Angina's been knocked out by the rebel's stone," Miky said.

"Oh Lud," I whispered, knowing that, unconscious, the

empath could not send courage to the big coercer. And if Hannay fell now, he would kill them both.

The rebel climber began to ascend again.

For a long time, the coercer did not move, but at last he began to climb again, too.

"Has Angina . . . ?" I began, but incredibly Miky shook her head.

That meant Hannay was going it alone. He went very slowly, testing handholds and creeping over the face of the cliff like an ant in a windstorm.

By contrast, the rebel climber rose with exultant speed, uncaring that his partner was being dragged and bumped against the poisoned rock wall. When he reached the top, he hauled up his trussed partner and gave a great shout of triumph.

This was echoed by the rebels below.

It was more than a half hour later when an utterly exhausted Hannay dragged himself onto the platform and pulled Angina up after him.

They were brought back down on kamuli. Angina had regained consciousness, though he had a lump on his forehead the size of a hen's egg and claimed to be seeing double. Kella drew the slight concussion out of him, and Miky went to where Hannay sat heavily on a boulder, staring at the ground.

"That was brave," she told him softly. "I know coercers hate heights. Are you all right?"

"That was the hardest thing I have ever done. But it was not bravery that moved me, Miky. It was blind terror."

"Not so blind," Miky whispered, pressing a kiss to his cheek.

A faint color rose in his face, just as Jakoby approached to summon us back to the dais. Miryum had wakened and joined us as we took our places. Bram looked closely at the stocky coercer before agreeing that she was fit to continue. Now we were ten again, but Malik had lost one player. The man who had been trussed and borne up the ridge wall had touched the walls too often, and he was seriously ill. There would be no question of his returning within two games.

"The rebel climbers clearly saw the object of the game as speed," Bram said. "Having identified their objective, they lost no time in pursuing it. It is also clear that the rebels have a second objective—that is, to destroy or harm their opponents. They have been equally single-minded in their efforts to fulfill this objective but so far have failed. Oddly, this does not appear to have excited a desire to retaliate on the part of the Misfits. They have done no more than use their unusual Talents to protect themselves when they were under attack.

"Neither did they use their powers to inhibit their opponents' progress up the wall," Bram continued, tugging at his earlobe. "They might have caused their opponents to jump from the cliff under some delusion. But they did not. They only appear able to use their abilities to help themselves or to defend themselves. There does not seem to be any capacity for aggression in them."

He straightened and the overguardian brought the dice again.

At the first throw, twelve marks faced up.

"The Pole," Bram intoned.

On the second throw, three marks faced the sky, and we gathered around Rushton to decide which three should represent us.

"I have some skill with the pole as a weapon, but twice I have failed," Hannay said despondently. "I am not afraid, but I think you should not choose me."

"You did not fail," Angina said. "I made you brave, and when I was hurt, you made yourself brave."

The coercer smiled wanly and ruffled the empath's hair. "Let us say you showed me the knack of it."

"I will do it," Miryum said stoutly. "Pole fighting is my specialty, and if it is aggression they want, I am the person to give it to them."

Rushton nodded. "I name myself as well to this, for I, too, have some skill at the pole."

"We need three," Miryum reminded him.

"I have not learned the pole, but I am strong," Daffyd offered diffidently.

"Why not," Rushton agreed, sounding almost cheerful. I guessed he was glad to be involved rather than watching.

"What if they are not to fight with the poles?" Dameon murmured, but Jakoby had called for Rushton to nominate his team for the third game. Malik spoke, and the chosen six were marched off to the armoring tent.

When Jakoby explained this game, my heart sank; we had misjudged yet again, for the game did not involve the common sport of pole fighting. The title referred instead to a long, slender piece of wood run between two high stands. Two of these scant bridges were erected before our eyes, to stand less than an arm's width apart.

The object, Jakoby said, was for the members of each trio to cross the pole from end to end, one at a time.

Hannay groaned. "Badly as we have done already, we cannot hope to succeed now. No coercer fears heights more than Miryum."

Our only consolation was that the rebel team seemed no happier. I kept my fingers crossed that at least one of their people would also be afraid of heights.

The six returned carrying short staves, which were clearly to be used for balance. Even at a distance, I could see Miryum was white and tense, as Jakoby told them each team must begin at opposite ends and proceed at their own pace.

"Begin," Bram shouted.

Rushton went first, crossing with an obvious lack of fear and the grace and balance that had served him so well aboard *The Cutter*. The first rebel had no hope of matching him and made his own crossing slowly and carefully, sweating and swearing at every step. By the time he reached the other side, Daffyd had already taken Rushton's place and was making his way carefully across the pole.

The second rebel was far more agile. He swarmed up the ladder and stepped out onto the pole with confidence. He looked across at Daffyd and smiled.

My heart pounded uneasily as he came level with the grimly concentrating Daffyd.

The rebel swung his stave out without warning and dealt Daffyd's a hard thump.

Panicking, the farseeker dropped his stave and swayed. The rebel laughed, holding up his own stave for another blow. But he stepped forward, failing to notice Daffyd's stave had fallen to straddle the two poles, just beneath the rebel's feet. He lost his footing and fell with a terrified scream.

"Lud help him," Miky whispered, but my eyes were riveted to Daffyd, who was still swaying dangerously.

"Use your arms!" Rushton cried.

Slowly, Daffyd lifted his arms, and after a long, tense moment, he stepped forward again, only to misjudge.

Kella screamed as he fell but, at the last second, he caught hold of the pole. He hung there for a long moment before beginning to make his way hand over hand to the other side.

There was dead silence as he climbed down the ladder and crossed to where the second rebel lay in the red-stained sand, motionless.

He looked up at the two rebels, who had made no move toward their fallen comrade.

"He's dead."

"Go!" snarled the first rebel to the third, shoving him. The red-haired man licked his lips, then began to mount the stand.

I looked across at Miryum.

She was trembling violently, her face paper white, her eyes fixed on the dead rebel.

Rushton cursed audibly and set his hands on the ladder at the finishing end.

"Look at me, Miryum," he urged from across the sandpit.

She lifted her head.

"Put your hands on the ladder. We'll climb up together. Do exactly as I do, and don't look down."

Seeming half mesmerized by his fierceness, she obeyed, putting her hands around the first rung.

And so they climbed.

The third rebel was halfway across now, but moving very slowly. The first rebel shouted and jeered at Miryum, calling her a great stupid sow, but her entire attention was focused on Rushton.

They had reached the top of the ladder and were facing one another. "Come," Rushton invited softly. "Walk across to me. Come as slowly as you wish and don't look down. Don't think. Just step out."

She did not move.

I closed my eyes, unable to bear the tension.

"Lud save us. She's doing it!" Hannay whispered incredulously.

439

I took a deep breath and opened my eyes to see Miryum had indeed taken up a balancing stave and stepped out onto the narrow pole. She walked forward, step by slow step, her eyes fixed on Rushton's as if they were her lifeline. She reached the center of the pole. The exact center.

Then I saw her eyes sweep down to where the rebel lay. She stopped.

"Come on," Rushton urged. "You've come this far." But she was like a statue, frozen with terror.

"Come on," Daffyd shouted from below. "Reach down and swing the rest of the way like I did."

"She can't," Hannay murmured, his own brow beaded with sweat.

"I'm strong!" Miryum cried in an agonized voice. "I'm strong!"

For one dreadful moment, I thought she was going to jump.

There was a cry of anger from the rebels, and I saw that Rushton had come out from the other end using his hands outstretched to balance himself. In moments, he and Miryum were facing one another. He spoke too softly for us to hear what he said, but it was clear that he was coaxing her. The third rebel had reached the end and was jeering and exhorting the coercer to join the dead rebel on the ground.

Miryum shook her head at Rushton.

He reached out, talking all the while, until he was also grasping Miryum's balancing stave.

"No!" Miryum moaned as he pulled her gently toward him.

"Yes," Rushton said calmly, firmly. "For Obernewtyn. Walk, Miryum."

And, incredibly, she did. He walked backward, leading her slowly, feeling his way with his feet and instinct.

When they were safe, I cheered myself hoarse with the others, blinded by tears of pride. Miky and Angina were nearly crushed to death by an elated Hannay, and there was not a dry eye among us.

The rebels roared, too, hissing that it was a cheat.

"How so?" Jakoby inquired of Malik, who had made the charge formal.

"He helped that fat cow. She would not have made it without him."

"That is true," Jakoby said, and for a moment her golden eyes were full of irony.

"The Misfits show great courage and great devotion to one another," Bram said. "Perhaps too much, for if the girl had fallen, she would undoubtedly have taken their leader with her. A wise leader does not risk himself in this way. Not for a lone warrior."

He went on to praise the single-mindedness of the rebels in trying to thwart their opponents but suggested they needed to temper zeal with thought, since they had lost another player and were now down to eight.

"There must be some warriors left in case a battle is only one of many in a war." He expressed regret at the dead rebel as the body was carried away, but none of the other rebels seemed overly disturbed by what had happened to their companion.

The next game to be played was called "the Ride."

✦ 41 ✦

"I AM FOR this," I told Rushton, for a swift probing had told me there were horses in a corral just behind a clump of trees.

For a moment, our eyes met.

"Yes," he said. "But, Elspeth, we have to do more than win this with speed and grace. We won the last game, I am sure, but we have to show some aggression. It sounds as if these Sadorians value that in the rebels, and we're losing because of it."

"I'll try," I said.

When Rushton named me to Bram, Malik named himself.

We were brought to the small herd of beasts I had farsensed and bade to choose our mounts. Malik immediately selected a huge gray gelding with intelligent eyes. He had clearly chosen the most powerful beast, but a race among horses sometimes had more to do with endurance than strength. I paused for a moment and swung myself into the corral to walk among the other horses.

I beastspoke at random, asking who was stronger and faster than all the rest. Suddenly I found myself face to face with the little mare Faraf, whom I had aided at the city gate the day I arrived at Sutrium.

"Greetings, ElspethInnle," she sent. "It seems our paths are twined. As you see/discover, my escape did not bring me to the freerunning barud."

"You were captured?"

"Yes, and sold to these. As funaga go, they are not bad/evil. Yet I dream of the freerunning."

"Choose," Malik snarled impatiently.

Ignoring him, I explained my need to the mare.

"The other/funaga has taken the strongest among us. But you had better choose me, for I am small and not strong," she advised.

"Why? Will the strong/wise other let us win? My need is very great."

"He would if I ask it, Innle, for he knows what you are. But they will feed us a garrug/a leaf that some call *prickleberry*. It causes a madness that infects/burns the brain. Better to ride a weak mad horse than a strong one."

I bit my lip to keep a smile of triumph from my mouth as I led Faraf out.

Malik looked down at the slender mare incredulously, but a servitor merely offered us a choice of saddles. The rebel chose a great solid armored thing with sharp metal spurs. On Faraf's advice, I took one that was light and deep-seated. I chose the simplest bridle but removed the metal bit.

When we were brought back to the isis pool, a space had been cleared, and Jakoby explained what Faraf had already told me. We would get onto the horses, and they would be fed the prickleberry, which would madden them temporarily. We would sit on them until the drug took effect. When one of us was unseated, the game would be ended.

"This weed will not kill the horses as it did the bear?" I asked, trying to recall what I knew of prickleberry.

Jakoby's brows lifted. "The bear did not die from the garrug. Its heart was weak and burst under the strain of battle."

The shadows were long now, and I prayed this game

443

would end the day. If we won, it would leave both sides equal, and perhaps that was the best way to win this fight.

"Courage," Faraf sent as I mounted her. The saddle felt stiff and hard against my backside, and the metal stirrups pressed my feet uncomfortably. A servitor brought a nosebag, and as Faraf ate, a thought came to me of how we might further impress the rebels.

"Faraf/littlesistermind, if you will let me into your thoughts/open to me, I can block the effect of this leaf so that it will not madden you."

"I will open, but already it begins to affect me."

This was true, for her whole body was already twitching. I sent a probe into her mind and examined the effect of the prickleberry. It moved swiftly, but I was faster, blocking nerve paths and sending it by innocent trails to the bowel, where it would be voided. Still, some of the drug remained in her system, so I took control of her nerves and immobilized her completely.

Gradually, the trembling faded, and she stood quietly.

Malik's horse, meanwhile, was pacing about, shuddering and shying at nothing. The rebel's face was pale, and he held the rein cruelly tight, ready to saw on the horse's mouth the minute it tried anything.

Without warning, the animal gave a shrill whinnying shriek and reared up.

The sound tore at me, and I tried to get to Malik's horse to ease him off. But the drug had taken hold, and his mind was inaccessible. The horse plunged and bucked violently, but the rebel kept his seat. He was a superb rider.

He gave me a look of patent fury, and I read his intention a moment before he kicked his horse into a maddened run—straight at me!

I could do nothing to move Faraf out of the way, because I had shut down her nerves. As Malik thundered past, the saddle spikes cut her neck and my leg deeply.

The horse bucked in a circle as Malik fought to bring him around. Then he charged again.

"Stop!" I screamed as this time the metal spur tore open the little mare's flank. I was trying frantically to restore her motor responses, but the drug was preventing me.

Again Malik fought his mount to turn it, and as he bore down on me, I saw that he meant to kill me if he could or to cut Faraf to pieces under me. The spikes missed, but he dug the horse with his heels and it kicked out, catching Faraf on the side of her head.

Blood streamed down her face, and she staggered sideways in a hideous parody of the first time I had seen her. He turned again.

"No!" I screamed, and threw my leg over her to slide to the ground. "I forfeit!"

There was a roaring sound in my ears, and my leg felt oddly numb, but I turned to slide my arms around the mare's bloody neck.

"I am sorry, ElspethInnle. I have failed you," she sent humbly.

"Never," I whispered, looking into her eyes. I kissed her soft nose and limped with her back to the pens. I did not look at Malik, who had jumped clear of his horse.

"There is nothing to be said since this game was forfeited," Bram said when we were all assembled again.

"Ye did th' right thing," Fian whispered angrily when I returned to them. Freya nodded and squeezed my arm. But I was not comforted. If only I had possessed the presence of mind, I might have coerced Malik, but fear for Faraf had stopped me thinking clearly.

I dared not look at Rushton.

Bram rose to throw again. The fifth game was named "Song," and the number of players from each team was two. We could not lose, and yet it was now impossible for us to win.

"A song! This is a joke," Malik snarled.

"I told you, the Battlegames test many qualities. Proceed, unless you would forfeit," Bram said tranquilly.

The two red-faced rebels Malik chose sang a bawdy battle song, probably the only one they knew.

In contrast, Miky and Angina's song dealt not with the glory of war but with the tragedy of it. It was an old song that told of two boys—brothers separated at birth and sent to war against each other. Only when one had killed the other did they understand what had come to pass. The song was supposedly a dirge, sung by the surviving man over his brother's body.

I had heard the song before, but never like this—never with such rending sorrow. Empathised, it became something greater and deeper than a song about two brothers. It became a song about all wars. I wept for the pity of two brothers, lost to each other until it was too late. But I also wept for my own brother, Jes; for Jik, Matthew, and Dragon; for the gypsy Caldeko; and for the nameless rebel who had broken his back on the pole. For all the victims of hatred and war.

And I was not alone. Kella and Freya and Dameon wept, but many of the Sadorians wept, too. Even some of the rebels wiped their eyes surreptitiously as Miky sang the final words: "Will there ever be a time when war does not kill the babes and the dreams of the world?"

446

When the final notes faded, the sun set in a dazzling golden haze, and it seemed to me that the radiant sky itself paid homage to their voices. Malik stood dry-eyed and contemptuous as Bram rose to speak, dabbing at his eyes.

"The rebel song offered humor, and this is a fine thing to bolster a warrior's courage," he said. "But the Misfit song is greater, for it reaches into the very soul of a warrior and causes him to question himself."

"What does it matter that a song brings tears to the eyes of the weak and the womanish? Will it win a battle?" Malik demanded.

"A song will not wield a sword of metal, my friend," Bram said softly. "But it can put a sword into the heart that will never rust or blunt. It can cause warriors to fight when good sense bids them surrender, raise an army, or quell the tears of a babe."

He rose and lifted his arms.

"The sun has gone, and the Battlegames are ended."

"Who won, then?" Malik demanded.

Bram cast a cool eye on the rebel.

"Impatience is not the least of your faults, Malik. It is a kind of greed, and someday it may see you undone."

He cast his eyes about to take in rebels, Sadorians, and Misfits alike.

"I have been asked to judge these Battlegames. I tell you now that this is not merely a matter of tallying points but of examining how each game was played. Sometimes this makes the judging difficult, for what seems a simple victory may be deemed less of one in light of our purpose."

My heart swelled in sudden hope.

"In this case, however, the judging is a simple matter," he went on. "The games were staged to determine who were the greater warriors and whether the Misfits and their unusual powers were worthy of alliance. The answer is that the rebels are clearly far more fitted to warfare than the Misfits. They have shaped their souls for aggression and quicken to violence as a gravid mare quickens with new life. The rebel legions, if they are truly represented by these men, are made for battle. No instinct of mercy would restrain them, no compassion stay their hand, no love of beauty keep them from destruction. The Battlegames have shown them to be swift, decisive, ruthless, and resourceful. They are filled with the warrior's desire to dominate and subdue.

"As for the Misfits, if they are truly represented by these before me, they are no warriors. They care too much for life and for one another. They are not stirred by the glories of war, and the shedding of lifeblood brings them sorrow, whether it be of beast or human, friend or foe. All their instincts are for defense, and so their great powers are all but useless in the cause of war. They are not cowardly or weak, but their minds appear incapable of allowing their great powers to serve them as weapons.

"Witness that they used the incredible ability that they call *empathy* to its greatest effect in a song, rather than to turn their enemies' hearts to terror. They will never have the rebels' single-mindedness of purpose, nor, therefore, their driving force, because they cannot see things in terms of simple goals."

He turned in the dead silence wrought by his oratory and faced the rebels. "We here in Sador value the earth above all life—humans and beasts alike are short-lived and unimportant. This you know. We have thought that Landfolk valued their own lives too much, regarding themselves as the chosen of their Lud. But these Misfits seem to value all life, and this is strange for us to contemplate. But think you this: You rebels opposed alliance with the Misfits, because you thought them monsters and inhuman. Ask yourselves now which team has this day shown the keenest humanity and which has shown itself to be more monstrous."

The old man paused; then he said in a voice drained of all vitality, "I declare the rebels the victors of the Battlegames."

The rebels cheered, but there was a puzzled, halfhearted edge to the sound. Malik's face was thunderous as he moved to join the other rebel leaders and receive their congratulations.

Rushton turned to us, looking much older in that moment than I had ever seen him.

"The old man's judging was fair," he said.

I stepped forward to tell him that if I must be like Malik to be a warrior, then I would not be a warrior, but my leg buckled under me. As I fell forward, Rushton opened his arms to catch me, but I slipped through them into the abyss.

I dreamed I was bound to the Zebkrahn machine and my legs were on fire.

I dreamed of the Agyllian healer, Nerat, telling me she would teach my body to heal itself.

I dreamed of a red-haired woman drowning in an ocean of blood, of Swallow raising a sword to salute me, of Ariel searching for me down long tunnels.

I dreamed of Maruman telling me I would lead the beasts to freedom, and of walking on the deck of *The Cutter*, watching the ship fish dance.

I dreamed of Rushton waiting at the doors of Obernewtyn and of Freya in his arms.

I dreamed of a shining river that called my name.

"Do not go into the stream, ElspethInnle."

"Atthis!" I sent. "At last you speak to me."

"*I have spoken often through the yelloweyes and the dreaming-woman you call Maryonfutureteller.*"

"Why did you never speak to me?"

"*Because the H'rayka would hear. He flies the dreamtrails. He listens to hear what I will say so that he may thwart me/us/you.*"

"Can he not hear us now?"

"*He would not dare come so close to the death/dreaming river for fear that it would swallow him. And so it might, for you are perilously close. You must come back from the edge now. I am holding you, but my strength fades.*"

"I like it here. There is no pain, and it sings to me."

"*It is not yet your time to hear this song.*"

"Then why am I here?"

"*A bloodpath in your leg was severed during this testing called Battlegames. You bled near to death. They have stopped this, but you are too close to the stream. Your body has learned to heal itself, but it cannot do so when you are so close to the stream. You must draw back if you would live.*"

I felt a great wrenching pull to return, but I fought it. I was not sure I wanted to live.

"*What you feel is the spiritcall of one who would have you live, ElspethInnle. Go back and let yourself heal, for the world has need of you. Go back, or the H'rayka wins. Go back, or the beasts will never be free.*"

I felt the pulling again and wondered whose spirit held me so tightly. Curious, I let myself be drawn away from the stream by it.

"Who are you?" I called, but there was nothing, only a roaring sound in my ears. There was a long rushing darkness, and then I opened my eyes.

A monster peered at me. I screamed and fled back to the darkness.

I opened my eyes and Kella smiled at me.

I opened my eyes and Dameon touched my cheek.

I opened my eyes.

I was lying in bed in a dark, cold room. Beside me sat the hooded overguardian.

"You are in the Earthtemple, Elspeth Gordie," said the voice from within the hood. "You have slept long."

· 42 ·

"Come," the Temple guardian murmured, his voice shuddering and whispering along the damp, echo-ridden stone tunnels that honeycombed the Sadorian cliffs.

"Where are you taking me?" I demanded, exasperated. "And when can I see my friends?"

"Soon," he answered. The same thing he had said for days in the same queer, breathy voice.

"I am no longer sick, and you are keeping me prisoner!" I snapped. "I know they were in here before, so why can't I see them now?"

He did not answer.

I glared at the damp walls resentfully. Maybe Rushton and the others had not come in to see me because they had left Sador. After all, I had been unconscious for five days and awake for three. Eight days in all since the Battlegames had ended. The Temple guardians had cared for me when I woke, weak and disoriented, and I was grateful for that. But I was fully recovered now. If the place had not been such an impossible warren of tunnels, I should have long since walked out myself.

I was about to repeat my question when we rounded a bend. Set into the side of the tunnel was a huge panel carved of wood; I had not come across it in my wanderings.

I stopped and gaped at it in amazement, for there was no

452

doubt in my mind that whoever had executed it had also carved the doors to Obernewtyn! The chisel work on the doors possessed a precision in angling that could not be mistaken, as individualistic as the markings on a person's palm.

"Come," the guardian prompted.

Dazed, I did not move. "Who did this?"

He came back a few steps, reluctantly. "Kasanda. Now will you come?"

I followed him. "Who is Kasanda?"

He did not answer, and my temper rose again. I wrestled it down.

"When can I see the overguardian?" I asked sweetly. Again he did not respond.

I ground my teeth and searched my mind, but before I could come up with something rude enough to fracture even a guardian's phenomenal composure, he stopped before a stone doorway.

"Go in. The overguardian will come to you here."

I opened my mouth to speak but thought better of it and went through the door. Behind it was an enormous lantern-lit chamber. Like most of the caverns, it was devoid of furnishings. The temple was, in fact, a natural labyrinth, and the guardians inhabited only a fraction of the chambers and tunnels. But unlike the other empty chambers, every bit of wall space in this one was taken up with huge panels of carved stone. I could see at a glance that they had been created by the same hand that had executed the wood carving in the hall.

"The sequence begins here," the guardian said, pointing to the panel nearest the door.

I nodded absently and moved to the first panel.

It was part carved, part daubed with mud and fiber to

raise up shapes, and tinted with darker and lighter tones. Little enough with which to create a world, let alone a lost world of unimaginable wonders, and yet the panel showed one of the Beforetime cities. I was reminded inevitably of the city under Tor, but the city depicted in the panel was vibrantly alive. The constructions were magnificent, reaching to the skies and embodying the greatness of their makers. The panel was a paean of praise to the Beforetimers.

I shivered, for surely such a vision could only come from one who had seen the cities of the Beforetime in all their glory.

After a long while, I tore myself from the first panel. The next also featured the towering Beforetime structures, but they were subtly different. After only a moment of admiration, I noticed not the buildings but the way they crushed and smothered the earth. I saw the caged and stunted trees devoid of sunlight. I realized that this panel spoke not of greatness but of soaring, overweening pride and, most of all, oppression. The Beforetimers had gouged and yoked and reshaped the very earth to their creations.

I shifted to the third panel. Here again were Beforetime structures. Above lay a pall of blackness such as rose chokingly from the smithy's forge. I did not know what purpose these buildings served, for no smith would need so much space, but the message was clear. Not content to despoil the earth, the Beforetimers had smeared the skies with their messes.

One after another, the panels depicted similar scenes—rivers clogged and poisoned, forests hewn down and transformed into salted deserts, mountains leveled to rubble. The Beforetimers had been masters of wanton destruction, and they had built their world regardless of the cost.

I moved to another panel and here at last were scenes of the

Great White. Seen thus, it seemed to me that the holocaust had been inevitable, given the nature of the Beforetimers. How else could their story have ended, but with men and women and beasts and birds fleeing in terror from the huge fiery mushrooms that rose in the skies behind them? And when the whiteness faded, there were panels of utter desolation—sere deserts and poisoned waters: the Blacklands.

"Truly this is a place of sorrows," a boy's voice said.

I whirled to see the tiny hooded figure who had sat at Bram's feet during the Battlegames. The overguardian's hands lifted and removed the hood.

I recoiled involuntarily, for the face revealed was grossly deformed. In stark, dreadful contrast, his eyes were the color of isis pools, sad and beautiful.

"I am sorry," I said. "I did not expect . . ."

He smiled, a grotesque twisting of his lips. "I am the over-guardian of the Earthtemple. That which poisoned the earth also poisoned my mother. It is so with all of the guardians here."

I took a deep breath, hiding my surprise at his age as much as at the fact that he was a Misfit. "I am glad to meet you. Thank you for healing me. . . ."

"I did not heal you. Your body healed itself. We do not know how."

His words evoked a memory of my dream and Atthis telling me my body could heal itself. Had it really been the old bird or a feverish delusion? Yet if it was true, it would explain so many things. Perhaps even the disappearance of Swallow's tattoo.

"There is a story," the boy said dreamily. "It tells of one who will come from across the sea in search of the fifth sign of Kasanda."

I frowned, drawn from my despair by curiosity. "The same Kasanda who carved these?"

He seemed not to hear. "There are many born with Kasanda's gift, here and even in your own Land. And it is said that when one comes in search of the signs, three companions will come also, one of whom shall be of true Kasanda blood."

"Why are you telling me this?" I demanded coldly. His talk of seeking and signs chilled me.

The boy shrugged. "Perhaps I dreamed that you would come and that I must say these words. I have Kasanda's gift of true dreaming, and so I am sometimes called a kasanda. But the first Kasanda is the one who dreamed of the Seeker."

"The . . . Seeker?"

He nodded. "After the signs. Kasanda told my people that the Seeker would bear the Moonwatcher and be borne by the Daywatcher, who is the color of shadows. You see the beauty and intricacy of the images? The Moonwatcher's daylight eye and the Daywatcher's shadow hue are complementary. Two sides of the spinning coin. The implication is that one may emulate the other in times of need. The interesting thing is that there is no information about the Seeker—as if that was too dangerous to be left."

I shivered, unnerved by his use of the name Atthis had given me. I thought of the disturbed youth outside the Earthtemple flinging himself at my feet. He, too, had spoken of the Moonwatcher. But the threads of my quest could not stretch this far, surely.

"It is said Kasanda took the signs from her dreams and strewed them across the lands so that they should not be found except by the Seeker. There are rumors that they lead to the deepest treasures of the Beforetimers. Still others say they are the key to a power that is great enough to shift the stars, and even to quench them."

Power again, I thought bleakly. That was what had brought about the holocaust. "Do you know what the signs are?"

He smiled enigmatically. "I know many things. I know that the Herders come bearing lethal gifts of disease and that they must be watched constantly to prevent them harming the earth or our people. I know that when the Seeker journeys forth with the Daywatcher and Moonwatcher, and with one of Kasanda blood, they will be looking for the final sign. Then may the kasanda, who is the overguardian, aid them."

I shook my head angrily. "This is nothing to do with me. I want to get out of here." I glanced around at the panels with loathing.

The boy sighed and resumed his hood. "Very well. Tomorrow your friends will come to the Temple for you."

He went out, and when I followed, he had vanished.

Left alone in my chamber, I sat on the edge of the bed. My mind was filled with pictures—the Herder torturing Iriny's bondmate, my parents killed for their beliefs, Malik's eyes filled with hatred, and the dark dreadful visions in stone left by the mysterious Kasanda for the Seeker.

Well, the Seeker had seen them.

I thought of the transcendent beauty of the first panel and tried to understand how the ability to create such wondrous beauty could have become so perverted, so destructive.

With power, my mind whispered.

I felt desperately confused and lay down, longing to be in the mountains. I closed my eyes and sent my mind out into the desert. It was night, and the pale changeless dunes undulated beneath the night sky, going on as far as the eye could behold without a sign of human life. So must the world have looked before the Beforetime and the demon-angels we named Old-timers. The Great White now seemed the least of their evils. Perhaps not evil at all, for if it had not come, then what would they have done next? Shaken by this thought, I tried to draw the calm grace of the desert into me, but the despair was too strong.

Again I felt a fierce longing for the clean coldness of the mountains.

"Then seek them," Maruman's voice whispered into my mind.

"Where are you?" I sent, trying to decide if his voice was real or imagined.

"Maruman/yelloweyes flies the dreamtrails. Fly to the mountains if you need them."

I sighed. "It is too far. You know I cannot send my mind over Blacklands."

"You can if/when you farsense you seek the dreamtrails. Come."

I let him take hold of me, but almost immediately I felt claws. Before I could summon the wit to struggle or fight, I had the uncanny sensation of hurtling through the air as if hurled from a catapult.

"Fly/seek!" Maruman's mindcry faded behind me.

"ElspethInnle. Come ride with me. . . ." Gahltha's mind-voice came to me.

I opened my eyes and was amazed to find myself sitting in my turret chamber at Obernewtyn.

Dazed, I crossed to the window and looked out. The black equine was standing in the moonlit garden below. I felt a surge of joy at the sight of him.

"I'm coming," I sent, and turned from the window to drag on riding boots and a cloak.

This can't be happening, I thought, hurrying down.

"It has happened, and anything that has happened can happen again. Life is filled with circlings," Gahltha sent as I mounted. He wheeled to trot down the drive. The air was cold and thin, and I shivered.

"Is this real?"

"What is real? You are here and I am here, but we are also far from here. Who knows which existence is more real?"

Which was no sort of answer, but as Gahltha traveled gently out of Obernewtyn's gate and along the road with its whispering green sentinels looming darkly above, it did not seem to matter very much. When the trail ran out, he broke into a wild gallop, crossing the long grassy plain like a creature possessed. His tail and mane streamed out behind as we sped through the gap in the foothills and climbed the narrow way into the valley above, and the one above that.

At last we reached the valley that lay at the feet of the highest mountains. Though it was not yet wintertime, the ground was hard, and snow lay spattered on the ground like ash. The peaks were already white.

We rested by a hot spring, and as I sat on a rock, warming myself, Gahltha grazed on the sweet grass that grew about the edge of the simmering water. "I will eat the grass and you will nourish yourself on the mountains," he sent, as if it were no more than biting into an apple.

Giving myself to the dream, I lay my mind wide open, seeking the detachment and clarity the mountains enabled. Their wild beauty always seemed to make a gentle mockery of brief human woes and lives. Had not these jutting bones of the world survived a thousand eons of human life? Could anything I or any human do really matter in the face of that?

But for once, I could not comfort myself and answer no. I had stood in the Earthtemple, and I had seen the panels made by Kasanda. In my mind's eye, I saw again the smothered and abused earth, the befouled waters and blackened skies. I saw again the desolation that lay on the other side of the mountains—the endless bleared deadness of the Blacklands—and I knew that even mountains could be killed.

It seemed to me then that I felt the earth's life, the cold sweetness of its breathing winds, the deep beat of its stone heart, and I understood the Sadorians' devotion to the earth. Everything lives, Powyrs had told me, and I realized he was right.

For the first time, it seemed to me that I knew the true evil of human wars and their instinct to dominate and oppress and subdue, for hadn't the Beforetimers poisoned great tracts of the earth with the holocaust? And if the Destroyer reached the hellish slumbering weaponmachines first, would not the task be finished for always? If mountains could die, and vast plains, then why not a world? Humans would perish, and perhaps it was no more than they deserved, but so would equines and bears and the Brildane. If the earth died, not a single blade of grass nor a cat with one eye would survive.

The moon rose, a thin sliver now, and shone its eldritch light through a haze of cloud and onto the mountain peaks, silvering their snowy mantles and transforming them into shimmering ghosts.

I clenched my teeth.

My resolve, shattered and confused for so long, became, all at once, blessedly strong. When the Agyllians called, I would leave Obernewtyn as I had promised. I would obey the prophecy the birds claimed I had been born to fulfill and all the strange strands of fate that sent me here and there seeking signs and ways; I would follow the sinuous, difficult, puzzling manywindings of my quest, whether they led me into the deserts of Sador, or over the vast dark seas, or into the very fires of hell—I would complete my quest so that what had been could not come again.

I would walk the dark road to its end and never return, for nothing was too great a price to pay for the earth and all its life. Not love or my own little life.

My quest was greater than fear or love, and it was greater than Obernewtyn and the fate of the Talented Misfits there, and nothing would ever make me question that again.

I slept then, dreamlessly, and when I woke, I was in the hard little Earthtemple bed. The terrible draining tide of sorrow that seemed to have defined my whole life had ebbed, along with the fears and murky apprehensions that had haunted me for as long as I could remember.

I felt as clear and light and pure as a glass of sunlit rainwater as the guardian led me through the tunnels to the outside. As I blinked into the fierce sunlight, I felt as if it pierced me and filled me up.

"Elspeth!" Kella cried.

She and Dameon had come to meet me. I let them hold me but felt a great distance had come between us. I had seen too much and flown too high.

"I am glad you are well," Dameon said gravely.

"The rebels have decided on their rebellion," Kella said, and a shadow passed over her features. "It is to be after wintertime."

I did not want to hear about rebels or rebellions.

"Is Maruman all right?"

Dameon chuckled. "He has made himself at home again

461

on Powyrs's ship. The old man dotes on him."

"Dragon?"

The healer sighed and shook her head. "There is no change in her condition. Maybe when we get back to Obernewtyn . . ."

I wondered suddenly if I *should* go back. There was nothing there for me now. I could just as well wait to hear from Atthis in Sador.

When we reached the tents, the others crowded around to greet me.

"Where is Rushton?" I asked, noticing abruptly that he was not with them.

A silence fell, and in spite of my new detachment, it made me uncomfortable.

I turned to Dameon and touched his arm. "Is he . . . he is not hurt?"

Kella looked exasperated. "Oh, Elspeth. Rushton has been odd ever since the Battlegames. He blames himself for our defeat."

"He walks alone and hardly eats," Miryum said. "He refuses to lead us."

As they settled back into their tasks, I looked around at the others. At Miryum brooding over our loss of the games as Hannay worked to cheer her; at Fian and Kella grinding leaves for herb paste; at Freya and Dameon, settling in to listen as Angina and Miky sat side by side, practicing a new song. Angina still bore the great bruised lump on his forehead from the Battlegames, but their faces were serene.

I thought of the song they had chosen for the Battlegames, and in a flash, I understood the power it had possessed. The empaths had sung it before, never knowing why the soldier sang. But now they understood. No wonder it had reached

462

even the hardened hearts of warriors, for there was truth in it.

I stared wildly about me, and the icy wall of detachment that had risen around me came crashing down.

Atthis had told me once that I should go to Obernewtyn and aid the Misfits in their struggle because it was worthy. I had gone and I had worked alongside the others, but I had always felt myself to be marking time, waiting for my true quest to begin. Now I saw that the two quests were parts of the same purpose. One without the other was meaningless.

Bram had been right to judge us unfit warriors. And perhaps in a world without threat of extinction from the weapons of the past, Obernewtyn would be free to usher in a new breed of humanity that would not take the same terrible path to destruction as the Beforetimers.

"What is it?" Kella asked, and I realized I had begun to grin like a fool.

I looked around and found they were all watching me. I took a deep breath.

Rushton had said we would learn about ourselves by taking part in the Battlegames and competing with the rebels. Well, we had learned all right. We had learned what it truly cost to be warriors. We had learned that the price was too high.

Losing the Battlegames had been the best thing that could have happened to us.

✦ 43 ✦

I FOUND RUSHTON sitting on a rock and staring out to sea.

"You haven't failed us," I said softly. "We haven't failed."

He was still for a moment. "Elspeth. I am glad you are well." His voice was dull, and he did not turn. I had never heard him sound so defeated.

"Listen to me—"

"I have called myself your leader," he said. "I thought to guide you all to battle, because I imagined your powers would fit you better for war, that all you needed was a leader to bind and direct you. But you are not meant for war. I failed you because I did not understand the truth of you."

"If there is any fault, it belongs equally to all of us," I protested.

He shook his head lethargically, but still he would not turn to face me.

"What will happen to you and the others when the Council sends its soldierguards to clear out Obernewtyn, Elspeth? Or when rebels like Malik come to wipe you from the earth? I wanted to protect you."

"Us," I said firmly, gently. "Us."

"I am not one of you," he said. "I have wanted to be and I have dreamed of it . . . but I know now that it will never be."

"Of course you are one of us," I said sharply. "Besides, leadership has nothing to do with your being a Misfit. You began this. You freed us and gave us a place and time to grow."

"But I was wrong. . . ."

"So were we," I cried. "*I* was the one who wanted to show the rebels our power and our might. If anyone is a fool, it is me."

"You have the right to make such decisions," he said more strongly. "Whereas I . . . I cannot even access my Talents without help."

"You think there is something wrong with needing help?"

"It is a weakness."

"Now you sound like Malik," I said hotly. "And maybe that's the point. Maybe there is a little of Malik in all of us. In spite of what Bram said, I have the feeling we could be like him if we wanted to badly enough. A Malik, after all, would never need help. Our need for one another is what makes us better than him!"

Now he did turn around. "*You* can say that? You, who never needed anyone in your life?"

"No one could say it with greater truth," I said sadly.

"And what happens when you cannot *have* what you need?" he demanded angrily.

That was a question I could not yet begin to answer. I knew only that, though Rushton might not love me, there was far more at stake here than my feelings. "Look, I'm trying to tell you that what we learned in the Battlegames was important. We needed to know what we couldn't do so that we could begin to think of what we can do. Remember Maryon said this journey had something to do with finding the right road? Can't you see that we've done that?"

He shook his head. "Will that knowledge show you how to deal with the soldierguards?" Rushton asked, apathy returning to his tone.

I held on to my temper with difficulty. "It might. Misfits are hated and persecuted because people fear us. The Herder Faction and the Council enhance that fear, just as Angina enhances Miky's songs. Maybe the answer isn't to fight and force and make, but to show. To empathise. To let them understand us so that they will see there is nothing to fear from us. I think we should try to reshape ourselves and our purposes around empathy."

"You are not an empath," Rushton said.

"No, but I can try to understand and care for the unTalents. Any one of us can learn to do that."

Rushton made a choking sound and turned away again. "You do not understand. How could you?"

A spurt of anger made me reach out and pull him back to look at me. "What do you know of how I feel? Do you think I am a machine like the ones the Beforetimers made?"

"I do not know," Rushton said with a sudden fierce bitterness. "I know nothing, because you have never *let* me know. Because I am not like you."

I gaped at him, my anger slipping away. "Not like you? What are you talking about? I have just been telling you . . ."

"Then why?" he asked softly, a world of pain in his voice. "Why will you never let me come near? Why do you reject me with every look and word if not because . . . I cannot reach my Talent, because I am not . . ." His voice faded away.

Had I understood correctly? "But surely Freya . . . ," I said faintly.

He nodded. "She is an enhancer. She has tried to teach me to use my powers, and we have had some success." He paused. "Though I don't know how you could know of it— but it is too little when you are . . . what you are."

I gazed at him, incredulous, my mind rearranging itself

466

like the colors of a kaleidoscope. He thought I did not love him because he could not use his Talent. He and Freya had been trying to reach his powers so that he would be worthy of me!

In that moment, I saw that if my quest to dismantle the weaponmachines and Obernewtyn's future were bound together, so were Obernewtyn and I bound up as one in Rushton's mind. In feeling he had failed one, he now felt he had failed the other.

But he had failed at neither. And I?

I understood that this was a moment that might never come again. I had learned the hardest way of all that beauty and happiness, like life, were ephemeral and could no more be saved up for later than a sunbeam could be hoarded. If I would have any life with Rushton, I must take it now, for now was all there ever was.

"What am I, Rushton?"

His eyes flared with a naked longing that seemed to suck the breath out of me.

He stood up suddenly, and I stepped back, almost frightened.

"You are everything," he said roughly, hopelessly. "Freya said to give you time, and I tried. But you have gone further and further from me. I have been a fool to imagine that you would ever care for me. . . ." He shook his head, and the light faded from his eyes, leaving them dull and sad.

"You are a fool, all right," I said tartly, half laughing.

He frowned at me, and my smile faded at the hurt in his face.

"You are a fool for thinking you failed Obernewtyn. You will go on leading us as we strive to find some other way to make our place in the world."

He began to shake his head, but I reached out my hand and laid it against his cheek.

He stood very still, and I let my hand slide around until my fingers were against his lips.

"I love you, and I have done ever since I saw you at Obernewtyn carrying that silly pig," I said simply, looking steadfastly into his eyes. "I just had to grow up enough not to be frightened of what I felt."

Rushton's face did not change, and for a moment, doubt flickered in me. But then I banished it, for surely nothing required courage so much as love, and I was equal to it.

Swallowing the fears of a lifetime, I reached out my mind, passing the barriers Rushton could not broach, and opened myself to him.

Only then did he move, and faintly, so faintly I could barely catch it, I heard his whisper inside my mind. "Ravek, my Elspethlove."

✦ Epilogue ✦

Maruman gave me a jaded look. "And what answer will that be?"

I leaned on the tower sill and looked out into the first flurry of wintertime snow, pulling my cloak about me.

"I don't know, Maruman. But we have begun to find it— Rushton and I, the guildmerge and beasts. And whatever it is, it will be the right answer, because it comes out of us and what we are."

"You will never make the funaga-li accept you," Maruman sent.

"Maybe that's the mistake we've made all along. Trying to make people accept us. I don't think *making* is going to be part of our answer."

I thought of Brydda. Just before we left Sador, he had come to the ship with Jakoby.

With them had been Miryum's Sadorian suitor leading little Faraf and the giant horse, Zidon, which Malik had ridden. He had gone to the Coercer guilden and held out the lead ropes to her. She had stared up at him suspiciously.

"They are a gift—" Jakoby began.

Miryum interrupted, stilted and awkward. "Well, that's all right, then. . . ." She took the ropes from the Sadorian's hand.

The man gave her a look of such burning intensity that her polite thanks faded. Then he turned and walked away.

Miryum looked even more bewildered.

"They are his bondgift to you," Jakoby had told the astonished coercer then. "That you accepted them means you have accepted him as your ravek. When he is ready, he will come for you. That is the Sadorian way."

Miryum's mouth fell open.

Jakoby then turned to Rushton. "I ask a boon of you, Leader of the Misfits."

This was the last thing we had expected.

"Bram and I ask that one of your empaths remain in Sador as a guest of the Earthtemple. We would have speech with you, for there is much about your people that intrigues us. This guest would be greatly honored and shown things none has seen before who was not of our people."

She and Brydda had withdrawn a little at this so that we could discuss it amongst ourselves.

"I will stay," Dameon had said without preamble. "This must be my task, for there has been nothing else for me to do. This must be why I was sent here."

Miky and Angina had chorused horror, offering themselves in his place.

"You don't understand," he said. "I *want* to stay. I am not sacrificing myself. It is . . . a selfish desire. I can learn much of these people, and perhaps teach them something. They have such a strange mixture of barbaric instincts and true wisdom. There is much in them that calls to me. The very fact that they regard empathy so . . . "

Rushton reached out and gripped his shoulder. "Dameon, I . . . I know why you would remain here."

To my surprise, the empath had flushed. "Then you must let me stay."

There was a long moment, and I wondered at this strangeness between them. Rushton expelled a breath of air. "Very well. One season. When wintertime is over and the pass is thawed, we will come for you. The two horses will stay here as well, for, in any case, they would not like the sea journey."

I shivered. So already there was talk of returning. I seemed to see the ruined face of the overguardian of the Earthtemple, telling me that the Seeker would come to Sador in search of some fifth sign.

"You cannot stay alone," Rushton was saying to Dameon. "Someone must stay with you to be your eyes and guard you."

"I will stay," Fian offered eagerly. "I will protect Dameon with my life and soul. And I can research this region for Garth."

"I can protect him best," Hannay said, flexing his muscles.

There was some more talk and more offers to accompany the Empath guildmaster, but in the end, Dameon and Fian stayed because it was felt there would be no need for guards. The Sadorians had too much honor to let anyone harm a guest.

Saying goodbye to Dameon had been harder than I could have imagined. I would have opened my mind and heart to him, but he had set a wall between us. Perhaps so that he would not be hurt by our sorrow at this parting; perhaps because he still felt Matthew's loss.

"It will not be the same without you," I had whispered, holding him tightly.

"Ever was Obernewtyn empty when you were not there," he had said. "Yet I survived, and you will survive."

"Rushton needs you, especially now."

"He does not need me, especially now," the empath said. "He has what he has long desired."

I felt the blood surge in my face.

He smiled, his blind eyes turned to me. He reached up and touched my hair and face, running his fingers over me lightly. Seeing. I made myself smile so that he would think of me that way. His fingers had reached my lips and seemed to tremble before he took them away.

He had embraced a tearful Miky and a pale Angina then, reminding them that they would rule the Empath guild in his stead.

"Only until you come back," Miky choked.

Dameon kissed her cheek and then farewelled Freya, who had not known him long and yet wept, too.

"I am ready now," he said. Smiling farewell, Fian had offered his arm to the empath. As they departed, Rushton put his arm around my shoulders and held me tightly. "He will be well, Elspeth. He . . . he needs to do this. It is but a season."

Then Brydda had come to bid us farewell. "I wish things might have been different."

"Perhaps this is for the best." Rushton clasped the big rebel's wrist. "I thought an alliance was the answer, but we would want such different things after it was over, and we will always be Misfits to them. We must be what we are."

Rushton's eyes had shifted to me fleetingly, and this time I had not flinched from the desire in them. If there was a loss in loving, I was learning that there was a finding in it, too.

Brydda had looked from one of us to the other and then had leaned across to embrace me. "Goodbye, little sad eyes, though they are not so sad now."

"You will always have our friendship, Brydda. No matter what," I said.

He had crushed my hand then. "Friends. Always," he said gruffly. "No matter what."

And so we had gone our separate ways. He to his rebellion, and we, first by sea to Sutrium, only to find that Domick had not yet returned, and then home to Obernewtyn—where I belonged; where Dragon lay in her endless coma; where Matthew might one day return; my home, which I must someday leave forever to take up the dark burden of my destiny.

"What if the oldOne calls before this answer is found?" Maruman asked. "Will you obey? Will you walk the dark road?"

I shivered as the bitter wind changed direction slightly, pressing its icy fingers through the folds of my cloak. The snow was falling more heavily now, blurring the jagged darkness of the mountains, making them seem far away. "All roads are the one road. I gave my promise," I sent soberly. Then I smiled. "But there are five secrets to be uncovered, and I must one day return to Sador, and I must stand in battle with a gypsy whose life is bound to mine. These things will not happen in a moment, and so there is time in the midst of this for me to live.

"Atthis has not summoned me yet, and perhaps the call to walk the dark road will not come until I am old and gray. I have promised to go, but I have not sworn to live out my life in the dark shadow of that vow. I have learned that happiness is like the sun. It must be enjoyed when it comes and while it shines."

But Maruman was not listening. He was looking up, searching for the moon's cold face.

THE KEEPING PLACE

for my many-talented sister Ellen

PART I

✦

THE WINDING PATH

✦ 1 ✦

IT WAS A chill, moonless night, the only light a raw glow from the fire in a stone-lined pit that reflected dully on the cobbles around its edge. Everything that lay outside the reach of the fire's brooding lume was lost in that blackest shadow that seems to attend any night light. Sometimes it seems to me that the dark is drawn to the light, as a moth to flame. Maybe it is the nature of all things to be pulled toward their opposites.

I dragged my eyes from the hypnotic lurching of the flames, determined to read on while I was yet undisturbed. Holding the pages instinctively to the light, though the marks on them would have been all but invisible even in daylight, I ran the tips of my fingers over the rough lines of holes in the paper. I had learned the code of prickings much as I once learned my letters, and I knew the words they shaped, yet skimming over what I had read before, it seemed that other meanings hovered above them.

Perhaps this was only because he who had made them did not see the world with his eyes but with his other senses. I could smell and hear and taste, too, of course, but not as well as Dameon. Since he lacked sight, his other senses had gained strength to compensate.

When he had pricked the pages he had been sending me, had Dameon realized more than the words he set down? Knowing him, I could not doubt it, for he was ever subtle. As an empath, he had the power to read emotions and transmit them, yet I had always attributed his keen perception to his blindness rather than to his Talent. Of course, it was impossible to try to separate their effect on him, for together they made Dameon what he was.

I missed the empath, and perhaps that was what made me strive for the essence of him within his letter, carrying it about with me despite its bulk and snatching what moments I might to read a few lines. With him gone, it was as if Obernewtyn had lost something vital to itself, some necessary spark so modest as to reveal its importance only in its absence. I did not know what name to give to it. Miky said we lacked our heart without him, and Angina said it was the soul we missed with their master away. Rushton called Dameon his conscience and regretted the loss of his sharp-honed ethical sense. But I thought it had some finer shading than all of those things. To my mind, Kella told it best when she said she missed Dameon's sweetness.

"Funaga-li need names for all things, even that which cannot be named," Maruman sent from where he lay on the bench seat behind me.

The old cat used the derogatory form of *funaga*, which was the thoughtsymbol beasts used for humans, but his mental voice lacked its usual bite. No doubt because he had been lolling in the sun all afternoon.

"Maruman does not loll," he sent indignantly. I turned to find his single yellow eye regarding me balefully, but the rest of him—his many scars, his battered head and torn ear, the empty socket of his ruined eye—was hidden in my shadow and the general darkness.

He was bad-tempered and difficult at the best of times, yet there was no beast so close to my heart. His had been the first mind I touched with my own. Later, he had followed me to Obernewtyn, convinced that I was destined to lead beasts to freedom from humans. I had long argued with him that I was not the Innle, or "Seeker," of beastlegend, but I had been called by that title now in too many strange circumstances to reject it outright. Nonetheless, I sometimes wondered why, desiring freedom from humans, beasts would want a human savior.

"One does not want a tree or the sky, but they are. No more do beasts desire a funaga to lead them. But we accept/know/see what is/will be. Unlike the funaga always asking whywhywhy," Maruman sent rudely. "Funaga-li rushrush body and mind here/there/otherwhere to prove they exist."

I made no response other than to give the old cat's intrusive probe a mental shove to shift it outside my mindshield, much as I sometimes pushed him from my lap when my knees had grown stiff from his weight. But he was right. We humans did seem to love our busyness for its own sake. Possibly it was the nature of our kind, for though our thoughts did flurry here and there, from that frenzy came whatever shaped us.

I smiled at myself wryly, for was I not guilty now of another human trait, which was to take ourselves too seriously, ever devising clever ways to prove to ourselves that all we do is vital simply because we do it?

My smile faded, for it came to me that this very characteristic was responsible for the doom that the Beforetimers had brought to their world. "Their" world—I always found it difficult to think of them as our ancestors, even though all who live in the time after the Great White were descended from the survivors of the holocaust and dwell in what little remains habitable of their world.

What we knew of them was incomplete and difficult to understand, being gleaned from ruinous bits and pieces left over from their time, most of it utterly disconnected from whatever context gave it meaning. We knew that they were very numerous and had divided themselves into a number of great nations. We knew their civilization had spanned the world and they had ruthlessly used nature for their gain and their amusement, to the detriment of all nonhumans.

We knew from the Teknoguild's researches that they had created machines that enabled them to think with incredible speed, fly and speak from one land to another, and build their cities of shining towers. This ability to make machines whose powers exceeded their own had been the secret of their might, but it had led them into folly, for they had made weaponmachines that had finally put an end to all their terrible cleverness.

I wondered what had possessed them to create the means of their own doom. How had they not lived in terror that the machines would be used? The Teknoguildmaster Garth said it was pride that led them to create such things and believe they could control them, but that did not explain *why* to my satisfaction. For their wars, Rushton said. To be sure they would win. But what good was a weapon that destroyed everything, including its user? There could be no winner in such a game. Yet they had made them and used them, and so had they severed themselves from us and become naught by the mythical beings of stories and nightmares.

Some said it did not matter that our memory of them was fragmented and fantastical, since their time was gone forever, along with all they wrought.

I wished that were truly so.

Chilled by where my pondering had brought me, I folded Dameon's letter into my pocket, arched my back to stretch the ache from it, and gazed about the company beginning at last to assemble. I could see only the parts of them that faced the fire, and at first glance it seemed that disjointed fragments of people and beasts were about me. Things that held the light caught my eye: the gleaming gold of the Beastspeaking guild-master's armband; the shining curls of the empath-enhancer Freya; the pale shimmer of Avra's mane and ear tips; and the ruff of the white ridgeback she-dog that sat between them.

I studied her with interest. The ridgeback had come to the mountains at the melting of the wintertime snow that each year blocked the narrow trail connecting us to the rest of the Land. She had led a great limping horde of half-starved domestic animals. One of the coercers on duty at the pass had notified Obernewtyn of their approach, and Avra had hastened out to meet the unlikely company.

The mountain pony explained that Obernewtyn was a secret refuge for humans and beasts. The newcomers could find food and healing there, and other help if they wanted it. At first, the travelers had refused the invitation, patently dismayed to learn that the freerunning barud the white she-dog had promised them was occupied by humans. Avra had explained mildly that the humans who dwelt in the valley did not interfere with them. As the travelers were exhausted and in need of food and treatment, she argued persuasively, they might just as well come to Obernewtyn and see for themselves.

It was the Beastspeaking guildmaster, Alad, who told me their story. They had all come from a farm just below the Gelfort Range. One day, the white ridgeback, Smoke, had turned on her master and killed him. Then she had convinced the other animals to come with her to seek the fabled freerunning barud.

It was a remarkable journey they had made, all the more

because the beasts had no survival skills, being bred and reared by humans. But for the will and determination of the she-dog, they would doubtless have been recaptured or killed by wild beasts, or they would have perished simply because of their inability to shelter and feed themselves. She had made them travel at night, fighting off predators, hunting for food, and forcing those who could not eat meat to forage for roots and grains to sustain them. When they would have given up, she drove them with threats that she would eat them if they fell by the wayside. Arriving in the White Valley at last, they managed to eke out a bare existence waiting for the pass to thaw.

After their initial disappointment, the beasts began to see that Obernewtyn was not like any funaga place they had known. They were nursed back to health by our healers, and they learned the fingerspeech devised by the rebel Brydda Llewellyn, through which humans could mimic the gestures and movements that animals used to communicate at the most rudimentary level. When Avra finally offered the choice of remaining and working as free beasts and members of Obernewtyn's community, with the right to speak in Beast-guild, many chose to stay. For those few who wanted to leave, the Beastguild appointed teachers to show them how to survive in the wild.

The ridgeback had been among those who stayed, though she was clearly capable of fending for herself.

Without intending it, I reached out to her with my mind. Immediately, I felt her awareness of me, but before I could address her mind, it spat out a rush of images that flowed so fast it took my breath away.

I saw a man cut the throat of a cow. The red line at its throat was like a gaping mouth, and when the beast fell, a bloody froth stained the snowy ground. I heard the keening anguish of its newborn calf and felt the departing mindforce of the dying cow brush me, felt the sweet sigh of its farewell to her calf and the watching dog. The man turned to lift the tottering calf's head back, baring its throat, and I felt the hot, terrifying fluidity of the dog's fury roar through her veins.

I tried to deflect her rage, but to my helpless horror, it drove down like a dark fist into the very deepest part of my mind, where my most lethal ability lay coiled and almost forgotten.

I felt her surprise as it stirred.

"No!" I cried in my mind, and thrust her violently from me.

I stared across the fire pit into her eyes, which were so pale a blue as to be almost colorless.

"The master-li killed the bovine and would have killed her calf because it lacked an ear," she sent in a powerful mental voice. "I do not know why. All beasts know not all of a kind are born alike/exact. None can know what darkness/madness drives the funaga."

"Why did you show that to me?" I sent, shaken to the depths of myself by the hot, hungry power that she had almost roused.

She ignored my question, sending, "Oldstories tell that the Innle who will lead beasts to freedom from the funaga has the power to kill by will alone."

"I have that power, but I do not use it," I temporized.

"I felt/smelled the use of it on you."

"Once only. Knowledge of it first came when the life of my mate was in danger, and I used it to save him. But not now/nevermore."

The dog gave the mental equivalent of a shrug. "It is nature to defend one's mate. It is nature for some beasts to kill and for others to be killed. The funaga are meateaters, and killing is nature for them, but they seldom hunt their meat with courage. They trap/breed/chain/fence until the killing, which is done without respect/dignity. Beasts eat flesh, but the funaga do what no beast would. Funaga eat freedom."

"No funaga here eats flesh. We/I think it is unnature for our kind of funaga to kill for any reason. Is it not unnature for your kind to kill in revenge/anger? Nature wills beasts to kill for food/protect the young. That cow was not your kind."

"She was not. I am unnatured, as are all beasts who dwell with the funaga-li. I am what the master/funaga-li made of me."

"Why did you come here?" I asked. "Why do you stay?"

She turned her pale eyes on me. "I came to seek my death."

"We all journey toward the longsleep, for that is where the road of life leads," Gahltha sent, his cool mental probe cutting between us. "But now Avra would speak, and we must listen."

As the black horse moved to stand behind me, I reached up to lay my hand against his long neck, disturbed by the white dog's chilly pronouncement. The pulse of Gahltha's blood beat soothingly against my palm, muted by his shaggy winter coat. The she-dog could not know it, but upon his arrival at Obernewtyn, Gahltha had shared her hatred of humans. Much had befallen him since then that had humbled him and soothed his rage, and he had appointed himself my guardian whenever I was away from Obernewtyn. Despite a hostile beginning, we have grown very close.

Avra began to address the beastmerge, and I noticed Alad lean near to Freya to translate softly. Though she could sense the emotions of beasts and communicate her feelings to them, Freya was no beastspeaker. If it was not beastmerge, Avra would, out of courtesy, use the signal language, but it was clumsy and limited compared to mindspeech. As it was, Avra left Freya to Alad and spoke mind-to-mind with the rest of us.

"Greetings. We welcome to this merge ElspethInnle, Alad Beastspeaking guildmaster, and Freya. Greetings also to those beasts who come new to this barud." Her gentle eyes fell to Smoke. "You have come far. We are glad/enriched by your coming." Then, to my astonishment, she asked if the dog wished to lead the Beastguild.

I saw the look of dismay on Alad's face, but none of the animals seemed even surprised.

"The whitecanine is strong-minded," Gahltha sent privately to me. "More than Avra, and so she offers her place. It is the beastway for the weak to yield to the strong."

"I will not lead," the she-dog responded gravely to Avra, "but I will stand with/by you."

Now there was a reaction. Gahltha sent that with these words, the she-dog had virtually appointed herself Avra's second-in-command.

The mare ignored the murmurous buzz and merely inclined her head gracefully. "Let it be that you will always run by me. Be strong when I falter. Lead if I fall."

"I will run by/with you, lead if you fall, but I think you will not, for the heartfire burns bright in you. I will be a gladshield to it."

Even I knew that this was a very fine compliment, and Gahltha snorted softly in pride, for Avra was his mate.

"I name you Rasial, if you will accept my naming," Avra sent. "Cast off the funaga leashname."

The white dog bowed her great head, and Gahltha told me with some amusement that the word literally meant "white shield" in human speech but could also be interpreted to mean "silver tongue."

"Enough sweetsaying," Maruman sent in irritation. "Speak less and say more."

There was a ripple of sound from the assembled company that was akin to laughter in humans.

"Peace, yelloweyes," Avra sent gently. "Things should not be said in haste, for swiftsaying means littlethinking."

She went on to speak of the truce among beasts that existed within the walls of Obernewtyn and asked that those not present be reminded that any who would hunt must do so beyond the barud walls.

One of the younger horses sent that Obernewtyn was becoming crowded, and before long they would have to turn beasts away.

"Before that day, Innle will lead us from this place to the freerunning barud where no funaga dwell," a little goat sent piously.

Some of the animals looked at me fleetingly, and to my discomfort, Alad gave me an amused grimace. He knew that Maruman had named me Innle, but he had no reason to believe I was the hero of that name foretold in beastlegend.

The merge moved on to discuss farms where beasts were raised in large numbers for butchering, and a mental cry went up to rescue those condemned to such places.

"I would speak, who am newnamed Rasial," the she-dog sent, and a respectful silence met her scything mental voice. "To save one beast or ten is useless. More will be bred to take their place. Avra has told me that you have a network of beasts throughout this land and that you perform rescues of beasts. We must use this network to destroy these deathfarms."

I agreed that the deathfarms should be targeted but warned

that open sabotage would rouse the fury of the Council.

"If they learned beasts had worked against them, they would rise up in fear and rage and destroy many beasts, and those that did not die would be chained and punished."

"Do you say we should not act against the deathfarms?" one of the younger horses demanded with some anger.

"I say only that your sabotage/rescues must seem mischance with no one to blame, beast or funaga."

I offered the help of the Farseeker guild, but there was a murmur of discontent at this. Some of the animals muttered that I was implying they could not act without human help. I pointed out that every human rescue and expedition we had undertaken had been accomplished with the help of beasts, so why should beasts not be repaid with our assistance?

Avra spoke then of gelding, and the meeting fell into uproar, for the practice of rendering beasts incapable of bearing young was horrendous to all of them. Freya rose and, using the signal language, explained that her father had been a horse trader. She had traveled about the Land with him before they parted company and had seen horses gelded.

"Beasts are bred for selling by the funaga-li, who desire strength or what they think of as the beauty of a certain color or other attributes. They think of breeding as an art."

Avra questioned Freya closely about the beast sales, learning they were held in the upper lowlands during harvest season and were attended by many hundreds of folk who traveled from as far away as the west coast. Once sold, most equines were gelded so that breeding could be controlled by the Council. I was interested to hear that pureblood gypsies also attended these harvest fairs but would buy only ungelded beasts and paid very high prices for them.

Rasial asked how one distinguished a Council funaga-li

from another funaga, but no animal could answer. I sent that there was no way to tell, for Councilmen were merely powerful humans descended from those who had united to take control of the Land after the Great White. Their original aim had been to establish order, which later grew into a determination that humans would not again go the way of the Beforetimers.

"Do they not?" the she-dog asked bitterly.

"They do, who most claim to prevent it," Alad sent sadly. "But we here at Obernewtyn oppose them and so do many funaga who are not Talented. If the Council fell, things might be different."

"If funaga fight funaga, whoever wins will still be funaga," Rasial sent.

They began talking about which beasts should labor in what manner during the planting season at Obernewtyn. It went on so long that I fell asleep.

The night was darker than any night I had known, and silent but for the sound of liquid dripping into liquid.

Then the sun came near to rising above a distant horizon, and I saw by the dawn's gray light that I was standing on a high, rocky plateau. Below the place where I stood, trackless Blacklands stretched on all sides.

I heard a cry in the distance and saw something rise above the horizon. It flew, and yet no bird was ever made that size or shape. I squinted my eyes and thought it looked red.

Could it possibly be a red-plumed Agyllian—those which Landfolk call *Guanette birds* and which Maruman called *oldOnes*—the very birds that now guided me in my destined task to destroy the Beforetime weaponmachines?

"It is no bird."

I looked down to find Maruman standing beside me, swishing his tail back and forth and gazing at the horizon. I knew now that I was dreaming, for he was in a shape he often took when he entered my dreams of his own will—far larger and stronger than in his true form, with slash marks on his coat. He looked very similar to those great cats that Before-time books called *tygers*.

"Mayhap this dream form is truer than that other shape I bear," Maruman sent, and he let out a roar that seemed to shake the stone under us.

"It is louder, in any case," I sent. "What are you doing in my dream?"

"The oldOnes sent me. They say you must not walk dreamtrails without me, ElspethInnle. I must guard you on them, as Gahltha guards your waking trails."

"I do not walk the dreamtrails. I do not even know how to find them. I am only dozing a little and dreaming aimlessly."

"Dreams may have purposes the dreamer cannot fathom. They are gateways to dreamtrails and may lead also to longsleep," Maruman sent. "Wake now and be safe."

"Soon," I told him. "Do you know what that was, flying above the horizon? You said it wasn't a bird."

"Is great winged beast, and its madness goes out from it along dreamtrails like a wind that shudders all it touches. Do not think of it, for doing so will summon it."

"Haven't I already summoned the beast, since it was in my dream?"

"You did not summon me, yet I came. Dreams touch other dreams, and things may travel from one to the other unbidden. That beast rides its madness like it rides the air, and it enters into those dreams which draw its notice—as will yours, now you think of it."

"I don't understand. How did I draw its notice in the first place? How could I have been thinking of its before I saw it?"

"Perhaps it thinks of you," he responded, but distantly, as if his mind wandered elsewhere.

I felt my arm being shaken, and all at once I was awake. Alad was smiling apologetically down at me, and behind him the yard was almost empty. Little remained of the fire but a few glowing coals in the pit.

"The merge is over, Elspeth," he said.

I rubbed my eyes and shook my head to restore my wits. "I wanted to hear what went on, but I did not sleep well last night."

"Do not apologize. I have slept ill of late, too. Maruman is wisest of us."

The old cat was still sleeping. Now I could see him in the ember glow. He looked very small and frail, and his whiskers shone gray.

"He walks the dreamtrails, as is his wont," Gahltha sent, coming over with Avra. "Do not fear for him, ElspethInnle, for he has long walked those strange ways."

"I am wakeful. I will watch over the yelloweyes," Avra offered.

I glanced at the mare's swollen belly and did not wonder at her wakefulness. She had to be very near to foaling.

"Will you walk back to the house with me?" Freya asked diffidently.

I nodded, and we left the courtyard just as a light snow began to fall.

✦ 2 ✦

WE ENTERED THE gate to the greenthorn maze that separated the main buildings of Obernewtyn from its farm and fields, walking somewhat awkwardly beside each other on the narrow track that ran between two thick-packed banks of snow. The nights were still painfully cold. I pulled my coat around me and sank my face into the collar.

Our progress was noisy, for the ground was covered in a crust of ice that cracked loudly when it was broken. For some way, we did not speak but only watched where we walked. It was very dark, and aside from the possibility of slipping, greenthorn stings were unpleasant.

Fresh snow fell like a dusting of flour on the black earth and on the evergreen foliage of the bushes flanking either side of us. The moon rose when we were halfway through the maze, and our shadows appeared on the path before us, deep blue and sharp edged. There was less need to watch our steps so intently, and Freya asked, "Do you miss Rushton?"

"He only just left, so it is less a matter of missing him than knowing I will miss him," I said wryly. "Certainly I already miss him as Master of Obernewtyn."

"I suppose it is no pleasure to have to stand in his stead," Freya said. "I would not like the responsibility."

"I doubt Rushton likes the responsibility of being master here, if it comes to that."

"But he *is* Master of Obernewtyn, and it is not his nature to question what is," Freya murmured. She knew him well because she had spent much time trying to help Rushton to reach his latent Talent.

I glanced sideways at the empath-enhancer, and it struck me that something was troubling her. My instinct was not to pry, yet this rose out of my discomfort with emotions. I had always found them cursed awkward things, but these days I was trying to be as receptive as a nonempath could be. The fact that I had noticed Freya's mood proved that at least I was honing my awareness somewhat. Nevertheless, I struggled a little with my own reticence before speaking. "Are you happy here?"

A fleeting smile bestowed on her plain features a quicksilver beauty. "If I could not be happy here, then I am incapable of it."

"And yet?" I sounded abrupt rather than sympathetic and regretted my clumsiness.

Freya sighed and blinked snowflakes from her lashes. "When Avra asked me to speak about those days traveling with my father, it all came back to me."

Freya's father sold her because her gift for soothing horses—the very Talent by which he had made his livelihood—had caused the Council to mutter of the black arts.

"Many poisons rise at night and seep away by morning," I said.

We came in mutual silence to the end of the maze path and parted in the cobbled area beyond its gate. The snow had stopped falling and was melting on the stones as I entered the Farseekers' wing of Obernewtyn. Mounting the stairs to my turret room, I felt as if I would sleep for a year.

Yet it seemed but a few minutes before Ceirwan was wak-

496

ing me with a tray of hot tea and toasted bread, and a list of matters to be dealt with at the Farseeker meeting to take place that evening after nightmeal.

"I thought ye mun want to go through th' agenda an' add a few things after last night's beastmerge," he said. "I'll pick th' list up later." I nodded sleepily, and he fussed about for a time with papers and the fire before opening the door to go. Maruman entered as he left, slinking across the room and leaping onto the window ledge.

I rose and splashed my face with icy water, then brought my tray to the ledge. Maruman refused any of my food, saying he had drunk his fill on the farms.

I ate, looking out upon the patch of garden clasped within the elbow of the rambling west wing of Obernewtyn. Over it, I could see a segment of the gray stone wall that surrounded our land, and past that, because the land sloped up, the mass of the forest that lay around us in the mountain valley. Most of the trees were still bare, and above them rose the high mountains—shoulder upon shoulder of them, still clad in their wintertime pelt and seeming almost to float in the sky.

They looked so pure and untouched, and yet the snow concealed the streaks of blackened earth left by the holocaust poisons, where still, centuries after, nothing could grow. In many places, the poisons were so virulent as to sear and blister the flesh at a touch, and more than the briefest exposure to them ensured a painful death. The world was full of such tainted places, some vast beyond imagining.

Maruman reached out a lazy paw and batted like a kitten at a strand of my hair caught up by the wind. I felt a rush of tenderness for him but resisted the urge to run my fingers over his soft belly fur, for he little liked to be petted as if he were a tame beast.

Thinking of beasts reminded me of Dameon's letter. In it, he urged me to press Alad to send a beastspeaker to Sador to teach humans and beasts there Brydda's fingerspeech. Unfortunately, the empath knew only a little of the signals and movements that made up the language, as it was ill designed for a blind man's use.

I ought to have mentioned Dameon's request at the beast-merge, I thought, and sighed. So much time was spent in meetings and merges, and in hurrying to yet another meeting to speak of what had been decided at the one before.

I pulled my shawl tighter, enjoying the delicate pink-gold quality of the light. It contained the promise of the brief, sweet season of spring. Each year, I both desired and dreaded the end of wintertime and the thawing of the pass that was our only access to the rest of the Land, for though it meant the end of the bitter cold, it also meant we were again accessible to our enemies.

It was the fear that we might be found and attacked by the Council that had led us the previous year to seek an alliance with their sworn enemies, a Landwide network of rebels. They had largely rejected us as freaks and mutants, so we had tried to prove our worthiness as battle companions, only to demonstrate to the rebels and to ourselves that our Talents did not incline to aggression or violence.

This had been a revelation, and instead of lamenting our inability to be warriors, we had rejoiced, determined to henceforth concentrate our resources and abilities on seeking nonaggressive means of defending ourselves from the Council.

We had parted from the rebels without anger, and I had been sure that we would see Brydda Llewellyn from time to time. Not only because he was our friend, but also because his parents had moved to Obernewtyn. But none of us had known what to make of his missive requesting that Rushton meet with the rebels in Sutrium. Rushton had gone out of friendship and curiosity, and because a journey to Sutrium was an opportunity to talk to the coercer Domick.

Domick had been changed terribly by his work as our spy within the Councilcourt, for in this role, he had been forced to witness and accept torture and other horrors. He had become strange and remote and had severed himself from his bond-mate, the Healer ward Kella. Just before the wintertime, we had received a letter in which he formally withdrew from the Coercer guild and from Obernewtyn, saying he could not accept our new oath of nonviolence. "It would be like a lamb declaring to a pack of savage wolves that he was a pacifist. What do the wolves care!"

Despite his estrangement from us, Domick had continued to send regular messages about matters he uncovered in his spying. I suspected he kept Brydda informed, too, for he had always respected the big rebel. But his messages had grown more and more cryptic.

None of us who had seen Domick in recent times could doubt that he needed healing. He had become a living symbol of what it meant to act against our natures. Rushton intended to bring him back to Obernewtyn, but I did not think Domick would come.

Thinking of Rushton made me feel his absence, despite what I had said to Freya. I missed him, not in the same way as I missed Dameon, but as if I hungered for food or water or some other essential need of life.

Rushton would be amused to hear himself compared to bread or water, and the thought of his laughter assuaged some of my longing for him. He would understand my missing Dameon, for they had been close friends. So much so that

Rushton had seemed to understand, far more than I, why Dameon had chosen to remain in Sador when we left to return to Obernewtyn.

I felt a sudden coldness, for the sun had shifted as I sat there. I pulled my shawl about me and resumed my seat by the hearth. Ceirwan had lit a little blaze to warm the chill from the stones, and I added a few sticks of wood. Then I took Dameon's thick letter and flattened it on my knees, and once again the dry whisper of my fingers over the paper rose into the air.

These Sadorians have memories that go back beyond the Great White. They are not passed on as written words in books but as spoken chants. This is a risky way of saving memories, it seems to me. But Sadorians do not believe the past should be remembered too well. The Temple overguardian says that if it is adored overmuch, the present is deemed less important.

I suspect this philosophy of holding lightly to the past arose from the Sadorians' own history. Their ancestors came from some distant place called Gadfia, where a savage Lud was worshipped. The Gadfians thought that if they were killed fighting for their Lud, they would be taken directly to dwell with him in splendor. Since there were many of them and they were very poor, I have no doubt heaven often seemed more attractive than life. Perhaps for this reason they held life very cheap. The only reason humans existed was to worship Lud and to force others to worship him, so men were counted important because they were warriors. Women were only the means of getting sons. They were considered much as the unTalents of our Land think of beasts and were owned utterly by the man to whom their father gave them. Daughters were considered worthless except as material for barter or to seal alliances, and many were killed.

Eventually, a group of defiant women and the men who dared aid them fled and journeyed to the desert country where they now dwell. They feared pursuit, so they dwelt as nomads to ensure they could no more be sieged or tracked than could the grains of sand that shift on the side of the desert dunes. I think much of their philosophy of leaving the earth untouched grew out of their fear of being followed. But their beliefs are no less profound for all that. They came to love the desert's barren emptiness, because there were no marks of human dominance on it.

In the end, it was the Great White that prevented immediate pursuit. The Sadorians think of it almost as the saving of them, because Sador was virtually untouched, though lands on all sides of it were laid waste. Unlike the Land, Sador was completely isolated by Blacklands and mountains and sea. No refugees came there, and they lived untroubled by the outer world. The Sadorians think of that time, which we call the Age of Chaos, as a golden time, but their chants reveal that they suffered internal struggles. They split into tribes, and there were skirmishes and a number of bloody engagements and then something worse. It seems there was a Beforetime weapon of some description, either found by the Sadorians or brought with them when they fled Gadfia, and this was used to devastating effect.

Left alone, the Sadorians may have gone the way of the very Gadfians they had fled. But their isolation was not to last. Eventually, during the one season that the tribes converged on the coast for fishing purposes, they were descended upon by five ships full of Gadfian warriors.

The Sadorians were completely unprepared. Many were killed, mostly men, and over a hundred women stolen. But the invaders had underestimated the Sadorians, for the tribes managed to prevent one of the ships from leaving, and they used this as a pattern to build two of their own. Eventually, the newly united Sadorians took warriors from each tribe and set off in search of the Gadfian settlement. They found the Land at this time, but for months all else they saw was Blacklands, including what had been Gadfia.

The Sadorians at last found small settlements along the coast, separated by Blacklands. A raid was made on one of them, and the Sadorians learned that these settlements were called New Gadfia. The men there were desperate for sons to carry on their holy war, for since the Great White, they had been unable to conceive healthy children—and as a result, they had beaten or stoned their own women to death for imagined offenses against Lud.

Of course, both the men and the women of Gadfia had been afflicted by the poisons of the Great White, so the stolen Sadorian women had also produced deformed babies. Unable to accept that their own monstrous seed was to blame, the men decided that Lud was offended by their use of unbelievers. The Sadorian women who had not been slain must be "instructed" in the faith. The birth of a deformed baby was taken as proof that Lud had rejected the mother. Already, many had been killed along with their poor, misshapen babies.

Horrified, the Sadorians attacked the three largest settlements on three consecutive nights and took them without losing a single person. They tried the leaders before a court of women and carried out executions. The Sadorians continued to plunder the smaller settlements, *until they had rescued every last surviving Sadorian, and more women besides, many of whom were pregnant.*

They returned to Templeport in triumph almost two years after they had first set out. The gravid women could not travel, and so the cliffs, riddled with caves and tunnels, became the first and only permanent dwelling in Sador. All of the children born of the stolen women were deformed and many died. Those who did not were cared for tenderly and later became the first Temple guardians.

Now I wonder if the slaver Salamander sells human cargo to whoever remains in New Gadfia, for the Sadorians did not destroy all the settlements nor kill all the men. Of course, lacking children, they ought long ago to have died out, but what if they gave up stealing women and bought children instead, to raise as their own? As Gadfians? The thought chills me.

I stopped reading, for a vision of the Farseeker ward, Matthew, rose in my mind. Dameon had been thinking of him as he bent over the page, and a wave of sadness flowed through me. Matthew's abduction by slavers had been a grievous blow, and my only consolation was that, though I mourned him, he was not dead.

I read on, but to my disappointment, Dameon wrote no more about slavery.

Elspeth, there are times when I am lost in these people and their lives. I work alongside the Temple guardians, caring for the sick, aware of the tragic irony that they themselves are dying slowly. Fian is sometimes shocked to see their deformities, and his emotional reactions tell me some are truly dreadful. I do not see them. I know the

*guardians only by their gentle hands or soft voices, and so
they are fair to me. Fian says that after a little, he cannot
see ugliness in them either, but I do not wonder why they
keep themselves covered when they move among outsiders.
Even now that they have lost interest in Sador, the Herders
might be driven by their fear of mutants to force the Council
to attack the Earthtemple if they learned the guardians are
all deformed. I have still not been able to find out why it is
so. Guardians are celibate by choice and so do not bear
children, which means the deformities cannot be hereditary.*

*Their recent history is one of gentleness and wisdom,
and this is due at least in part to the influence of a woman
they rescued from the New Gadfians—whom they call
Kasanda. She was very ill when they brought her to Sador,
for she was not young and had been savagely beaten over
and over. Not for failing to bear a normal child—she was
too old for that—but for defending the women. I wish I
could learn more of her. She was no Gadfian; that much is
clear. She had a profound effect on the Sadorians, teaching
them to heal even as they healed her, but whence came the
knowledge she taught them of healing and of other things?
What did she say to unite the tribes and draw them finally
away from the warlike path of their ancestors, and how did
she convince them to establish the cliff caves as the
Earthtemple? For that was her idea as well. The Sadorians
will not speak of her to me, and I do not know why, for they
are entirely open about all else. I have even been taken to
their precious spice groves.*

He went on to describe the immense trees and the many
uses of the spice they produced. I let my fingers slide over the
long description, eager for more of the mysterious Kasanda.

In the labyrinthine tunnels of the Temple the previous year, I had been shown a chamber that housed a series of relief carvings of the Beforetime made by this Kasanda. Seeing them, I had understood for the first time that the Great White had not been a terrible accident but the inevitable conclusion to the arrogant, greedy, self-centered age of the Beforetimers.

The stone carvings had been true works of art, but I had been struck by their resemblance to the *wood* carvings on the front doors to Obernewtyn and wished the latter had not been burned, so I could compare them. I had intended to look into their history, but more immediate matters had always demanded my attention.

"It is your path/purpose to bring the funagaglarsh to the longsleep, ElspethInnle," Maruman interrupted the flow of my thoughts pointedly. *Glarsh* was the beast thoughtsymbol for "machine." I felt there was reproach in his single yellow eye.

"I have sworn to find the glarsh and bring them to the longsleep, but the oldOnes have bid me wait," I sent.

Maruman merely laid his chin on one paw and closed his eye.

I shrugged. I needed no reminder of the dark road I must walk, for it was foretold that if I failed, one would come whose destiny was to resurrect the Beforetime weaponmachines and their deadly potential, bringing the poor, battered world to a final doom. I could not imagine why this Destroyer would wish to unmake the world, since it must mean his own doom as well. Perhaps, like the Gadfian fanatics Dameon had spoken of, he believed his reward would come after death.

Or maybe he was no more captain of his fate than I of mine.

✦ 3 ✦

"ROLAND BEGAN IT," Ceirwan said over his shoulder as he preceded me down the narrow spiral of stairs. "He accused Miryum of pursuin' a selfish vision of glory to th' detriment of Obernewtyn an' said she mun as well be takin' coin from th' Council fer her work against us."

"He *said* that?" I muttered, but I did not doubt it. Roland was blunt and choleric at the best of times.

"Miryum asked if he was calling her a traitor, and he said he was calling her a fool but that she was too stupid to realize it. She said she pursued glory in order to make unTalented folk revere Misfits. You know how pompous she can be these days. . . ."

I knew. Since our return from Sador, we had applied ourselves to the problem of rendering ourselves less abhorrent to the unTalented folk of the Land, in the hope that they would someday come to accept us. Each guild had found its own means of approaching the matter.

The Empath guild had decided that they would use their abilities wherever they traveled to encourage people to feel compassion for others. More dramatically, they and the coercers had worked together to manipulate dreams so that unTalented people could momentarily experience life as hunted and reviled Misfits. During the last guildmerge, there had been a long discussion about the nature of dreams and

506

whether or not manipulating them was any more immoral than writing a song about events that had passed, reshaping them for effect. The matter was yet unresolved, but it had become a favored topic of debate.

The Coercer guild had begun creating teaching entertainments for unTalented children using simple songs and jokes, good puppetry, and acrobatics, which made use of their hard-won physical skills. The few times they had so far performed, they had disguised themselves as halfbreed gypsies and called themselves *magi*. Unlike true gypsy performances, the magi show had hidden depth; beneath the jokes and stories there was always some subtle lesson designed to make the audience examine their prejudices.

Miryum had devised her own way of changing people's thinking after reading a Beforetime book about warriors who rode about their land performing noble deeds. Inspired by these knights, who had lived by a system of ethics called *chivalry*, Miryum had begun riding out regularly wearing a black mask, performing good deeds, and preaching her code of chivalry to anyone who would listen. Before long, several of the younger and more volatile coercers, chafing under our new vow of pacifism, had joined Miryum's expeditions.

No one had done anything at first, in the hope that her zeal would fade. But gossip about her eventually reached even Sutrium, and a warning came from Domick that the Council was becoming interested in talk of the mysterious coercer-knights.

Ceirwan and I came onto a narrow path that ran from the kitchen garden to the maze courtyard, and we heard Roland bellowing. "Blasted woman. You will see us all dead with your antics!"

Coming round the corner, I had a clear view of the craggy

Healer guildmaster glaring ferociously at Miryum. Behind the stocky Coercer guilden were two of her coercer-knights, identifiable by the black scarves around their necks that doubled as masks. Beside Roland stood the Healer ward, Kella, a long-suffering look on her delicate features. A group of goggling youngsters stood around them.

"What is going on?" I demanded.

Roland jabbed his head toward me. "You try to make her see sense!" he growled. "She dares to claim that she is doing no worse than my healers in galloping about the Land playing the heroine!"

"Do you say we should not help people in need?" Miryum asked frostily.

"I am saying you might consider the value of a little discretion!" Roland shouted.

"To be discreet would defeat our purpose," the Coercer guilden said with composure.

"You are naive beyond belief," Roland said.

"Miryum." I intervened firmly before the Healer guildmaster gave up on words and throttled the coercer. "Is it not true that at the last guildmerge, the coercers agreed to restrain the activities of the knights, given that they could cause the Council to resurrect its plan to set up a soldierguard outpost in the highlands?"

"Gevan agreed to that suggestion, not the knights," Miryum said.

"Are your blasted knights not coercers, who should obey their guildmaster? Or do you think to replace him?" Roland raged.

Miryum did not rise to the jibe. "I do not wish to take Gevan's place, but my philosophy and that of my fellow knights sits uneasily within the charter of the Coercer guild.

I do not wish to undermine the guild's work, but more is needed to change the status of Misfits than teaching plays. If people fear us because they see us as superior to themselves, we must ensure they know that we will use our abilities for the betterment of all who dwell in the Land."

Roland almost danced with fury. "Gevan's plays are subtle, and people will not resist what he teaches because they do not know they are being taught. But your performances are as delicate as a hammer blow! Not only that, but they also indicate that we see ourselves as an elite. Do you think that will incline people to look on us with favor?"

"The people we aid are genuinely grateful," Miryum said with rather touching dignity.

I could not help but admire her aplomb, but like Roland, I thought exaggerated heroics far too simple an approach to an old and complex problem.

"Miryum," I said sternly. "Gevan is guildmaster of the coercers, and in your guild's name, he made an undertaking to Rushton. As a coercer sworn to that guild, and an office bearer within it, you are bound by its rulings. Are you not also bound by your own code of chivalry, which demands that your word be as enduring as stone?"

Miryum was silent, and the color rose slowly in her cheeks. "You are right," she said simply. "We will not ride out again until this matter is resolved." She bowed to me and then to Roland, and departed, followed by the two other coercer-knights.

"Say what ye will of Miryum, but this code of hers bestows great dignity," Ceirwan murmured as the children drifted back to their games.

Roland gave the Farseeker guilden a black look before stalking away.

"What on earth started it this time?" I sighed.

"Roland went into Darthnor and was questioned by a rabble of miners as to whether he had seen this band of murderin' masked rebels sent out by Henry Druid," Kella said softly.

"But Henry Druid is dead!" I said, taken aback. The rebel Herder priest had perished in the White Valley in a terrible firestorm that destroyed most of his followers along with his secret encampment. "Where would such rumors come from?"

"I dinna ken, but Roland is right in sayin' it will make things difficult in the highlands if people start becomin' jumpy," Ceirwan said.

A young teknoguilder had been among those watching the confrontation. I called him over before he could leave and asked if he or others of his guild had noticed anyone snooping about the White Valley. The Druid's encampment there had been secret, but there had been rumors aplenty. If there were soldierguards in the highlands looking for him, that was where they would go.

The teknoguilder said that he had not heard of anyone wandering around, but that in any case Garth had most of them in the city under Tor. They had learned that the Reichler Clinic had kept its most important records in the basement of the building that housed the Reception Center.

I was puzzled. "Then they are lost to us still, for the bottom of the building is under water and earth. Unless Garth has found some way to transform people into fish."

The teknoguilder opened his mouth, then shut it again. But I received a clear visual image of someone swimming beneath the water.

"What is Garth up to?" Ceirwan sent to me, for he had seen it, too.

I told the teknoguilder to let his guildmaster know that I would call on him in the Teknoguild cave network that afternoon. But he flushed and said apologetically that Garth had gone down to Tor three days before. This surprised me, because Garth seldom left the caves just outside Obernewtyn's wall.

As the teknoguilder hurried away, I turned to speak to Kella, but she had slipped away. "That girl is like a wraith," I muttered.

"She grieves," Ceirwan said gently.

My fleeting annoyance at Kella dissolved into pity, for I knew Ceirwan was right. The young healer still mourned the end of her relationship with the estranged coercer Domick.

This brought me back to the Coercer guild, for I felt sure that it was Domick's defection that had paved the way for Miryum and her knights to consider forming a splinter group. The guild had always been somewhat troubled because of the mind-controlling aspects of its members' Talent, and the shift to pacifism had been more difficult for them than any other.

More than ever I missed Dameon, for he had the gift of seeing to the heart of such impossible disputes.

Taking a side corridor, I came out of the building onto a path that ran along the west side of Obernewtyn. A wall constructed too close to the other side of the path meant that almost no sun reached the narrow walkway; as a consequence there were still deep drifts of snow along each side. The path would originally have been used by servitors bringing wood to the front-room fires, but there were now more convenient ways in and out.

The wall enclosed the area that had once held Ariel's wolf pens. Bars and gates had long since been removed and an herb garden planted in the enclosure, but it still had a grim feel, as if tainted by the cruelness of our nemesis long after he had left Obernewtyn and become a Herder agent.

I went straight through the garden and out a gate on the other side of the enclosure to a flat patch of grass, as gray and dull as an old man's hair. This was where Ariel had tortured the wolves and half-wolves he had bred. "Training them," he had called it, curling his pretty lip.

On the other side of the grass was the outer wall that surrounded all of Obernewtyn. A scraggy line of dead-looking shrubs ran parallel with it, continuing to the greenthorn wall of the maze. At a glance, it looked as if the maze and outer wall were one, but in fact there was a hidden lane between them.

I pushed my way through the shrubs to where a weathered bench stood against the wall. Behind it, a creeper hung in spidery tendrils that spring would transform into a thick, shiny tapestry. Beside the bench grew a small rosebush that offered the deepest crimson blooms right through spring and summerdays and even the Days of Rain, if it was not allowed to run to seed.

I did not know how the seat or the rosebush came to be there, and I could not ask without giving away my secret retreat. Only Maruman knew of it. Sitting, I realized I had half hoped the old cat would be here, but no doubt the snowdrifts had put him off.

I never thought of Maruman as intruding on my solitude. He spent so much time with his mind curled around mine that my shield took him as part of my own self and would not keep him out unless I concentrated on excluding him.

The lane was choked with weed and tough shrubs gone wild, but cleared, it would make a swifter route to the farms than the maze path, which had been designed to confuse. The maze was now clearly marked by carved posts, and some sections of the wall had been removed for ease of access on the other side of Obernewtyn, but it was still slow going during wintertime when the snow clogged every turn. My conscience pricked me, and I knew that I should mention the path. It would mean the loss of my retreat. But, after all, it was only a matter of time before one of the teknoguilders discovered it. A greater number of them explored the grounds of Obernewtyn more than even the submerged ruinous city beneath Tor.

Ever since we had stumbled on the Reichler Clinic Reception Center in the Beforetime city, the Teknoguild had been obsessed with learning more about it. We knew that the clinic had been a Beforetime organization devoted to researching Talented Misfits, then called *paranormals.* This was proof that Talents existed before the Great White and were a natural development in human evolution. Our amazement was redoubled when we discovered that the Reichler Clinic had been founded by a woman whose second name was the same as Rushton's—Hannah Seraphim. Hannah had had some dealings with a man named Jacob Obernewtyn, who we believed had constructed a home, the ruins of which provided the foundations of our current Obernewtyn.

The real Reichler Clinic, too, had been sited in our valley, although there had been an earlier Reichler Clinic in a different location, which had been destroyed. The establishment of a "reception center" in the city under Tor had been a ploy to divert the attention of the Beforetime organization called *Govamen,* which had developed a sinister interest in the use of paranormal abilities as weapons. The Reception Center served to distribute what Beforetimers named *misinformation.*

Anyone who tested paranormal was immediately spirited away to the real Reichler Clinic.

Hannah and her people had begun publicly to falsify their researches, claiming the abilities they had detected were weak and generally uncontrollable, but Govamen continued its surveillance. This led Hannah to undertake her own inquiries, whereupon she discovered that the destruction of their original headquarters had been contrived by Govamen to cover the kidnapping of a group of paranormals. The Teknoguild had found documents detailing the prisoners' whereabouts and the various experiments performed upon them—documents that indicated Hannah had had a spy within Govamen. The last clear information the Teknoguild had compiled suggested Hannah had intended to rescue the paranormals. Whether or not she had done so, we had no idea, for the time of the holocaust was nigh.

Most of us accepted that we would probably never know the true history of the Reichler Clinic, and Rushton openly disapproved of time being spent on historical puzzles. He could not see any point in learning more about Beforetimers, because they were all dead and gone. What did it matter if he was related to Hannah Seraphim? It neither helped nor hindered us in our struggle to find a legitimate place in the Land.

But the teknoguilders continued to pick at the mystery like an old scab. Suddenly I had no doubt Garth had deliberately timed his trip to the White Valley to coincide with Rushton's absence. Which meant the Teknoguildmaster was almost certainly up to something he knew Rushton would not like.

There was a crackling sound, and I glanced up to see the Futuretell guildmistress, Maryon, push her way through the shrubbery. Her expression was so blankly preoccupied that I thought she was in a trance. But then her eyes widened in surprise.

"Elspeth! I was just thinkin' of ye."

I did not much like hearing that. I was all too conscious that I appeared often in the futureteller's inner journeying.

"Do ye mind if I sit by ye?" she asked.

"Of course not," I lied.

Sitting down, she gave me a wry sideways look, and I was uncomfortably reminded that she discomposed me.

I did not dislike her. I did not know her well enough for that, and this fact alone said much, for I had met Maryon at the same time as I had met Roland, Alad, and Gevan. I thought of the latter three as friends but not Maryon. I had almost hated her when the young Herder novice Jik was taken on an expedition at her futuretelling insistence, only to die. In addition, she had allowed the young empath Dragon to follow me secretly to Sutrium, knowing this would lead to her current comatose state. All because her visions demanded it.

It was this quality of remoteness from the things she foresaw that disturbed me. Possibly I was being unfair, for many novice futuretellers lamented their helplessness in the face of what they saw. Older futuretellers were silent, perhaps becoming resigned to what they had learned could not be changed. Certainly it seemed that futureteller remoteness was not a personal trait but part of what they did with their minds and Talent. Like all coercers and some farseekers, futuretellers used the Misfit ability known as *deep-probing.* But whereas coercivity used a deep probe to dig into the unconscious of other minds and bend another's will, futuretellers delved only into their *own* minds.

Their training focused on enabling them to descend through the conscious and subconscious layers of their own minds, all the while shielding themselves at the levels where minds lose individual focus. Here, dreams and longings both dark and bright swim like exotic fish in a thick, seductive soup. A descending mental probe could easily become lost in a memory or a nightmare or some delicious imagining. It was their goal, and I sometimes thought their addiction, to descend to the point where the barriers between all minds faded. This was the level at which myth moved from mind to mind and generation to generation. Beneath this level lay the glittering mindstream, which called to all minds to merge and surrender their individuality. This surrender would mean individual death, but twice in my life I had come so dangerously close to it as to hear the unearthly loveliness of its call-song to a final merging.

Futuretellers spent a good deal of their time hovering above the mindstream, and perhaps it was the effort of resisting the longing for that lovely death that caused their remoteness. They saw much as they hovered in this way, for the mindstream threw up bubbles of memory from the minds absorbed. Occasionally, bubbles of what *would be* rose, since the stream contained both all that had been and could be, but it was not the express purpose of their delving to see into the future. The futuretellers' desire, as far as I understood it, was to know themselves deeply and, through this, to know life. They claimed that thinking intensely of a matter at this level drew thoughts from the mindstream of others, long dead, who had pondered the same questions. They believed that knowledge could be best obtained on the brink of dissolution of the individual.

Their purposes seemed strange to me, and oddly self-centered, but it was not my place to judge them. Indeed, their ability to penetrate minds had profoundly enabled them to draw healers deeper than they could go alone, and on more than one occasion, this had saved someone's life or sanity.

"I have sometimes wondered who made this wee garden," Maryon said, breaking her silence at last. It seemed an innocuous enough comment, but I was not deceived. Futuretellers took charge of the dreariest household duties, because the monotony allowed their minds to soar. If Maryon was talking of gardens, I had no doubt her attention was on something far more complex.

"I suppose it must have been part of Lukas Seraphim's design," I said blandly.

"No. The maze existed before Lukas Seraphim had Obernewtyn built. He simply had the maze replanted."

I stared at her in surprise, for I had always assumed the maze had been the creation of Obernewtyn's reclusive first master.

"I dreamed of Rushton last night," Maryon went on, and now her eyes were distant and fey. "I saw him swimmin' in dark waters. . . ."

Her words made me think of the image I had seen in the young teknoguilder's mind. "Was it a true dream?"

She gave me a long look. "If ye mean was he truly in th' water, I can nowt say. Of late, clear futuretellin' has been difficult."

"Difficult?" I echoed.

"It happens from time to time that there are disturbances. Lately, much of our futuretellin' is of th' past. 'Tis as if a storm rages above th' mindstream, wrenching up what has been an' drivin' it at us like rain afore wind."

"Do you think Rushton is in danger?" I pressed worriedly.

Maryon sighed. "I said nowt of danger."

I debated telling her of the picture I had seen in the young

517

teknoguilder's mind that so disquietingly paralleled her dream, but she went on before I could speak.

"I have been wantin' to speak wi' ye on th' subject of dreams," she said. "All folk dream, an' most sometimes dream true whether they ken it or no. Even unTalents. We recognize a true dream because it recurs. If it comes only once, whether or no it feels true, we dinna mull on it. But lately I have come to believe that true dreams can recur in a number of people, rather than in only one, an' so my guild has begun to create dreamscapes that show th' patterns of our dreams. T'would make the dreamscapes more accurate to include the dreams of those of other guilds, but it is impractical for my guild to record all dreams. Dell suggests that each guild keep its own dream journal."

"So long as it does not require another meeting," I said. Maryon's mouth curved into a rare smile, but almost immediately a breeze blew up out of the stillness, and as the bare branches of the trees clattered together, the futureteller gazed up at them, her expression once again distant and serious. My own vague apprehensions hovered and refused to settle.

I wondered if Maryon knew anything about the dreamtrails Maruman spoke of and, on impulse, asked. She gave me a long look. "*Dreamtrails* is too tamish a name fer them. It suggests some windin', pleasant path to wander on. *Dreamrapids*, I would sooner call them, or *perilous dreamslopes*."

"Have you traveled on them, then?" I persisted.

"Traveled? I would nowt say so. I have stumbled onto them by accident, an' sometimes I have been affrighted by encounters on them. But I will nowt speak more of them. There are many things better left unsaid. Ye'd ken that well enow, Elspeth Gordie."

Her eyes were again on my face, as pure and direct as a

beam of sunlight. I felt suffocated under her intense regard. I told myself that she must once have been a child, playing and singing, a girl who had loved and hated and feared as passionately as half-grown folk do when trying out their emotions. But it was impossible to imagine her as anything but a lofty futureteller. Wanting to break through her shell, I asked how she had come to Obernewtyn.

She lifted her dark brows, unperturbed by the personal nature of my question. "A man desired me, but I rejected him. I had foreseen he was cruel an' violent behind his honeyed mouth an' pretty eyes an' made th' mistake of sayin' so aloud. He gathered friends an' tried to take me. My family defended me an' died fer it. I saw my sister killed by his hand, an' my wits left me. I remembered nothin' more until one day I woke here. I found that I had been condemned defective, but rather than sendin' me to th' Councilfarm, I was sent to Obernewtyn. Or sold mebbe."

Maryon told her story without any visible emotion, but I could not blame her for that. I had seen my parents slain in front of my eyes, and when I thought of it, something in me turned to stone, too. More gently, I asked if her family had known she was a futureteller.

She answered in the same clear, distant tone. "I had no name then fer what I was. I nivver considered that seeing what would come from time to time made me Misfit any more than peepin' round a corner ahead of friends. My family knew of it an' did not speak of it as evil but only warned me nowt to tell anyone. We were seldom among folk, as our farm was remote, so there was little danger of givin' myself away. Th' night before they attacked our farm, I had a nightmare that my sister would die. It was so terrible, I could nowt believe it. I was even ashamed of it, because I had quarreled with her over a length of ribbon th' day before an' thought th' dream some nastiness of mine comin' out. If I had spoken, my father would have acted, fer he trusted my visions mebbe more than me. I could have saved them, but I didna speak."

"I'm sorry," I said inadequately.

She looked at me calmly. "There is no need fer sorrowin'. I ken now that my nowt speakin' out back then was fer a reason, as was th' death of my family. I dinna ken what that reason is, but I have faith that life's purpose is finer an' more profound than th' purposes of me or my sister or father, an' I serve it with my whole self willingly. That is what bein' a futureteller means."

She was silent for a time; then suddenly she said, "'Tis cold here without th' sun. I will go in now."

I watched her depart and found myself pitying her for the first time. I could see that she had given herself to fate as its instrument as a way of bearing the destruction of her family. Possibly, learning to see things in the way she did now was all that had enabled her to return to her senses.

I shivered, realizing she was right. The breeze had developed a sharp edge. Pulling my coat tight around me, I rose and made my way back inside.

✦ 4 ✦

"CAN'T YOU HOLD on!" Zarak gasped aloud.

The young coercer beside him glared. "I could, if you would keep your mindprobe still and not shake it all over the place. It's like trying to hold a fish!"

"I wasn't shaking!" Zarak sent indignantly.

"You were," Aras sent gravely.

"You were, son," Khuria murmured in his quiet rasp of a voice.

Zarak reddened. Ignoring his father, he turned on Aras furiously, but Ceirwan forestalled his outburst by directing them all to make their minds quiet. "There is no point in accusations," he sent firmly. "It didn't work, an' that's that. I ken yer all tired. So am I, but let's try one last time an' concentrate very hard."

"I *was*," Zarak cried aloud.

"There is no point trying again unless Zarak can see he was not concentrating and remedy it," Aras sent.

"It's a stupid, impossible idea anyway!" Zarak snarled at her, a tide of red rising in his cheeks. "You think you're so smart!"

At that moment, Freya entered with a gust of wind that slammed the door behind her.

"I'm late," she said.

Ceirwan went to take her by the hands. "It doesna matter

that yer late. It's wonderful that yer here. We were just about to have a last try."

I saw Zarak's mind shape a continuation of his attack on Aras and sent sharply that I would speak with him after the practice. This transformed his anger into alarm, for Ceirwan handled all guild matters except ones considered serious enough to warrant my direct intervention.

The boy's lack of concentration itself was not usual. He had been something of a handful since we had permitted his transfer from the Beastspeaking guild to the Farseekers, but he was not usually given to temperamental outbursts.

Whatever was bothering Zarak, his lack of concentration and his silly refusal to admit it were ill-timed, as they interfered with what was clearly the most promising group we had assembled to attempt Aras's unusual mindmerge. What had come to be named the *whiplash* would be a great achievement if we could ever make it work, for it would enable us to farseek farther than any of us could manage alone or even within a traditional merge, which increased power but not range. Theoretically, Aras's merge could enable us to reach mentally from one end of the Land to the other.

The merge required groups of three to form traditional mindmerges, which would be linked to one another to form a line that could be used as a conduit and directed by a farseeker with coercive abilities. But so far, every attempt to put it into practice had failed. The difficulty was in having each participant hold consciously into both triple and line merges while also making themselves passive enough to be used as a conduit. What kept happening was that the moment they attempted to become passive, the conscious links relaxed their connection, and the whole thing fell apart.

We had been seeking a complementary combination of

minds for over a year, first trying with farseekers and then ranging into all the other guilds. The current merge was the most harmonious yet.

"Let's try again," Ceirwan said. "We'll form up in a circle around Freya." Those attempting the merge had been physically linking in the hope that this might help retain the connection when their consciousness faded.

I was not taking part in the actual merge. I would monitor it. If they succeeded, I would attempt to use them as a conduit.

"Let's begin," Aras said aloud.

Again the triple merges formed, and with Freya's enhancing presence at their center, the links were flawless, even those formed by members of other guilds.

Aras worked to connect the triples into a continuous line. One by one, the triples were joined, and finally Aras came to the team made up of Zarak, the young coercer Hari, and Ceirwan. It was to link into the meld containing Zarak's father, and then from within, Ceirwan would smooth the individual merges into a single long strand.

Whether or not Freya's presence was enhancing my confidence as well, I began to feel we really might manage it at last, for as the last triplet was linked in and Ceirwan began to smooth the merges into a single strand, the line remained stable instead of falling apart at once.

Then Zarak's mind skittered, and the whole thing crumbled again.

"It's not my fault!" Zarak shouted.

"Control yerself," Ceirwan sent sternly. Then he said aloud and more gently, "Dinna let's be disheartened. Th' process was completed fer th' first time, no doubt due to th' encouraging presence of our visitor." Freya smiled wanly. "I am certain we have th' right combination, but it will take time to perfect. We'll meet again in a few days."

Ceirwan thanked those of the other guilds for coming, telling them he would speak with their guildleaders to ensure they would be free henceforth for practices. Zarak's father left last, with a worried glance at his son, who stood mutinously to one side, avoiding his eyes. When only farseekers remained, the guilden directed everyone to take a short break before the guild meeting started.

Then I was alone with a pale-faced Zarak.

"What is the matter with you?" I snapped. "You *know* it was your fault the merge could not hold."

He hung his head.

"I do not blame you for failing the meld, but it was nasty and cowardly to attack Aras, especially when she only spoke the truth."

"She thinks she's so perfect," he said angrily. "I'm sick of her always telling me what to do. She can't even farseek as well as me, and she can hardly coerce at all. I don't know why you would make her into a ward—" He stopped, aghast.

I stared at him coldly. "How did you know that we were considering making Aras a ward?"

"It was . . . I overheard it. I didn't mean to. Lina and I were in that tunnel that runs alongside the main wing and . . . you and Rushton were going past. I heard you tell him that Aras was a brilliant theoretician, and you wanted her to be a ward."

I cursed myself for having failed to sense their presence, but I tended to focus on Rushton's so strongly, I could be somewhat deaf and blind to anything else.

"I'm sorry," Zarak muttered.

"Sorry?" I said icily. "I don't think so. I think you don't

care at all that you violate privacy when you creep about in the walls. I don't think you are sorry about anything except being caught out. Your behavior tonight was abominable, and your reasons for it disgusting. You are jealous of my considering Aras as a ward, and you have no right. She is not a strong farseeker or coercer, as you say, and she would never presume to pretend she is. Unlike you, she is very aware of her limitations, and she strives hard to overcome them. Unlike you, she does not secretly covet wardship. In fact, she refused when I proposed it."

Zarak looked stunned.

"Yes. Because she does not have the conceit to think she deserves it. You might be interested to know that she suggested *you* be made a ward instead."

Zarak paled.

"Had I offered you the wardship, which you so clearly feel you deserve, you would have accepted it without ever wondering if you were worthy. Being gifted as a farseeker and being crossguilded does not qualify you for the position. You must also have a refined sense of responsibility and genuine concern for the guild. You think of nothing but yourself, and you spend too much time involved in Lina's silly pranks."

I stopped, anger threatening to make me cruel. "Go away now. I don't want you at the meeting. Go to the kitchens and tell Javo you are his for two sevendays."

When Ceirwan returned, he frowned. "I could feel yer anger from outside th' hall."

"Zarak learned that I was offering Aras a place as a ward, and he was jealous," I said tightly.

"Ahh. Did ye tell him ye were considerin' him, too?"

"I did not, and his behavior tonight has shown that he's not mature enough."

"I dinna know, Elspeth. Some people need responsibility to grow. I think Zarak will remain a child until he is treated as somethin' else."

My anger faded, for Ceirwan had some small ability to empathise, and if he thought Zarak needed responsibility, maybe he was right.

"Zarak needs th' chance to prove himself to himself." Ceirwan hesitated. "Ye know, part of his problem is that he reminds ye of Matthew. Yer too careful of him, an' somethin' in him knows it an' interprets it as lack of faith."

I stared at Ceirwan, stunned because I realized Zarak *did* remind me of Matthew. Was it true that I had held him back because of my own fear that he would go the same way?

The others filed in for the guild meeting. When they were seated, Ceirwan made an opening speech mentioning various matters, then told them of Maryon's request for a record of dreams. An elderly woman named Sarn, who had come to us with her pregnant daughter, offered to establish a dream journal for our guild. Next, Ceirwan invited Tomash to deliver a report.

The plump, good-looking Tomash rose, pushing back his dangling mass of black curls. "You asked me to put together all the information we've gathered on the rebels and on the Council in some easily accessible form. I've made a chart." He unrolled a large sheet of paper showing a list of towns and villages in the Land. Beside each was a series of names.

He looked at me. "I ought to begin by telling you all that there are now Councilmen in the highlands."

The hair on my neck rose.

"Where?" I asked.

"In Darthnor, there is Councilman Moss. And in Guanette, another called Bergold."

526

"Honorary Councilmen appointed from among th' locals?" Ceirwan ventured hopefully.

"No. Both came up from Sutrium." He hesitated, and I sensed there was worse to come. "They are both sons of Radost."

Worse than worse, I thought. Radost was the head of the Council.

"They have each been given land to go with their appointments," Tomash went on. "This may be not so much an attempt by the Council to strengthen its control over the high country as a move by Radost to extend the territory he controls. But it seems the catalyst at least was the rumor of Miryum's knights."

I suppressed a burst of fury. In fairness, I knew Miryum's deeds alone would not have caused Radost to send his sons to the high country, but they had certainly given him a good excuse. "The number of soldierguards they brought might give us a clue as to what they mean to do," I said.

"Enoch said that both have small bands," Tomash said. "Ten armsmen each."

"Doesn't sound too threatening," I said. "But we had better keep an eye on them."

Ceirwan made a note, then nodded to Tomash to continue.

"Radost is one of three Councilmen ruling in Sutrium. He has a daughter as well as the two sons, but our information says she is estranged. Most Councilmen have children or other blood relatives as official assistants. So far, there is no Council representation set up in Arandelft or Rangorn. They are administered by the representatives from Kinraide. And we don't know the name of the Councilman or the assistants on Norseland. Everyone else is named on the chart. Here"— he unrolled another sheet showing a map of the Land covered in blue and red circles—"these blue circles indicate each Councilman's personal farm holdings. The red circles are Councilfarms."

We pored over chart and map with interest. It was the first time I had seen clearly how the Council divided up the Land, and I was amazed that almost all farm and grazing land belonged to individual Councilmen or to the Council as a body.

Tomash laid aside the map and returned to his chart. "Now, beside each Councilman are the names of rebel leaders in the same area. I've also noted whether the rebels there tend to align with Malik in Guanette or Bodera in Sutrium. There have been some interesting developments in the west coast bloc among Radek in Morganna, Cassell in Halfmoon Bay, and Serba in Port Oran—"

"Wait," I said. "I thought Madellin ran the Port Oran rebel group."

Tomash nodded. "He did, but he has taken ill. Serba is his daughter. She assumed his place and has become very popular. In fact, it looks as if she might achieve what her father desired and unite the west coast bloc at last."

"Radek and Cassell agree?"

"I don't know about Radek, but she's to bond with Cassell," Tomash said.

"Madellin probably proposed th' bondin' as a way of unitin' th' bloc finally," Ceirwan murmured.

I was not so sure. Cassell had struck me as a clever, strongwilled man. "Perhaps the idea was Cassell's."

"They might be in love," Aras said rather shyly.

Ceirwan smiled at her. "So they might. What a terrible lot of cynics we are nowt to think of that first."

"All of our information about the west coast is sketchy at best," Tomash said. "I will try to fill the gaps."

"You have done a wonderful job," I said warmly. "This is invaluable. We will present it to the next guildmerge and let it do the rounds of the guilds to see if anyone has anything else to offer before you make a fair copy."

Tomash nodded and sat down.

"Wila?" Ceirwan sent. "Ye have a report due about th' Herder Faction?"

The woman rose. "I'm afraid I have not been so successful as Tomash," she said diffidently. "I have some information, but I am expecting more. I would like to defer presenting my report until the next meeting."

I nodded. I had scarcely expected much, for the Herders were notoriously secretive. Rising, I made my own report of the beastmerge; then Ceirwan dealt quickly with the few minor matters remaining. We ended the meeting just as the nightmeal bell rang.

"Have you seen Maruman about?" I asked Ceirwan. Usually, the old cat joined me during guild meetings.

"Isn't he asleep in your turret room?" Ceirwan asked.

"Excuse me, Guildmistress," Sarn said. "I saw him in the Healer hall just before I came here."

"The Healer hall? Now what was he doing there?" I muttered.

The Healer hall was actually two long, narrow rooms joined at one end by a chamber with an enormous hearth. Both of the long rooms were filled with beds, and there were small sleeping chambers running off from one side.

Walking past empty beds, I noticed a healer and the Futuretell ward Dell sunk in concentration over the sickly babe born to Sarn's daughter. Dell's presence indicated that things were not going well. I passed quietly into the connecting room, where a group of healers were seated in front of the fire on low stools, talking softly and plaiting what I took to be some sort of herb garlands.

As I approached them, a tiny pile I had taken for another garland stirred at the foot of an empty bed, and two huge orange eyes opened to survey me. I realized it was an owlet when the diminutive creature hooted in fright.

Kader turned to greet me, smiling. "Welcome, Guild-mistress. You have just missed Roland."

"I wanted to see Kella, actually."

"She has gone to fetch some more dried reeds. We are plaiting prize wreaths for the moon fair." He gestured at a basket full of leafy coronets. "Shall I go and get her?"

"No. I'll sit with Dragon until she returns." I glanced over to Dragon's bed and saw with shock that it was empty.

"She has been moved," Kader said, his smile fading. He ushered me down one of the long rooms and into a smaller chamber, where a candle burned low on a table beside the sole bed. The red-gold mass of Dragon's hair, spread over the white pillow, glowed in the dim light. I was startled to see that Maruman was nestled in it. The sight of two I loved so dearly lying together brought me close to tears.

Kader had strong empathic abilities as well as being a healer; he merely touched my arm gently and withdrew.

Kella believed Dragon's long coma was the result of Dragon's decision to retreat into the blocked part of her mind and resolve what was hidden there. If she had not done so, the healer argued, the block would have burst, filling her mind with poisons and rendering her defective.

If Kella was right, Dragon was inside her own mind, reliving over and over again whatever it was that had caused her to forget her past and trying to resolve it. One of us might have entered her mind and tried to help, but Dragon's Talent was so strong that it would almost certainly have trapped any intruder inside the recurring memory until Dragon recovered.

If she recovered. The brutal truth was that she might wake in a day or a year or ten years—or she might never wake.

Sitting on a low stool by the bed, I took her limp hand in mine. It was white and the nails pale and long. I remembered how she had reached out a filthy paw to touch my clean skin the first time we had managed to communicate. I envisaged her playing with Maruman and brushing Gahltha's coat, or gazing at Matthew with an adoration he could not return. Again I saw her fall to the ground as my augmented mind-probe smashed through her mental shield, knocking her unconscious in my desperation to keep her safe from soldierguards.

It is my fault she is like this, I thought bleakly. Yet another occasion on which the lethal killing power of my mind, even muted, had shown its malignancy.

I looked into her pale, still face and fought a blur of tears, resting my head on her hand.

"Elspeth?"

I sat up to find Kella gazing down at me concernedly, the owlet perched on her shoulder.

"I started to fall asleep," I muttered, surreptitiously brushing tears from my cheeks.

Kella gazed down at Dragon. "I sit with her a lot," she murmured. "I can't bear to see her lying here alone. I'm glad Maruman has taken to keeping her company."

I looked at the old cat, wondering uneasily what had brought him to her bed. Dragon had no ability at all to communicate with beasts, though they were drawn to her and had given her a name of their own—*mornir*, which meant "brightmane."

"Kader said you had to move her."

"Any healing is difficult with her near," the healer said. "When you begin to focus on your mind and shape a probe, she . . . well, her mind pulls at you. Like an undercurrent in a river. You feel yourself being tugged toward her." She shrugged. "It is easy enough to resist, of course, but it's impossible at the same time to focus properly on healing. It's like having someone shouting numbers at you when you are trying to add up."

"Is she getting worse?"

"I don't know," Kella said. "She could be getting worse, or maybe this is a prelude to her getting better."

Hope must have shown in my eyes, for she went on. "You should not make too much of it, Elspeth, because she has been like this before. There is a strong pull, and then her mind just suddenly goes passive again. I think she gets like this when she is close to resolving her memories, but something goes wrong and she has to start all over again."

I noticed Maruman beginning to twitch.

"Chasing mice in his dreams, I suppose," Kella said fondly. "No doubt he is faster in them than in real life these days. He's not supposed to kill anything within the grounds, but I know he hunts mice when he thinks no one notices. I do not think he catches many, though."

But in his dreams, Maruman is not slow nor old nor even really a cat, I thought. I shaped a probe to dip into his dreaming mind, but there was a muted cry of pain from the other end of the hall.

"The child is failing," Kella murmured. "I fear we are losing him."

"Poor little baby," I said, and sat back down.

Kella sat beside me. "Sometimes it seems that life is nothing but struggle and sorrow, and yet we spend our time remembering moments in which we experienced joy and believing they are what life is meant to be."

"You are thinking of Domick," I said, giving up any attempt at subtlety, since I was so bad at it.

"I never *stop* thinking of him," Kella admitted dully. "I accept he no longer wants or needs me as a woman. When I was with him, I thought that meant I had become unlovable. But you were right in bringing me away, for I now see his loss of love is no true judgment on me—it is a symptom of his sickening spirit. Because I loved him, I failed him as a healer. But I would not fail now. I have been thinking of it more and more, and I might as well tell you I have spoken to Roland about going to Sutrium again."

I wanted to argue, but I could not. Would I be any different if Rushton were in trouble? Kella smiled a little. "Now you look exactly as Roland did when I told him."

I stiffened as Ceirwan farsent me to say that the pass watch warned of riders headed for Obernewtyn at a fast gallop. At least two riders were Sadorian by their attire.

"What is it?" Kella asked.

"I have to go. Ceirwan sends that riders are coming up the pass." Kella looked frightened, and I laughed. "Don't worry. Ceirwan says some of them are Sadorians."

Kella's eyes blazed with delight. "Dameon must be home!"

533

✦ 5 ✦

Fortunately, Ceirwan had shielded his farseeking, otherwise the steps of Obernewtyn would have been crowded with people longing to welcome the Empath guildmaster home. As it was, only Gevan, Kella, Ceirwan, and I were at the front doors to greet him and his escort.

Because it was a moonless night, it took some moments to discern the Sadorian tribeswoman Jakoby and her daughter, Bruna. They dismounted and bowed low, palms against their chests, while the teknoguilder Fian leapt from his mount and hurried across, beaming with pleasure.

"It is good to see ye all. My only regret is that it's too dark to see th' mountains. Ye have no idea how often I have missed them these last months."

"I am glad to see you again, Elspeth Gordie," Jakoby said warmly.

"And I you," I said. I had forgotten how tall she was. "I did not imagine you would accompany Dameon home yourself."

"Where is he?" Kella asked, squinting into the darkness, where two other riders dismounted.

"Dameon did not come," the tribeswoman answered. "I will let Fian explain, but it is Dameon's own choosing. Is there somewhere we can water and feed the horses before we talk further?"

Gevan looked somewhat embarrassed. "Lady, I am sorry to

say this, but here we do not think of horses as belonging to people; in fact, if they desire it, we must offer your beasts asylum."

She burst out laughing. "I think you will find them willing to return to Sador." She turned to me. "Dameon will have let you know that I am hoping to bring back a beastspeaker with us when we return to the desert lands—one who knows the fingerspeech better than the asura. There have been changes in Sador that he will not have had time to relate."

"Asura?" Ceirwan echoed.

"That's what they call Dameon in Sador, an' it's partly why he's nowt here," Fian offered.

"Wait," I said. "This is not a story for a drafty front step. You have ridden far, and as you say, the beasts must be shown to the farms, where they can find food and water."

"I will take them," Ceirwan offered.

Jakoby thanked him and turned to the other riders, two Sadorian men. "Harad, you and Straaka will go with the horses." She turned back to me, the beaded strands of her midnight hair clinking together.

"There is no need to send your men. The Beastspeaking guild will take good care of the beasts," Gevan said.

"I send them only because it would pain them not to go. I will tell you more of these matters inside. I dare say we need a wash, but I would be glad to drink and eat first if you can tolerate our travel sweat."

I said heating water for a bath would take some time in any case. "We had best go somewhere quiet, and I'll have something brought to us. In the dining halls, one look at Fian and we would have no peace until all knew why Dameon had not come."

"I will go and organize some food," Kella said. "But it will not be long before the rumor is out."

"We will have a little respite, at least, while rumor pursues fact," I said.

Gevan and I led Fian, Bruna, and her mother through the central hall and down a passage to a small room where once I had waited to see Madam Vega after my arrival at Obernewtyn. That was now only a shadowy memory overlaid with many others.

"You said Dameon chose not to come?" I said the moment Jakoby had laid aside her dusty travel coat. I was unable to ignore the prompting of my heart any longer.

"He wrote ye a letter, Elspeth," Fian said. "I have it for ye. But I can guess th' gist of it is that th' Sadorians are makin' him an honorary tribesman, an' he can't come until th' ceremonies are complete."

"It is rarely done," Jakoby said, suddenly sounding grave.

I did not know what to say. Apart from the honor of it, it would cement our alliance with the Sadorians. But I was bitterly disappointed.

"The ceremonies and celebrations last a month," Jakoby said gently.

Fian rummaged in his pockets and withdrew a rolled sheet of paper. "There are two letters. One for ye, an' t'other fer Miky an' Angina. Have ye sent for Rushton?"

I took the letter and thrust it into my pocket with the same resolution as I pushed my disappointment to the back of my mind. "Rushton has gone to Sutrium. Brydda sent a message asking him to meet with the rebels," I said.

The teknoguilder blinked at me in bemusement. "With th' rebels? Why?"

"That is what I would like to know."

"Perhaps I can guess," Jakoby said. "There was much discussion about your people after you left, for the rebels were beginning to realize very clearly what sort of leader they would have if Malik took charge of the rebellion. No one said it aloud, but it was clear few liked the idea of being ruled by him after the war. Your offer, along with your superior behavior, became increasingly attractive. And Malik knew it. He may have defeated you, but maybe he showed his nature a little too explicitly, and that has gone against him."

I never doubted that the rebels would succeed in their struggle to overthrow the Council, having witnessed firsthand the raw ferocity and single-minded drive of Malik and his followers. I had not needed the Battlegames verdict, delivered by the Sadorians, to know the rebels were gifted warriors—if the ability to wage war could ever truly be called a gift. They surely did not need us to win, but in accepting our aid, they would have gained victory more swiftly and gently.

But men like Malik did not want a gentle victory.

"We will learn soon enough what transpires with these rebels," Bruna said firmly.

Jakoby's eyes rested enigmatically on her daughter. "Bruna felt she must accompany me to Sutrium."

Bruna lifted her chin a little but said nothing.

"The tribes still mean to take part in the rebellion?" I asked.

"We promised aid and broke bread with the rebels over it, and so we must aid them if they desire it, although now that the Council has lost interest in possessing Sador, we no longer have any real need to involve ourselves. The Council's new indifference is Dameon's doing, and that is partly why he is to be made a tribesman." Jakoby's golden eyes were more catlike than ever when she smiled. "It never occurred to us to allow Landfolk to see how difficult it is to harvest spice, for we did not understand that much of their desire to control

Sador lay in a greed to increase its production. Dameon also told us that the Council believed there were great fertile valleys that we were concealing beyond the desert."

Dameon had told me some of this in a letter, but not all. "What did you do?"

"We took them on a kar-avan tour," Jakoby said, grinning. "Within days of their return, they took ship for the Land. I do not think they will be back."

"Tell her about th' horses," Fian urged.

Jakoby nodded and smiled again. "Dameon will have told you that he taught us what he could of the fingerspeech, but being blind, he could not tell us how to understand beasts. That was Fian's task, though he warned us he was not very good. Nevertheless, we were able for the first time to communicate with beasts. We had thought them less than humans, but quickly we understood that most are easily equal to humans in intelligence. Our previous treatment of beasts seemed base and terrible in the light of this, and our community changed almost overnight. Ownership of animals is now called slavery in Sador, and I am sure Dameon has told you enough of our past for you to understand our hatred of that trade. Henceforth, horses and their riders are comrades and allies, as equal as man and woman."

"What about horses who don't want to be ridden?"

"They need not. But life is difficult in Sador for human and beast alike, and we survive only by our unity. Seeing this, most horses are content to remain among us, as long as they are free to come and go as they please. Even so, some do not choose a rider and have formed a wild pack to defend themselves from the giant cats that prowl the desert."

"Do they regard the tame horses as traitors?"

Jakoby shrugged. "I do not know enough animal speech to

ask such a question, but the wild herd leader has just proposed that all horses run with the herd as foals, then submit themselves to a period of learning with humans, after which they may either choose a rider or return to the herd. We decided we would no longer buy horses from the Land, but the herd leader has asked that, in repayment for the occasional labor of horses, a certain number of enslaved beasts be brought from the greenlands and freed in Sador each season.

"Next year, we will make a treaty of honor with the herd leader. This makes it imperative for us to learn more of the fingerspeech so that there will be no misunderstandings between our kinds."

"What about other beasts?" Gevan asked.

"We hope to use the fingerspeech with them, too, in time. The kamuli are as wise as horses, but although they prefer to remain among us, they have no wish for closeness and ask only that we use no rein or whip on them and that we do not take their calves from them. We still hunt wild beasts for meat and for leather, but it has been decided that the tribe will hunt only those that are hunters of men and eaters of meat. Of course, we will not hunt beasts that are pregnant or with young. Some beasts are less wise—chickens are nearly brainless, and snakes reject all approaches. There is a sort of desert dog that is completely insane, and the big desert cats refuse to respond."

There was a clatter at the door, and Kella entered with Katlyn, both bearing laden trays. Gevan made space on a sideboard and helped them lay out bread and cheese, a vegetable slice, and pots of butter and mustard. There were also little pancakes dripping with mountain-clover honey, fruit dumplings dusted with sugar, one of Katlyn's famous preserved berry pies, and a jug of cream.

Jakoby gazed at the food appreciatively, as Katlyn drew a

pottery urn and some mugs from her voluminous apron pockets and poured a measure for the tribeswoman, saying, " 'Tis a fement brewed by my bondmate, Grufyyd."

Jakoby studied her so intently that Katlyn's smile faded. "What is the matter?"

"Nothing is amiss, good woman. I merely saw in your face a flash of another's. It is my guess that you are the mother of Brydda Llewellyn."

Katlyn beamed and agreed that she was. She began to press food on the tribeswoman and her silent daughter, telling them how this or that was cooked or baked. She left only after being assured there was enough for twenty people.

After Katlyn had gone, Kella said, "I went to tell the futuretellers we needed some beds made up, but they had them ready. They foresaw—" Without warning, something flew in the open window and crashed into the wall beside her. With an exclamation, she hurried over and picked up the small owl I had seen earlier on her shoulder.

"I'm sorry," Kella said, tucking the dazed bird into her pocket. "It will follow me in the most exasperating way."

"You speak to birds?" Bruna asked.

"No," Kella laughed. "A nest full of these fell out of a tree, and I fed them until they could fend for themselves. The others have all flown away now, but this one will not go."

"You cannot beastspeak it?" Jakoby asked.

Kella shook her head. "Birds are almost impossible to reach, and in any case, I am not a beastspeaker. I can merely empathise to them a little."

After everyone had eaten their fill, Kella and Fian took the trays away. Jakoby sat back with a groan and belched loudly. "That was a true feast. These greenlands offer a richer harvest than the deserts."

Gevan refilled our mugs and insisted on drinking a toast to Sador. Jakoby responded by drinking one to Obernewtyn. They would happily have gone on, but the jug ran out. We talked a little more of beasts in Sador, and Jakoby told me the Battlegames had been modified to ensure animals were not harmed. If they participated, it was of their choosing, and for this service they might ask a boon or payment. Then she spoke of Dameon. "I think he saw the true beauty of the desert more quickly than those whose eyes see only barren white dunes shimmering in the heat. Dwelling among us, he lived with the desert, and that is a powerful thing. Maybe he will not find it easy to leave."

"We have need of him," I said.

"I do not doubt it. I have never known anyone so strong and yet so gentle."

"I don't look forward to telling everyone that he has not come, truly," I sighed. "The Empath guild has spent many hours preparing special performances to honor him at our moon fair."

"Moon fair . . ." Jakoby frowned. "A celebration of the new moon?"

"No, it is a celebration like the bazaar week after the annual Battlegames," Bruna said, stifling a yawn. "There is feasting and competitions. . . ."

"Since we cannot easily or safely attend fairs, we have our own," I said. "Of course, there are no outside traders or jacks, and competitions are more displays than anything else. But there is feasting and dancing and music and a couple of our own ceremonies."

"Is it permitted that we remain?"

"We would be glad if you would," Gevan said, and I could see he was pleased to think of showing his magi to the Sadorian.

"The moon fair will not take place for a few days," I said. "If Brydda is expecting you . . ."

"I am in no particular haste," Jakoby said easily, but her eyes flicked to her daughter. Bruna was fast asleep, curled like a long, thin cat into the side of a deep armchair. All of the haughtiness had gone out of her, and she looked vulnerable and little more than a child with her fingers curled under her cheek.

"I cannot say as much for my daughter," Jakoby sighed. "It was her suggestion that I should travel in person both here and to Sutrium. She then asked if she could accompany me, to 'learn more of the barbarian customs of Landfolk.' She also professed to be curious to see Obernewtyn with her own eyes, and well she might be, for Dameon has told us much that is fascinating about this valley.

"But underneath all of these fine-sounding reasons, Bruna hungers to see Bodera's son, Dardelan. When they first met, she called him a pale, soft boy more like to a woman than a man, but I think her harsh talk against him hid a sweet barb that he had set in her the first time she beheld him. She would like to tear it out of her, my little wildcat, but such a barb is not easily removed. I think she comes to the Land to show herself Dardelan is unworthy of her, but under that she longs to see him. But if he can love her, what then? Her spirit belongs to the desert, but he must take his father's place in the Land. No matter what comes of this journey, I fear Bruna will suffer . . . and perhaps Dardelan, too."

She sighed again, and I thought that for all she was an accomplished warrior and tribal leader, she was also a worried mother.

She rose then and asked where they were to sleep.

I took her cue and said I would show her. Gevan rose, too,

542

and bid the Sadorian farewell. When Gevan had gone, Jakoby bent to touch Bruna's cheek. The girl woke instantly, reaching instinctively for her knife.

"Come, child," Jakoby said firmly. "We have yet to bathe before we can sleep."

I conducted them to the chamber that had been prepared for them and showed them where the nearby bathing room was. The barrels of water steamed, and Jakoby sighed in pleasure at the sight.

"So much water!"

I had barely taken off my boots in my own chamber when Ceirwan arrived. "I sensed ye were awake, an' I had to tell ye."

"What?"

He grinned, his eyes alight. "One of those two Sadorian men with Jakoby says he is betrothed to Miryum."

"Oh dear," I said, remembering Miryum knocking a Sadorian warrior to the ground because she thought he was making fun of her when he had actually been proposing. The tribesman had later presented her with two horses, and Jakoby had broken the news to us that, by accepting them, the stocky coercer had unknowingly accepted an offer of bonding.

Ceirwan giggled. "I can't wait to see her face."

I was less amused. "Did he bring the horses he gifted her?"

"Zidon an' Faraf. Yes. They both asked to see Innle, an' Alad started tellin' them ye were nowt th' Innle out of beast-legend, but they seemed to ken ye in reality."

I nodded and quickly changed the subject by asking Ceirwan to announce the news of Dameon's delay at midmeal.

Ceirwan sighed. "I might have guessed I would end up havin' to break th' news. Ye ken that in th' Beforetime, they killed messengers bringin' unwelcome tidings."

"That sounds very shortsighted," I said.

The guilden yawned widely. "Well, it is late, an' I am weary."

On the verge of sleep once he had gone, I heard a scratching at my door and Maruman's mental demand to be let in. He was indignant because as he'd slept on Dragon's bed, Kella's owlet had landed on his tail and had tried to carry it off, apparently thinking it was some variety of furry worm.

Suppressing laughter, I patted the bed invitingly. "I missed you today."

That was the nearest I dared come to questioning him about his visits to the Healer hall, but he made no attempt to explain himself. I had known him too long to try asking again and merely shifted over to give him room. The old cat leapt up and coiled himself into the curve of my hip; at the same time, his mind cuddled to mine, ignoring my mindshield.

I lay listening to him snore until I, too, slept.

I was walking through the maze, but it was different—made from some bitter-smelling hedge mounted up on a frame. The mountains in the distance were too steep and jagged to be the mountains ranged about Obernewtyn. Nevertheless, I was trying to get through the maze, because I wanted to look at the doors of Obernewtyn, although a part of me knew they had been destroyed.

Maruman appeared beside me, swishing his tail and yawning to show off his fangs. Muscles rippled along his flank, and the saber markings on his tawny coat gleamed. "You can see the doors if you want," he sent languidly. "They exist still on the dreamtrails."

"Shhh," I hissed, for now I could hear a woman's voice beyond the hedge wall.

Maruman gave an offended growl and faded.

"... can't explain why," the woman said, her words strangely accented. "I just feel as if we should go. Something is going to happen here. Something bad."

"As bad as in Turka?" The voice belonged to a man, and it was sharp with anxiety.

"No. Not that ... but something. We need to go somewhere else."

Suddenly, a nightmarish beast appeared before me, massive and red, tearing through the shrubbery and screaming in fury. Its raking claws barely missed my face as it slashed at me in a swooping pass.

"Beware!" Maruman sent urgently. "It comes again. Wake!"

Instead, I sank and found myself brushing against a memory of walking in the woods with Rushton. It was so pleasant that I allowed myself to be absorbed.

"I love you," he said, and kissed me long and softly on the lips. Then he drew back and looked at me so intently that I felt shy. "Are you sure you do not mind that I am unable to use my Talent?"

I took his face between my hands and kissed him. "I would not reshape you in another mold, else you would be another person."

His green eyes glinted. "I hope you will always feel that way."

Always, I thought, wondering dreamily what it meant for mortal creatures to use such a word.

There was a screaming cry, and the great taloned beast dropped suddenly from the clear sky and plunged toward us.

"Wake!" Maruman sent.

"Look out!" I screamed at Rushton. I threw myself to the

ground, but Rushton did not, and the thing lashed out at him before flying away.

I stared up in horror at his bloodied arm. Rushton swayed and fell to the ground. I had started toward him when Maruman leapt between us in his tyger form.

"Let me go to him!" I screamed.

"He is a dream, but the beast is not. Wake!"

The beast uttered its chilling cry, then plunged, claws outstretched.

Again I sank instinctively, only to find myself drifting in darkness.

I heard a roaring sound and the unearthly singing that told me I was deep enough inside my own mind to hear the mindstream and to feel its pull. I waited passively for its magnetism to equalize with the desire of my mind to rise to consciousness, knowing that I would then not go up or down without exerting will. I did not fear the beast would follow, for it could not do so without risking its own destruction. Perilous safety, though, for the mindstream's lure was so powerful as to tempt me to succumb to its call.

Below, I could now see its silvery flicker. A bubble detached itself from the roiling surface and floated up toward me.

I had no hope of avoiding the memory it contained, and all at once I was in a strange, noisy machine speeding above the earth. There was a young girl in it and beside her a man. I had done enough reading to recognize that they wore Beforetime garb, even if the flying machine they rode in had not made it clear that I was seeing into the past. In front of them was a third man with a strange contraption on his head. He was peering intently out of the bubble that separated us from the air, touching this dial or button. I guessed he was directing the course of the machine. Outside, the sky was very blue and clear, and the sun shone down on a mountainous terrain.

"You can't afford to get mixed up with Tiban fanatics," the man said.

The girl responded hotly. "The Chinon Empire—"

"Have closed themselves off, and they are no concern of ours. That is their choice."

"It wasn't the choice of Tiba to be swallowed up by them. But you don't care about that, do you? You're like everyone else who doesn't care what atrocities the Chinon Empire commits, as long as you don't have to witness them," the girl said with cold fury.

"I'm afraid I'm not a schoolgirl with the leisure to go on peace marches. I can't do anything about what happened hundreds of years ago in Chinon. I am simply doing what I can in practical terms to stop the world from destroying itself."

"Helping to stabilize the balance of terror?" the girl muttered scathingly. "What sort of solution is that? The weapons industry must be beside itself with joy."

"The weapons industry has nothing to do with it. A balance of terror crosses all ideological and religious boundaries. It is the only thing no one can argue with."

"What about these accidents that everyone knows are not accidents?"

The man's face developed a closed look. "You know perfectly well my people have been asked to prepare a program that will eradicate the possibility of such accidents. The Guardian program will have access to all world information sources, and it will be able to evaluate danger swiftly and without bias. If it deems that one country has aggressed on another, it will activate the Balance of Terror unit, and BOT will retaliate, targeting the perpetrators without any country having to make the decision."

"Eye for an eye? What if your precious Guardian makes a mistake?"

"It is far less likely to make a mistake than a human being."

"That's not an answer. And if the Uropan government is designing the computer, it will think as a Uropan would, so it will still be biased."

"The program developers are of all nations, including Gadfia and Chinon, and it has been designed to evaluate and take into account the varying cultural differences. In a sense, the Guardian program will be the very first world citizen. Not only that, but it is also capable of learning, and as time goes on, it will continue to grow and mature. It will be the most sophisticated program ever created, and it will be a buffer between humans and the BOT retaliation unit."

"I suppose it will walk on water as well."

The man gave her an exasperated look. "The World Council believes that Guardian and BOT will protect us from human greed and stupidity."

"Nothing can save us from that. . . ." There was a note of sorrow in the girl's voice, and the older man seemed taken aback.

"Cassy, is it so bad to spend the summer at the institute? The mountains in Old Scotia are very beautiful once you are accustomed to the bareness of them. We can spend some time together hiking, and you can do some sketching. . . ."

"Sure thing," the girl broke in bitterly. "Only you'll be too busy directing your precious projects. What is it you're researching there, anyway? It's not just this Guardian thing. What's with those weird red birds?"

A shutter closed over his eyes. "Forget the birds. You shouldn't have seen them."

"I suppose you're doing some sort of disgusting experiments, dissecting the poor things or spraying perfume in their eyes."

"Don't be absurd. The institute is not a cosmetic laboratory. As far as I know, the birds are part of a genetic research program."

The girl crossed her arms. "Why can't I go to Mericanda with my friends?"

"Your mother does not want you there and neither do I. Especially not in the border region."

"The only thing you two manage to agree on is repressing me as much as possible."

"After the devastation of Raq and Turka, I don't think anyone could be blamed for worrying about the state of the world."

"It's all right for *you* to worry, but when *I* worry, I'm being childish."

The flying machine now hovered over a collection of flat, square buildings, and it began to drop toward a pale circle drawn onto the grass among them.

"This place is a prison," the girl said sullenly.

The older man gave her a strange look.

I felt a pain in my head so sharp it made me cry out, and the dream faded as I rose quickly through the levels of my mind to consciousness.

✦ 6 ✦

I OPENED MY eyes to find Maruman staring balefully into my face. At once the mental pain lessened.

"What is the matter with you?" I sent, sitting up with a groan and rubbing my temples. "You've given me a terrible headache jabbing at my mind like that."

"You desired/wished to wake early," Maruman sent. He began to wash his ears industriously.

I looked out the window. It was still dark but more blue than black, which meant it was nearly dawn. I thought with a shudder of the creature that had flown at me in my dreams. It had seemed so real.

"Beast is real," Maruman sent, ceasing his ablutions to stare at me. "It can kill/wound, but last night it sought only to vent rage."

"On me? Why?"

The cat gave the mental equivalent of a shrug. "Maruman-yelloweyes does not know. Dreambeast screeches/is mad with pain from some old injury/hurt. Lives in fortress with no door."

With a sudden fear, I wondered if it was possibly a form assumed by the H'rayka, but Maruman heard the thought and sent that it was not the Destroyer.

That was some relief, at least. "I dreamed that Rushton was injured by it. . . ."

"He/Rushton-mate was not real. Your memory Rushton only. He cannot be killed/harmed."

Relieved, I climbed out of bed. The flagstones were cold under my bare feet, but the air felt warm and smelled sweet with new growth and blossoms. Suddenly I was eager to be outside when the sun rose. I poured some water into a bowl and washed myself, toweled briskly, and dressed. Maruman leaped onto the windowsill and gazed out.

Brushing my hair, I became aware that Ceirwan was trying to farseek me and hastened to open the door.

"I brought ye a bit of somethin' to eat," he said, maneuvering a small tray past me. "I meant to wake ye on my way up, but yer mind was closed to me."

"Maruman saw to my waking," I said, casting the old cat a wry look.

There was a roll with some cheese, as well as a bowl of egg and milk for Maruman. I took up a steaming mug and sniffed appreciatively.

"Choca. Th' Sadorians brought sacks of it as a gift, an' everyone is to have it with firstmeal this morning. Hopefully it will make them feel better about Dameon not comin'," the guilden said. He sighed. "Well, I had better go back to th' kitchen. The Sadorians might get up early after all, an' I ought to be there to fend off questions so they can eat in peace."

I nodded. "I want you to take them to the farms after they have eaten. Alad can give them a tour and arrange for them to spend time with the beastspeakers, learning more of the fingerspeech. I'm off to Tor soon, but tell Jakoby I will be back by tomorrow evening at the latest."

Ceirwan opened the door, then turned back. "Did ye dream? Ye should write it in th' book afore ye go. . . ."

"I'll start tomorrow," I said, knowing already that I would

have to leave out a good deal of my dreams. "But ask Sarn to make sure everyone else starts filling it in today." I hesitated. "Did you dream last night?"

To my surprise, Ceirwan blushed. "I did, but it is nowt that would need to gan in any dream journal."

I realized then that Maryon might have asked more than she guessed in wanting a record of dreams. After all, many were no more than expressions of private desires.

When he was gone, I farsought Gahltha to ask if it would trouble him to leave Avra when she was so near to foal. He responded wryly that Avra would be glad to see the back of him for a while.

I put Maruman's bowl on the sill, but he stared pointedly at my roll until I took out a slice of cheese and offered it to him. I took up my mug of choca and sipped at the rich, sweet brew. It was hot and burned my lip, so I set it aside to cool. I chafed at the delay, but choca was too rare a pleasure to leave.

I laced my boots and gave more thought to dreams, remembering Maryon saying our maze had been reconstructed from the remnants of an older version. Could that original maze be what I'd seen in my dream? Yet it had been surrounded by unfamiliar mountains.

"Were the people I heard talking in the maze real?" I sent to Maruman, but he did not respond. I puzzled a moment before remembering that I had bluntly shushed him in my dream. I sighed. "I'm sorry I told you to be quiet, Maruman, but tell me, was I remembering something that really happened from the Beforetime, or was it just a dream?"

He lapped at his milk, and I resisted the urge to shake him. "Well, did you mean what you said about being able to show me the doors of Obernewtyn on the dreamtrails?"

Still he did not answer.

"Maruman!" I said aloud and with my mind. He yawned rudely in my direction and began to lick his paw and wash his face with it.

I became sly. "Well, you probably can't do what you boasted, and that's why you are silent," I sent with the faintest suggestion of condescension.

He regarded me coldly. "Maruman knows dreamtrails. Knows where doors are/were."

"You mean your *memory* of the doors," I sent.

"All that is/was/could be can be reached by dreamtrails. Real are things on them," he sent haughtily. But at once his manner changed, and he gave me a long grave look. "Maruman could take/bring/show ElspethInnle. But flying beast may scent/see/seek you."

I frowned. I wanted to have the chance to study the doors again, but my memory of the beast plunging from the sky and savaging Rushton was shudderingly fresh.

I drank some choca pensively. "Could it really hurt me?"

"In dreams/memories, you can be hurt/pained/bruised, but dreamhurts do not become reality. On the dreamtrails, spirit and flesh of dreamer are one. Flying beast is not the only danger. Maybe H'rayka watches for chance to hurt/harm Innle. Watches for moment when Maruman is not watchful/wary."

"But you could show me the doors?" I persisted.

The old cat merely coiled himself into a ball, and I knew there was no use in going on at him. He would raise the matter if he decided to show me the doors, or he would refuse to discuss it again. I did not know whether to be sorry or not. I was certainly in no hurry to risk the dreamtrails. But the likeness between the doors and Kasanda's panels in Sador haunted me.

With a sigh, I finished my choca in a few greedy mouthfuls and sent to Gahltha that I was on my way.

Fian met me in the courtyard that led to the maze path. He confessed he had been lurking in wait. "I saw Ceirwan in th' kitchen, an' he said ye were goin' down to Tor to see Garth," the teknoguilder explained. "Would ye mind if I ride wi' ye? I'm curious to see what they've bin doin'."

Me too, I thought. "Come if you like. I wanted to ask more about your time in Sador anyway. Dameon was well when you left him?"

Fian slipped on the melting crust of snow at the maze's threshold and righted himself before answering. "I have never seen him look better nor be more fit. He spent much more time than I ridin' about on those foul-tempered kamuli. 'Tis a funny thing about Sador. To start with, th' sun is oppressive an' ye can hardly bear it loomin' over ye. But after a time, ye learn to move slow an' to savor th' lovely cool evenin's, an' ye discover th' flowin' robes worn by the Temple guardians are cool and soft. Ye learn to like the way they lick an' flap at ye heels, an' in th' evenin's, the dunes go from bone white to violet an' rosy pink an' deepest blue, an' the tribesfolk's fireside chant songs seem to fly over them. . . ." He fell silent.

"You sound as if you miss it."

He gave me a quick look. "Ye know, I guess I do at that, though if ye'd predicted it when I was there, I'd have denied it. But th' desert gans into yer blood." He laughed. "But still th' mountains are rooted deeper, an' it's glad I am to see them. I am even glad to see a bit of snow, for it dinna fall once in Sador during all th' long wintertime."

Fian's words summoned up my own time in the desert

lands, and I could see them clearly in my mind's eye.

"I've been hearin' all about Miryum's coercer-knights," Fian said.

I groaned. "This Sadorian who claims to be betrothed to Miryum . . ."

"Straaka," Fian said.

"Straaka," I tried. The highlander corrected my pronunciation, rolling the r and lengthening the a sound. "I just can't believe he would regard the few words he said to Miryum as a serious proposal. They had only just met, and she had hit him."

Fian grinned. "No doubt that is why he proposed, for there is a streak of wild in th' tribesfolk that makes them as volatile an' sometimes violent in love as in hate." The highlander sobered. "But Miryum ought to ken that Straaka regards th' proposal as a serious bond. By Sadorian lore, she accepted him. But it's more complicated than that."

"Is that possible?"

"Straaka would ordinarily be here to bring Miryum back to bond with him. But his betrothal gift is now morally repugnant to him."

"The horses?"

"Aye, them. Now th' Sadorians are committed to fair an' equal dealin's between human folk an' beasts, Straaka feels th' giving of them as not only a shame on him but a grievous insult to Miryum. He has brought th' horses here personally—escorted them, he says—because he wants to explain to her why th' gift is withdrawn an' ask what she will have in their place."

"You mean . . ."

"That he expects her to name another gift he can gan to replace th' first, an' it has to be a difficult enough thing to obtain to restore his honor. If she simply spurns him, he will take it

555

that his shame is too great to be wiped away, no matter how she puts it, an' he will have no choice but to kill himself."

I was appalled.

"I'm afraid Miryum is goin' to have to say no in some very clever, tactful way or have th' life of th' fellow on her hands," Fian went on.

I felt like throwing my hands up at that. Miryum was famous for her lack of tact, and the devising of her code of chivalry had made her as absurd on the subject of honor as her suitor was. Straaka would certainly seek Miryum out before I returned from Tor, so the only solution was to take her with me.

I farsent to Ceirwan, who said that he would put it to her that I ought to be guarded.

"Don't encourage her!" I sent, exasperated.

We came to the end of the maze path just as the sun slid free of the mountains. All of the extensive farmlands enclosed by the walls of Obernewtyn were bathed in glistening morning light, and here and there, remaining drifts of snow glowed against the grass.

Fian stopped and drank in the vista with a sigh of appreciation. His eyes traveled lovingly from the orchards on our left to the rich brown fields on our right. Everywhere pale green shoots had pushed through the ground, and leaves on the trees were beginning to unfurl. I had been to the farms only a few days past, yet, all at once, spring seemed to have arrived.

Alad emerged from one of the farm sheds to greet us.

"Greetings, Guildmaster," Fian said. "I am pleased that ye acknowledge my importance by comin' in person to welcome me home."

"Don't get too excited, lad," Alad laughed. "I was keeping an eye out for you, Elspeth. One of Rushton's birds just flew in, and I thought you'd want to know about it at once."

Alad was smiling, so it could not be bad news, yet my heart constricted with anxiety. "What does it say?"

Alad held out a tiny soiled scroll, and I unrolled it and read: "A request made by a friend was gently refused. Leaving today after meeting with Domick. Home by moon fair. R"

I blinked, cursing Maryon for frightening me. "It seems we were right about the rebels wanting us to join them. It will be interesting to hear why when Rushton gets back."

We made our way along the orchard path toward the buildings that both Beast and Beastspeaking guilds used for their merges—four barns built around a paved, open courtyard. Alad brought us into this area, where the fire pit now gaped empty and smoke-streaked. Up one end of the courtyard, a vine-covered trellis formed a natural roof, and I saw that there were trestle tables set up under it, laid with cloths and what were clearly the remnants of a substantial meal. Katlyn and a couple of beastspeakers were collecting mugs and plates on trays.

"What has been going on?" I asked.

Alad grinned. "It's been too long since you worked on the farms, Elspeth. It is seeding time, and today we begin to plant the far fields. The Beastspeaking guild and everyone assigned to us ate a hearty firstmeal before dawn, and they've been hard at work for an hour now. But I daresay there is a morsel of one of Katlyn's pies and some choca left, if you fancied a bite or three."

Fian gazed wistfully at the food. I left him to it and went to collect Gahltha.

Avra whinnied a greeting as I approached. She made a pretty picture of impending motherhood, framed in trees laden with blossom. Gahltha was by her, nuzzling her neck. Someone must have brushed him, for his winter shagginess had given way to the sleek gleam of his summer coat.

Avra nuzzled my hand affectionately, and I stroked her swollen flank and asked how she felt. She seemed very big to me, but I supposed it was because she was a small horse, as free mountain horses tended to be.

"I feel I carry a galloping herd inside me rather than one foal," she sent wearily. "I would that it were done, but the oldmares say it is longer with the first foal."

"You're sure you don't mind me taking Gahltha?"

"Rasial will protect me should I need it, but I have nothing more dangerous to do than eat. But *you* will ride into the lands of the funaga-li. Take care, ElspethInnle."

"We will not go far into them nor be gone long," I assured her. "I doubt any funaga-li will even see us."

She whickered softly in approval and sent that she had found Zidon and Faraf illuminating. "Many beasts say perhaps desert lands are the true freerunning barud. Some equines talk of joining that wild herd."

"Some should go and report back to the rest," I sent. "But we will talk later of this." I gave her a final pat and turned to find Faraf, who had trotted up in the soft grass.

"Greetings, ElspethInnle," she sent softly, her great, dark eyes reverent.

I smiled and reached out to run my fingers through her mane. "I am glad to see you here at last, little sistermind," I sent. "It has been a long journey since first we spoke. I wonder that you left the desert lands, though."

"The funaga there seek/desire fair dealing, but I longed for the greenlands and steephills of my youngdays. It is fair/beautiful here, as you promised/told."

"It is," I sent. "And I am glad you've come." She looked well, though somewhat thin from the ride. That could be healed by a few good days of grazing. But her flanks were savagely scarred from Malik's attacks during the Battlegames, and those marks would never fade. Faraf did not blame me for her injuries, but that only made me blame myself the more.

"Alad beastspeaking guildmaster says you ride this day?"

"We can talk when I return," I promised.

"If you permit, I would ride/go with you."

I thought she probably needed rest more than another ride, but it was not so strenuous a journey to Tor, and I did not have the heart to say no to her.

"Let us begin, then," Gahltha sent.

✦ 7 ✦

By the time we left Obernewtyn, it was far later than I liked, and we were seven riders and eight horses. A number of Miryum's coercer-knights had decided to accompany her, and Ceirwan had farsent to Alad for more horses. The knights had been waiting at the gates, clad nominally as gypsies but also wearing their black scarves. Rather than delay us further, I made no protest.

Miryum knew nothing of Jakoby's arrival, because she had eaten a hasty firstmeal in her chamber when Ceirwan had sent that I wanted her to ride with me. I let Fian explain Dameon's delay and was interested to see that she showed no reaction at learning of the Sadorians' arrival. She had apparently forgotten the strange proposal of the year before, and Fian had tact enough not to blurt it out.

I had hoped to discuss Straaka with the coercer during the ride to Tor, but with her four followers hanging on her every word, it was impossible.

We traversed the stretch of tainted earth just beyond the pass; then the track widened to become the main road, which wended its way right through the Land and down the coast, broke at the Suggredoon, and recommenced on the other side, running all the way to distant Murmroth. In that sense, the road we now rode along was the road to all the Land. I would have preferred to diverge immediately and enter the White

Valley, but the road traversed a high stone spine, which fell away so steeply on the Valley side that we had no choice but to keep to it until there was a safe descent.

Soon we passed the smaller road leading off to Darthnor and its mines. My anxiety increased, for there was now the danger of running into other travelers.

We increased our pace, and I noted with consternation that several of the places where it had once been possible to enter the Valley were now almost cliffs, with crumbling edges. It occurred to me that we might be wise to somehow improve access to the Valley closer to the pass.

Faraf had fallen behind, and glancing back, I noticed she was favoring a leg.

"She tripped/stumbled in a pothole," Gahltha sent as we lingered to allow her to catch up.

"I hinder you," Faraf allowed regretfully.

"Never, little sistermind," I assured her. "I was just about to suggest a stop."

Miryum and one of her knights rode ahead to find a place out of sight of the main road. They returned and led us to a grassy glade to the east of the road, where there was a fresh-water spring. The coercers built a scratch fire and boiled water for tea while Fian and I mixed a poultice of herbs and mud for Faraf's leg.

"We will definitely have to stay th' night at Tor," Fian murmured as we applied the poultice.

I shrugged. "We'll wait until this dries, and by then the swelling will have gone down enough to bandage it. See if anyone has cloth with them."

Miryum brought me a mug of tea, and seeing everyone else preoccupied, I seized the opportunity to speak to her.

The coercer shrugged when I asked if she remembered the

tribesman who had proposed to her in Sador, but she paled when I explained that he had escorted Faraf and Zidon to Obernewtyn with the express intention of claiming her as his bondmate.

"He must be mad!" she said incredulously. "I could not believe it was meant as anything other than a joke. How could a man offer a proposal to a stranger?"

"Well, it seems he did. Fortunately, given the Sadorian's new attitude to beasts, his betrothal gift displeases him, and he means to ask you to name some desire that he can fulfill to replace the horses."

"I will tell him there is no need for him to honor a betrothal promise to me."

"I'm afraid he does honor it, and if you refuse, it is very likely that he will kill himself out of shame."

She gaped at me, and seeing the flush play over her cheeks, it occurred to me for the first time that Miryum might want to accept the proposal.

"Do you *want* to bond with him?" I asked bluntly.

She looked mortified. "I did not even know his name until you said it!" I caught enough of her thoughts to see that she had ruled out love, feeling herself too plain to inspire it.

"The trouble is that you accepted the horses, so as far as Straaka is concerned, there is only the matter of the gift to be cleared up."

Miryum shook her head and seemed to wake from a dream. "I will not bond with him nor any man. I am a knight and am sworn to chastity," she said.

My temper frayed at her sudden reversion to grandiose heroine. "What in blazes is chastity?"

Her color deepened, but she said with less pomp, "It means we cannot give our bodies or minds or hearts to one person, for we are sworn to love all people equally." Now it seemed there was a pleading look in her eye. "But I do not want him to die."

I sighed. "At least you need not worry until the moon fair, for I asked Alad to relay the message that you would not give an answer until then. I will speak with Jakoby in the meantime and see what she can suggest."

Miryum nodded and withdrew to sit, frowning and shaking her head as if she were conducting an inner dialogue.

I was bandaging Faraf's leg when Gahltha sent a sharp warning that strangers approached. I cautioned the others to do nothing but act like gypsies and bid Gahltha lead the horses out of sight. I was not unduly bothered, since there was more than enough coercive talent among us to deal with trouble.

Five men and one woman leading saddled horses emerged from the trees. The woman had cropped yellow hair and was clad in peasant boots and fawn trousers, a loose tunic belted at her hips. The young man beside her had similarly colored hair and was dressed much the same but with a gorgeous green silk cloak, heavily embroidered at the hem with Council symbols, thrown over his shoulders. Three of the other men wore soldierguard cloaks, and the fifth was a thin, cringing fellow who looked like a farm worker.

"Here be gypsies," he announced, as if no one would have known it without his saying so.

I rose up and bowed to the young Councilman in the perfunctory way gypsy halfbreeds had with such gestures.

"What are you doing here?" he demanded.

"As you see, we drink tea dangerously," I said.

"What is she saying?" he asked the woman, as if I spoke another language and must be interpreted.

"She said they are only drinking tea," she said seriously, but her mouth twitched as if she was trying not to laugh. Her hair, though cut unusually severely for a woman, accentuated the beauty of her face and eyes.

"Who gave you permission to drink tea?" the Councilman demanded. The woman leaned forward and whispered in his ear. "Oh yes. I mean, who gave you leave to drink tea *here*!"

"I did not know this clearing was claimed to any farm holder. It is not fenced," I countered mildly.

"It is not fenced," one of the soldierguards snarled. "But it is claimed sure enough. By Bergold, son of Radost. All the land above Guanette to the western mountains is his, and any who goes there without permission will answer."

"Fenced land is forbidden to us gypsies, but we may camp for up to three days wherever there are no fences," I said, quoting Council lore.

"Filthy halfbreed. You dare to speak that way to Councilman Bergold?" The soldierguard unhooked his whip. "I will teach you to mind your manners."

The young Councilman frowned and waved the man back. "Hold. Are you sure she is being insolent? After all, what she says is true. The land isn't fenced." He looked at the woman, and she came forward to his shoulder. "Do you think she is being insolent?"

Her eyes smiled, flickering above sober lips. "She is saucy, brother, but I think not insolent. Gypsies have that in their nature, so they cannot be blamed for it."

"Yet Father blames you for *your* nature," Bergold said. The woman made no response, but the yellow-cloaked soldierguard regarded her with fleeting hatred, which he swiftly masked.

"Well, I suppose one cannot have her whipped if sauce is in her blood," the young Councilman decided.

"She should be whipped to set an example," the yellow cloak snapped.

"I think you love your whip more than your manhood, Sestra; perhaps because it performs more willingly," the woman said. She gave him no chance to reply to her insult, turning back to her brother. "I would release her with a warning, brother," she advised. "After all, she can spread the word among her kind that this land is now yours, and no one else will trespass."

Bergold brightened. "That's so. Well, hear this, halfbreed: I will spare you, for gypsies can't help their sauce, it seems. But you must show your gratitude by publishing my claim over this land."

"I will let it be known among such of my people as I meet, and none who know will trespass, but I cannot promise to speak to every halfbreed."

"The ones you know will do," the woman said carelessly, now sounding bored. To her brother, she murmured that the word would spread soon enough regardless. "But it might be useful to have Sestra bang a few signposts into the ground along the road."

"A good idea. See to that, Sestra," the youth said imperiously. "In fact, we should post notices to ensure that my brother knows where my land ends and his begins."

Thoughts running loudly under his words told me that Bergold's older brother, Moss, resented not being given entire charge of the high country and both plots of land, and might well try to take more than his share.

The young Councilman scratched his head vigorously as if having his thoughts read itched him. I withdrew hastily in case he was mind-sensitive, then spoke to distract him.

"Shall we leave the fire alight for you to brew your own tea, sirrah?" I asked, rising.

Bergold shook his head. "I don't like tea. I don't suppose you have any ale?"

I caught the eye of his sister, who grinned at me. It was such a mischievous look that I was taken aback. She was entirely unlike any woman I had ever met.

"Well, what do ye make of all that?" Fian asked after we had parted from them and were mounted up on the verge of the road.

"Bergold is clearly a simpleton, but the sister is not, and it seems as if she will keep a tight check on the soldierguards and her brother," Miryum said.

I was less sure the sister could be so easily summed up, but I only said that I thought Bergold less a fool than simply young and not terribly bright.

"If th' brother is anything like him, I'd say we have nowt to worry about," Fian said.

But one of the coercer-knights said rather grimly that the two brothers were as different as night and day. "I lived in Sutrium before I came up here, and I knew Moss by reputation and sight. He was cruel and brutish even as a child."

"Remember, too, Bergold may be relatively harmless, but Radost is his father," Miryum pointed out.

Sobered by this, we rode silently until we came upon a place where the cliff had tumbled into a broken ramp that allowed us to leave the main road and make our way at last down to the White Valley. Through the trees, I caught the distant glitter of the upper Suggredoon, and beyond it, the Gelfort Range. There was neither a proper road nor a track once we reached the valley floor, but I was glad to dismount for a while. I loved riding, but I felt far more in touch with the land with it pressed against the soles of my feet. All of my senses seemed to sharpen. I heard small animals scurry away from us and the occasional bird call. Leaves rustled and branches creaked as we passed, twigs snapped underfoot, and whirring insects fell silent. The whole valley seemed significantly more overgrown than when I had last been there.

Reaching the river, we followed its bank until it switched back toward the road; then we set a straight course for Tor. Before long we came upon clear evidence of wagon ruts and recent passage. The coercers who always traveled with the teknoguilders were careful to erase all tracks before this point, but this was deep enough into the valley not to bother since no one would stumble upon them by chance. Here and there along either side of the track, among the tangle of fire-spawned regrowth, dead and utterly blackened trees rose up like shadowy accusers. It seemed the reek of smoke still lay over the place.

Eventually, the river looped back to meet us. When the undergrowth became less dense, we mounted up and alternated between trotting and walking, reaching the base of Tor late in the afternoon. Here the Suggredoon poured itself into the mountain via the gaping tunnel that led to the huge underground cavern housing the drowned Beforetime city.

We dismounted when we were within sight of the campsite, just as two teknoguilders came stumbling out of the tunnel, both blue to the lips and deathly pale. At first I thought something terrible had happened, but the coercer who had been on guard merely wrapped them in blankets, shaking his head.

I noticed both had wet hair. Without saying a word, I

turned and strode into the tunnel, where the Teknoguild had chiseled a walkway above the water level. It had been widened considerably by the teknoguilders, but I was too outraged to pay much attention to this or to any other improvements.

I heard footsteps behind me. "What is the matter?" Miryum asked, her voice bouncing oddly from the stone walls.

"I don't know, but I mean to find out," I said grimly.

There were rush torches set into wall grooves, and these provided light as daylight faded behind us. We came into a newly widened section of the tunnel, where a shallow inlet had been created. Several rafts were tethered to a small wooden ramp. Here the walls were damp enough to provide habitat for the glowing insects that fed off tainted matter.

Miryum, Fian, and I boarded a raft, but the coercer-knights declined, preferring to walk. Miryum shrugged and poled us from the makeshift shore until the current picked us up and propelled us along the curving tunnel to the main cavern. She knew the currents, having been into the caves several times before. She did not like boat travel, but time on a raft did not affect her as sea travel had when we had gone to Sador.

As ever, I felt both wonder and horror at the sight of the Beforetime towers half submerged in the dark, oily-looking waters. From a distance, it seemed they had been untouched by the ages, but up close, their eroded surfaces resembled rich embroidery. Here and there were glowing patches of insects, and in other places gaping holes, or jagged sections where segments had fallen away.

I ran my eyes over the crumbling buildings, trying to envisage how they had looked when people had dwelt in them. Even now, flooded and cloaked in shadow, the city was an awe-inspiring creation. The horror was to understand that a people who had risen so high could have fallen so low.

The failings of the Beforetimers brought me back to Garth, and my anger swelled again. I was tempted to ask Fian if he had any idea what his master was up to, but I held my tongue, thinking I would give the edge of it to the Teknoguildmaster soon enough.

There were lights down at the end of the cavern, where the building that housed the Reichler Clinic Reception Center stood. Unlike many of the dead towers, this was built up at the shallow end of the cavern and had escaped the drowning. Or so we had imagined. If what the young teknoguilder said was true, what we thought of as the Reichler Clinic building was only part of it. The Teknoguild concentrated their activities here, not just because of our interest in the Clinic, but because the relative shallowness of the water meant there was less of a current and access to the dry parts was easier.

Miryum let the current carry us toward the light and wielded her pole only to prevent our being beached on the rubble islands created by fallen buildings. But when we were closer, she bid Fian take a pole, and between them they brought the raft out of the main channel and into a quiet canal that, far below, would be a side street. To go farther with the current would be dangerous, for it led to the hole where the water plunged steeply to the lowlands. Having miraculously survived that journey once, I had no desire to repeat it.

Gliding between the empty buildings, I imagined Hannah Seraphim hurrying along this very street with a book under her arm, or peering out one of the windows above.

Looking around, I spotted a haze of lights on a small pile of rubble partly obscured by other buildings. I pointed, and

Miryum nodded and directed the raft that way.

As we drew nearer, I saw there was a great mass of things heaped about the edges of the isle. Some I recognized as equipment from the Teknoguild caves, but more looked as if it had been salvaged from the drowned city. The teknoguilders were all up at one end, clustered around a mass of tubes and lines of rope running from a square metal instrument down into the water. Several teknoguilders seemed to be working very hard operating the machine, while the rest stood by the water, looking down.

Garth was almost facing me as the raft made landfall, but so intent were they all on what they were doing that they did not even notice us.

"Do you see her?" I heard the Teknoguildmaster ask.

I signaled for Fian and Miryum to be silent so that I could listen, and stepped carefully from the raft.

"I think I see a light." That was Louis Larkin's voice. He was on his knees, peering into the water.

"There!" a girl cried. "It is a light. She's coming up."

"Silly little fool," Garth muttered, sounding more exasperated than relieved.

I stepped up behind him and peered over his shoulder into the water just in time to see a pale, glowing face rise out of the depths. I gasped, for the body emerging was terribly bloated.

Garth clutched at his chest in fright and whirled to face me. "Elspeth! You gave me a fright coming up behind me like that!"

I couldn't speak, though it was clear now that the girl was not gross from immersion but was clothed in some strange fleshy-textured suit, which even now Louis and the others were peeling from her. As with the two teknoguilders I had seen outside, her lips were blue and she was trembling violently. Around her neck swung a pair of glass goggles.

"What are you doing here?" I demanded of Garth.

"Do n-not bl-blame the guildmaster," the young tekno-guilder said through chattering teeth. She took my wrist in an icy grip. "It is my fault for st-staying so long. G-Garth warned me but you cannot imagine how w-w-wonderful it is down there. You don't even re-realize how cold you are get-ting." She turned back to Garth. "It is lucky the glows started to fade—not a disadvantage after all th-that th- . . ." She could say no more for shivering, and Garth told her to go back to the camp with the others.

"We've done more than enough for the day," he said, and looked at me cheerfully. "I hope you brought some food. I'm afraid there is not a great deal left to eat."

I was speechless with outrage that he would dare to bab-ble of food instead of explaining and defending his activities.

"I'll gan out an' light a fire," Louis said with a laconic glance at me. He helped the shivering teknoguilder onto one of the rafts, and some of the others climbed aboard before Louis threw off the tether rope. Everyone else began to move about, covering equipment or winding tubes.

Garth sighed. "I know you are troubled, Elspeth, but they *will* push the time limit. Let us get back to camp."

Fian and two more teknoguilders were already on a raft, and Miryum helped Garth and me aboard a third. When we were under way, he asked with infuriating calmness what brought me to Tor.

I gritted my teeth. "I came because I suspected you were having people try to swim down to this wretched cellar you've discovered. I couldn't believe you would condone something so dangerous!"

"It is not terribly dangerous. The divers are well protected by the suits, and if they obey the time limits, they do not even become very cold. We did a great deal of research before anyone went down. Tomorrow I will show you how the air pump works. I assume you are staying the night. We have found a few interesting bits and pieces you might like to see. . . ."

My anger gave way to a kind of exhaustion. Talking to Garth was like trying to build a sand bridge in the path of the sea.

Miryum brought us swiftly to the small bay where the other rafts were tethered, and we were soon walking toward what little remained of the daylight. Garth was questioning Fian about Sador.

"I hope you have made proper notes," he said at one point. "I am always having to impress on you young people that being a teknoguilder is not just exploring and digging. It is good careful records. . . ."

I decided it was simply a waste of energy to be angry with the Teknoguildmaster. Let Rushton rage at him. But I would learn exactly what the teknoguilders were up to, and unless I was satisfied there was no danger, I would exercise my power as interim master and demand the entire guild's return to Obernewtyn.

An hour later, it was full dark, and we were all seated around a roaring fire, which threw an eerie dancing light against Tor's weathered rock face. I felt somewhat calmer since Garth had explained that in the Beforetime, many people had dived deep in the great sea out of sheer pleasure at seeing the world beneath the water. It was an ancient science of submerged exploration, and there were many ways in which people had carried air with them. There were tanks, which had somehow compressed air into pod-shaped metal cylinders that were strapped to divers' backs; there were entire sealed vessels that could be driven beneath the water; and there was also something called a *hookah*, which allowed air to be pumped from the surface. This was the simplest method and the one used by the Teknoguild. They had constructed a simple pump that could be worked by hand to force air down long, flexible tubes constructed from the same material as the suits.

Of course, it meant the divers could not venture anywhere the tubes could not freely follow. If they were bent or snagged, the air supply was instantly cut off. This had happened, but additional air lines were always sent down with the divers, and in an emergency, several could take turns breathing from the same tube.

The flabby suit I had taken for grotesquely waterlogged flesh had been constructed by the guild to preserve heat and had in fact been formed from melted and remolded plast. Three divers went down in a strictly timed sequence. They wore thick belts into which were sewn heavy lumps of metal or stone. Before pulling themselves back up by a knotted rope, they could remove the belts and place them in a basket with the small glass bulbs of glow insects they took down for light. The basket of weights and glows could then be retrieved separately.

Garth explained that each of the divers had a teknoguilder monitoring their air hose above the water, ready to stop the air three times, by the simple means of pinching the tube closed, if there was a need for the divers to return quickly to the surface.

"Yet you said they stayed down longer than was safe," Miryum said.

Before Garth could respond, all three of the Teknoguild divers began talking at once of how the world shivered green and mysterious far below and of how it felt to fly down and down to it. There were many incomprehensible machines to be puzzled over in the Beforetime roads. One had seen a skeleton inside a machine, and another had seen what appeared to be a face but had been a monstrously deformed statue. Another talked of savage eels that lurked in the water, and another had been frightened by a strange glowing snake coiling in and out of the wavering purple forest that rose from the streets. I found myself envying them their unique experience, though in truth I had no desire to descend into the cold, silent darkness of that long-dead city.

But even as these thoughts passed through my mind, a vision rose before my eyes of Rushton swimming in darkness. I shook my head. No doubt I was putting things together wrongly. My every instinct told me that Rushton would never make such a dive.

I caught Louis Larkin's eye, and he came around the fire. "Not often ye gan away from Obernewtyn these days," he said.

I smiled ruefully. "I wish I could do it more often, but it becomes harder to justify it. Rushton and guildmerge always speak against guildleaders putting themselves in danger."

Louis shrugged. "It makes sense not to let yer head gan chopped off, if ye can lose a hand instead."

It was a harsh philosophy, but I made no comment about the ill fortune of being a hand. I had wanted to see Louis for another purpose than to complain about my lot.

"You know the great carved doors that used to be at Obernewtyn's front entrance?" He nodded. "Do you remember anything about them being installed?"

Louis chuckled. "I remember they were a memorable pair that brought them."

"Brought?" I could not help a note of excitement entering my voice.

"Well, it was nowt th' doors they brought," Louis corrected himself. "Them carved panels that was in th' midst of th' doors came in a wagonload of carved work. Th' idea of havin' them made up as doors came from th' master's bondmate." He curled his lip in memory of Marisa Seraphim, whom he had feared and disliked. "She turned those yellow eyes on th' master an' said she would like two grand front doors fashioned about th' panels. She said she had some special idea fer the border carvin', if it could be done. Th' gypsies said it would take a while, but they was happy to stay an' do th' job."

"Gypsies?" My voice was so sharp that Miryum looked over at us. I lowered my tone. "Are you saying that the people who brought the carvings were gypsies?"

Louis nodded. "Nowt just gypsies. Twentyfamilies gypsies, though I didna truly ken th' difference back then. I was just a lad, an' my mind was more on fishin' an' catchin' sight of Guanette birds than on gypsies."

I thought of Swallow's elaborately carved gypsy cart and remembered his saying proudly that such work was a specialty in his family. The style of carving had even reminded me of the Obernewtyn doors.

I forced my reeling mind back to Louis, who was watching me expectantly. "Do you remember if these gypsies seemed to offer the panels for sale especially, or did Marisa simply choose them of her own inclination?" I was not sure what I was groping for.

The old man screwed up his eyes as if he might pierce the veil of time and see back to that day. "We didna have many visitors in th' mountains, an' any were occasion fer interest.

But it's long ago just th' same. I recall us young 'uns was all about crawlin' over th' wagon an' pettin' th' horses an' gawkin' at th' carvin's. There was th' old man almost like a carvin' hisself, an' a sturdy young lad with dark curly hair an' dark eyes. Th' old man was kin to th' boy, I'd guess. His grandfather, mebbe." His forehead crinkled. "Now I think back, I wonder that an old gaffer like that made such a trip. In them days, all above th' Gelfort Range was wild country, an' th' road little more than a rutted animal track, yet up they come uninvited, sayin' they'd heard there might be work fer carpenters an' carvers. Th' master was pleased to have them, of course, fer it were hard to get any workers up here. Then Marisa come out an' . . . yes. I do remember. Th' old man sparked up suddenlike, though he'd let th' lad do most of th' talkin' afore that. He said as how they had a couple of special panels as she mun like." He nodded, confirming his memory. "Yes, th' old man offered them in particular."

I could barely take it in, let alone respond in any sensible way to Louis's obvious curiosity.

Louis interpreted my silence as the desire for more information. "They stayed all winter, carvin' th' design th' mistress wanted round th' edge of the doors an' tappin' tiny sheets of gold into th' gaps. It was a thing she had seen in one of them books she was always gettin' sent to her, an' she worrit an' worrit at them gypsies till they did it exact as she wanted. They finished all th' chores th' master wanted th' first sevenday, but he was glad they were about workin' on Marisa's doors when this or that cropped up, an' they ended up doin' a lot of small jobs. They was here fer ages, but they pretty much kept to theyselves. To my mind, th' oddest thing was that there was just two of them. Gypsies always travel an' camp in troupes."

Unless they had been sent to perform a special mission, I thought. "What about the panels? Did they say anything within your hearing about why they offered them to Marisa? Or about who had carved them?"

Louis reflected for a while. "It's funny ye should ask. At th' time, I supposed th' old man had done th' work. But thinkin' back, I dinna recall either him nor th' boy ever sayin' th' work was their own. You could see th' panels were finer work than th' rest of th' doors, though. Pity ye burned th' doors, else ye could see fer yerself. To tell ye th' truth, I always felt it was a shame to destroy them fer a bit of gold." He scratched at the fluffy tufts of hair rising from either side of his bald pate until they stuck out comically.

I took another breath but still felt breathless. I watched Miryum bring more wood to the fire, wondering if it was madness to speculate that the panels had been carved by Kasanda. Yet the overguardian said she had possessed futuretelling abilities, and so might she not have foreseen Marisa and her desire to hide her map to the weaponmachines?

But how had gypsies become involved? There was no doubt that they were the perfect messengers because of their wandering ways, but under what circumstances could Kasanda have encountered them? And when?

Then an incredible thought smote me: If the panels had been brought to the mountains with the gypsies at Kasanda's behest, then how that had come about was less important than why. And there was only one answer to that.

She must have wanted me to see them.

✦ 8 ✦

"WHAT IS IT?" Louis asked.

"Nothing," I said, forcing myself to be calm, though I felt like riding to Obernewtyn at once and demanding that Maruman take me on the dreamtrails to see the doors, for I was suddenly certain they contained the first of the clues I had to uncover before returning to Sador to learn the fifth clue from the Temple overguardian. What a terrible irony that I had ordered them burned! Maruman was now my only hope of learning what message Kasanda had left for the Seeker.

"What has you so pale and thrilled?" Garth demanded, coming to join us.

"Gypsies," Louis said, giving me a sharpish look as if to ask if that was still what we were talking about.

"Ah well, they're fascinating enough for a study all on their own," Garth grunted. "I should certainly like to speak with that fellow you met. What was his name? That Twenty-families pretending to be a halfbreed."

"Swallow," I said. "He only called himself that when he was disguised as a halfbreed, though. I don't know his real name, nor much else about him except that he is the son of the leader of the gypsies."

Garth shook his head. "It is a dangerous game he plays, given that purebloods are supposed to be estranged from halfbreeds."

"Did you ever find out anything about that Govamen mark the Twentyfamilies wear?" I asked.

"Not much, save that it is called a tattoo. Such marks were mainly decorative in the Beforetime, though occasionally they signified allegiances just as our guild bands do. Possibly the gypsies descend from those who supported Govamen and decided to adopt their mark."

"But why Guanette birds?"

"Perhaps the Govamen people thought the birds striking. Who can know? But they were at hand, because Govamen was experimenting on them."

My heart jerked in my chest. "Are you certain of that?"

"I am," he said. "Jak came upon some mention of the experiments in the plasts. There may be more about it once we get into the records kept in the basement."

The Teknoguildmaster was staring into the fire now, his eyes full of reflected orange light. "On the next expedition to the lowlands library, I will instruct my people to look specifically for mentions of Govamen and the Reichler Clinic and also of the city under Tor—which seems to have been called *Newrome*," he murmured dreamily.

"You mean to mount another expedition to the lowlands?"

He gave me a bland smile. "I thought quite soon, while the weather is fine and people are too busy planting and basking in the warmth to be suspicious of travelers or to spend time gypsy baiting. I will be proposing it at the next guildmerge."

"Rushton will be back by then, and I can't see he will gainsay it, though he might have a word to say about this business of diving," I added tartly.

Garth leaned forward. "Did he say what Brydda wanted?"

I repeated the brief message and my interpretation, with which he concurred.

"I am not sorry that we are out of this brewing confrontation," Garth said. "War is a terrible waste of time and life. When I think of the Council and this Malik, I fear that people learned nothing from the destruction of the Beforetimers."

" 'Twas a lethal lesson that killed all its pupils, so none were left to teach the lesson on," Louis said.

I shivered as a breeze stole under my hair to the back of my neck, and Garth shrugged massively and said, "War or an accident. Either way, they did it with their weaponmachines."

"Were there many accidents with weaponmachines?"

"Well, there were accidents and things made to seem so," Garth said. "Accidents the books say, but you can feel the writers believe they were often deliberate attacks blamed on weaponmachine errors so countries did not have to take responsibility for the killing and destruction they had wrought. We know that the Beforetimers were doing a lot of writing and talking about how such incidents might be monitored and punished. . . ."

"Computermachines," I murmured.

Garth's brows rose. "Yes. There was talk by the World Council of all the computermachines concerned with defense being linked into one great, neutrally located computer with the power and intelligence to evaluate information and retaliate against any country that attacked another, whether the aggressor claimed it was an accident or no. The Sentinel project, it was called, if my memory serves."

The man in the flying machine had spoken of the Guardian program, but it had to be the same thing.

"What did the Beforetimers fight over?"

"Land mostly, or for coin or power."

"Not religion? Dameon told me that the Sadorians are descended from Gadfians, and I read that Gadfians wanted to kill anyone who didn't believe in their Lud."

Garth's eyes sparkled with interest. "So the Sadorians hatched out of that fiery egg, did they? Yes, the Gadfians were very violent and ruled by their religious mania—which was also, in a way, a desire for power."

I told him in more detail what Dameon had said of the connection between the Sadorians and Gadfia, and he wagged his head judiciously. "It fits neatly with what we have been learning. It seems the world was mostly divided into five powers in the Beforetime, and Gadfia was one of them—the largest in terms of land and people, but it was very poor in resources. We believe that our Land was once part of another of the five powers called Uropa. If Dameon is right in saying this land mass links with Gadfia, then we have further proof of that, for we know that Gadfia bordered Uropa—or it did before one of those 'accidents' turned the border land between them into an impassable Blackland. Jak says both nations were probably quite glad to have that buffer between them, which makes me wonder if one or the other was responsible for it. Of course, that border area had once been a country, and every single person in it died. . . ."

And was that country called Turka? I wondered. "Garth, do you have any idea of the location of the very first Reichler Clinic? The site that was destroyed?"

"It was in Uropa, near to a place called Inva, which was the capital of Old Scotia."

"Was this Scotia mountainous?" I demanded.

Garth nodded. "Very much so. But Hannah did not hail from there. She was not even Uropan. She belonged to another of the five powers, Tipoda—an awkwardish melding of very different islands and cultures on the other side of the world. But Tipoda and Uropa were allies, probably because both their peoples, as well as the peoples of Mericanda, spoke the same language—urolish. They hadn't always, though. In ancient times, there were hundreds of languages, particularly in Uropa."

"Strange to think of people living in adjoining lands not being able to understand one another," I mused.

"Indeed. It is very possible that the different languages led to misunderstandings that, at least in part, ended in the five powers being established and only three main languages being spoken. Other than urolish, Gadfians spoke gadi and Chinon spoke chinanka. But even with only three, trouble invariably erupted regularly on borders where one language group met another, because the language difference was only an obvious mark of vast cultural differences. You might talk to Fian about that; he has some interesting ideas. We do know that Gadfia and Chinon each had as many people as there were in all three urolish-speaking powers put together."

"How does anyone know how many people were in Chinon if their borders were closed?"

Garth smiled approvingly. "Chinon continued to send diplomats to meet with the other powers, because all of the countries traded with one another. There were people in each of the powers who made it their business to understand the other two languages because of the advantages it would afford them in trade, or for diplomatic reasons."

"Do you know anything of a Beforetime people called *Tibans*?"

Garth frowned and sank into his multiple chins for a moment. "I seem to remember some mention of a small mountainous land called *Tiba*, which was swallowed up by the Chinon Empire. Would that be what you mean? But that was long before the five powers were established."

He was looking at me so oddly, I felt he would ask me at any moment what book I had got that from, so I cast about for a diversion. "I wonder why the Sadorians speak as we do if they started out speaking gadi."

"Maybe your Sadorian friends would know. Otherwise, you might talk to Fian. Always assuming that his adventures in Sador and his enthusiasm for the deeps have not erased his previous interest in languages." His eyes flicked in amusement to the young highlander, who was still enthralled in his guildmates' talk of diving.

We fell into a companionable silence, lulled by the buzz of their talk and the crack and hiss of the fire. I stared up at the dark mass of Tor and shivered.

"You are cold," Garth said. "You should get some sleep, and so must I."

He heaved himself to his feet with a grunt, threw the piece of wood he had been using as a bolster onto the fire, and bid everyone good night.

I considered a walk to see how the horses fared, but a brief probe revealed that they were all asleep, so I said good night, too, and climbed into my bedding. I missed Maruman coiled onto my stomach and hoped he was not annoyed with me for leaving without saying goodbye.

My last sight before drifting to sleep was of the flames licking the night sky between me and the teknoguilders, still deep in their conversations.

I woke with a faint start to broad daylight, surprised to realize I had not dreamed for the first time in many days. I sat up and found I was alone except for Miryum, who was squatting by the fire, feeding it twigs with a faraway expression on her wide, flat face. I yawned aloud to let her know I was awake.

"Garth told me not to wake you," she said, as if expecting me to reproach her.

I stretched languorously. "I have not slept so soundly in ages."

"It is always easier to sleep away from Obernewtyn," Miryum murmured, hanging a pot above the flames. "Here, on the rare nights you dream, the dreams are comfortably dull."

I stared at her. "Are you saying the dreams you have here are different from those at Obernewtyn?"

"Of course. And it's getting worse. I think dreams are grown vivid and strange at Obernewtyn, because so many Misfits dwell there."

I thought of what Maryon had said about her guild finding it hard to futuretell clearly and wondered if there could be a connection between this and what Miryum was saying. Then there were my own dreams. I had never experienced so many dream-memories from the distant past. I had put it down to my dwelling on the past in my waking hours, but what if it was more than that?

I made up my mind to speak to Maryon as soon as I returned. Perhaps her guild's dreamscapes would give us some clue as to what was going on. Very likely she had no idea there was a difference in the way people dreamed away from Obernewtyn, since she and those of her guild seldom traveled.

"Do you want some food?" Miryum asked.

I groaned and pressed my stomach. "I ate too much last night to feel hungry now. But if there is choca . . ."

She nodded at the pot swaying languidly over the flames.

"It is brewed already. I did not think you would say no to that." She poured a mug of the frothy brown mixture, and I sat up, wrapped in my blankets, to drink it. The grass sparkled with dew, and the day seemed to glisten. Gahltha and the other horses were grazing peacefully by the water's edge, and I had a brief, vivid memory of the day we had gone on rafts into the mountains to escape Henry Druid's armsmen. Gahltha's fear of water had forced us to leave him, and he had fled into the highest mountains to escape what he perceived as his shame and perhaps to seek his death. Instead, he had met the Agyllians.

"I will stay on here until the teknoguilders return for the moon fair," Miryum said abruptly. "The other coercer-knights will escort you back to Obernewtyn."

I sighed inwardly. I would have been glad to ride with just Faraf and Gahltha for company, but to say so would have offended the coercer-knight's very substantial sense of dignity, so I merely thanked her. She set about washing up the few firstmeal pots and dishes, and I drained my cup, saying I would have a quick bath before going into the caves.

Carrying a towel and fresh clothes, I went to relieve myself in the refuse pit that had been dug some way from the campsite. After shoveling fresh earth over the pit, I ran to the water's edge. Throwing off my night shift, I immersed myself in the icy river water, gasping at the chill and taking care not to go deep enough for the current to catch hold of me. I splashed about lazily, enjoying the sparkle of sun on water and wishing somewhat wickedly that Rushton was with me and naked, too.

That thought was so pleasant, I daydreamed of it, and imagined pressing myself against him and feeling his hard hands on my hips.

A concerned call from Miryum recalled me to myself. Hastily, I got out, dried, and dressed, and returned to the campsite.

"I thought you had drowned," Miryum said repressively.

I ignored her disapproval as we went together into the mountain, but my lightheartedness dimmed as shadow swallowed daylight.

The Teknoguildmaster greeted our approach with an echoing shout of welcome and helped me from the raft. "Come and see how it works, Elspeth. Zadia and Yokan are down already, but Qwinn is just about to dive."

Fian was watching the two teknoguilders monitoring the hoses. They paid no heed to us at all. Qwinn was being helped into his suit.

"Give me the glows," he said to his aide.

The younger teknoguilder handed him two small bulbs. Qwinn clipped them deftly to his weight belt, drew on gloves and goggles, and sheathed a knife in a knee pouch.

"Be careful," the Teknoguildmaster said, passing him a breathing tube. There was a loop of rope around it, which Qwinn slipped over his head. After a brief general nod, he backed down the mound, pulling the tube after him. As he vanished into the water, I seemed to feel myself sinking into that chill depth.

"How did you learn that the building had shifted?" I asked.

"Some of my people dug down after we learned of the basement storage and found the bottom was broken away. We knew the building could not have shifted too far from the base, since it was still intact. But it will be no easy matter to locate the base, even though we know pretty much where it must be. It is such a mess down there, and add to that the pitchy darkness and the forest of water weed, grown to fantastic heights. . . ."

"Surely th' basement would have been crushed when the buildin' tore apart?" Fian said.

"Since the upper levels are intact, it is very likely that the base is as well," Garth explained. "It was buried in the ground before the city was flooded, and it will have been heavily reinforced to bear the weight of its upper levels. The chambers themselves may even be dry if they were sealed and secured. The real problem will be getting in."

"How long has this diving been going on?" I asked.

Garth tilted his head and gave me a faintly challenging look. "We began preparing the apparatus over a year ago. We have been diving since thaw, mostly to test the equipment. Our initial intention was casual exploration, but then we learned about the Reichler Clinic's basement storage."

"All this preparation, and you never spoke of it to guild-merge?" I asked with only a tinge of mockery. "What if something had gone wrong?"

"All life is danger, and you cannot be judging every action by that alone," he responded, a trifle brusquely.

"You can make that point at the next guildmerge."

Garth heaved a long-suffering sigh. "I would have made a report in time; I hope you know that."

I said nothing to that, aware that he would have done so only when he had something valuable enough to prove that the end justified the dangerous means.

"I will let Rushton know that you will present a report to guildmerge once you find this cellar, *before* you do anything," I said pointedly. He nodded with obvious reluctance. Having forced this concession, I left to return to Obernewtyn.

Though I thought nothing would drag Fian from the dive

site, he wanted to come back with me. Miryum had coercively summoned the coercer-knights, and under cover of their preparations for departure, she begged me to find some way of dealing with the Sadorian that would not drive him to suicide.

"You want to refuse him, then?" I asked, still sensing an ambivalence in her.

She flushed. "I was . . . charmed, I admit, by the idea of a man coming so far for me. But my life is given to Obernewtyn and our cause here."

I wanted to say what I had learned—that happiness must be taken when it is offered. But some wisdoms can only be recognized if they are come upon after a hard climb. I promised I would do my best to have a solution when she returned to Obernewtyn.

As we mounted, Faraf came over. She was still limping slightly, and it had been decided that she must rest and return when the others did. "We have not had much chance for thinktalk," she sent regretfully.

"Very soon we will walk into the high valleys and think/run together, little sistermind," I promised, stroking her mentally and physically.

She nuzzled my knee and sent shyly that this would please her very much.

"She is sweethearted as Avra," Gahltha sent privately as we turned our backs on Tor. I waved to the little pony and Miryum until the trees blocked them from us, wondering to the black horse if Avra had foaled yet.

"Not yet," Gahltha sent with such certainty that I asked how he could be sure. He answered that heartmates could always sense how the other felt if they wished. This made me ache anew for Rushton. The bird-borne missive from him had eased my anxieties, but it was a long way from Sutrium to Obernewtyn.

No one was in sight when we rejoined the main road. A smudge of smoke from Guanette was the sole reminder that we were not all alone in the world.

The air was very clear, and as we turned our noses to the high mountains there were rank upon rank of them visible for once, and behind them, what appeared to be banks of clouds were in fact more mountains.

Gahltha dragged my thoughts down to earth, sending that the horses wanted to stretch their legs. We rode at an exhilarating pace for some time, trotted a bit, and then galloped again. It was only early afternoon when we stopped to rest at a public spring just before the turnoff to Darthnor. The horses were thirsty, and there would be no more drinkable water until we had got through the pass. Technically, we were on public property, but boundaries had a way of shifting when gypsies negotiated them, and the memory of Bergold and his sister prompted me to set a watch. Half the coercer-knights posted themselves in trees, perching in branches that gave them a good view of both the road and the turnoff.

Leaning against a mossy fallen log, I realized I was weary.

"I had forgotten," Fian groaned. He flung himself flat on the ground not far from me.

"Forgotten what?"

"How much I hate to ride. Every bone in my body aches, an' I know it will be worse tomorrow."

Smiling, I advised him not to think of riding, since more of it lay ahead. "Fian, do you know why the Sadorians do not speak gadi?"

A true teknoguilder, Fian's fidgets ceased as soon as his mind was engaged. "They do speak it, but they have chosen to communicate in urolish. A lot of Gadfians actually learned urolish back in Gadfia, and they simply taught the others after their exodus."

"Why didn't they just go on speaking gadi?"

"Partly because they wanted no one they encountered to know where they had come from, in case they were followed. But also I think rejectin' gadi were part of rejectin' their country an' their heritage in a broader sense," Fian said. "But they still teach gadi to their children, an' they use it for ceremonies an' in songs." He rolled onto his side. "Ye know, when I first figured out that them codes I was findin' was actually ancient languages, I remember wonderin' why dinna th' Beforetimers choose one language an' all of them speak it? But when I was learnin' th' jerman code, I found there were things I could say in that language that there were no words for in our language. I realized a different language is nowt just different words fer th' same things, it's a different way of thinkin'. . . ." He shook his head. "I'm nowt bein' very clear."

I thought I understood. "You're saying that you think the Sadorians want to remember gadi because it lets them say things that our language doesn't?"

He nodded eagerly. "Exactly. I think there is a part of th' Sadorians that can only be expressed in gadi, an' that bit of them would die if they let their language gan. Of course, there's a lot th' Sadorians feel is bad about their Gadfian heritage, so they only use it in poetry an' songs. There is some sort of rule they have about never usin' it in anger. But still, some of th' Sadorians say gadi ought to be let die, because although it is a language of poetry an' passion, it can also express perfectly th' rage of th' Gadfian fanatics."

One of the coercer-knights interrupted to report that she had detected a group of miners traveling from Darthnor to

Guanette. Their leader planned to bring them to the spring.

"I could coerce him to change his mind, but then we'd have to stay hidden for ages until they have gone out of sight down the road," the coercer said. "It's better if we go now."

I told Fian, who sighed and struggled to his feet. "Let's gan, then. Sooner begun's soonest ended."

We arrived at Obernewtyn late in the afternoon. The coercers dismounted by the main gate, thanking their mounts, and Fian took himself off, too, when we came to the grassy track leading to the Teknoguild cave network. His horse offered to carry him there, but he said wryly that he had better walk the remainder of the way or he might never walk again.

I continued on the outer trail running along the wall to the farm gate. I jumped down from Gahltha outside the barns, and he rubbed his head on my chest, then went in search of Avra. I did an attuned scan of Obernewtyn seeking Rushton, but to my disappointment it did not locate.

I was halfway across the furrowed field on the other side of the orchard before Alad spotted me and left his team of planters to greet me. His shirt clung damply to his shoulders and back, and his face gleamed with sweat.

"I see you are exercising the guildmaster's privilege to watch others carry out your orders," I said dryly.

He grinned and said he could use a drink and a bit of shade. He led me to where a spreading eben tree grew in one corner of the field. Here, in shadow, a bucket of water and a dipper were half buried in a vanishing snowdrift. He poured himself a drink and asked how the trip to Tor had gone.

I told him about the diving project, and he shook his head and advised me to leave scolding Garth to Rushton.

"I had decided that already," I admitted. "Have you heard anything more from Rushton, by the way? I had half hoped he would be here by now."

"He would be riding easy, as traveling jacks do. I'd not be looking for him before tomorrow morning."

I repressed a sigh. "How are preparations for the moon fair going anyway?"

He beamed. "I think this will be the best we've had yet, what with all the displays and Gevan's magi. You must see the wagons. Grufyyd has crafted them. . . ."

As he talked, my mind drifted back to Miryum's assertion that people slept unquietly in the mountains. When Alad gave me a quizzical look, I did not pretend I had been listening to him. Instead, I asked if he slept better when he was away from Obernewtyn.

He blinked at the change of subject. "I leave Obernewtyn too seldom to know if I would sleep better away."

"Do you sleep well in general?" I persisted.

Alad looked puzzled. "What are you getting at, Elspeth? No, I don't sleep well. I toss and turn and can't switch my mind off for thinking of planting this seed, or pruning this row, or cutting down on tubers."

"Do you dream much?"

He snorted. "Now you sound like the novice we have nagging me to fill our dream journal. The thing's a damn nuisance." His exasperation dissipated in resignation. "All right, I do dream, if you can call them dreams. I'd call them distorted memories. Last night, for instance, I dreamed that Domick, Roland, Louis, and I were racing to the Teknoguild cave network to rescue you and Rushton from Alexi. That was pure remembering, but then it turned into a nightmare." He shook his head.

592

"A nightmare? What do you mean?"

"One minute we were running through the trees just as we did in reality, and the next this giant dragonish beast flew at me. I screamed, and then I was awake and covered in a muck sweat." He noticed the expression on my face. "What is the matter? You look as if *you* just had a nightmare."

My lips felt numb. "The . . . the monster that came at you. You called it *dragonish*?"

"Oh, well, I meant no offense to our poor wee Dragon," Alad said. "It's just that the beast looked so much like those visions she conjures."

I was flabbergasted at the sudden realization that it was not a critical mass of Talent distorting dreams and making sleep difficult at Obernewtyn. It was one Talent in particular.

"Things wear different shapes on the dreamtrails," Maruman had sent to me so many times.

Different shapes.

✦ 9 ✦

"How HAVE YOU all been sleeping lately?" I asked.

"Are you joking?" Gevan demanded bluntly. "You called me in the middle of a vital rehearsal of the magi to answer questions about my sleeping habits?"

"I was mixing a difficult preparation," Roland growled.

"And I am Mistress of Obernewtyn in Rushton's absence," I responded coldly.

There was a startled silence.

"Well, then, if it matters so much, I slept badly," Gevan said. "Last night and for as many nights past as I can remember. But no doubt it is because of the moon fair preparations. I was up until—"

"Dreams?" I interrupted.

His irritation faded, and he nodded. "Now that you ask, I dreamed of Ariel and his wolves going after Selmar all those years ago. I dreamed I could hear her screaming. I seem to be dreaming a lot of the past lately."

"Roland?"

The healer nodded. "I sleep little, and I toss and turn and can't seem to settle. It is the same with all my people. Last night, I dreamed of trying to heal people with the plague. Hundreds of them, and as quickly as they were healed, they were ill again."

"Angina?"

The young empath said softly, "I dreamed of Hannay climbing up the cliff during the Battlegames in Sador. I dreamed of how scared he was of falling."

I looked at Maryon, who did not answer but spread out what appeared to be a large, beautifully dyed, woven map.

"What land is this?" Gevan asked, striding across to peer over her shoulder.

"Not any land such as ye will walk upon in wakin' life," Maryon answered. " 'Tis a dreamscape." She flicked me a darkly knowing look. "Ceirwan did nowt say what ye wanted it fer. We have many 'scapes coverin' different periods. But I had th' feelin' ye might want this one, which covers dreams experienced by members of my guild from wintertime to last week. An' to answer yer question, I have slept restively over that period, as has everyone in my guild. We dream vividly as ever, but it is growin' more difficult to futuretell, an' there are more ancestral memory dreams."

"At Obernewtyn, people are dreaming more, particularly of the past, and are sleeping badly," I concluded flatly. I let my eyes rove over them all, seeing they were now intrigued enough to have forgotten that I had dragged them from other matters. "Away from Obernewtyn, however, we sleep well and dream little." I brought my gaze to Maryon. "Would I be right in saying that if you compared an older dreamscape to this one, there would be a substantial increase in dreams?"

"We have only just begun to monitor everyone's dreams, but that is certainly true fer th' Futuretellin' guild. Assumin' this is so, th' amount of dreamin' at Obernewtyn has increased dramatically." She swayed over the dreamscape and touched a slender finger to an inky blot. "This signifies dreams that we would generally call *nightmares*. There has been a marked increase in them as well."

I pointed to a red blotch overlapping the black. "What does this represent?"

Maryon held my gaze as she answered. "It is a recurrin' nightmare."

"By recurring, you mean . . ."

"In this case, it means a nightmare experienced by many people. We noted it only because recurrent nightmares usually plague a single dreamer. If a number of people share the same nightmare, 'tis generally a warnin' of an event that will affect many—like a firestorm, or a roof fallin' in. But this particular nightmare does nowt concern anythin' like that. It centers on a great flyin' reptile that swoops or manifests suddenly in some threatenin' manner, then vanishes."

"Wait a minute," Alad said. "Maryon, are you saying other people have dreamed of a great red flying beast?"

Gevan gaped at him. "You? A couple of my people dreamed of a savage red-winged beast, but I thought it was because of the masks we have been making for our plays. . . ." He frowned at Maryon. "I think you might have told us about this."

"To what end? Until recently, I knew only that my guild were dreamin' of th' same beast. But knowing we are all dreamin' the same thing doesna help in learnin' what it means."

"Still . . . ," Gevan began, but Roland rose with an unusual look of mingled embarrassment and worry.

"Perhaps it is I who should have spoken sooner," he said. He glanced at me in apology, and I nodded for him to continue. "I had no idea others were dreaming of this creature. I thought it was only healers. Because of the proximity . . ."

"Proximity to what?" Gevan demanded.

"To her . . ." Roland sighed. "To Dragon."

"Dragon? Little Dragon?" the coercer said. "Are you telling me we are all dreaming of a monster created by a comatose girl?"

"If I am understandin' correctly, Roland is saying that the beast *is* Dragon," Maryon said. "And we are nowt so much dreamin' of her as bein' invaded by her."

Roland inclined his head gravely. "We believe the beast is the shape her mind, or part of her mind, has assumed. As I said, we had no idea anyone else was encountering her, and there seemed no point in upsetting everyone by speaking of it. You see, at first we thought it was her reaching out to us— asking for help. But very soon we learned that the flying beast does not know it is Dragon"

"I should have guessed," I said sorrowfully. "I have dreamed several times of it. Maruman sometimes wanders in my dreams, and he saw it, too. He said it lived behind a fortress with no gates."

Roland looked interested. "I don't know about any fortress, but it is highly likely that it represents the barrier that divides her madness from her sane mind."

"If this beast is part of Dragon, why can't we reach her through it?" Miky asked.

"Don't you think we've tried, lass?" Roland asked wearily. "It's no use. The beast is mad. It can't be reasoned with, and when we tried, it fled or swooped at us."

"It is dangerous," Maryon said. "And if I do not miss my guess, it is getting stronger."

Roland nodded morosely. "I'm afraid that's true. As the beast gains strength, so Dragon must be losing the battle she fights behind her fortress wall."

"Maryon, what do you mean by saying it's dangerous?" Alad asked.

"She means dangerous to Dragon, surely," Angina murmured.

"I mean to her *an'* to us," the futureteller said.

The others all spoke at once then, objecting to the idea that Dragon's manifestation as a mythical beast in our dreams could do more than disturb our sleep. Maryon cast a brooding glance at me, then spoke coldly and clearly. "Th' delvin's of my guild are difficult an' dangerous in themselves, but th' disturbances we have encountered, which seem to be a direct result of this dream dragon's presence, would be fatal if we had nowt all but ceased our activities. In addition, you, Roland, have just been sayin' that th' dragon is interferin' with your healers' work. Isn't that a real danger? I think it will not be long before this beast disrupts th' coercers' activities an' possibly th' empaths as well, which means we would have trouble defendin' ourselves or keepin' a watch."

"I can see that," Roland said impatiently. "I was under the impression you were trying to say the dragon could harm us in our dreams."

"Maruman seemed to think so. If he hadn't been in my dream when the dragon attacked . . ."

"Attacked!" Roland barked. "The beast has not attacked anyone in my guild. The worst it did was shriek at us or swoop. . . ."

"Dragon wouldn't attack ye, Elspeth," Ceirwan objected. "She loves ye."

"That is exactly why she *would* attack Elspeth," Maryon said. "Think on it. Dragon was abandoned as a wee child. We can assume that because she was little more than a savage when Elspeth found her and brought her here after winnin' her trust. Now Dragon is again severed from all she has come to care about. From us an' from Elspeth."

"But *she* did the severing," Roland objected.

"The part of her that is still that tiny abandoned child doesna ken that. It only grieves an' rages, an' th' red beast is th' child of that rage. If Dragon can nowt reach Elspeth, whom she loves, it can only be that Elspeth has deserted her. The greater th' love, th' greater th' rage."

I could have wept at the unfairness of it. "What can we do to help her?" I asked, my voice a dry rasp.

"Nothing," Roland said flatly. "That is why we did not speak of this to you. Dragon is unreachable. Knowing she is appearing in our dreams changes nothing."

"That is nowt true," Maryon said. "Since th' child's manifestation as a dragon is affectin' our dreams an' indirectly our Talents, nowt to mention th' fact that she is a danger to Elspeth, we can no longer afford to look upon her as simply a sleeper. Dragon must now be considered a problem that we must resolve."

I felt a surge of anger at the futureteller's cool summation. "She has not harmed me," I snapped.

"Not yet," Maryon said.

"What do you suggest?" I demanded. "Should she be killed so that you can futuretell unhampered and I can feel safe?" They all stared at me, and I felt my face drain of blood at the awfulness of my words. "I'm sorry. That was unforgivable and unfair. I . . . I just can't bear to think of her having suffered so much and now . . . Is it nothing that she saved Obernewtyn?"

"I am nowt suggestin' any hurt be done her," Maryon said. "I would merely advise that she be moved away from th' building. Mebbe she could be kept in th' Teknoguild caves, since th' teknoguilders' work is unlikely to be affected. . . ."

"Her range can easily encompass the distance back to the main house," Roland objected.

"What about the city under Tor?" Alad said slowly. "I'm sure Garth would jump at the chance to build a permanent safe house there. Or maybe we could take her to Enoch's farm."

"There is no need to send her away just yet." I heard the pleading note in my voice.

"Not yet, but, Elspeth, you must be sensible about this," the Healer guildmaster admonished.

"With your permission," Angina said, looking from me to Roland, "I'd like to sing to her. Maybe she will hear. Or the red-beast part of her will."

"I have no objection," Roland said. "But maybe you should wait until Maruman has wakened."

Angina shook his head so decisively that in spite of my despair, I wondered if the soft-spoken empath was finally feeling at ease in his interim duties. He said, "I'd like to begin immediately, because if Maruman is watching her somehow in his dreams, he can tell us if the music has any impact." He looked at me, a question in his eyes.

I nodded. "Play. Sing to her of the princess that will be wakened by a kiss. . . ."

He sent a surge of gentle comfort and left with Miky at his heel.

I composed myself and turned to Gevan. "I would like one of your people and one of the futuretellers to sit with Dragon constantly and monitor her."

"I'll have Dell set up a roster," Maryon said, rising. I asked if she would leave the dreamscape for me to examine, and she shrugged elegantly and left it.

"I'll never understand that woman," Gevan said when the door closed behind the futureteller. "Well, I must get back to my rehearsals. I am sorry about Dragon, though. Is there anything else my guild can do?"

I forced myself to smile. "I think not."

Roland took my hands and said, "Do not give up hope for Dragon, Elspeth. Maybe Angina's music will reach her. Will you come with me to see her?"

I shook my head and asked him to send Maruman to me when he awakened. I could not bear the thought of seeing Dragon lying so vulnerable, falling deeper into madness, and that in her madness she hated me.

"I must get back to the farms," Alad said, his eyes compassionate. "I'll ask Rasial to find out if animals are also dreaming of the dragon. Who knows, maybe it communicates with them better than with us funaga. After all, myth or not, it is a beast."

I nodded and changed the subject. "How did Straaka react when you told him Miryum would speak to him at the moon fair?"

Alad shrugged. "The mere mention of her name renders him silent. I daresay he hopes she will ask him to bring her a mountain stone by stone for the sheer delight of doing so in her honor."

I frowned. "As far as he's concerned, he must provide something to replace the horses as a betrothal gift. And Miryum is supposed to decide what, right? And there is no limit to what she can ask?"

"Not so far as I understand. In fact, I gather he would be insulted if it wasn't sufficiently difficult. But, Elspeth, what are you cooking up? Miryum won't set a task for him if she does not mean to bond with him. It would be dishonorable, and her code would forbid it."

"If it was an impossible task, he would never complete it. And if her sense of honor is bothered by such a ruse, then she must either keep the promise she inadvertently made in accepting the horses or let him die."

Alad shrugged. "Tell that to her, not me."

I sighed. "I'm sorry for snarling at you. It's this business with Dragon on top of everything else."

He relented and gave me a quick hug. "I'll see you tomorrow on the farms."

When he had gone, I sank into a chair as Ceirwan attended the fire.

"Elspeth, ye smell of a hard ride, an' ye look pale an' faded," Ceirwan said. "Why don't ye bathe an' relax. I'll organize a meal on a tray." Before I could respond, there was a knock at the door, and Ceirwan slapped his forehead. "That will be Wila. I fergot she wants ye to see her notes on th' Herders in rough before she prepares them for th' next guild-merge."

"I'll talk to her. In the meantime, maybe you could have Javo send up something light to eat."

Ceirwan nodded and let Wila in on his way out.

The older farseeker arranged a pile of notes on the table and sat diffidently on the edge of her chair. "You understand these are just rough notes, Guildmistress?"

"Ceirwan explained," I said, as ever discomfited to find myself deferred to by a woman old enough to be my mother. I had tried to be less formal, but it only made the older folk at Obernewtyn uneasy. Now I reminded myself that the deference was to my office and tried not to let it bother me.

Wila had riffled through a sheaf of scrawled notes and was now peering at one page in apparent dismay. This was an expression she often wore, so I simply sat back in my seat and waited.

"As you can imagine, we found it difficult to discover much about the upper ranks of the Faction because of their secrecy. But we have managed to get some vital information.

The leader of the Faction is a man known as The One. He is served by a group called The Three. They, in turn, are served by The Nine. Theoretically, The Nine serve all of The Three equally, but in practice they seem divided up among them. That might be less a matter of faction and more to do with the various areas of responsibility of The Three. We have some of their names, but not that of The One, of course."

"This One. Does he ever leave Herder Isle?"

"Never, and no one but The Three and a few trusted servants see him even on the Isle. Now, we call this group—The One, The Three, and The Nine—*the inner cadre.* They are the core of the organization. . . ."

"What about the head priests of the cloisters?"

"They form the upper rank of the outer cadre. There are thirty-nine of them, and each has the power of a One over the hundred and seventeen senior priests who are next in rank. Lesser Threes. You see, it follows the same pattern as the inner cadre. The head priests are Ones, the senior priests are Threes, and under them are Nines—in this case, the ordinary, un-ranked priests."

"You said there are thirty-nine head priests, but there are not thirty-nine cloisters in the Land. . . ."

"There are fifteen on the mainland. But Sutrium has a double set of priests in residence, as has Morganna. Then there are two cloisters on Norseland and three on Herder Isle—training cloisters." She paused as I added up in my head. "The extra ones are on Herder Isle, waiting to be rotated for their turn in a cloister. That turnaround happens every year, just like they shift orphans in the orphan homes."

"Thirty-nine sets of thirteen comes to . . . over five hundred priests!"

"Not counting acolytes, novices, and bonded servants, of

course," Wila said. "Nor the thirteen who make up the inner cadre."

I stared at her, wondering if she had grasped that her figures represented real priests. If she was right, there were nearly a thousand people in the Herder Faction. I would have guessed a few hundred at most.

Wila was talking again, and I forced myself to listen. "All wear gray habits but novices, who wear white. Then there are the bands. Head priests wear gold armbands, and senior priests wear red. The rest wear brown. Just before they go up a rank, the band is edged with the color of the next band. There are also priests who have other colored bands; most of the Sadorian priests wear green. On Herder Isle, there are a lot of priests who wear black bands. We have no idea yet what these colors signify."

"So very complex," I said.

"If you'll pardon me for saying so, Guildmistress, those who have been researching the Herders believe the complexity and the secrecy are designed to keep the power and knowledge at the center of the Faction."

"I wonder what they are hiding in their unassailable core," I muttered, all of my old distrust and fear of the priesthood reawakened. I looked at Wila. "How did you learn all this about the inner cadre?"

"Nhills of The Nine happened to visit the cloister in Guanette when we were scrying it out."

"You farsought this man?" I asked worriedly, for the upper-rank Herders were often mind-sensitive.

"Not him. A novice assigned to be his servant during the stay. He overheard a bit here and there, and we were able to put it together with other bits and pieces." She looked justifiably pleased, and I forced myself to smile, although I was filled with dismay.

I could not imagine why Herders had not taken over the Land if there were so many of them. It was almost as if they were biding their time. But biding their time for what?

I rose. "You and your helpers have done some important work, Wila. It would be useful to have your report in full by next guildmerge. It is not necessary to come up with charts and lists as Tomash did. Just make sure the numbers are clear. Rushton will be back tomorrow, and he should know how matters stand."

After she had gone, I sat thinking of the way no one really looked at Herders. Especially the ubiquitous brown bands. You saw the bald heads that came after banding, the gray whispering garments; you heard the reproaches and exhortations. But you didn't notice how many faces there were, because in a sense, one Herder was the same as any other. The stealthy increase in their numbers was like a secret invasion, like the rotting sickness that had destroyed Pavo's body, only revealing itself when he was riddled with its deadly spore.

I shivered and looked at the table before me. Under Maryon's quarter-year dreamscape were Tomash's chart and map, which I had yet to examine properly. In my cloak pocket were Dameon's letters, one still unopened. So much to do, and I felt suddenly exhausted.

Sighing, I lifted out the chart Tomash had made and began to examine it.

When Ceirwan brought me a tray a little later, my appetite had vanished. The number of Councilmen, soldierguards, and their collaborators was not as shocking as the Herder figures, but it was still high. I was overwhelmed by the sheer number of our enemies, and that did not count the rebels and ordinary folk who feared and loathed Misfits.

"Ye mun rest," Ceirwan said, sounding exasperated.

Ignoring his fussing, I told him of Wila's findings, and he looked as stunned as I had felt. "So many Herders? Does Rushton know?"

"I doubt it," I said. "He does not consider the Herders a specific threat, but only an aspect of the threat posed by the Council."

"The thing that always shivers me is that Ariel is a Herder acolyte," Ceirwan said.

Incredibly, I had forgotten that, and it was not a thing to be forgotten. Nor was it wise to forget that the ruthless slave trader Salamander also had some mysterious connection with the Herders.

After Ceirwan had left, I allowed myself to long for Rushton. Nothing would be changed by his presence, really, but just having him slide his arms around me would comfort all the vague and nameless fears that haunted me. And where was he? Riding still, perhaps, as it was not yet midnight. Or more likely he was sleeping under a tree, curled up by the equine that had volunteered to carry him to the lowlands. Or sitting at a bench, drinking ale in some roadside hostelry, sifting through gossip and drunken maundering for useful information.

"Rushton, love," I whispered to the fire. "Time you were home."

PART II

✦

THE ROAD TO WAR

⋆ 10 ⋆

SLEEP DID NOT come easily that night. I tossed and turned for an age, thinking of the Herders and how ruthlessly they had dragged me from my bed to watch my parents' burning. At some point, the face of my father became Rushton's face, and this was too much. I got up again and stirred the fire before wrapping myself in a blanket on the chair. Before long, I sank deeply into sleep, past disjointed images from the day, and down into the chaotic swirl of dreams and imaginings. I sank as if something pulled at me. And I dreamed.

I was in a sunlit garden. It was cold, and there were mountains in the distance beyond a high wall. A girl was seated on a low stool with her back to me. She wore a mustard-colored woolen coat and a scarf. Long dark hair flowed down her spine in a thick plait. Before her was a square, white sheet of paper, clipped to a board held aloft by a three-legged metal stand. There were a few lines on the paper, and as I watched, she reached up with a stub of black charcoal to scratch another line that intersected the others. I was amazed to see the essence of the dark, bare mountains emerging in these few simple lines.

All at once, there were footsteps, and when she turned to see who was approaching, I found myself staring into the face of the girl from the flying machine. I was startled to see how dark her skin was away from the winking lights and tinted glass. She could easily have been taken for a Twentyfamilies gypsy. Her look of curiosity faded into a scowl, but it was not aimed at me. The man approaching was the target of her displeasure. Clad much as the man in the flying machine had been, he was younger and very handsome, but his eyes were the same flat gray as his coat, and the smile that lifted his curved mouth did not change them.

"Good morning, Cassy," he said in a smooth voice.

"Mr. Masterton," she responded coldly, and turned back to her drawing.

His smile did not falter. "I have asked you to call me Petr."

Cassy made no response. Instead, she began rubbing one of the lines on the paper, smudging it with quick, finicky movements.

"The director showed me the sketches you made of the flamebirds," he went on, still smiling. "They're very good."

"He shouldn't have done that," Cassy said icily, still rubbing at her line, still looking obstinately away from him. "I don't like anyone seeing unfinished work."

"Of course. Artistic temperament is permissible when there is true talent. But you do understand that his allowing you to paint the birds is an infringement of the rules here?" There was a hard note in his mellow voice now, as if velvet was laid over stone.

Cassy turned at this, standing and facing him squarely, her expression defiant. "What do you want?"

He ignored her manner and went on pleasantly. "It is an infringement of the rules, which, as head of security, I have to regard seriously. It was agreed you could spend time here only if you were kept under control. This is, after all, a top-secret establishment, and there is a great deal of delicate research going on. Those birds were part of a very sensitive project, and although they are no longer being used, your painting them is a serious breach of security. But there is a solution. I am sure the director mentioned that we have engaged a firm to design a logo for our organization."

"He doesn't tell me anything." Cassy's voice was rudely uninterested.

"Then he will not have told you that we were displeased with the designs. I would like to suggest to the director that your drawing of the flamebirds would serve very well as a logo. You would even be paid for your efforts."

"Me design a logo for this place? You must be crazy," Cassy sneered. "I'd as soon design a logo for a gang of axe murderers!"

The man smiled, and if anything, his eyes became flatter. "That is a pity, because I am afraid, in that case, I will be obliged to convey news of the director's transgression to our superiors. I am sure you are aware that they are also your mother's superiors, and they might well be interested to know of your . . . liaison, shall we say, with a Tiban rebel?"

"That is blackmail, Masterton," Cassy snarled.

"Petr, please," he said suavely. He unrolled a sheet of paper and handed it to her. "You will produce a full-color work of this. It is my own design."

I peeked over his shoulder and gaped to see, sketched crudely, the now familiar Govamen logo of three Agyllian birds flying around one another in an ascending spiral.

"I'll need to see the birds again," Cassy said sulkily. I could not see her face, because her head was bent over the design.

"I'm afraid that is impossible."

"Then what you want is impossible," Cassy said, still looking down. "I work from life. The drawings I made are quick, thoughtless sketches. I would need to do a detailed study if you want anything worthwhile."

The man was silent, his expression still. At last he nodded decisively. "Very well. I will see what can be arranged." He turned and walked away, and Cassy lifted her head to stare after him. I expected to see her look ashamed or angry, but her expression was of ferocious triumph.

I heard a screeching cry overhead and looked up to find the red dragon, its scaly wings outlined by the sun.

"Dragon!" I cried, and lifted my hands, but even as I spoke, the creature swooped, madness glittering in its eyes.

I flung myself sideways and out of the dream. Almost immediately, I was absorbed by a memory of myself as a young child in Rangorn.

I was in the little wood on the hill behind our home. My brother Jes was with my father in the fields, and my mother was hunting an herb she used to season our soups in wintertime. I had gone with her but had wandered apart, drawn by a golden butterfly. I lay passively inside my child self, enjoying my own wonder at what I had imagined was a piece of flame that had escaped the fire. The butterfly vanished from sight behind a tree, and I ran after it on my short legs.

I stopped, for behind the tree lay Maruman in his dreamtyger shape.

"Greetings, ElspethInnle," he sent languidly, yawning and baring his red mouth.

"Maruman!" I cried, and the child self fell away, leaving me in my own form. "I'm so glad to see you. I was worried that Dragon had done something to you."

"Marumanyelloweyes is safe. But Mornirdragon seeks ElspethInnle," he sent.

I gaped at him. "You knew the dragon was her/Mornir?"

"Now know," Maruman sent succinctly. "Wake now, for the beast seeks you."

I shook my head. "I don't want to wake yet, Maruman. I need to see the doors of Obernewtyn. You said they still exist on the dreamtrails."

"They do," he sent.

"Take me there now," I requested.

He looked troubled. "Dreamtrails danger filled. Mornir-dragon confused by feelmusic but seeks ElspethInnle."

"I have to see those doors, Maruman," I sent. "It is part of my quest to destroy the glarsh. The oldOne would wish you to help me."

He gave way suddenly. "Come, then. You must prepare/change to travel the dreamtrails."

I did not argue, though I had no idea what he meant me to do. The thoughtsymbol he had used for *prepare* was unfamiliar to me. I drew close enough to his mind that I could see him rise nearer to consciousness—he took on his true, one-eyed form. But he did not wake.

I sensed a surge of energy and gasped as a silvery snake arose from his body like some fantastical umbilical cord. Light began to flow along the cord as water through a hose. It ran from his sleeping form and spilled from the end of the cord into a widening pool of silver that soon assumed the dimensions of Maruman's tyger shape. But it was a form of pure light with no substance and remained attached by the cord to the body. Maruman's consciousness was still within his flesh, but all at once, I felt his will flow away from it, up the silver cord and into the shape of light. Then the eyes of the shining tyger opened, and golden light flecked with blue swam in one, while a diamond-bright white light shone from the eye that had been removed in his true form.

"Must do same as Maruman. Only in such form/shape can fly dreamtrails." Maruman's voice sounded far away and oddly distorted.

I brought myself close to waking as he had done, then tried to coerce a silver cord out of myself. Nothing happened.

"Must draw on mindstream," Maruman's voice whispered.

I did not know what he meant, for surely the mindstream could only be accessed from deep below consciousness, yet he had remained close to wakefulness. Then I remembered that in Maruman's strange mind, all levels merged and flowed. I sank swiftly through the levels of my mind—too swiftly to attract the dragon, I hoped—stopping only when I could hear the humming song of the mindstream. I locked myself in balance between the pull to rise and sink.

I thought of the way the silver light had run up the snaking spirit cord like water up a tube. I thought of how bubbles of past existences rose from the stream and concentrated on visualizing a tiny tributary flowing up toward me.

At first, nothing happened. Then a silvery thread rose from the mindstream. It moved very slowly toward me, and each fraction of its journey cost me a tremendous outpouring of energy, as if I pulled the entire stream from its natural course. I became afraid as the tendril approached, for to merge with the stream was death, and maybe this was just another form of merging.

Steeling myself, I reached out a hand to grasp both my courage and the silvery thread. A cold clarity filled my mind, as if I stood atop a mountain buffeted by icy gusts of air. I let the stream flow into me until I felt as if it were running through my veins in place of blood. Heady delight filled me, but instinctively I forced myself to remain passive and very slowly willed myself to rise until the upward urge to consciousness was strong enough to overcome the urge to sink. The thread linking me to the mindstream paid out behind me as I ascended through the levels, thinning until it was no more than the wet glimmer of moonlight on a spiderweb. I became aware of my flesh again and vaguely sensed Maruman's presence nearby, but I dared not let it distract me.

I concentrated on calming myself and then tried again to coerce the thread to run from my being. This time, I felt it slip through me and rise like a snake from my belly, wavering and coiling. I had the distinct sensation of the mindstream and all of those levels of my mind that it ran through. It was like hearing the distant prattle of many voices, and I realized this must be what Maruman heard constantly, this mad seductive babble.

Steadying myself, I felt the distant mindstream flowing upward and spilling light out the end of the cord. For some reason, the gathering whiteness made me think of the soft downiness of Kella's owlet. I waited until it seemed the form of light was complete—humanoid but somehow indistinct—knowing I must now take the final step and transfer my consciousness to it. I was not sure how to do this, but the light-tyger had opened its eyes when it assumed Maruman's consciousness, so I willed myself to see through the eyes of the silver shape.

There was a rushing sensation, and I opened my eyes.

I gasped, for now I was floating above my body, which slumped awkwardly sideways in the chair before the dying fire. It took some time to realize what I was seeing, because it was not so much a body as a human-shaped shadow surrounded by a shifting halo of light. Everything in the room was thus, glowing in a wash of shimmering color, although far brighter halos surrounded other forms, perhaps because my will was now contained within the detached spirit shape. Though my body's aura was dullish, it was chiefly gold and a deep violet, with a single flash of white marred by a seam of dark crimson.

"That is the life you took," Maruman sent, his voice now quite clear.

"Life?" I echoed, but even as the question formed in my mind, I understood that the red stain had been caused by my killing Madam Vega when she would have cut Rushton's throat.

The halo's various colors gradually merged into the thread of light that connected me to my sleeping form.

"If the link/cord is broken, mindspirit will flow into stream and you will be longsleeping," Maruman warned. "Ride on me. I will fly to dreamtrails. Mornirdragon will not be able to follow/smell/see/distinguish you from me."

I moved awkwardly onto the tyger's back and wondered if in time my use of this strange new form would be less clumsy. I seemed to have no proper feeling for it, but the second I touched Maruman, I felt myself absorbed by his form and grace. He gathered himself, leaped, and went on rising. It struck me suddenly that I had never used my Talent to rise from the point of consciousness before. Always I had descended. How much would our minds be capable of, I wondered, if we only knew them better?

The air around us was full of colors merging and reforming, but as we ascended, they faded into pure white.

Then all at once, I was indeed sitting on Maruman's broad furred back, my hands wound in the ruff of thicker fur at his neck, my legs locked around his belly. We were flying through the blue sky, and the wind tugged my hair and chilled my flesh. I seemed to be naked except for some sort of heavy cape weighing me backward. I would have liked to shrug it away but dared not loosen my hold on Maruman.

Thinking about the gradual shift from flowing, weightless color and light to this semblance of solidity, I reasoned that we had reached a place so light and high that even our current evanescent forms gained substance by comparison.

"See," Maruman commanded.

I lifted my head and saw a broad glimmering pathway set into the clouds like a road through undulating hills. Maruman landed lightly upon it, and at his bidding, I climbed gingerly down. At once, my sense of individuality and separateness established itself as clearly as the unfamiliar drag of the heavy cloak down my back. Irritated, I reached up to unfasten it from my neck, but I could not find cloth or fastening. Instead, my hand encountered a hard bony protrusion covered in feathery down. I twisted my head and gaped to find I was looking at a set of wings.

"Things take their shape from your mind on the dreamtrails," Maruman sent complacently. "You may change if you wish/will it but must first master trick of it." His tyger shape darkened to pure black and became longer and sleekly lean. "No time now for you to practice shape-shifting."

I wondered at the wings. I had no particular affinity to birds, except for my relationship with the Agyllians. I had thought very fleetingly of Kella's little owl, and that might have been enough to give me wings, but I had had no conscious choice or desire for them. Thinking of the wings caused them to shift fractionally as a hand might flex its fingers. They were as much a part of me as a hand. With a flash of wonderment, I thought I might even truly fly.

"Come," the now shadow-hued Maruman sent impatiently. The path was solid underfoot, but the dust glittered unnaturally. On either side, clouds swirled, as insubstantial as smoke.

"This is a dreamtrail?" I asked. My mental voice had a strange echo, as if I whispered underneath speaking.

"Many trails there are," Maruman sent cryptically. His almond eyes glowed gold and diamond white. "Think of the doors now, ElspethInnle. I remember them not, and so you must recall. Think of looking at them. . . ."

I thought of them as I had last seen them, and at once I became aware of the heat and sound of flames. A huge bonfire with the doors in the center began to take shape.

"No," Maruman sent sternly. "Think of before burning. Think of first time you saw."

The sensation of crackling heat faded, and the skies darkened dramatically. I cried out in fright, but Maruman merely stood by my side, swishing his midnight tail. All around us, clouds ran through the sky at an impossible speed. They boiled and churned as though an entire day of slow progress through the skies was crammed into a few seconds. The sun set in an instant, the clouds dimming rapidly from wild rose and crimson to violet and deepest blue. Then it was night.

The moon rose and was lost in cloud, then showed again through a ragged patch of darkness like an eye peering through a tear in cloth. A cold wind blew, and I heard the rustling of leaves and branches. Trees began to materialize around me, full of creaking gestures. They formed up along both sides of the road behind us, but ahead, on one side, they gave way to a high, neatly trimmed hedge.

Everything slowed and was all at once so real and solid that I truly felt myself to be standing on a road at night. I could hear the howl of a wolf in the distance. The chill in the air told me it was not far from wintertime.

"Come," Maruman sent, and padded swiftly up the road, a black shadow barely visible in the night. He stayed close to the high, smooth-trimmed hedgerow and frequently lifted his black muzzle to sniff the air. I followed, leaning forward to compensate for the weight of the wings.

"Be swift," Maruman demanded. His lambent eyes shone back at me. I hurried as best I could, and when I stood by him, I saw that, around the bend, the road vanished into what seemed to be a mass of dark cloud. But even as I watched, a building took shape. It was enormous—more like a number of buildings awkwardly joined together than a single construction. In some places, it was two or three stories high, and on either side, turrets rose up, with steep little roofs ending in spires.

Obernewtyn, I thought, incredulous. It was Obernewtyn exactly as I had beheld it the very first time. The road ran around in a loop, circling the now familiar fountain and lantern. Its flame shuddered in the wind, casting shadows that lurched fitfully along the walls.

"This is—" I began, but Maruman threw himself hard against my hip, forcing me to stagger sideways.

"Away," he snarled with enough urgency to make me obey without question. I slipped between the trees opposite the hedge and dragged the wings through after me. Turning back to face the road, I heard the sound of horses' hooves and the grinding scrape of metal wheel rims against stone and gravel. A coach drawn by two horses burst into sight just as Maruman leaped into the trees beside me.

"Whoa, there!" the driver cried softly, pulling on the reins with a practiced hand. The coach slowed, and my mouth fell open—for the driver was Enoch, but a younger Enoch, his unbuttoned Council livery jacket flapping untidily about him. I saw fleetingly the dull flash of an enameled Council emblem on the window of the coach door and above it a girl's pale face pressed to the glass.

Only then did I understand, for I had seen that face too many times in the mirror not to know it. The girl peering out was little more than a child to my sight now, her green eyes enormous in a thin, remote face. Yet she was me as I had been the night of my arrival at Obernewtyn.

The shock of realizing that I was seeing my own past caused the world about me to waver, and the dark trees took on a vague and cloudy look.

"Hold to dreamtrail," Maruman warned me urgently.

"In the carriage . . . ," I sent. "It was . . ."

"Yes. ElspethInnle comes to mountains," Maruman agreed. "Dreamtrails hold all things. Look. Remember."

The carriage had lurched to a stop beside the broad entrance steps, and the tall, too-slender girl that I had been climbed out. She stood, and I saw fear and loneliness in her rigid stance. The girl's hair fluttered freely in the rising wind.

My hair, I thought.

I watched myself look around, remembering vividly how forbidding Obernewtyn had seemed that first night. I watched myself study the stone walls, the fountain, and then the trees, full of blustering wind and murmurous hissing. Momentarily, my own moss-green eyes looked right at me, and an irrational fear smote me.

She can't see me, I assured myself, not really knowing why the thought of being seen by my younger self unnerved me so. But I also remembered how, on that first night, the trees had seemed to whisper of incomprehensible secrets.

"She/you could see you if you desire it," Maruman sent. "But if she/you did, all would distort/take on new form. Dreamtrails are not keeping place for untouchable memories. Imprints of life they are, but have their own existence and can be affected/changed."

I did not understand. "I was really watching myself when I arrived back then?"

"Yes and no," Maruman sent. "We visit past on dream-trails. The past passed. It was."

"But . . . ," I began.

"Watch," Maruman sent again.

The younger Enoch's passengers mounted the broad, low steps to the front doors to Obernewtyn. The inconsistent lamp-light played over their backs as the guardian who had escorted me reached up to ring the bell. I heard it very faintly, or perhaps I was only remembering how it had sounded. There was a long wait; then the doors opened to reveal a tall, bony older woman carrying a candelabrum: Guardian Myrna.

They were speaking now. I could not hear as the door closed behind them, but I could remember. The guardian had dismissed me as defective. *"You'll get no sense out of her. . . ."*

"Do not remember this way, or you will merge," Maruman warned, and the sound of his voice pulled me back to an awareness of the trees shivering and rustling around us.

The door banged open and the plump guardian emerged. She crossed to Enoch, who opened the coach door to let her inside, then climbed back onto his seat and took up the reins. The carriage lurched forward, and the horses drew it back down the drive and out of sight.

I glanced at the huge building, conscious that, somewhere inside its walls, I was now being conducted to a stone cell and a night of frightened dreams.

But I was not here out of nostalgia, I reminded myself. "I must see the doors," I sent. Hurrying by the fountain and lamp, I halted before the steps and gazed up at the deeply recessed doors. It was too dark to see them clearly, and I wondered if, after all, they were the plain ones with which we had replaced the originals after the burning.

"Hold to the moment," Maruman warned, padding up beside me.

I pictured the doors as they had been the night of my arrival. By the time I reached the top step, I could make out the scrolled panels and the shallowly carved borders. Marisa had hidden directions to a cache of Beforetime weaponmachines in the borders, but I concentrated my attention on the panels, shifting to one side to allow the lantern light to illuminate them. Now that I was looking for it, I could see clearly that the wood of the central panels and that of the border and outer frame were quite different. The panels were formed of a darker, more finely grained timber, and studying the queer half-human beasts they featured, I felt absolutely certain Kasanda had carved them. The intricacy of the work resembled the sculptures in the Earthtemple in too many ways for it not to have come from the same hand. I squinted, trying to see if there were any words written within the figures.

"If only it was daylight," I murmured, frustrated.

At once, the wind rose, and I turned to see the clouds speeding up again. In an instant, the sky lightened to a deep violet, and the distant mountain peaks brightened to a paler blue. Realizing my wish had hastened the night, I focused on the blue-black chilliness of predawn, and the clouds slowed.

"Commands on the dreamtrails send out loud signals," Maruman sent in stern disapproval. "Mornirdragon will hear/smell/come soon. Must go/fly."

"But now that it's near morning, I might be able to see." I turned back to the doors and saw there were letters inscribed on a banner behind the figures. They were incomprehensible but similar to the exotic lettering I had seen in Sador. Could the message possibly be in gadi?

"If only I had some paper," I muttered frantically, reaching instinctively for my nightdress pocket. To my amazement, I discovered I was clothed, and my hand closed around Dameon's letter. Paper! But of course I had nothing to write with. Remembering what Maruman had said about thoughts being answered on the dreamtrails, I visualized the stick of black charcoal the girl Cassy had been using to draw with. Immediately, I was holding a stub of burned stick. I laid a page of the letter over the carved script on one door and brushed the burned end of the stick gently over it, hoping the makeshift rubbing would take over the pricked lettering.

"I smell Mornirdragon," Maruman warned. "She comes."

"One second more," I said, laying a second sheet of paper over the lettering on the door and rubbing the stick over it.

"No more time!" Maruman urged. He sank his teeth into my clothing and tugged me back from the doors as a screeching cry rent the air. Then I felt a sickening pull that seemed to wrench my guts inside out.

It was blazing daylight, and I was standing with Maruman on the gleaming cloud-road. I was naked again and carried neither stick nor letter, but there was no time to lament, for the red dragon appeared, hovering above us on huge scaly wings. I was thunderstruck by its sheer enormity. Its eyes stared into mine, and it gave a guttural scream of such hatred that all strength seemed to run from my legs. I was too terrified to move, but Maruman leapt forward without hesitation, butting me roughly from the path. I fell through the clouds with a scream of terror.

I tumbled mindlessly over and over before remembering that I was now a winged thing. The wings flexed, and I thought about opening them wide. I felt them move and went from falling like a stone into a flat, gliding trajectory.

As I slowed, I was overcome by a vision.

I was standing somewhere outside, and it was a chill, pitch-black night. All at once, I had the distinct sensation that someone was behind me. I whirled, and there was Ariel as he had been when I first encountered him: a boy with a face like an angel and eyes bright with malice. I could see him, because he glowed with an eerie pallid light.

My skin crawled at the nightmarish vision as Ariel gave a high-pitched child's giggle, then dissolved. Before my eyes, his shining matter reformed into an exquisitely handsome young man with long fair hair and a lithe form. He looked exactly as I had seen him on the deck of the Herder ship that had carried Matthew away, even down to his cloak.

"What do you want?" I demanded.

"Want?" he asked, and now his voice was deeper, and his features shifted slightly, growing older. If it were possible, he was more beautiful than he had been as a child. Despite all I knew of him, I was dazzled. His eyes flashed with amusement, as if he heard my thoughts and reveled in them. "I want you, of course," he whispered, and a warm wind blew softly, as if his words and breath swelled to fill the air around me, caressing my face, playing with my hair.

I felt the blood churn in my cheeks. What was he saying? What was I thinking? "You hate me. Us."

"There is no *us*, Elspeth. There is only you. And I do not

hate you. I need you." He laughed again, and his laughter grew and thundered around me.

"Leave me alone!" I screamed.

He smiled and stepped toward me. Then, all at once, his face changed. He glanced over his shoulder furtively, then vanished.

I was falling again, struggling to use my wings to right myself.

"Go down/wake!" Maruman's voice was so urgent that I obeyed instantly, angling downward and letting myself pick up speed. Reaching the region of amorphous color, I felt my physical substance dissolve into the floating etheric light shape. Now I could see the silver thread running away from me, and I willed myself along it as if it were a rope.

In seconds, if time can be measured in such a state, I was hovering over my sleeping form. I knew I must resume my body to be safe from Dragon, but I hesitated, afraid for Maruman. What if the beast turned on him? To my amazement, thinking of the old cat transported me instantly to the Healer hall where Maruman's body lay with Dragon's. The real shapes of things were again only vaguely apparent beneath their shifting halos of color, but these auras seemed far less stable than the ones in my turret room. They lurched and swayed in constant dizzying movement, mingling weirdly at the edges so it was difficult to be sure where one thing began and another ended.

The center of the disturbance was the boiling mass of red and orange light shot through with livid streaks of dark red and yellow, which could only be Dragon's aura. I was literally seeing the effect of her mental disturbance. The tumultuous swirling of fiery light about her slight form was creating a suction that violently disturbed all auras within range. Obviously, the effect would diminish the farther things were physically from her, but it was no wonder our dreams had been disturbed.

I turned to study the human forms by Dragon's bed. The aura of the nearest person glimmered pink and gentle lavender, flecked with misty blue. Strands like spiderwebs ran between this form and Dragon's. Without thinking, I reached out a hand to touch them. I had no sense of flesh meeting flesh, but as my hand of light entered the pale strands, I knew the form belonged to Angina and that some sort of link had been forged between Dragon and the Empath guilden. There was another thickish thread of light running away from Angina and out of the room. I dipped my hand into it and learned that it was an etheric connection to his twin.

The form alongside him had a very pure blue-white aura that reminded me of moonlight on snow or sea foam at night. I did not need to touch it to guess that it was the futureteller Dell. Beside her was yet another person with an aura of green shot through with a single festering streak of red, shading to purple at the edges like a faded bruise. I reached into the green light and discovered it belonged to Kella. The streak of red was her sorrow and guilt over Domick.

I located Maruman's shape within Dragon's sickly dominant aura. At first, I was frightened by the way the two auras appeared to merge, but even as I thought of the old cat, his aura sharpened and became more distinct. There were whorls of opalescent color in it and pure threads of silver, but livid streaks of yellow also tangled with the other colors. His intermittent madness, I guessed. There were seams of black, too, but before I could touch them to find out what they were, Dragon's aura began to flow around me.

626

Alarmed at the thought that the dragon beast might even now be flying toward me, I willed myself to my turret room and let the silver thread of light draw me back into my flesh. Picturing my hand plucking away the thread of light and flinging it loose, I felt a sharp stinging pain, and then it fell away as I rose to consciousness like a cork bursting explosively to the surface of water.

I gasped and opened my eyes.

I was in the chair by my hearth, my skin clammily cold. I sat up with a groan. The room seemed incredibly drab after having seen it with spirit eyes.

I forced myself to get up, marveling at the extent of my exhaustion. Traveling the dreamtrails was much harder work than traversing any true road. I threw a few sticks of kindling on the fire, hooked a pot of water over it to boil, then pulled on my jacket. Resuming the chair, I held my fingers out to the flames and wondered anew at my strange adventure. I was fascinated at the way in which auras revealed not only the nature of the thing they shaped, but also even what ailed it. Surely a healer who could use the dreamtrails would be better able to treat illnesses.

It was some time before I remembered the purpose of the night's adventures. With an exclamation, I groped in my pocket and withdrew Dameon's crumpled letter, unfolding the paper and gaping at the streaks of charcoal on it. Maruman had insisted that what happened on the dreamtrails could have an impact in life, and now here was the proof of it.

Drawing the candle near with shaking fingers, I flattened the letter carefully. Of course, I could no more read the rubbed letters now than when I had been on the dreamtrails, but I could see I had managed to get a good, clear imprint of them.

Whether it was clear enough to translate, only time would tell.

The water began to boil. I laid the pages aside and set about preparing an infusion of herbs. Feeling weary, I coerced a small mental net to trap my fatigue so that I would not unwittingly fall asleep. Dragon was sure to be waiting. It hurt me to think of the killing hatred I had seen in her eyes as she attacked me. Ironically, every time I evaded her, it increased her feelings of abandonment. Yet I could not stand and let her kill me to prove I loved her.

I shuddered, and the movement rustled the charcoal-rubbed pages of Dameon's letter on the table. I remembered I had yet to read it. Stirring honey into the scalding liquid, I settled myself back in the chair.

✦ 11 ✦

THE PRICKED WORDS on the previous page had been obliterated by the rubbing, but the last page was untouched. It began halfway through a sentence:

the Sadorians have offered to make me an honorary member of their tribe. An asura. This will allow me to become privy to all that is known to the tribal leaders and to the Temple guardians. Fian has probably said as much to you, but he will not have told you that the overguardian is dying. Fian does not know it, nor does Jakoby or anyone outside the Temple. Traditionally, such knowledge is kept within the Temple community, and it says much that I have been given access to it. That is the true reason for my delay in returning to Obernewtyn. The overguardian tells me that one day his successor will simply appear in his stead to the tribes. There is no beauty or peace in his dying, and maybe that is why they choose to shroud it in secrecy and ritual. He will suffer great pain before the end, which no drug will be allowed to alleviate. Other guardians use a spice drug that gives them pleasant dreams when the pain of their deformities is beyond enduring. But he cannot have recourse to it, because in the worst extremity, he is supposed to see a vision that will reveal his successor. Maybe it is true, but the thought of his suffering horrifies me, for already he undergoes certain agony. That is why I could not refuse him when he asked if I would stay with him at the end. He asked it in a time of terrible pain, and it was as if a child begged me. He is frightened of what he must endure, and he knows I can empathise a calmness and acceptance in him, without affecting his clarity of mind. It will mean sharing his suffering, and truly I fear it for this reason. Yet I will endure it. Witnessing his dying fills me with the determination to learn why the boy and the other Temple guardians are so terribly afflicted. I have asked him openly about their deformities, and he says that I may know the truth of that only when I am named asura. So I am patient, or try to seem so.

I must finish this now. But it lightens my heart to think I will see you and Obernewtyn very soon, and I pray that all is well there.

My love,
Dameon

I sighed, my fingers lingering on his name. Given what we had learned about Dragon, I wished more than ever that the empath was on his way to Obernewtyn.

There was a knock at the door, and I opened it to find Roland with Maruman in his arms. As the Healer guildmaster set the old cat carefully down, I noticed with alarm that his hind leg was heavily bandaged.

"What happened?"

"We don't know," Roland said soberly. His eyes met mine. "Claw marks, left by no animal that exists. I fear they can only be the dragon's doing. . . ."

I bit my lip at the memory of Maruman leaping between

Dragon's beast and me, and of the odd black streaks I had later noticed in his aura. Claw marks!

"It is my fault he's hurt," I cried.

"Don't be absurd," Roland growled impatiently. "To blame yourself for this . . ."

"Roland, last night the dragon appeared in my dreams and tried to attack me. Maruman was with me, and he deliberately got in the way."

Roland stared at me. "This cannot go on. Dragon must be taken away from Obernewtyn."

"It may not be necessary. Maruman said Angina's music had an effect. I know it didn't stop Dragon last night, but perhaps, given time . . ."

"One more night may be all it takes to cause some irretrievable harm."

"At this stage, I am the only one in danger. Dragon wasn't attacking Maruman last night. She was after me." I told him that I would eat firstmeal and then seek out Angina.

He nodded and took his leave, but he stopped at the door. "By the way, Dell said she needed to speak with you today. Or to put it more exactly, she said she had foreseen that she *would* speak with you today."

After he had gone, I lifted Maruman gently into my bed. The cat gave a soft buzzing snore, and I rubbed his soft belly and rested my head beside his on my blanket.

Even before I was washed and dressed for firstmeal, dark clouds had blotted out the sun, and the smell of rain was in the air. If the morrow was like this, most of the outdoor events and displays planned for our moon fair would have to be canceled. On top of Dameon's absence, it was almost too much, and when I reached the kitchens, I saw that I was not alone in thinking so. The tables were surrounded by gloomy expressions.

Spotting Angina next to Miky, I went over to join them. He looked exhausted and downcast. "I feel so bad about Dragon scratching Maruman," he told me. "I had the beast mesmerized, but then I fell asleep."

"That is very good news," I said. "If the dragon attacked only when you stopped playing, we know it can be controlled."

"We've been talking about it," his sister said eagerly. "Last night, I dreamed Angina was playing his gita beside a big gray wall of stone. The dragon was sitting atop the wall, but after a while, it came and laid on the grass beside him, listening. It was only when the music stopped that it flew away." She frowned. "I saw Maruman, too."

"Maruman?" I was startled to think mine were not the only dreams the old cat wandered through.

"He was watching the dragon, too," the empath explained. "He looked like a big striped cat with queer shining eyes, but I knew it was him the way you do in dreams. He went away before Angina stopped playing."

"Do you and Angina often dream of each other?"

"We dream *next* to each other," Angina said cryptically. Seeing my puzzlement, he went on. "I can go into Miky's dreams if I want, and she into mine. Sometimes we just dream together, but it's not always easy to tell whether we're dreaming of one another, or if we're sharing the dream. Not until we wake up and talk."

One of the kitchen helpers interrupted us to bring bowls of steaming oatmeal. I poured creamy milk over my oats and added a dollop of honey, wondering what the effect would

632

have been if I had entered the twins' dream. Would the music have counteracted the creature's violent response to me, or would the sight of me inflame it enough for it to brush aside the music?

"What do you think of a rota of musicians playing to her constantly?" I asked.

Angina shook his head decisively. "The others might not be able to hold her. I don't mean to sound conceited, but it's very difficult. You have to . . . to reach her somehow, as I've done. It's not just the music." He paused, and suddenly I thought of the strands I had seen linking his aura to Dragon's. "Miky and I have talked about it, and we've decided it's best if I keep watch and play my gita. Some others can take turns watching me so I don't fall asleep, and a healer can draw off a little fatigue if I get too tired."

"You can't do that forever," I said. "You will need to sleep sometime."

"I will sleep in the daytime," he answered. "After all, the dragon can't get into someone's dream unless they are asleep."

As I left the kitchen, I debated going the longer way round to the Futuretell wing, under cover, but in the end, I pulled my cloak over my head and ran across the yard. I burst into the futuretellers' hall at a run, startling a young man and two girls sitting around a frame that hemmed a splendid tapestry.

Each year, the futuretellers made a tapestry depicting a part of our Misfit history and presented it to Obernewtyn at the first moon fair following wintertime. Usually, Rushton unveiled the work and made a speech about our future.

I averted my eyes as the futuretellers covered their work,

but I had seen enough to know that they were depicting the Battlegames. I let myself be patted down with a towel and fussed over, trying to recall the names of the embroiderers. The two girls were sisters who had sought refuge with us after being freed from an orphan home by the farseekers scrying out their forbidden Talents, and the young man had been sent to us by Brydda the previous year to save him being dragged to the Councilcourt and sentenced as a dreamer. His mother had begged the rebel leader's help.

Valda! His name came to me at the same time as the memory of gossip that he was paying court to Rosamunde, who had once loved my brother, Jes.

Like many condemned to Obernewtyn in the old days, Rosamunde was unTalented, but her association with Jes had cast enough suspicion on her to have her tried by the Councilcourt. Since then, she had always regarded me with hostility. I was never sure whether she saw Jes in me and it pained her, or if she hated me for meddling with her mind when we were both at the Kinraide orphan home. To my surprise, she had elected to stay on after Rushton took over Obernewtyn. To begin with, she had worked in the kitchens, but now she dwelt in the Futuretell demesnes.

The three futuretellers were regarding me with the discomfiting intensity of their kind.

"Maryon said to ask you to go up when you arrived," Valda said.

Repressing a flash of irritation, I thanked them and made my way up a flight of stone steps to the guildmistress's turret room. But when the door opened, it was Dell who looked out at me. She said that she had just brewed choca, and, cheered by this, I allowed myself to be ushered into the turret room that was a mirror image of my own.

"It is not often you come here, ElspethInnle," Dell said.

I was startled at her use of this form of my name but decided to make nothing of it. "Roland said you wanted to see me."

"Did he say that?" She smiled, a slow quirk of the lips. "Well, it is true in any case. We have a gift for you."

"A gift for me? But why?"

"Does there need to be a reason fer a giftin'? Can it nowt simply be of itself?" Maryon asked, gliding from behind the stone wall that divided the chamber.

"A gift can be for no reason, I suppose, but seldom are they, or so I have found."

Dell's smile deepened, but Maryon's face remained gravely courteous. "Nevertheless, our gift is fer no reason other than that it pleases us." She reached for a basket under the table and drew from it an astonishing swatch of red-dyed heavy silk of the sort lately shipped from Sador. I was coerced by its loveliness to stroke it.

"We procured it last year and embroidered it throughout this winter just past," Dell said. "Only yesterday did we finally sew the fringing on."

As she spoke, they spread it out, and I saw that it was a shawl worked in silken thread. Here and there, mirror beads and glass balls glimmered like sunlight dancing on water. But it was the design that thrilled me more than the exquisite fabric, for it featured a multitude of intertwined beasts. A tyger with flaring eyes, a rearing black horse and a small pony, a dark dog and a white one, three silver-eyed wolves, and, most astonishing, a dragon hovering over all the rest. The fringe was long and moss-green, and this color found an echo in the delicate subtheme of interwoven leaves behind the beasts.

"It . . . it is the most lovely thing I have ever seen," I whispered, overwhelmed.

"Th' design came to me in a trance," Maryon said, and even now, the remoteness in her tone stopped me from expressing the warmth her gift deserved.

Yet this gift did not serve life's purpose and could come only out of some specific individual wish to please me. I did not understand and admitted to myself that knowing Maryon's past did not truly explain her nature. I watched her fold the shawl with graceful economy that reflected her desire to have no gush. She restored the lovely thing to the basket, saying offhandedly that her people had also made me a moon-fair dress and slippers to complement the shawl, and they were in the basket as well.

"I thank you, Maryon, and all who had a hand in this magnificent gift. It is a work of art whose skill even the Twenty-families must envy," I said, determined to thank her properly, even if it had to be very formal.

Maryon inclined her head and then nodded to Dell, who poured choca into three small silver goblets. Taking one, I asked how she had fared in her night vigil over Dragon.

"You know about Maruman being wounded, of course," Dell said, handing one of the goblets to her mistress. "And of Miky's dream of the beast listening to the music?" I nodded. "Then you know everything."

"You didn't dream anything yourself, then?"

Her eyes flickered, but she said, "I regret sleeping very much. I made the mistake of forgetting how powerful Angina's ability is to empathise through music; his gentleness is the secret of his strength."

"You didn't dream, then?" I persisted.

"Well, I did," she admitted with the faintest irritation. She turned to her guildmistress, who nodded. I felt a pang of alarm and wished suddenly that I had not been so insistent.

636

"I dreamed of you, ElspethInnle. I saw you walking with a great horde of animals into the deepest Blacklands."

I could not think of a thing to say.

"It is clear to Dell an' I, at least, that yer truly th' Innle th' beasts tell of in their stories," Maryon said with a certainty that was all the more devastating because it was so casually put. "Ye need nowt fear we will speak of it, nor question ye about it, fer there is a deep and needful silence laid about this matter."

I made myself sip the choca, though I was too rattled to taste it. The silence between us lengthened, and I cast about for a change of subject. "Have any of your guild seen whether Dragon will wake?" I had never dared ask this before so bluntly.

Instead of speaking, Maryon reached under the table and withdrew a rolled cloth. She opened it to reveal an elaborate dreamscape and pointed to a small, irregular blue shape. "This represents the sum of dreams within which Dragon wakes, but in every one of them, th' dreamer has nowt been able to say how th' child is when she wakens."

"You're saying she will definitely wake, but you don't know if she'll be defective. . . ."

"Nor how long before she wakens," Dell elaborated. "But you might be pleased to know that a lot of our people have been seeing Matthew as they delve."

"Futuretellings?" I asked.

"Most of the seein's of Matthew were memory dreams," the Futuretell guildmistress said. "Th' rest might be true seein'. They correspond in detail. Yer welcome to read our dream journal if you wish. But what Dell has nowt told ye is that in almost all the dreams where Matthew appeared, Dragon—or rather her dragon beast self—swoops an' tears

Matthew to pieces. Of course, it's a dream manikin she destroys, but it shows all too vividly that he rouses in her th' same violent rage as ye do.

"Th' other thing to consider is that none of us dreamed of th' lad until Dragon fell into her coma. This suggests she is somehow responsible fer th' dreams, or for somehow openin' a connection between us an' him."

"I should like to read your dream journal. May I take it now?" I asked eagerly, wondering if it would be possible to deliberately reach Matthew using the dreamtrails.

"You could not carry it alone," Dell said. "I will have two of our lads bring it to your chamber when the skies clear."

As I departed, I glanced over at the window, where rain continued to fall hard. The drumming roar of it seemed constant, for all Dell's certainty that it would abate.

✦ 12 ✦

"It is beautiful here," Straaka said, turning in his saddle to look back at the mountains through a gap in the trees. Wan afternoon sunlight poked through the tattered edges of fraying storm clouds, giving the Sadorian's skin the gleam of old wood polished to blue-black with beeswax. His eyes had a rich amber glow within the brown and were fringed by very long lashes.

I was aware for the first time that Miryum's suitor was an attractive man measured by any standard. Miryum must have felt this, and I thought again of her hesitation before she had announced her decision to reject him.

"It rains so cursed much, my mount is hard-pressed to keep her footing," Jakoby growled from behind. "Never would I have thought to hear myself complain about rain, but by the Earth goddess, this is a sodden land!"

"I think you would like it even less in the wintertime, when the ground is hard as stone under layers of snow," I said, slowing Gahltha to let her draw alongside. "This soft, wet land has its harsh face, too."

The tribeswoman grinned at me. "Like its people?"

I smiled and transferred my gaze to the sky, willing the clouds to depart entirely rather than massing again before morning. It was not so much the wet ground that troubled me as the thought of the moon fair being washed out.

Without warning, Gahltha moved into a slow trot, and I adjusted my seat to the motion. He and the Sadorians had been ready and waiting to go when I arrived on the farms, which meant we would be able to reach the Teknoguild cave network in daylight. It was a rare occasion, the guild opting for a formal meal in honor of the Sadorian guests—usually they stopped working only long enough to have a hasty bit of this or that.

But, in fact, research was on my mind at least. Fian was my best hope for translating Kasanda's writing from gadi. Hoping to avoid awkward questions about what exactly I'd based a rubbing on, I'd transcribed the text, making a careful copy by hand.

We passed into a dip containing a thicker belt of trees. Their leaves were still small and pale enough to let the sun through, and it seemed to give a shimmer to every wet leaf. I thought for the thousandth time how much I loved the mountain valley that had become my home and refuge. As always after rain, the world seemed fresh and sharp-edged. Rushton loved the forest after rain, too, and we had taken many wandering walks together when we could steal the time.

Bruna urged her mount forward to speak in a low voice to her mother. I found myself pondering her passion for Bodera's son, Dardelan. Could such a violent desire become real love and affection? It was as if a lamb were loved by a wolf. But perhaps she was not all wolf, nor Dardelan all lamb, despite his gentleness.

Straaka's horse floundered slightly in yet another boggy patch on the trail, and the other horses fell back to give it room to find its feet. As we waited for the others to catch up, I asked Jakoby's horse Calcasuus how he liked the Land.

"Green/wet lands seek the sky, ElspethInnle," he responded.

"Slippery/high/climbing lands lead to the freerunning barud," Straaka's horse suggested as he joined us.

"Our barud is the freerunning land," sent Bruna's fiery, high-stepping mare, Domina. I thought in this case that mount and rider were certainly matched in temperament.

"Funaga dwell in our barud and in this barud. The freerunning-barud-ha will not be ruled by them," Calcasuus sent, his long-fringed eyes mild. *Ha* was an obscure thought-symbol that suggested reverence for the subject to which it was attached.

"It is good that the drylands are free, for not all beasts will follow Innle to the barud-ha," Gahltha observed.

"Some beasts will remain. All roads lead to different barud," Calcasuus agreed.

"But only one path will lead to the barud-ha," Gahltha sent softly.

Chilled by their certainty of my future course, I was glad when we reached a straight, firm stretch of the path, and Bruna announced that Domina desired to canter. I thought it unwise for the desert-bred equines to go so fast over unfamiliar ground, but despite some close calls and wild skids, no horse fell or lost its rider. The sun was nigh to setting when we came to the fold in the low granite hills swelling out of the earth that marked the Teknoguild caves. There was a new mosaic around the entrance we were approaching, glinting with pieces of mirror and green and blue glass. I was somewhat surprised, for teknoguilders were inclined to the functional.

As we dismounted, Fian emerged to welcome us. With him were two young teknoguilder boys with beastspeaking abilities, both eager to tend the horses. I stroked Gahltha's flank fondly, noting the devotion with which the Sadorians examined the hooves of their horses for stones. Once they were done, I suggested we go inside and leave the Teknoguild lads to feed the horses. The others agreed, but Bruna would let no one else attend Domina. She bade us go in, saying that she would come along when she was finished.

We were not many steps into the tunnel before daylight faded, and our way was lit by bottled bulbs of glowing insects hung from potmetal hooks imbedded in the walls. When Jakoby expressed her curiosity about them, Fian explained that the Teknoguilden Jak had smeared the inside of the bulbs with a substance that attracted the insects. The creatures were quite free to escape, but there was no reason for them to do so. They had very short lives—a few brief months to make the journey from larvae to death. Not wanting to disrupt their life cycle, the teknoguilders had elected not to plug the dribbles of slimy water in any of the tunnels connecting various parts of the cave network, for the dampness was an essential part of the insects' habitat.

Fian was obviously well at ease with the tribesfolk, and conversation flowed easily between them. The Sadorians were more formal with me, though that might simply have been because of my position as temporary leader of the Misfits. When the tunnel narrowed, Straaka fell in beside me. A split second before he spoke, I caught a flow of subconscious thought that told me he wanted to ask about Miryum.

"May I ask you a question, lady?" he asked.

I decided to slice straight to the heart of things, for subtlety was no gift of mine. "You wish to speak of the Coercer guilden, Miryum."

He nodded gravely. "She was well when you parted?"

"She was, but I must tell you that she is troubled about the oath between you, because it crosses another oath she made."

642

Straaka frowned. "She had promised herself to another man?"

"Not to a man, but to Obernewtyn."

"I do not understand."

"Miryum leads the coercer-knights, and they are vital to our safety here. She fears that leaving would constitute a betrayal of her oath to Obernewtyn."

"In accepting my gift, she agreed to wive with me."

"In our Land, such a gift is only a step toward bonding. When she took your betrothal gift, Miryum did not realize that things were done differently in Sador. She did not imagine that her promise to you would take anything from her oath to Obernewtyn. She assumed one oath would be fulfilled and then, in time, another."

Straaka nodded. "I see. What was the nature of her oath to Obernewtyn?"

"You must ask that of her," I said gently, deciding I had said enough to lay the groundwork for my plan.

Fian brought us from the tunnel into a newly excavated part of the cave network, and I looked about with interest as he pointed out a section of Beforetime wall that had been exposed. A mass of twisted, silver metal poles and wires poking up from a heap of dirt and rubble drew all of us near, and Fian explained that this had been a moving stair. Harad asked incredulously where such steps could have led and was told that the caves, and indeed the whole untidy tumble of granite about us had once been an imposing Beforetime building that had climbed twelve levels above us into the air, as well as many levels below. During the upheavals of the Great White, the building had collapsed. I gazed around the enormous half cave with its rocky walls and earthen floor sprouting mushrooms in the damp crannies and corners. The remnant of the wall and stair looked utterly misplaced in the midst of it, yet the entire network was a combination of rough present and lost past.

Fian ushered us all through a short hall into the main cavern, and the Sadorians gaped at the immortal glowing sphere that lit the entire cavern, with its silvery floor and walls and row upon row of laden bookshelves. There were also numerous mismatched tables and chairs piled high with notes and scholarly paraphernalia. Above hung thick stalactites, dry now, for the cavern was kept heated to preserve the precious Beforetime books. Several teknoguilders were seated at the tables, while others pored over the bookshelves, but Fian made no attempt to interrupt them.

Bruna appeared with one of the lads who had tended the horses, and stared at the globe of light in fright. "That is not natural," she hissed at her mother.

"It is not, indeed," Jak said, coming out from between two high bookshelves to introduce himself. "In my master's absence I welcome you to our hall."

Bruna eyed him suspiciously. "I do not like the earth around me and over my head. It is like being buried."

"Having heard Fian talk of your deserts, I do not wonder that you would feel that way," he said.

"I like the mountains and the trees and the streams of this Land. Even the stone dwelling you call Obernewtyn has its beauty," Jakoby observed. "But I must say I agree with my daughter that there is something about this place that creeps the flesh."

"If you think it gloomy now, you should have seen it in the beginning," Jak said cheerfully. "Slime running down the walls, stinking mold everywhere, and any time we dug, we had to carry out by hand twisted metals and masses of rotten stuff. It is a good deal more pleasant now, and I hope that by the time you have taken a meal with us, you will feel less oppressed." He glanced at Fian. "Why don't you have the meal laid out, and I'll take our visitors on a tour of my museum."

Fian hastened away, leaving Jak to lead us through another door. I was astounded at how much the teknoguilders had extended their network and asked how they had managed to shift such masses of earth as must have filled the new caverns.

"Oh, the rooms that were intact were not packed full of earth. Only their entrances were blocked. The hardest work has been in constructing the tunnels to link the rooms, but again some of them were passageways in the Beforetime, so the earth was not hard packed in them either."

We entered a small cavern. Rock walls were hung with tapestries at regular intervals, depicting simple mountain scenes. Window-like, they made the cave less claustrophobic than the other parts of the network, and the Sadorians visibly relaxed.

Tables had been placed around the walls of the cavern, their surfaces slanted down slightly at the front so you could better see what was on them: stone pillars and metal poles, a figurine of a woman, half-melted flat square plates stamped with numbers and letters; and all manner of unknown gadgets. Jak took up one of the plates and explained that it had been taken from a Beforetimers' metal vessel on the submerged roads of Tor.

On another table, a number of badly damaged books lay under a glass plate. I recognized one as the diary of the man who had built our Obernewtyn, Lukas Seraphim.

Beside me, Jakoby took up a small brown tube with a bowl at one end and studied it with interest.

"We think that was a device to encourage a new-lit fire," Jak said, coming to join us. "There are traces of smoke in the bowl and in the pipe."

Jakoby looked amused. "We have a similar implement that is used during certain vision dances. We press a sort of spice into the end and then light it, inhaling the smoke through this end of the tube. The smoke enhances the ability to meditate before ritual battles."

Jak looked intrigued and began to question her while the rest of the group drifted away. I had seen much of the display before, though not laid out so accessibly. I complimented Jak on his museum, but he shrugged off my praise, saying that what lay in the room was in a sense the Teknoguild's least important discoveries. "This is a collection of mere curiosities and incomprehensible gadgets. It sometimes even depresses me. The more we learn of the Beforetime, the more I can see that it is a lost civilization and we will never regain it. To me, this place is a graveyard as much as anything else."

"We of the desert believe humans worry too much about remembering their past," Jakoby said equably. "What does it matter that many of these things are unknown to you now?"

"If all that we learn is forgotten, each generation must re-learn the same things over," Jak said. "You must build upon what is known in order to reach up to what is unknown."

"I do not say things ought not to be remembered. Some things. Some knowledge. In Sador, our remembering lies in music and poetry. What is not remembered in these ways ceases to exist. In our experience, people remember what they need and forget that which is no doubt better forgotten."

Jak looked inclined to argue, but I caught his eye and shook my head firmly. He shrugged and said he would like to hear one of the tribal memory songs. Jakoby grinned and said she could manage it if they had a bit of Grufyyd's ale to wet her tongue.

Jak smiled, too. "We do at that." He suggested we move on to the guild's dining room, and we made our way back through the main cavern and along an older tunnel to a small, dry cave. To my surprise, the room was full and the tables covered in snowy cloths upon which lay a veritable feast— flat vegetable pies and dishes of runny cheese sauce and spicy chutney to accompany them, fragrant baskets of fresh baked bread, pots of butter and honey, and platters of dried fruits and slabs of cheese. At the center of each table, a cream pie concocted with choca had a place of honor. Teknoguilders usually subsisted on bread and cheese and apples between visits to the big house, so the food must have been brought in for the occasion.

We took our seats, and Fian poured mugs of ale or cordial, then made a speech welcoming the Sadorians. We drank a toast to them; then we ate.

In between mouthfuls, the teknoguilders questioned one another about their projects. Harad and Bruna asked Fian many questions about Teknoguild expeditions and about the guild's slow work in trying to gain access to the older chambers upon which the caves rested. Jakoby and Jak talked to one another, their voices raised in argument from time to time as they disagreed over the concept of remembering and the importance of knowledge, but there was no open row, because the Teknoguilden sat beside me, and I prodded him with a hard toe whenever things became too fiery. Straaka sat between Bruna and me and was chiefly silent. I did not need to read his mind to know that he was thinking of Miryum.

After we consumed the last sweet crumbs of pie, Jak requested the promised song from Jakoby. The tribeswoman laughed and withdrew a small flat rectangle of very pale fine-grained wood from her shirt pocket. Three taut strings ran from end to end, passing over a raised ridge. Jakoby plucked three surprisingly somber notes before settling herself and beginning to sing. I had heard the tribes sing in Sador, but that had been a far more formal rendering of music. Now, her strong deep voice swelled in a less lofty way.

When she was finished, I asked her if she had sung in gadi. She nodded, explaining the song told of a man sitting in the desert night and pondering the battle he must fight the following day. I asked if she could read something written in gadi for me, but she gave me a peculiar look and said that she could not read the language.

Fian leaned across and asked if I had the piece of writing I had wanted him to translate. After a slight hesitation, I produced my copy of the rubbing. He leaned close to a candle to study it.

Jakoby bent over his shoulder. "What does it say?" she asked the teknoguilder.

"The lettering is not very well scribed," Fian complained. "There's something about a way, and that word means 'need' or 'must.' I think that is a name. Ka . . . Karada?"

Alarmed, I said quickly that a feast was no place to begin a translation and that I'd thank him to put the paper away until he was sober.

"I haven't had any ale," Fian said, giving me an injured look, but to my relief, he returned the copy to its wax pouch and slipped it into his pocket. I had probably overreacted, but I had feared he would translate aloud the name Kasanda.

"Where did you see these words?" Jakoby asked.

"I dreamed them," I said lightly.

"What was the dream?"

"I was looking at . . . at a carving," I said, deciding to stay as close to the truth as I dared. "That's where these were scribed. When I woke, I wrote down what I remembered. I don't suppose it will make much sense, but it irks my curiosity."

"Maybe you saw words in the Earthtemple when you were there and remembered them in your dream," Bruna said.

"I believe the overguardian would not have shown me anything I should not have seen," I said, responding to her somewhat accusatory tone.

"That is so," Jakoby said. "The Temple is very protective of its secrets."

Bruna tossed her shapely head, making the beads and clips in her hair clank together, and I pitied Dardelan if he did care for the moody little hellcat. A strong longing for Rushton smote me.

Jakoby gracefully declined requests for another song, volunteering Bruna instead. The girl acquiesced with bad grace, but her voice turned out to be surprisingly sweet. Her manner might be brusque and arrogant, but her voice was pure sunlight and honey.

Rising sometime later, I asked Jak if we could see his workshop before we returned to Obernewytn. Harad and Bruna immediately protested that they were too full to move, and after some discussion, it was decided that the Sadorians would stay the night. I took my leave and followed the Teknoguilden back down the short hall to his museum room. On the other side of it, behind a long tapestry, there was a doorway.

"The tapestry keeps the dampish air I need in my workroom from getting into the museum," Jak explained. His workroom

649

proved to be a small, dank cavern with one flat wall against which his workbench and a host of shelves were built. Clusters of bottles hung on hooks, filled with coruscating masses of glows. Their combined light was dazzling. "I am trying to breed them," Jak said. He indicated a series of tanks, where more glowing insects crawled over several lumps of metal.

"What are they doing?"

"Feeding," Jak said. "That is mildly tainted metal."

"Tainted!" I drew back in alarm.

"*Mildly* tainted," Jak stressed. "You would have to handle it a great deal before the skin would absorb enough to do any harm. And it is a lot less tainted now than when I brought the stuff in."

"Where did you get it?" I asked disapprovingly.

"Ah, well. I got it from the ruins on the edge of the Blacklands, but they are not dangerous unless you spend a lot of time there. I am not so in love with the idea of my death to lie about that. I've too much work to do to waste time even being sick."

"All right, let's say for the moment that it's true the ruins are not very dangerous. You should still not be there, because guildmerge forbade it."

"I know," Jak said, but he did not look contrite. "I wanted to see what would happen if I bred some of the insects to tolerate a drier climate—hardier insects that could live out in the open if need be. We could set them to cleaning up the Blacklands. The problem is that any sun is quite deadly to them, so we would have to breed them to be nocturnal feeders." He gave me a penetrating look. "Years ago, I dreamed of the Great White destroying the land, spilling its poisons. It has haunted me since, and if I can help heal what has been done, I would count my life well spent."

I nodded, understanding even better than he how much harm had been done. "You ought to put in a formal request to spend some time in the ruins."

I asked then if I could look at the plasts his guild had unearthed that had any mention of flamebirds. He rummaged obligingly in a trunk under the bench and handed me a slippery pile.

"There are only a few mentions, and they're scattered. Why don't you just take the plasts back to Obernewtyn with you? Someone can collect them later."

I said good night and, donning my cloak, farsent Gahltha. Outside, mist swirled along the ground, wet and heavy, and my breath came out in white puffs.

Gahltha appeared like a dark ghost.

"I am sorry I was so long," I sent once we were on our way. "You must be worried about Avra."

He tossed his head. "Avra had no fear/worry for the foaling. Maybe it is the mother/nature to feel so, but I am no dam calmed by nature." I sensed he did not wish to speak of Avra anymore, and I looked up at the sky. We had come high enough on the winding forest trail to rise above the cloying mist, and I was pleased to see the spine of stars running across a cloudless night sky.

Gahltha interrupted my meandering thoughts to ask if I would mind if he galloped. When I agreed, he leapt forward, and for a time the pace was too great for any thought other than those connected with riding. I flattened myself against his back, my cheek pressed to his hot neck, and concentrated on becoming a part of his flowing movement. Time seemed to blur and ceased to have any meaning as we sped over the ground. We might have ridden hours or minutes before we broke out of the trees, but still Gahltha did not slow. We galloped along the open path and plunged through the farm gate at a speed that would have been dangerous at any reasonable hour.

Outside the barns, Gahltha reared up and pawed the mist with a whinny of exaltation before stopping.

I slid from his back, laughing. "That was a wild ride!"

"There is no better way to chase fears away," Gahltha sent, nudging me affectionately before trotting off to find his mate.

✦ 13 ✦

I WOKE THE next morning with Maruman patting a velveted paw against my cheek. My first thought was that Angina had succeeded in constraining Dragon's mind, for my sleep had been undisturbed.

"You must not go back to sleep. Mornirdragon grows restless as feelmusic weakens," Maruman advised.

I rolled over to stare at the old cat. He was curled into my pillow, his single yellow eye gleaming in the dimness of the shuttered chamber. "I'm glad to see you awake. I was worried."

"Mornirdragon did not mean harm/hurt to Maruman-yelloweyes," he sent.

"But she did hurt you," I sent. "You saved me and I thank you for it."

Maruman made a sniffing sound. "ElspethInnle came late last night. I wakened. . . ." He sent a picture of Ceirwan and Freya, whom I'd asked to watch him in my absence. They were sitting side by side before the fire, their heads close together. The image shimmered with his irritation, but I smiled to see Freya's head droop into the curve of the young guilden's neck.

The picture vanished in another flash of irritation.

"Human mating," Maruman jeered. "So longwinding."

I lay watching him until I remembered what day it was.

Not only moon-fair day, but also the day Rushton would come home! Suddenly wide awake, I slipped out of bed and hurried across the room to open the shutters. The day was as fair as we could have wished, the sky blue and cloudless. I grinned and hugged myself.

Traditionally, on moon-fair mornings, Ceirwan sent some of the younger farseekers up with a special firstmeal for me, a mark of honor to the sender, even though it was truly my pleasure. But it was much too early to worry about disappointing them with an empty room. I slipped on my robe and padded in woolen slippers down the stairs and along the halls. The bathing room was empty, which pleased me, and although it usually meant I had to stoke the furnace and wait for the water to heat before bathing, it had already been done. No doubt Javo and Katlyn had been up since dawn and had sent one of their kitchen helpers to tend to it.

I turned a spout and undressed as the end barrel nearest the window filled up. Closing the valve, I threw in a handful of sweet-scented bathing spices and climbed in with a sigh of pleasure. I thought blissfully that any worry that could not be eased by a gallop with Gahltha or a hot bath must be truly grim.

I returned to the turret room with my hair wound into a sodden turban and pulled a seat into the sun. I forced myself to concentrate on toweling it, combing the tangles out and rubbing in a slippery herbal liquid Katlyn had given me as a gift to make it shine. Then I fetched the pile of plasts Jak had lent me, Tomash's rough chart, and the heavy dream journal Dell had sent up. Settling myself so that the weight of my hair caught the sun's direct rays, I grabbed the pile of plasts resolutely. I did not feel like reading them, but better that than worrying endlessly about Rushton.

He will come, I told myself, and focused my mind on the plasts. A brief riffle through made it clear most were similar to other Reichler Clinic plasts, ostensibly advertising the Clinic while downplaying its successes. Written between the lines was the offer of friendship and help to anyone with Misfit abilities. They were cleverly composed missives, and I wondered exactly who had put them together.

I spotted a mention of Govamen and flamebirds.

Govamen are using flamebirds for their experiments, which naturally outrages animal welfare groups, as the birds are virtually on the edge of extinction. The director of the institute handling the research says that scientists chose the bird for the very qualities that have endangered it and that their team is not the cause

The plast ended suddenly, indicating that it was part of a longer document. There was no telling who it had been to or from, nor its purpose.

I glanced over the other plasts until I found another mentioning the birds.

Demands by animal welfare groups for a review of the breeding program and for the opportunity to monitor the experimental use of the flamebirds were met with a refusal by head of security at the institute, Mr. Petr Masterton. He reminded reporters that as the research was being conducted by an organization employed by the World Council, it must be assumed to have the highest moral and ethical standards.

Petr Masterton! I reread the name in disbelief, thinking back to my memory dream. Seeing the name here was proof

655

positive that Cassy had lived at the same time as Hannah and the Reichler Clinic and that she had been connected to the Govamen that had kidnapped Misfits from the Reichler Clinic.

I flicked through the remaining plasts but found only one other mention of the birds, a description that confirmed conclusively that they were the Agyllians in the Beforetime, if I had doubted it.

I laid the plasts aside and turned my attention to Tomash's work. Unscrolling his rough-inked map of the Land, I looked for the information he had added about individual Councilmen's holdings. Radost's sons, Moss and Bergold, were written in neatly, their territories marked out to show their common border. Tomash had written in tiny script that Moss had elected to extend Darthnor's mining into his holding and eventually to open a smelter that would process his private mine yield as well as that of the Darthnor mines. Currently, Darthnor mines sent all their ore to the west coast to be processed.

Bergold had elected to transform his holding into orchard land. Later he would sell the fresh fruit, as well as dried and bottled fruit and sauces. In brackets, Tomash had written that his sister, Analivia, dwelt with him.

I let my eyes run farther over the map. The Councilmen used their holdings in a variety of ways, from farming, logging, and horse breeding to establishments for dye works and smelting. Radost operated a slaughterhouse in Sutrium. On the west coast, where there was little arable land, fishing was key, with Councilmen owning small fishing fleets and fish-drying plants.

At the map's bottom were further notes explaining that in addition to their land holdings, all the Councilmen had interests in numerous smaller concerns that brought them a small but steady trickle of coin. Many Councilmen also had money sunk in businesses within the cities they ruled. They used their positions shamelessly to advance their interests and to extinguish rivalry and competition, with the notable exception of Noviny in Saithwold, a man who seemed, by all reports, to be just and good and widely respected in his area.

A timid knock at the door roused me. I sat up and farsent an invitation, whereupon a beaming Aras entered, accompanied by a wide-eyed child with cornflower blue eyes and a curly mop of dark hair. I racked my mind to think of the child's name as they deposited their trays.

"Twyna," Ceirwan farsent, for, of course, he had been following their progress. "She is Lina's younger sister an' has slight farseekin' Talent."

I invited them to drink a sip of preserved berry juice to celebrate the start of moon-fair day. The toast was a tradition, and the tray Aras bore held a tiny silver jug and three glasses kept especially for this purpose.

I suggested Aras make the toast, and she flushed with pleasure. "To this day, Guildmistress. That it be bright, and with it, all the days thereafter."

It was gracefully said, but a grim part of my mind knew that all days were not ever going to be bright. The most you could expect was that there would be more bright days than dark ones. Repressing a swirl of superstitious unease, I clinked glasses with them and we drank. Twyna drank so fast she almost choked, and Aras pounded her between the shoulder blades.

"Killing yourself would be a bad omen to bring to the day," I chided.

"She's nervous," Aras explained, putting her arm about

the smaller girl. Then she smiled shyly. "I am, too, a bit. I did not know I would be the one to come up in Ceirwan's place. It's too great an honor for me."

"Never," I said firmly. "We are very pleased with how hard you have worked and how much you have put into the new mindmerge, not to mention coming up with it in the first place."

Aras's eyes sparkled. "I really think we are on the verge of it working," she said. "Zarak and I have been practicing and practicing in our spare time."

"Zarak?"

She nodded, her smile disappearing. "I know you are angry with him because of how he was last time in the practice, Guildmistress, but he is very good usually."

"He lets ambition cloud his mind," I said coolly.

"No, indeed," Aras said earnestly. "In fact, just yesterday, he was at me to agree to be a ward, because he thinks I am the only one fit for filling Matthew's shoes. I said he ought to be one, because he was more Talented, and he said Talent was the smaller part of being a ward. He said you had to be fit for it in your heart and soul, and he was the least fit of all in those things." She shrugged her bemusement, but I was well pleased.

When they had gone, I lifted the cover on my tray and smiled to find a stack of golden pancakes dripping with butter and honey-syrup, and another jug of preserved blackberry cordial. There were also bowls of cream and soft cheese for Maruman. I set these on the ground near the fire, thinking he would sniff his way to them when he was hungry enough.

I sipped at my cordial and flipped over the more recent pages of the futuretellers' master dream journal. Individual dreamers were only identified by guild and Talents—perhaps

I had misjudged Maryon's ability to recognize people's sensitivity about their dreams. There were a good number of entries featuring the dragon, though never in any particularly threatening way unless Matthew or I were also in the dream, in which case we were the only targets of the beast's aggression.

I read:

> *I dreamed of Matthew, who was Farseeker ward before he was taken away by slavers. He looked older than I remember, and he was standing with a girl who had long moon-pale hair and a sad face. The girl was weeping, and he was comforting her. A big stout man with a beard came to them. "You can't stand out here like this," he said. "They don't like seeing us acting human. It makes them feel guilty, and that makes them angry because to them, we are dumb beasts who have no right to feelings."*
>
> *"One day they will learn that neither we nor beasts are dumb," Matthew said.*
>
> *The big man scowled at him. "Such talk will get us all whipped or killed."*
>
> *Then the dragon flew at them, and I woke as it caught hold of Matthew.*

Leafing on, I came to another mention of Matthew.

> *I dreamed of a building like the Councilcourt, only twenty times more grand and made of reddish stone all carved into lions and bears and other beasts. It stood in the midst of a dense city with packed-earth streets rather than proper paving stones or gravel. All of the buildings looked to be of reddish stone or mud bricks, and none ever rose*

more than two levels above the street, except this one. It was so hot you could imagine they never had to think of mud or slush or even snow. There was no grass or trees anywhere.

I saw the Farseeker ward Matthew with some other men. They were all carrying heavy loads of rocks in baskets and wore sandals and short skirts belted at the waist. They brought their loads into the courtyard of the biggest building, and as they laid them down, Matthew gave a gasp. He was staring at one of the walls, but I could not see what had caught his attention.

"What's the matter with you?" one of his companions asked him.

"Th' woman in th' carving . . . she . . . she reminds me of someone . . . ," he stammered.

The other man laughed, but his face was so sad it seemed more like weeping. "Would that you had seen that woman, for she is our queen vanished these long years past. It is said she will return to us one day."

"Get moving, man," another man said, shoving Matthew. He glared at the other. "And you shut that stupid mystical babble about the Red Queen coming back. Everyone knows she's dead."

Then the dragon appeared, smashing through the wall and howling. It snatched Matthew up, and he screamed as it bit into him.

I shuddered but forced myself to read on. There were two more brief entries within which Matthew appeared, breaking rock with a mallet in some sort of quarry, and a third entry of him staring at boats in a harbor. Finally, I laid the book aside, thinking of the similar details reported by the dreamers. It could only mean that they had seen Matthew in reality—a slave in a hot, red land over the sea.

"Are you coming, Elspeth?" Gevan's coercive mental prod hammered into my mind.

I sent that I would come as soon as I had visited the Healer hall.

"Make it fast, then. You can collect Roland and the twins on the way."

I gave my almost dry hair a shake to loosen it and dressed hurriedly. The shawl I had been gifted was incredibly soft against my skin, and the slippers fit perfectly. I dabbed on some rose oil and ran downstairs, leaving the door ajar for Maruman.

Roland and Kella met me at the entrance to the Healer hall, their eyes widening as they took in my finery.

"Oh, Elspeth! You look beautiful!" Kella sighed, fingering the embroidered shawl. She was dressed in her normal drab gray and white skirt and shirt, the little owl fixed to her shoulder like an oversize shawl brooch. Seeing my amusement, she said it was less trouble to let it use her as a perch than to have it fly about, banging into things looking for her.

Miky and Angina came out of their borrowed chamber, clad in matching lavender tunics with violet trimmings.

"You did a good job last night," I told them warmly. "The dragon did not once visit me in the night."

"It was more tiring than I expected," Angina admitted.

"Oughtn't you to be sleeping now?"

"I had a couple of hours when I was sure everyone else was awake," the empath said. "But I don't want to miss the moon fair."

"But tonight . . . ," I began.

"He will be fine," Roland rumbled. "I'll siphon off fatigue

until I can't stay awake, then Kella will relieve me. It's just a pity the dragon isn't as charmed by Miky's music. It would have been a lot simpler for them to alternate."

"I wonder why it prefers your music, Angina," I said. "After all, Miky is a fine musician as well."

"Better than I am," Angina said firmly. "Stronger."

"Maybe so, but strength is obviously not what Dragon needs," Miky said.

The subject lapsed as we came out into the sunlit courtyard where Maryon and Dell, clad in palest blue tunics, waited with Garth. The Teknoguildmaster merely wore a cleaner version of his normal brown tunic, and Gevan was dressed in a shining black robe trimmed with rather gaudy red cloth flowers, but beside him, Miryum looked no different than usual, her clothes as somber as her expression. I guessed her mind was less on the moon fair than on the meeting she must later have with the Sadorian, Straaka. I would have to find a moment during the day to let her know what I had told him.

"I have the potmetal bracelets," Garth said. "I also have some exciting news!"

"Let's get moving while you talk," Gevan pressed, and ushered us into the maze. Most of the snow was melted now, and the leaves were losing their numbed look.

"You found the base of the Reichler Clinic building?" I guessed.

He nodded. "It was buried under a mass of silt and mud, and though that is going to be cursed difficult to shift, there is at least one level above the ground intact. This means the main entrance is accessible."

"What about the basement?" I asked.

"Well, that will be trickier, but I think we will manage it," Garth said, looking positively demonic in his enthusiasm.

Alad was waiting for us at the farm gate, clad in moss-green velvet. With him were Gahltha, Faraf, and the pale-eyed Rasial on behalf of the beasts, and Louis Larkin on behalf of the unTalents. He had even brushed his wild mop of hair, which made him look only slightly less ferocious than usual. The rest of Obernewtyn's populace was arrayed by the barns in the distance. The sight of them, Talents, unTalents, and beasts assembled together, brought a lump to my throat.

Alad welcomed me to the farms formally as Master of Obernewtyn in Rushton's stead. Then he welcomed the other guildleaders and our Sadorian guests, and led the way down the orchard path to the crowd assembled around the small grassy patch under a pear tree where Rushton traditionally spoke to open the festivities. I made a short speech praising everyone for their work during the year and inviting them to enjoy the day of rest and celebration. My words felt uninspired and brusque. In truth, I felt rather nervous having to talk to so many people all at once.

Dell then retold the story of the Battlegames in Sador with simple eloquence, pointing to the self-knowledge we had acquired in losing to the rebels. When she unfurled her guild's annual gift to Obernewtyn, there was a universal sigh. The tapestry was truly magnificent. None of the futuretellers had ever seen the desert lands, yet they had managed to capture perfectly the burning dryness and blinding salt-white heat of the sand dunes, contrasting them with the carved stone cliffs and the dazzling blue of the sea. They had even included a ship and several ship fish at one corner.

I thanked them for their gift, managing to be slightly less stilted, because most of the audience were concentrating on the tapestry. "We have made many efforts to redefine ourselves since the Battlegames. Let us hope that we will soon see the fruit of our efforts ripen. Let us hope that just as Gevan's magi are applauded and admired, Misfits, too, will someday be accepted at last." I paused, searching for a way to end my speech, but I realized there was one important thing yet to be said.

"This tapestry also reminds me of another thing, and that is the absence of our beloved Empath guildmaster. I know you are all as disappointed as I am not to have him with us today. He remains with the Sadorians in order to receive high and deserved honors from the tribes, which will further cement our friendship with them. But our honored Sadorian guests have promised to faithfully render a tapestry of words to him of this day so that he can share it with us."

There was a spontaneous burst of clapping, and I stepped back with relief, my task done. Alad took my place and invited everyone to find a soft piece of grass and wait for oiled groundsheets to be handed out. After everyone was seated, midmeal would be served.

The guildleaders traditionally sat together at the celebratory moon-fair midmeal. We spread two large canvases and a scatter of cushions under the pear tree and were soon joined by Enoch and Louis Larkin and by the Sadorians. Miryum slipped away to join her coercer-knights, and I saw Straaka's eyes follow her with longing, but he made no move to go after her.

Katlyn's helpers handed out plates and knives and sturdy mugs, and I leaned my back against the pear tree and breathed in the delicious savory smell of pies and pastries and herbed soups.

"You seem very self-satisfied," Alad said, looking amused.

"And why not," I said, smiling lazily at him. "It is a beautiful day, and a splendid feast is about to be laid out for us.

And although my words were less impressive than Rushton would have managed, they are over and done with."

"Truly no one has his gift for speechmaking," Roland said. "But I daresay he'll make up for it tonight at the guilding ceremony. And I am very curious to hear what news he'll bring from the lowlands."

Gevan said, "I might just as well tell you all that Enoch has just brought me news that the Councilman of Sawlney wants the magi to play at his daughter's bonding ceremony. The invitation and a request to see that it reaches us was made to a group of halfbreed gypsies who, of course, knew nothing of us. By sheer chance, Enoch heard them deliberating about which troupe it could be."

"You want to accept it?" I asked.

"I do. It is too good an opportunity to miss."

"You will have to present the whole thing to guildmerge," I said.

Gevan nodded and reached for a slice of pie.

As soon as the main part of the feast had been consumed and we had moved on to little preserved-berry pies and lemon tarts, a good number of empaths vanished into the barn.

"What is happening now?" Bruna demanded.

"We are about to see a performance," Alad told her. "Each guild has an offering for this moon fair, a sort of gift. There are displays from the Teknoguild, and—"

A bell clanged, and Miky and Angina emerged from the barn wearing billowing violet cloaks over their clothes. They bowed in unison; then Miky spoke in a clear, strong voice. "Our moon-fair offering is not a story of things that truly happened but a created story under which slumbers a deeper truth than can be told with mere facts."

The twins bowed again, and Angina withdrew to one side to sit on a small stool set against the barn wall. He was joined by several other empath musicians, and some moments passed while they set themselves up with stools and tuned their various instruments. Then there was complete silence.

Still standing, Miky nodded her head slightly. Nothing happened, or so it seemed, but one of the musicians had begun to play very, very softly. The other musicians joined in, swelling the sound, and at last Miky sang.

The strength and purity of her tone caught my breath, and then I sensed Angina begin to empathise his sister's music, enhancing and projecting the emotional tones in her voice so that they thrummed in your heart as well as your ears. I was so entranced that I scarcely noticed three black-clad coercers slip from the barn to stand behind Miky.

The twins had written the song based on Dameon's retelling of a Beforetime story, but it had been much developed and elaborated since the last time I had heard it. I was trying to pick out the initial tune from the rest when all at once, a beautiful young woman clad in a lavish white dress, all sewn over with tiny pearls, appeared on the grassy stretch between Miky and the audience.

There was a loud gasp, for of course she was a coerced illusion. Ordinarily, I disliked any sort of tampering with my perceptions, and I could easily have blocked the vision, but I was riveted. With her mass of fiery red hair all wound through with pearls and roses and hanging to her slender waist, and her bright blue eyes, the woman reminded me inescapably of Dragon as she might grow to look in womanhood.

"Incredible!" Alad muttered beside me.

The emotions being empathised became more complex, and I realized that I was feeling the princess's boredom with the privilege and selfishness of court life. I experienced in song and empathy her concern for all the poor of the kingdom who would never have a full belly, let alone a pearl-encrusted gown.

Next I felt the young woman's fear as a wicked Beforetime scientist appeared, boasting to the court of his machines and abilities. Everyone laughed and praised him except the princess, who feared what would come of his dark manipulations. Inevitably, the Beforetime scientist went too far. Driven mad by his lust for power and angered by her reproaches, he ended up cursing the princess to sleep forever. As she fell, the court wailed in horror. But a woman with shining silver hair rose up and announced herself to be a futureteller. She promised that the princess would not sleep forever, but only until one came who knew the secret of healing her.

Weeping servants lay the princess on a carved golden bed studded with jewels, and surrounded by a bed of roses. As years passed, the roses grew up over her in a bower, and then a room, and then a castle of flowers with thick thorns, as dark as claws.

Then the story shifted to a prince, and I cried out in delight, for whose face should the prince wear but Dameon's! Blind Prince Dameon sat on his balcony, listening to a bard sing all we had just heard of a princess asleep these hundred years.

That night, the prince dreamed that the sleeping beauty was calling to him, singing in a beautiful voice. The sweetness in it caught his soul and bound it. In the morning, he set out, determined the sleeping princess would be his bondmate. With him was his faithful companion, a horse that would be his eyes.

He heard more of the story from innkeepers and jacks as they traveled toward the dark forest of thorns. Numerous princes had tried over the years to reach the princess, but neither they alone, nor the entire armies some of them mustered, had succeeded in hacking their way through the forest to the princess. Many died painfully, for the thorns were poisonous and sharper than daggers. One king had tried to set the thorns ablaze in a rage, though he might well have burned the princess, too. But the forest only smoldered, giving off a poisonous smoke that had killed the king and his men at arms.

Prince Dameon was disheartened, for the more he heard, the more he wondered how one blind man could go where an army could not. When he reached the impenetrable thorn forest, he fell silent, for though he could not see it, he felt the heaviness of its shadow looming over him, and he understood that it had its own sentient life. He took out his dagger but did not wield it.

He sat beneath the thorns to think, using the knife to peel an apple. His horse trembled beside him, begging him to come away, but Prince Dameon bade the horse wait for him at a stream they had passed. The prince loved his companion too dearly to risk him as well.

When he was alone, he stood and turned to address the brooding presence of the thorn forest. "Are you not there to protect her from all the wrong princes who came before?"

The forest did not answer, but he felt it listening.

"If so, then how did you know they were wrong for her?" Miky sang blind Prince Dameon's words to the forest. "The stories tell that they came with swords and knives and tried to fight their way through you to her. They saw you as a barrier to their desire, and they were ready to destroy you to get what they wanted. They did not try to understand you."

The forest was still silent, but it seemed to the prince that its suppressed fury had quieted.

"You are here to protect her," the prince repeated, "but maybe you are part of her as well. For are not the thorns as natural to the bush as is the lovely rose? Maybe you must be courted, forest, just as she would be, and maybe you must be allowed to say no to me, for does your princess's heart not have a choice to wake or no?"

All at once, a bird sang a long peal of music.

The prince realized this was the same tune sung by the princess in his dream. He took a simple reed pipe from his vest and played back the tune. Then he embroidered it, adding his own depth and dimensions. Beneath and above the loveliness of the princess's melody, he wove the song of his own yearnings. There was a great rustling as if the entire forest sighed, then utter stillness.

The prince ceased to play and stood wondering. Then a scent arose about him sweeter than a thousand blossoms. Slowly, he walked forward, without even lifting his hands to defend his face from the thorns. But rather than thorns, blossoms caressed his cheeks and hair. He felt the forest sigh again, and he lifted the pipe to his lips and began to play. The scent of roses became so powerful as to make him drunk, yet he played and walked slowly, allowing the forest to lead him this way and that, into its deepest heart.

Only when he stepped into the open did he cease to play. Almost he ceased to breathe, for he sensed that he was near to the princess of his dreams. He walked forward, now with his hands outstretched so that he should not strike her bed. As he touched the edge of it, smothered in roses, he heard her soft breath, and it brought him to her face. Laying aside the pipe, he touched her hair and cheeks, her eyelashes and lips, marveling at their delicate beauty and softness, and at the sweetness that flowed from her as surely as the scent from the roses.

Then, because he could not help himself, he kissed her.

The princess opened her blue eyes and spoke to him. "This gentle tune I dreamed of all through my long sleep," she whispered. "Play on, my love."

The vision of Prince Dameon bending over the red-haired princess faded, and I realized I was weeping. I was not alone. Even Bruna and the other Sadorians were scrubbing at their cheeks.

"By the goddess, how to render a song worthy of such a performance!" Jakoby exclaimed huskily over the applause.

"That was beautiful, truly," Bruna said. "But it is just a story. The thorns of the real world would not be turned aside by a song."

"Not th' song of one man, mebbe, even if he were a prince. But mebbe a song sung by many in harmony could blunt th' thorns if that were its desire," Maryon said. "Unfortunately, most of th' world sings a song of hatred an' violence." She rose and walked away into the orchard.

"What is the matter with her?" Bruna demanded.

"Those who see visions are not as others," Harad said respectfully.

Bruna shrugged in dismissal and turned back to finish her tart.

Gradually, people began to rise and move about. Cramped from sitting so long, I rose, too, and strolled over to where the various competitive guild games were beginning. Organized and judged by my own guild, they were the farseekers' contribution to the day. Ceirwan was too busy to do more than wave. I watched for a time, noting with approval that the emphasis of the games was on the demonstration of hard-won skills rather than competition. These were followed by a series of games designed to amuse and entertain. They were successful, judging by the laughter of the watchers, but the empaths' performance had left my emotions oddly raw, and before long, I drifted away.

In the center of a ring of blossom-laden trees in the orchard, each guild had set up a display of the handicrafts they had amassed during the wintertime. Of course, everything was bartered rather than exchanged for coin. Any item left over at the end of the day would be sold by the magi when they were on tour, and this would allow us to increase Obernewtyn's supply of coin. I noticed Rosamunde and Valda, who were standing on the other side of the stalls talking earnestly. I turned away to give them privacy and found myself looking at Freya and Ceirwan, who walked by holding hands, entirely absorbed in each other.

Jak had come to stand beside me, and he chuckled at my expression. "It would be interesting to do a survey on the number of relationships that are formed on moon-fair days."

"My own parents met at a moon fair in Berrioc," I said.

"You must be wishin' Rushton would hurry up and arrive," the guilden said. "I bet he feels no less impatient to get here, but he's sure to arrive soon."

"I hope you're right," I muttered. I had managed not to worry about Rushton for a time, but Jak had brought my suppressed anxieties to the surface. Where was he?

Suddenly, Miryum shrieked for me in such a panic-stricken mental summons that I was compelled to go to her at once, leaving Jak openmouthed behind me.

✦ 14 ✦

"WHAT HAPPENED?" I demanded, staring down in dismay at Straaka. He lay motionless and unconscious at the Coercer guilden's feet.

Miryum lifted her hands helplessly. "I had to knock him out or he would have killed himself. He came up and asked if I meant to honor my vow to him. I couldn't not answer. I had to tell him the truth," she said defiantly, seeing the look on my face. "I told him I had taken the horses as a gift without understanding what it meant, and in all honor, he could not hold me to an agreement made without understanding."

"What did he say to that?" I asked, cursing myself for failing to speak to her sooner.

"He told me he understood, but by his people's customs, he had no choice but to kill himself. Then he took out his knife!" Her voice rose on a note of horror. "I didn't know what to do."

I sighed. "Miryum, do as I tell you now. Drag him inside the barn and put him into Alad's spare bed. Take his knife away."

"That won't stop him," Miryum said.

"Look, you have to—"

"It's too late now for any plan!" she cried.

"Not if you erase his memory of your conversation with him," I said firmly.

She stared at me in shock. "But that is—"

"Unless you want him to die," I continued ruthlessly, "you will erase his memory. When he wakes, tell him only that he fainted before you could exchange a word. If you have to, coerce him to believe you."

"But he will simply ask me the same thing again."

"He will," I said calmly. "And you will hear him out. But this time, you will tell him that you have every intention of keeping the oath you made in Sador."

"No! It is not true," Miryum cried. "I will not lie."

"Then speak and watch your precious truth kill him."

She gulped. "Elspeth . . . I can't bond with him!"

"I didn't say you must," I snapped. "But he needs to believe you will. Once you have agreed in principle to come with him, you explain that you must first honor a prior oath to Rushton and Obernewtyn. Tell him you swore to serve Rushton until Misfits are safe in the Land. Tell him that you are not free to come until that oath is fulfilled. Say that he has the right to withdraw his offer. With luck he will do so."

"If he does not?"

"Tell him to return to Sador to wait for you. If he threatens to kill himself over the delay, you might just as well fight fire with fire and tell him that if he does, you will have to do the same."

"Wha-at!"

"He is besotted with you," I said sharply. "Do you think he would want you dead?"

She shook her head. "What if he agrees to wait?"

"Then he will spend his life in Sador waiting for his heart's desire. There could be worse fates. It is more likely that he will change his mind after some time, though, and we can come up with some Land 'custom' that will allow him to withdraw after a period with no hurt to your honor."

"It hurts my honor to lie to him," she said sullenly, and added that it seemed she was being punished by my solution. "It is not as if I set this matter in motion."

"Didn't you? If you had listened courteously to his offer in Sador and answered him in the same way, rather than hitting him, you would not be in this predicament now." I pulled the shawl about my shoulders, goaded to fury by her endless talk of honor. "Now, I am going to rejoin the festivities. You can make your own decision whether you do as I have suggested or find your own way of dealing with all of this."

I turned on my heel and headed back to the orchard, where everyone was now sitting in a semicircle facing a daz- zlingly elaborate gypsy wagon I had not seen before. The magi performance was about to begin. The sun hung low in the sky, and the air had grown so misty that when torches were lit about the wagon, the whole scene took on a mystical air. The show began with a roll on the coercers' own favored instrument, a flat, round, one-sided drum like a tambourine, played with a two-ended club and a wrist-rolling movement. Three empath musicians were seated in a cluster beside the wagon, playing a soft fanfare underneath the rolling grum- ble of the drums that gradually grew louder, as with thunder approaching.

At their roaring peak, Gevan stepped onto a small plat- form jutting out from the edge of the wagon and hinged so that it could be swung up when the conveyance was in mo- tion. The Coercer guildmaster wore a smooth black mask now, the eyes and mouth exaggerated with red, demonic strokes. He bowed elaborately, then began to juggle woven balls of flowers that he seemed to pluck alternately from thick wax candles on either end of the stage. Empath musicians played a popular tune in time to his movements, skillfully embellishing it with all manner of amusing loops and beats. After a time, Gevan switched to juggling hoops and ribbons of silk and finally to balls of fire. He finished by tossing them into the air and apparently swallowing them, belching a cloud of multicolored smoke at those seated nearest.

I smiled, wondering how the Teknoguild had felt to be asked to produce chemicals for such a use. Of course, Gevan could have coerced the fireballs, but the aim was to use as little true coercivity as possible. As far as I could see, they had succeeded. So far, the performance was no more than a sophisticated jongleur might provide at a city moon fair and cleverly fell short enough of brilliance to be unthreatening.

Some of the younger coercers appeared out of the wagon black-clad but for colored, dragonish masks. They performed a tumbling acrobatic dance, again to a familiar tune, while Gevan orchestrated them as if they were music.

The tumblers turned away, baring black-clad backs so that they seemed to be swallowed up by the growing shadows. Gevan stepped through them, now wearing a hideously beaming mask, and gave a flamboyant and nonsensical speech about the known and unknown mysteries of nature; he asked how people behaved when they did not understand a thing.

"Like chickens with no heads! Like clover-drunk sheep! Like fools!" he answered himself.

He began doing more tricks, simple, obvious things one saw at every moon fair and festival. He asked his audience to spot the trick, and before long, he was revealing pockets in his gown and vials of powder and black strings attached to silk scarves. He began taking an astonishing number of objects from an inner pocket. When he brought out a chair, everyone howled with laughter, for the person passing it to him from behind the cloak pretended clumsiness and was clearly visible.

Gevan berated the assistant, who explained in a tremulous voice that she was afraid the tricks were making use of the black arts. The assistant spoke in such a silly, cowardly way that I had to laugh. It was hard to believe the clowning pair were really the formidable Coercer guildmaster and his guilder Merret.

I glanced about to discover everyone laughing except for Miryum's coercer-knights. They had drawn apart and were standing together watching without expression as, on the wagon stage, Gevan loomed over his cringing assistant.

"Only when fear is suppressed can we truly see what we see," he announced.

There was a blaze of fireworks, and he twisted so the cloak covered him and he seemed to vanish. Though the trick was quite obvious, Merret gave a credulous squawk of terror and pretended to faint. Two black-clad coercers dragged her back into the wagon, and her place was taken by three older knife-throwing coercers, who used a trickle of Talent to ensure their knives did not slice off someone's ear or nose.

As each trick dissolved seamlessly into the next, Gevan appeared here and there, mocking blind ignorance and praising those who stopped their screams long enough to notice the trickery. I could see quite clearly the shape of the lesson evolving, about fear making people foolish.

The show ended in a burst of applause and shouts for more, but Gevan merely made a short speech outside of his flamboyant role, thanking us all for our attention. Soon he was in the thick of an excited press of performers and admirers all chattering and laughing. Waiting for them to disperse, I walked about the wagon. Truly it was worthy of awe. Almost every stretch of board had been lovingly and minutely carved and smoothed and polished or painted in intricate patterns. Who would have thought that silent Grufyyd would have such a lavish talent? It was funny what could be hidden inside people until some circumstance arose to let it out. Katlyn had said that before this task, her bondmate had merely liked a bit of whittling.

"Phew, these masks make you sweat. They'll have to have more air holes," Gevan gasped, mopping his forehead and coming to stand by me. "What did you think of the show?"

"You were all marvelous," I said. "Merret was so funny."

Gevan grinned. "She's splendid, isn't she? I take it you don't feel the show holds our abilities up to ridicule as Miryum and her coercers-knights do?"

"I don't," I said. "But I saw the knights looking rather disdainful."

"They can't see that the Talent of coercing is separate from how it is regarded. I am no less powerful because I use my abilities to make people laugh. You know, as much as I regret the thought of it, I really think I will have to let Miryum form a splinter group."

"It saddens me to hear you don't think it can be held together."

Gevan shrugged. "Oh, I can hold the split off indefinitely, if that's what you want. But it's disruptive to feel the knights silently pulling against the rest of us. It's not as if they disobey me, but a guild can't be divided in its heart."

"Just don't do anything until we see what Rushton says," I asked.

Gevan frowned suddenly. "Speaking of Rushton, it seems as if you'll have to fill in for him again after all. It's time for the Choosing Ceremony."

Only then did I become aware that we were standing in near darkness, with a single guttering torch left alight by the wagon. All that remained of the day was a few streaks of golden light on the underside of the clouds near the horizon. My heart gave a nasty lurch. Fear for Rushton coursed through my veins.

Gevan squeezed my arm in sympathy and said he was sure there was some good reason for Rushton's delay; nevertheless, the Choosing could not be put off.

And so, as the sun fell behind the mountains, Valda and several others formally chose the Futuretell guild, a young lad called Kally chose the Coercers, and some teknoguilders were promoted. Both Aras, bursting with pride and red as a beet, and an astonished Zarak were elevated to the rank of ward. Offering congratulations, bestowing bracelets and armbands, and lighting their candles, I waited until they stood with their various guilds before expressing my regret that I must again speak for Rushton. I implied that his delay had been half anticipated, and rather perfunctorily, I enjoined them to strive to be their best in all things.

Now that the sun was gone, it had grown distinctly chilly, and I was shivering in my thin silk dress and shawl. I farsent Miryum, who told me glumly that the Sadorian was yet to wake. I then farsent Gahltha and learned that Avra was in labor but all was going well. He refused my offer to keep him company as he waited, saying there was naught I could do. In any case, as a wild mountain equine, Avra preferred her foal to be born without human presence. His tone was apologetic, but I sent that I understood perfectly and asked that he give her my love.

I found Jakoby to let her know that I would ride on the morrow with her to the pass. Then I briskly bade her good night and walked away from the light and laughter of the moon fair.

✦ 15 ✦

By the time I climbed into bed, my eyes were closing of their own accord, but contrarily, the minute my head was on the pillow, I could not sleep.

"Rushton!" I sent his name in a probe that stretched far into the night, but of course there was no answer.

What if he had been more than delayed?

Fortunately, sheer exhaustion claimed me before my self-control faltered. I fell asleep and eventually into a memory dream of traveling with my father.

"Now, you mind your manners," my father said, sitting by me on the wooden carriage bench and holding the reins. "This is not our little village where everyone knows everyone else. A city is a hard place, and people who dwell there have grown so to match it."

"Is that why we live in Rangorn, Da?"

"It is, but it's not the only reason. Now, that's enough questions from you. A city is a bad place for idle chatter. You hold your tongue while we're there and don't go speaking out of turn."

Something in his voice frightened me. "Will there be a moon fair, then, Da?"

"There will at that, but it's not for pleasure that we're going, lass. We'll be doing some serious trading and one or two other bits of business. But you'll have time enough to hear a few tunes and see a puppet show."

"And have some sweets?" I asked urgently.

He laughed. "Oh, you'll fill yer belly with muck just as your brother does and will moan and puke all the way home."

"Da!"

I sat silently, listening to his thoughts bubble and mutter in his mind like a stream running under the earth. He was worrying about whether he would be able to find a man he needed to speak with. He was thinking he ought not to have brought me into danger but that a child stopped people giving a man the evil eye the way they did a lone stranger. Normally, he would bring Jes, but the boy was fevered. Mother had said to take me, because she didn't want me coming down sick as well. She would be furious with him if she knew he was still feeding the odd bit of news to his rebel friends in the city. Well, he couldn't do much else with the responsibility of a family, but cursed if he'd sit back while the filthy priests charged innocent folk so as to steal their lands.

He drew the wagon to a halt to water the horses at a stream, and I forced my mind to close itself to his thoughts, feeling shamed. Somehow, without being told, I knew that listening to his private mind was as wrong as eavesdropping, and maybe worse.

"Sometimes you have to eavesdrop," a familiar, piping voice said.

I looked down to find Ariel, as a child, too, standing by the side of the road and looking up at me. He tittered with malice and became a man before my eyes.

"Greetings, Elspethelf," he said in caressing tones. "That's what your brother used to call you, isn't it?"

681

"What do you want?"

He held out a white, long-boned hand. "Come down, and we will talk. Come."

I shook my head, unaccountably frightened.

"Are you afraid?" he whispered. Darkness began to pour from him like smoke, and in seconds it was as night. Dimly, I saw his form change. He was a child again; then he was something huge and writhing. A pallid tentacle crawled toward the stream where my father was still filling a bucket.

"Da!" I screamed, and began to climb down. Then something smashed into the wagon, toppling it violently sideways, and I was thrown into the air with a shriek of terror.

I sat up gasping in fear. It was still dark, and it took me a moment to calm down from my nightmare enough to recall that the Sadorians were departing at dawn, and I had set my mind to wake me. I stepped out of bed onto stones that felt like slabs of ice, and dressed in thick trousers, socks, and two undershirts, all the while wondering why I had dreamed of Ariel yet again. Pulling on my riding boots and an oiled jacket, I glanced out the shutter and was relieved to find it hadn't snowed, despite the icy feel of the air. I dragged a comb through my hair and farsent to Alad, who was sharing a predawn meal with the Sadorians, and told him I would meet them.

"Oh, you should know that Avra had a filly as coal black as her da about an hour ago," he sent.

"Are they well?"

"Avra is tired but triumphant, from the tenor of her thoughts, and the foal is staggering about wondering what it is. Gahltha doesn't want to leave them yet, so Zidon will carry you to the pass and back."

I caught a brief image through his mind of the Sadorians rising from the table and realized I had best get a move on if I was to be at the front door when they came past.

Waiting at the end of the curving moonlit drive, I had an eerie sense of déjà vu, for it reminded me of the night I had visited Obernewtyn on the dreamtrails. The stillness of the mountain predawn made it seem as if the world held its breath. There was not a whisper of wind to disturb the trees. Not a leaf rustled nor a frog croaked, and a thick frost glimmered over everything. Then I heard the sound of horses.

As the riders emerged like shadows from the darkness, I saw Fian and Rasial as well as Alad and the Sadorians. Fian was mounted on Faraf.

"I'm just on my way back to th' Teknoguild caves," Fian said. "It was so late, I figured I mun wait until mornin' an' ride along wi' ye a way. Faraf offered to carry me to give her leg a bit of exercise."

I greeted Faraf and asked if her leg was truly well enough to bear the lad.

"The boy is light and will soon dismount," she sent.

Alad interrupted to say he was freezing without a proper coat and must get indoors. He got down from Zidon, and I took his place. As the horses turned their noses to the lowlands, Jakoby invited me to ride by her.

When she again praised the empath singers' moon-fair performance, I took the opportunity to tell her we had decided to send an empath and two beastspeakers to replace Dameon.

She looked pleased. "Any of your people would be welcome among us, particularly empaths and beastspeakers. Which reminds me: You have shown us great courtesy here, and I hope you will not mind extending it further. Straaka

683

took ill yesterday, and we have had to leave him behind."

I assured her that we would be happy to host the tribesman until he was fit to travel.

"He was alone with Miryum when it happened," she mused. "She said he was in the midst of greeting her when, without warning, he apparently fainted. It is puzzling for, as a rule, he is not a sickly man."

Realizing she must have questioned Miryum, I felt uneasy. The coercer would not lie well. "Perhaps the mountain air affected him," I murmured. "It is thinner up here than at sea level. But whatever happened, we have accomplished healers. I'm sure it won't be long before he follows you."

"I think that might depend more on your Miryum than on Straaka's health," the tribeswoman said, giving me a sideways glance.

"Perhaps Straaka will return to Sador to await Miryum's arrival."

Jakoby shook her head decisively. "He will not return to Sador without her. Either he will wait as an exile here, or he will take his life. No tribesman could prepare for a wife and then fail to bring her without being ridiculed."

"That seems very harsh," I said, beginning to wonder if I had been too clever for my own good.

We rode in silence as the sky grew steadily brighter. The moon stayed high but faded to a pale sliver against the blue, and by the time Fian left us, the sun was close to rising, and the mountains glowed gold and magenta. Riderless now, Faraf trotted alongside Zidon, and behind them Rasial padded tirelessly, offering no clue as to why she had decided to accompany us. In sight of the pass, I asked if Alad had given them a brace of homing birds so they could send back a message if they encountered Rushton or at least heard news of his passing. Bruna held up the wicker cage tied to her pack, where two birds on a swinging perch looked phlegmatic and unimpressed.

"If you don't hear anything on the way, would you ask Brydda to let us know what happened when Rushton was there? Who he met and spoke to, and especially who saw him last and when."

"You need not worry for him, surely. Your seers would foresee harm to their master," Bruna said so loftily that I felt an urge to slap her.

We trotted slowly down the last stretch to the pass, hailing the coercers on watch in their fortified hut. I farsent to ask if there had been any activity on the road and learned that there had been no sign of anyone as far as Guanette since the previous day.

"That is good news," Jakoby said. None of us dismounted, for it was not the Sadorian way to do so at partings.

"Travel safely and give Dameon my love when you see him. Say we miss him sorely," I said.

"I will," Jakoby promised. Then she put her arm across her chest and half bowed in Sadorian fashion. "I hope Rushton comes home safe and soon."

"So do I," I said.

Watching the riders break into a gallop and diminish in the distance, I wished with all my heart that I would see Rushton riding up toward me, but of course he did not appear. As Zidon turned his back on the pass, I glanced down at Rasial, wondering again why she had come.

"The loss of a mate is a hard thing," Rasial sent morosely. "The funaga-li killed my mate before he could sire pups on me."

"You are not old. Perhaps you will find another mate?"

Zidon sent compassionately. As usual, animal exchanges were on an open band, so I could understand what they said to each other as well as what was directed specifically to me.

"I will bear no pups," Rasial sent, her strange eyes burning with a queer zealotry that reminded me of the way Herders looked during burnings.

"I don't see how you—" I began, but Rasial began to growl a warning. "What is it?" I demanded. When she did not respond, I sent out a probe to discover what had alarmed her. I could find nothing, though she continued growling and all the hackles were up on her neck.

I noticed Faraf was trembling and had drawn nearer to Zidon. "What is it?" I demanded of them both. "What do you sense/scent?"

"Funaga," Faraf sent tremulously.

"Impossible. I don't sense any human nearby."

"No sense funaga. Smell," Rasial sent, lifting her lip to bare her teeth in a ferocious grimace.

I did not understand. A human who could be scented ought to be easily found with a probe. Unless whomever the animals scented was cloaking themselves coercively.

I thought of the killing power that lay slumbering in my mind. I had drawn on it before to enhance my other abilities. Carefully, I delved down into my mind, drawing on a shred of the dark power and sheathing my farseeking probe in it. Casting it out again, I had a sense of exaltation, for it made my probe far more potent. This time, the probe located two human minds beneath a strong coercive shield.

Asking the animals to wait for me in the clearing, I pushed through the trees toward the minds I had sensed. It did not take me long to find them physically: a girl of about twelve and a much younger boy, cowering in the bole of a huge dead tree. The boy burst into tears at the sight of me peering in at them, and the coercive cloak that had hitherto hidden them dissolved.

"I'm sorry, Seely!" he wailed to the girl.

"You are runaways?" I asked calmly.

"We are, and what of it?" The girl's belligerent answer was belied by her frightened eyes. "Who are you?"

"I live near here," I said ambiguously, registering that the girl was an unTalent.

Her eyes widened in a different kind of fear. "We heard that no one lives up in the mountains, because the people who dwelt here got burned in a firestorm and them that survived died later of the plague."

"I don't have the plague," I promised, spreading my hands. "Come out. I won't hurt you. I'm unarmed."

The girl hesitated before urging the boy out and crawling quickly after him. She wrapped her thin arm protectively around his chubby shoulders. There was a delicate cast to her face and frame that suggested she was not the child of a rough peasant household. The sturdy little boy might have been a peasant child, but he had a mass of golden curls and soft skin under the dirt and scratches, which marked him the son of wealthy parents, too. A prickle ran up my spine, for here was a riddle—and maybe a dangerous one.

"Do you have food?" the girl asked, an edge of desperation in her voice. "I have a few coins. . . ."

"Are there soldierguards after you?" I asked.

"They might be looking for us, but not up here," the girl said with a glint of malice in her eyes.

"You're not highlanders, are you?"

She glared at me with a mixture of defiance and fear. Clearly, she knew they needed help, and I could almost see

687

her trying to decide how much of their story to tell. "I'll help you," I said bluntly, "but I need to know for certain that no soldierguards are on your trail."

"I swear no one knows we are here. Gavyn has hid us from soldierguards and other travelers on the road."

"Well and good, then. Come along with me. There's a clearing just over here where you can have a drink, and then we'll ride to my home."

"Hooray! A drink!" the little boy caroled. He turned his guileless eyes on me. "I don't mind at all that you found us."

The girl looked at him, then at me. "How *did* you find us?" she demanded suspiciously.

There was no point in prevarication, so I told her.

"You are like Gavyn?" She gaped. "I thought the poor lad was a lone freak and pitied him for it. You are up here hiding from the Herders as well, then?"

"You could say that," I said, repressing a smile. Then I realized what she'd said. "Here, a moment past you said the soldierguards weren't after you, but what about the Herders?"

Her brown eyes flared with hatred. "The bastards would like to have us, but they don't have any idea where we are."

I stared, for the curse had been the sort she would never have heard in a wealthy house. When the pair of them had quenched their thirst, I felt the girl decide she might as well tell the truth of their story. Having made up her mind, she told their tale quite simply, with a weariness that was all the more poignant because it was too heavy for her years.

Seely's parents had died when she was very young, and she'd been adopted by distant relatives. She said little, but enough bitter visions flickered through her mind to show she had been more maid than daughter to the family that took her in. Nevertheless, she formed a friendship with the daughter of the house, who was some years older than her and who'd been promised by her parents to a Councilman. When the daughter went to her man's house and bed, Seely went with her as her companion and personal maid.

She had a better time of it then, living in luxury and traveling when the couple went about on Council business. The man had turned out not to be such a bad sort, though obviously he was too old for his bondmate. Nevertheless, he'd got her with a child. Seely helped birth young Gavyn. She had held him, weeping her eyes out, as her friend died in the bloody childbed. She stayed to care for the boy, on whom the father doted.

Things went well enough until the man got another bondmate, Lady Slawyna; she was older and unpleasant, with a grown son from a previous bonding. Though the woman cooed and praised Gavyn in his father's hearing, Seely quickly saw she hated the child and wanted him dead so that her bondmate's rich holdings would go to her own son. He was a Herder, and though he could not inherit himself, his order would receive whatever he would have inherited, paving the way for his promotion within the Faction.

Things went on in that uneasy way until Gavyn's father died. Then Lady Slawyna took over as guardian of the heir to all her man's wealth. Seely knew the woman would not dare to harm the boy openly, but still the girl never let Gavyn out of her sight, for she'd sworn to her friend a deathbed oath to protect him. But Gavyn grew to be a strange child, and Lady Slawyna began to cast a fishy eye on him, watching him like a cat watches a bird hopping closer and closer to its claws.

"One night, I heard her speaking to her Herder son about Gavyn," Seely recalled. "The son said he'd have to be

689

examined, but if he was truly Misfit, there'd be no question of him inheriting. He promised to set the process of investigation in motion. I knew then we'd have to run." Her eyes clouded with memory. "I never knew how hard it would be. Ye gods, we've run from one end of the Land to the other, and if there's no refuge for us here . . ." She finished on a sob that made the boy look at her anxiously.

"There's a place for you here," I promised. I was glad to think of her finding refuge after all she must have gone through, but more than that, I was excited at the thought of how much invaluable information she might have absorbed about Councilmen and Herders, given the exalted circles she'd moved in.

She went on. "Gavyn's abilities caused us a lot of difficulties, but they also hid us. The last time we were spotted was in Sutrium, near the ferry port. None could know whether we were trying to get over it to the west coast or had just come from it. Gavyn made it so that people could not see us." She ruffled the boy's curls tenderly. "After that, we traveled by night and stole what food and clothes we needed, always heading away from the coast, for I thought maybe we could find some remote hamlet where Herders and soldierguards never came. It was our last hope, truly."

I saw a bleak vision of her feeding the boy poison and then herself and realized she was at the end of her resources.

"You have done an incredible thing keeping him safe and going so far," I said gravely. "But now you need to eat and rest. Can you ride?"

"I've never," Seely admitted, staring with frightened eyes at Zidon.

Gavyn toddled over to Faraf and patted her nose clumsily. "Gavyn ride Faraf?"

I gaped, but Seely misunderstood my concern. "He's not afraid of any animal that ever lived, and they never hurt him no matter how savage they are," she said.

"Your Gavyn is a Talented little boy indeed," I said, wondering if she had missed the significance of the boy using the mare's name without being told it. As well as being a strong coercer, he was probably a beastspeaker, too. "Faraf will carry Gavyn, then, and you can ride with me." I lifted the child up onto the mare's back, asking her to be careful.

"I will not let him fall," she promised.

I climbed onto Zidon then and pulled Seely awkwardly up behind me. "Don't fear. We won't go at more than a walk."

"Do you live alone?" Seely asked with a renewed wariness that told, more than any tale, how hard a time she'd had of it. I said I did not live alone but that she need not fear my friends.

"Who were those men hiding up on the mountain?" Gavyn piped up. "Are they your friends?"

When I did not answer immediately, Seely said, "He probably imagined them."

"No," I said. "There are two men watching the pass. They will be very surprised when they learn that you two escaped their notice."

"They're Misfits?"

I turned to look over my shoulder at her. "There are more of us about the Land than you'd guess. Most of us start out thinking we're lone freaks. Gavyn is lucky, because he'll grow up among his own kind, never feeling an outcast. But there are ordinary folk like you up here, too."

"We heard a group of riders go by just now," Seely said slowly. "I thought maybe they were hunters, though I'd heard no one comes up here because it's haunted."

"Well, the haunts and shades are the watchers' doing," I said, letting a smile infuse my voice. "And the riders you heard were friends. But it's true that very few people come up here. You are the first in ages, and I would not have known you were here at all if it hadn't been for Rasial." I nodded at the ridgeback.

"She smelled us," the boy said, his eyes fixed on the white dog. Rasial lifted her head, and an extraordinarily long gaze passed between her and Gavyn. I had a feeling some communication had taken place between them, though my senses detected nothing.

As we rode through the gates to Obernewtyn, Seely's arms tightened around my waist. "This is the place they said was burned out by firestorm."

"I'm pleased to tell you that there never was any firestorm, nor plague either," I said. "Those were all illusions to keep the Council and Herders from taking an interest in us. Some of the Misfits here can make a proper building seem like it is in ruins, just as Gavyn can make people see nothing where there is something."

When Obernewtyn came into sight, Seely gasped aloud. "What sort of place is this?"

"Home." I smiled as Zidon came to a quiet stop alongside the stone steps leading to the entrance. I slid down and helped Seely off. Gavyn dismounted before I could help him, agile as a squirrel. He patted Faraf and kissed her nose before squatting in the dirt beside Rasial and staring intently into her silver-white eyes.

Without warning, the front doors banged open and Ceirwan rushed out. Seely shrank back with a cry of fright.

"I'm sorry," Ceirwan said in contrition, holding up his

hands to her, "But when th' guildmistress farsent me to say she'd found ye both, I was burstin' with curiosity." He held out a hand to her with a friendly grin. "Ye mun be Seely."

She shook his hand gingerly. "You . . . you're a Misfit, too?"

"I am," Ceirwan laughed. "But listen, I fergot how overwhelmin' this place can be. I near burst into tears the first time I saw it."

"I'm not far from it, truly," Seely said with a watery smile.

Zidon sent that he and Faraf would return to the farms, and I turned to thank them. The boy's mind chimed in clear as a bell alongside mine, saying goodbye. There was a strange sweet ringing in his tone that reminded me somewhat of Angina empathising.

"His mind sings," Faraf agreed.

I stared at the boy, wondering if he could be an empath as well as a beastspeaker and a coercer. No other Misfit had a combination of coercion and empathy, and I had always imagined the two could not coexist. Ceirwan was ushering Seely inside, and she called over her shoulder to Gavyn. Still kneeling in the dirt with Rasial, he told her that he wanted to stay with the dog.

Before Seely could argue, Rasial beastspoke the boy. "I will come with you."

I watched in wonder as she mounted the steps. Gavyn followed contentedly, his fingers wound into her thick fur. Seely shook her head wearily as if this sort of thing was common to her and asked if I minded that the dog came inside. Though she was aware of Gavyn's affinity with animals, she seemed to have no idea that he could actually communicate with them.

"You'll find that beasts have pretty much the same status as humans here," I told her mildly, thinking it would be better not to give her too much to take in immediately. She was looking white and stretched beyond her limit. I farsent to Ceirwan to get them both some food and ensure they were not bothered by questions until they had had a chance to rest.

"Go with Ceir now," I told Seely. "We'll talk again later, but don't worry about anything. Consider Obernewtyn your home for as long as you wish."

"I do not know what to say, my lady," Seely whispered.

I ignored the honorific and said, "There is no need to say anything. Go and be welcome."

Eating a very late bowl of somewhat lumpy firstmeal porridge, I refused to let myself dwell on Rushton's continuing absence, knowing it would lead me to despair. Instead, I turned my attention to the day ahead and the things that needed doing. Gevan must be told about Gavyn, given the boy's Talent. Alad would need to examine him as well, and perhaps Angina and Miky. Wila would be the best person to question Seely about the Herders, and Tomash was the obvious choice to question her about the Council.

I would also ask the coercer-knights to note any rumor of a couple of runaway children in the high country. Seely had been sure no one knew where they were, but in my experience, someone always noticed what you did not want seen.

Zarak came out of the kitchen carrying two large, steaming apple puddings in a basket. Catching sight of me, he came over. "Guildmistress, I did not get the chance to thank you for . . . for the wardship," he said. "I know I did not deserve it, truly, but I will strive to become worthy of it."

I smiled. "I'm sure you will bring pride to us all in your

new role." I nodded to the basket. "You are taking those to the farms?"

"They're for the nightmeal. I'm going with some of the other farseekers to help with some planting, but I'll be back before our guild meeting," he said earnestly.

He went, leaving me feeling glad that I had changed my mind about promoting him. It seemed that already he had matured with his new position.

Then Maryon entered the dining halls, looking pale and stern. Her eyes settled on me, and as she came across the room, a cold hand closed around my heart.

"What is it? Is it Rushton?" I babbled, half rising to meet her.

"I fell into a trance this mornin'. I have foreseen a time of great upheaval an' strife."

I sat back heavily. "Is Obernewtyn in danger?"

"Trouble comes to th' mountains, to th' highlands, an' th' lowlands. I have seen fightin' an' bands of riders warrin' throughout th' Land. I have seen death an' blood an' tears." Maryon's voice was a fey monotone.

"It must be the rebels," I whispered. "They have decided to rise. Can you say when the strife will begin?"

"Three sevendays, perhaps sooner," the futureteller said. "I wish I could have had some earlier warnin', but I suspect Dragon's mind got in th' way."

Knowing sooner would alter nothing, I thought. After all, the rebellion itself no longer had anything to do with us. It was the aftermath we must concern ourselves with, and Maryon's words about strife coming to the mountains suggested we did have something to worry about.

I took a deep breath and looked at Maryon. "Is there anything more?"

She inclined her head gravely, and my heart sank. "I saw treachery, but I dinna ken how or by whom or when. Only that it is connected to th' strife."

I swallowed welling terror at the thought that Rushton's failure to return meant he had been betrayed. What if the rebels had kept him prisoner in Sutrium since he had refused our help? Brydda would never participate in any treachery against us, and I did not believe Dardelan or his father would harm us, but Malik certainly might.

"If what you have foreseen is the rebellion, we'll know about it soon enough," I said grimly. "I'll call a full guildmerge for this evening, and you can tell the others what you have just told me. Do not mention it before that. The last thing we need is a panicked wave of rumor."

She nodded and withdrew, but I barely noticed her departure, for my mind was already flying, farsending the news to the other guildleaders.

✦ 16 ✦

"LET'S TRY TO have some quiet," I said with enough of a co-ercive snap to stop the conversations that had erupted. "Now, the first thing to remember is that we don't know for sure if Maryon's futuretelling refers to the rebellion."

"What else could it refer to?" Gevan demanded. "Are we to sit and wait for confirmation when danger is coming for us at a gallop?"

"I don't say we should sit and twiddle our thumbs," I said crossly. "There is much that can be done. But we need infor-mation if we are to make effective plans. I agree that it is al-most certainly the rebellion Maryon has foreseen, but it troubles me that we have had no news of it from Brydda."

"Maybe the rebels don't know yet themselves," Alad said. "Maybe whatever will spark the rebellion off has yet to take place."

"Perhaps. The thing is, we are not only assuming a rebel-lion, but also that it will be successful and that Malik will then lead his people up to attack us. But what if it is not his peo-ple who win?"

"After seeing them in the Battlegames, who can doubt it?" Miryum asked in a low, flat voice. "Most of the soldierguards are lazy mercenaries who have never been in a battle in their miserable lives. All they do is torment defenseless farmers and merchants."

I sensed the anger she was repressing but knew it had more to do with Straaka's decision to wait at Obernewtyn until she was free to come with him to Sador then with the matter at hand.

"I do not doubt they have the ability to win," I said coolly. "But if you recall, when we entered the Battlegames, we did not doubt our ability to win either. Yet we failed." I let my eyes rove around the table. "What I am trying to say is, what if the threat is not what we are expecting?"

"Information is needed, you are right, Elspeth, and the magi will be in the perfect position to gather it," Gevan announced briskly. "As some of you know, we have been invited to Sawlney to play at Councilman Alum's bonding celebration for his daughter in ten days. There will be both Herders and Councilmen from all the Land in attendance and a great swell of ordinary folk drawn by the fair and the promise of a good feast. In such diverse company, we ought to be able to get the flavor of whatever is brewing."

There were nods from most seated round the table. "Very well," I said. "The magi will go to Sawlney. What else can you suggest?"

Miryum stood. "I should like to ride out with the knights and see if we can learn anything," she said.

"Where's the need if Gevan is going with the magi?" Roland demanded gruffly. "Besides, your knights are unlikely to be discreet enough for our purposes."

Miryum gave him a long, measuring look. "We were not indiscreet by mistake, Guildmaster, but because it fit our purpose. If we are to gather information now, obviously we will act in a manner that best serves the defense of Obernewtyn."

I rose, waving Miryum to sit before the pair of them got into another argument. "I don't see why the knights can't go out as well. After all, it will be some days before the magi will be ready to move, and they will be focusing on Sawlney. Miryum's knights can ride at once and make inquiries in the highlands and upper lowlands. They will not be clad as gypsies, so they may be able to mingle less conspicuously than Gevan's people. Furthermore, they can be back here before the magi depart, enabling Gevan to set off with some knowledge of what he and his people are likely to encounter."

"It would be useful to know if there are any places we ought to avoid," Gevan admitted.

"In that case, with your approval, Gevan, I will command the knights for the time being?"

His eyes flashed with understanding that I was offering him a way out of his guild difficulties with the knights. "I formally release them from my guild to the Master of Obernewtyn."

I nodded. "Your magi should travel directly through the high country and make your initial camp at Arandelft. Spend a day there and learn what you can about why they have neither cloister nor Councilman. You'd best take some birds. Send one every twoday or so with reports. All messages sent must be in the code devised by the Teknoguild, so everyone should familiarize themselves with it. Garth, can one of your people give extra lessons to anyone who needs them?"

He nodded and scratched a note on a piece of paper at his elbow. "Someone ought to go into Sutrium," he said.

"Someone will," I answered. "Kella will travel with the magi to Sawlney and then on to Sutrium to see Domick. She will remain there for several days and learn what she can of the rebellion before returning to Obernewtyn." I looked at the healer. "Kella, the only condition I would put on your trip is that you return within the three sevendays Maryon allows us.

The last thing we need is to have you stranded there alone."

She nodded, but I clearly heard her behindthought that she would not be alone because she would be with Domick. I resolved to speak to her again before she left and get her promise that she would return as I had bidden her, whether or not she managed to convince Domick to accompany her.

I shifted my eyes to Alad. "In the meantime, I want the Beastspeaking guild to look at provisioning two possible journeys: one overland to Sador and another higher into the valley. The Teknoguild will examine the logistics of moving us in either instance. Garth, your people should look at those caves you located higher in the mountains and decide what needs to be done to ready them for a long stay."

"What about the planting program?" Alad asked worriedly. "There's still quite a bit to go, and it will be difficult to last through the next wintertime unless I have enough workers to plant all we'll need."

"I'm afraid you must try to fit it in as best you can around these other preparations. The other guildleaders will assign whomever they can spare to help you. But remember, we may not be here to harvest what you plant."

"It's sheer madness to think of us going to Sador," Garth declared. "It would be an immense undertaking, and we would be leaving behind everything we have fought for. Have you even spoken to the Sadorians about the possibility?"

"No decision has been made yet about what we will do, and when it is, we will all be making it. I just want us to have all courses covered when we do decide. Now, I want you to figure out roughly how long it might take to reach Sador in laden wagons. Alad's people will need some sort of time frame to work out supplies."

Jak stirred in his seat beside Garth. "If we do go to Sador, it will mean moving while the rebellion is in progress. That could be difficult."

"Truespoken," I said.

"Between Radost's sons, the Herders in Guanette, and the presence of Malik's people, gannin' to th' coast road with a line of wagons will be difficult even without a rebellion," Ceirwan pointed out.

"What about beasts?" Alad demanded, scowling. "Ordinary Landfolk and Councilmen alike are notorious for sequestering beasts from halfbreeds, claiming they must have been stolen. Since a good many of the animals that live with us are runaways, a strong case could be made against us."

Angina said, "Maybe it would be best to evacuate smaller groups, some with wagons and some without, taking different routes. If we travel at night, we might manage to escape notice altogether."

"We could make sure no one remembers any of us going by," Miryum said.

"I think we will not need to worry about Councilmen or soldierguards or rebels stopping us from leaving," Aras said rather shyly, for this was her first guildmerge. "Isn't it more likely that they will all take their forces to the lowlands for the rebellion?"

"You're right, of course," Gevan grunted thoughtfully. "The rebellion will certainly start in the lowlands, and that will give us a free run up here for some time."

"Maybe they won't care about us going anyway," Miky said. "They want us to, after all."

"Malik wants us dead," Miryum said flatly. "He wants us wiped out as abominations against nature. If it's known we're leaving the Land, he will come after us."

There was a silence across which her harsh words skipped like a stone.

"What about Rushton?" Zarak asked. Of course he would ask what no one else dared.

I felt their eyes on me and fought to remain cool. "He has been delayed, obviously. We cannot wait until he comes to decide how to act. He would not want it. Until we hear from Jakoby or Brydda, we will not waste time speculating. Leave worrying about what will come to the futuretellers, who will be doing their own delving for information."

I glanced at Maryon and Dell, who nodded as one.

The guildmerge broke up soon after that. Many of us lingered, but Garth and his people left in a huddle, their expressions serious. I had no doubt they were already worrying about how to continue their work if we were forced to leave Obernewtyn.

"Couldn't we try again to reach some sort of agreement with the rebels once the rebellion is over?" Miky asked me. "I do not want to leave Obernewtyn."

"Nor I, and with luck, it might not come to that," I said. "But I doubt Malik will agree to leave us in peace. Miryum is right about his hatred of us."

Alad said, "Maybe Malik won't rule the rebels. After all, the Sadorians said they had been having second thoughts about him after the ruthlessness he showed in the Battlegames. Perhaps other rebels won't wish to appoint him to lead in the end."

I was aware that Alad's thoughts were more on the beasts than on the rebels. And he was right to be troubled. So many would be unfit for the hardship of moving, particularly on the grueling, treacherous road to Sador, and once there, some would find it difficult to adapt to the arid land. Yet those that could not travel with us would inevitably become prey to wild animals or die of exposure, unless they were gathered up and sold or returned to former masters. If we were to move higher in the valley, most could follow, but what cave would hold all of us and food enough for the wintertime?

I touched Alad's arm. "We must not make the mistake of thinking it is our place to decide how to care for the beasts who have made their home with us. You will let Avra know what has been foreseen, and doubtless she will call a beast-merge. Ask her if you can attend, and let me know what happens. And ask her to send representatives to our next guildmerge."

Miryum approached as we left the chamber. "I have been wondering if the rebellion might only be part of the strife Maryon has foreseen, Elspeth," she said. "If the rebels win, and the others refuse to take Malik as their leader afterward, I doubt he will tamely accept their decision. They would resist any attempt of his to dominate them all the more, because they have only just thrown off one yoke. . . . What I am trying to say is that there could well be war between rebels, after the rebellion."

"It did occur to me Malik might try to force himself on the rebels as their leader, but I had not thought of their resisting," I said. "It may even be that Brydda called Rushton down to Sutrium not to take part in the rebellion but to aid in a civil war that might follow."

Miryum shrugged. "Either way, he refused."

"I just wish we knew exactly what went on at that meeting," I muttered.

Later that night, Miryum came to my chamber to tell me that her knights were ready to ride if I would give them leave.

She looked fiercely determined in the orange fire glow.

"What does Gevan say?"

"He says that the knights are now commanded by the Master of Obernewtyn."

"Very well. Did Gevan have any idea when the magi will be ready to leave?"

"A threeday. We can be back before then even if we wait until morning to leave, but going now will give us a few more hours." Miryum went on to say the knights would ride as a group rather than in pairs and would claim to be a band of mercenaries hired by a Councilman. "Of course, we will not name him, and we will create enough unease coercively to stop anyone inquiring too much."

"What of Straaka?"

Frustration showed in the stocky coercer's eyes, but she merely answered that the Sadorian had insisted upon riding with them. "I told him that his appearance would draw too much attention. He said he would ride into the towns separate from us but that he must be close to protect me." Irritation flitted across her face. "It is useless to tell him that I do not need protecting."

I said mildly that he would learn that soon enough. "But I wouldn't worry about him standing out. There are enough Sadorians in the Land these days for him not to look out of place. The Council welcomes the Sadorians for the sake of the spice trade, so it is unlikely anyone will start trouble."

Miryum conceded grudgingly. "We also plan to look for Rushton, if you are agreed," she said.

My heart lurched, but I only suggested that if they had to ask questions, they should not align themselves with Rushton, in case he had been arrested.

"I thought of that. We mean to say that we are searching

for the jack who seduced our master's daughter, and then describe him. . . ."

"Seduced?!"

Miryum shrugged. "Most folk will have a bit of a laugh at the thought of a common jack dallying with a Councilman's lass. We thought it would be safer that way for Rushton, in case he rides up after we have been through. And it will explain why the Councilman would hire mercenaries rather than simply calling in soldierguards."

She was right, though I disliked the idea of spreading such a scurrilous rumor and suspected this was her mild revenge over the business with Straaka. "You might as well go tonight, then," I said. "But be careful, Miryum. The last thing we want is to find we have set into motion the very strife Maryon has foreseen. It seems to me that is a very real danger when you act upon futuretellings."

"We will be careful," she promised. She strode to the door, then hesitated and looked over her shoulder. "I would take it as a favor if you would let Linnet sit in on any meeting that takes place in my absence."

I lifted my eyebrows, for it was known that the coercer Linnet was considered by the knights to be Miryum's second. But it was too late now to be worrying about the knights splitting away from the coercers.

After she had gone, I stared into the fire, feeling drained. Angina had gone straight to Dragon after guildmerge, so there was nothing to stop me from climbing into my bed and sleeping, but I was too unsettled. Besides, Maruman had curled up in my lap, and I did not want to disturb him.

I had not had the chance to tell him yet about Maryon's visions, for though he had awakened to eat, he had been groggy and hard to reach. He would hate to leave Obernewtyn. Much as I was loath to admit it, he was getting old and sleeping rough griped his bones and ached his scars.

Pondering the cat's ills, I eventually drowsed off in my seat.

I dreamed of walking alone along a road. I did not know where I was, but I had a feeling of urgency. I noticed someone a little way ahead perched on a rock. My footsteps slowed to a stop as I recognized Ariel. He gave me a dazzling smile.

"You see? All roads bring you to me," he said in a caressing voice as he slid down from the rock. "Come, we'll walk the road together. There are many things I would like to ask you."

I shook my head, and a sense of danger gripped me.

His smile grew, and to my horror, I saw that his mouth was filled with sharp teeth. I screamed and turned to run, but something dark ran at me and knocked me down.

I woke with a thundering heart. Ceirwan entered only moments later with a laden firstmeal tray. He grumbled at the dimness as he opened the shutters. At once the room was full of sunshine and the scent of blossoms, and my night terrors began to seem foolish.

"Ye slept in th' chair again," Ceirwan said disapprovingly. "Truly, Maruman has more sense than ye."

I turned to see that the old cat had indeed shifted during the night from my lap to the bed. I stood up, groaning and feeling sorry for myself.

"Did ye dream? I've brought th' book up just in case," Ceirwan said.

"I had a nightmare about Ariel," I murmured.

"After yesterday, it's no wonder," Ceirwan said. "But

nightmare or no, ye best put it in th' book or Sarn'll be chasin' ye down."

Resignedly, I scrawled in a few lines about the nightmare, then frowned at the words I had written. I had dreamed of Ariel far too often. What on earth could my subconscious be trying to tell me? Ceirwan set about stoking up the fire, and I laid the book aside and sniffed a pot to find he had brought a sweet ginger infusion. Pouring a cup, I asked, "Do you know if any of the beastspeakers have managed to coax Kella's owlet to leave her?"

It did not surprise me when the guilden shook his head. It was uncanny how a tiny detail could so thoroughly thwart more important things. Kella dared not carry the bird with her to Sutrium. It would not matter while she traveled with the magi, for it would be assumed the owl was part of the performance. But once she left the troupe, the bird would draw suspicious mutters, for it was commonly believed that users of the black arts kept beasts as familiars to aid them.

"Here, I dinna suppose young Gavyn might have a chance at befriendin' it?" Ceirwan said suddenly, straightening and rubbing the soot from his hands onto a rag.

"It might work," I said. There had been little time to judge the exact nature of Gavyn's Talent yet, but there was no doubt he had some special affinity with beasts, quite aside from his ability to communicate with them. "Why don't you take him into the Healer hall and see how he fares with the owlet? Speaking of Gavyn, where are he and Seely now?"

"In th' kitchens. I introduced them to Javo an' some of th' others over firstmeal. Zarak is showin' them around th' big house an' grounds. I thought I'd take them down to th' farms this afternoon. But ye need to eat. It's bad enough that ye won't rest properly without ye starvin' yerself as well."

"I hardly starve myself," I said.

Ceirwan shook his head in exasperation as he moved toward the door.

Restless, I soon decided to go down to the kitchens. Maruman woke and sipped a bit of milk while I was dressing, saying peevishly that he might as well come with me since I would not have the courtesy to tell him if I decided to go riding off somewhere again. He leapt onto my shoulders, and I winced as he used his claws to arrange himself around the back of my neck.

I carried the tray down the halls and into the kitchen, where Javo whisked it out of my hands and greeted Maruman like a visiting prince. From the corner of my eye, I saw a young healer washing dishes with a long-suffering expression that I understood all too well. I had cleaned hundreds of greasy pots and plates when I first arrived at Obernewtyn.

Zarak and Seely were sitting by the window in the sun, but there was no sign of Gavyn. I sauntered over to them and asked Seely where the boy was.

"Gavyn went with Ceirwan just now to see the healers, lady." She was wearing a pale green dress that suited her, and her brown hair had been brushed and lay clean and shining over her shoulders. Her heart-shaped face had a winsome quality that an unhealthy diet of fear and meager food had left pinched and overly taut.

I took a seat beside her. "You need not address me so formally, Seely," I said as gently as I could. "I am no more a lady than you."

Abruptly, Seely asked if Obernewtyn was about to be invaded. "I heard people talk of it this morning." There was an accusing note to her voice.

"You must understand that as established as we seem to

be, we are no less fugitives than you and Gavyn, and as such, we have always lived with the possibility that the soldierguards could come for us."

"Zarak said it was not soldierguards who would come," Seely said, and Zarak farsent apologetically that he had reassured her, because she had overheard enough to be badly frightened.

"The fact is, we are not sure of anything but that trouble of some kind is coming to the mountains," I told her firmly, assuring Zarak mentally that I was not annoyed with him for speaking frankly to the girl. "It is possible that it will be soldierguards. But given what we know, it seems more likely that our tormentors will be rebels. You understand that a rebellion is brewing in the Land and has been for some years?"

She nodded, wide-eyed. "I heard talk of it as we traveled, though I paid no mind to it then. Such talk is as common as leaves flying in the wind. Yet maybe all the talk has some center after all."

"It does, I'm afraid," I said.

"Why are you so worried about the rebels? Why should they care about Misfits and suchlike?"

"Rebels are also ordinary people," I said. "How often have you seen decent common folk stand to cheer on a burning or whisper a bit of slander in the ear of the authorities to ensure someone's child is dragged away in the night to the Councilfarms? Whether the rebels win or lose, they will feel the same way about us as always. But if they win, they will be in a position to do something about it."

She bit her lip. "I guess it is not just the Councilmen and Herders who want Misfits killed."

"Most ordinary folk hate Misfits as much as Herders do, because they've listened their whole lives to the preaching that makes us scapegoats for anything bad that happens. And unfortunately, there are powerful rebels who loathe us like poison and dream of wiping us off the face of the Land."

"I thought you said no one knew about this place?"

"None but friends do, but we have friends among the rebels, and things have a way of leaking out."

Without warning, Seely's eyes filled with tears, and she seemed to shrink into herself. "I knew it was too good to be true," she whispered. "I should never have brought Gavyn here."

I heard her behindthought that they were prisoners now, because we dared not let them go since they knew the whereabouts of Obernewtyn.

"You need not stay if you don't want to," I told her gently. I did not tell her that knowledge of Obernewtyn would be erased from their minds if they chose to leave.

Seely brushed the scatter of tears from her cheeks and stared into my eyes. Evidently, whatever she saw there reassured her, for at last she said, "Well, we had no other choice truly, and we still don't. We will stay, but if things look dark, I will take Gavyn and go."

"No one would dream of hindering you. But I am wondering if you would think of helping us in the meantime."

"How?" Wariness flared in her eyes.

"You've had quite a lot to do with the Council one way or another, and a bit of a glimpse at the Herder Faction as well. All we want from you is any information you've picked up."

"But I don't know anything," Seely said, looking dismayed. "Nothing important. I was in the Councilcourt only twice—once when I was given to my relatives after my parents died, and once again when Gavyn was a babe."

"Seely, you lived in the house of Councilfolk, and you

lived with the mother of a Herder who visited and had long conversations with her. You will have soaked up a lot of information." I leaned closer. "How do you think you have managed to evade the Council's soldierguards so cleverly all this time? It's not just Gavyn's Talents. It's outthinking them. Isn't it logical to assume that you can do this because, at some level, you know a great deal about them?"

Now Seely frowned in doubt. "Maybe I heard things from time to time, but if I did, I don't remember them. . . ."

Zarak touched her hand. "You don't need to remember," he assured her. "You'll just be asked a lot of questions, and without your meaning it, you will remember things. The coercers will help you."

"Will it hurt?"

The lad grinned and squeezed her hand. "Not a bit. Listen, it happened to my father and me when we first came up here ages back."

"It's not like what Gavyn does sometimes?" she asked uneasily, the memory of pain darkening her eyes.

"Gavyn has a Talent that we call *coercivity*, and it's a very strong and aggressive ability. Because he's so young and completely untrained, he can misuse it. Sort of like when a very small child squeezes a puppy too tightly," I said. "No doubt he hurt you sometimes trying to tell you things?"

She nodded vehemently. "He gives me the worst headaches sometimes, and once, in a tantrum, he hurt me so bad I fainted. I woke up to him sobbing his eyes out thinking he'd murdered me. He's never done that since."

"Painful for you but a good hard lesson to him not to hurt people just because he can. Well, rest assured he'll learn to use his abilities properly here. But the coercers who will help you to remember are well trained. A couple of people from my own guild who already know a lot about Herders and the Council will question you. You probably won't even notice the coercers in your mind."

Zarak nodded over my shoulder, and I twisted in my seat to see Ceirwan entering the kitchen, holding Gavyn's hand. Rasial was padding along close behind, and Kella's owlet was firmly affixed to the lad's shoulder. Rasial laid herself along a wall in the sunshine as Seely gawked and admired the owlet. The Farseeker guilden farsent privately to me that all Gavyn had needed to do was pet the bird.

"I suppose Kella was relieved?" I said aloud.

"Well, she was an' she wasn't. It was a nuisance, but I think she quite enjoyed th' bird's devotion to her. When it went so willin'ly to Gavyn, she felt a bit bereft."

"It might fly off looking for her in a bit," I said dubiously.

"Not if Gavyn wants it to stay," Seely said with evident pride.

Just then, Maruman noticed the bird. Hissing, he dug his claws into my shoulder to stand and arch his back. The bird seemed completely oblivious to anything but Gavyn, and Maruman leapt to the ledge and yowled to be let out into the garden. At my request, Zarak manhandled the window open, and the old cat disappeared with an angry twitch of his tail.

"That was Maruman," I said dryly.

Seely frowned. "He's the first animal I've ever seen who didn't go to Gavyn."

"Well, he's a moody thing at the best of times," I said dismissively.

Gavyn turned to Ceirwan. "Can we go to the farms now?" he asked. "You said we might if I could get the owl to come with me."

712

I laughed. "You should go at once. You might as well enjoy the sweet weather while it lasts."

Zarak said he would walk down with them, since he had promised a few hours of planting to Alad, and Rasial joined them as well. Watching them all go, it came to me suddenly that we might not see another wintertime safe in the mountains. I was glad when Javo distracted me by bringing a morsel of something to taste. The square cake was dry and not very appealing, and I said so as politely as I could.

Javo laughed, the rolls of fat around his neck wobbling. "You won't offend me by saying it tastes foul," he boomed. "This is a meal cake for traveling. We're trying to come up with a biscuit full of nourishment that is dry enough neither to rot nor get stale on a long journey, and compact enough to take up very little space. This is our first attempt."

I grimaced. "Well, I'd say you wouldn't die from living on this, but living won't be much fun either."

His laughter was infectious, despite all the things looming over our heads, and I grinned back at him.

As Javo returned to his work, a mental probe blundered against my mindshield without warning, rocking me back on my heels. I sat heavily, my head throbbing. "Calm down and identify yourself," I sent sharply.

Another clumsy prod followed, but this time I recognized one of the younger Beastspeaking guilders, a girl with coercive Talent named Rori. I sent a probe, which located her in a far field where she had been planting.

"What is it?" I demanded, irritated that courtesy required that I did not simply enter her mind to learn what I wanted.

"I . . . we've found a dead bird, and it's got a message in the tube on its leg. The others are looking for Alad, but I . . .

we think the bird is one of those the Master of Obernewtyn took with him to the lowlands."

I swallowed a lump of fear. "What does he say?"

"The note is not from Rushton, Guildmistress. It is *about* him." Rori's mind quivered, and my own control faltered. "It says he'll die if . . ." Her mind slipped out of my grasp.

I clenched my teeth so hard my jaw ached and found her again. "Rori, I want you to bring the bird up to the maze gate. I'll meet you at the farm end."

My legs trembled as I hurried to the maze. I felt sick with apprehension. What had happened to Rushton? And who had sent the note? Was it a warning or a threat? How long had the bird been dead, its message undelivered?

What if it was already too late?

✦ 17 ✦

Ceirwan and the others were walking through the maze when I overtook them.

I farsent a brief explanation to the guilden. For the benefit of Seely, I said aloud that I was on my way to retrieve an important message, and hurried on.

By the time I reached the farm gate, young Rori was there, looking apprehensive. The Beastspeaking guildmaster stood beside her, so grim-faced that dread rose up in my throat.

"I'd say it's two days dead," he said, holding out the mangled bird. "It looks as if it was hit by an arrow and managed to fly back here, but the poor thing didn't make it to the coop."

He sent Rori off to fetch his ward. When we were standing there alone, I asked him bluntly what the message said.

"You'd best read it yourself." He handed me a tiny roll of parchment that had been dipped in wax to stop the ink on the scribing from being washed off if it rained. I spread it out with shaking fingers and read the tiny crabbed script.

To who may care.
  I have your precious Master. If Misfits do not aid the rebels in their fight against the Council, he dies.

The world spun dizzily about me. "Elspeth," Alad cried, catching me by the arm.

"It could be some sort of h-hoax . . . ," I stammered.

Alad held out a black twist of hair I could not fail to recognize. "It came with the note, and the bird was Rushton's. It might be fake, but they wouldn't dare send it and make demands if Rushton was around to deny it. Unless . . ."

I shuddered at what he did not say: unless Rushton was dead.

Dead!

"Elspeth . . . ," Alad murmured worriedly.

I waved him back and waged a short, savage battle with my emotions for control. I won because of the knowledge that if Rushton lived, and I could not bear to think of anything else, then his life might well depend upon my being able to think clearly.

"It doesn't make sense," I muttered. "No one but the rebels could want us to join them, but they refused us when we offered ourselves."

"From Rushton's earlier note, they had changed their minds," Alad said. He took my arm and led me firmly toward the main house. "The note says that he will be killed if we don't help the rebels, but there is no sense of violence or anger in the words so far as I can see. It's rather an emotionless statement, and for all we know, it's no more than an empty threat. Maybe they are trying to bluff us to force our hand."

I lifted the note but could sense no thoughts adhering to it nor any trace of its writer's personality. That was unusual in itself.

A bluff, Alad had said.

An ugly suspicion reared its head.

Brydda and his closest confidants within the rebel movement knew that Rushton was the Master of Obernewtyn. Brydda and his allies wanted us to join them in their fight against the Council. Brydda had summoned Rushton to ask for our help and had been refused.

Common sense told me that if Rushton had been kidnapped by rebels, Brydda might very well have heard about it, even if he was not the instigator.

I felt sickened by my thoughts, for even entertaining them seemed a kind of ultimate mistrust. Yet nothing else made any sense of the few facts we had.

And if it was true?

No harm might be meant to Rushton, but it would still be a betrayal. Just as Maryon had foreseen.

It was late afternoon before the guildmerge was assembled to discuss the kidnap message. I needed to decide what to do, and I could not decide alone.

Yet, in the end, all we could agree upon was that we knew too little. "We don't have information enough to reach any final conclusions," I said after a long and fruitless debate. "We need to know what happened in Rushton's meeting with the rebels, and we need to know exactly when he left the coast. Someone will have to travel to Sutrium."

"I'll go," Linnet offered promptly. "I can take one of the other knights with me as backup. We can search for Rushton. He's bound to be somewhere in the city if the rebels have him. We can also question the rebels about his meeting with them."

I stifled a mad urge to say I would go myself. "It's one thing to probe for information, but I don't want you to make direct contact with the rebels just in case there is some sort of treachery afoot."

"I don't like the way you keeping hinting Brydda is a traitor," Gevan said sternly.

"The message makes it very clear that whoever has

Rushton knows where we are. And no one knows that but Brydda," I said.

"And Reuvan. And the Sadorians. And maybe a couple dozen others, for all we know," Gevan added.

Aras sat forward. "I don't mean to interrupt, but does whoever wrote that note really know where we are? After all, a homing bird flies to its roost, so whoever released it knew the message would find us, whether or not they knew our whereabouts. And any rebel would have known the bird was a homer by its leg capsule."

"The note called Rushton the Master of Obernewtyn," Alad said.

"It didn't," Aras said shyly. "It only said 'your Master.' And since the rebels knew Rushton as the leader of the Misfits, the note might simply mean that."

"Truespoken." Gevan gave the young ward a look of approval that made her blush with pleasure.

Jak nodded. "In any case, it doesn't change the fact that whoever wrote the note wants us to work with the rebels. And that puts us right back to wondering who it is and whether the threats against Rushton are real."

The others exchanged dismayed glances, and I sensed our thoughts roiling around in the air about us like an invisible thunderstorm.

"I think we must act as if they are real," Angina said. "Rushton's captors must believe that we take them seriously."

"We should organize a meeting with the rebels," Gevan said. "That's what we'd do if we meant to obey, and indeed, it's the only way we can show that we accept the terms of the note."

"We ought to send a note requesting a meeting," Garth suggested. "One without any specific information or mention of the kidnapping. If Linnet leaves it at a drop in Sutrium, it will take time for Brydda to get the note and respond to it. In the meantime, she will have had the chance to nose around."

Merret spoke up next. "What if the meeting took place in Sawlney during the bonding celebrations?"

"I don't think it is a good idea to draw rebel attention to your magi," I said.

"The magi need not be involved in the meeting," Gevan offered. "But it might be the perfect location, given the influx of moon-fair visitors. Sutrium is so much of a rat trap these days, I'm sure the rebels won't object. You'd have to come in Rushton's stead of course, Elspeth. You can ride to meet me there, and the two of us can represent Obernewtyn. If there is treachery afoot, we should be able to sniff it out between us."

Gevan gave me a hard look, and I pulled myself together. "Very well. I will compose a note to Brydda immediately. Linnet, choose a companion from your knights and prepare to leave for Sutrium before the sun sets."

Later that evening, I went to the dining hall, deciding I had best let everyone see I was not falling to pieces.

I made a point of talking and looking purposeful and de-termined, though in truth my will felt as insubstantial as smoke in the wind. Unexpectedly, I found myself comforted by the bustle. It reminded me of all that Obernewtyn meant to Rushton. No matter what happened to him, I knew he would want me to put Obernewtyn's welfare first. In a funny way, by trying to reassure the others, I ended up feeling stronger.

Javo, Alad, and their people were discussing provisions, and I eavesdropped shamelessly, glad of the distraction. They already knew from usual winter planning how much food would be needed to take us through thaw to first harvest if we were to withdraw to the caves higher in the mountains. They seemed to feel that, with strict rationing, we would manage well enough. But they foresaw trouble if the siege continued beyond thaw, because there would be no way to restock.

The meeting moved on to the more vexing problem of provisioning an exodus to Sador.

"I wish I'd thought to ask Jakoby a bit more about the route," Alad grumbled.

Lina tapped his arm and said thoughtfully, "You know, Guildmaster, I've been thinking. If people only thought we'd left the mountains, there would be no one searching for us. There'd be no siege."

"No, but someone would take over Obernewtyn, and that would be the same as being sieged, since we couldn't return," Javo said.

Lina looked crestfallen, and Alad said gruffly that they ought to stick to the matter at hand. Talk veered back to bags of dry grain versus prepared ration cakes, but I was struck by what Lina had said. I realized with some excitement that she might have hit upon the perfect compromise between two difficult solutions. To remain, yet make it seem we had gone. The only trouble was that Javo was right; Obernewtyn was too grand a prize not to be claimed by someone.

The best answer was to turn it into a tainted ruin again. That, after all, would tally with the last official report. Of course, we no longer had Dragon's ability to create massive illusions, but all the coercers working together could make sections of Obernewtyn appear ruinous, while strategic parts could be damaged to prevent access to intact sections.

If we could manage that, and convince anyone searching for us that we had left the mountains, we could avoid any sort of confrontation and return to Obernewtyn when wintertime cut off the pass. I was sure Jakoby would help us by spreading the rumor that we had come to the desert lands.

A hand descended onto my shoulder, and I started violently.

"I'm sorry, Guildmistress," Tomash said. "Ceirwan said you might like to know what came out of my talk with Seely. But I can just give you my notes later, if you'd prefer."

"No, sit," I said, waving him to the seat opposite.

"I'm sorry about Rushton," he said with such graceful simplicity that my eyes blurred.

"I'm sorry, too, but I don't want to speak of it now. Tell me what you learned from Seely."

"The main thing is that the Council seem to know the Land is on the verge of an uprising, because there is at least one traitor among the rebels."

I felt a thrill of dismay. "The Council must know about us, if they know what the rebels know."

"It's hard to be sure. Most of Seely's memories revolve around the west coast, so I'd say the traitors are there. In which case they're less likely to know in detail what Brydda and his people know of us. But I think we can assume that the Council is aware that Talented Misfits, disguised as half-breed gypsies, offered their help to the rebels and were refused, since all the rebels know that much. And they probably know better than we do what took place at that meeting Brydda had with Rushton in Sutrium."

"How much of this did you get out of Seely's mind?"

"She had a lot of overheard scraps of information that were meaningless to her and meaningless in themselves, but they fitted with other scraps we already knew. I'm just giving you the bones of it, of course. Another interesting tidbit is that Cassell and Serba are bonding out of genuine love. It seems the two of them are working brilliantly together, much to the Council's chagrin."

"The Council know even that, yet they wait like spiders for a fly to shiver their web," I murmured.

"One other thing: there have been unofficial meetings between soldierguards and Herders on the west coast . . . the sort that happen at odd hours in peculiar places."

Immediately, I thought of my nightmares. "Did you find anything in her mind about Ariel?"

"I didn't, and you can be sure I looked as soon as the Faction came up."

Relieved, I said, "We know a lot of soldierguards are in the pay of the Faction. I wonder, if it came to it, which side would they choose?"

"Whichever they judged to be the winning side, I expect," Tomash said.

"These meetings occur only on the west coast?"

"They're the only ones Seely knows about, and Wila has no knowledge of similar meetings this side of the Suggredoon. She's going to talk to Seely tomorrow, so she might learn something further. I'll write up my notes and let you have them tomorrow."

"It would be interesting to know if the rebels are aware that they have traitors in their midst," I murmured to myself as he got to his feet.

"I was thinking that's probably why they changed their mind about wanting us with them," Tomash said mildly as he departed.

I stared after him, certain that he was right. If the rebels knew they were being betrayed, who better than us to scry out their traitors?

Deciding that I had made enough of a display of confidence to withdraw, I got to my feet. Ceirwan caught up with me as I reached the door of my turret chamber.

"Freya wants to go wi' th' magi to th' lowlands," he puffed, having sprinted up the stairs after me.

"Gevan will decide who is to accompany him," I said.

"I ken that, but if ye tell him, he'll take Freya. An' I think ye should. She wants to help find Rushton, an' though she's no coercer, she kens his mind. I was thinkin' that she an' I could go with Kella to Sutrium," he said, flushing. "Freya an' I can look for Rushton while Kella tries to get through to Domick."

I frowned. I didn't like the idea of anyone going to Sutrium with things in such an ambiguous state, but on the other hand, a young man escorting his betrothed and her cousin to the city would be a far less provocative cover than a young woman traveling alone. And maybe it would be just as well, given that we had no idea how Kella would react upon reuniting with her bondmate.

"I'm not saying yes or no right now, Ceir, but I will think about it," I promised.

"My thanks for that at least," the guilden said earnestly.

I froze as Gevan's coercive voice boomed in my mind, warning that his people at the pass had reported riders approaching the mountains at a gallop.

"Soldierguards?" I farsent sharply.

"Too soon to say, but as there's only four or five, I doubt it. It's more likely to be some of the knights, and from the way they're riding, I'd say they have news."

"Did you catch that?" I asked Ceirwan breathlessly.

"Of course. But if it is the knights, then why are there only four or five when more than ten rode out?"

✦ 18 ✦

Resisting the urge to hurry down and wait at the front gate, I told myself it would be some time before the riders arrived and busied myself stoking the fire and closing the shutters. As I did so, I realized that it had started to rain.

The door creaked, and I turned to see Maruman slink into the chamber.

I asked if he knew a bird had been found carrying a message from someone who claimed to be holding Rushton captive.

"Marumanyelloweyes knows many things," he sent with infuriating ambiguity.

I sighed and slid onto the chair, pulling him onto my lap. "So many people have been killed or lost to me since I first came to Obernewtyn. Cameo and Selmar and Jes. Jik and Matthew and Dragon."

"I will not leave you," Maruman sent, and he turned around and around, needling my legs through my clothes before he settled himself.

Touched, I blinked back a scatter of tears and gazed into the fire, trying not to think about the riders approaching, trying not to hope. But it was impossible.

To stop myself, I asked Maruman his impression of Gavyn.

"Adantar is beastspeaker-enthraller—" Maruman began.

"What is 'adantar'?" I interrupted, having a vague impression it meant something like "joined" or "linked."

"No funaga words for this word," he responded tersely.

"Why does Rasial/silvertongue follow Gavynadantar?"

"What she seeks, she sees in the adantar."

I frowned. "She told me she came up here to seek her dying."

"Just so," Maruman sent.

I stared at him. "Are you saying Rasial follows Gavyn because she sees her death in him?"

Maruman sniffed, signaling the topic was closed. Then I remembered the nightmares about Ariel. I described them to Maruman, and his eye flashed. "Marumanyelloweyes knows. Who else overturned wagon? Marumanyelloweyes watches the dreamtrails. Protects ElspethInnle."

I gaped at him stupidly. "I don't understand. You . . . you were in those nightmares?"

"No nightmares. ElspethInnle on dreamtrails," Maruman sent. "Marumanyelloweyes watches/follows. Protects Elspeth-Innle."

I licked dry lips, feeling as if I were slicked in ice. "Are . . . are you saying that I need protecting because I wasn't dreaming?" I sent with incredulity. "That Ariel was . . . is after me in my dreams?"

Maruman closed his eyes. I felt like shaking him, but Gevan sent to tell me the riders were approaching Obernewtyn and suggested I meet him at the front entrance. I slid the old cat unceremoniously onto my seat, ignoring his indignant protests, and got up to put on boots and a shawl, asking Gevan if the riders had been identified.

I was on my way down the halls when Gevan answered. "It is Miryum, and Brydda Llewellyn rides with her."

"Brydda?" I sent with surprise. "But she can't have told

him about the blackmail note—the knights rode out before it arrived."

"Good," Gevan sent. "I want the chance to see Brydda's reaction when we tell him about the note."

"I thought you trusted him." I was walking toward the front hall now, and my senses told me Gevan was waiting in a small chamber off the front entrance hall.

"I trust him not to be the instigator of the kidnapping," Gevan said. "But if he was aware of it, he could think he was sparing us the worry by keeping it a secret. Remember last year how he didn't tell us some of the rebels were opposed to an alliance with us until you forced it out of him? He didn't have a bad motive then, but he was still lying by omission in hopes of resolving the problem himself."

"Lying about Rushton's kidnapping would be rather more than a thoughtful attempt to smooth things over," I said aloud, striding into the antechamber.

Gevan nodded. "Truespoken, but let's wait and see, shall we? They should be here any minute."

I went to lean on the mantelpiece, where Gevan had lit a fire in the hearth, and told him what I had just learned about a traitor among the rebels.

He looked at me sideways. "Let's see what Brydda has to say before we tell him anything."

We both stiffened at the sound of horses and hurried to open the heavy front doors. Through the rain-swept darkness, I saw Brydda dismounting from his white mare, Sallah. Miryum and the coercer-knight Orys were on the ground already, as was Brydda's right-hand man, Reuvan. But Straaka stayed on horseback, shouting over the rain that he would go with the horses down to the farms.

"We've a fire blazing. You can dry out while we talk," Gevan said by way of greeting, closing the main doors behind us.

"Elspeth." Brydda smiled, taking my hands. "I'm glad to see you again." Looking up into his kind brown eyes, his long molasses curls and beard all dripping wet, I felt like howling.

Instead I swallowed hard and said, "I'm truly glad to see you, too, Brydda, but I wish it was under happier circumstances."

"You've still had no news of Rushton, then?"

Gevan interrupted smoothly to deflect the question, hustling us all into the antechamber and suggesting everyone remove their wet top clothes and drape them about to dry.

"I've farsent Ceirwan," I said. "He will be here soon with food, and we've got water heating for baths and chambers made up for you to sleep in."

"I won't say no to food, but we won't be staying the night," Brydda said. "Reuvan and I rode out as soon as Jakoby told me Rushton hadn't got back to Obernewtyn. We decided to ask after him all along the main road. This afternoon, we walked into a roadside tavern a few hours below Guanette, and who should we see but Miryum and a couple of her knights drinking and playing darts."

"We were probing the crowd for news of Rushton . . . ," Miryum said, then hesitated. I sensed Gevan warning her coercively to say nothing of Maryon's futuretelling, if she had not done so already.

"I suppose she told you we got a bird he sent after leaving Sutrium?" I said.

"I was there when he released it from the outskirts of Sutrium. He rode off safe and well after that. He should have been back well before your moon fair, by my reckoning."

"So far, we're found no one who even saw him coming up the road," Miryum said.

"Nor did we, but if he rode at night, it's possible he'd go unnoticed," Reuvan said.

"There was no reason for him to be so furtive," I protested.

"Unless something happened at the meeting he had with the rebels to make him so," the Coercer guildmaster interposed blandly.

Brydda shrugged. "I can't think what. We invited the Misfits to join us in the rebellion, and Rushton declined."

"Why did you decide to ask us to join you after everything that has happened?" Gevan asked. "I can't believe Malik changed his mind about us."

"Well, he didn't, that's true. But since Malik has no more say than anyone else, he was outvoted."

"Malik was glad we refused, then?" Gevan asked.

"Yes, though he claimed it was a deadly insult that Misfits would refuse anything to 'true humans.' His words," Brydda added wryly, twisting his lips as if he had tasted something unpleasant.

"What about the other rebels?" Gevan asked. "Were they angry that we would not join them?"

"Not so much that as plain bewildered," the big rebel admitted. "They could not understand why you would refuse when you'd tried so hard to join us before." His expression grew serious. "You are wondering if any of the rebels went after Rushton on the road because he spurned our offer of alliance?"

"Isn't it a reasonable assumption, since he seems to have disappeared right after the meeting, and no one but your people and ours knew where he was?" Gevan countered.

"You are assuming he was attacked by someone who knew who he was, but there are those on the road to whom a jack would seem a good target. But I can see why you might wonder about the rebels, and I admit to wanting to make sure none of them are involved myself. That's why I want to get back as soon as possible." The big rebel looked at me from under his lashes, and I caught his unsaid thought quite clearly.

"He's not dead," I said flatly.

"It is a possibility, if he was waylaid by robbers," Brydda said.

"Tell him," Gevan sent to me.

I nodded and took a deep breath. "Brydda, you might as well know that we have had news of Rushton since Miryum left."

Brydda stared at me. "*Of* Rushton? From whom?"

"From whoever is holding him captive."

The big rebel looked stunned, as did Miryum and Orys.

"Captive?" Miryum muttered as if she didn't understand the word.

"A note came with Rushton's second bird. You will remember he carried two?" Brydda nodded impatiently. "There was no identification on the note. It said only that Rushton was being held and would die if Misfits didn't aid the rebels."

Brydda looked completely taken aback.

"You can see why we suspect it must be rebels who have him," Gevan said.

Brydda ran blunt fingers through his curls. "I see that it seems so, but it makes no sense, truly. For Rushton to have been kidnapped so efficiently, with no one seeing anything, a plan would have to have been organized well in advance of the meeting. But why would anyone have bothered, since none there imagined that Rushton would refuse us?"

"But who other than a rebel would want Misfits as part of the rebellion?" I asked.

There were footsteps outside the room, forestalling Brydda's response. Ceirwan entered with Merret, both of them carrying steaming clove-scented jugs of mead, platters of bread and cheese, and cold slabs of pie. Their entry broke the tension that had been growing between us. When we were all settled about, sipping hot, spiced mead, Brydda spoke about what had led the rebels to offer an alliance to us.

"You impressed people far more deeply than even they realized at the time. They had not really thought about the cost of winning the rebellion before. After returning from Sador, they started looking at what they really wanted. Rather than revenge or power, most wanted simply to live in peace. In our meetings, the rebel leaders began talking seriously of how to keep the death toll down, and we spoke of preserving the structures that govern the cities while removing the corrupt Council and Faction network. Plans were made to introduce a popular vote to establish leaders in each town, and someone suggested a sort of law-keeping force that the town leaders could draw on at need. We thought the force could be made up of men and women for some period of their lives, rather than of a constant body, because all that law-keeping can warp a mind after a while so they can't draw the line between keeping the law and oppression. Another suggestion was drawing up a charter of laws so that the people of the Land could have the chance to modify or at least discuss them before they came into force. It'll be up to us rebels to keep things running and peaceful until everything is in place, of course, but we now see ourselves as a sort of interim peacekeeping body, rather than ultimate rulers."

"I can't see Malik being pleased by the idea of communal decision making," Gevan said.

"He isn't, and he wasn't the only one to oppose a lot of the new ideas, but the majority of us feel the same, and our numbers were enough to carry the vote. I daresay it riles Malik that, despite his win in the Battlegames, only his cronies wanted him running anything."

"What did Rushton say when he refused your offer?" Merret asked.

Brydda drank a deep mouthful of ale, then said, "He told us that Misfits couldn't be part of any war, because it meant consenting to the violence and abetting it even if you did none of the bloodletting. He said you'd seen your true nature in the Battlegames and had made an oath not to go against it."

"Would that be enough to provoke foul play?" Gevan asked.

"Malik or his cronies would be malicious enough to hurt Rushton for daring to refuse us, but there would be no gain whatever for him in this kidnapping. As to the others, I just can't see that any of them would be dishonorable enough to do it," Brydda said.

"Perhaps dishonor would be seen as a small price to pay for finding out who is betraying your secrets to the Council," I said coolly. "It might be considered a lesser evil than the knowledge that on the eve of your uprising, every step you take will be anticipated and thwarted by your enemies. Isn't that the *real* reason the rebels decided to ask us to join them? Your need to flush out your betrayers?"

Brydda set his empty mug aside carefully before responding. "So you know about the traitors."

I said nothing, and neither did anyone else.

The big rebel sighed and leaned back into his seat. "It's

true that knowing there are traitors among us was one of the reasons the subject of an alliance with your people arose again. But if you had not made such an impact during the Battlegames, no one would have suggested it." He smiled disarmingly. "You are annoyed because I did not speak of the traitors. I understand that, but the only way we are surviving right now is by telling no one anything other than what they absolutely need to know. It has become a habit."

"Don't you think the need to find your traitors puts Rushton's kidnapping in another light?" Gevan asked.

"Maybe you see it as a good enough reason to bury would-be allies. I don't," Brydda said. "Besides, think of it. If the kidnapping was committed to make sure the traitors are caught, you would almost certainly unearth the kidnapper when you were scrying out the traitors."

"But who did it, if not the rebels?" Merret asked. "You are the only ones who will benefit if we do what that blackmail note demands."

Brydda ran his hands over his head. "That is a cursed good point, but I don't know the answer. But I refuse to see us benefit from this—I would not accept a forced alliance. We will turn the Land on its head to find Rushton. If rebels have him, I swear I will sniff it out."

"Like you have sniffed out the traitors in your own ranks?" I asked with more bitterness than I intended.

"What would you have me do, Elspeth?" Brydda asked with a flash of weary irritation. "I did not kidnap Rushton, nor am I trying to take advantage of this situation, despite the needs of my own people."

I took a deep breath before answering. "I'm sorry. Search as you said, and so will we. But in the meantime, help us make it seem that we will obey the kidnapper. We meant to organize a meeting with you as a display of obedience. When you get back to Sutrium, you'll find a message from us asking for a meeting with the rebels in Sawlney."

"Why Sawlney?"

"A moon fair and Councilman Alum's bonding ceremony for his daughter will take place there in just over a sevenday. There will be a lot of coming and going, and it will be easy for our people and yours to converge there without anyone wondering why."

Brydda tugged at his beard in a familiar gesture. "The rebel leaders are due to meet soon anyway. I'll simply name Sawlney as the venue. Malik won't object since it's Brocade's territory, and you can just turn up. I'll announce you then and there. That will be safest."

"I appreciate your trying to protect us," I said, "but the whole point is to let the kidnapper know that we're doing what he wants."

Brydda pondered that. "Very well, I'll mention your desire to meet and make sure the news gets passed around, but I don't think you need feel too frightened that the kidnapper will do anything suddenly, since he can't know if you will obey or not until the rebellion is in progress. He will want to keep his hostage safe in the meantime."

There was little more than that to say, and since Brydda still refused to stay the night, he and Reuvan decided to visit the farms to see Brydda's parents. I walked with them, for the rain had stopped.

The air felt damp, and the ground squelched underfoot as we wound our way through the sodden greenthorn. Not wanting to talk any more of Rushton, I sought some less painful topic and asked if he was disappointed with the Sadorians' decision to send only a token force to aid them.

"We were, of course, but since it was always uncertain how many the Sadorians would send, we had not got used to counting on them." A smile ghosted over his face, lit by the lantern he carried. "You know Bruna remained in Sutrium when her mother left this morning?"

"I didn't. I suppose she is staying with Bodera?"

"She is, and again she is playing merry hell with poor Dardelan. To look at his face, you can see he's neatly and uncomfortably balanced between longing for peace and plain longing."

"He cares for her, then?"

"It's obvious to everyone but Bruna. He has sense enough not to give her the knowledge, for she's the sort to use it as a whip on him. He treats her with perfect courtesy even when she behaves like a spoiled brat."

"And how is Bodera?"

The rebel sighed. "Some days are bad, and others are worse. Very few of his days can be called good anymore, sadly. It must be hard to die so slowly. He does not want to die while he is needed, but I think he is utterly weary of his existence. It's my belief that he means to live until the rebellion is won, and with his will, he might do just that."

We had come to the end of the maze path, and I farsent to locate Katlyn and Grufyyd. They were waiting eagerly for their son in Alad's kitchen. Katlyn burst into tears at the sight of Brydda, but he swept her into his massive arms and gave her a long hard hug and a dozen kisses, until she stopped weeping and started laughing and protesting. Releasing her, he gave his father a heartfelt hug and sat down between them.

Katlyn's face fell when he told them he would not stay even one night, but Grufyyd patted her arm and said she was not to fuss, as he doubtless had to hurry back because of Rushton being kidnapped.

"Oh, of course." Katlyn pressed a plump hand to her mouth. "Poor dear Rushton. It's too much on top of the trouble Maryon's foreseen."

Giving Alad a swift warning glance, I said casually to Brydda that the futureteller had foreseen strife throughout the Land, which we had taken to be the rebellion.

"Did Elspeth mention about Sawlney?" Grufyyd began. I instituted a swift, gentle coercive block to stop him from going on to mention the magi as he'd intended, and the wagons he'd so lovingly created.

"She did, and it seems to me a good safe meeting place what with the moon fair dragging strangers from all over." Brydda did not notice a vaguely puzzled look flit over Grufyyd's wrinkled face as he wondered why he felt suddenly reluctant to speak of what was on the tip of his tongue.

"It is my hope that by the time the fair comes, we'll have found Rushton and you won't have to go there," Brydda added.

Alad opened his mouth, then closed it at my warning kick under the table. Fortunately, Brydda didn't catch his pained expression, because Katlyn was offering to pack a basket of special food for the journey back to Sutrium.

"Mam, we'll be riding fast, and they have food aplenty in Sutrium," Brydda objected.

Katlyn said that it wasn't *her* food and that she could tell by his looks that what he'd been eating was nowhere near as healthy. I grinned in spite of everything, because Brydda had never looked undernourished. He caught the look and lifted his hands in helpless obedience as Katlyn hurried off.

"I'm sorry I can't stay longer, Da," the big rebel told his

735

father. "I would like to think I'll be back soon, but I don't know when, with the rebellion about to turn the Land upside down. And I'll have to be part of sorting things out afterward. I just don't know how long it will be before we can resume our own lives. I've had my fill of cities and crowds these last few years; when this is all over, I might move back to Rangorn and rebuild the old farm. How do you like the idea of going home after all this time?"

"Well now, we wouldn't want to go back, truly," Grufyyd said. "Me and your mam're settled here, and here we'll stay until they put us in the ground. Unless we're driven out."

"I'd never let that happen," Brydda said. "Well, then, maybe I'll ride up here and build a farm instead." He gave a surprised sort of laugh. "It's funny to hear myself talk of afterward. All those years of plotting and scheming, and the rebellion always seemed so far away you couldn't imagine an afterward."

"What about you, Reuvan? What will you do when it's over?" Alad asked the blue-eyed seaman.

Reuvan gave a rare, dreamy smile that made him look older rather than younger, as if somehow all the worry and fear had arrested his development. "I'd like to go to Sador again," he admitted. "But before that, I'll get a small boat and a crew, and we'll go off looking for the place that buys slaves from the Land, in memory of Idris. I'll find Matthew and the others Salamander took and buy their freedom if I can't help them escape."

That reminded me of the dreams everyone had been having about Matthew. "Reuvan, have you ever heard seamen talk of a land where it's terribly hot and where the ground is red and hard, and there are steep, rocky hills of reddish stone?"

Reuvan stared. "Can't say I've heard of such a place."

"A lot of us have dreamed of Matthew lately, and that's the kind of terrain we see around him. He is in a port city, but it's not like any in the Land."

"I will ask around," Reuvan promised, looking interested.

Katlyn returned with two enormous baskets, and Brydda said that he and Reuvan could not possibly ride as swiftly as they needed with such a load. Protesting and clicking her tongue, she repackaged some of the food into two smaller bundles, and we followed Brydda out into the chilly darkness.

"Don't lose hope, little sad eyes," he said to me as I hugged him. "Miryum said none of your futuretellers foresaw any danger to Rushton, and whoever the kidnappers are, they need him healthy, so he is safe for the present. And he must know that we are all searching for him."

The rebels mounted up, their coats flapping in the rising wind. He blew a kiss to his mother before galloping away. We stood there until the hoofbeats faded and all we could hear was the wind and Katlyn's soft weeping.

"It's long past our bedtime," Grufyyd said, and led her tenderly away.

Alad walked me to the maze gate, but I would not let him escort me up to the house. "If I'm not safe at Obernewtyn, I might as well give up."

"Let's hope Obernewtyn will always be a safe haven for us," Alad responded seriously. "Elspeth, I might as well tell you now that I mean to vote against our leaving the mountains. And if the choice is made to go to Sador, then I will stay here on my own with the beasts that cannot travel."

"I don't want to leave any more than you," I admitted. "In

fact, I may have a plan that would enable us to stay here."

"I can't say how it relieves me to hear you say that," the Beastspeaking guildmaster confessed. "I have always loved Obernewtyn, but until we began talking seriously of leaving it, I never knew how much. Before I came here, I was a lone fugitive with nothing to hope for. Here I found purpose and friends and a life that I love. What I am today, this place made me."

"We will hold on to Obernewtyn with all of our strength," I promised him and Rushton both.

✦ 19 ✦

IN THE DAYS following Brydda's visit, my determination not to fall into despondency remained firm, and I threw myself into the business of running Obernewtyn and planning its protection.

To begin with, I spent some time speaking to the other guildleaders and listening to general talk, only to learn that Alad's passion to remain in the valley was universal. Therefore, even without any formal decision being made in guild-merge, I allowed the emphasis to shift from the idea of abandoning the Land to a strategic withdrawal to caves higher in the mountains.

The proposed exodus to Sador became part of a sleight of hand to produce the illusion that we had quit the Land once and for all. I spoke of the need to prevent anyone occupying Obernewtyn while it stood empty, and Gevan agreed that, while no one could reproduce Dragon's incredible illusion, quite a lot of imaginary damage could be induced by a prac-ticed team of his people. Miky suggested that the Empath guild could contribute to the illusion by projecting feelings of unease and edginess verging on nausea into anyone who looked at it. And Garth promised that his guild would pro-duce a cluster of huts that would make it appear as if we'd been living rough in the valley and that Obernewtyn itself had been an uninhabitable ruin for years.

Alad and Javo prepared complete provision lists for our proposed sojourn in the mountain caves and had begun readying supplies to be transferred when the refuge was complete. Crops were planted bit by bit, and Grufyyd finished the magi wagons and began constructing others to be used as decoys in the apparent exodus to Sador.

Miryum rejoined her knights and continued to scour the highlands for news of Rushton. Straaka insisted on accompanying her. But they found only a persistent rumor of impending rebellion.

Maryon's people were also hard at work, delving into their minds for information about Rushton and the rebel traitors; unfortunately, they came up with nothing more than vague visions of danger and betrayal. Or they dreamed of Matthew in his strange, red-stone city.

Avra and Gahltha left Obernewtyn with their foal to run for a time with the wild herd, but Gahltha had promised to return in time to convey me to the meeting in Sawlney. In a previous beastmerge, the matter of the beast sales and gelding practices had been raised again. But with the rebellion looming, no one could say when the next sales would occur, so there was nothing for it but to wait and see.

As far as my own guild was concerned, a slight variation of the whiplash mindmerge was achieved successfully, though it would take many hours of practice to perfect it. Zarak and Aras had taken over organizing the practices in order to free Ceirwan to run the farseekers, since I was increasingly engaged in other matters.

The morning the magi were due to depart Obernewtyn, a note arrived from Brydda by bird saying the rebels had agreed to allow us to speak at their meeting in Sawlney. He had not enlightened them as to the subject we wished to address and had informed only his most trusted people of the kidnapping, because he had needed them to help search Sutrium for Rushton. Despite their best efforts, no trace of him had been found. It was, Brydda wrote, as if Rushton had vanished off the face of the earth.

When I saw the three lavishly decorated magi wagons loaded up outside the entrance to Obernewtyn, I had the sudden premonition that our lives were about to change forever. A small crowd of well-wishers had assembled to see the wagons depart, including Rhianon, a silent blue-eyed woman who had been left in charge of the Coercer guild. Her shoulders were bowed as if already she felt the unaccustomed weight of her new responsibility. Gevan had confided to me that he had intended to raise her to wardship during the next Choosing Ceremony but that he had hastened the promotion informally. It was significant that he did not leave Miryum in his place and that she did not protest.

It was a beautiful day, and the elaborately carved wagons decorated with ribbons and garlands of herbs and flowers lent the whole occasion a brave, festive air.

"Don't look so woebegone," Gevan said. "You'll be riding after us in a few days."

"It's seeing so many of you leaving that makes me feel sad," I murmured.

"There are a motley lot of us, to be sure." He grinned, casting his eyes over his troupe. There were ten magi, including himself, Merret, and Hannay; three empath musicians; and Freya, Ceirwan, and Kella. There were also six horses, two apiece to a wagon; two goats that had offered to provide milk and take part in the tricks; and three chickens, as well as a small cooing flock of homing birds. The birds and fowls had no minds to say whether or not they were willing to join the traveling show, but they looked content enough.

Gevan wanted to ride straight by Guanette without stopping. The magi would then stay three nights in Arandelft, perfecting their performance before the rustic locals and investigating the area we thought might be a prime location for a safe farm, since it lacked both rebel and Council affiliates. Leaving the forest village in the afternoon, they would arrive in Sawlney with a day to spare before the bonding of the Councilman's daughter. The rebel meeting was to take place the following night, when the festivities were at their height. I would time my own journey to arrive the night before the meeting.

"Be careful," I said softly.

"Always." Gevan squeezed my arm and gave the whistling gypsy signal for his troupe to ready themselves for departure. Watching him scold and chivvy everyone into their places, I could see he was already becoming the irascible halfbreed gypsy-troupe leader. He looked every inch the part, and I had no doubt the magi would be safe under his guidance.

"Ri-ide," Gevan sang in the gypsy way, and the travelers broke spontaneously into a well-known gypsy song as the wagons rolled away down the drive. I heard the faint trill of pipes and the soft thunder of a coercer drum as the last wagon passed out of sight around the curving drive. The sound of the music lasted for some minutes after the wagons had gone out of view, but eventually it faded, too, until there was nothing but the murmur of wind in the trees bordering the drive and the intermittent trill of birds.

With faint melancholy, I reflected that I seemed to be always bidding friends farewell these days.

"Well, that's that," Alad sighed beside me. "It's funny how you always feel so flat and dull when people go off on a journey and you're left behind. Yet, I don't envy them, truly."

I was only half listening, for I had caught sight of young Gavyn over near the tree line, standing very still and holding up a small, chubby hand. He smiled in delight as a bird came to light on his finger and tilted its head to study him.

"He is an odd one," Alad said softly. "It's often said of people that they charm the birds off trees, but he really does. All he has to do is focus his thoughts on them and they can't resist him."

"Are the animals in thrall to him somehow?" I asked.

Alad shrugged. "He's not capable of deliberately enthralling anyone. Indeed, I can't make him sit still and concentrate long enough even to finish a sentence. The best I can say is that it is some rare combination of empathy, coercion, and beastspeaking Talents."

When Alad left, Gavyn trotted after him with Rasial at his heels. The others drifted away, and presently I was alone. Enjoying the rare solitude, I stood drowsing pleasantly in the sunlight.

At supper that night, there were a lot of empty seats with the magi and coercer-knights absent. People sat in little clumps looking subdued and talking softly until a couple of empaths, picking up on the general melancholy, played some comic songs inviting participation. The atmosphere lightened perceptibly.

I was sitting with Aras and Zarak and had been explaining that they must run our guild while Ceirwan and I were away. The duties were not onerous, since the majority of those left would be youngsters needing only to be encouraged to practice, and older folk with work of their own to be getting on with. To my surprise, Zarak said he thought it would be better if I left a small council of farseekers in charge, since he and Aras were working very hard on the whiplash variation. He had drawn up a list of names, saying the job of leadership would be better shared out among all of them.

Impressed with his reasoning, I conceded and bade him let those on his list know. I noticed Aras give him a glowing look and experienced a prickle of unease, for he was all but betrothed to Lina of the Beastspeaking guild. Since the tragedy of Dragon's feelings for Matthew, I was wary of unrequited love.

"Guildmistress?" Aras said timidly. "A few of us were talking, and we were wondering why we don't just shut the pass altogether. It wouldn't be too hard for the teknoguilders to cause an avalanche to block it. Then no one could get to us."

"Who is taking my guild's name in vain?" Garth boomed, coming up to the table behind the wards. Aras yelped in fright, but Zarak pulled a seat out for the big man courteously and repeated Aras's suggestion.

"We could do it, and don't think for a minute that we have not thought of it," the Teknoguildmaster said, grunting as he lowered his bulk into the seat. "The trouble is that no beast or human wanting refuge could find their way to us once we had done it. And we have our own reasons for wanting and needing access to the rest of the Land."

"I didn't mean we should cut off access altogether," Aras said shyly. "I thought maybe we could make another way to come up here. Something smaller that would be almost impossible to find by accident. We could have the beasts pass on the location."

Garth waggled his beetling brows at her. "You're a clever

744

little puss, aren't you? Unfortunately, to create another way would require boring through the mountains. Apart from the sheer impossible weight of stone that would have to be shifted, they're still tainted enough to do us harm."

"Oh." Aras looked deflated.

"If the pass wasn't so big, now, we could obscure the opening with a false rockfall to deter anyone looking for a way in. We're using that technique on our Teknoguild caves."

"False rockfalls? I thought you were going to close up the caves with *real* rockfalls. I hope you're not envisaging creeping back and doing a bit of work when the valley is occupied by hostile forces?"

"Of course not," Garth said blithely.

I gave him a stern look. "I know your research is important to you, Garth, but you cannot put it before our need to make it look as if we have abandoned the mountains. If just one of your people is seen or caught, we would all be exposed."

He looked faintly penitent. "I see your point, but our current research—"

"Will not go anywhere!" I snapped. "It is the past you are researching, Garth, not a bird about to fly away. . . ." I broke off at the sight of Fian approaching.

"Greetings, Guildmistress," Fian sent courteously; then he turned to his master. "Alad says he can talk now about which beasts are willing to help us dig or haul dirt."

Garth heaved himself to his feet to leave. Fian made to follow, then swung round to me. "I almost fergot." He dug in his pocket and withdrew a sheet of crumpled paper. "Here's that translation ye wanted, but it doesna make much sense."

I was glad that Garth had walked out of earshot, immediately aware how hypocritical it seemed for me to pursue my own research of the past. And, of course, it couldn't be worse

745

timing in a way. But I had long ago accepted that, to some extent, what happened at Obernewtyn was connected to my larger secret quest to find and disarm the weaponmachines. The two might seem to be separate matters, and even at times opposing, but if I succeeded, then Obernewtyn must survive to become the seed that would change forever the way Landfolk lived their lives.

I took the sheet, and though I was aware of Zarak and Aras watching me curiously, I could not resist a glance. Fian had given me back the copy I had made of the rubbing, having written between the lines and along the edges of it. My heart sank to see gaps and question marks, and in some places, two or three possible meanings. I folded the sheet and slipped it into my sleeve as if it was nothing very important and went on speaking to the two wards of other guild matters until Zarak's father appeared, giving me the chance to escape.

In my chamber, I cursed and struggled to light the fire. I had grown accustomed to Ceirwan doing it. He had been concerned enough about leaving me to offer to instruct another farseeker to serve me, but I had not wanted to be bothered getting used to someone new fussing around me when in only a few days I would be away to the lowlands myself.

With the fire lit at last and a lamp glowing at my elbow, I flattened the paper. There were the six lines that I had copied out as exactly as I could from the dream rubbing.

Fian had written above the top line,

I, [Carandy?], have left [steps/signs/things] behind me that the [leader/wanderer/searching one] must find before

Fian had tried a couple of spellings of "Carandy" in the

margin, but I did not doubt what was meant.

I had been right about the doors. They *did* contain a message from the mysterious Kasanda. And "the searching one" could only mean "the Seeker." A cold finger ran down my spine at the thought that I was reading words left by a dead woman who had long ago foreseen my coming.

I studied the abrupt end of the first line, where there had to have been a gap in my rubbing. The seeker had to find the signs left by Kasanda before . . . what? The overguardian of the Earthtemple in Sador had claimed that I must find four signs before seeking the fifth there, so the end of the line probably said something like that. But was this message to be counted as the first sign, or was it merely a notification of where the signs would ultimately be found? I read on.

> *That [key?] which must be used [before all else?] is [with/given/sent to] she who first dreamed of the [leader/wanderer/searching one]—the hope beyond the darkness to come.*

Fian was clearly unsure about the word *key*. Did it mean I had to find an actual key, or was it a key in some other sense? And who was the "she" referred to? If Kasanda had kept it with her, then it must lie in Sador with her body. But the overguardian had said that the four signs were to be found in the Land.

Perhaps "she" referred to some other woman who had dreamed of me. The fact that Kasanda referred to herself as "I" in the first line suggested that she did mean someone else, but how was I to know who, much less find her? If Kasanda had known her, she would be long dead now.

I sighed and turned my attention to the third line. Over it Fian had written:

> *Who [would/must] enter the [sentinel/guard/watcher]*
> *will seek the words in the house where my son was born.*

I frowned. If Kasanda had borne a son, how on earth was I to learn where he had been birthed? The only people who had known her were the Sadorians, and she had been past childbearing when they rescued her from the New Gadfians. If she had given birth to a child, it must have been long before she came to Sador.

I bit my lip. The overguardian had said that on my return to Sador, I would be accompanied by one of Kasanda blood. I had thought at the time that he was using the word as a title, for the Sadorians called any person with futuretelling ability "kasanda." But if I read the word *blood* literally, he could have meant that I would travel with someone descended from Kasanda.

I blinked into the fire, considering the possibility that Kasanda had been in the Land as a young woman. It would explain how she had been able to distribute her signs. But why and how had she left the Land to end up in the hands of the Gadfians?

I set that aside and continued to read.

> *That which will reach the [heart/center/core] of the [sentinel/guard/watcher] seals a [pact/promise/vow] that I did forge, but never [witnessed/saw].*

I frowned, for this was less clear. Was this "guard" a person? Was I to somehow seal a pact that Kasanda had made? Or was I to find something that had already sealed the pact?

A carved monument could sometimes be used to symbolize a pact between parties. Such a thing would make use of

Kasanda's talents, and it would be much more likely to endure than an agreement on paper. If Kasanda had left a physical symbol of some allegiance that I was to find, it would have to be something that would endure for generations.

The final section was longer than all the others and had in fact been the hasty second half of the rubbing.

That which will [open/access/reach] the darkest door lies where the [?] [waits/sleeps]. Strange is the keeping place of this dreadful [step/sign/thing], and all who knew it are dead save one who does not know what she knows. Seek her past. Only through her may you go where you have never been and must someday go. Danger. Beware. Dragon.

The paper slid from my fingers at the realization that the final words could only mean that the futureteller had foreseen Dragon's dream beast attacking me at the very instant I was reading her message on the doors.

I took up the page again and read the lines together, striving to reduce all the words and possible meanings and nuances to simple essentials.

I was to find something left with a woman who had dreamed of me. Possibly an actual key. I was to find some words in the house where Kasanda had birthed her son. I was to find something that sealed a pact, possibly some sort of carved monument. Finally, I was to find another thing with the help of a woman who did not know what she knew, in a place where I had never been. That could only mean the farthest reaches of the west coast, for I had been everywhere else in the Land.

I sat back in my chair, confounded. For the life of me, I could not see what these cryptic signs, nor indeed Kasanda

749

herself, had to do with my finding the weaponmachines left dormant by the Beforetimers.

My heartbeat accelerated as I remembered where I had heard the word *sentinel* before. It was the name of the computer system being developed by the Beforetime World Council to gather information about patterns of aggression and violence among countries. It was supposed to be capable of eventually deciding for itself who was to blame if any incident occurred. In the final analysis, it was to have sole power to activate a worldwide retaliatory system known as the Balance of Terror.

Cassy's "Guardian" and Garth's "Sentinel" had to be the same thing. And what if it had been completed before the Great White? The whole point of the system was that it could operate outside of human influence; so, what if the deadly computermachine was even now standing somewhere in the world, needing only to be activated? Learning of the devastated world, wouldn't Sentinel then rouse BOT?

I felt truly sick at the thought of a second Great White initiated by a mindless machine and cursed the Beforetimers with every foul word I knew for making an evil that would outlive their own rotten lifetimes.

I ran my eyes down the page.

A key that must be used before all else . . . Words that would let me enter Sentinel . . . Something that would reach its core . . . Something that would open a door.

My mouth felt dry as I saw that Kasanda's "signs" could in fact be the means by which I gain access to the site of Sentinel and to its weaponmachines. No wonder I needed to find what Kasanda had left before walking the dark road.

But why had she made it so difficult for me? Even as I thought of the question, I knew the answer. She had foreseen the existence of my fated opposite: the Destroyer, destined to activate the weaponmachines if I failed to disable them.

Kasanda must have known she was making it difficult for me as well as for the Destroyer. Of course, nothing about futuretelling was certain, and Kasanda could have overestimated my abilities. But knowing what was at stake, she would have done her best to transform possibilities into probabilities.

That meant the balance of chance was in my favor. It struck me that the purpose of the message I held might even have been to ensure that I understood that. I felt awed at the thought, for in a way, she had also been telling me that no matter how lonely my quest seemed, I was not alone.

I laid the page aside.

The quest before me was no less dark than it had ever been, but the feeling that I was not alone was new and welcome. Staring into the glowing embers on the hearth, I had the feeling that I need find only one clue, and it would lead me inevitably to the rest.

◆ 20 ◆

I DID NOT sleep until Maruman came into my room looking so shifty I suspected he had been chasing mice. Instead of scolding him, I lifted him onto the bed and curled my body around his furry warmth. On top of everything else, I was worried about the old cat. He had been behaving oddly for days, and though he had not fallen into one of his mad states, his mind had been unfocused. We had last communicated normally just after my nightmare about Ariel, and his confusion in the following days reassured me that it had been merely a period of mental instability that had led him to suggest my nightmares were anything out of the ordinary.

I shivered and pulled his body closer. I could not imagine life without him. I lay listening to the slow soft buzz of his breath until I drifted into unconsciousness.

That night, I did not dream at all, but the evening before my departure for Sawlney, I sank through the layers of my mind until I was just above the mindstream, and a memory bubble rose from it to engulf me.

I was hovering beside Cassy, who was painting a flamebird in a very white room with plain, shining surfaces. There were no windows and only a single closed door. The lighting in the room was the same radiant kind as the immense globe that lit the main cavern in the Teknoguild network but on a much smaller scale. The only color in the room was Cassy's orange shirt, glowing brightly against her brown skin, and the brilliant scarlet plumage of the bird in its cage on the table before her.

I studied the bird in wonder, for though much smaller, it was otherwise astoundingly similar to the Agyllians.

Cassy was absorbed in her painting, but suddenly she looked up, a stunned expression on her face. For a second, I thought she had sensed my presence. Then I realized she was looking at the bird.

"What?" she whispered, leaning closer to the circular air holes in the glass cage.

It said nothing, of course, but I opened my mind and heard its thoughts reaching out to hers. To my astonishment, I recognized Atthis's voice.

". . . can/do you hear?"

Cassy looked around the room in suspicion.

"Do not fear," the bird sent calmly. "It is I/we who reach you. I/we need your help."

Cassy licked her lips and spoke aloud, though very softly. "I . . . I *did* hear you the other day, didn't I?"

"Did," the bird sent with obvious satisfaction. "Felt you could/would. Not all funaga do/can hear." Now I realized that though the voice was Atthis's in a sense, it was like one strand of it, and that reminded me that the Elder of the eldar retained the memory of its ancestors.

"How is it that you can . . . can do this?" Cassy stammered.

"Many things they did to us/me. Many wearypainful things." The bird's tone held a residue of anguish that was almost palpable. "Funaga do not think birds feel/fear/think."

"You . . . you're using telepathy, aren't you?"

"Something like. Something very like. But word too little. Too limited."

"You *made* me want to paint you, didn't you?" Cassy asked with a touch of fear. "You put the idea of it into my head."

"Not put. Found thought. Amplified and nourished. Cannot/will not make."

Cassy licked her lips doubtfully. "You . . . you said you wanted my help. Do you want me to set you free?"

The bird gave the avian equivalent of a sigh. "O freedom. Yes. But there is a more important doing needed. In this place there are others."

"I might manage to get you out, but I doubt I could get to your friends and free them without being arrested. All of the experimental animals are locked up in the labs."

"Friends yes. Not beast. Not avian. Human/funaga."

"You have *human* friends here?"

"Telepaths, you would say/call them. Like you."

"I'm not telepathic," Cassy laughed self-deprecatingly. "Believe me, I'd love it if I was. I even went to one of those centers. They tested me and found zilch."

"Do not know tests. Not know zilch. Know only could not reach your wakingmind if not receptive."

"But I'm telling you I tested as dull normal!"

The bird made no response.

"All right. Let's just say I am telepathic, or at least I'm receptive to telepaths. You say there are people here who are telepathic? Volunteers?"

"Prisoners. Like me/mine. Stolen."

She looked shocked. "You can't steal people. There'd be inquiries."

"Stolen, yes, but cleverly so no searching. Most dark

of skin/hue like you. But no money. No family. No position/place to make for wondering."

"Trashers," Cassy said. "That's what people call poor folk who live in the rim slums. . . ." She spluttered to an indignant halt.

"Your anger burns me," the bird complained.

Cassy looked discomforted. "I . . . I'm sorry. It's just that the whole thing makes me so mad. It's just dumb luck my mother was able to get herself educated, or I'd just as likely be in those rim slums right now. All the progress we've made, and still no one does anything about the disadvantaged . . . uh, sorry," she said, seeing the bird ruffle its feathers in reaction to her anger. "Look, these people. Why are they being held here?"

"Experiments. Like on I/we."

"Oh hell. What can I do? I mean, I'll help, but I'm nobody here. I'm only here because I was dumped on my father at the last minute. He's the director of this place," she added. "I barely move without Masterton treading on my shadow, the bastard."

"No one knows they/human telepaths here," the bird sent.

"No one . . ." Understanding dawned in her eyes. "You want me to let people know? The electronic bulletins would jump at the story, but I'd have to have proof. . . ."

"There is a woman who must be told they are here. If more know, they would be moved or killed."

"A woman? Who?"

For the first time, I sensed uncertainty. "Not know name. I/we dreamed of her. Find her. Tell her."

"I can't find her without knowing more than that."

"Woman searches for telepaths," the bird sent with a touch of desperation.

"Hell, lots of people are interested in telepaths. Or they were a couple of years ago. There were all those mobile clinics roving around testing people, though it all came pretty much to nothing. At least, that's what the bulletins said. . . ."

The Agyllian sent a swift warning, and Cassy barely had time to snatch up her sketch pad before the door burst open and the gray-suited Petr Masterton appeared.

"Time's up," he said.

I was only slightly less shocked than Petr Masterton appeared to be when Cassy smiled at him. "Damn. I haven't worked nearly as fast as I'd hoped." He blinked, as well he might, for her tone was several degrees warmer than usual. As if realizing that this might require some explaining, she said blithely, "It's just been the first good subject I've had in ages. I've been in such a bad mood. I really enjoyed today, so I guess I owe you one for hustling me into it."

Petr Masterton gave her a stiff smile, as if it was not an expression that often crossed his face. "I'm glad you are having a pleasant time," he said.

"I know I shouldn't ask when I've been such a bad-tempered brat to you, but do you think I could have some more time in here tomorrow?" Cassy directed a pleading look under her lashes, and I all but felt the man melt under its impact.

"Not tomorrow. There are World Council representatives to be shown through the compound. They will want to see the birds."

"You said they were useless." Her response was a fraction too swift and sharp, but her face was so guilelessly open and friendly that he didn't seem to hear it.

"The birds are the remnants of an older phase of a long-term experiment that continues to this day. Flamebirds are actually the result of cloning in the last century. They possess certain natural properties that make them ideal for the genetic manipulation of the frontal lobe. That is the seat of paranormal abilities. Unfortunately, cloning is costly and the bird is unable to reproduce efficiently, so it is on the verge of extinction." His voice had taken on a lecturing tone, and Cassy adopted an expression befitting a favored student receiving the wisdom of her acknowledged master. "The birds were subjected to various treatments, but it was discovered that you can only develop a bird mind so far. Ultimately, they lack certain qualities that exist in, say, the human mind. This bird and the others you saw were not subjected to the more drastic phases of experimentation, because they were the control group."

"What happened to the experimental group?"

"They were vivisected and subjected to autopsy. The few birds left are a pretty but bitter reminder that even the most promising experiments can come to nothing. That's how science is. A lot of dead ends before you find a fruitful lead."

Even I felt Cassy's rage, and the bird shuddered slightly in response, but she only said lightly, "I guess it's lucky I'm an artist, then, since there are no dead ends and certainly no dead birds."

Petr Masterton's eyes flickered, and I wondered if she was underestimating him. She must have felt the same, for she began packing up her notepad and pencils, chattering about the sort of colors she would like to see as part of the design. After she had gone, he stood staring at the bird, frowning.

"Wake." Maruman's mindvoice lifted me from the dream. "Angina wearies. Mornirdragon restless. Wake lest she comes. . . ."

It was still early enough to be chilly when I left Obernewtyn later that day, but by the time I reached the outskirts of
Guanette, it was very bright and sunny, and I was hot enough
to want to peel off a few layers of clothing. Stopping by the
road, I slid from Gahltha and stripped off a thick shirt and
jumper before replacing my jacket. I stuffed the extra clothes
into my pack and rummaged for a couple of apples.

As Gahltha munched contentedly on his, I ate mine, then
fed the core to him. At the same time, I sent out a wide-
ranging, fine-grained probe attuned to Rushton's mind. I was
not surprised when it failed to locate. The coercers had covered the highlands very thoroughly by now.

"Let us ride," Gahltha sent, and I mounted him, watched
by a wide-eyed clutch of children making mud pies by the
public well. They were too young to have learned to throw
stones at halfbreeds, and there was not another soul in sight.

I rode down past Berryn Mor, clear for a rare change, and
between the dun Brown Haw Rises and soaring Emeralfel at
the end of the Gelfort Range, without ever seeing another
rider. In the late afternoon, the road curved toward the forest,
beyond which lay Arandelft. I was half tempted to ride to the
little village to see what gossip the magi had generated. But I
would hear the whole story from Gevan soon enough.

Some hours of uninterrupted riding later, the way grew
abruptly busier as we neared the turnoff for Sawlney. Well-
loaded carts trundled along slowly, and men and women on
horseback or mule and groups of people afoot threaded
around them.

Slowing to an amble, I used a trickle of coercivity to cloak
us lightly and joined the crowd. I sensed Gahltha greeting
other beasts on the road and exchanging information, and

this prompted me to let my mind rove among the human travelers. Predictably, most were bound for Sawlney, either to sell or trade goods at the bonding fair or simply to join the festivities. Two were thieves hoping to filch a few fat purses.

I focused the probe more tightly using Rushton's face, but there was no corresponding memory in any of the minds I skimmed. Beginning to feel my energy drain, I withdrew and prayed to whatever forces of good there were to let me discover some clue to his whereabouts at the rebel meeting.

The traffic slowed to a crawl at the Sawlney turnoff. The congestion was increased by the customers surrounding a couple of stalls whose enterprising owners were offering food and drink to ravenous travelers at exorbitant prices. Most did not seem to mind the pace, but here and there someone grumbled.

I had not gone far down the Sawlney road when an argument broke out, and we came to a standstill. I sent a probe to find out what was happening and discovered with a touch of excitement that the mind I had accessed was one of Malik's men. He was not high in his master's hierarchy, but I dug about thoroughly in his mind just the same. Unfortunately, I found no memory connected to Rushton, though I did find a hatred inherited from Malik of Misfits, Brydda Llewellyn, Tardis of Murmroth, and, interestingly, Sadorians in general and Jakoby in particular.

Even after I had withdrawn the probe, the hatred into which I had dipped clung like a film of grease, and I resolved to stop farsending for the time being. I also decided to walk; after all, it was sheer laziness to ride when we were virtually standing still. Gahltha suggested we leave the road altogether and try threading our way through the thick trees alongside it. Given the look of the road ahead, clogged with wagons for as far as I could see, I decided he was right.

Pushing our way through the undergrowth and ducking low-slung branches was tiresome, but it was faster than staying on the road. Still, it took another hour to reach Sawlney— or the temporary outskirts of Sawlney created by the number of visitors who had set up tents and wagons around the perimeter of the town. I threaded through the makeshift streets, leading Gahltha by the rein for the sake of appearances, my mind seeking Gevan's. It took some time to locate him, for the magi were on the far side of town, in an area so empty of people that I guessed it must be set aside specifically for gypsies.

Once we reached the town proper, we took a path that ran between the outermost dwellings and a dense forest. By the time we reached the far side of the town, the forest was almost an impenetrable wall of green. A wide path had been cut through it, fortunately, and I entered, sensing that this path would bring me to the magi encampment. Before long, the noise of the town faded and I was struck by the silence of the forest. I could hear neither bird nor insect. The trees grew so close that even the wind seemed unable to penetrate to stir their foliage. Enormous twisted trunks were covered in a greenish moss that gave them a dusty appearance. I had the feeling that the trees were immeasurably ancient and found myself remembering the empath song of the prince who had discovered a forest that was a living extension of his slumbering princess. As a child, I had been sure that trees communicated in some way unknown to humans. It was not hard to imagine that this was a forest that lived and breathed and watched.

The path curved slightly and I came suddenly to the end of the forest. I caught my breath, for before me lay a broad

green veldt and beyond it the glimmering indigo of the endless ocean. A wave-scented wind whipped the hair back from
my face and tugged at Gahltha's mane and tail, and I took
several deep breaths of its exotic fragrance. Sharp and briny,
it reminded me vividly of the memorable sea journey to
Sador on Powyrs's fat-bellied *Cutter*. Inevitably, Rushton's
face came into my mind, for it was on this journey that we
had first spoken of love to each other.

Gahltha shifted impatiently beside me, and I pulled myself
together and sent out another probe. The grassy plain ran
clear to the edge of the land with nothing more than a few
clumps of scrubby brush to break the relentless sea winds. I
spotted a bluish smudge of smoke above a straggling cluster
of bushes, and as I approached, Gevan pushed through them
and lifted his hand in greeting, sending that he had felt my
probe. As usual, his rough-hewn coercer contact made my
head ache.

"I gather this windy corner is kept especially for important performers," I farsent dryly.

"Halfbreed performers," he responded sardonically. "The
townsfolk appreciate our tricks and pitch coins willingly
enough, but they don't see us as more than clever beasts." He
flicked his fingers expertly to welcome Gahltha and advise
him where oats and bran mash could be found. I rubbed at
my buttocks as the black horse trotted away, asking Gevan
aloud if someone had had the foresight to include some of
Kella's soothing salve in their medicine box. It had been some
time since I had ridden so far.

"I'm afraid not," he said sympathetically. "But come and
sit down and have some food. We're about to eat."

The others of the magi troupe were involved in various
small tasks or seated on upended logs or low stools about a

ined with stones. They hailed me and called lazy

gs with the same informal air that always seemed to

n expeditions but never at Obernewtyn. Perhaps that

ne reason I enjoyed them so. Vegetables and fruit and

l were skewered in pieces over the flames, and one of

coercers was brushing a honey sauce over them, while an-

er turned the sticks constantly.

"How was your trip anyway?" Gevan asked. "You don't

ook any the worse for it."

"The parts that are the worse for it are not necessarily visible," I said tartly. "But the trip was uneventful. I trust the same
can be said for your time here? How was the Councilman?"

"A tight-mouthed old bastard with a hard eye is the best
that can be said of him. But he was pleased enough with us
because his guests were pleased. Fortunately, they were as
enthusiastic as Alum was dour. And they thanked us with
coin, which was a good bit more welcome than sweet words,
since everything here is double the usual price." He snorted
in disgust. "We'll spend every cent we've made on supplies,
though we do recoup a fair bit by performing in the main
square each day."

I frowned, accepting a hot mug of spiced milk from Merret. "Is it wise to be making yourself so visible with the rebels
coming into town?"

His dark eyes glinted. "It might not be, if they were able to
recognize us. Instead they even throw the odd coin. Brocade
strode by yesterday without our having to deflect so much as
a glance of curiosity."

"I hope you know what you're doing," I said, shaking my
head. "Did you see anything of Alum's son, Jude?"

Merret's face darkened. "Jude the monstrous, his servants
call him behind his back, and I'm surprised they dare, be-

762

cause he'd have the skin off their backs if he heard it. I don'
much believe in simple evil, but that man comes close. His
wife had a black eye and bruises she claimed came from a fall.
His children cringe every time their father looks their way,
and one of them had a broken arm I'd bet was his doing. His
horses are better kept because they're worth coin, and they're
watched constantly because of a band of brilliant beast
thieves operating throughout the Land." She grinned mis-
chievously. "Of course, they can't imagine that the animals
are escaping by themselves, so there has to be a gang behind
the disappearances."

"How did Jude react to you?"

She shrugged. "He felt we lowered the tone of the occasion. And he seemed concerned that the Herders officiating
saw our performance as a mortal insult. They looked like
they'd bitten into something rotten when we were performing, but I think they hate us just as a matter of form. It's the
purebreeds they really loathe."

"Jude favors the Faction?"

"He's thick as thieves with the local cloister's head priest,"
Gevan growled.

That was worth knowing, and I made a mental note to
mention it to Tomash.

Night fell as we ate and the others talked of this trick and
that customer. I enjoyed the simple meal and the sound of the
fire crackling over the muted roar of the sea. Afterward, when
the empaths and coercer drummers began softly to practice a
new tune they had heard musicians play at the fair, I wondered whether it would ever be possible to learn where gypsies had come by Kasanda's carvings—and whether she'd
produced any more such works in the Land.

I asked Gevan if he had seen any carvings in his travels.

?" he echoed blankly.

onuments or maybe wall friezes."

cer looked as if he thought I had lost my mind. "I
even whittle in Arandelft. It is not the sort of place
s and crafts flourish," he said at last.

et said, "If you're interested in carvings, Elspeth, the
ast is where you should be looking, not Arandelft or
ey."

Vhere on the west coast?" I asked eagerly.

he coercer licked her fingers and wiped them on a ker-
ef as she considered. "I've never seen it myself, but I've
ard talk of a place outside Aborium on the Murmroth side,
ight on the sea cliff, which used to be where stone-carvers
were trained."

"Used to be?"

"Well, there's still a quarry there, and stonecutters are ap-
prenticed to learn their trade, but these days the emphasis of
the place is on cutting and dressing stone for the facades of
Council buildings and the houses of rich traders. Cloisters,
too. The only true carving that gets done is on gravestones,
but in the past the place was famous for its fine work. The
carvers did everything from statues of Councilmen to public
monuments. The fashion now is to have them made of fancy
blown glass from Murmroth."

"A stone-carving works . . . ," I said doubtfully, thinking it
did not sound like the sort of place where Kasanda would
have worked.

"Anyway, there is still a display of stone carvings there, if
you want to see the sort of stuff they used to do," Merret said
with a shrug.

"What makes you ask about such things?" Gevan asked
curiously.

"Perhaps we'll want a monument ourselves sometime," I said blandly. I gave him no chance to question me further, saying I would stretch my legs for a bit and then turn in. I strolled out of the cozy circle of wagons. The wind was stronger, and the sound of the sea had grown insistent, as if night had whipped it into a state of turbulent agitation. I dared not walk to the edge, as the cliffs were unstable with the sea constantly gnawing at their base. Nevertheless, the now inky expanse drew me. I went a few steps toward it, admiring the way it mirrored the shimmering band of stars my father had liked to call the sky road.

I looked up, craning my neck. There was no moon, and I was glad. I had spent so much time with Maruman over the years that I had grown to dislike the sight of it looming over me, especially when it was full and looked like a burning white eye peering mercilessly down. I had no idea why Maruman felt as he did, but his loathing of the moon was as much a part of him as his legendary bad temper and queerly distorted mind.

I turned to walk parallel to the cliff. Maruman had elected to stay at Obernewtyn, saying Gahltha would watch over me until I returned. I had taken that to mean he saw no particular danger in my journey. I yawned deeply, hoping that were so.

Then I heard a soft footfall behind me.

I whirled to find Gahltha approaching.

"You should sleep," he sent.

"I am planning on it."

We walked side by side back to the magi campsite. I could hear that the empath musicians had given up practicing and were now playing a simplified version of the song that had accompanied the sleeping beauty story. The sound wound into the night, frayed at the edges by the mournful sigh of the wind, and I stopped, entranced by the way it seemed to absorb the sea noise.

Again, I thought of Rushton, remembering the first time we had danced together with the wind in our hair and the night sky above.

"It is hard to be away/separate from a mate," Gahltha sent wistfully.

I glanced at him. "You miss Avra and your foal."

"I do," he sent. "But seeing them with the freerunning horses made me see what I am not."

I felt his pain as if it were my own and laid my head against his neck. "Dear one, you are yourself, and your spirit is free no matter that humans used you ill and bound and rode you. Perhaps in escaping the funaga-li, you are freer than the wild equines, because your freedom was hard-won. Can anyone really know freedom who has not known the lack of it?"

I felt a tremor go through his body, but he said nothing. After some time, he moved and I let him go, knowing he would wander alone rather than join the other horses, for that was my own instinct when I was troubled. I understood the brooding aspect of his nature that had been shaped by his past. Even now, I sometimes felt myself to be crippled by my years in the orphan home system. Yet, these days, I no longer anguished over them. I was what the harsh years had made me and was perhaps better prepared for my dark quest than I would have been with a gentler life.

✦ 21 ✦

I DREAMED OF Cassy in a building that could only be a Beforetime library. She was accompanied by a young man with slanted eyes and golden yellow skin. He watched as she collected a pile of books from the shelves.

"Cass, I don't understand what you think you're doing. Marching with us is one thing, but this is likely to get you killed," he finally said.

"Don't be ridiculous." Cassy sat at a table and unloaded the books, skimming through their pages. "All I'm doing is looking for information about people interested in paranormal abilities."

"In the public library, where every book you remove from the shelf records your thumbprint? And right after you return from a holiday on a top-secret government base where they are experimenting on human beings to learn whether telepathy is possible?"

She ignored this to ask, "You think I'm being watched?"

"I think everyone is being watched all the time."

"That's because you're Tiban, and where you come from, everyone probably *is* watched all the time."

"Don't be flippant, Cass. I think you're out of your depth in this. If there really are people being held prisoner in that compound, you should go to the bulletins and let *them* expose it."

"There would be nothing to expose if I did that. The evidence would evaporate. I just have to find this one woman and tell her they're there. I told you."

"A woman! Hell, Cassy, that's just narrowed it down to half the human race! I don't see why whoever you talked with couldn't have told you more about her."

"It wasn't possible," Cassy said shortly. "All I know is that she's interested in telepaths. Maybe a scientist, or . . ." Her eyes blazed. "I know!" She leapt up and walked along the shelves; then she knelt down and withdrew a book I recognized: *Powers of the Mind*.

Trembling with wonder, I watched her open to a random page and read the very words I had first seen in a dark Beforetime library in a ruinous city on the west coast.

The Reichler Clinic has conducted a progressive and serious examination of mental powers and has produced infallible proofs that telepathy and precognitive powers are the future for mankind. Reichler's experiments have taken mind powers out of the realms of fantasy and set them firmly in the probable future.

"What have you found?" the young man asked, coming to stand beside her.

"This book was written by that man who funded the Reichler Clinic."

"The Reichler Clinic! That organization was totally discredited over falsification of results."

"I remember reading this book," Cassy said dreamily. "I even went to one of those mobile testing clinics. . . ."

"You weren't the only gullible one," the man said gently.

"It was not long after that there was the scandal," Cassy

768

went on thoughtfully. "And then their whole place was destroyed. I always thought it weird how that happened."

"It was hinted that they did the job themselves for the insurance money. A lot of people being tested there were killed in the explosion. The only reason no one was charged was because they were trashers bused in for the day."

Cassy tapped the book with a fingernail. "The clinic was set up again somewhere else, wasn't it? Somewhere in central Uropa, and they've kept a very low profile since."

"Wouldn't you, with that much muck in your past? Besides, they'd have no money for the sort of splashy campaign they ran the first time around. Now all you see is the odd advertisement asking anyone who thinks they have paranormal abilities to contact them by calling a toll-free number."

"Why?"

"Why what?"

"Why would they bother testing people for paranormal abilities when they publicly admitted they had no credible proof that they exist?" Cassy asked.

"Who knows? Some sort of scam maybe."

"It doesn't make sense that they'd run a scam under the name of a discredited organization. And surely not all the people connected to the Reichler Clinic were charlatans. Even if the clinic was faking results to keep research money flowing in, there must have been *some* people who genuinely believed in what they were doing. What if they're the ones who reestablished elsewhere in a modest fashion?"

"Even if you're right, so what?"

Cassy pushed the book back in its place with unnecessary force. "What if the woman I'm meant to find is working there?"

"Cassy, this is so far-fetched that you ought to write scripts for holodramas!" He put his arm around her. "Let go of this and come have some lunch with me. I have to go back into Chinon in two days. . . ."

Cassy looked at him in dismay. "After what happened last time?"

"They need hard evidence of what is happening in Tiba. Photos, holos, tapes . . ." He shrugged. "But I don't want to talk about that right now. Come and eat with me, and let's forget about everything but us for a few hours. Okay?"

They dissolved into a dream in which I was swimming in the star-flecked night sea, waves breaking against me with enough force to slap the breath out of my lungs. Rushton was floating just out of reach. I tried catching hold of him, but I was always a fraction short of the distance. I called to him and gradually realized with horror that he was not swimming but was being dragged away from me.

Hannay woke me, looking so worried that I guessed I had been thrashing about in my sleep. But he merely said tactfully that porridge had been made if I wanted some.

Gevan toasted himself a chunk of bread and buttered it lavishly, explaining that since the magi would not be putting on a show until evening, Merret had walked into Sawlney with some of the other coercers to perform informally in the square.

"It troubles me that we haven't found a single sign of Rushton," he admitted.

My appetite vanished, for I knew what he must say next. "Gevan—"

He cut me off gently but firmly. "I know you don't want to talk about this, Elspeth, but I'm afraid we must. If and when we find no evidence that any of the rebels have taken Rushton tonight, what then? Do we agree to a forced alliance as the kidnapper demands, or not?"

"We made an oath." I swallowed hard.

"If we stick to our oath, then we must pretend compliance to the kidnapper's demand. The trouble is that I doubt there's much time left to pretend, with the rebellion looming so close."

"Truespoken," I sighed. "And how do we explain the reason we have changed our minds about joining them?"

"We tell them we all discussed it after Rushton returned and overruled his unilateral refusal. We decided we could give the rebels limited help, if it was wanted. We will offer to find their traitors for them. It will give them a nasty surprise that we know about the traitors, I warrant. We will offer to facilitate their communications; we will help in direct battle only when there is a surety that our help will prevent bloodshed rather than cause it. That sounds finicky enough to have been hammered out over a few long sessions, and it even fits with our oath."

"I expect they would want our people dispersed among them almost at once."

"I think we must plan on actually sending people out," Gevan said. "It will give us the chance to keep an eye on the rebels, and, more importantly, it will mean we can search for Rushton. We should send mostly coercers, as they can protect themselves if things become dangerous. It would mean some of our people going a long way from home."

"This sounds as if we are planning a real alliance. What if the rebellion breaks out while they are still away?"

"I'm afraid that is very likely at this point, but if we stipulate very clearly what our people will and won't do, we can keep our oath. In a way, we are offering an alliance, I suppose, albeit a limited one, but . . ." Gevan broke off and slapped his head so hard that the others looked up from what they were doing to stare at him. "Oh, curse me for a fool, Elspeth. I forgot to tell you that the Herders are selling a thing they call a *demon band,* which they claim will protect decent folk from demons and the black arts."

I shrugged. "What does it matter? It will only be another scheme aimed at parting the gullible from their coin. . . ."

"But you don't understand," Gevan cried. "The blasted bands work on *us*! They must be impregnated with some slightly tainted material or some such. The Herders at the bonding ceremony handed them out to Alum and Jude, and when I attempted to probe them, it was like trying to read over tainted ground. Of course, the priests wore them as well, so I could get no information about the bands out of them."

"Are you saying the Faction has invented a way to block our powers?" I demanded, half shouting myself.

"I'd like to believe it is an accident that it works on us, but we know the Faction are interested in Misfits and that they take those they can catch away to Herder Isle. The likelihood is that they have developed the bands specifically for use against us."

I felt shuddering cold all over. I could not doubt that the Herders knew as much about us as the Council did, and thanks to the rebel traitors, that meant they were aware that the rebels had asked us to join them. That had obviously been enough of a spur, on top of whatever else they knew, to send the Faction scurrying to invent a way to block us.

Gevan went on. "Luckily, the demon bands don't seem to work on empaths, whose Talents are much different than our own. And they are cursed expensive, so I doubt most folk could afford them. But I think we can expect the more powerful priests to be wearing them from now on, and maybe whichever Councilmen support the Faction. Maybe even all of them if the bands are given as gifts, though I don't see the Herders giving away something when they can sell it."

I took a steadying breath before responding. "Even if these bands are distributed in limited ways, they will make things difficult for us."

"I agree. I think we need to keep a close eye on the Herders, though I don't see them being a serious problem ultimately. If the Council loses its hold on the Land to the rebels, the Faction will have no standing at all."

I thought again of the figures Wila had outlined but decided against bringing that up now. "Does Brydda know of these demon bands?"

"No doubt he has heard of them, but he'd have dismissed them as flimflam. How should he know any different? Of course we will tell him, but again it might be wise to keep it from the rest of the rebels lest they decide we are useless to them as a result. We haven't had much trouble with natural mindshields here, though they seem cursed common among the gypsies."

"You've had no trouble passing?" I asked.

"Not since you learned so much about their culture during your time in Sutrium. I even took a stroll over to a nearby camp when we first arrived, to exchange useful gossip. I told them about Bergold and Moss up in the highlands. The other leader was courteous enough, and he was a touch curious when I told him about our show. Seems he'd heard of it. He asked if it was a good coin spinner. I told him the truth, and when I left, he was looking very thoughtful."

"Maybe your troupe won't be the last magi show on the road."

"I hope we're not," Gevan said with surprising earnestness. "I'd like to think I had done something to improve the prospects of halfbreeds, for they have a lousy time of it. And unlike us with our dyes, they can't wash their skins when they're weary of being spat on and starved and told to go where decent folk won't be contaminated. If they can come up with some acts and sell their skills, good for them. It makes my blood boil to think of the Twentyfamilies hoarding their pureblood and skills to save their own necks and letting kin go begging."

"I don't think it's as simple as that. . . ."

"Maybe not," he conceded. "I suppose not all the Twentyfamilies feel so sanguine about the division anyway. That Swallow you met at least tried to help."

There was the sound of hoofbeats, and we stepped clear of the wagons to see Brydda riding over the grass to us. Sallah pranced a bit and waved her hooves in a showy fashion before settling to let the big rebel dismount; then she galloped off, farsending for Gahltha and the other horses to run with her. We watched them race off, their hooves sounding like distant thunder. Brydda laughed with sheer pleasure at the sight of them streaking along with their tails and manes flying like flags behind them.

"She loves being away from the city," he murmured fondly, coming over to us.

We exchanged greetings, and the rebel explained the meeting would take place in a grain barn owned by Brocade. "It is early yet, but you may as well come with me now."

"Who is coming?" Gevan asked.

"As usual, Malik does not see fit to let anyone know if he will appear or not," Brydda sighed. "It is a favorite tactic of his, but I think in this case he will come, because it is the last meeting we will have before the rebellion begins. He will not want anything to be decided without him. He distrusts his own people almost as much as he distrusts his enemies.

"Lydi of Darthnor and Vos of Saithwold are here already. They're cronies of Brocade's, and the three of them are thick with Malik, of course. Also Elii of Kinraide is on his way with Zamadi, who was one of Malik's too, but they had a falling out. Cassell and Serba have come from Halfmoon Bay and Port Oran, but both Radek and Yavok sent seconds, as did Tardis. You've met Gwynedd before, of course. It was he who swayed the White Lady in your favor."

"White Lady?" Gevan echoed.

Brydda smiled. "Well, groups tend to give their leaders informal titles. So, as I am the Black Dog, Tardis is the White Lady."

I gaped. "Tardis is a woman?"

Brydda smiled. "Until the Battlegames, we all thought Tardis a man, which was as she wanted. But you saw her in Sador. She was the very beautiful, severe-looking woman with long fair hair."

"What is Malik's title?" I asked softly.

The big rebel's smile faded. "Generally, titles are bestowed as a sign of affection and respect. Malik's people fear him, so none would dare risk angering him by giving him a title that suits him. But I saw you frown when I named those rebel leaders who would not be coming to the meeting. I would not regard that as reason to suspect them of being kidnappers. Especially in the case of the west coast rebels. They often do not come to meetings this side of the Suggredoon. They claim with some justice that it's unfair that most meetings are held here, though they can see it makes more sense to have them where fewer need to travel far."

"I take it you don't object to our probing the rebels who are here," Gevan said.

"We have no desire to pry into rebel business, private or otherwise, nor to work against your people in any way," I said quickly. "We will only be looking for thoughts connected to Rushton."

"I don't object because I trust you, but I'd not let the others know you would enter their minds for your purposes, if you take my meaning."

Gevan explained our decision to offer limited aid to the rebellion.

"A sound ruse to test how close an eye these kidnappers are keeping on you. If they dislike this limitation, I'm sure they will let you know, and how long that communication takes and what form it comes in might give us a lead on where they are holding Rushton. But I haven't had a whisper of anything that would suggest any of the rebels had aught to do with the kidnapping. The only unusual occurrence is that Domick seems to have disappeared as well. No one has seen him since Rushton came to Sutrium."

I stared at him. "Are you saying Domick had something to do with Rushton's kidnapping?"

He looked taken aback. "Of course not. I am saying only that when two men vanish about the same time, it is curious. I don't imagine the lad crept after him on the road, but . . . Well, it nags my mind that maybe somehow there's a link."

I opened my mouth to protest, and then closed it again, for I had long suspected that Brydda had latent Talents that he drew on unconsciously, calling them a "knack." And it *was* odd that Domick had vanished around the same time as Rushton. Or before, in fact, since he hadn't responded to Rushton's note.

"Brydda, you made a good point about using the offer of

limited alliance to force the kidnapper to show his hand again," Gevan cut in, "but you should understand that when we talk of limited help, we mean it. We are prepared to help with communication between rebels, and in finding your traitors as well as with healing, but we will not fight."

Brydda looked from the coercer to me. "You mean to offer us aid in reality?"

"Limited aid, unless we manage to flush out Rushton's kidnapper today, and somehow I doubt that will happen," I said. "What is the rebel purpose of this meeting anyway?"

"Not a lot. To clarify a few aspects of the first part of our plan. The meeting is more an expression of final solidarity than anything else."

"The *first* part of your plan?" Gevan asked curiously.

"That's right. There are three distinct phases. The first deals with this side of the Suggredoon. That's another reason you should not worry too much about west coast rebels not coming to the meeting in person."

"Why three phases?"

"We do not have the numbers to attack everywhere simultaneously, so our plan will be like a snowball rolled down a hill. It will gather mass and force as it moves. But tell me one thing—if you do join us and then find Rushton, will you immediately withdraw your help?"

Gevan and I exchanged a glance and a brief mental dialogue.

"No," I said at last. "If we commit ourselves, we will remain until we are not needed."

Brydda nodded his approval.

The rebel meeting took place late in the afternoon when the sun was as fat and golden red as a ripe peach suspended above the horizon. The barn was old enough that the daubing had crumbled away between the horizontal boards, leaving gaps that allowed a multitude of crisscrossing beams of sunlight to stripe flesh and bales of hay and illuminate the dust rotating slowly in the air. The gaps meant that although no one glancing at the barn would realize it was full of people, we would see anyone long before they came close enough to hear us.

As Brydda had predicted, Malik attended the meeting. When we entered, he was deep in conversation with the silk-clad Brocade. Tardis's representative, Gwynedd, sat a little apart from the rest, his muscular arms crossed and his long fair hair loose except for a plait on either side of his austere face, in the Norseland fashion. Dardelan smiled and lifted his hand in greeting, looking subtly older than the year before, and I wondered idly where Jakoby's daughter Bruna was. Beside Dardelan was Elii, and I let my eyes rest for a time on the stern face of the young Kinraide rebel leader, wondering if he truly had no memory of me as one of the orphans he had led in search of the deadly whitestick.

Gevan and I seated ourselves near Brydda just as the prematurely white-haired Cassell came in looking frailer than ever beside a handsome, heavy-browed woman with a mass of crisp black hair: Serba.

Before the meeting began, several more unfamiliar men and women arrived and seated themselves on hay bales or stood lounging against the thick frame beams that supported the roof. The barn was near to full when Brocade rose to give a flowery speech of welcome. He then invited Gevan and me to speak on behalf of the Misfits.

My mouth dried instantly, for I had not expected to be named at once. Since Gevan had suggested I do the talking while he coerced and probed those assembled, I stood and took a deep breath, then explained that we were representing Rushton, who was ill. I was trying to be alert to anything untoward in people's faces, but I saw only what one might expect if they had known nothing of the kidnapping. Surprise, interest, disinterest, but no furtive guilt or glee. No half smiles. Malik and his cohorts sneered of course, but that was as much a reflection of innocence as anything else.

"Is Rushton mortally ill?" Elii asked with a bluntness I remembered from childhood.

"No," I said, thinking, *Not mortally ill, but maybe in mortal danger.*

"Would you have us heal him?" Malik sneered.

"I do not think you would have more skill than our healers," I said. "In fact, I come to make an offer. You met with Rushton and proposed an alliance, which he had to refuse given our oath of pacifism. But we are prepared now to offer limited aid."

"Limited aid," Malik mimicked. "I think *any* help your people could offer would be limited."

"I do not think the limitations we impose on our offer will trouble any but you, sirrah," I said coolly, "since they are designed to prevent mindless slaughter."

"What exactly are you offering?" Elii demanded impatiently.

"We will not kill or fight. We will nurse and help to heal your wounded. We will aid in capturing enemies where this can be done without bloodshed. We will pass messages between your groups so that you can remain in constant contact. And, last but not least, we will seek out the traitors in your midst."

There was a stir at this, which I had anticipated. I let them

779

mutter and mumble until Gwynedd asked how we knew about the traitors.

"Brydda told them, of course," Malik snapped. "He tells his pet freaks everything."

"We learned about the traitors by chance in the course of our own activities," I said.

Elii called immediately for a show of hands as to whether our offer could be accepted. Predictably enough, Malik and his allies voted against us, while the rest voted aye. Vos cursed Zamadi, who growled an insult back at him, and as a babble of argument and recrimination rose, I took the chance to farsend to Gevan to see if he had found anything.

"Not yet," he sent.

Serba rose, demanding silence in a contemptuous voice. "We did not come to squabble. Surely, on the eve of war, we are beyond that. The show of hands means we accept the Misfits' offer. Of course, any rebel leader may refuse the offer of aid if they wish. I, for one, will be glad of help in flushing the traitors out of Port Oran. My only question is how soon before one of your people can arrive?"

This was directed to me.

"It will take a minimum of three days for someone to reach Port Oran," I said. I turned to Gwynedd. "It will be five days for Murmroth, if you want our help."

"I voted aye," Gwynedd said levelly.

"How long will it take for your people to reach Guanette?" Malik demanded. When I gaped, he said, "I did not want Misfits with us, but I will obey the decision of the majority."

I realized the need to obscure that we would be coming from the mountains. "It would take three days for one of our people to come to you there," I lied in a flat, unfriendly voice.

"But you will remember our aid does not come free of obligation, Malik of Guanette."

"I will keep that in mind," he agreed so smugly that my mind churned with suspicion.

Brocade gave an exaggerated sigh and said he supposed he could bear having Misfits around if it would flush the maggots from his band, and Vos concurred. I boiled inwardly but only repeated that we would send Misfits to all who desired our aid.

Serba rose and suggested tersely that we proceed to the next matter. I resumed my seat beside Gevan, careful not to let my anger show.

"I would like to go over the first stage of the entire plan one last time," Serba began.

"Are these Misfits to remain and hear our plans?" Vos interrupted in a voice as thin and hard as his frame.

I opened my mouth to speak, but the rebel woman spoke first. "Fool. How can you keep the Misfits ignorant of the very information they will be passing on for you? Do you blindfold your horse when you would gallop?"

Vos gave her a look of intense malice, but she outstared him, hands on hips, until his eyes dropped. She reminded me very much of Jakoby, and I could not help but admire how smoothly she had assumed control. Malik made no effort to prevent it. He seemed more inclined to jeer and heckle, which might simply be evidence that the dynamics of the rebel struggles had altered radically since the Battlegames. Yet the mocking half smile he wore troubled me. I could easily believe he was up to something, though I could not convince myself that he had kidnapped Rushton. It just didn't make sense.

"None of them did it, far as I can tell," Gevan concluded, catching my unshielded thought. "I can't read Gwynedd, because his mind is naturally shielded, but my instincts rule against it. And your Elii's mind is too sensitive to meddle with inconspicuously. Other than that, nothing."

"Malik?"

"He is wearing one of the demon bands, and very pleased it is making him, too. I agree that he's unlikely to be Rushton's kidnapper, but he must have *something* to hide."

"Probably he's plotting to take over the Land after the rebellion and doesn't want us warning Brydda."

I shook my head fractionally then, for I wanted to listen. Serba was speaking in detail about the rebellion, saying that phase one was to begin after dusk, with each group taking control of the Councilman's holding and cloister within their area. The cloister cells were to be used to hold prisoners, because these could be secured by only a few guards. If possible, the local populace were to be kept in ignorance of what was happening in their midst. At midnight on the same day, the soldierguard stronghold below the Gelfort Range would be targeted.

"The aim of phase one is to consolidate all the territory this side of the Suggredoon, excepting Sutrium. It would be disastrous for Sutrium to get wind of what is happening, because the soldierguard force in the two camps outside the city is formidable enough to give us trouble, especially if they manage to get messengers over to the west coast. Of course, as agreed, we will not discuss plans about the individual operations each of you has evolved even at this eleventh hour, for security reasons, but it is vital that you contain your areas," Serba said.

Someone asked what was to be done with the prisoners already in the cloister and Councilcourt cells.

"They will have to be held until after the rebellion, although they should be separated from our prisoners. It is unfortunate, but the last thing we need is to free a brigand chief who will see the opportunity for a bit of looting," Serba said.

She went on to remind everyone that the soldierguard encampment would be the focus of a two-pronged strategy. First, a diversion organized by Malik would draw the majority of the resident soldierguard force out of the camp and up into the White Valley, where they would be surrounded and taken prisoner.

Malik signaled his desire to speak, and Serba ceded her place to him. "As you know, the problem of creating a diversion has occasioned much discussion. My idea was to use a rumor that Henry Druid's people have been seen massing in the White Valley to draw the soldierguards into our trap. Some of you have mewed and squeaked in horror at the idea, because it would require human decoys, but no one has come up with a workable alternative. I now propose an alteration that should please the most squeamish pacifists among you."

There was a murmur as Malik glanced around the barn. "I propose that these Misfits who have offered us aid gather a group of their people in secret outside the soldierguard encampment the night of the rebellion and use their powers to lure the soldierguards out. They can then ride and lead the lot of them into our ambush in the high country."

I blanched. It seemed Malik would waste no time in putting us in harm's way.

"YOU PROPOSE TO use the Misfits as bait after opposing them as allies?" Serba asked.

"Why not?" Malik said with a bland smile. "I have agreed to honor the majority decision. And no harm would come to them. They can use their powers to slow the soldierguard horses and confuse their riders' minds. With their aid, the loss of life in the entire operation will be nil. That should please them and the rest of you," he added with a hint of a sneer. "I don't care about the soldierguards' lives, but I will be glad to know that no rebel will die."

I thought of the ease with which Malik had sacrificed his followers in the Battlegames and doubted he truly cared for anything except winning. I could not fault his argument, though, for it was true that a group consisting of empaths, farseekers, and coercers would be easily capable of leading the soldierguards into a trap.

"The plan is sound," Elii said slowly. "Zamadi and I are to lead our people to take over the encampment once the majority of soldierguards have gone, but there was always a danger that not enough would ride out to render the place vulnerable. If the Misfits can do as Malik suggests, my people could attack without fear of meeting an impossible force. . . ."

"I do not like the idea of using anyone as bait," Dardelan volunteered in a troubled voice.

"Nor do I," Elii said. "But someone must do the decoying, because our whole strategy depends on taking that camp. If we fail, we will have a war at our front and rear, and the rebellion will drag on for months with no certainty of victory. Given the Misfits' abilities, it seems to me that Malik is right in saying they would be in less danger than anyone else."

"This is not fitting," Gwynedd said.

"Why?" Malik asked with a cold smile for the Norselander.

Gwynedd rose and said with quiet dignity, "It is not meet that we should discuss the merits of this idea until the Misfits have been asked if they will do it. They are not servants but free participants and allies."

"Truespoken," Serba said. "What say you to Malik's proposal?"

Gevan and I conferred.

"Why not agree?" the Coercer guildmaster sent. "We can do this without violating our oath and with as little risk as that bastard Malik says. Think of it—if we do this and find their traitors, the rebels will have trouble discharging their debt to us in any way other than to give us the right to live in freedom in the Land. They have said outright that their entire strategy could fall if this phase fails."

"I don't trust Malik, but I think you are right," I sent.

I told Serba that we were willing to decoy the soldierguards as proposed. "But I want Malik's word that the soldierguards will not be summarily slaughtered once we have brought them to him."

Malik smiled. "My oath on it, Misfit. Not one rebel I command will be permitted to harm any soldierguard."

Instead of feeling reassured, my misgivings redoubled. "What penalty would there be for breaking such an oath?" I asked Serba.

"Death or exile from the Land," she answered promptly. "That is the fate of any traitor who would break a sworn oath to an ally."

"Do you allow this Misfit to insult Malik by implying he will not keep his word to her?" Vos snarled, springing to his feet.

"Since this Misfit has all but agreed to risk her people in Malik's plan, though he makes his loathing of them insultingly apparent, I cannot blame her for wanting his sworn word and our surety that he will abide by it. I think it wise rather than insulting," Serba observed. She turned to me, and I was gratified to see respect in her deep-set eyes. "We will accept your aid in this matter with gratitude, of course, but I will leave it to you and Malik to sort out the finer details privately, as is our policy these days."

"My people will make their own plans and execute them," I said, looking past her into Malik's stone-gray eyes. "All we need to know from Malik is where and when the rebels will be waiting in ambush."

"I will show those of your Misfits that join me in Guanette," Malik countered.

"I don't trust him, but I can't see that he will dare break this oath," Gevan sent. "Maybe we should ask outright why he wears the demon band."

"If I raise the subject, it will mean admitting we tried to probe him without his permission. And worse, it will let him know that the wretched things work. I would rather say nothing and force him to wonder. But I would like to get hold of one for Garth to examine."

"If we send an empath to Guanette, we should be able to confound Malik into thinking the band is useless," Gevan suggested.

Serba was continuing the rebellion strategy, and I listened

786

with interest as she reminded everyone that after the soldier-guard camp had been secured, all able to be spared would ride to Sutrium for phase two of the plan. Once these rebels had joined Dardelan's groups throughout the city, a simultaneous attack would be made on the main Herder cloister, the two soldierguard encampments, the Councilcourt, and the holdings of Radost, Jitra, and Mord, preventing the possibility of any group aiding another. This was to be accomplished with as little noise and bloodshed as possible, thereby keeping the general populace unaware of what was going on. Serba would have some of her people from Port Oran watching the ferry port to ensure no one slipped away to warn the west coast Councilmen.

If all went according to plan, Sutrium would be in rebel hands by dawn. But Serba admitted frankly that the Sutrium phase of the plan was most likely to go awry.

"The possibility that someone will sound an alarm is a real danger, though with Misfit aid, getting the timing right—our other main concern—will no longer be a problem."

"I would like to remind everyone that the Councilmen and soldierguards we take prisoner are not to be harmed," Elii said firmly. "No bruised or broken noses. Nothing. We want them fit for their public trials so that we can demonstrate the difference between our justice and theirs."

"What of their families and children?" Dardelan asked.

"I'm afraid they must be taken prisoner, too," Serba said. "I don't like the idea of it, but what else can we do? Children are better with their parents, in any case, and it won't be for long."

"What about keeping wives and children together somewhere other than the cloisters?" suggested Tilda, the effeminate young man who represented Yavok.

"I'd prefer that, but it might not be possible the first night," Serba said. "Not when speed is so vital. Better the children get a fright than be dragged into a bloody battle that rages for months."

Dardelan spoke then, explaining the measures he had devised to keep a lid on Sutrium so that the third phase of their plans could proceed smoothly. Once the city was under control, rebels would occupy all soldierguard posts, clad in their telltale yellow cloaks. Notices would be posted throughout the town warning that someone suspected of suffering from the plague had entered the town and advising people to remain indoors until the cloister bell was sounded, signaling that the culprit was in custody. It was a clever idea, and with luck, the notices would drive people to cower in their homes.

"Phase three will begin after nightfall the next day," Serba said. "We will go over that again in Sutrium in detail, but for now, you know we will be taking one city each night by attacking from outside while the town's own rebels move from within. Morganna is almost as big as Sutrium, but we will have a considerable combined force at our disposal by the time we get there, and hopefully we will still have the element of surprise on our side."

She paused, her eyes sweeping the room sternly. "Up until tonight, no one but the rebel leaders and a few trusted confederates have been privy to these plans, and we have circulated misinformation among our own people as a way of thwarting the traitors in our midst. We have no choice but to let at least a portion of our true plans be known now. This is our greatest danger, yet with the Misfits' help, that danger will not trouble us for too much longer. Just the same, I suggest each rebel leader delay speaking of these plans in detail until the Misfits assigned to him or her have arrived. Anyone may refuse to have the Misfits penetrate their minds, but I suggest those who do be given no vital information."

Something made me glance at Malik. I found him staring at me, his masklike face giving no clue of his thoughts. I kept my own expression bland and was pleased to see a ripple of doubt cross his hard features.

"Elspeth?" Serba said. I stared at her blankly until Gevan sent sharply that she had asked me if Misfits could speak to one another from one part of the Land to another.

"Our mental reach is limited, and some of us have a shorter reach than others, just as some among your rebels are stronger physically than others. With enough of us spread throughout the Land, we should be able to efficiently relay messages. But our abilities do not work over tainted areas like the water and the banks of the lower Suggredoon, or over very large physical barriers like the Gelfort Range. Also, heavy rain or storms make it harder for us to make contact with one another."

"If you cannot send your mind across the Suggredoon, then perhaps we could have one Misfit on either side," Cassell suggested. "They could take turns crossing by ferry at regular intervals to exchange news."

"What of Herder and Norse Isles?" I asked.

"We have not included them in our immediate plans. Ultimately, we mean to offer the priests exile on their island if they prefer it to being defrocked, but first we will have to take it over to release anyone who wishes to leave," Serba said. "That will require boats and will be the fourth phase of our plan, along with the taking of Norseland." Her eyes flickered to Gwynedd, who had stiffened slightly at the mention of his birthplace.

"Can we finally set the day?" Malik asked loudly.

"I believe we should make our move one sevenday from today," Serba said decisively, and the others nodded.

"That will give the Misfits time to join our groups," Elii approved.

"A good night for secrecy," Zamadi added. "The moon will be a mere sliver in a sevenday."

"Very well, then, in a sevenday from now, the rebellion will begin," Serba announced. "Speak of this date to no one outside this room, for all of our sakes. I have no doubt the traitors among us wait for just this information. Now, I suggest we finish this meeting. The time for action looms."

"Truespoken," Elii said, standing immediately. "If all goes as we have planned, we will meet again in Sutrium when it belongs to us."

There was a murmur of approval tinged with excitement, and people began to leave, slipping out at staggered intervals. Malik and his cronies departed first, with Brocade asking Brydda to ensure the door was closed after everyone had gone.

I thanked Dardelan for defending the Misfits' honor. "You are beginning to make a habit of it," I said.

"Malik is a disgusting man," he answered. "He has no scruples, and I am more than glad the Battlegames showed him for what he is. It will be purely thanks to your people that this rebellion will not become a slaughter. I truly feared it, especially when it looked as if Malik would become our leader."

"I just hope that whatever help we give will be remembered afterward," Gevan said.

"It will," Dardelan promised. "But we have not met yet. I am Dardelan, son of Bodera, rebel chief of Sutrium."

"I am Gevan," the Coercer guildmaster said, standing to

bow formally. "I have heard much of you and your father."

Serba interrupted to bid us farewell, and when she departed, Gwynedd, Cassell, and Yavok's proxy, Tilda, went with her. Whatever their inner struggles, it seemed that the west coast rebels were far more united than those in the rest of the Land.

As Brydda secured the barn, he told Dardelan he would collect Sallah and meet him at the crossroads on the other side of town. Then Brydda, Gevan, and I walked back to the gypsy encampment together.

"You found nothing," the big rebel said as we picked our way over a shadowy wheat field with the wind in our faces.

"Nothing in those we were able to probe," Gevan admitted. "We could not touch Elii's mind or Gwynedd's, and Malik was unreachable because he wore one of those demon bands the Herders have been selling."

Brydda gave him a startled look. "These bands block your powers?"

"Unfortunately. Though, given our lack of reaction during the meeting, I bet Malik is wondering now if they work or not."

"Do you suspect him of the kidnapping because he wears the band?"

"Not truly," I said, sighing. "As you said at Obernewtyn, it just doesn't make sense that he would force us to join you."

We walked in silence on the narrow track running along the cliff, listening to the churning roar of the sea at its base. The wind was chilly enough to make me draw the edges of my coat together, but its astringency revived my flagging spirit.

"What now?" Brydda asked when the magi wagons were in sight.

I shrugged. "I'll leave for Obernewtyn tonight, and Gevan can follow in the morning. Then we'll send some of our people to each rebel group as promised and go on looking for Rushton. There is nothing else we can do until we have some clue as to who took him and where."

He nodded absently. "You did not need to agree to be decoys in Malik's foray. You realize it makes you sworn allies, for all your talk of limitations."

I wondered if I ought to feel we were betraying Rushton and our ideals, but instead I felt we were doing the right thing. We had talked in guildmerge of abstaining from violence, but we had never considered that we might actively work against it.

The rebels seemed genuinely committed to a bloodless rebellion, and with our help, this might be possible. Wouldn't helping them be a different sort of adherence to our oaths?

Gahltha and I cut around the perimeter of the town as before, avoiding the narrow, winding streets clogged with revelers. Getting through the cluster of tents was less easy. The moon fair was drawing to an end, and there were twice as many as when we had gone in the other direction. People were becoming increasingly uninhibited. Everywhere there were campfires and clots of people laughing and singing, blocking the makeshift roads.

After I passed the outskirts, the road became easier. Most travelers endeavored to reach their destinations before dusk, given the robbers who prowled the dark hours. There were only one or two men driving empty carts, and they eyed me suspiciously.

The stalls at the crossroad were boarded up, their owners having presumably joined the revels. I passed them and took to the main road. Far ahead, the Gelfort Range was a jagged smudge.

The moon rose slowly, at first low and golden and then fading to white. It was odd to think that right now in Sutrium, Kella or Ceirwan might be looking at this moon, and in the high mountains perhaps the Agyllians gazed at it, dreaming past and future dreams. Maybe Jakoby looked up at it, too, somewhere in the Sadorian desert, and far out to sea, ship fish would be leaping out of the silvery waves into its faint light.

There was no secret from the moon. Perhaps even now, it illuminated Rushton's face.

The thought of Rushton came to me as the weary ache of a bruise that has been bumped too many times. I asked Gahltha to gallop, but as we thundered along the empty road, I seemed to hear Rushton's name over and over in the beat of his hooves. We galloped until Gahltha wearied, and then he walked and trotted alternately, following his own inclination.

After some hours, exhausted by emotion, or the repression of it, I stopped to get some food at a roadside tavern, a rough ale pit reeking of spilt drink and vomit. The customers leaning over the bar were all male and glared at me suspiciously or with repellent lust, so I did not linger. Taking my purchases, I rode another hour up the road to the Brown Haw Rises before stopping. I climbed a low hillock that overlooked the road in both directions, laid my travel blanket under a single ravaged Ur tree that stood on a jutting mound, and sat down with a sigh. Emeralfel was a looming black shadow whose presence I could discern only because it blotted out a great jagged triangle of stars. The moon had gone behind a cloud, and I hoped it would not rain before I got home.

I had brought oats and carrots for Gahltha, and he munched hungrily as I unwrapped bread and soft cheese for myself. It grew colder, and as I gazed down at the shadowy world where everything was so eerily still, it seemed it was holding its breath in the calm before a storm. By the time I finished eating, Gahthla had wandered away to graze. I lay back against a tree root and stared up at the dark canopy of leaves, silvered here and there where the moon penetrated the clouds.

"Rushton," I whispered, feeling the name in my mouth and on my tongue.

I wept a few useless tears out of frustration and sorrow and confusion before falling into a dull mindless state. I did not mean to sleep, but sleep I did, and deeply.

I dreamed of Matthew walking under the glaring sun along a red-earth street bordered by slablike buildings of red stone with small windows and flat roofs.

At first I barely recognized him, for his hair was very long and hung in a gleaming tangle around broad shoulders. His upper torso was naked, and he was impressively muscled and very brown. For the first time, he looked a man rather than a boy stumbling into manhood. His face had a new maturity, and the lines etched between his brows told me he had suffered.

He seemed to be searching for something, for his eyes scanned the street on both sides constantly. A number of times he cast quick glances over his shoulder as if he feared he was followed. He stopped outside a brown door set deep in a stone wall and looked about again before knocking just once. The door swung open and a girl beckoned him inside.

I gasped, or I would have if I had mouth or breath to do it with, for the girl was unmistakably Gilaine, the mute daughter of the renegade Herder Henry Druid, and the long-sought beloved of our ally Daffyd. She had since been sold to the notorious Salamander by none other than my own nemesis Ariel. I opened my senses and heard her welcome Matthew telepathically. The light inside the hall was dim, falling from a set of slits near the roof. In it Gilaine looked older than I remembered, though no less lovely, her moonbeam-pale hair bound into a long plait.

"You were not followed?" she sent to him.

"No. But, Gil, I saw something. A carving on the temple wall . . ."

"It is the lost queen of the people who once ruled here."

"What happened to her?" asked Matthew.

Gilaine shrugged as they entered a windowless room containing two low, worn couches and a simple wooden table. The only ornament in the room was a square of green cloth fastened to the wall. The light from slits near the roof fell directly onto it, causing it to glow and cast its cool hue over the room.

"Some say Salamander sold both her and her daughter over the waters," Gilaine sent. "Our masters don't tear down the temple wall that shows her face, because they know the people will not revolt so long as they believe she will return."

Matthew had a queer expression on his face. "How old was the daughter when she disappeared?"

"A child," came a new voice. A dark-eyed woman with long, unbound, blue-black tresses entered the room, carrying a tray of tall glasses. "Five or six years old."

"Bila, how are you?" Matthew asked gently.

"As well as I can be," the woman said almost indifferently, but there was a quiver in her voice and raw pain in her eyes that told another story. Gilaine came to take her hand and pressed it to her cheek.

795

"Perhaps he lives . . . ," Matthew began.

The woman shook her head. "No one lives who enters the pit." A tear rolled down her cheek, and she dropped her head and wept without embarrassment. Gilaine and Matthew exchanged a worried look over her head.

"This can't go on," Matthew sent to Gilaine. "They have to find the courage to stop this."

"You don't understand," Gilaine sent gently. "It is not that they fear to rise. They simply believe they must not until the queen comes again. That is their prophecy, and it is all that holds them together."

"Their prophecy keeps them enslaved!" Matthew sent. "And it's only a matter of time before I am sent to the pit, too. . . ."

I blinked and squinted to find I was lying on my back with the sun full on my face. I sat up, bewildered, and realized the whole stony face of Emeralfel was shining in the sunlight.

Cursing, I stood, finding my clothes wet with dew. Gahltha was nearby, cropping contentedly on a clump of clover. I reproached him for failing to wake me.

"You needed sleep," he sent.

I wet my hands on the dewy grass and washed my face as best I could, then changed into a dry shirt. It was still very early as we rejoined the road, and my annoyance faded.

The road curved around behind the Gelfort Range to avoid the sullen mists of Berryn Mor, and I pondered my dream. It had felt like a true dream, but it would be an incredible coincidence if Matthew had ended up in the same place as Gilaine.

Yet perhaps it was not so extraordinary, considering that they had all been taken by Salamander. No doubt he returned to the same markets to sell his wares, like any trader. Matthew had never met Gilaine when they had dwelt in the Land, but he might have sensed her abilities, as he had mine when we'd first met.

I wondered if Matthew ever dreamed of us or of a dragon flying at him in the night. Then I reminded myself that for now I must focus on the rebellion and the need to find Rushton. Once the Land was secure in the hands of the rebels, and Rushton in his rightful place as Master of Obernewtyn, I could pursue the signs and dreamtrails with renewed purpose.

PART III

◆

THE DREAMTRAILS

✦ 23 ✦

ALAD TOLD ME that there had been no news of Rushton, not by bird nor from the returned coercer-knights nor from the futuretellers.

"We will find him," I said, dismayed to hear that I sounded more desperate than determined. I turned away from the flash of pity in his eyes, saying he had better come up to the house as soon as he had a chance.

By the time I was through the maze, I had composed myself; after all, it was hardly as if I had been expecting news from Rushton. I had hoped for it, but a dashed hope had not changed the situation for the worse or better. Walking along the stone passage leading to the Farseeker hall, I farsought Ceirwan before remembering that he was still in the lowlands.

I sent a tuned probe to locate Zarak and found him in the Healer hall. I returned his greetings, then asked him to summon the guildleaders.

"It will take some time for Garth to get here from the caves. Shall I tell Roland and the twins they are to come to your chamber once he arrives?"

"There is no need for them to come at the same time," I said.

When the contact between us was severed, I farsent Miryum to ask her to attend a meeting with me in Gevan's stead. She responded by saying she would come to represent the knights but that Rhianon should represent Gevan. She said they would come directly.

As I climbed the stairs to my chamber, I realized Gevan had been right in seeing that Miryum would use the situation to separate the knights from the Coercer guild. I could not decide if it was a bad thing, for she and the knights were proving to be a very useful mobile force and would no doubt continue to do so in the coming conflict.

I was disappointed to find my turret room empty, but it was hardly a surprise that Maruman would be elsewhere, for the air was dank and chilly despite the sun shining outside. It was strange how rooms deprived of their occupants developed a neglected air. I lit a fire, washed the travel dust from myself, and changed into a long dress and soft slippers, throwing a shawl over my shoulders to ward off the chill of the stone until the fire could warm the room. All the while, I mulled over how to explain to the others what had transpired at the rebel meeting.

Strictly speaking, our agreement to take a limited role in the rebellion should not have been made without guildmerge approval, but we had agreed in principle that there would be times when it was impossible to meet and vote before making crucial decisions. Even so, I kept my fingers crossed that if Maryon disagreed with our decision, she would merely be personally opposed rather than offering a definite future-telling against it, because I had virtually committed us to involvement in the rebellion and the reshaping of the Land that would follow.

There was a timid knock at the door, and Aras appeared with a welcome tray of food. "I thought you might be hungry," she said shyly.

"You read my mind," I quipped, half expecting her to

laugh as Ceirwan would have done, but she merely looked shocked and said she would never do such a thing. Sighing a little as she set out the utensils, I found myself missing Ceirwan more than ever. How I wished he and Rushton and all the others were safe at Obernewtyn and the pass blocked with wintertime ice. It was a childish wish, given what was unfolding. Very soon, many more of our number would ride out into danger, and it was I who had initiated the exodus. We were approaching the end of an era. Once the rebellion ended, there was no knowing how our lives would be changed. The only certainty was that they *would* be changed. I made another fruitless wish: that I would not have to face this moment without Rushton.

"Guildmistress?" Aras looked up from pouring some steaming herb tea.

"It's nothing," I said, realizing I must have sighed. I accepted a mug from her and sipped at its contents, enjoying the underlying flavor of ginger. My mother had seen it as a purifying herb, but it always made me feel more comforted than purified, perhaps because of its association with her.

As Aras smeared a wedge of vegetable slice onto a chunk of crusty bread and passed it to me, there was another knock at the door, and Alad entered without waiting for a response, puffing slightly. "I'm sorry, I thought you were in the library." He helped himself to some food, declining Aras's offer of tea. "I forgot to mention to you on the farms that I had seen the refuge that the Teknoguild has created. They have done a fine job, but there is still much to do."

"It may be that—" I began, but there was another knock at the door. Miky and Zarak entered.

"Dell has gone to fetch Maryon, and Roland will be here soon," Zarak said.

"He's finishing a foul preparation for Javo's bunions," Miky reported with a grimace. "I didn't wake Angina because Zar said it wasn't a proper merge."

I waved them to get stools and sit and, without preamble, outlined what had happened at the rebel meeting, including Malik's use of the Herder-designed demon band. "I have not brought you here to vote on anything but merely to tell you what was decided and to ask you to compile a list of suitable candidates from your guilds—preferably those whose primary or secondary skills are empathic, coercive, or farseeking. . . ."

"So we are to join the rebellion after all," Alad murmured. "The animals will be glad, for it will give them the opportunity to organize more escapes."

I told him of the rumors circulating the lowlands of a band of beast thieves, and he grinned but absently, for his mind was audibly running over the members of his guild and their secondary skills. I was a little surprised that he did not dispute our decision.

"So this demon band does not work on empaths?" Miky asked.

"That's what Gevan said, but you can question your own people when they return with him. We'll have a proper guild-merge tomorrow to decide on who will go where," I said. "With less than a sevenday before the rebellion begins, we will have to move swiftly. The rebels are literally awaiting our arrival to be able to reveal their plans to their own people. Those sent to the west coast will need all that time to reach their destinations. Those going to towns or villages in the upper lowlands and highlands won't need to ride out for a couple days, though."

"Gahltha will have told Avra by now, but we'll still have to make a formal request to the Beastguild for support. How many people will be needed altogether?" Alad asked.

"Gevan and I thought at least three of us should join each of the thirteen rebel groups," I said. "Thirty-nine altogether. We felt that three could look after one another better than two if something went wrong."

"Sort of like the whiplash," Zarak put in eagerly. "They'll all be working for the same thing, but they have to be able to mesh as lone units as well."

"A good example," I said appreciatively. "Speaking of which, how is the whiplash progressing?"

"I think you'll be surprised," Zarak said with a sideways smile at Aras.

"I can see why we are offering help to the rebels, but I do not like our people being decoys for Malik," Alad said.

"I don't trust him either," I admitted. "That's why I will be one of the three going to his group in Guanette."

"No one is going to agree to that, and you know it. You can't risk yourself, not with Rushton lost to us."

"Given Maryon's prediction, I doubt Obernewtyn is going to be any safer than anywhere else for the next little while. And I can handle Malik. I am easily as strong at coercing as Miryum and Gevan, and I have other Talents."

"All of which will be useless, given that Malik wears one of these demon bands," Miky said. "What is needed is an empath. I will go."

"I'm afraid it can't be you, Miky," I responded. "Your first priority has to be helping Angina with Dragon."

There was another peremptory knock, and Miryum entered with a grave-faced Rhianon.

Once they understood what was happening, Miryum suggested that as many knights as possible be included. They were well used to roaming the countryside and fending for themselves, and they could fight with their minds and their bodies.

"How many of you are there?" I asked.

"Ten, counting Straaka."

I made no comment on this surprising addition. "Very well. Then I suggest that one of your knights travels with each of the groups going to the west coast. That makes five. . . ."

"The other five ought to act as Malik's decoys," Miryum said, but I shook my head.

"I think more than five of us will be required, and we will need empaths in case some of the soldierguards are wearing demon bands."

"The decoy team ought to have beastspeakers as well," Alad interjected. "To quiet guard dogs and to slow the horses carrying the soldierguards after us."

"It might be wise to have the west coast group traveling together in magi wagons," Rhianon suggested. "The rumor of the magi is bound to have reached that far by now, and it will ensure them a warmer welcome than halfbreeds usually get."

Maryon entered so silently that none of us heard the door. I was struck by her calm expression.

"You *knew* we would end up helping the rebels," I murmured, speaking aloud without intending it.

Her dark eyes met mine. "There were indications. An' this mornin' I was certain."

"So the rebellion is definitely the trouble you foresaw?" Zarak asked.

"That I cannot say. But I believe Elspeth's decision to involve us in the rebellion has changed the future. I still see bloodshed, but far less, an' much of it is far from here."

"So we did the right thing?" I said, feeling almost giddy with relief.

"I dinna ken if ye acted wisely or no. I still see treachery close at hand."

We all stared at the futureteller, but she sat silent.

"Can't you tell us if we are victims of betrayal, or only witness to it?" I asked, trying to control my irritation.

"I have said what I have said," she offered so evasively that I had the sudden certainty that she was not saying all she saw. Instead of being angered, I felt chilled, and for this reason I could not bring myself to ask about Rushton.

But Maryon said, "I have seen naught of Rushton other than that he lives."

"You've seen that he lives?" I demanded.

She nodded.

I told Maryon that I did not think her people should take an active part in the rebellion. To my surprise, she disagreed. "One of us will gan to th' west coast. It shall be Dell."

"Why Dell?" Alad demanded. "Why the west coast?"

Maryon gave him the blank stare that meant she had no intention of answering, and he swore under his breath and turned to add wood to the fire, though by now morning sunlight warmed the small room. A surge of claustrophobia drove me to stand by the open window. The others were talking together as Roland entered and crossed the room to join me.

"I'm sorry for the stench," he said perfunctorily as I gagged at the smell rising from his hands. "It is treatment for Javo, and effective if pungent. It will wear off in a few days. What is happening?"

Trying not to breathe through my nose, I told him.

"A healer should go with each group as well," he said.

"Only if they have a second ability. The rebels will have their own herb lorists, after all."

"You think that will be enough if there is a war?" Roland demanded. "I hope you do not believe that the desire for a bloodless rebellion will mean it is assured."

There was no answer to that. "Make a list of those you recommend and note any second or tertiary abilities the healers have," I said.

He nodded. "We must also find some way to ensure a swift flow of information between Obernewtyn and the rebel groups," Roland said.

"We can use the whiplash variation," Zarak offered eagerly. "If some of our whiplash people go with the rebels, they can relay messages from one group to the other, and if you wish, Guildmistress, you could use us as a conduit and farseek the groups directly . . . at least up to the Suggredoon."

"Elspeth means to be among those who go to Malik's rebel group," Alad said loudly, ignoring the look of annoyance I sent him.

"Well, that's something guildmerge might vote differently upon," Roland declared. "Rushton ensured that even the Master of Obernewtyn can be outvoted by a full guildmerge, and I for one won't agree to your putting yourself into Malik's hands."

I glared at the healer, but he shrugged and said if there was nothing further, he had work to do. As he left, Jak entered, red-faced and wild-eyed. "Garth sent me to see what was happening."

"Where is he?" I countered.

The guilden gestured vaguely behind him. "We found a map of Obernewtyn that indicated there was a path between the maze and the outer walls. The guildmaster assigned some of the younger teknoguilders to clear it out as a punishment for some mischief they had got up to. He is with them now."

I glanced furtively at Maryon, and she smiled slightly.

"I don't see why that requires Garth's attention," Alad said. "And if he wants to punish his people with physical labor, then they ought to be sent to the farms to help with the planting. Clearing some obscure path is a waste of—"

"But you don't understand," Jak interrupted. "They found a grave."

My heart thudded with excitement. "Hannah Seraphim's grave?"

Jak shook his head. "It took us ages to clear enough moss away to read it. It's Jacob Obernewtyn's grave. We are going to open it up, for there may be records or—"

"What if there are?" Miryum asked sharply. "There is no time for this now."

"But . . ." Jak looked bewildered.

"She is right, I'm afraid," I said. "It is fascinating that you have found his grave, but right now we have some serious matters to discuss. I want you to go and inform Garth that I must speak with him immediately."

Jak nodded and backed out.

"They can't help the way they are, Guildmistress," Aras said earnestly. "They want to know things more than they want to breathe or eat. It is a hunger in them."

"I dinna think Garth should open this grave," Maryon said. "It is nowt a box but th' restin' place of a man."

"I agree with Maryon," Miky said. "It's disgusting to think of opening a grave just because he thinks there might be something inside it. If there is, it is not meant to be looked at by anyone."

Divided by my own need to know more about Hannah Seraphim for my quest and the feeling that Miky and Maryon were right in their belief that a grave ought not to be disturbed, I said, "It certainly shouldn't be done without guildmerge agreement, and I'll tell Garth so when he gets here. In the meantime, you have lists to compile."

Everyone but Zarak and Aras departed. I sank into my fireside chair and bade the hovering wards sit and tell me what had been happening in our guild during my absence.

An hour later, Garth appeared, disheveled and dirty. "I would have bathed, but Jak said you needed me to come immediately," the Teknoguildmaster said reproachfully.

I sighed, fatigued as ever by Garth's single-mindedness. "I am sure by now that you know why I wanted to see you?"

"I did happen to go by the kitchens for a morsel of food before coming here," he said blithely. "I must say I think it a bad thing that we are to be mixed up in this rebellion. I thought Rushton had refused Brydda."

Rushton's name acted like a knife stab, but I repressed my reaction. "I am mistress in his absence, and there were reasons for the change that you would have heard if you were not so busy burrowing into the past," I said severely.

He lifted his brows. "Oh, I do not dispute your right, Elspeth. What's done is done. I am assuming you will not want teknoguilders to be assigned to the rebel groups?"

"There would be no point—"

"I agree," Garth interrupted. "However, I would propose that a group of teknoguilders travel to the ruins where you found Dragon and the Beforetime library."

I gaped. "You . . . you can't be serious! You would propose an expedition when—"

"Not just an expedition. I would have them set up a refuge for our people. You must admit it would be useful to have a haven on the west coast where our people can gather. A healer can be part of the team, and one of your guild can keep

810

contact with the others spread out on the coast. They will be a long way from home, after all, with no easy way of contacting us this side of the Suggredoon."

I bit back a sharp comment about Teknoguild opportunism, because he was right. It would be useful and perhaps even necessary to establish such a refuge. Much as I hated to admit it, there was no reason why the teknoguilders shouldn't continue to investigate the ruins at the same time.

"Present the idea to guildmerge tomorrow," I said at last.

"A proposal is being put together even now," Garth said tranquilly.

My ire faded, and I gave him a weary smile. "You are incorrigible. Now tell me about this grave. I hope you realize you will have some opposition if Jak was serious about your opening it up."

Garth's grin dissolved. "Jak shouldn't have mentioned it. . . ."

"Until it had been done, you mean?" I finished his sentence for him.

He flushed. "Sentiment has no place in the gathering of information. . . ."

"Unfortunately, it does," I said. "You will not open that grave unless a vote allows it."

"This is intolerable!" Garth stalked back and forth in agitation. "It's not as if anyone knows the man! He's been dead for hundreds of years!"

"We may not know him, but his name is that of our home, and people are bound to be sentimental about him because of that. Quite apart from the fact that some might say a grave is a sacred place."

"*Knowledge* is sacred," Garth snapped.

"Nothing else?"

He glared at me. "Don't you understand, Elspeth? There might be records in that grave! Records of the Reichler Clinic and of the Beforetime Misfits!"

"In a grave?"

"The map we found led us right to it. Why would a grave be put in such a place? Why would it be marked on a map?"

"I don't know, but the fact remains: You can't open the grave unless everyone agrees to it. Or at least a majority."

"This is absurd!" Garth declared furiously.

"Apart from all else, there is no time for it right now. Your people should be out helping Alad on the farms. I'm afraid when winter comes, people are going to be far more interested in food than records or knowledge."

The tension left his face. "I know you are right."

"You can continue your researches afterward," I said gently.

The days following my return passed in a blur. Gevan and the magi came back without the three from Sutrium but with word that they planned to take a public coach to Guanette in a few days.

The guildmerge met to approve the final list of people to be sent to work with the rebels, and my request to go to Guanette was unanimously refused, as was Garth's request to open Jacob Obernewtyn's grave. But the Teknoguild was given permission to mount a limited expedition to the west coast, where they would set up a refuge in the Beforetime ruins, on the proviso that they were ready to leave almost immediately. This resulted in all the Teknoguild's single-mindedness being mobilized. Jak was to lead the expedition, and with him would go three other teknoguilders; the knight-coercer Orys; the healer Kader, who was also a farseeker and an empath; and the futureteller Dell. Also traveling with them was the newcomer Seely. I learned that during my absence, she had become interested in the guild's work and had begun spending more and more time in the caves. Of course, most of the teknoguilders had little Talent other than an affinity for machines, so she was less conscious of herself as being different among them.

"What if soldierguards are still seeking her and Gavyn?" I had objected.

"Orys can deal with anyone who recognizes her," Jak said. "And she does offer the advantage of having a very good knowledge of most of the coastal cities, as well as having a real feel for Teknoguild work. I'd like to have her along."

Despite my own reservations, I let myself be convinced. I half expected to have to argue against her young charge going too, but Gavyn was more than content to remain at Obernewtyn, and in fact spent most of his time wandering in the wilds with Rasial and Kella's owlet. He was not even present the day the expedition departed, but Seely was unperturbed.

"He doesn't really seem to understand properly how time works," she said. "He never gets impatient, and he always knows if he is being told the truth. I told him last night that I would come back, and that was enough for him."

Kader and Orys had been drilled over and over by Aras and Zarak in a simple mindmerge. Alone, neither of them would have had enough farseeking strength to receive news in the ruins from Murmroth or Aborium, but together they could just manage it.

The farseekers in both Aborium and Halfmoon Bay would have to ride some distance toward one another in order to pass messages on. This would slow the passage of information, but the alternative would mean having a farseeker camped at a halfway point between Aborium and Halfmoon Bay.

The two Teknoguild wagons departed, and with them a third wagon carrying those Talents bound for Murmroth and Aborium.

The next morning, two magi wagons departed, also bound for the west coast. They might have traveled with the others, but five wagons were likely to draw the less-than-friendly interest of the soldierguards. Besides, ordinary traders, such as the teknoguilders appeared to be, would never travel with gypsies.

The magi wagons would travel as the performing troupe that had delighted Councilmen in Sawlney, but Merret would be its leader rather than Gevan. They planned to offer performances in Port Oran, Morganna, and Halfmoon Bay, gathering information and shedding Talents as they went. Merret would eventually join Serba's rebel group in Port Oran, and each day she would farsend to Orys and Kader in the ruins at a prearranged time, drawing on the coercer-knight with her to increase her range. Zidon had offered to carry Merret, and she looked genuinely magnificent on him, clad in her scarlet and black mage cloak.

"Be careful," I told her. "Do not play the rebels' game."

"I will not be used," the coercer promised, her dark eyes glimmering with the suppressed excitement I had often felt as an expeditioner. Despite all the dangers and uncertainties facing the magi, in that moment I envied her the adventures and freedoms of the road.

Several days later, I was with Miryum, listening to her outline her strategy for decoying the soldierguards from the Gelfort encampment. According to her, no more than ten would be needed, but I disagreed, saying that Malik had specifically requested a group.

"Why not let more ride than are needed. They will be in no danger, and no one will know that they are simply padding," I argued. "It will allow a lot of the older and younger folk here to feel they are contributing, and it won't hurt for Malik to believe we need that many."

Straaka agreed in his soft, deep voice. "Always best if enemy is misjudging strength."

I did not disagree with his assumption that Malik was an enemy, for so I felt him to be, despite our agreement.

Miryum regarded the Sadorian seriously before saying she would let me decide who else would ride. I wondered at the smooth, almost wordless communion between the coercer and her unwanted suitor. I saw no sign of tenderness between them, but she had clearly grown to respect the Sadorian. Indeed, all the coercer-knights regarded him highly. Though unTalented, Straaka was a canny fighter, and yet he did not boast of his abilities. In fact, he spoke of war as if it were an expression of a deep philosophy, its physical or aggressive elements being the least important part of the discipline. Miryum and her knights were fascinated by his attitude, and often at night in the kitchens, I would see them listening to his stories, as wide-eyed as children.

"Someone farseeks, Elspeth," one of the other knights interrupted.

I opened my senses to hear from Ceirwan that Enoch had brought him up from Guanette. Delighted, I farsent that I would come directly. Before I had even turned to go, Miryum, Straaka, and the other knights were bent over their maps again.

"I am more than glad to see you back safe," I told Ceirwan. "Where are Kella and Freya?"

"They're havin' something to eat in th' kitchen. I thought ye might come an' join us so that we could tell you what happened in Sutrium. Ye look as if ye could use a meal," he added pointedly.

I did not say that I had not eaten firstmeal or midmeal that day. Without Ceirwan to fuss at me, my eating habits were precarious, and I had lost weight I could ill afford. Worrying about Rushton did not help matters.

Ceirwan's eyes flicked at me suddenly, and the compassion in his expression told me that he had caught my thought. "We dinna find a whisper of him," he said gently. "We probed th' rebels left in Sutrium without their knowin', an' just like Brydda said, so far as anyone kens, Rushton rode out in fine health. We left messages an' searched in all th' places Kella could think of fer Domick, too, but he didna contact us. The three of us walked for hours together and separately trying to pick up something from either of their minds, but it would take a hundred farseekers to cover th' whole of Sutrium properly. Especially down near th' river wharves, where th' tainting is as bad as I have ever felt it, an' the streets are wound together like a tangle of wool."

"Maryon says Rushton is alive," I said aloud, suddenly wanting to say the words as if they were a talisman.

Ceirwan's eyes lit up. "Where is he bein' held?"

"She saw only that he is alive. Even if his mysterious kidnappers have spirited him to the moon, he is unhurt."

In the dining hall, the tables were empty except for Freya and Kella. I had to work hard not to show my dismay when I saw how haggard the healer looked.

"Welcome home," I said brightly.

Kella's lips twisted in a ghastly attempt at a smile. "I know what I look like, Elspeth. You needn't pretend. I suppose Ceir told you we couldn't find a trace of Domick. We tried and tried. . . ."

I turned to Ceirwan to give the healer time to compose herself. "I assume you know that we are taking part in the rebellion after all."

"What?" Ceirwan asked, but Kella and Freya nodded, saying Javo had told them.

"What has been happenin', then?" Ceirwan asked in some asperity.

I told him in between mouthfuls of stew. I had not felt hungry, but now that food was before me, I was ravenous. I had finished my tale and my stew when I noticed that Kella had done little more than shift hers around the plate. I touched her arm, and she looked up at me blankly. "I know how you feel, but you must eat," I said gently.

"Oh, I know," she said, looking into my eyes. "Believe me, I am not giving up. I was actually wondering if I could go back to Sutrium with the team you send there."

"You haven't listened properly," I said gently. "Rhianon, Zarak, and Noha have already gone to join Bodera's group in Sutrium. It's a wonder you missed them on the road."

"Noha?" Ceirwan echoed.

"He's a musician and an empath," Freya reminded him.

"But no healer," Kella said. "I could join them."

"Let me think about it," I said firmly, remembering her tainted aura and wishing I could have a second look at it. "Tomorrow, we will be sending teams to Saithwold, Sawlney, Kinraide, and Berrioc. But, Kella, you do realize that Domick could be anywhere in the Land. And every one of our people has instructions to look for him and Rushton both. You might be better here, ready to go to them when they are found. You won't be able to just leave if you are stationed with the rebels."

Kella frowned. "Truespoken."

"Think it over," I said.

✦ 24 ✦

"Can you hear me?" I farsent.

"Loud and clear," Duria responded. Aras and I had ridden through the mountain pass in order to reach him in Guanette. I had a fleeting vision of the farseeker staring into a fire. Focusing on flames or water always helped steady a farseeking probe. I could sense people moving around him and talking, but they were mere shadows to my perceptions.

"Rebels," Duria explained with a dryness that told me more than words how it was among Malik's people.

"Where is Gevan?" I settled myself more comfortably on the blanket Aras had laid out.

"With Malik." There was a clear sensation of distaste. "Explaining that there are no traitors among his people. It's not surprising, for they are far too afraid to betray him. Tonight he will let his people know the full plan, or as much of it as he deems they need to know."

"How is Lirra bearing up?"

"Not too well. She said Malik stinks of ill will, but when I spoke of the decoy and reminded him that no soldierguards were to be harmed by his people, he agreed, and Lirra didn't get any sense that he lied. She says he is wary of the other rebels turning against him, though. Every time a message comes, he emanates distrust. I'm not sure how long she can bear being here. The fear of Malik's men for their leader is almost as hard for her to tolerate as his loathing of us."

"Have you managed to connect with Ceirwan yet?" I asked.

"Yes. If you like, I can link with him now, and you can go through me to speak to him yourself."

"Let's try," I sent.

The Farseeker guilden had been sent to establish a camp in the Brown Haw Rises, because the distance between Guanette and Sawlney could not be broached in a single farseeking leap, given that the Gelfort Range lay between them. Without Ceirwan to connect them, Duria and Wila would have had to ride toward one another to exchange information. It had been decided that, as well as speeding up the time it took for messages to reach us, a halfway camp would be a useful rallying point for Miryum's decoy team.

The camp was set up well back into the Rises to avoid being visible from the main road. So far, only Ceirwan, Freya, two other farseekers, and a healer were in the camp. On the morrow, Miryum and her remaining knights would join them.

Duria bade me hold myself ready while he formed the necessary link with Ceirwan and made himself properly passive. When I sensed his readiness, I allowed myself to slide along the link he had established with the guilden.

"Ceirwan?" I sent tentatively, for we had only ever tried this separated by short distances.

"Elspeth!" Ceirwan sent in excitement; then he quickly damped down his elation, for he knew well that too much emotion would shatter the delicate connection. I could sense that it was no easy matter to communicate with me while retaining his link with Duria.

"How is it there?" I sent simply.

"It's beautiful here," Ceirwan sent, but the brief picture I received from his thoughts was of Freya. I smiled and asked if he had made contact with Wila.

"Just a little while ago. She says the empath there is having the same sort of trouble with Brocade and his people that Lirra is having among Malik's. The worst of it is that the rebels seem to know they're hurting the boy, and it just spurs them on."

I was careful to remain cool, but it was a struggle. "Tell Wila . . . Better still, can you hold on to Duria and make the same sort of whiplash connection with her, so that I can talk to her directly?"

Ceirwan sent regretfully, "Th' others have gone to get water at a spring a ways back. I'd have to wait 'til they're back, so I can use their energy."

"Perhaps I can help," I said, and bade him try to make the connection. He did so doubtfully, but as he threw out his mental spar, I allowed some of my own energy to infuse the link. I felt Ceirwan's mind connect and slipped my probe down his to Wila.

"Greetings, Guildmistress," Wila sent. Her mind was full of distortions and interference, and I exerted more of my own energy before instructing her to tell Brocade that the Misfit team assisting his people would be withdrawn if he did not prevent his men from tormenting the empath.

"Thank you," Wila sent. "Poor little Feay is beside himself, and Harwood is about to break his knightly vows to give these men a taste of their own medicine."

"If it does not stop immediately, the three of you will leave. Warn Brocade once, then do it. Any sign of traitors there?"

"None so far as Harwood or I can find," Wila sent.

"Have you had a chance to scry out any of the priests?"

"No," she sent, sounding frustrated. "The cloister here is all but empty. Most of the Herders have gone off to some sort of religious ceremony in Sutrium. It is a pity, because this would have been the perfect opportunity to further investigate the Faction."

It seemed too much of a coincidence that the Faction should have a religious ceremony right when the rebels were on the verge of rising. More likely the Herders knew something of what was to come and were absenting themselves strategically. Quite likely they even knew who the rebel traitor was. On the other hand, why choose to congregate in Sutrium, which was likely to be the center of the strife? I asked Wila to find out what Zarak and the rest of the team in Sutrium knew of the Herder ceremony there.

"Tomash farsent me from Kinraide," Wila continued. "He scried out a traitor in Elii's group—a woman who was thinking of betraying them for money. She was taken prisoner, though Tomash argued against it, saying it was no crime to think about betrayal as long as you didn't go through with it. But Elii said they couldn't afford to take the risk."

I frowned. The traitors we were looking for were not merely *contemplating* betrayal. "Try to link with Khuria," I sent. "I will feed you energy."

"I'll try," she responded. When it anchored, I slid along Wila's probe to Khuria.

"Greetings, Guildmistress," came very faintly. The slight echoing effect told me the older beastspeaker was linked into a small traditional merge, drawing power from the young farseeker who had gone with him.

"Any traitors found?" I sent quickly.

"None here . . ." The voice faded. ". . . Zarak . . ."

"I'm not getting you. Try again," I sent.

"Zarak contacted me . . . No traitors found there yet, but . . ."

I realized Zarak's father was at the end of his strength, even drawing on a merge. I sent thanks and drew back to Wila.

"I'm sorry," she sent, sounding exhausted. "It's hard to hold a two-way distance link."

"You've done well," I sent. Without warning, Duria's link dissolved and my mindprobe was wrenched back into me with painful force.

"Are you all right?" Aras asked anxiously.

My head was pounding with the worst imaginable headache, and everything around me wavered alarmingly. "I . . . I'm all right," I stammered, the words enough to set my teeth aching. I closed my eyes and erected a block to catch the pain I was feeling, knowing I could not possibly ride in such a state.

Back at Obernewtyn, I went to the Healer hall to have Kella draw off the pain that had accumulated during the whiplash link. Too much was at stake for me to take the time to let myself recover naturally.

"That was severe," she commented when she was finished. "What happened?" I told her, thinking she looked better than she had on her return from the lowlands. I had argued against her being immediately swept into her guild's preparation of full herbal kits for those healers traveling away, but Roland had assured me it was best for her to be active. It seemed he was right.

"I'll come with you tomorrow when you farseek," Kella murmured. "That way I can drain off any pain as it accumulates."

"I'm just going down to the Brown Haw Rises, and I'll be

farseeking any group I can reach from there. Hopefully I won't need you this time."

"Somebody else might. Those soldierguards you mean to lure into Malik's trap, for instance. I would not trust him to keep his word to leave them unharmed," Kella responded darkly.

Angina came out of Dragon's room. "I thought I heard you out here, Elspeth. Did you farsend to Duria?"

"Lirra is fine," I said. "But I think being close to Malik is taking a severe toll on her. Duria seems to think she might not last out. What do you think? If all goes according to plan, she'll only be there another night and day. The battle will shift down to the lowlands, and she can return to Obernewtyn."

"Miky and I would like to ride with you tomorrow as part of the decoy operation. It won't be so bad leaving Dragon alone for a night if you're away, and if Lirra is too exhausted, one of us can fill in for her. Apart from all else, we need a break."

"Very well," I said, suspecting the twins disliked sending out their guild members while they remained safely at Obernewtyn.

I made myself go into Dragon's chamber then. She lay as beautiful and motionless as ever, and useless tears pricked my eyes.

"Elspeth?" Aras murmured apologetically at my elbow. "We had better go to the farms. The beastmerge is due to begin."

I let her draw me away, feeling guilty, because at some level, I was always glad to leave Dragon's sick room. As we hurried along the halls, Aras questioned me about what had happened with Duria.

"I can feed more energy if you start in my mind and let *me* link with Duria," she offered. "And I can organize a team to act as an energy source. That way, as long as the others can form the whiplash linkups, we can feed them whatever energy they need."

I smiled at her enthusiasm. "Remember when you first told me about this idea? I little knew how valuable it would come to be."

She smiled. "I am glad to see it works."

"Works! Without it, we would be forced to use an old-fashioned relay of messages. This is almost miraculously swift."

"It is hard to believe that this afternoon your mind went all the way from the highlands almost to Sutrium," she admitted, beaming. "It's a pity about the Suggredoon or eventually we could go right to Murmroth."

"Having someone travel back and forth on the ferry will not cause too much of a delay. Tomorrow we will see if Zarak has heard anything from the west coast. I won't stop feeling anxious until I have heard from all the teams."

That night, I dreamed of Cassy again. She was with the Tiban rebel who had gone with her to the library.

"You did *what*?" he demanded, stopping and staring at her. They were in some sort of park.

"I got a tattoo," Cassy said flatly, continuing to walk.

He hurried to catch up to her. "You know this won't just wash off when you're sick of it, Cass. You'll get bored with it in a few years. . . ."

"I want it to be indelible, and I won't get bored with it," Cassy said, pushing her hands deep into her coat pockets. "It's a symbol of a promise I made."

"To that crazy woman?"

825

"She's not crazy."

"You know every nutcase swilling synthetic metho in the street prophesies doom and the imminent end of the world."

"Maybe they're right," Cassy snapped.

The young man sighed. "Don't let's talk about doom when tomorrow—"

Cassy gave a groan and leaned into his chest. "I swear, every time they send you in, my heart dies a little bit. I don't know what I'd do if anything happened to you."

"Nothing will happen. Any more than the world will end no matter what your precious Hannah says she foresees. . . ."

My shock was so great that the dream dissolved, and I woke. It was still deep night, and the fire was alight.

Knowing I needed my strength for the next day, I tried going back to sleep, but hearing that name was too jarring, for it told me that Cassy had contacted Hannah Seraphim. Even more stunning was the dream's implication that Hannah had foreseen the Great White, for what else had that been but the end of her world?

I blinked, struck by a queer thought.

One part of Kasanda's message had bade me seek a woman who had first foreseen the darkness that would come. Was it remotely possible that this referred to Hannah Seraphim? Or was I forcing impossible connections? After all, there must have been other futuretellers back then, and who was to say that Hannah had been the first to see what would come? And in any case, if she was, how on earth was I supposed to seek a woman so long dead?

Unless that was what the message meant. Go where that woman's body lay. Her grave.

My mind skipped sideways, and I thought of the crumbled cairn the teknoguilders had found. Jacob Obernewtyn's grave. Where, then, was Hannah Seraphim laid to rest?

There was a strange poetry in the thought that part of the key to saving the world from a second Great White lay with a woman who had foreseen the first. Certainly there were some tenuous connections between Kasanda and Hannah. The doors to Obernewtyn, for instance . . .

"Sleep," Maruman sent crossly.

"I'm sorry I woke you," I sent back.

"Too late to be sorry," the old cat grumbled. "Shortsleep is like young mouse to old feline. Hard to catch."

"I'm sorry," I sent again, feeling an ache of love for the battered cat. His mind had grown clearer, but he was little inclined to communicate these days. I stroked him tentatively, and for once he did not object. Soon he was snoring softly, and I drifted back to sleep, too, wondering what promise Cassy had made to Hannah.

The following day passed all too slowly, for none of us could concentrate on anything but the rebellion, which would begin that very night.

Far from being nervous, I was only too glad when it was time to ride down to Ceirwan's camp. Aras, Kella, Roland, Miky, and Angina were also mounted up and attired as gypsies, as were several beastspeakers with empathic or coercive secondary abilities. Lina and another group had ridden down earlier in the day. We had been wary of advertising our presence in the high mountains, and small groups were less remarkable than large ones. Malik had been told that we intended to gather near the soldierguard encampment from all over the Land. Under no circumstances must he learn that we dwelt at Obernewtyn.

We rode steadily, and passing Guanette, I farsent Duria to

let Malik know we would be in position to make our move at midnight as planned. "Has he told you exactly where we are to bring the soldierguards?"

"He has, but there is no need for me to explain, because I will be in place with him, so you can use me as a guiding focus. The location of the ambush is perfect—a cul-de-sac with steep sides and a single narrow entrance. Whatever else Malik may be, he's a strategist," Duria added with grudging admiration. "I don't think anyone will even have to fire an arrow, because once inside, the soldierguards will see immediately that they have ridden into a trap. Malik will step out of cover with all his men and announce that no one will be harmed if they surrender, and that should be that."

"It sounds too simple," I sent.

"Simple plans are best," Duria sent so confidently that my own fears were somewhat allayed. "Oh, I wanted to apologize for letting go so suddenly yesterday. . . ."

"There is no need," I cut him off. "I didn't suppose you did it on purpose. How is Lirra bearing up?"

"We've sent her back to Obernewtyn. It was too cruel to keep her here any longer."

I relayed this to Miky and Angina who, after a swift consultation, decided Miky would ride to Guanette to replace the younger empath. I sent as much to Duria, who was obviously relieved. "I don't like that we can't gauge Malik's mind at all with Lirra gone," he admitted. "I told him no traitors had been located this side of the Suggredoon so far, and he's already ranting that they must be in the west coast groups. But from what Zarak said yesterday, I don't know."

"You've heard from him?" I asked.

"I got word from Wila this morning. The only lot who haven't reported yet are in Murmroth. I decided not to pass this on to Malik, because he's bound to turn around and start accusing us of incompetence."

"I wouldn't give him any information outside the necessary. But it's odd news, just the same."

"Of course, every rebel hasn't been tested, because some of them are out in the field," Duria stressed. "But they won't be in a position to hamper tonight's activities."

"Let's hope," I sent.

"I will ride with Malik until his people reach Sutrium, if you don't object. He repels me, but watching him is like watching one of those deadly spiders they have on Norseland. It's horrible, but it's fascinating as well. He never uses reason where he can use fear or intimidation instead. What makes such a man?"

"Who can know? How is Gevan?"

"Pretty much as I am. He wants me to stay with the rebel group who will take over the Guanette cloister. Malik is leading another group on to the Darthnor cloister, because Lydi's people may need the support. Gevan will be going with them. The plan is that we must take over the cloisters and be back here ready to ride to the White Valley well before midnight."

"Farsend when you're on the verge of leaving for the Valley. And be careful," I sent seriously.

Several hours later, we went down the little-used track that ran between Berryn Mor and the Rises from the main road to the coast. When we had gone far enough to ensure we would not be seen ascending the slopes of the Brown Haw Rises, we set a course for the camp. Ceirwan and the others had erected a small series of canvas huts patterned after the nomadic dwellings that the Sadorians called *tents*. Though constructed of waxed cloth and hollow poles lashed temporarily together, they were surprisingly good protection against the weather, in addition to being light and easy to carry.

Ceirwan was preparing an evening meal when we rode up. Before long, we were all eating and talking about the coming night, the horses clustered nearby grazing and communing with the beastspeakers. Miryum and her coercer-knights had arrived, the guilden said, but they had ridden out almost at once to station themselves close to the soldierguard encampment. Miryum wanted to scry out its inhabitants and gain a working knowledge of the daily operation of the establishment. Only then had they carefully constructed, within the minds of key figures within the camp, the illusion that a small band of soldierguards had taken Henry Druid prisoner in a brilliant coup. The soldierguard captains believed a daring rescue attempt would be made by some of the Druid's men. They had been convinced coercively that this escape must be allowed so that the soldierguards could learn the whereabouts of the Druid's secret camp in the high mountains.

It was a meshing of rumors set in motion by Malik's people and pure coerced illusion, and it played hard upon the ambition of the head soldierguard to become a Councilman. He reasoned that capture of the notorious Henry Druid would make him famous, but the taking of him and all his followers would be a success so spectacular as to make it impossible for the Council to refuse to make him one of them. Whether or not this was true, he believed it, thanks to Miryum's manipulations. The main problem was convincing the soldierguards that they had Henry Druid in a cell within the camp. The capture and all else could be built of implanted memories, but Miryum had had to create a physical illusion of Henry Druid in the minds of anyone who looked into the cell where he was supposedly being held. For this reason, she had made the soldierguard captains decide to keep their infamous prisoner a secret from the majority of their people for the sake of security. This ensured that only the few entrusted to guard the empty cell would need to be constantly coerced into seeing what did not exist.

The part the rest of us were to play was ludicrously simple. At some point around midnight, upon a signal from Miryum, we were to erupt from concealment in the forest nearby the encampment and ride wildly up into the high country. Miryum and her team would ensure the soldierguard force followed us.

Since they could not coerce all the soldierguards individually and constantly, the knights intended to focus on the leaders, both formal and informal. Being soldierguards, the majority would obey their superiors without question, but because there were always men and women who were less slavishly obedient, the coercers had spent a lot of energy locating them and tampering with their minds as well. It was a plan that relied less on brilliant mental strategy and subtlety than on the sheer ability of Miryum and her coercers to control minds. It struck me rather as one of the card houses that moonfair conjurers liked to construct, but I trusted Miryum's abilities and her determination. Those, at least, were no illusion.

"They'll be so full of the hunger to win glory an' a fat coin bonus that they won't wonder why we would allow ourselves to be followed back to our secret camp," Ceirwan said.

"Bonus?" I echoed blankly.

"Miryum means to plant th' notion at th' last minute that there is a large reward fer each armsman's brought in," the guilden explained. "Greed really is a good emotion to work on, because it almost entirely overcomes the ability to think clearly."

"Making sure their greed does not find a target will take a terrific lot of energy. We won't be able to stop them shooting at us forever," Angina warned.

"We won't need to," one of the beastspeakers said eagerly. "We'll be out of their reach for most of the ride, and once we get them to the ambush point, their minds will be on other things."

Ceirwan stiffened and looked at me. "It's Wila, Elspeth. She's ready to link ye to th' others."

I nodded, and we moved a little aside from the fire as Aras arranged her team into a simple merge. When Ceirwan had established contact with Wila, the young ward connected the two merges with her own probe. I waited until they were all securely engaged, then sent my probe smoothly along the path to Wila.

"You are so clear!" the older farseeker exclaimed in a startled mindvoice. "It's like someone is pouring energy into me."

"That's exactly what's happening, but let's not waste any time just now on explanations. Can you try linking with Khuria?"

The connection was established, and as with Wila, Khuria's surprise shivered it dangerously, but he quickly collected himself. I asked him how matters were proceeding in Saithwold. He explained that Vos had decided to secure Councilman Noviny's holding before taking over the cloister.

"I was there last night, scrying to see if there was any sort of alert," Khuria sent. "It seemed a very peaceful place to me. The servants and bondservants and even the animals are content with their master. I had a brief look into Noviny's mind, and to tell you the truth, I like him somewhat better than Vos."

"He is a better man, by all accounts, and that's all the more

832

reason to make sure no one gets hurt. You might remind Vos that he will have trouble afterward if he hurts someone as well liked as Noviny."

Khuria agreed. "I have been in touch with Zarak, by the way," he added. "He wants to speak with you. Maybe you can try going through me?"

The merge felt strong and stable with Aras's input, so I concurred. I felt him link with Zarak, and at once the Farseeker ward responded. "I'm glad to hear from you," he sent.

"It's an amazing thing that you and Aras have done," I sent. "I hear you've scried out no traitors in Sutrium?"

"Not a one so far, though a few of Bodera's people seem to have considered pulling out from time to time, and a number of them are secretly in favor of Malik's hard line. But I suspect you'd find a few of Malik's people preferring Bodera's ideas, too. I told Brydda, but he said that other than outright traitors, he was not interested in knowing people's doubts. He said they have a right to doubt and question in the privacy of their own minds. He wanted me to tell him who is most firm in their support of Bodera and who is most trustworthy and faithful. They're the only ones he's told the whole plan."

"He was ever a canny man," I sent in admiration. "You've been in contact with the west?"

"I have, and everyone's in place. The teknoguilders have found all sorts of subterranean tunnels. It seems like what you see aboveground is only the tip of the city. Anyway, the good thing is that they haven't had to set up on the surface, so there's almost no chance of their being spotted. Dragon's illusions all that time ago still keep folk from poking around."

I thought of Dragon with a stab of pain and wondered if it

833

would not have been better if she were still there now, rather than comatose in the Healer hall.

Zarak went on. "The only problem is that someone always has to be aboveground in case anyone tries to reach them. Oh, they said Dell has been dreaming of treachery, but she doesn't know to whom or what."

"Helpful," I sent tersely.

"She said she's trying her best."

"I know, but it is frustrating to be given such vague warnings."

"Dell said to say this is specifically to do with the west coast. She dreamed of treachery when she was at Obernewtyn, like a lot of the other futuretellers, but she says that it's different here. She thinks it is another matter entirely."

"Treachery on two fronts. That is troubling, but I suppose given the number of people involved in this rebellion, it's not surprising. Speaking of which, did any of the west coast people scry out traitors?"

"One or two apparently, but no one really important. They don't account for the kind of information that was leaked out. Some of us are starting to think that, without a highly placed traitor, the only way the Council can have got hold of some of the things they know was to have had a Misfit working for them."

I felt my mouth drop open. "A Misfit traitor?"

"I hate to think any of our sort would help our enemies, but it makes a sort of sense."

Little as I liked contemplating it, he was right.

"I told Brydda, and he's going to try to get some of those demon bands for his key men and women to wear, just in case. But if the Council already know what we've got brewing for tonight, there'll be no helping us."

834

"I doubt they know that," I sent. "Not one of the futuretellers has foreseen the rebellion failing."

"Truespoken. Anyway, Radost doesn't know the rebellion begins tonight. He has a demon band, but he doesn't really believe in it, so he doesn't always keep it on or properly fastened. He knows the rebels plan to rise soon, but he has no idea when."

I frowned. "Maybe we should try backtracking the source of the information he *does* have."

"We've tried, but it didn't make sense. Some of the information that ruined one rebel operation supposedly came to Radost from Kana of Halfmoon Bay, who supposedly got it from Rorah of Morganna. But when I checked with the farseekers there, both Rorah and Kana think the same information came from Radost. It's as if whoever is feeding them intelligence wants to stay hidden."

"Maybe it's the Herders," I mused. "Far more likely they'd be using a Misfit, given their interest in them, and this sly secrecy smells like them, too. And they must be worried about what will happen to them if the Land falls from Council hands."

"Speaking of the Faction, today I tried scrying out the Sutrium cloister to discover something about this ceremony they have been having. The walls around it seem to be tainted like those demon bands, so it's impossible to farseek through them. But at midday there was a huge parade as the priests escorted some important visitors from Herder Isle back to the ships. I managed to get into the minds of some priests, but anyone with rank was wearing one of those demon bands."

"Hmph. Did you get any idea what the ceremony is for?"

"It's their annual banding ceremony. Brydda says they don't usually draw so many priests from all over the Land,

835

and normally only one of the inner cadre comes from Herder Isle to officiate. He reckons it's bigger because someone has been promoted to the inner cadre. That only happens when someone dies and his place becomes vacant."

"You didn't get any inkling that they know what is brewing among the rebels?"

"Everyone I probed was thinking only of who had been raised a band and who had been demoted."

"If Brydda's not bothered, I guess that's good enough," I sent. "Tell him I will farsend as soon as the decoy operation is complete. Ceirwan will stay here with Freya so that I can go through him to reach you in Sutrium."

"I'll be ready," Zarak sent.

Thanking Khuria, I withdrew gently to Wila, asking her how matters stood with Brocade's people.

"Pretty much the same as the others. Brocade means to take Jude's and Alum's holdings before he tackles the cloister. We'll move on the two farms after dark, because they'll be relaxing and unlikely to leap up and start waving a knife or bludgeon around."

"I'm gratified to hear that Brocade is trying to avoid blood," I sent.

"Don't be. He just doesn't want to risk his own neck. He's a coward, and he'd much rather run things from a pile of cushions in his own holding, but he can see that he has to make some sort of masterly display if he wants to be taken seriously as a leader."

"You seem to have matters well in hand. Can you link with Tomash?"

Mindful of her fatigue, I did not communicate longer than necessary to assure myself that Tomash and the other two sent to Kinraide had been well received by Elii. Unlike most of the rebels, he treated the Misfits assigned to him as trusted allies rather than loathed tools. Elii had mustered his own people, and as soon as it grew dark enough, they intended to make their way up to the Weirwood. There they would rendezvous with the Berrioc group to storm the soldierguard encampment after we had lured the majority of its forces away. By the time Malik rode down with the soldierguards as his prisoners, the barracks should have been transformed into a prison, which some of Elii's people would oversee until the rebellion ended.

I broke contact first with Tomash and then with Wila, to the older woman's clear relief.

"She is doing well considering she finds it hard to hold a dual link," Aras said as I came back to myself.

The ward dismissed her own now weary team with lavish praise, and they went off at her behest to eat and rest. I ate a bit of bread and cheese smeared with a tart chutney Katlyn had sent; then Ceirwan suggested sensibly that we all try to get some sleep, given that we were unlikely to get much of a break once everything began.

I felt too overwrought to sleep, and it was still too light, but I lay down on a blanket anyway and pulled my coat over me. The sooner the rebellion was under way, the sooner I could devote myself entirely to finding Rushton.

Thinking of him filled me with a bitter loneliness, for despite Maryon's certainty that Rushton lived, not once had she mentioned seeing him return.

✦ 25 ✦

I DROWSED AS the daylight faded, memories of Rushton, Dragon, Dameon, and Matthew mingling until they became muddled together in my head. I must have drifted off, for when Ceirwan shook me, I sat up in startled fright.

"I'm sorry, but I thought ye would want to know: Duria farsent that Malik an' his people are musterin' fer th' ride to th' White Valley." The guilden was carrying a small lantern, for it was now full dark. His pupils in its light were huge with excitement or fear, or maybe some of both.

Despite my surety that nothing much could go wrong, I felt a sick sort of agitation course through my veins at the knowledge that, for better or worse, the rebellion had begun.

"I presume they took over the cloisters in Darthnor and Guanette without any difficulty," I said huskily.

"Duria said it were less trouble than their fondest hope, because th' cloisters were both empty."

I stopped in the midst of pulling on a boot and stared up at the guilden in astonishment. "How do you mean, empty?"

"I mean empty as in abandoned. Every one of the priests an' all their underlings had gone down to some ceremony in Sutrium, apparently. There were only a couple of half-witted servants left behind. And it was almost as smooth fer th' rebels to take over th' Councilmen's holdings, because thanks to Gevan an' Duria, they were able to time th' attacks fer when th' households were in th' middle of nightmeal. I guess we can be sure Radost knows nothin' of what is comin', else he would have let his sons know to be alert."

"Maybe," I murmured, thinking that Radost was the sort who would jettison his sons in a moment if it suited him. "What of Bergold's sister?"

"She was out on some errand when they took th' holdin'. One rebel has been left in waitin' to take her when she returns to her brother's house."

"She went on an errand that would keep her away an entire night?"

"Bergold claims his sister is nowt given to explainin' herself, but she often visits th' sick. Apparently, some woman living out a way from th' town was near to givin' birth."

Dismissing thoughts of Radost's enigmatic daughter, I asked if there had been any injuries.

"Nowt other than th' odd scraped knee or banged elbow, an' them from stumblin' round in th' dark rather than from fightin'. Duria said Malik an' Lydi are crowin' with delight an' brimming with confidence, for they see their success as an omen for th' rebellion."

Ceirwan looked so delighted himself that I kept my misgivings to myself and finished donning my boots and coat. It was chilly and the air smelled damp. Wrapping a scarf about my throat, I went over to the fire where a few of the others stood about looking wide-eyed and edgy. The rest were still sleeping in the tents or wrapped up in their blankets. Freya handed me a mug of something hot, and though it tasted bitter, it warmed me. Sitting on an upended log, I stared into the fire and farsought Wila.

"Alum's holding fell easily enough, but there has been some fighting at Jude's place and it's not over yet," she reported.

"Two of the rebels have been killed and one of Jude's people, though that was more an accident than anything. I don't think it will be too much longer before the rebels round them up."

"Just so long as no one gets out to give the alarm in Sutrium," I said, thinking morosely that the three dead were unlikely to be the last. "What of the cloister?"

"Now there's an odd thing," Wila sent. "There was not a soul inside other than two beaten prisoners locked in cells. One was unable to speak, and the other had only just been taken and knew nothing more than that he had been left days without food or water. He thought it was part of their torture, poor devil. We were expecting that at least a few priests would have been left behind, but I suppose the whole order went off to this ceremony in Sutrium without caring if their prisoners lived or died while they were away." She sounded disgusted.

I wondered if the priests would leave their cloister completely uninhabited, unless they had no intention of returning to it. "Can you link with Khuria?"

"I will, but I might have to cut you off suddenly, for Brocade is on the verge of having us ride down to Sutrium."

This reminded me that we would be completely cut off from the rest of the Land after Wila rode out.

"Truespoken," Wila sent, catching my thoughts. "I wish I could say I'd stay behind to act as a relay, but Brocade insists we ride with him. He says it's our duty, and I feel that since we've given our word to stay with his group, he's right." When I made no further response, Wila sent out a probe for Khuria, but to her surprise, it would not locate.

"Maybe they have already ridden out to Sutrium," she said.

"Try Tomash."

This time her probe found its mark, and I slid along her link to the young farseeker.

"Is something wrong?" he demanded anxiously.

"Naught, I hope," I sent. "But tell me, has Elii taken over the Kinraide cloister yet?"

"He has, but it was not much of a task after all our worry and planning. It seems all the priests went down to Sutrium days ago. There were only three or four servants looking after the place, and they knew nothing except that their masters had bade them tend their work carefully or they'd be whipped."

"These servants were under the impression that their masters would return?"

"You might well ask. I thought it mighty queer that none of the priests had remained to watch over the place, but when I said so, the elder of the servants said it was not the first time all the cloisters had been emptied for a banding ceremony."

"It's almost too much of a coincidence," I muttered aloud, though I was somewhat mollified by Tomash's information. Besides, I still could not see how gathering their members in Sutrium would serve the Faction during the rebellion.

I felt an urgent tug from Wila and bid Tomash be careful before withdrawing to the older woman's mind.

"I didn't want to interrupt, but we're about to ride. Jude's people have been rounded up."

I bade her ride safe, and withdrew.

Gradually, the others began to wake and gravitate to the fire, but Ceirwan shook his head when he was asked if it was time to ride yet.

"It sounds mad to say it," Lina said, "but sitting here waiting to ride is fearsome dull."

"It's an odd thing, but it always feels like that on the edge of danger," one of the other beastspeakers mused. "It's like you can only take so much fear before there's just no more room for it, and you stop being afraid."

"I don't see there's so much to fear," Lina responded. She looked over to me, her eyes glimmering with reflected flames, and asked if I had been in touch with Zarak.

I told her I hadn't and explained that we would not be able to contact him or anyone below the Gelfort Range since Wila had ridden out of Sawlney with Brocade's rebels.

"Someone ought to gan down to take her place," Ceirwan observed.

I smiled slightly. "We'd still be out of contact once we ride into the White Valley."

"Not fer long," Ceirwan said. "I could go. Freya could keep me company."

In a short time, the guilden and the enhancer had made up a bundle of supplies, folded one of the tents, and ridden out, planning to establish themselves in the forest around Arandelft, not far from the road. This would enable Ceirwan to farseek to Sutrium directly, and I was strong enough to make the farseeking leap to him once I was clear of the Gelfort Range.

We set about packing up the Rises camp and stowing the tents away, and then Miryum sent that it was time to move. Extinguishing the fire, we mounted up and retraced our steps to the main road.

A thin moon appeared as we rode warily toward the encampment, our ears and minds straining to ensure we did not run into anyone unawares. Clouds in the sky moved high and fast, and Emeralfel loomed intermittently above the treetops to the west, its weathered face split with deep crevices.

I prayed the night would remain overcast, for even a sliver moon could cast enough brightness to illuminate pale skin or a buckle at the wrong moment.

Before long, I sensed that we were quite close to the outer perimeter of the encampment, though we could see nothing through the surrounding screen of trees and scrub. When we were close to the gate, I signaled everyone to dismount. We left the track and pushed through the trees to a clearing Miryum had suggested, where we could leave the tents and other equipment. We would have to gallop hard once the soldierguards were behind us and wanted nothing to hamper us, but neither did we want to abandon good equipment.

As we divested ourselves of our gear, I sent out a probe to locate Miryum. She suggested we move as near the front gate as possible, in order to give strength to the illusion that we were riding out of the camp, having rescued our master, Henry Druid. Miryum assured me that the dogs would give no alarm until the beastspeaker with her signaled them.

"Be careful, though, because both the watchtower above the main entrance and the gate booth are manned."

I wondered why it mattered, for surely the soldierguards had been instructed by their superiors to let us enter as if we had been unseen. Otherwise, how could they plan to follow us back to our camp?

"Only *some* of the guards know what is to happen," Miryum sent. "Also, since you won't actually be going inside the encampment, it's better they don't see you until you're riding away. Otherwise, the reality of your actions might break the coercive illusions we have set up in their minds."

She sounded so fatigued that I asked worriedly if she was capable of the ride to the highlands ambush.

"Of the ride, yes, but not much more," she admitted.

"We're all exhausted. We've had to work hard to set all this up, especially since some of th' bastards wear those blasted demon bands. Fortunately, it doesn't seem to have occurred to them to wear them in their sleep. And once the chase begins, it should be no more than a chase."

"How much longer?"

"I want to wait until the guards change shifts on Henry Druid's cell; otherwise we'd have to convince the current guards that they were witnessing an escape. The new guards will only have to discover the empty cell. We have set everything up to ensure a domino effect that will create the maximum fuss. No one will be in the right frame of mind to coolly question anything. I had better pay attention now. You need to be mounted and absolutely ready to ride hell-for-leather, because once we trigger this, there will be no stopping it. You'll know when it begins, because the dogs will start barking. But wait for my signal to ride."

Breaking contact, I whispered to the others that we needed to get closer to the gate. We crept forward, humans first and horses following, until we could see the watchtower strung with lanterns through a break in the trees. The actual gate beneath it was hidden behind thick brush. Holding my hand up to signal a halt, I sent a probe up to the watchtower. The guard there was worrying about staying awake, because anyone who slept on watch was whipped. Gently, I coerced him to remember the whipping of a friend that he had been forced to witness, and while he was distracted, we flitted to the patch of trees almost directly under the tower.

Now he would not see us unless he hung over the edge and looked straight down, but we had a clear view of the gate. Two more guards stood near it, lounging against the wall and talking in low voices. Using Talent to enhance my hearing, I found that they were talking, predictably enough, about the capture of Henry Druid and the rumor that his armsmen would try to break into the camp that night.

"All I'm asking is why they'd do it, when they know we'll follow them back to their hideaway?" I heard one of them ask.

"Maybe they're desperate because he's their leader," the other muttered, but I could feel his mind begin to fret at the inconsistencies of Miryum's scheme. Swiftly, I planted a modifying thought about how seldom the captains told anything to rank-and-file soldierguards, and I strung this to a suspicious conjecture that there was something vital he hadn't been told.

"Ah, curse it!" someone hissed behind me, and I opened my mouth to silence him when I felt a drop of water fall on my cheek and another on my hand. All at once, the foliage was full of the whisper of falling rain. I mouthed a curse myself, for the last thing we needed were rain-slick roads. Worse, rain could interfere with farseeking and coercivity.

Suddenly, a dog began to bark furiously, and in a minute, it sounded as if twenty dogs were in a frenzy. The watchtower guard poked his head out and peered around, and the two gate guards snatched up bows and swords and rushed out into the open to shout up at him.

"Do you see anything?"

I felt Miryum give the man in the tower a coercive shove.

"Yes! Yes," he cried. "People running across the yard. Lud curse them, it's the Druid's people. They've broken him out! Tell the captains!"

After a hurried consultation, one of the gate guards ran off into the darkness and the other withdrew into his booth, believing he had been instructed by his masters to let the prisoners go by. I was fascinated to witness implanted "memories" burst open so he would believe he had seen and heard the Druid and a group of his armsmen run past.

The frantic barking of the guard dogs had grown louder, and now I could hear the shouts of men and the sound of heavy boots.

Then I heard the whinny of a horse.

"They're mounting up," Gahltha sent, and I realized we were supposed to be mounted already.

"Quick—we have to ride," I hissed, cursing my stupidity.

"Are you ready?" Miryum farsent with painful coercive force.

"We are," I sent tersely.

"Ride, then, and go as fast as you can," she sent. "We're right behind you. Go!" This last was a general coercive command, and we burst from the bushes onto the track heading for the main road.

"They've got out!" bellowed the man from the watchtower; then I heard no more over the thunderous sound of Gahltha's hooves. Luckily, the horses could see better than their human mounts, for it was pitch dark away from the lantern lights. I loosed a probe to warn me of any obstacles, just in time to avoid an overhanging branch. If I fell—if any of us fell—the coercers had too little strength left to prevent the soldierguards killing us.

Fortunately, everyone taking part in the decoy could ride well. Lina was alongside me, leaning low over her horse's neck, and behind us I sensed Miryum and her team catching up.

"Ride!" her mind commanded. "The soldierguards are coming, and we need to open a gap between us."

We reached the main road, and the horses swung their noses to the highlands. There must have been some moonlight showing through the clouds, because I could see the road and the trees on either side now. I shook drops of water from my eyes and risked a glance over my shoulder. Beyond Miryum and her knights, I could see the dim outline of distant riders. Their horses were deliberately running more slowly than they could to enable us to get far enough ahead that no arrow or knife would cover the distance. Since our horses were moving at full speed, we were steadily drawing away.

But we could not go on at that pace forever. As soon as there was a decent gap, Gahltha signaled the other horses and we slowed to a fast canter.

After some time, I farsought behind us and discovered that a small number of soldierguards had drawn away from the rest and were gaining on us. I cast about in their horses' minds and learned with horror that their leader was flogging his horse mercilessly with a whip to force her to run faster. I tried to coerce him to stop, only to find he wore a demon band. Three other captains were wearing them, too, and they were also flailing their whips, not only at their own horses but also at the horses around them. Against their will, the horses were increasing their speed.

"Bastards," Miryum sent impotently, cursing herself for failing to foresee this possibility and implant coercive instructions for the soldierguards not to notice tardiness in their mounts.

"They'll kill the horses if they don't increase their speed," I sent to Gahltha. "We have to ride faster."

Agreeing, he sent a command to the others and our pace redoubled. "We have enough lead that they will not catch/stop us before we reach the White Valley," he sent reassuringly.

I concentrated on being as little of a burden as I could, knowing our lives depended upon our winning this race.

"There!" Lina shouted over a mighty crack of thunder.

I squinted through the rain to see the familiar outline of Guanette in the distance, illuminated by streaks of lightning. This meant we were close to the turnoff into the Valley. I had just begun to fear we might have missed it when Gahltha signaled that he scented it ahead, past a slight bend in the road.

When we reached it, I stared down in dismay. Little used at the best of times, the access track was fiendishly steep and narrow and badly eroded at the edges, but the downpour had turned it into a rain-slicked death trap descending into pitch blackness. Ordinarily, the horses would have gone down riderless, with us following on foot, but there was no time. The soldierguards were bare minutes behind us, and I prayed Avra had been right when she had told me that the horses who had volunteered for the decoy ride were sure-footed.

Lina pulled up beside me, her hair plastered to her neck and cheeks. She looked down at the track, then up at me in inquiry.

"Can you do it?" I asked.

Her eyes narrowed, and all the mischief and irreverence in her sharp little face became a tough determination. "Can a wolf howl?"

Swallowing my fear, I bade her go. She was an excellent rider, and if she could not descend safely, I knew some of the others would have no chance. I watched with my heart in my mouth as she and her mount negotiated the treacherous path, descending until they were out of sight, swallowed by foliage and shadows. I waited with bated breath, following the rest of her descent with my mind and gasping aloud in relief as I felt her touch bottom.

The other horses followed her route carefully, one at a time. I wanted to urge them to hurry, but dared not.

I watched Angina ride over the edge fearfully, knowing he was not as good a rider as the others, but his horse assured me that she would not let him fall. Kella went next and then several of the knights. Trusting their prowess, I took the chance to glance back. Miryum and Straaka were just riding up with three beastspeakers.

"These are the last. You go next," the coercer shouted to me after chivying the first beastspeaker down.

"No. The other beastspeakers, then you two."

"You are Master of Obernewtyn. . . ."

"And you have sworn to obey me as a coercer-knight. Now do as I say. You can't coerce those banded captains anyway."

"Nor can you," Miryum cried.

"No, but I can beastspeak their horses," I snapped. "Now stop wasting time!"

The second beastspeaker vanished over the edge. I sensed dimly that someone had fallen farther down but not badly. There was no time to probe further.

"I see them," Straaka shouted, pointing back along the road.

"Go!" I shouted to him and Miryum. Then I turned my attention to the leading soldierguard's horse. "Help us! Lose your rider if you can/will."

"I would have thrown/trampled him/funaga-li weary years past, but he rides like/with the soul of an equine. If I succeeded, his pride will desire me dead," the mare sent.

"We need your help," I sent. "Do this, and it will be the last time you will ever bear a rider."

"I obey, Innle."

I saw her stop and shy spectacularly in a flash of lightning, bringing the pursuit to a confused and milling halt. But her rider stuck to her back as if he were part of her flesh, and as the mare dropped wearily back onto all fours, he uncoiled his whip, his face contorted with rage. I prayed he would strike only once and then turn his attention back to us, but he slashed at her raw flanks as if in a frenzy. I felt only the dimmest edge of the pain it gave her, but it was enough to make me cry out in agony.

"The way is clear now," Gahltha sent urgently.

The mare stumbled to her knees, and the soldierguard leapt from her back and turned to lay into her with such abandon that I could see he meant to whip her to death.

"We cannot help her," Gahltha sent.

Fury ran through me like hot fire, and I reached instinctively for my deadliest ability. Everything seemed to slow down around me as it wakened. Even the rain fell with monstrous lethargy.

I sheathed my coercive probe in the power and hurled it at the soldierguard captain's mind. Dimly, I envisaged it making enough of an impact to distract him. But to my astonishment, the probe sheered through the storm static and the demonband block as if they did not exist.

Knowing the blow would kill the soldierguard, I tried to soften it, but, incredibly, the probe bucked and writhed, refusing to obey my will. It had been formed of uncontrolled fury and would respond to nothing else. It fought to strike at the soldierguard along the worn trajectory of my hatred for all abusers of beasts, and the effort of holding it back took all my energy.

I felt my grip falter, and the partly tamed probe slipped sideways and struck its target. *My* target.

Gasping as that dark power recoiled into me, I watched the soldierguard captain arch dramatically backward, the bloody whip falling from his fingers. With a terrible, inhuman shriek of pain, he pitched sideways, his mouth stretched with agony. When he fell, he did not move.

Trembling with exhaustion and shock, I reached out with my mind. He was alive, but only barely.

The soldierguards were beginning to bellow, and some were pointing at me as others tried to lift their captain to the roadside. The mare staggered away into the trees, but I had no energy left even to beastspeak her.

"I will send her directions to the barud, but we must go *now*," Gahltha sent. Without waiting for me to concur, he plunged over the edge onto the valley path. I was too shattered to be afraid of falling or of being shot in the back by the soldierguards. My body felt weak and hollow, and my mind was so spent as to render me unTalented. I felt witless at having nearly killed a man.

"He meant to kill the equine," Gahltha sent firmly.

"Misfits . . . don't kill," I sent. Even in physical contact with the horse, it took a great effort. "We don't kill or maim or hurt anything. . . ."

"You did not will to kill him/funaga-li."

"You don't understand," I wept. "Part of me did!"

"What happened?" Miryum demanded. "You were so long, we thought . . ."

I dragged my wits together, realizing the others were clustered around me in the dark, wet foliage instead of taking advantage of our lead.

We all froze at the sound of a scream from above, and moments later, a riderless horse came stumbling down the path, its eyes showing white. Obviously, her rider had not anticipated how steep the path was and had trusted his own instincts over those of his horse. We heard him cursing foully and calling up to his comrades that he'd broken his leg.

"Let's go while we can," Miryum urged.

As we rode on, I tried to farseek Duria, but my mind was incapable of even locating him let alone of communicating. Fortunately, he linked with one of the coercers to guide us to the ambush point. We were perhaps twenty minutes away, and there was no need to ride fast now. Ironically, we had to make sure we left a good clear trail so that the soldierguards would not lose us in the dark.

The storm had faded away without my noticing it, and the rain had almost cleared, but we were soaked to the skin. The long, hard ride had kept us from feeling the cold, but with the slower pace, I could feel it beginning to gnaw at my bones. By the time we came to the narrow track leading into the cul-de-sac where the trap was to be sprung, my teeth were chattering so hard I could not speak.

The track opened up into a broad clearing surrounded by high walls of stone, and I knew we had reached our destination. Sliding from Gahltha's back, I staggered.

By the time we were all sheltered under several clumps of trees down the far end of the canyon, the rain had ceased completely and the clouds began to fray and separate. The moon showed through their ragged edges, revealing the full extent of the cul-de-sac limned in silvery blue. Duria had been right in saying it was the perfect place for an ambush.

"Can you contact Duria?" I asked Miryum. "I used up all my energy delaying the soldierguards."

"I'm afraid I have nothing left. I couldn't coerce them if my life depended on it," she admitted.

At her words, a terrible premonition smote at me, but

before I could grasp what it might mean, the soldierguards arrived. They galloped wildly into the clearing, one after another, until there were dozens milling about.

"This is not Henry Druid's camp!" a soldierguard cried.

One of the captains dismounted and drew a short, businesslike sword. Moonlight slid along its blade with liquid grace as he peered toward us. "No, but those seditioners are skulking in the trees. I daresay they hoped we'd give up before this."

I expected Malik to announce himself then, but instead a peculiar awkward silence fell. On our part, it was an expectant silence, but on the part of the soldierguards, it was infused with puzzlement. They had caught sight of us now, and we were not behaving as penned prisoners ought. The soldierguards dismounted and came toward us slowly.

"Something doesn't tally," one of them muttered, peering into the shadows under the trees. "Look at them. Gypsy halfbreeds by their clothes and skin. Oldsters and women and children, mostly. These were not the armsmen who rescued Henry Druid."

"This lot were set up as decoys, to draw us away so that the Druid and his men could vanish," one of the captains snarled.

I wondered why Malik was holding his hand for so long. Miryum must have felt the same, for without warning, she took several strides into the space before the horde of soldierguards and faced them boldly. Straaka followed smoothly as her shadow.

"Surrender your weapons, for you have ridden into a trap," she said boldly.

The huge, bearded soldierguard captain holding the sword fairly goggled at her. Then his eyes slitted. "I do not think there is any trap," he sneered. "The only thing you have led us to, woman, is your own death." Without warning, he lifted a small crossbow and fired.

It would have taken Miryum in the head, but moving like a snake, Straaka twisted to place himself in front of the coercer, and the arrow took him deep in the chest. The Sadorian fell without a sound at her feet, and Miryum gaped down at him in disbelief. She knelt, seeming at once to forget where she was, but the rest of us watched in horror as the soldierguards nocked arrows and drew their knives and swords.

"Leave a couple alive. We'll torture the Druid's whereabouts out of them," the bearded captain said.

Instinctively, I tried to coerce him to stop his men, but my Talent would not function. Taking a deep breath to steady myself, I stepped out into the open, ignoring Gahltha's attempt to catch my arm in his teeth.

"Stop," I commanded. "The woman spoke truthfully. We have led you deliberately into a trap. Even now, you are surrounded by rebels, but they will spare you if you do no further harm."

Some of the soldierguards looked around uneasily, but the captain who had shot Straaka smiled scornfully. "Let your allies reveal themselves, if they exist," he challenged.

Now we all looked up, Misfits and soldierguards alike, but there was nothing; not the slightest rustle or glimpse of light on skin to suggest there was anything above but wet foliage and stone.

Only then did I understand.

Malik was in place, listening even now. He and his rebel force. But they would no more move to save us than grow wings and fly.

Malik had sworn to do no hurt to the soldierguards, and

854

none of the empaths had found a lie in his vow, because he had spoken the truth. He had never intended to murder the soldierguards.

It was *us* he meant to harm.

I understood clearly that this was no momentary impulse of treachery. It had been planned, perhaps even from the moment Malik suggested that Misfits act as bait. He knew from the Battlegames that our Talents were limited by our energy, and his plan had been designed to ensure any Misfit taking part would be drained before the ambush.

"Where are you, Malik? Show yourself!" Lina yelled, coming out to stand beside me, but her only answer was the mocking echo of her own voice. "I don't understand," she muttered. "The horses say the rebels are all there hidden above us. What are they waiting for?"

"They are waiting for the soldierguards to kill us," I said, loudly enough for Malik and his men to hear my words and know that I understood their treachery. Strangely, I was not afraid, though death was all about us in the night and in the cold purposeful eyes of the soldierguards.

I lifted my hands to show that they were empty. "Do not kill us, for we are unarmed," I said. I sensed the others behind me, coming from under the trees to show their empty hands.

One of the soldierguards lowered his bow a fraction. "They're half of them little more than children," he muttered. "I can't kill unarmed children in cold blood."

"They are foul demon spawn created by the loathsome experiments of Henry Druid," the bearded captain warned. "Their faces are innocent and young precisely to sway you to pity. But behind these winsome guises, they are monsters. And do not think them weaponless either. Remember the demonish tricks they played to slow our horses under us, and look what happened to Tarick back there on the road. One of these 'children' struck him a mortal blow without even being close to him."

The faces of the men around him hardened with revulsion, but even as they lifted their weapons, there was a flurry of movement. Before anyone could act, a mass of horses—both those of the Beastguild and the soldierguards' own mounts—had made a fleshy barrier of themselves between us and the soldierguards. Gahltha had positioned himself directly in front of me, and I fought to push past him, but he stood resolute.

"Very well," the soldierguard captain snarled. "If the beasts are possessed by these demons, then let them perish."

"No!" Angina cried, wriggling through the line of horses to stand in front of his mount. "Please don't hurt them. Give us a moment, and we'll make them go. . . ."

But the captain barked a command to fire.

My heart leapt into my mouth, but Gahltha was not hit, nor the horses on either side of him. For a second, I thought perhaps the arrows had been shot high to frighten us. Then I heard horses begin to scream, and Angina fell with dreamlike slowness. A coercer-knight who had also broken through the line of horses groaned and staggered with an arrow in her groin.

I stepped forward on rubbery legs, but Gahltha's teeth closed painfully on my shoulder. "Do not expose yourself, ElspethInnle!" he sent urgently. He insisted with brutal clarity that far more would die than those gathered here if I were to perish.

Gahltha commanded the other horses to guard me with their lives, and I felt him gather himself to attack the soldierguard captain.

"No! No, Gahltha!" I screamed as he moved toward the soldierguards, and I flung myself after him, grasping onto his mane.

"Fire again!" the captain's voice rang out.

I heard the thrum of bowstrings, preternaturally loud despite the keening of dying horses and the groans of Misfits, and knew that both Gahltha and I were too clear as targets to miss this time.

It seemed many minutes before the arrows struck. I saw Rushton's face, grave and ardent, and Maruman's dear, battered muzzle. Gahltha's flank was warm against my belly, and I had the muddled thought that it was good to die so close to one I loved.

But I did not die. Instead, the soldierguards cried out in shock and pain. They were falling.

I gaped at the sight. A line of archers had entered the cul-de-sac, firing upon the soliderguards from behind.

But they were not rebels. They were gypsies, pureblood and halfbreed alike, and foremost among them was the tall Twentyfamilies prince whom I knew only as Swallow.

He nocked another arrow, training it on one of the captains.

"Don't kill them!" I cried.

Swallow arched his brows. "As you wish," he said in his rough velvet voice.

◆ 26 ◆

MALIK'S FACE WAS heavy with thwarted rage. Incredibly, he seemed oblivious to the sounds of suffering around us, blind to the fact that dozens of Misfits, soldierguards, and horses lay dead or injured. It was as if they did not exist to him.

"Is this what you wanted?" I whispered. "Does it please you to see children and innocent beasts lying in their lifeblood, as well as soldierguards who need not have died?"

"No one was killed by my men," Malik mocked as his men rounded up uninjured soldierguards to rope their hands behind their backs.

"What happened this night arose because you planned to let the soldierguards slaughter us before you took them prisoner," I said.

The rebel gave a hateful sliver of a smile; then his expression became cool and lofty. "Doubtless it looks that way to one with diminished mental capabilities, but it is merely that my people were longer in assuming position than we had calculated. Unfortunate, but—"

"You were in position when we arrived," I snapped.

"You will tell your story, and I will tell mine. We will see which is believed," he responded, actually sounding bored.

"You betrayed us."

His eyes glittered. "One can only betray one's own kind, Misfit," he hissed. Then he said loudly, "I will take the soldierguards capable of walking with me to the lowlands. I leave the rest to your mercy, since it is your friends who injured them." He cast a malevolent glance at Swallow, who had insisted on remaining at my side with a bared sword throughout the confrontation. The Twentyfamilies gypsy met the rebel's gaze with wordless contempt.

Malik turned on his heel and strode away, and his men followed, prodding a line of bewildered-looking soldierguards to march. Distantly, I noted that a few rebels looked about in furtive shame as they trailed after their leader, but most ran their eyes over the carnage with as little expression as if the dead were fallen leaves at the end of summerdays. Malik's hatred was contagious.

When they had gone, I felt paralyzed. Swallow touched my arm gently. "You are not hurt?"

"No . . . no," I said, and my voice was surprisingly calm. He hesitated, then went to help his people with the wounded.

I heard the sound of running footsteps, and Miky burst from the path into the cul-de-sac. She stopped dead at the sight that met her eyes and at the moans and cries that rose on all sides from the darkness like some nightmarish chorus. Her face was white as paper in the moonlight.

Gevan and Duria were close behind her. They stopped as she had done, to stare about in disbelief.

"Elspeth, thank Lud you are not hurt," the Coercer guildmaster said fervently. "Malik convinced us to move some way back with a handful of his men, in case any of the soldierguards tried to escape. It was Miky who sensed something was wrong, so we disabled the rebels. But we were too far away. . . ."

"If the gypsies had not come, you'd all be dead," Duria said.

"Too many are dead because of my blindness," I said.

Gevan gave a snort of fury. "Because of Malik's treachery! But he will not get away with it. The other rebels will punish him."

"That will not bring back the dead," I said.

Swallow appeared out of the shadows, frowning. "Come, this is no time for talk. There are wounded who need attention. My people's wagons are nearby, but the way into this pass is too narrow to admit them. We must carry out those who can be moved."

"Who are you?" Gevan asked.

"I am known by many names, but you may call me Swallow."

"You are the Twentyfamilies prince?"

"I am the king of the Twentyfamilies now, though we do not use such archaic terms. I am the D'rekta, and my people are at your disposal. But people and beasts suffer as we speak. Let us save our talk for the campfire."

Gevan nodded decisively. "You are right. Duria and I will find out how many can be moved. We'll need someone to show us the way to your wagons." Swallow nodded and turned to speak with a gypsy hovering at his elbow.

I knew I should help, but I felt both weak and queerly indecisive. I walked through the clearing, feeling as if I were drifting rather than setting my feet on the ground. It was dark enough that bodies were merely crumpled shapes until I came close, and then, as in some nightmare, they seemed to form before my eyes to become someone I had known and loved. Many more than Angina and the coercer-knight had tried to shield the horses. At least a dozen horses lay dead, too, and the same number again were wounded, some mortally. One horse was screaming piteously in pain, and I saw that Lina was trying to staunch a bright red gush of blood from its neck.

I should have stopped, but my legs carried me past them to where Kella was bent over the recumbent body of Straaka. I kneeled and touched his ankle where his flesh showed above the boot. His skin felt soft and warm. I managed to raise a weak probe that told me Kella was operating internally on the Sadorian, encouraging nerve and muscle tissue to knit in such a way as to stem massive internal bleeding around his heart. But his life force ebbed dangerously low.

My vision blurred, and I realized that even this mildest form of probing was too much for my ravaged mind.

Kella continued to work, but after a little, she sat back with a sob and shook her head.

Miryum was kneeling beside us, an arrow she had taken in the soldierguards' second volley protruding from her own shoulder, though she seemed oblivious to it. Her eyes were fixed on Kella. "He jumped in front of me," she muttered.

"He saved your life," Kella said gently; then she got to her feet and moved away to find another who needed her.

I rose, too, and the movement caught Miryum's feverish gaze. "Elspeth," she rasped. "He would not listen when I told him to stay back. He never listened."

I did not know what to say. Eventually, Miryum's eyes fell to Straaka's body, and I followed Kella, who was now kneeling beside Angina. He looked so dreadfully young, and Miky was clinging to his hand, her face streaming with tears. I needed no probe to tell me Angina was near to death.

"Leave her to do what she can," Swallow said, coming up beside me. "We need your help to carry one of the wounded."

I let myself be led to where an enormous soldierguard lay, an arrow in his back. With a shock, I saw that it was the man who had shot Straaka—the bearded leader of the soldier-guards. Seeing my reaction, Swallow said noncommittally, "He will die if he is left to lie here."

I took a shuddering breath and shook my head. "We can't carry him alone."

"No," Swallow said, and he waved his hand to summon two ragged halfbreeds. Aras came over, too, and between the five of us, we struggled to lift him. He gave a deep groan and then was silent. We were all panting hard and sweating by the time we were halfway down the trail from the cul-de-sac. Fortunately, more gypsies waited, and they took him from us. One of them was Swallow's half sister, Iriny, but she did not notice me.

"The arrow has not gone deep enough to kill him," Swallow told her.

"Maire will have a look at him. But here, do you want any of our herbalists down there?"

"One," he answered. "The horses will have to be treated where they fell. Where is Darius?"

"He comes as fast as he can," Iriny said with faint reproach.

Swallow nodded and bid Aras and me return with him to the clearing. By the time we reached it, rain fell again.

"Twenty-three horses dead and seventeen wounded. Ten people dead and the same number wounded," Gevan said when all who could be moved had been taken to the gypsy rigs.

It was just on dawn, and those of us who remained in the clearing were clustered around a small fire. It had been built when the rain stopped, but the air was still clammy with damp, and drops fell steadily from the leaves all around us onto the sodden ground. Only three injured humans remained, too seriously hurt to be shifted, and all of the surviving horses. The dead had been covered with blankets.

Small makeshift canopies had been set up above the injured to keep them dry, and Kella and a gypsy herbalist were even now working on a soldierguard who had been arrowed in the stomach and in his hand. It was likely that the hand would have to be amputated. As I watched, Kella rose, moving away to examine a coercer-knight I had seen fall. There was little hope that she would survive, and I watched the healer settle a gentle hand on the girl and close her eyes as she drained away the girl's pain.

Farther down the clearing, the gypsy beasthealer Darius limped toward Lina and two other beastspeakers who were sitting with a badly injured horse. Several other bandaged horses stepped aside as the old man drew near. He had a painful lurching walk, because, aside from a crippled leg, his spine was twisted so that his back rose up into a hump. Nevertheless, his skill with beasts was formidable. Many more would have died without his help, and already both the beastspeakers and beasts regarded him with reverence.

"Seven of ours dead," Aras murmured, as if she needed to say the words aloud to begin to believe them. I turned to see that she was hanging another pot of sour-scented herb water, which Darius used in his healings, over the flames to heat. Her face was filthy except for the tracks made down it by tears. She had taken an arrow through the fleshy part of her thigh, but the wound was not serious.

"Eight if you count Straaka," Gevan said wearily, nodding to where the Sadorian lay. Miryum was still sitting a lonely vigil beside him, stroking his limp hand and muttering to herself.

"How could Malik do such a terrible thing?" the young

ward asked. She poked a stick needlessly into the fire under the pot.

"I don't know," I said truthfully. *But I should have known*, I thought bleakly.

"Humans seem ever capable of exceeding the lowest expectations," Swallow said, coming to stand by the fire.

Aras gazed up at him, her face transformed by an adoring awe. "You saved our lives," she said breathlessly. The gypsy made a negating gesture.

"She is right," Gevan said stoutly. "You did save our lives, Swallow, and you have our heartfelt thanks for it. Malik would have stood by and watched us hacked to pieces if you had not happened along."

"So that is who he was," Swallow murmured. "Malik's name is well known among the halfbreeds for his brutality. I only wish I'd been a bit quicker in getting here, but we had trouble finding a way to bring the wagons down into this cursed Valley."

I looked over to where Angina lay.

He had not yet regained consciousness, and it was possible that he never would. An arrow had grazed the boy's temple, and though seemingly a slight wound, it had caused internal damage, much of which could only be repaired by his own body. Miky had not left his side, and seeing the desperate intensity in her expression, I sensed she was using all her empathy to bind her twin to life.

I knew I ought to go to her, but when I tried getting up, Swallow caught my arm, pulling me to sit back down. "Just stay there, Elaria. You are in shock."

I had no energy to resist him. It was all I could do to lift a hand and push back a strand of hair. I noticed that my fingers trembled violently and understood that if my body was weak, my mind was worse. It was possible that what had happened back on the main road had permanently harmed me in some way, but I could not summon up enough concentration to care. What use were all my powers if they could not keep those I loved safe?

Swallow dippered a mug of warm water from the pot and handed it to me. "It's not hot yet, but the herbs in it will help to steady you."

I drank only because I sensed he would force me if I refused. The liquid tasted foul, but my mind did seem to clear somewhat.

I knew that, given the time, the rebels would be in the midst of taking Sutrium. I had intended to ride down to the coast after the decoy operation to join them, but the night's events had sucked all meaning from the rebellion. Soon we would light funeral fires for the beasts and beastspeakers, who preferred their bodies to be disposed of as beasts were, and later, all the remaining human dead, including the two soldierguards, would be buried. Too much death.

The only thing that raised a flicker of emotion in me was the possibility that other Misfits were among treacherous rebels, perhaps soon to be betrayed and slaughtered, because I had underestimated the loathing of unTalents. They had to know what the rebels were capable of.

Of course, Ceirwan must have seen Malik ride by. If so, he would have wondered at the absence of Misfits among the party. He would have probed their minds to learn what had transpired; therefore, he would know that we had been betrayed by Malik, and he would have warned Zarak.

Or would he? The terrifying swish of arrows and the screams of humans and horses rose in my mind with such ghastly clarity that I felt myself near to fainting.

After the funeral fires are lit, I will ride, I vowed.

I heard Aras ask, "How did you come to be in the Valley, uh . . . Swallow?"

The gypsy shrugged. "Luck guided us to your aid." The pot of water began to boil, and he asked Aras to take it to Darius.

When she had gone, I said softly, "It was not luck that brought you to our rescue."

He smiled, his teeth white against his dark, shining skin, but his eyes were serious. "I told you once that I had a vision we would stand together in battle when next we met."

"That doesn't explain how you came to be here tonight," I persisted.

"A voice in my dreams bade me ride to the highlands with all haste, lest you perish and all promises be broken," he said in a low, intimate tone.

I shivered. "A voice . . ."

"The same that sent me to save you from being whipped to death in Sutrium. And again I obeyed."

I had once felt sure that the mysterious voice that had sent Swallow to my aid in Sutrium belonged to the Elder of the Agyllians, Atthis, and that the gypsy's babble about my involvement in his people's ancient promises was no more than some sort of coerced vision, implanted by the bird to make him biddable. But knowing that Twentyfamilies gypsies had carried two panels of wood to Obernewtyn containing a message to me carved by the mysterious Kasanda, I had to accept that our lives might be truly linked.

"These promises . . . to whom were they made?"

"To the first D'rekta, who led our people from the lands that were destroyed by the Great White to the country of the Red Queen."

I gaped at him. "The . . . the Red Queen?"

He nodded. "The first D'rekta brought our people to her land. The Red Queen gave them refuge, but after many years, the D'rekta had a vision and asked the people to travel yet again with her. Many refused, for they had intermarried with the Red Queen's people, and the D'rekta would not reveal her vision to any but those who had sworn to go. It is said that those in whom she confided walked silent and pale until the boat that the Red Queen commanded to be built was completed. But they did not tell what they had learned, for the D'rekta forbade them to speak of her vision henceforth, even to their own children."

"Then you can't know what her vision was," I murmured, fascinated to discover that the first D'rekta had been a woman. But I was more intrigued by his talk of a Red Queen. I wanted to know the whereabouts of her land very badly, but some instinct bade me not to come upon it too bluntly. I asked, "Why did the Red Queen build the D'rekta a ship?"

"The two had become as sisters when the D'rekta bonded with the Red Queen's brother," Swallow said. "He died not long before the D'rekta had her vision, and many of the people who refused to go thought the vision a product of her grief."

"What happened to her bondmate?"

Swallow shrugged. "He was killed by sea raiders. It is said that the queen wept as the boat was launched. Some say she did so because she grieved still for her brother, and others claim she wept because the D'rekta had revealed the vision to her. Still others say she shed tears for she knew that the D'rekta carried within her a child of royal blood when the ship set forth on its perilous journey to this Land."

"The D'rekta's vision brought them here? Why?"

"I cannot say," Swallow said.

"Are the ancient promises about the vision?"

"In a sense, they are, but I cannot say more than that."

"But you once said you saw me speak those promises," I protested. "You said I was involved in them."

He nodded gravely. "That is so. But I do not know how the knowledge of them comes to you. Only the D'rektas know the words, and you have never met my father. Nor would he have told you, for we were bade keep our secret."

Weary of his mystical talk, I remembered that I had questions of my own to ask. "Did you . . . did you ever hear of a woman named Kasanda?"

"No. Who is she?" The gypsy's face was blank.

I sighed. "She was a woman who made a wood carving I have seen."

Swallow's dark eyes glimmered. "Perhaps she was a student of the D'rekta, then, for carving was her greatest skill. She learned it as a girl in the Beforetime, but she perfected her ability with the stone-carvers in the Red Queen's country. When she came to the Land, she took students and taught carving throughout her pregnancy."

I gaped at him, an incredible thought forming in my mind. "The . . . the D'rekta was a carver?"

"A master carver," Swallow said, giving me a curious look.

I struggled to compose myself, dizzy at the possibility that the first gypsy D'rekta and the mysterious Kasanda might be the same woman!

Swallow misunderstood my reaction. "Is it so shocking to you that a woman shaped stone? It is true that here in this Land it is not common, but our stories tell that in the Beforetime and also in the land of the Red Queen, many women did so. Of course, it was not only stone that she shaped. All substances became graceful beneath her fingers. Glass and jewels and wood as well as metals. It was she who taught the Twentyfamilies the skills that allow us to tithe to the Council for safe passage."

"What was the D'rekta's name?" I asked, hoping I did not sound as breathless as I felt.

He shrugged. "I do not know that I ever heard it spoken."

I wanted desperately to ask if the D'rekta had sent her people throughout the Land with her works—the signs—but feared this might come into the forbidden area of the ancient promises. "The original D'rekta brought your people here, and she negotiated with the Council to pay a tithe that let you have safe passage. Then what?"

"The D'rekta did not bargain for safe passage, though the statue that marks that pact is her work. . . ."

His words were virtually a paraphrasing of the fourth line in the message left on the doors of Obernewtyn!

"Why didn't she make the pact?" I asked tensely.

"A vision took her from us before the day of the pact-signing came," Swallow said simply.

"She . . . she was not taken by slavers, then," I muttered, wondering how else she would have come to be with the Gadfians.

Swallow gaped at me in disbelief. "How could you know that?"

It was some seconds before I could speak, for the desire to do so warred with Atthis's warning to tell no one of my quest. "I, too, have dreams," I managed finally, taking refuge in mystery.

"You dreamed of the D'rekta?" Swallow asked very deliberately.

"You said a vision took her," I countered.

He frowned. "There is dispute among the older ones over this matter. You see, slavers took her as she walked alone on a beach one night. But the day before, she had announced that she must go on a journey from which she would never return. The Twentyfamilies mourned her loss to the slavers, believing that evil chance had stolen her from her intended journey, but the D'rekta's son argued that his mother had foreseen the coming of the slavers, that she had walked upon the beach alone deliberately, knowing that it was their unwitting task to take her where she must go. He named himself D'rekta and vowed to honor and abide by the ancient promises, lest her vision be corrupted." Swallow shook his head. "I have sometimes wondered what it must have been like, driven by visions into the hands of slavers. I do not think I could have given myself to them so wholly."

You could, I thought somberly, *if you knew what would come should you fail to obey the visions.* I knew very well what the D'rekta's quest had been. Was it not my own now?

"The D'rekta's son . . . ," I murmured.

"He took her place as the leader of my ancestors, and he made the pact of safe passage with the Council in his mother's stead."

"Do the ancient promises have anything to do with the things the D'rekta carved?" I asked, hoping to surprise a response from him. His eyes flickered, but he only gave me a bland look, and it struck me that he had been more forthcoming when last we had spoken. Perhaps becoming D'rekta had made him more circumspect.

"Can you at least tell me if any of her stone carvings remain in the Land?"

"They do, but I may not reveal what they are or where they can be found," Swallow said.

"Can you tell me where the D'rekta's son was born?"

He considered this, then said, "He was born on the west coast, where our people dwelled for a time before we began to travel the long road."

Suddenly a thought occurred to me. "You . . . you are a descendant of . . . the D'rekta," I said. "You are of her blood."

"I, and others of the Twentyfamilies," Swallow agreed, looking puzzled.

But you have seen yourself standing beside me, I thought; and all at once I knew, as if I were a futureteller, that Swallow would be the one to go with me when I returned to Sador to seek the fifth sign—the one of Kasanda blood.

"I wish I could help you further, Elaria, but I must obey the ancient promises made to the D'rekta," he said heavily. "I am no longer a man who may obey his own whims and desires."

"I am sorry about your father. . . ."

"There was no love between us, and I mourn him less than the loss of my freedom. He was neither a good father nor a particularly good D'rekta." He gave me a long measuring look, then gestured about the clearing. "What will you do now?"

The despair that had sapped my will and wits had largely abated during our conversation, but my heart sank a little as I thought of what lay ahead. Yet, as Swallow had his responsibilities, so I had mine.

"I must ride down to Sutrium," I said. "The rebels will have secured the city if their plans have progressed as they hoped, and tonight they will move on the west coast. My friends are among them, and they must know what happened here."

"It surprises me that you would ally with these rebels when they would betray you because of what you are."

"And what do you think we are?" I asked warily.

He smiled sardonically. "I believed you and your friends to be escapees from the Councilfarms when last we met, but our seers tell me that you are Misfits of a special kind. And Malik's loathing of all Misfits is well known."

"We had no choice," I said.

"There is always choice. But perhaps in some things, no choice is good."

"Not all of the rebels are like Malik. . . ."

"Fortunately, it is not something I need concern myself with," Swallow said.

"Unless the rebels win control of the Land."

"Then we will negotiate safe passage with them," he said.

I could hardly believe he was so indifferent about the rebellion. But on reflection, I realized he was right in feeling it had little to do with his people. If the rebels failed, life would continue as before for the gypsies, and if they succeeded, there would still be a market for the gypsies' remarkable wares.

Aras returned with the empty pot and said that the beastspeakers were ready to light the funeral fires.

A little later, standing in the midst of a haze of smoke shot through with wan sunlight, I decided it was time for me to go. When there was time, Obernewtyn would mourn for its dead, but now there were the living to think about.

"You will leave?" Swallow asked.

I turned to him. "How did you know what I was thinking?" I demanded.

He smiled with an echo of his old mockery. "I cannot read your mind, if that is what you are asking." His lids drooped secretively over his dark eyes, and I understood he had no intention of explaining himself to me.

I shrugged. "Well, the answer is yes." I hesitated. "I know that many more of us, perhaps all, would have died if you had not come to our aid, Swallow. We owe you a debt of gratitude."

He bowed his head in acknowledgment. "There is something else you would ask of me?"

I was confounded by his perceptiveness but knew there was no time to puzzle out this riddle of gypsy awareness. "I have to ride for Sutrium, as I told you. But the sick and wounded have to be taken back to our refuge in the high mountains."

"You wish us to take them?" His brows lifted in a questioning arc.

"Few are fit to ride, let alone walk, and you have wagons. I can't offer you any payment, but you will be well provisioned for your troubles."

He smiled. "I will do as you ask, and perhaps there will come a day when I will ask a thing of you in return."

Originally, I had thought that Gevan, Miryum, and I would ride down to Sutrium after the decoy operation, but Miryum had vanished in the early hours with Straaka's body. The knights believed she had ridden with it to Sador.

Kella proposed that she take Miryum's place. Unspoken was the possibility that she might be needed if there was further treachery.

"I am not against your coming," I told her. "But what of Angina?"

The expression that crossed her face chilled me. "I can do nothing for him, Elspeth. He is stable enough to survive the journey to the mountains, and that is all I can say."

"Well, come, then," I told her shortly, thrusting my anxiety about the young empath to the back of my mind with my fears for Rushton.

As we were mounting, Lina strode over and demanded to come with us, saying she could be of use. I was on the verge of refusing, when it struck me that I had so long regarded her as a wayward child, I had failed to see she was almost a woman. And not just a woman. Her courage during the night was undeniable and deserved its due.

She looked surprised and gratified to be simply told to find a horse who would agree to carry her.

In an hour, we were riding back along the road that we had last traversed in the dark and rain. The sky was blue above us, and the sun shone, but there were long straggling lumps of gray, sodden-looking cloud along the horizon. By tacit agreement, we did not speak of what had taken place in the White Valley.

"It rains on the coast," Gevan said.

"I would be glad if getting wet was the only problem we had to face there," I said morosely.

Once we reached the Brown Haw Rises, I tried to farseek Ceirwan, as nervous of using my abilities as a fallen rider mounting up again.

"Where have ye been?!" he responded. "Malik's crowd rode by hours an' hours ago an' so fast that I could barely make head nor tail of their thoughts. There was somethin' of betrayal an' gypsies an' dead Misfits."

"All too many dead and not just Misfits, but I can't speak of them now," I farsent bleakly. "The simple truth is that Malik betrayed us."

"This mun be th' treachery Maryon foresaw," Ceirwan sent in a subdued mindvoice.

"Undoubtedly. But now let us speak of Sutrium. Do you know what is happening?"

"Elii's rebels took th' soldierguard encampment as planned. Once it was secured, he left a few of his people to watch over the prisoners, an' he an' the rest rode down to rendezvous with the other rebels and those of ours what went with 'em."

"Have you farsent Zarak?"

"I managed it just after the rebels took over th' three Councilmen's holdin's. Two rebels were killed an' three wounded at Radost's place. From there, I ken they took one of th' soldierguard camps without a hitch, an' also th' Councilcourt, but I dinna ken about th' others."

"What about the cloister?"

"They've put it off, because th' place has been locked up since yesterday mornin'. Zarak says not a soul has gone in or out of th' cloister. Brydda reckons th' Faction got wind of what was happenin', an' the priests've barricaded themselves in to sit it out. Of course, none of our people can scry past th' outer walls, so no one knows what they intend."

"They will have to come out when they run out of food."

"I'd say they are countin' on th' rebels losin' th' rebellion. Brydda is nowt worried anyrate. He says their lockin' themselves in saves him appointin' guards to do the job. He says we can deal with th' Faction when th' rebellion is over."

"Maybe," I said, privately wondering if the Faction was going to be quite as easy to deal with as everyone supposed. I told Ceirwan to meet us at the Sawlney turnoff.

"Ye want us to come with ye?"

"Only you. I'd like Freya to return to Obernewtyn to let everyone there know what has been going on in Sutrium."

After collecting Ceirwan and bidding farewell to Freya, we ate a rough meal of bread and cheese on horseback rather than lose time stopping. Even so, we did not reach the escarpment overlooking Sutrium until dusk. The city spread below looked as it always had: a demented labyrinth of streets and stone and thatched buildings running to the sea on one side and to the Suggredoon on the other, all flattened by the perspective from which we viewed it. A light rain was falling yet again, blurring and darkening everything slightly.

There was no sign that anything untoward was happening, but the streets and roads leading up to the town gate were deserted. The fact that the gate itself was unmanned brought us all to a halt.

"Weren't there supposed to be rebels disguised as soldier-guards here?" Ceirwan wondered aloud.

"Dardelan's plague notices might have worked so well there was no need of gate guards," Kella said.

"Or maybe the rebels couldn't spare anyone to play the part," Gevan offered.

"Let's keep going," I said. "We'll ride to the Councilcourt. Brydda said they'd use that as their command center."

"Ye know I have th' distinct feelin' we're bein' watched," Ceirwan observed nervously.

"I wouldn't doubt it," I muttered.

As we made our way toward the center of the town, I saw several curtains twitch. Kella spotted the first of many Councilcourt notices warning people to stay in their homes to avoid contracting the plague. The notices advised that the cloister bells would be rung when the plague-carrier was caught, and they looked absolutely authentic to me, right down to their Council seal.

But knowing why the streets were deserted did not stop the ride through them being a profoundly eerie business. I experienced an immense rush of relief when the Councilcourt came into view, even though, as ever, it brought back vivid memories of my being committed to the orphan homes after my parents had been executed. The streets had been silent then, too, but only because people always fell silent at the sight of children with the lurid red paint on their faces that marked them as the offspring of seditioners.

What a long way I had come since that day.

I sent out a probe to Zarak. It did not locate, but I was not troubled, for he could well be over tainted ground. There was enough of it in Sutrium. I was shaping a probe to Tomash's mind when Gevan pointed out the lack of a guard at the door.

"You'd think there would be someone here, if only for the look of the thing."

We dismounted, and for once there was no need to dirty Gahltha or pretend to tie him up to ensure no one would steal him. He sent to me that he could smell other horses round the back of the Councilcourt and suggested he question them. Before I could agree, Brydda's white mount Sallah trotted around the corner.

"Greetings, ElspethInnle," she sent, coolly as ever. "I trust/hope you come to ensure that no funaga-li will have the right to bind equines in this barud-li." Without waiting for my response, she invited our horses to join a beast council taking place. The horses trotted after her without a backward glance, though Gahltha invited me to call when I needed him.

As we mounted the steps to the entrance, I wondered whether there would be any serious attempt by the rebels to institute beast rights. Brydda was committed to changing the way humans dealt with animals, but he was just one man. Most of the rebels would not feel as he did, and common sense told me that any law that divested humans of beasts that they regarded as rightful property would be unwelcome.

Especially since so many human livelihoods depended on the enslavement or even death of beasts.

I lifted my hand to open the door to the Councilcourt, but it swung open on its own to reveal the dear, longed-for face of the blind Empath guildmaster, Dameon.

"Elspeth," he said, a world of gentle loving in that one word.

Unable to speak, I moved into his waiting embrace.

"I am so very glad to see you," I sighed, my mouth against the rough linen of his shirt collar. "Rushton . . ."

"I know, my dear," Dameon whispered into my hair. "Zarak told me. But you know he will let nothing keep him from one he loves so dearly."

✦ 27 ✦

"SHE LIES!" MALIK snarled.

"She is mistaken," Brocade said pompously. "She claims that Malik deliberately prevented his men from announcing their presence to the soldierguards in order to see her people slain. But she also admits that her powers and those of the other Misfits with her were exhausted, so how could she know if Malik was there or not?"

"The horses smelled that he was in position," I said tightly. I wished uselessly that I had not had to plunge so swiftly into this particular confrontation. My emotions were too close to the surface, and an outburst of anger or sorrow would weaken my argument.

"The Misfits called Duria, Gevan, and Miky were brought some way from the ambush point so that they would be in no danger," Malik said, spreading his fingers. "It was while my men and I made our way from where we had taken them that the soldierguards arrived on the heels of the Misfits. Sadly, we were not yet in place."

Before I could undo myself by voicing my rage, I felt a surge of such sweet calmness and certitude that I knew Dameon was directing his considerable ability to calm me. I bathed gratefully in his essence for a moment, and when I spoke again, my voice was as mild as I could have wished.

"Malik emerged from his hiding place conveniently after

the gypsies had stopped the soldierguards firing on us. It is well known that he loathes Misfits, and it was his suggestion that we act as bait in a trap that he claimed to be infallible. I have no way to prove that he maliciously watched beasts and Misfits die, but if you look at what happened, you must see the truth. If you cannot, I wonder how your new order will fare. Your words sound very fine, but it is your deeds that will reveal your truest intent."

Brocade got to his feet with a grunt. "What I would like to know is where these gypsies came from. They must have been told the location of the trap, and if that is so, then the only treachery was Misfit-born."

Elii stood. "I, too, should like to know the answer to this question, but I am fully mindful that Malik hates the Misfits and would like them eradicated despite their invaluable aid in putting his plan into practice. Maybe Elspeth is mistaken, and maybe not. I do not see it as out of character for Malik to have held his hand at the crucial moment, knowing he broke no sworn oath to us in doing so."

"If you agree that I broke no oath, then why are we sitting here discussing treachery?" Malik demanded.

Dardelan stood, and the others fell silent.

"I think this is ultimately a matter of ethics, and such a debate is never out of place, especially among those who would depose an oppressive order so that they can institute a better one. If you deliberately planned harm, Malik, then treachery it was, whether or no you swore not to harm the Misfits."

"I did not harm them," Malik growled.

"You broke an obvious unspoken trust if you did not act as soon as they appeared in the clearing."

"I have told you already what happened." He sounded bored.

Dardelan looked about at the other rebels. "We have before us two conflicting stories and no way of proving which is true."

"The word of my men should be enough," Malik said coldly. "They will tell what happened."

"If you betrayed the Misfits, would you not also threaten your people to keep them from bearing witness against you?" Dardelan asked. "As host of this meeting, I say that there can be no fair judging at this point. But people and beasts died, and this matter is not ended. When the rebellion is over, we will investigate the incident more deeply."

"But what of these gypsies?" Lydi demanded.

Dardelan gave me a look of inquiry, and I decided to be as truthful as I could. "I once did a favor for the gypsy leader, and when he had a true dream of my need for aid, he rode to the cul-de-sac. He has no interest at all in this rebellion."

"Another Misfit," Brocade sneered.

I regarded him icily, ignoring the curious look Gevan was giving me. "Many in the Land who are not called Misfits occasionally dream true."

"Perhaps the gypsy who came to Elspeth's aid may speak for himself of what happened when this matter is judged," Brydda suggested from the back of the chamber, where he sat by the door. "It would be interesting to know exactly what he dreamed, would it not?"

Malik lurched to his feet and jabbed his great blunt-ended finger into the air toward Brydda. "Of course you would speak for your monstrous pets." He swung to face Dardelan. "As for this Misfit gypsy, obviously he will side with his own kind."

Dardelan let a silence grow before he spoke. "If I use your reasoning, Malik, then we can call no non-Misfit to vouch for you, for your own kind would not speak ill against you either."

"I speak of Misfits, who are as amoral as beasts, not of humans," Malik said haughtily. "A rebel would not lie in council, even to protect his leader, for true humans understand honor."

"I think Malik's understanding of honor was shown very clearly in the Battlegames, was it not?" Jakoby asked blandly, her slanted yellow eyes gleaming. "When it comes time to judge this matter, let all here remember how both parties behaved then and who showed the deepest morality."

Malik looked apoplectic, but before he could speak, Dardelan held up his hands. "I know these are grave and sorely disputed matters, but right now, we must look to the west coast, for the rebellion is not yet over. Elspeth, will your people continue to aid us and allow this matter to be deferred?"

"Our people will remain with the rebels they were assigned to, but none will serve with Malik and his men," I said.

"I desire no aid from monsters," Malik snapped.

"If you—" Dardelan began, but there was a loud banging noise and the sound of shouts from the back of the chamber. Everyone turned to see a bloody-faced Serba enter, supported by Zarak.

"What in blazes—!" Brydda exclaimed, leaping to his feet. He helped Serba to a seat and bid someone bring water.

"What has happened?" Malik demanded.

"Treachery," Serba gasped. "They knew all the plans. The rebellion. The Misfits helping us. Everything . . ."

"They? The Council?"

She seemed not to register the question. "The soldier-guards burst in on a secret meeting we were holding in Port Oran. It was to be the last between the leaders of the west coast bloc. Cassell and Radek, Tilda in Yavok's place, their seconds, and mine. All of our best fighters—trapped like rats . . ." She shook her head in disbelief. "They took no prisoners. They simply fired their arrows and slashed with their swords and knives. So many dead . . ."

"Strange that the Misfits with you failed to foresee the attack," Malik sneered.

"No," Serba said. "It was not possible for them to know the soldierguards were coming, for all wore strange metal headbands that prevented their minds being detected. I only escaped because the empath Blyss became agitated and claimed that we were in danger. She wanted me to tell everyone to leave. I drew her aside with me into a small tunnel leading to the roof to question her. Merret came out, too. She is a coercer, and she told Blyss she sensed no danger; the empath became weak, overwrought by whatever she sensed. Then we heard the sound of wood smashing.

"I ran back and we saw . . . I saw the slaughter. I heard the soldierguard captain in charge of the operation taunt Cassell with the knowledge that the Council knew the rebel plans. He knew a rebel force would be coming from this side of the Suggredoon tonight. He said there would be no rebels to meet them, because none would be left alive on the west coast by then. Soldierguards would be waiting in Port Oran. Hundreds of them, from all the other cities.

"I wanted to go in, but one fighter would make no difference to the outcome, and if I was taken, then no rebel would remain to warn you and . . . and to avenge my . . . the others. We got away from the building by jumping from roof to roof, then losing ourselves in the crowd that had gathered to investigate the disturbance."

I glanced at Zarak and farsent a question.

"She was alone when she came to the ferry," he responded grimly. "She told me that she separated from Merret and Blyss when the pair insisted they ride outside the city to warn the other Misfits. I suppose they meant to farseek Orys and the teknoguilders. They were supposed to meet her afterward, but they never showed up."

"It was not just the meeting they targeted," Serba was saying, tears flowing unchecked down her filthy cheeks. "They attacked all our refuges and hiding places. It can only have been the same in Morganna and Halfmoon Bay. Perhaps also in Aborium and even Murmroth. I went to several safe houses, but they were all burned out and filled with dead rebels. The soldierguards caught me in one of them. They . . . they questioned me about the Misfits who had escaped from the meeting. They even knew their names!" She gasped and rubbed a ragged sleeve over her face. "I fought my way out. I had to. Now I must go back. There will be others like me who escaped, and I must . . . must find . . ."

She fainted dead away into Brydda's arms.

Kella pushed through the rebels and lifted the unconscious woman's eyelids. "She must be carried to a bed so that I can treat her."

Malik caught at Kella's arm. "You can't take her away. She has information we need."

She gave him a look of scathing distaste. "If Serba cannot speak of her own will, will you torture her to do so? I know all too well how cheap life is to you, Malik; both the lives of my people and of yours. But this woman can give you nothing until she is well."

The gray-eyed rebel looked as if he wanted to strike her, but Brydda scooped Serba up and pushed past him. Kella followed him out.

884

As the doors swung shut behind them, Elii said, "You realize that if the soldierguards made no attempt to take prisoners, it means they have no need for any information. They know everything they need to know."

"How convenient that the Misfit warning should come too late to save hundreds of rebels, but not too late to save themselves," Malik sneered.

Zarak took a step toward the big man, his face cold. "What advantage do you imagine would come to us in betraying you?"

"Enough," Jakoby said. "This is not the time nor place for such squabbles. Let the boy tell his story."

There was a mutter of agreement, and Zarak took a deep breath. "I went across the Suggredoon to the other bank so that I could make contact with the west coast Misfits. Brydda suggested I let them know how things had gone here to lift their spirits. I had barely stepped off the ferry when Serba came running out of the trees, saying all was lost. She bid me return to the other bank with her before the soldierguards came.

"At first I thought she was delirious, but there was no lie in her mind. I . . . I saw it all there. The slaughter and her escape with Merret and Blyss. I got the rebels looking after the ferry to help her aboard and make ready to depart; then I went away from the water and tried to scry out Merret. I couldn't reach her. I might have tried again, but I heard the sound of horses approaching. A great horde of them. I went back aboard the ferry and ordered the men to bring it over to this side. We were only just out of reach when they arrived on the shore. Soldierguards. Over a hundred of them."

Dardelan laid a hand on the ward's arm. "Zarak, let us be clear on this. Were they following Serba?"

"I don't know," Zarak admitted. "She said they were after her, and they came. But maybe they were sent there to seize the ferry."

"I think we can assume that if a great horde of soldier-guards rode up to the ferry port openly, they know she had reached us and that we are alert to the trap that was to be sprung tonight in Port Oran," Reuvan said.

"Why did the Misfits not foresee this in the minds they probed?" Brocade demanded.

"I don't know," I said evenly. "It may be that these bands Serba spoke of prevented our people from entering the trai-tors' minds. Or maybe the traitor is not a rebel but someone intimately connected to a rebel, someone who would not be tested. Or perhaps the traitor simply has not submitted him or herself to be tested yet. Even on this side of the Suggre-doon, we have not probed every mind." I looked now at Malik.

"The one thing we do know is that the traitors are on the west coast, else what happened to the rebels there would have happened here," Gevan declared.

Some of the others nodded, but Elii said sharply, "Right now, the identity of the traitors is the least of our worries. What's more important is to know what the Council plans to do."

"Obviously they will attack us," Brocade said shrilly. "We must post a heavy force along the Suggredoon immediately."

Zarak shook his head. "You forget that the ferry is on our side of the river and is the only way across. No one would dare swim with the water being so tainted."

"Of course, by the same token, we cannot sally out and engage them since the ferry is too small to take more than a meager force," Elii said. "I daresay that is what the soldier-guards came to prevent. Of course, they will have to guard their shore constantly to prevent our sending over spies."

"In time, they will try to send their own spies using small vessels at night," Brydda rumbled. "They would no doubt have done so already, except for this huge trap they planned. Fortunately for us, they obviously focused on the west coast, just as we concentrated our first moves this side of the Suggredoon. If not for Serba and the Misfits with her, we would have fallen into a deadly trap."

There was a grim silence.

"Brocade is right. We ought to set up a shore watch along the Suggredoon," Dardelan said.

Jakoby rose, saying she would post some of her people while we decided on a course of action. I caught her thought that this development could have definite consequences for her people.

"What of seagoing vessels?" Reuvan said when she had gone. "They could come straight in from the ocean and land hordes of soldierguards somewhere this side of the river. We ought to set up a shore watch everywhere a ship can anchor and let off passengers."

"A good point," Zamadi said. "But we need not worry about that so swiftly. Such a venture would take time to organize."

"Of course, we could turn the tables and send our own ships out," Dardelan said, calling all eyes in the room back to him. "The Council cannot possibly guard all of that western shoreline, for you could beach a ship almost anywhere along it without difficulty and without being seen because it is so sparsely settled."

"Now there is a truly cheering thought, because even if we don't do it, the Council can't afford to overlook the possibility that we might. They will be stretched dangerously thin trying to guard that shore," Brydda said. "But I think sending out ships of our own is a brilliant idea. Elspeth, I know your people cannot scry over the tainted waters of the river, but could a farseeker scry to land from the deck of a ship?"

"Perhaps," I said. "If the shore has not been tainted and if the vessel was very close in to shore."

Dardelan nodded. "We will speak further of plans to attack once we have made sure of our defenses. Brydda, you and Reuvan can look into a preliminary strategy for sea approach to the west coast. Zamadi, will you and your people take charge of patrolling the riverbanks? The Sadorians are too few to watch the whole shoreline, and I'm afraid that is what will ultimately be needed."

"I will, but that's a cursed lot to watch. We'll need to have people set up right away along the bank past the Ford of Rangorn to the Blacklands," Zamadi said.

"I'll assign more people to you when we are organized," Dardelan promised.

"Good enough," Zamadi said, and sat down to mutter to a couple of his people.

Malik rose, and I half expected him to challenge Dardelan's authority. But this time there was no talk of Dardelan being too young or being Brydda's pawn. Instead, the gray-eyed rebel offered his force, Vos's, and Brocade's to arrange a watch of the vulnerable places along the sea coast. This was less of a job than it sounded, for the combination of sheer cliffs and impassible shoals meant that there were only a limited number of landing places.

"Done, then," Dardelan said. "You should begin by setting

up a watch on the wharves in the city, too. A spy could easily come in that way under the cover of dark."

"I can organize that," Reuvan offered.

"Very well," Dardelan said. "I'll assign you some of my father's people. And, of course, aside from watching, we must devise plans in case they do attack in force either here or somewhere else on our coast."

"Dardelan, I'd like to try getting inside the cloister as soon as possible," Elii said. "After all, the demon bands that block the Misfits' powers are of Herder making, and they obviously knew at least a day before what was going to happen here. Maybe they also know what happened on the west coast."

"Truespoken," Dardelan said. "I am not opposed to your making an attempt at getting in, if no one else objects." He looked around but no one else spoke. "Very well. Lydi, I am afraid it lies with your group, then, to take control of watching the prisoners."

"I assume you mean the prisoners here and elsewhere?"

"All the prisoners ought to be brought to Sutrium eventually for the trials, but let's leave the ones outside Sutrium where they are for the time being. Have someone go up and let the rebels guarding them know what has transpired and set up watch rosters. We should know better how we stand in a few days. Besides, when we do collect them, the locals will want to know what is going on. We will have to be prepared to talk to them. I will give some thought to it."

"What about the city?" Lydi asked. "This plague ruse won't last forever. . . ."

Malik cut in brusquely. "We cannot spare the forces to control civil unrest nor the time to institute alternative systems right now. I will have some of my men dress as soldierguards and patrol the streets shouting that several people disobeyed

Council orders and therefore plague is now rampaging through the city. That will keep them in their houses for at least another day or two."

Dardelan looked around at the others and, seeing no dissent, nodded. "I don't like it, but we can't afford for anyone to get wind of what is happening on the other bank of the Suggredoon yet. There will be a panic if people fear the city is likely to become a killing ground. We must begin to take some sort of visible control of the city soon, though, or matters will slip out of our hands. That means we will have to make decisions I had hoped might be made after all the fighting was done. But let's get moving now. We will meet here again in the morning."

There was a general movement toward the door, but Tomash sidled through the crush to me. "Elspeth, Elii wants me and some of the others to come with him when he tries broaching the cloister walls."

"Go, then," I said. He departed with Wila in tow, and as other Misfits approached, I instructed most of them to remain with the groups they had been assigned to. Others, I decided, would return to Obernewtyn. There were more than enough of us to help the rebels, and given what had happened with Malik, I preferred there to be less rather than more of us working with them.

I asked Zarak to let everyone at Obernewtyn know what was happening. I suggested Dameon return as well, but he said gently but firmly that he would return when I returned, and I was selfish enough to be glad.

I told him who I wanted to return to Obernewtyn, and when Zarak heard Lina's name, his eyes lit up. "She is here?"

I realized then that he had no idea what had happened in

the White Valley. Rather than tell him of Malik's treachery, I bade him talk to Lina and work with her to gather the others who would ride back to Obernewtyn. I knew she would explain everything.

Promising to see me before they departed, Zarak went to find Lina. I turned to Dameon. "We have had no chance to talk, and there are so many things I want to ask you about."

He found my hand unerringly. "Do not concern yourself with me right now. I will go and sit with Kella and her patient. We will have plenty of time later."

I hugged him impulsively, at the same time instructing Ceirwan to take him to Kella. By the time the guilden returned with Brydda, the council room was virtually empty.

"What now?" Ceirwan asked.

"You stay with Dardelan," I decided. "Everything that happens will be relayed back to him, and you can farsend it to me."

Brydda ran his fingers through his hair in a gesture of frustration. "This is a cursed mess."

"It is," I said.

"I have not had time to tell you how sorry I am about what happened in the White Valley. Rest assured that Malik will be brought to answer for what he did, though I know that can be no consolation to you."

I said nothing. The deaths in the White Valley and now the news that the Misfits sent to the west coast were trapped in a hostile situation, utterly beyond our help, was almost too much to bear.

"Despite everything, it is good to see Dameon again," Brydda went on.

I smiled wanly, for it was true. "When did he arrive?"

"On a ship yesterday evening with Jakoby and her people. He wanted to go up to Obernewtyn when you did not arrive, but Malik said you would come."

"What exactly did Malik say when he arrived here without us?"

The rebel scowled. "He said there had been a mishap." He strode about restlessly, then suggested we go to Dardelan's home, saying he wished to speak with Bodera.

As we made our way along the street, I was struck again by the silence that lay over the metropolis. For all its appearance, there were hundreds of people on all sides, many times outnumbering the rebels occupying the city. Dardelan was right in saying control could slip from the rebels' fingers all too easily if they did not tread very carefully.

"You won't be able to keep these people penned up forever," I said aloud.

"Dardelan said in the meeting that he would think about how we might assume peaceful control, but the reality is that he has been giving it considerable thought for some time. He has a plan."

"A plan?"

He nodded. "He believes we should begin by organizing a series of trials of soldierguards and Councilmen as a way of demonstrating our disinclination to rule by brute force. This will allow us to remind the people of the tyranny and greed of their erstwhile masters. The trials will also focus people's attention on what comes next. I should let him explain, but I can say Dardelan wants to institute other changes."

"Will he be able to do so with the west coast situation?" I asked.

He sighed, and his stride slowed. "First we have to consolidate our position this side of the river. We must ensure that what we have won cannot be taken back. Then we must find a way to wrest control of the west coast from our enemies. I am afraid what has gone before will be nothing compared to what will come, for there will be open confrontation."

"You are speaking of civil war," I said.

He nodded morosely. "I am afraid so. Of course, we will not speak those doubts very loudly. If we are to hold what we have gained, we must instill confidence in people by showing them we can run things competently. Otherwise, they will collaborate against us for fear of what will happen if the Council resumes control."

"I wouldn't let people know much about the situation on the west coast to start with, then," Reuvan opined.

"Exactly my feeling," Brydda agreed.

"You won't be able to stop people realizing that something is going on when they can't use the ferry," I said.

"Truespoken, but we can make it seem as if the port is held in a desperate move by a few soldierguards," Brydda said.

The big rebel stopped outside a small house and knocked softly. It was opened by the scarred blond woman I had first met long ago with Domick. Instinctively, I probed for news of Domick or Rushton in her mind, but there was nothing. She had not seen Domick in many sevendays, and she had never seen Rushton.

She paled to hear Brydda's news but asked calmly enough what he wanted her to do.

"Help Reuvan set up a watch of the city piers," the big man said.

Reuvan lifted his head and grasped the big rebel's arm.

"What is it?" Brydda asked impatiently.

"Smoke," the seaman said. "Can't you smell it?"

Now that he had pointed it out, I could smell it, too. Reuvan pointed to the sky, and I turned to see monstrous billows of black smoke, streaked with orange and red, rising over the buildings.

"It's coming from the wharves," Reuvan said. "One of the sheds must be on fire."

Brydda groaned. "Not the sheds, curse it! The ships!" He broke into a run.

· 28 ·

"THE STINKING BASTARDS," Brydda cursed as we stood help-lessly on the pier, watching every ship in the port burn, in-cluding the ancient Sadorian vessel, *Zephyr*. Dirty black smoke hung in a thick veil over the sky, and the angry red of flames was reflected in the waves as a blighted dusk.

"Who did this?" Reuvan said incredulously. "The Coun-cil?"

"Who else could it have been?" Brydda raged. "They must have set someone up here to burn the ships. Who would think they would be far-sighted enough to consider the possibility that their plan might fail?"

Other rebels were arriving now, Dardelan among the first, with Ceirwan at his heels.

"I saw th' smoke an' turned back," the young rebel panted.

Jakoby came running up. Seeing the conflagration, her eyes sought out the *Zephyr*, which Dameon had told me had been among the ships that had carried her people on their raid of New Gadfia. She swore coldly.

"Why didna th' crews sound an alarm?" Ceirwan asked.

Dardelan said, "Hiding inside their homes for fear of plague germs, I suppose."

Reuvan said in a queer, flat tone, "No ship would ever be left unwatched. There would always be at least a skeleton crew aboard."

"My people had no home in this place but the *Zephyr*," Jakoby said very softly, her eyes shimmering with reflected flames.

No one said a word, for we saw then what we should perhaps have realized immediately. It was not just the boats that had been destroyed. Anyone who had been aboard them had been murdered.

Suddenly Ceirwan spoke. "Isn't that a ship way out there?"

"It's going out," Brydda muttered. "I would bet my life that the people who did all of this are aboard and are even now bound for the west coast to report to their masters."

Reuvan shook his head decisively. "That ship is bound for the open sea."

"Open sea . . . ," Brydda echoed blankly.

"That, or Herder Isle," Reuvan murmured.

"Herder Isle," Dardelan repeated. "But what has Herder Isle to do with this?"

"Maybe nothing," Brydda said slowly. "That ship might simply have turned back when it saw the smoke."

"What if th' Herders are th' ones who fired th' ships?" Ceirwan said breathlessly. Then he shook his head. "No, that's stupid. Why should they?"

"Why, indeed," Brydda said darkly. "I think we had best go and see how Elii is faring with the cloister."

"What about the ships?" Reuvan protested.

"There is no saving them," Jakoby murmured.

"I must speak to my father," Dardelan said. "I will come to the cloister after that." As he turned away, I bade Ceirwan mentally to stay with him.

"I will wait here," Jakoby murmured, her eyes on the burning *Zephyr*. "I can do nothing to help her, but some things must be witnessed to the bitter end."

"I will stay, too," Reuvan mumbled. Brydda gave him leave with a look of compassion. He knew that, as a seaman, Reuvan would have known most of the men and women killed.

On our way to the cloister, Brydda strode so fast that I had to run to keep up, his face set in a mask of cold rage.

I was more frightened than angry. There seemed something nightmarishly sinister in the possibility that the Faction were involved in the destruction of the ships and their crews. I thought again of the nightmares of Ariel and wondered if he could have anything to do with what was happening.

Soon we came in sight of the cloister. I had not clapped eyes on one since I had tried to rescue Jik from the clutches of his former masters. But this was larger than the cloister in Aborium. Set apart from other buildings, the cloister and its grounds were surrounded by a high wall of hard stone. Greenery showed above the wall, and though I could not see it, I pictured the manicured gardens and lawns surrounding the square buildings where the priests lived and went about Faction business.

I tried to farseek beyond the wall, but my mind could not penetrate the perimeter. As Zarak had described, it felt exactly like trying to scry over badly tainted ground. I frowned up at the walls. Once I might have thought the use of tainted material an accident, but that had been before the Herders manufactured their demon bands. Now it seemed very likely that the stone had been chosen and used specifically to thwart Misfit powers.

"There," Brydda said, pointing. Elii and a group of rebels had come from a nearby street, carrying lanterns and dragging a log they clearly meant to use as a ram. Seeing the big rebel, Elii hailed him cheerfully and asked if he had come to lend his muscles to the ramming.

"Let me try the muscles in my tongue first," Brydda said.

Elii shrugged. "Call them if you like, but we have tried and they respond to nothing."

Brydda walked up to the gate and hammered boldly upon it. The sound of his blows was a loud, flat clangor on the still night air, but not a sound came from beyond the wall other than the hoarse barking of dogs.

"Come out, priests! The boats are burned, so there is no going back to Herder Isle," Brydda bellowed.

Still no response.

He came back to where the rest of us stood. "Don't bother with the ram. The doors are too heavy. Get ropes and hooks, and we'll go over the walls."

"No!" I said, and they both stared at me. "I am sorry but . . . it's possible the walls contain tainted stone. If anyone climbs onto them, and the taint is strong enough . . ."

Brydda nodded. "Very well. Then have someone find two long ladders and lash them together. We'll construct a bridge that will clear the walls."

Elii sent a few of his people off to fetch ladders and leather thongs but said he did not think ladders a good idea. "They'll just as likely shoot arrows into anyone who shows his head above the top," he said.

"We'll use shields, but somehow I don't think anyone will be shot," the bearded rebel said.

"There may be no soldierguards in there, but the priests will defend themselves," Wila said. "They don't fight as a rule, but many of them can."

"The priests would attack intruders, I know," Brydda agreed, "if there were any there."

Elii stared. "Are you saying that you think the cloister is empty of priests?"

"That is exactly what I am saying," Brydda said grimly.

The ladders came, were fixed together, and then scaled. Elii insisted on being first to mount the makeshift bridge. He carried a small shield of stiffened leather before his face, but not an arrow was fired from beyond the wall.

"I can't see anyone," he cried down to us. "Just a couple dogs over by the stable gate."

Brydda called him to come down, saying he would go over the wall first. But I caught at his arm and suggested I go first. "It's not a matter of sacrificing myself," I said. "The dogs can be trouble. I can calm them down and scry out the whole place from the top to make sure this is not some sort of trap. And if there is someone waiting when I climb down, you know I can defend myself."

He tugged at his beard but finally nodded. "Very well. But take no risk, Elspeth. If you sense anything untoward, come back at once. Enough Misfits have been lost already in this rebellion."

To satisfy him, I carried a wretchedly awkward shield and nearly fell off the ladder for my pains. Once I topped the wall, the breeze flicked my hair irritatingly into my eyes. The dogs Elii had seen were tied up, and when I beastspoke them, they projected ravenous hunger, saying they had not been fed for days. Bidding them be patient, I turned my mind to the dark buildings connected by stone corridors that formed the main part of the cloister and sent out a broad probe. It did not take me long to discover that there was not a single human mind in the place. I turned to shout my findings, then climbed down into the grounds.

It was even darker under the trees, but I sensed a dog bounding toward me before I had taken two steps. I used both coercion and beastspeaking to stop him from attacking me. He sniffed my leg, then lay on his belly in a sign of respect, addressing me reverently as ElspethInnle. As ever, I wondered how it was that beasts knew me. He promised to let the other dogs know not to attack anyone coming over the wall.

"I will tell them you bring food," he sent with a hopeful wag of his tail.

Repressing amusement, I agreed that we would certainly provide food while we searched the buildings.

"You seek the funaga-ra who dwell here?" he asked, adding a suffix I had never heard of. I agreed that we were seeking the inhabitants of the cloister.

"Many funaga-ra came. Then some went out the gates. Many more went/were eaten by the ground."

I asked what he meant, but he could explain it no better. I heard a noise and turned to find Brydda coming down the ladder. He eyed the dog warily, but I assured him it would not attack.

"They're half starved, especially the ones tied up," I said, and told him what the dog had said about the priests.

"Maybe he means the cells," Brydda said. "There is a great network of them beneath the buildings."

My heart skipped a beat. "Under the ground?" I echoed. "I cannot farseek under the ground. Maybe I was wrong about there being no one here."

Other rebels and Misfits were coming down the ladder now, and Brydda directed some of them to go and open the front gate and others to tend to any animals needing care. I asked the dog to accompany them in case any other dogs were minded to attack.

"I have warned them," he sent, "but I will go with the funaga."

He trotted off amiably.

900

I was hesitating outside the door to the main building when Tomash and Wila joined me.

"What I don't understand is how the priests got away without anyone noticing," Tomash said, following me inside. "They must have gone under cover of night. Or perhaps it was all that coming and going to the ships from the cloister. Maybe there was a lot more going than coming."

"It is so dark," Wila said, looking back longingly at the door. "Are we looking for something?" she asked in a subdued voice.

"Prisoners," I said. "Brydda told me there is a network of cells beneath the grounds, and if the priests are gone, I doubt they would have bothered freeing their prisoners."

We went randomly along several halls and through a number of doors, until we came to one that was bolted from the inside.

I focused my mind and forced the lock, then pushed the heavy door inward. A foul reek rushed out, and after an initial recoil, I felt my way warily into the room.

Only it wasn't a room. It was a stairwell. I realized we had found a way down to the cells, but it was idiotic to think of descending without light. I sent Wila and Tomash to find one, and a little time later they reappeared, both carrying candles in unadorned metal holders.

"There don't seem to be any lanterns about," Tomash said apologetically.

"Candles will serve," I said.

He insisted on taking the lead, and I followed, with Wila coming along behind.

"What is that terrible smell?" she whispered, for indeed the offensive odor seemed to increase in potency as we descended. I did not dare say what I thought it was, and the

901

fact that Tomash did not venture a guess suggested he had made the same dreadful assumption as I.

"I think this must be the bottom," he said when the stairs ended in a low-roofed corridor running away into shadow. His voice sounded flat, as if the weight of earth above us were pressing down on his words.

"Let's keep going," I said.

We continued slowly along the corridor. It turned sharply, and just beyond the corner, there was a metal door, locked crudely with a beam. The door was so heavy that it took all three of us to move it, and when it opened, the smell was horrendous. Wila reeled back, retching, and I held my nose.

"Give me the light," I said, gesturing impatiently to Tomash.

Gulping audibly, he brushed my hand aside and stepped through the door. I followed, and we both stopped at the sight of what appeared to be a room full of bodies.

"Mercy," Tomash whispered.

Suddenly a filthy hand clawed at the light. It belonged to an emaciated man with a rash of red weeping sores over his face.

"I will tell you," he rasped. "I will tell you everything. Don't leave me here."

Fighting horror, I forced myself to step forward.

"We are not priests. We have come to help you," I said.

The man cowered back. "Please! Please," he begged, struggling to his knees.

I took a deep breath and regretted it instantly as the odor of the cell filled my nostrils. Forcing myself to calmness, I reached out mentally in an attempt to probe the man's mind, but it was so shattered by his ordeal that I could find nothing to hold on to. I tried sending reassurance and compassion, but I was no empath. Finally, I simply resorted to sending images of the open sky above white-capped mountains.

To my relief, the man grew still. Then he looked up, his face twisted into a dreadful parody of a smile. "Sky." He sighed it as a prayer.

"Come," I said in the gentlest voice I could muster, and I held out my hand. "Let me help you to find the sky."

The man climbed unsteadily to his feet and stared for a long time at my outstretched hand. I kept on sending images. Day skies gray with cloud, dusk skies swirling with dramatic color, skies rent with lightning. Gradually, the crazed wildness in his eyes faded into a kind of devastated hope.

"The others died, you know. They couldn't wait."

"I am sorry we took so long," I whispered, fighting back tears.

The man nodded and put his hand into mine. It was so thin that it felt like I was holding a handful of dried twigs. "Come," I said again, warning Wila and Tomash mentally not to do anything lest the man be frightened back into his witless state.

Taking the candle from Tomash as I passed, I instructed him and Wila to see if there were other cells occupied by living prisoners.

"There are," Tomash sent in a shaken mindvoice. "I sent out a probe."

"Then try bringing them out. I will be back with help."

Leaving them, I led the man back to the stairs and, step by careful step, up to ground level. He flinched at the sight of the open door and the hallway beyond, and I tightened my grip on his fingers to make sure he did not pull free and hurl himself down the stairs.

"Soon you will see the sky," I promised over and over until

it became no more than a soothing chant. After what felt like an eternity, I brought him to the outer door. He shuddered violently at the sound of a dog barking, but at last he stepped through the door and looked up.

It was a brilliantly clear night. The stars were like diamonds fallen in a random spill over midnight velvet.

The man gave a long sighing gasp, and his hand twitched convulsively in mine.

"I thought I would not see the sky again," he whispered. "I forgot how beautiful it is. I told my daughter stories of the sky, but I never got it right. We have to show her. She's down there, too, you know. I was lying beside her, but she went to sleep."

I swallowed hard and could find nothing to say. He showed no inclination to move, and so I stood there holding his hand and farsent to one of the other Misfits to fetch Kella. Only then did I learn that herbalists had been summoned already, for I was not the only one to discover prisoners in subterranean cells.

When I had left the man in an herbalist's care, I returned to help Tomash and Wila search. I met them bringing out two young men who were crippled from what looked like a combination of torture and infection. I noticed that above the smell of filth and decay, there was a sweet acrid scent that reminded me of old grapes on the verge of rotting.

There were many dead in the cells, and I wondered how the priests had been able to stomach descending into their self-constructed hell and how often the bodies had been cleared out. When we came upon a number of chalky skeletons, I understood with revulsion that perhaps they had never bothered. After all, what better way to break prisoners than to put them into a cell that was serving as an open grave?

Of those we found alive, many were completely insane, or so close that there was little difference.

In one cell, we found three people alive, but barely—one of them a child whose face was so wasted she looked like a wizened little woman. I could not believe even the Herders would condemn a child to such a fate.

"Who are you?" she whispered, cowering against two women who stared at me in abject terror.

"I am a friend, and I have come to bring you out of here," I said. The last thing these people needed was emotional hysteria, and in the face of what they had endured, I felt my tears could only be a self-indulgence.

Neither of the women moved, but the child tottered forward on spindly, black-streaked legs to look up at me. "You are so pretty," she said, and reached out a dirty hand to touch my wrist. This reminded me so vividly of Dragon, touching my belly with her filthy hand when we first met, that I had to fight the urge to snatch the child up and run from that foul place with her.

"I am only clean. But soon you will be clean, too, and your mother . . ." I looked at the women.

"My mother went away with the gray men," the girl said with owlish gravity. Her eyes had begun to water from the candlelight, dim as it was. "She didn't come back. But these are my friends."

"Then perhaps you can help me to bring your friends out of this terrible place into the fresh air."

It took some persuading, but eventually I managed to get all three of them out, though they cringed at the sight of Tomash, and no amount of talking would convince the girl that he was a friend as well.

"I suppose it was men who tortured them," the farseeker

said shakily after I had taken them to the healing center that had been hastily established under the trees. Gazing up at the pinkening sky, I could scarcely believe that a whole night had all but passed.

There was a surge of flame through the trees, and I turned my head to see a shower of sparks fly up. More wood had been thrown onto the massive funeral pyre for the dead. There were far too many to consider an ordinary burial.

By the time we had cleared the buildings of the dead and wounded, it was late afternoon. Altogether, we had brought out thirty-three people alive. Two were children. Every one of them was suffering from thirst and malnutrition, and most had been tortured.

I thought it a miracle the whole place was not rife with plague and other diseases, but Wila explained that the Herders had used certain whitestick-based substances to disinfect the cells. This explained why so many of the survivors had strange, purplish burns over their bodies.

Dardelan had arranged a work crew to clean out the largest of the halls and fill it with beds. Ironically, the cloister was to become Kella's healing center. The young rebel leader had encouraged her to arrange it as she pleased and to consider herself mistress of the herbalists he sent. Kella had accepted the responsibility of leadership with surprising ease, and although I had been concerned that the herbalists would resent her being given control, it was quickly clear that this was not so. Under Council reign, none but Herders were permitted to heal or prescribe medicines, so most herbalists had practiced in secret and in constant fear for their lives. This meant they had much in common with our Misfit existence.

And seeing Kella heal, they had come to regard her with genuine admiration.

Brydda and Elii had found what they named the torture chamber. There was horror in the big man's eyes as he told me this, and I was glad that he did not go on to describe what he had seen. Perhaps the most important discovery was a tunnel at the back of a locked cell, leading from the cloister right under the city to the seashore. Obviously, the priests had used their prisoners to construct the tunnel, and, of course, it explained the mystery of their disappearance. They would have slipped aboard Herder ships after night fell and been taken out to Herder Isle. We had no doubt now that the priests had fired the boats to prevent anyone coming after them. Indeed, Brydda was convinced that the whole elaborate banding ceremony had been no more than a cover for the mass exodus of the priests. He also suspected that it was the priests who had alerted the west coast Council to our plans.

"Why didn't they let the Council here know, then?" I asked.

He shrugged and stood up. "Maybe it was simply a matter of timing, and they wanted all their people out before they did anything else. Or maybe they made some sort of deal with the west coast Council, which involved getting rid of their counterparts this side of the Suggredoon. I'm going to take a look at the head priest's chamber now."

I rose, too, but he shook his head. "You've been up for two nights without sleep, Elspeth. You need some rest, or you'll end up in one of Kella's spare beds. The meeting has been postponed until tonight, and Gevan can sit in for you. You go to Bodera's place and get some food and sleep."

It was not until he spoke of fatigue that I realized how

bone weary I really was. Horror and pity and disgust had kept me going through the long night and day, but I was at the end of my strength, and so I agreed to Brydda's suggestions without argument.

Nevertheless, I went to see Kella first. She was in her element, moving from bed to bed, consulting herbalists and volunteer aides in her soft voice. She emanated serenity, and I wondered what I would see if I looked at her aura now. Surely in healing, she healed herself.

Seeming to feel my eyes on her, she glanced over to the door, then hurried over, looking concerned. "Are you all right, Elspeth?"

"I am, I just . . ." I stopped, not knowing what I had intended to say.

She nodded. "I know. I cannot believe it either. I have never seen anyone in such a wretched physical state as these prisoners, and their mental state . . ." She shook her head. "Some of them will never recover." She hesitated. "But you know what I keep thinking about?"

I shook my head.

"It is terribly self-centered, but I keep remembering when they brought Domick and me and Jik to their Aborium cloister. If you had not rescued us, we would have been like these people. I was so frightened back then, but I had no . . . no idea what the Herders were capable of."

Jik did, I thought bleakly. He knew, or suspected anyway. No wonder he had been so terrified.

"You should get some sleep," Kella said gently. "Or do you want me to drain you?"

"I will let myself sleep," I said. "I need to get away from all of this for a while. I don't want to think anymore."

She touched my arm. "I will give you a potion that will help you to sleep, then." I barely registered her going away and returning to press a small leaf pouch into my fingers. "Chew it and spit it out. Don't swallow it," she cautioned, and gave me a push toward the door.

On my way out, I passed people carrying stretchers inside. The men and women on them were injured but looked too healthy to be prisoners from the cells. I realized they were probably bringing in rebels wounded during the various skirmishes.

The streets were still virtually deserted, though there were more faces at windows now, and they did not draw back so quickly as before. I guessed that suspicions were growing that there was no plague. The burned ships and funeral pyres were probably the only reason there were so few people out. The smoke would have reminded them of the Herder fires once lit to cleanse plague-ridden houses.

There was a great deal of coming and going and general bustle around Bodera's dwelling. A rebel at the gate directed me through the building and into the central gardens, where a small path wound among the trees and bushes to a timber folly, open on all sides and furnished with a square table and several chairs. Dardelan was seated at one of these, surrounded by papers and squinting in the late afternoon light at what looked to be various maps. He stared at me blankly, then jumped to his feet.

"Ye gods, Elspeth. You look near to fainting. Sit down and eat!" He burrowed beneath the mountain of papers to unearth a platter of sliced fruit. "I suppose you haven't had a bite all day?"

"I haven't," I admitted, sinking into the seat beside him.

"But I could not eat right now if you paid me in gold to do it."

Dardelan's expression became grim. "Of course. You've been helping clear out the cloister?"

I nodded, and tears blurred my vision. "I think you would need only let people see what we saw last night, and they would vote for all priests to be weighted and thrown into the sea."

"They will not see, and, unfortunately, people have a way of doubting the veracity of anything they do not witness with their own eyes. Especially something like this. But we will have as many of those prisoners as can stomach it talking of their ordeals, and I daresay their stories will be harrowing enough."

I nodded again, weariness sweeping over me.

"You must be exhausted. Why don't you go in and bathe, then sleep if you cannot eat," Dardelan suggested.

I went inside. There in the kitchen, seated in the late afternoon sun, was Dameon. I felt a rush of simple joy at the sight of the empath, and he turned to face me as if I had shouted his name.

"Elspeth. I have just been thinking of you. You are tired."

"Less tired now that I see you," I said, and it was true. Just being in his presence sloughed away some of the darkness that clung to my mind. I crossed the long room to sit beside him. "What a mean welcome this is for you."

He took my hand, and I gasped to feel the full strength of his gladness, more vivid and lovely than any words.

"Ah, Dameon, I missed you so. We all did. Obernewtyn was not the same without you."

"I missed you, too," he responded softly, his voice sounding oddly sad.

"You did not wish to leave Sador?" I asked.

He smiled. "I belong at Obernewtyn, if I belong anywhere, though I came to love the desert—the strange fierceness of the Sadorians and their love of song and poetry. The peace of their land steals into your blood and heart."

"I wish you could have come home to us in a better time."

"I know that terrible things have happened, but some things have also been gained. The rebels have won the right to live without Council tyranny this side of the Suggredoon, and I believe in time they will claim the west coast as well."

"The cost of their win was very high," I said bleakly. "Not just here, but on the west coast. So many of our people are trapped there now. And I have just been speaking to Dardelan and realizing how difficult it is going to be for the rebels to set change in motion."

"Difficult, yes, but not impossible, and Dardelan is young and idealistic enough to go on trying when others might give up."

"If anyone can establish a new order, I think it is he. But there are still those like Malik who will have to be restrained."

"I think Dardelan may well give them the task of guarding the borders and planning war against the west coast Councilmen, and they will not demur. Such men who are violent and warlike to their very marrow lose their sense of purpose in a time of peace."

The empath smiled a little, and I asked why.

"I was thinking how strange it feels to be here. My senses are still too full of Sador, and the Land seems cramped and chilly and damp to me." He sighed. "The overguardian died." He spoke so mildly, it took me several heartbeats to absorb his words.

"You were there?"

He nodded, and I saw a shadow of pain cross his face. "I

did what I could, but he suffered dreadfully. He had a vision in which he named his successor; I do not know if it was a true vision or a hallucination. But it was a good choice. At the very end, he was lucid, and he told me what lay behind the Temple guardian deformities. Sadorian women immerse themselves in the isis pools one year after their first child is born. The water carries a particular taint that causes no harm to the woman, but if they are with a second child, as some are, those children are deformed in the womb."

Horrified, I thought of the strange, lovely rifts in the barren desert where flowing water allowed a subterranean oasis to flourish. I even remembered being warned by one of the Sadorians neither to drink from the pools nor taste any fruit growing near them.

"But who makes them do that?"

"There is no force involved. Indeed, some women do refuse, and some men beg their partners not to go to the pools. But the majority of Sadorians concur with the practice. It is their repentance. Their sacrifice, if you like."

"Repentance for what?"

"I wrote to you, I think, of a Beforetime device either found or brought by the Sadorians from Gadfia, which they used in their internal wars. The poisoning of the isis pools is one of the effects, and their immersion is the way the Sadorians share the harm they dealt to the Earth. The overguardian told me the practice would end only when they had the power to actively heal the Earth rather than simply to exist peacefully and lightly on it. He said he had seen that one would soon come to bring that means to Sador."

I shivered. "What did Kasanda think of the practice?"

"I did not ask," he said. "There were many questions in

912

my mind, but the boy was dying and it seemed more important to care for him than to sate my curiosity."

We were silent, perhaps both thinking of the glittering isis pools and of the tiny Temple overguardian. At length, Dameon asked when I thought to return to Obernewtyn.

"I want to know what the rebels plan to do about the west coast before I can make any decision about the future. I can't just go back to Obernewtyn and forget about Merret and Blyss and all the others trapped behind soldierguard lines."

"Perhaps they are safe in this Teknoguild shelter that Zarak spoke of."

"I hope so with all my heart. Maybe Merret and the others got there. It is even possible that some of the rebels evaded the traps and are in hiding with them. The worst thing is not knowing."

"We know they are smart and resourceful, and they have their Talents to aid them. We know the hideout is beneath the ground in ruins where people seldom go. We know that the rebels were unaware of the shelter, so we can assume that the Council is as well. And our people will be aware that we are doing our best to get to them."

"If only we had not agreed to be part of the rebellion," I muttered. "If I had not sent anyone to the rebel groups, we would all even now be safe at Obernewtyn."

"And perhaps Rushton would be dead," Dameon said with uncharacteristic bluntness. He shook me a little. "Dear one, don't crush yourself between impossible burdens. It is a conceit of yours, I fear, to see yourself as the center of things, but it is not true. You were not alone in making the decision to send our people to work with the rebels. Indeed, from what Zarak said, you had more than enough volunteering to go."

I laughed shakily, for he was right in saying I saw myself too often at the center of things. That was my secret fate, of course, distorting my thinking.

"I only wish I had not been Master of Obernewtyn when all of this happened. I wish Rushton had not disappeared. I . . . I miss him so," I said, and realized I was weeping.

Dameon gathered me into his arms. "My dear girl . . . Elspeth . . . I know. I am humbled by your courage in taking charge of all this when he is so mysteriously vanished."

"Who took him, and why? We still haven't figured that out. It doesn't make sense, but if the note was real, then where is he? We did what it bade us."

"If the note was real, it is possible that whoever holds him is also trapped on the west coast. Or maybe they don't consider the rebellion over yet."

"Or maybe they never meant to release him at all!" I was crying so hard now I was almost incoherent.

"Elspeth, you are beside yourself with grief and exhaustion. I heard a little of what has been found in the cloister—I am going over there this evening to see if I can help—but you need to rest. Come."

He stood and took my hand and led me carefully into a nearby chamber. "This is where I have been sleeping. I do not know where other bedrooms are. But sleep here. Later I will bring you some food."

I let him pull off my coat and shoes and bundle me into bed. He smoothed the covers over me and kissed me on the cheek. Dimly, I was aware that he retained his shield between us, and I realized my grief and guilt were probably hurting him. I made an effort to gather myself and thanked him.

"Sleep," he said, and withdrew from the room, closing the door behind him.

I did not need Kella's potion after all. One moment Dameon was closing the door, and the next I was sinking into unconsciousness.

I fell into a dream in which Dameon was leading me through the labyrinthine Earthtemple in Sador.

"This is the way," he said, leading me as if he were sighted.

"Where are we going?" I asked.

"Kasanda is here. She has something to tell you."

I tried to stop, but Dameon held my hand tightly and was drawing me inexorably after him. "Dameon, I can't come now. I have to find Rushton."

"It is too late," Dameon said, only now he was Domick.

"Where have you been?" I asked him.

He gave me a strange, darkling look. "You want to find Rushton, don't you?"

"But . . . he can't be here."

He did not answer, and I pulled my hand free. "Domick, where are you taking me?" I demanded, for now I was realizing that we were not in the Earthtemple at all.

He turned to face me, and though there was no visible source of light, his face seemed to glow with its own livid, greenish hue. "I am not a torturer," he whispered.

"Where is Rushton?" I asked, but my voice came out as a frayed thread of sound. And then I was alone in a dark tunnel. I heard a sound and realized with a dreamy sense of familiarity that it was water falling into water. Then I saw a yellowish flash of light far away in the distance and understood that I was where I had been many times before.

But this time, instead of going forward, I hesitated.

"Why do you hesitate?" Atthis's voice asked, deep in my mind.

915

"I . . . I'm not ready," I said, and there was a pleading note in my tone.

"If you hesitate, all will be lost."

All at once, I felt a grip again. But not Domick's. It was Ariel.

He laughed when I tried to pull my hand away from his.

"You are not strong enough to resist me," he said, and began to pull me toward him. I struggled, repelled and frightened.

"Maruman!" I screamed.

Ariel's smile faded, and his hand squeezed mine painfully. "That creature that protects you will not be here forever. His aura weakens no matter what form he takes on these dreamtrails. And he is too far away to help you now."

Furious for Maruman's sake, I tore my hand free. "He will never let you get me," I cried.

"Not on the dreamtrails, perhaps, but eventually you will have to face me in reality. Then who will save you?" Ariel hissed.

I gaped at him, suddenly realizing what he was saying.

A look of fury passed over his beautiful face. He held up his hand, and a torch appeared in it, the flames leaping high. "Let me give you a token of my regard," he snarled.

I backed away as he advanced; then I heard the sound of a horse neighing.

Ariel's eyes went past me, and his face was transformed by terror. He vanished.

I turned to find a half-man, half-horse towering over me.

"You are safe now, ElspethInnle."

"Gahltha! That . . . that was Ariel. He . . ." I swallowed, scarcely able to say what I knew must be true. I had been a fool not to have seen it before.

"Ariel is the Destroyer."

"Ariel-li is H'rayka," Gahltha agreed. "He hunts Elspeth-Innle, but nothing will be decided on dreamtrails. The glarsh wait in the land of realthings. You must wake now. I/Gahltha am not strong on dreamtrails. Not as Marumanyelloweyes."

"He asked you to look after me, didn't he?"

"That is so. Marumanyelloweyes is seliga, so Gahltha watches. But Gahltha is Daywatcher. If Ariel had attacked, I/Gahltha might have been unable to defend us/you."

"You are the Daywatcher, and Maruman is the Moonwatcher," I murmured, remembering what the Earthtemple overguardian had told me: I would return for the fifth sign accompanied by one of Kasanda blood, with the Daywatcher and the Moonwatcher. Swallow, Gahltha, and Maruman . . . But where was Maruman? I had not recognized the beastword Gahltha had used: *seliga.* I thought it meant something like "behind" or "back."

"Wake," Gahltha prompted urgently, and I saw that he was fading.

"Ariel is the Destroyer," I told myself bitterly, and willed myself to wake.

It was dark in the room, and my instincts told me it was deep night. My tongue felt swollen with thirst, and as I pulled the blankets aside, I grimaced at the smell rising from my clothes and body. How had I slept with the foul reek of the cells all over me? Nauseated, I groped about for a lantern and then for a washing bowl and a jug of water. Stripping off my befouled clothes, I cleaned myself thoroughly, longing for a deep barrel full of hot water. When I had dried myself, I found Dameon's clothing in a bag and borrowed loose Sadorian trousers and a woven tunic.

All the while, I thought about my nightmare. Except it had not been a nightmare. I had been on the dreamtrails. Somehow, Ariel had drawn me there. Ariel. The Destroyer, and a defective Misfit. I should have guessed. And I had no doubt he was mixed up in whatever the Herders were doing.

Gahltha had said nothing would be decided on the dreamtrails. So why did Ariel keep seeking me out on them? Why was he haunting me? The answer came immediately, and it was chilling. He had said it himself: He needed me. Needed what I knew and what I would learn from Kasanda's signs. Without them, he could not reach the weaponmachines.

A terrible thought occurred to me. What if Ariel had Rushton? And what if he offered me a choice: Rushton's life for the knowledge that would let him activate the weaponmachines . . . ?

Unable to bear my thoughts, I dragged a blanket from the bed and flung it round my shoulders as a shawl and left the bedchamber.

I expected to be met by the silence of night, but instead I could hear the sound of voices. I made my way to the kitchen and found Ceirwan, Brydda, Dardelan, Reuvan, Jakoby, Bruna, and a number of rebels seated about the table, talking in low, intense voices.

They looked up as I entered, and Brydda bade me join them.

"The clothes of the desert suit you," Jakoby said.

"I had to borrow some of Dameon's things," I mumbled, forcing myself to set aside thoughts of Kasanda and Ariel.

"Tomorrow we will find something more appropriate," Dardelan promised. "Sadorian clothes are not heavy enough for the Land. In the meantime, you must be starving."

The rebels bustled about producing bread and honey and

cheese, a bottle of milk, and a skin of sweet mead. As I ate, the conversation I had interrupted resumed, and I gradually learned what had been decided at the rebel meeting.

On the morrow, at a public meeting, the citizens of Sutrium would be informed that the rebels had taken charge of the Land and would administer it for one year. During that time, a charter of laws, based on the ones Dardelan had devised, would be formulated with the input of all people in the Land, and trials would be held in which the crimes of soldierguards, Councilmen, and Council collaborators would be addressed. In the meantime, a set of interim laws would be publicized and enforced by the rebels. The people would be told that the west coast was still in dispute, but they would not be given specific details just yet.

After a year, there would be a people's vote to decide who would lead each community, and these elections would be held every year in the same way at the same time throughout the Land.

I gathered there had been some dissent on this point.

Some of the rebels had wanted leave to rule for longer periods before their community could vote. Still others had opposed the notion of a year limit on the tenure of the chosen leaders. But in the end, Dardelan had argued successfully that to give any man or woman prolonged power over other people was to introduce a system where injustices would be bound to occur. Those who would rule must be accountable to the people they ruled, he had insisted. They must only rule by the will of the people rather than by their own arrogant desires.

It was fascinating to see how the young rebel's words permeated the conversation ebbing and flowing around the table. He had a powerful ability to wind words together persuasively, and I envied him, for it seemed akin to the empath's ability to sway people, and in that sense it, too, was a Talent. Dardelan was anything but proud or conceited, and that made him all the more appealing. I was interested to see how many of the rebel leaders deferred to him despite his age.

And what then of Bruna, who, for all her apparent coolness, never shifted her eyes far from his face?

Brydda moved to draw some ale from a stone jug and reseated himself beside me. There were dark rings of fatigue under his eyes, but the eyes themselves were bright. He took a deep pull from his mug. "I never imagined such things as we saw today; though, when I think back, Domick mentioned the cells a number of times."

"You think he had any real idea what it was like?"

"I think more than any of us gave him credit for," the rebel said sadly. "Perhaps, in that sense, we failed him."

When Brydda turned to talk to another rebel, Ceirwan took the opportunity to speak to me. "I heard from Zarak," he said. "He and Lina are camped outside Saithwold, because the town is bein' held under siege by Noviny's people. Apparently, they broke free from their rebel guards an' locked them in th' cloister as hostages before taking control of th' town an' blockin' th' road. Khuria sent to Zarak that Noviny intends to discuss terms with th' rebels, which is a good sign in its way. But th' whole matter is lookin' very sticky, because Vos will certainly complain if we negotiate with Noviny."

"Does Noviny know Khuria is in contact with Zarak?"

"No. He thinks Khuria is just another rebel."

"What does Noviny want?"

"That is th' interestin' thing. He wants nowt fer hisself. Just a guarantee that his family an' th' soldierguards loyal to him will not be harmed, an' he wants assurances that we are not goin' to rape an' pillage Saithwold's inhabitants. He wants to ken th' rebels' intentions."

"Reasonable enough. Even admirable in its way. Was anyone hurt when they took control?"

"One man got a bump on th' head, Zarak says. I'd say Vos simply didn't leave enough guards, because he underestimated th' old man with his usual arrogance."

"I don't see there is any serious problem, then. Noviny is a fair man by all accounts, and his wants seem absolutely modest to me," I murmured.

"Ironically, that's th' trouble. It would have been easier if he were a tyrant. Th' rebels could simply rush in an' liberate th' town. But Noviny is not seen by his people as a tyrant. Indeed, th' locals are with him, which means that if th' rebels want to take Saithwold by force, they'll have to fight ordinary Landfolk."

"We won't be doing that," Brydda said, returning to the conversation. "Dardelan is going to Saithwold tomorrow after he gives his speech, and he will offer Noviny the assurances he wants about his family and the locals. But the soldierguards must be handed over. And, of course, Noviny himself must surrender and face trial for his support of the Herders and his toleration of their atrocities, as all Councilmen will do. Of course, quite a bit of what Dardelan will say is saber-rattling. Privately, he wants to come to an arrangement with the old man, because it will be very useful to have an ex-Councilman recanting the Council's hold over the land. It will take some clever talking to sort it out, but Dardelan can do it if anyone can. Truly he seems as wise as his father in these matters, which is fortunate."

I opened my mouth to speak, then sensed Tomash was struggling to make contact.

"What is it?" I farsent, locating him just outside the cloister grounds.

"I . . . Elspeth, you'd better come," he sent in a queer tone.

"Why? What is the matter?"

"It's . . . it's Rushton," he sent shakily. "He . . . he was one of the people brought from the cells. Kella didn't recognize him until she was bathing his wounds. . . ."

I was already on my feet. The others about the table looked up at me in astonishment.

"What is it?" Brydda demanded.

"Ruh-Rushton," I stammered. "He was in the Herder cells. I . . . I have to go."

"It's the middle of the night. I'll go with you," Brydda said firmly.

I didn't care who came. I hurried out into the chill night, repressing a hot slither of fear.

✦ 29 ✦

WHEN I REACHED the cloister gates, Tomash was waiting.

"Where . . . where is he?" I panted, hurrying through the gates and into the dark, dew-wet gardens.

The farseeker took my hand and led me wordlessly into the healing center. Once inside, I felt him. Pushing off Tomash's restraining hand, I passed through the beds in the large hall and entered into a second, smaller chamber. All the beds were occupied, but my eyes went unerringly to the one nearest the window.

Rushton lay on his back in a pool of candlelight, his eyes closed. A blanket was pulled up to his chest, but aside from being pale and slightly thinner, he seemed otherwise un-marked. He bore neither the chemical burns nor the bruises and sores that every other prisoner had in common. His dark hair lay long and black over the pillow, damp as though freshly washed, and I stared in wonder at a streak of prema-ture gray at one temple.

Without thought, I reached out to touch it. Rushton's eyes snapped open, green and luminous.

"Rushton, my dear love," I breathed, and cupped his face in my hands.

But instead of smiling, he began to laugh—a terrible howling cackle that threw my hands back and turned my blood to ice.

Kella appeared at my side. Pushing me away, she forced a piece of wadded cloth between his teeth as he began to convulse violently. The blankets slipped away, and I saw with horror that Rushton's arms and legs were held down with leather restraints.

Kella grasped his head between her hands and focused her healing Talent on him, but still it took a long time for the maniacal struggles to fade. At last his eyes closed, and he was still again.

Panting hard, the healer turned to face me. "I'm sorry. I would have warned you, but I didn't see you come in."

"What . . . what is wrong with him?" I whispered. She reached out to me, but I batted her hand away and repeated my question.

"Physically, very little," she answered. "Unlike most of the other prisoners, Rushton has not been tortured physically. But his system is full of drugs. I'd say they've had him on something for as long as he has been here. I don't recognize the drug traces, but it must have been something powerful to have had this effect in such a short time. I went into him, but he's . . . Well, it's as if his personality is torn to shreds. Nothing connects properly."

"What are you saying?"

Kella's face was grave and sad. "I am saying that, right now, Rushton is completely insane."

I was standing on the cloud-road that was the beginning of the dreamtrails, trying to understand how I had got there without creating a body of light as Maruman had shown me. There was no sign of Ariel. I looked over my shoulder and was relieved to find that at least I was not burdened with wings. I was merely my own self, though my skin appeared

924

to be a pallid lilac color and my hair a vibrant blue.

All at once, the old cat manifested before me in his tyger form, his eyes gleaming.

"Did I dream you up by thinking about you?" I sent.

"Maruman is no more tame to dream masters than to any other," Maruman sent with his usual contrariness. I felt like singing, because his mindvoice was clear and incisive again.

"Where have you been? Ariel has been trying to get me. Did you know he is the Destroyer?"

He ignored my questions. "OldOnes drew you from deep unconsciousness onto the dreamtrails so that I/Maruman-yelloweyes can give their message to you," he sent, licking a great, tawny paw.

"What message?"

"ElspethInnle must return to barud," Maruman sent. "Must bring all Misfits back, for one is needed."

"Needed for what?"

"To help Innle fulfill quest."

"My . . . But you can't mean I am to leave now to seek the weaponmachines?"

"The oldOnes said return to Obernewtyn to discover/ possess last sign, else too late."

"The last sign is at Obernewtyn?" I echoed stupidly. "The fifth is in Sador. Do you mean the fourth sign?"

"Come swiftly/now, or will be lost."

My mind whirled with questions. "How can the fourth sign be in the mountains? It is supposed to be somewhere I have never been. . . . And what about the other signs? I haven't found . . ."

The road began to lose definition.

"You fade!" Maruman sent, though to my eyes it was he who was fading. "Come. Obey your vow. . . ."

925

"Maruman! Maruman!" I cried, but the road disappeared, and again I was falling and falling, but this time there were no wings to save me.

I fell into a dream in which Rushton and I were on the deck of *The Cutter*, watching ship fish at play. I was leaning back against his chest, clasped securely in his arms, and it seemed that I was truly and utterly content for the first time in my life, wishing for nothing but what I had and uncaring of what would come.

"It is said that ship fish have aided seamen who fall overboard by carrying them to shore," he murmured into my hair.

I turned and wound my arms about his neck, loving the feel of his body against mine. But his green eyes seemed as fathomless as the ocean and as unknowable, and there was a terrible sadness in them that smote at me. Then he began to fade, too, until he was no more than a translucent shimmer in the sunlight.

"Where are you going?" I cried. "Don't leave me."

The sunlight seemed to brighten, absorbing his glittering outline, and then once again I was falling into the light.

"Wake, Elspeth," someone murmured softly.

I opened my eyes and found it was morning. Dameon was leaning over me. He smiled, sensing that I was awake. I thought of my dream, and a babble of words burst from me.

"Dameon. I had such strange dreams. Maruman was there, but he faded before my eyes, and then Rushton vanished, too. You aren't a dream, are you? You won't disappear? Everyone disappears in the end. Matthew and Dragon, Cameo and Domick . . . I always thought I would be the one to leave, but instead it's I who am left." I realized I was sounding hysterical, and with some difficulty, I made myself stop.

"It's all right," Dameon promised huskily. "I am here, and I will not leave you." I registered the distress in his voice with sudden dread.

"What is the matter? Am I . . ." I looked around in bewilderment, not recognizing anything.

"You are fine. You just fainted," he explained. "You were . . . very tired."

"Tired? No . . . There was something. . . ." A thrill of fear ran through me as shadows flickered around the edges of my vision. I was tempted to let them fold around me like a cloak and draw me away from the knowledge that seemed to be pressing just outside the edges of my consciousness.

"What is the matter?" I made myself ask, but before he could speak, it came back to me.

Rushton!

All the strength in me seemed to trickle out like water from a leaky pot. Dameon laid his hand on my cheek, and I saw that his eyes were wet, though whether from my empathised grief or his own, I did not know.

"I have heard it said more than once that you are a woman ruled by her mind to the detriment of her passions, Elspeth. But those who say so do not know you," he murmured.

"Rushton is—"

"Ill," Dameon interrupted firmly. "Very ill. But he lives. And while he lives, there is hope he can be healed."

I brushed my cheeks dry, loving the empath for his gentle optimism. "It was such an awful shock seeing him like that."

He nodded. "Kella said she could bring you round but that it would be better to let you wake naturally. You're in one of the smaller rooms of the healing center."

"Healing center," I echoed bitterly.

"Forget what it was. It is now a center for healing, and in

time, all of the dark memories imbedded in this place will fade."

"I can only think of it as the place where Rushton . . ." I swallowed a hard lump in my throat. "Kella said he had been drugged. I remember that much."

"Bruna has had some training in Sadorian medicines, and she thinks Rushton was given a powerful derivative of their spiceweed. It does not so much cause unconsciousness as a state of vivid hallucination through which the mind blunders until the drug wears off. In effect, if she is right, Rushton has been lost in an endless nightmare for so long that his conscious mind or his sense of himself has disintegrated under the strain."

"What will happen now?"

"The drug is terribly addictive, and that convulsion you witnessed was a withdrawal symptom. But the physical withdrawal from the drug, though painful, is short-lived. The trouble is that a mind is not able to withdraw so easily from its influence."

"I don't understand."

"Having existed in a delusional state for such a period, Rushton's mind is simply mirroring it endlessly back to him. He now perceives it as normality."

I sat up and pushed away the blankets. Someone had left new clothing by the bed, good sturdy Land attire, including new boots.

"You should rest," Dameon protested when I swung my feet out of the bed.

"I am not sick," I said, pulling on the trousers. "What time is it? How long have I slept?"

"It is near midday."

"Dardelan's speech?" I threaded a belt through the waist loops and tucked in my undershirt.

"Was made this morning. I have a scribed copy of it that you can read. It is to be posted all through the Land and contains a list of laws by which all people will temporarily be ruled. The list ends by asking people to make any suggestions that would better the laws."

Dameon shook his head in admiration. "They are fine and fair laws, truly, and I doubt much would better them, but they made less of an impact on the general folk than did Dardelan himself. The lad understands people and their deepest hearts the way sea folk know the hidden currents. I was monitoring the crowd. I saw hope rise in them with every sentence he spoke—and not just hope, but a kind of yearning for integrity and a cleaner way of living. He appealed to what was best in them. I could feel that they wanted to *be* their best, if only to please him. There is not a shred of cynicism in him, and people knew it."

"I am sorry I did not hear him," I said. "Has he gone to Saithwold yet?"

"He rode out about an hour past."

"Too bad. I should have liked to say goodbye."

"Goodbye?"

I nodded. "We are leaving for Obernewtyn this afternoon." Dameon looked startled, but I did not give him time to speak. "I want to get Rushton home to the mountains. If he heals anywhere, it will be there. And I want to see how the others are faring."

"Shall I let the others know we are to leave so soon?" he asked.

"Tell anyone in the cloister. I'll go outside the grounds and farseek everyone else when I've finished dressing."

Dameon nodded and withdrew. I pulled on the boots, thinking of what he had said about my being perceived as unemotional.

I poured myself a glass of water from a jug and drank it, staring out at the cloister grounds without seeing anything. The water had an unpleasant metallic taste, but maybe that was shock distorting my senses. I did not feel myself, for all my apparent self-control. Every action seemed to require too much thought and effort.

Brydda knocked at the door and entered the chamber.

"Dameon said you want everyone to leave this afternoon. Is it true?" he asked.

"As soon as possible," I said.

"You risk losing all the ground you have gained," the rebel protested.

"That can't be helped. We need time to withdraw and reflect so that we can decide how to proceed," I said.

Brydda flung himself into a seat by the bed. "I hope you know what you are doing," he said morosely. I said nothing, and he sighed, his expression softening to resignation. "'Little sad eyes' I named you when I first saw you, and your eyes are sad now. Maybe more sad than I have ever seen them."

"If I look sad, it's because I have seen too much pain and death and plain hatred in the last few days. It fills me with despair," I said. "It makes me wonder if anything will ever truly change."

"Elspeth, the Misfits need not feel tainted by their part in this rebellion. In fact, the low number of casualties and injuries is entirely your doing, and Dardelan intends to make very sure the general populace realizes it. That's why your staying is important. No matter what he says, people will

930

think 'monster' when he mentions the word *Misfit*. If your people were here, Landfolk would be able to see that you are far from monsters. But with you gone . . . Elspeth, I wish you would reconsider. Can anything at Obernewtyn be more important than securing your place in the Land?"

"If all we have done is not enough to ensure us a place in the Land," I said brusquely, "I doubt our presence here over the next sevendays will change that."

Brydda shrugged. "You are resolved, and so I must respect your decision. It seems we always part this way, does it not? We should have at least shared a mug or two of mead to celebrate what we have achieved. It is no small thing to free half a land from black tyranny."

"I am glad for you rebels that the rebellion thus far is a success, but I do not know yet whether to be glad for Misfits," I said. "Will you walk with me? I want to get outside the walls so that I can beastspeak the horses."

Brydda rose with a grunt, and we walked together from the healing center. There were many people about the gardens and outside the cloister gates; the streets were suddenly as busy as ever. Foolishly, I had thought the city would feel different with the rebels in control, but there was nothing at all to tell that the rebellion had even occurred.

As if reading my thoughts, Brydda said, "If it looks the same, it is only on the surface. Underneath, everything has changed."

I sent out a probe to locate Gahltha and found him on his way to the cloister. "We are being led, for free horses are still liable to be enslaved," he sent disparagingly.

I looked at Brydda. "I did not have the chance to ask Dardelan what he intended to do about ownership and treatment of beasts."

931

He scowled. "He agrees that beasts must have their freedom, but he thinks we must introduce the subject of their emancipation slowly, lest we make our own position untenable. He says we cannot give power back to people by commanding them to do what they do not wish to do. We must find a way to change how people think about animals so that they will not want to own them any more than they would choose to own a human."

"If we wait until people learn to care about more than their own species, beasts will be slaves forever, and Misfits outcasts," I said.

"I feel the same and so does Sallah, but I understand Dardelan's point, too. If the changes are made as he plans, they will be true and enduring changes. But if changes are made in swift heedless passion, people will resist them. Why don't you speak to the others at Obernewtyn? Especially to Alad and the beast council. See if they can come up with any ideas. Dardelan is as eager as we are for change, Elspeth, but he is wise enough to see that it must be done carefully."

In less than an hour, Rushton was settled in the small covered wagon that would convey him to Obernewtyn with Kella seated by him. The healer had not wanted to leave the healing center, but she had agreed that Rushton could not be shifted without her.

I did not want to think about Rushton and what it meant that he had been found in the Herder cloister. The others were silent on the matter as well. I was glad for their reticence, but trying to stop myself thinking about what had happened to him was like trying to keep a secret from myself.

It made no sense that the Faction would force us to work with the rebels. Had they thought to turn us against the rebels entirely? Had it all been a diversionary tactic to distract us from some other plot? Unless the entire aim had been to capture Rushton and ruin him. But why?

The only thing I could think was that if Ariel was part of what had happened, he might have arranged to have Rushton kidnapped as a way to manipulate me.

If that was so, I had barely missed being given that dreadful choice.

"How soon before this sleepseal wears off?" I asked Roland.

It was late in the afternoon, several days after our return to Obernewtyn. Despite Maruman's urgent summons and all that had befallen us, life had resumed a numbing regularity. It had been all I could do to function under the weight of a growing depression.

Roland shrugged. "Kella was right to impose it on Rushton for your journey, but it is always hard to predict the effect of a sleepseal on a damaged mind." He gave me a slanting glance. "I was thinking of speaking to Darius about him," he added.

"Darius?" I echoed blankly.

"The gypsy beasthealer. It is a pity I could not persuade the gypsies to stay up here."

"Since you were unable to do so, I don't see how you can consult Darius," I said tersely.

"I will ride down to the White Valley and see him," the healer said.

I gaped at him stupidly. "Are you telling me the gypsies are still there?" I demanded.

"I thought you knew," he said. "One of Garth's people was in visiting the big house this morning, and he mentioned that your friend Swallow had dropped into the Teknoguild camp.

The gypsies are building a monument to those who died in Malik's decoy."

My heartbeat quickened at the mention of a monument, but at the same time, I felt a twinge of shame. I had not thought of the dead in the White Valley since riding to Sutrium. Malik's treachery in the cul-de-sac, the screams of dying humans and horses, the whine of arrows, and the funeral fires in the misty morning had assumed a half-remembered nightmarish quality. Not even the recovering soldierguards and Misfits in beds in the Healer hall nor the injured horses on the farms could bring it into focus properly. More and more, I seemed to be seeing life through a fog, but I fought against it now to ask what Darius could possibly do for Rushton, given that he was a beasthealer.

"That name is too narrow for what he does," Roland said. "Better to say the kind of healing Darius does is especially useful to beasts. You see, when a beast suffers an injury, both mind and flesh are wounded, and the inner wound is the more dangerous of the two. Darius made me understand that a wound healed physically can still cause a beast to die, because the inner wound has been left to fester. At the same time, an inner wound that is healed can almost miraculously help a fleshy wound."

I thought of the livid red streak I had seen in Kella's aura with my spirit-eyes and wondered if such dual wounding did not also happen to humans.

"My point about asking Darius's advice is that Rushton's spirit and mind seem far more wounded than his body, so that is what needs healing. His spirit."

"It's worth a try," I murmured.

"I'd like to take Gavyn down to see him anyway," Roland

went on. "Alad says he has been asking about Darius, and he so seldom even seems to notice humans, it is worth putting them together again. Oh, by the way, did anyone tell you that Gavyn foresaw that Seely was in danger?"

That caught my attention. None of the futuretellers had foreseen anything of our people on the west coast. "Was the hideout attacked?" I demanded.

"I doubt Gavyn could tell you," Roland said regretfully. "His vision seemed entirely focused on Seely. Not on her surrounds."

"What exactly did he see?"

"She was hiding somewhere and watching men searching. She was frightened. Gavyn thought the bad men were looking for her. That's how he put it. 'The bad men.'"

"They must have been soldierguards," I murmured. "Was Gavyn very distressed?"

"Not truly. He told Avra and Rasial what he had seen, and then suddenly he smiled and said she was all right. Then he seemed to forget about it completely."

"What did he mean, she was all right?"

"He would not say. I'd guess that the soldierguards left without finding her."

I made up my mind to have Avra speak with Gavyn about his vision. Anything we could learn of the west coast would be invaluable, and perhaps the boy had seen more than he said.

Roland began to unwind an unconscious man's bandage. I recognized him as one of the soldierguards from the White Valley. His foot had been amputated at the ankle, and Roland examined the livid pink flesh of the stump with professional interest, grunting with satisfaction before rebandaging it. The

Healer guildmaster had asked Kella to delay her return to Sutrium until the soldierguards were fit for the journey, and she had agreed.

"I have been thinking about Dardelan's laws," Roland said presently. "I've scribed a couple of suggestions of my own, which I want Kella to offer him."

I was ashamed to admit I had not read Dardelan's proposed laws. Alad had told me that the beasts approved of them, though they felt that very specific laws would have to be made as to the use and abuse of animals by humans.

"But they can see how the ground for such laws is being subtly laid," the Beastspeaking guildmaster had said.

I had been genuinely surprised to find that the animals understood Dardelan's dilemma. Their only immediate requests were that the Council's practice of gelding not be resumed and that a law be made to forbid deliberate physical and mental abuse of animals. They did not demand that all beasts be freed by their masters, as I had expected. Avra merely commented that this must come in time, but her primary concern was to ease the lot of animals in captivity. Pragmatically, she pointed out that many animals would need to learn how to be free, and that would take time, too.

Alad had further suggested that in addition to learning to read and scribe their letters, all children ought to be taught both Brydda's fingerspeech and the simplest of the animals' physical movements upon which it was based so they could understand what beasts were saying. His hope was that, as in Sador, once people understood that animals were intelligent, it would be harder to mistreat them.

"Elspeth?" Roland said.

I realized I had been standing there lost in thought. "My apologies. What did you say?"

He sighed in exasperation. "Honestly, Elspeth. I said why don't you ride down with us to see the gypsies? At least you could be assured of some good, deep sleep."

"There is that," I said noncommittally, thinking that I must look as badly as I felt. Angina's condition had improved, but he was far from able to resume playing for Dragon, and nights were again dangerous for me. Only Maruman's constant vigilance enabled me to avoid her dream beast, and I relied on Roland to drain me of fatigue, for I was unable to manage more than a few hours of sleep a night.

Of course, I could not tell him that I did not dare leave Obernewtyn for fear of missing whatever it was that had caused Atthis to summon me back to the mountains.

But I didn't have to wait much longer for a clue. When I rose the next morning, a message had been slipped under my turret room door. Taking it up, I read:

My dear Elspeth,
*   We have found a monument in the waters under Tor*
that will be of particular interest to you. If you would see it,
you must come at once.

Garth

✦ 30 ✦

LATER THAT MORNING, Roland, Gavyn, Dameon, Zarak, and I rode down to the White Valley. I had been surprised when Dameon chose to accompany us, for he was not a good rider. But Gahltha offered to carry us both, so he was safe enough behind me.

He admitted sheepishly that he had less interest in our destination than in knowing he would have a decent sleep, since we planned to stay the night. Like the rest of us, he had been sleeping badly since his return to the mountains.

"It is hard to believe Dragon is causing such lurid nightmares as I have experienced," he murmured.

"Nightmares?" I echoed.

"Matthew is in them," Dameon said. "He is somewhere hot and dry."

"What do you see in the dreams?" I asked.

"I do not see anything," Dameon told me gently. "I dream as I live; I dream of words spoken, of smells, and of feelings. It is always the same dream. In it, I am standing with my bare back against a stone wall. I feel heat radiating from it and from the sun above. I am, I think, in some sort of stone quarry, for I can hear the stone being broken with metal picks. I smell the sea somewhere at a distance, when the wind blows, and from another direction, the smells of a city like Sutrium, only more spicy. I smell the sweat of workers and the sweet oils worn by their masters. I hear the crack of a whip, and I hear Matthew's curses. That's how I know he is there—I hear his voice. Then I hear something else: the roaring of some indescribable beast." He shuddered against my back. "Then I wake."

Avra had drawn level with us, and Gahltha turned to nuzzle affectionately at her neck. The mountain pony was carrying Gavyn and his owl, and her pitch-black foal pranced behind alongside Rasial, shying playfully at every leaf that fell and darting skittishly sideways in little wild outbursts of excitement. The tiny equine was so full of bright-eyed mischief that, looking at him, it was impossible to feel downcast.

We made an exotic group. It was queer to think that, for the first time, we need not hide our oddness, since no authority existed to persecute us. Just the same, none of us could be sure exactly what would happen the first time a Misfit used their Talent openly among unTalents. I feared there would be trouble, unless the occasion and the Talent had been very carefully chosen.

It was growing late in the afternoon by the time we reached the Teknoguild camp at the foot of Tor. It was deserted, which meant everyone was still inside the mountain. Divested of their loads, the horses wandered off to graze, and Gavyn and Rasial vanished into the trees.

Roland had brought a number of parcels and baskets of delicacies conjured by Katlyn and Javo, with the intention of inviting the gypsies to share our campfire later in the night. Zarak volunteered to find them and render the invitation, and Dameon elected to accompany him, saying he needed to stretch his legs.

"Elspeth! I am glad you have come," Garth said, helping me to clamber from the raft onto the island of rubble. It looked much as I had last seen it, piled high with equipment and rusting metal boxes. Even the three divers were the same ones I had met before. I waved to them where they sat wrapped in blankets and drinking from steaming mugs, and instead of responding, they gave looks of such profound wonder that I grew uneasy.

"This monument . . . ," I began.

Garth's eyes virtually glowed, and he nodded violently. "Yes. The monument. It's under the water, of course, but we managed to break off a section and haul it up. No easy task, I assure you, and furthermore—"

"Garth. What is so special about this monument?" I asked warily.

"It's better if you see," he said, moving to what I thought was a rock draped in stained canvas. He drew the sheet carefully away to reveal what appeared to be a great, ragged chunk of ice, glimmering in the torchlight.

Then I realized it was not ice, but glass, and far from being randomly jagged, it was hewn roughly into the face of a woman. Then I gaped, and my skin rose into gooseflesh, for I realized the face was *mine*.

It was not a carving of a woman who looked somewhat like me; it was me. It even looked to be my current age.

What sort of sign was this?

"But . . . but how can that be?" Roland stammered.

"That is what I should like to know," Garth said almost smugly. "How could a Beforetimer carve the face of a woman who had not yet been born?"

"The carver had to have been a futureteller," Roland murmured.

"Of course. But why did he see Elspeth's face?" Garth asked.

940

"Where did you find this?" I whispered, still unable to tear my eyes from my own decapitated head.

"The monument is in the foyer of the Reichler Clinic building," one of the divers said. They had all drawn about us now, trailing their blankets and staring down at the glass head.

"The foyer? Not the basement of the building?"

"No. It was in the public domain. We have not yet figured out a way to enter the basement. It might be impossible," Garth admitted in a disgruntled tone. "We've spent the whole blasted day trying to figure it out, but time is running out."

"What has time to do with anything?" I asked.

"There is an unstable airlock in the foyer."

"Like this," one of the divers volunteered, cupping a hand and holding it upside down. "The base of the building is watertight, so when the city flooded, the air stayed where it was. But our clearing the rubble from the entrance has destabilized the lock, and so each hour a little more air is lost. Eventually, the lock will give way completely, and water will rush in with such force that it will tear loose anything that is not firmly fixed. The monument is already badly cracked and will almost certainly be destroyed."

"This woman who looks like me," I said carefully. "What is she doing in the monument? I presume it is a statue of a full person?"

"Zadia?" Garth prompted the diver.

"The foyer is constructed on two levels," she said, her breath steaming in the chill air. "The first is already underwater, so you have to swim in and up a set of steps, which brings you above to where the air is still trapped. The statue looms above the steps. It would have been designed to be the first thing you would see coming in the door of the place. It is enormous. You . . . I mean, the woman is all wound about with a great serpentish beast, but there are many animals carved into the monument as well. It is like a rendered dream or maybe a kind of nightmare."

I took a deep breath. "Was there . . . were there any words on the statue?"

She nodded. "There were: 'Through the transparency of now, the future.'"

"It has to have been a futureteller who carved it," Roland said positively. "They dreamed of the future, and they foresaw Elspeth."

"So it seems," Garth said, but there was a dissatisfied note in his voice.

I took a deep breath. "I must see the whole monument," I said.

"I felt the same, but—" Garth began.

"No, you don't understand," I interrupted brusquely. "I must . . . dive down and see it for myself. And right now."

Garth stared at me in horror. "Now! But . . . but you are not trained to dive. . . ."

"You said yourself it could be destroyed at any moment," I said determinedly.

"I will take you," Zadia said.

"Are you both insane?" Roland raged. "I forbid it!"

Garth stuttered, "Elspeth, you can't be serious. He's right. Rushton would . . ."

"Rushton is in no condition to approve or disapprove anything, and right now, I am Master of Obernewtyn. Zadia, you are ready?"

"Ye gods!" Garth exclaimed, wringing his hands and looking truly distressed.

"You must not do this," Roland said.

Zadia ignored him and shed her blanket. She found two of

the flabby gray suits, still wet, and ordered me to strip down to my underwear. I did as she bade, trying not to shudder at the clammy feel of the material as it was rolled up over my skin. Once sealed into the suit, I warmed up very quickly. Despite its bulk, it was remarkably light. Zadia gave me a weight belt, and I fastened it with trembling fingers.

There was no time to worry about consequences. If the monument was a sign from Kasanda, nothing Zadia or Garth had said suggested what it might mean. Perhaps the message was one that I alone could interpret.

Zadia donned the other suit and her own belt, then handed me several small bulbs of glows and a little pair of goggles shaped to seal to my face and keep water from my eyes. As she passed me one of the breathing tubes, she asked, "You're sure?"

In answer, I took the leather loop fastened to the end of the pipe and slung it around my neck.

Zadia said, "The important thing is not to panic down there. You must breathe normally. It will feel as if you can't get enough air, but that is only an illusion. I will lead you, and we will go down the rope."

"Elspeth!" Garth pleaded.

"Let's go," I said.

The other two divers gave me somber nods and went to the pumps. I followed Zadia to the water's edge, my heart pounding with trepidation. We were up to our necks before Zadia pulled on her goggles. Then she put the mouthpiece of the hose between her lips. I did the same, resisting the urge to gag as it pressed against my tongue and the roof of my mouth. Zadia made me breathe until she was satisfied that I was doing so normally; then she went under the water.

I glanced back at Garth and Roland and the others

standing on the rubble shore, faceless shadows with the light behind them. Forcing myself to be calm I, too, sank beneath the impenetrably dark surface of the water, and silence pressed on me from all sides.

I was terrified into complete immobility and immediately felt myself to be suffocating. The only light came from the bulbs, and it seemed feeble and inadequate faced with all that liquid darkness. My heart thudded in my chest, and I was on the verge of catapulting myself back to the surface when Zadia floated up to me, her face pallid and greenish.

She lifted a thumb and pointed upward, tilting her head in inquiry.

I had never wanted anything so much in my life as to nod and rise into the world of light and sound and warmth. It took an immense effort for me to shake my head and point down. Zadia gestured to a rope running from the surface down into the lost depths; then, taking hold of it, she began to descend hand over hand.

I followed.

The sensation of weightlessness and the numbing silence were so alien as to feel like a dream, and I tried to summon the accepting passivity of the dreamer as we descended. I realized very quickly that the rope was only a guideline, for the weight in the belt dragged me gently downward without any effort.

I concentrated on breathing calmly, looking neither up nor down, and so it was a shock when I noticed buildings appear out of the murk and then vanish again, as the feeble light shed by the glow bulbs brushed them and rendered them fleetingly visible. A strange pity filled me at the sight of those once mighty towers, green-furred with algae and hidden in endless shadow.

We descended through the wavering tips of giant plants that danced in the slight currents, and as we penetrated deep into the watery forest, glimpses of buildings were less frequent. The plant foliage looked leathery, but it felt smooth and silky against my cheeks. Gradually, the stems thickened until they were as wide as tree trunks, and then we were at the bottom, hovering above what must once have been a Beforetime road. The water plants grew alongside the road, but not on it—as if the substance of the road was inimical to life.

I watched as Zadia removed one of her glow bulbs and attached it to the end of the rope we'd descended. Then she swam to another rope, which ran alongside the Beforetime road. This time, she did not take hold of the rope but swam directly above it.

Emulating her slow writhing movements, I followed, glancing back nervously to ensure the air hose was in no danger of being snagged. It snaked away and up until it vanished in the gloom and the wavering fronds of the towering water trees. I squashed another spasm of panic at the thought of how much water lay between me and the surface.

Zadia had stopped to wait for me, her eyes calm but watchful behind the glass goggles. When I caught up, she turned and swam on.

Eventually, we came to a clearing where a single level of a great windowless building stood half buried in rubble that had obviously fallen when its upper levels had been wrenched away. What was visible of the upper edge was jagged, and here and there, twisted pieces of metal protruded at wild angles. The ruin was also partly covered in a rampant waterweed.

A path had been cleared through the broken stone and vegetation running down to a broad door, really little more than a metal frame with thick grooves that must have once held glass.

Passing through the doorframe, I checked my hose again before paying attention to my surroundings. The glow bulbs revealed that the floor was a pale, shining stone flecked with something that sparkled. Like the road, it was smooth and bare, suggesting no plant had been able to gain a foothold. On the other hand, perhaps it was simply that there had not been enough time for anything to grow, since the foyer had only just been exposed to water.

Zadia stopped, and I saw that we had come to the steps she had described, leading to the upper part of the foyer. I glanced up and saw the surface of the water shimmering not far above. Instead of swimming straight up as Zadia did, I made my way to the steps, put my feet on them, and walked up out of the water. As I climbed, the sound of water dripping from me and of my soft, slushing footfalls echoed as if in some vast cavern.

Zadia had removed her mouthpiece and goggles, and I did the same apprehensively. The air was icy cold and tasted of metal, but there was nothing else to say that it had been trapped for so many years.

When we reached the top of the stairs, the teknoguilder lifted the thong from around my neck so that she could remove the air hose. She tied both to an ornate post set into the floor and attached another bulb of glows to it. "They're not long enough to stretch any farther," she murmured.

I looked around, squinting against the impenetrable darkness and wondering where the monument was.

As if I had spoken my question aloud, Zadia pointed straight ahead. Only then did I see that there was something in the center of the foyer. That the monument was constructed of glass prevented its being solidly visible.

"Are you all right?" Zadia asked, laying a hand on my shoulder.

"I am," I said.

I went forward, and when I was close enough for the glow light to reach the monument, it suddenly took on a brilliant life, its many facets catching the light and throwing shimmering knives to illuminate all corners of the massive foyer. Now I could see flat soaring walls set with metal plates, and an ornate, vaulted ceiling high above. The foyer took up the entire floor of the building, and its only furnishings seemed to be the monument and a table constructed of the same stone as the floor.

I walked forward, stopping only because I noticed that the ground around the plinth sparkled with millions of slivers of broken glass, and my feet were bare. A splintered crack ran its full length, branching off to where the head had been fixed.

Zadia murmured that the monument had probably been damaged when the upper stories of the building were torn away. It was a miracle the foyer had not been destroyed and the statue crushed. There was no doubt in my mind that this would happen when the airlock failed.

I walked around the statue.

As Zadia had described, it was the figure of a young woman encircled by what looked to be some sort of snake. But when I saw its head, I sucked in a breath of astonishment, for surely the serpentish beast was an elongated dragon! But rather than being given a threatening mien, the dragon was curled about the woman's figure protectively, and one of her hands rested gently on its scales.

My hands, I thought, and shivered.

The remainder of the glass was carved into a seething free-form mass of beasts that reminded me of the shawl Maryon and the futuretellers had made.

"It is very beautiful," Zadia murmured. "It is a pity it cannot survive, but I am glad to have seen it."

I took a few careful steps forward and studied the workmanship. Being created of glass, it was difficult to compare the style with that of a stone or wood carving. It seemed as much melted into shape as chiseled, but I felt fairly certain that the artist had not been Kasanda. There were similarities, but the work was raw and unpolished compared to the mastery revealed in the doors of Obernewtyn or in the Earthtemple reliefs. It was as if a talented student had emulated a master.

"There is the name of the piece," Zadia said, pointing to a glass plaque set into the floor.

I read: "Through the transparency of now, the future." Beneath this, in smaller lettering, were other words, and I knelt down to make them out. They read: "For one who has the courage to see what will come, and hope." Under this dedication, in still smaller lettering, was the name of the monument's creator: Cassy Duprey.

Cassy. I thought of the dark-skinned girl from my dreams. She had been an artist.

There was a slight creaking sound, and I looked up at Zadia in alarm.

"We should not stay too long," she said, looking around uneasily. "It is not safe in here."

I had an image of the airlock giving way before a great dark gush of water that would smash the monument into lethal spikes of glass. But I refused to let fear hasten my examination of the monument. I knew I would never have another opportunity.

Fian's translation of a line of Kasanda's message came into my mind: "That key which must be [used/found] [before all else] is [with/given/sent to?] she who first dreamed of the searcher—the hope beyond the darkness to come."

Surely the plaque was a paraphrasing of these very words, and if so, whomever the statue was dedicated to—the "one who" saw the future—was also the "she" referred to in Kasanda's message. And if the creator of the statue and dark-skinned Cassy of my dreams were one and the same, then it was almost a certainty that the "she" in question was Hannah Seraphim.

The trouble was that even if I could guess that Hannah had possessed some key, I was still no closer to learning its whereabouts.

Unless the key was somehow contained within the monument.

A thrill of excitement ran through me at the thought that Cassy might have sent the key to Hannah—perhaps secretively, given that Govamen must have been watching Hannah closely.

I circled the monument for the seventh time, searching for niches and crannies. Unfortunately, if anything was concealed in or on the statue, I could not find it.

I froze as a long, ominous cracking sound rent the silence, followed by the sound of something snapping. Then all was quiet again.

"Elspeth . . . ," Zadia said anxiously.

I glared at the statue helplessly, willing it to reveal its secrets; but it remained transparently beautiful, utterly mute. There was another creak, and cursing under my breath, I turned to Zadia and nodded my readiness to go. Looking infinitely relieved, she grabbed my hand and all but dragged me down the steps to where the air hoses were fixed. Thrusting one at me, she pulled her own about her neck and positioned her goggles. I did the same, all the while looking back longingly toward the nearly invisible statue.

Zadia swam ahead, looking relieved to see me emerge through the metal doorframes. We swam back through the trees and along the black road, following the horizontal rope, collecting glow bulbs as we went. Watching the teknoguilder remove her belt and lay it in a weighted basket attached to another rope, I was already regretting that I had let fear pull me from the foyer.

Zadia gave me a look of inquiry, and I realized she was holding on to the rope and waiting for me to remove my weight belt. I did so, at the same time turning to cast a final look around. It was impossible to imagine that once people had walked here and smiled and talked, yet so they must have done. Hannah had walked along this very street, and maybe Jacob Obernewtyn as well.

Wearily, I turned back to Zadia, but she was no longer looking at me. Her attention was riveted to something over my shoulder, and I turned with a thrill of terror, half expecting to find one of the aggressive eels that dwelt in the depths.

But there was nothing. I calmed down, and only then did I realize what she had seen. Through the wavering water trees, a great cloud of dirt and filth was visible in the distance, rising up along with huge, shining bubbles of air. I did not need Zadia to tell me that the airlock had given way.

She gripped my arm with trembling fingers and pulled me to face her, gesturing determinedly upward. I nodded, and we released the rope and began to float swiftly up. Taking my cue from the teknoguilder, I caught the rope and rested whenever she did, but in what seemed bare minutes, we had risen above the swaying submarine forest. Then I could look above and follow the snaking hoses to a patch of light far above. It grew larger and closer, and white blobs appeared, resolving into faces peering into the depths.

Bursting into the air, I spat the hose out and sucked in several long, sweet breaths of fresh air. Roland and Garth caught hold of me and dragged me none too gently onto the rubble island.

Garth glared at me, his face a pasty white. "Curse you, Elspeth. You near sent me to my grave!"

I tried to stand and found my legs would not support my weight. Roland caught me. "Are you all right?" he shouted, as if he thought I might be deaf as well as weak.

"I . . . I'm fine," I panted. "I just feel so . . . so strange."

"It takes you like that before you grow accustomed to it," Zadia said. She was puffing, too, but she seemed not to be suffering the same dreadful lethargy that had suddenly overtaken me. The other divers rolled me out of the suit expertly and threw blankets around me.

"A hot drink, and you'll be good as new," one of them said with a grin that told me my mad venture had made me one of them, despite my status.

"We saw a great mass of debris and air bubbles and feared that the airlock had collapsed with you inside the building," Garth said fiercely.

"We were outside when it happened, obviously," Zadia commented mildly, pressing a mug of steaming liquid into my numb fingers.

Garth looked horrified. "Are you saying the lock *did* fail?"

Zadia nodded, and Garth looked from one to the other of

us in helpless fury. I gave him a bland look, thinking it served him right. I knew exactly how he felt, having been all too often faced with teknoguilder determination that disregarded all else but its own desire.

"Let's get outside," I said. "I need to see the sky."

✦ 31 ✦

It was night when we emerged into the open, and I was reminded of the man from the cloister cells as I looked up at the stars. They dwarfed me, but I was glad to be diminished by their greatness.

The waxing crescent of the moon hung above the trees. It was the same moon that had lit the clearing the night of Malik's betrayal, the same moon that had witnessed the end of the Beforetime. No wonder it seemed so remote and cold. How small and ugly humanity must seem to it.

"What in blazes is going on?" Garth muttered.

I followed his gaze to the campsite, which lay just visible beyond a clump of trees. A huge bonfire blazed at the center of what seemed to be a great crowd of people.

"The gypsies have accepted our invitation," Roland said, and hurried ahead.

"Hmph," Garth grunted, though it was unclear if this signified approval or not.

As we drew closer, I smelled cooking food and burning wood, and I could hear the thin strains of musicians tuning their instruments. Every sound and smell seemed vivid after the chilling graveyard that was the underwater city, and despite my fear that I had failed Atthis and Kasanda, I could not help but feel a thrill of joy that I lived.

The minute we were in sight, Zarak came running over.

"We have prepared the most incredible feast, but Swallow wouldn't let anyone eat a morsel until you came. I'm starving!" He frowned. "Your hair is wet. . . ."

"Enough talk! Lead me to the food, boy, for I am famished!" Garth declared, propelling Zarak before him.

"Elaria!" a voice cried, and Swallow's grandmother, the tiny white-haired healer, hobbled from the crowd to take my hands in hers. "It is good to see you; though now you look more Landborn than gypsy. And as troubled as ever." Her eyes passed about me rather than resting on me—a disconcerting habit shared by every Twentyfamilies I'd encountered. I was glad for my sleeves, which hid that I no longer bore the gypsies' tattoo.

"It is good to see you again, Maire," I said. "I had hoped to find you all at Obernewtyn when I returned from Sutrium."

She shook her grizzled head. "Twentyfamilies do not dwell within walls nor under roofs. We have lived like this for so long now that I suspect we could not live any other way." She made a sweeping gesture encompassing sky, forest, and mountains. "What palace or mansion could better this roof, these walls?"

A hand descended on my shoulder, and I turned to look into the familiar face and strange two-colored eyes of Swallow's half sister, Iriny. For a few heartbeats, we stared at one another solemnly; then she said, "I never thanked you proper-like for saving me all that time ago."

"There is no need for thanks," I said. "Especially when your people just saved our lives."

"Maybe that's why I can finally thank you. It should have been said sooner, but it's hard for us halfbreeds. And for a long while, I could not see the saving of my life as any good fortune."

"You were mourning your bondmate," I said.

"I will ever mourn him," she admitted. "But I have learned to love life again. I am glad to have lived to see the end of the Great Divide and my brother assume the role of D'rekta."

"If only he would bond a maid," Maire snapped.

A faint smile passed over Iriny's face. "He knows his duty, Grandmother," she said fondly.

"Elaria!" Swallow called, and I turned to see him on the other side of the fire with Dameon.

"Go," Maire said, giving me a little push. "He is eager to speak with you. Sit, and we will serve the food."

"I am glad to see you," Swallow said, standing to offer me his own stool. Knowing a little of gypsy manners, I accepted, and he waved for another to be brought.

"Well, now," he said, reseating himself. "I have heard that these rebels have won the Land up to the Suggredoon, but they have lost what lies beyond it, and now no one may pass over to the west coast. A pretty mess."

I nodded. "They have lost it for the time being, but I do not think they have any intention of losing it forever. It will take some time, though—we may have no news until after next winterime."

"You are worried for your people trapped there?"

"Very much so. But worrying won't help them."

"We must trust to their courage and wisdom," Dameon said. "If it is possible to survive, then Merret will find a way."

"Dameon here has been telling me of Dardelan and his charter of laws." Swallow smiled at the blind empath, who felt his regard and smiled, too.

"I told you that not all of the rebels were like Malik," I said.

"Perhaps not, but in my deepest self, I doubt life for gypsies or Misfits will differ greatly under these rebels. People do not easily relinquish their scapegoats, for if they accept us, who will they blame for their misfortunes?"

I shrugged. "I have to hope change is possible; otherwise, why strive at all? But change won't come easily, and maybe there will always be some places it is better not to go. Yet I think you will find that some areas do change, depending on which rebel rules them. If Dardelan runs Sutrium, as I think he will, gypsies and Misfits will receive fair treatment there."

"Better to continue to live warily everywhere," Swallow said.

Iriny interrupted to give Dameon and me platters laden with spiced vegetables and covered in a delicious-smelling sauce. I was feeling almost dizzy with hunger. The divers had spoken of their appetite after dives, and I marveled that my own, shorter immersion had the same effect.

One of the other gypsies came up to speak with Swallow, and between mouthfuls, I took the opportunity to ask Dameon where Gavyn was.

"He went trailing after Darius hours ago," the Empath guildmaster said. "He seemed quite drawn to the old man."

"What did Darius make of the boy?"

"He did not say, but they went off together to where the horses are grazing. Rasial went, too. 'Following Gavyn like a pale shadow' was how Zarak described it." The empath shook his head. "It is a curious thing, but there are times when I cannot tell the boy apart from Rasial. It is understandable in Rasial's case, for my beast empathy is very slight. But I have the same opaque sense of Gavyn. . . ." He trailed off, clearly troubled by his inability to express himself more accurately. "His . . . affinity with animals has nothing to do with Talent. It is as if he aligns with them somehow, as if he is not quite human."

"These Talents your people have," Swallow said, having heard the last words. "I am interested to know more about them, for as you know, my people also have abilities not possessed by ordinary folk."

"Your people can futuretell," I said.

He nodded. "They can, though we call it *seering*. And we can scry out truth and lies when people speak."

"Truly?" Dameon murmured.

Swallow smiled in his wicked way. "Well, it's more of a trick than a Talent. We have learned how to see and read the patterns of energy that hover about all things. One can read many things in the fluctuations of pattern and color as a person speaks. Seeing is the easy part, though. Anyone could be trained to it, I think. The real ability lies in learning to read and interpret, and that's a lot of long, hard work."

Auras, I thought incredulously. Surely he was speaking of seeing auras with his ordinary eyes.

"What else can your people do?" Roland asked. He had been standing, but now he brought a stool and came closer.

Swallow frowned. "Naught but those two things and healing, although we have an affinity for beasts. But I think that rises from our love of and our respect for them. We cannot beastspeak."

Roland explained that only some Misfits knew how to beastspeak but that all of us could communicate with animals using a form of signal language. Swallow grew excited at this, and for a time, the conversation centered on Brydda and his fingerspeech.

Someone came to refill our plates and pour mugs of ale. I asked for water, though, ever preferring to have my wits solidly about me. Swallow tossed back a deep draft and said that he would like to learn the signal language but that his people would be on the move within the next few days.

"There are matters that must be attended to on the west coast," he said.

"But you can't get to the west," Roland objected. "The whole of the Suggredoon from the coast to the Blacklands will be guarded on this side by rebels and on the other by soldierguards."

"The best guards are slack from time to time."

"If you're determined, you'd best speak to Dardelan," I said. "The rebel guards this side are like to think you a spy if you are caught trying to sneak by them."

"I don't doubt we can elude clumsy Landfolk, but maybe I will speak to this young rebel. I'd like to get his measure."

"How will you get across the water?" Roland demanded. "A boat of any kind would make you an easy target, and you could not swim, for the water is poisonous."

Garth said, "Well, you could swim in tainted water with a diving suit, if you could keep your head out."

Everyone stared at the Teknoguildmaster.

"Are you telling me diving suits would protect a person from being poisoned?" I asked.

"For a limited time, if it were completely sealed and thick enough, yes."

"Brydda would be interested in this," Roland said.

"*I* am interested," Swallow said with an imperious flash of his dark eyes. He looked at me. "You said before that you were in our debt. I would take one of these suits as fair discharge of that debt."

"You don't understand," Garth spluttered. "I do not have such a suit just lying about. It would have to be made and tested. That would take time."

"I am a patient man," Swallow said, his saturnine features

alight with purpose. "I will send someone to collect it once it is ready."

"This is madness," Roland said.

"Sometimes success demands a certain refined insanity," the gypsy responded.

A sudden burst of music made further discussion impossible. The gypsy musicians had finished their meal, and their first song was greeted by laughter and clapping from gypsies and Misfits alike. In no time, men and women were up dancing in the wild gypsy style. I saw Zadia hauled to her feet by one of the halfbreeds, and even Roland was drawn into the dance by a Twentyfamilies girl with a bewitching smile.

At length, everyone had risen, leaving me alone with Swallow.

"Will you dance?" he asked, holding out his hand.

Rushton's face rose in my memory, asking the same thing, and I shook my head. "I am not truly in the mood for dancing. But if you could bear a walk, I would like to see the monument your people have been constructing. I understand your camp is not far. . . ."

"It is being constructed within the cul-de-sac, but that is not more than an hour's walk, if you are willing."

The rollicking music faded into the sounds of the night as we left the merry campfire scene behind. We walked some way without speaking; then I said, "This Red Queen's country—do your people have maps of the journey from there to here?"

"There was never any map. The D'rekta led us here by her visions."

"What about a diary?"

"There is no written record, but there were songs. Some of the old people might recall the words."

"Perhaps when you come for the suit, you could bring me the words of these songs."

He looked at me. "You need no map to find the Red Queen's land, if you are meant to find it," he said.

I blinked at him. "You really believe that no matter what you or I do or don't do, we will end up where we need to be?"

He nodded without hesitation.

I sighed. "I have never found it easy to give myself into the hands of fate."

"I do not think it is a matter of giving," Swallow said. "I see fate as more of a ruthless tyrant than a gentle supplicant."

"You think we have no choice?"

"I think our choices are irrelevant. I also think that only a fool would try to pit his or her puny human will against fate." His expression became more serious. "But even if it were possible, I would not fight my fate in this. It would be to turn my back on the ancient promises and to spurn everything that my life has meant, for I am as I am because of the D'rekta's vision. Because of my obedience to it."

I realized the conversation was beginning to loop uselessly back on itself, and I wondered why I persisted in trying to get Swallow to name the ancient promises. I was more than certain that his D'rekta's vision dealt with my quest to locate and disarm the weaponmachines, and the ancient promises were no more than a means to protect the signs and portents she had left for me—the Seeker.

"What will you do now?" Swallow asked.

I shrugged, suddenly dejected. "Return to Obernewtyn and hope that Roland has learned enough from your Darius to help Rushton," I said. "Wait for news from the west and also from the rebels." I gave him a straight look. "As to the rest, we shall see."

"It is better not to speak of matters that involve fate," Swallow agreed. "Our old people say that to do so is like discussing the affairs of the wind. I will send Darius with you tomorrow, if you like. Aside from helping your Rushton if he can, he could learn this beast fingerspeech you spoke of earlier." Now his voice was businesslike rather than fey, and he was every bit the leader of his people.

All at once, we came upon the track leading into the cul-de-sac. I followed Swallow wordlessly and drew in my breath when we came to it. Fresh burial mounds were limned silver in the moonlight.

"There," Swallow said, pointing to a pale pillar at the end of the mounds. It reminded me eerily of a Beforetime column that stood on the way from the Kinraide orphan home to the Silent Vale and had always caused our Herder escort to gibber prayers and make fierce warding-off signs. I went closer to read the lettering and realized the stone was finely carved into an intricate stylization of fire.

"It is beautiful," I murmured, noticing despite myself that the work owed much to Kasanda's style.

"It is fitting that their deaths should be marked," Swallow said.

I read through the list of names again, noting that the soldierguards had been listed as well. No doubt their names had been scribed on the small silver tags they wore on chains about their necks.

"Let us return," Swallow said after some time.

That night, I dreamed I was back in the dark foyer with the glass monument, only this time the statue contained the faces of Selmar and Cameo, Matthew and Dragon, Jik and Pavo, all wound dementedly together. The severed head was

Rushton's, and it lay at the top of the steps. I tried to pick it up, but as my hands closed around it, I found it was all jagged edges. I gasped and drew back, my palms covered in blood. Without warning, an inexorable flood of water swept the severed head from my sight. I struggled against the onrush, groping for the head, somehow knowing that unless I could find it and restore it to the monument, Rushton would be lost to me, like all of the others.

✦ 32 ✦

"HIS MIND IS gone," Darius said decisively. "I cannot help him."

I stared at the hunchback in disbelief. "What do you mean? He has been drugged to madness, but—"

He shook his head. "He is not mad. I could help him if he were. His mind—his spirit—is gone. There is nothing to work with but flesh, and that is not sickened."

I looked at Rushton lying in the bed between us. His face was calm, and his chest rose and fell smoothly. He looked as if he had simply fallen asleep. I had a mad urge to kiss him on the lips.

"When we left Sutrium, he was having fits, raving and frothing at the mouth," Kella said. "Someone without a mind does not rave."

"That is true," Darius said. "But if he was mad when you left Sutrium, then something further has happened since he has been here."

"He came out of the sleepseal late last night, but instead of waking, he has lain like this ever since," Kella said. "Just like Dragon."

Darius asked curiously what a sleepseal was, and Roland explained. They were too calm. I could feel myself beginning to shake, when Kella gave me a look of profound pity and sorrow.

"I am afraid I can do nothing," Darius said again. "But this Dragon you mention; she is the comatose girl whose restless spirit torments your dreams?"

"Her mind went into a passive state last night, so there is not much for you to examine," Kella said softly. "It seems to go in cycles, running from this state to some sort of powerful agitation. That's when she troubles our minds."

"I should like to look at her, just the same."

Roland nodded to Kella, who led the old gypsy from the tiny chamber. The Healer guildmaster made to follow them; then he hesitated and returned to press my shoulder. "Elspeth, don't take this too much to heart. Darius is a healer of beasts, after all. Perhaps he is wrong."

"Rushton lives," I muttered. "If he lives, he can be healed."

Roland sighed and said that he would return later. Left alone, I sank to the floor at the side of the bed and laid my hand on Rushton's cheek. He did not stir, and though his skin was warm, there was a waxen lifelessness to it.

"My love, don't leave me," I whispered, and tears I had not felt gather spilled down my cheeks.

Later, I heard Roland and Kella speaking outside the door.

"Let her stay with him until it's over," I heard the Healer guildmaster say in a voice roughened with sadness. "Darius says a body cannot live long when its mind is gone."

I wept until there were no more tears in me, only a rusty kind of dryness. Then I whispered into Rushton's deaf ears all the thousand endearments I had been too shy or stubborn to say to him in life. It seemed that I had withheld the deepest part of my love from him, giving only what mean crumbs I had felt I could dispense with. I had been a miser, taking all that he lavished and giving little in return.

✦　✦　✦

When sleep stole me from his side, I dreamed again of the city under Tor. I was swimming through the murk, searching for Rushton. I knew he was trapped somewhere under the rubble, and if I did not find him quickly, he would suffocate. But the harder I swam, the more slowly I moved, and the submarine foliage seemed to clutch at me with flabby fingers. Then a swift current caught hold of me, and I was propelled upward. I came suddenly to the water's surface, but I had not reached the outside. I had come up inside a cave.

Dragging myself from the water, shivering and gasping, I struggled to my feet. The only source of light was the ghostly glow of the insects clustered on the walls. It was enough to illuminate several tunnels leading from the cave.

I chose one at random. Some way into it, I heard a noise and stopped to listen. It was the sound of water dripping into water.

"No!" I cried. "I can't be here. I have to find Rushton!"

I turned back, but the tunnel behind me had become a great, carved niche, and within it stood a stuffed Agyllian bird. Not Atthis, as in the old nightmare, but the smaller Beforetime equivalent I had seen in my dream of Cassy.

"I made no promises to *you*," I said in a weak, sullen voice that shamed me.

The light around me faded until I was standing in darkness.

"*You* are the promise," a voice whispered into my mind. "You are the end of all the promises."

"What of *my* promises?" I cried.

Then a familiar mindvoice called my name.

"Come, ElsepthInnle," Maruman sent. "There is not much time."

I woke to find myself slumped over Rushton's bed in the healing hall. Sitting up, I saw that Maruman was crouched on Rushton's chest and peering intently up at me. His single eye flared brilliantly in the candlelight.

My heart seized in terror. "Is he . . . ?"

"He lives," Maruman sent calmly. "But Rushtonmind far from here."

I gaped at the old cat. "Wh-what? They said his mind was gone."

"Rushtonmind hurt. Fled to dreamtrails. Did not know where belonging. Could not return to flesh."

"I will travel the dreamtrails and bring his mind back!" I cried, springing to my feet.

"Rushtonmind no longer on dreamtrails. Is with Mornir-dragon."

"With Dragon? I don't understand."

"Mornirdragon took Rushtonmind beyond gray fortress wall."

"She *what*?"

"ElspethInnle must follow."

"But . . . you said before that I shouldn't do that."

"OldOnes say ElspethInnle must go beyond gray fortress wall. Summoned ElspethInnle from lowlands for this journeying/signseeking."

"Signseeking?"

"Sign! What else?" Maruman demanded irritably.

Was it possible the glass monument under Tor had not been the sign I was summoned from Sutrium to see? I had no doubt that the glass statue had been created by Kasanda who was both Cassy and the first gypsy D'rekta. So what was the statue if not a sign?

Unless it was one of the other signs?

"But I thought . . . " I stopped, remembering Kasanda's enigmatic words.

966

That which will [open/access/reach] the darkest door lies
where the [?] [waits/sleeps]. Strange is the keeping place of
this dreadful [step/sign/thing], and all who knew it are dead
save one who does not know what she knows. Seek her past.
Only through her may you go where you have never been and
must someday go. Danger. Beware. Dragon.

The words had fit the glass statue, but incredibly, they also
fit the current situation. Dragon's *mind* was the strange keeping place for the sign. Her lost memory contained something
that I needed for my quest.

"Must go," Maruman sent firmly. "Search for Rushtonmind
will bring ElspethInnle to Mornirdragon for signseeking."

I understood all too clearly from this what he did not say:
that bringing Rushton back was not the point. That he was irrelevant.

"Did the oldOnes say how I get back?"

Maruman chilled me by ignoring this. "Marumanyelloweyes will come," he sent.

I opened my mouth and then closed it. I wanted to argue
with him. He was my dearest friend, but he was also an im-
placable guardian of my sworn quest, and maybe his presence would tip the balance in my favor. That he would not
speak of returning revealed how dangerous this journey was.
If I failed to return, Rushton, Maruman, and probably Dragon
would die; and because I would die, too, then the world
would fall to the Destroyer.

I took a deep breath. If Atthis had not foreseen my success,
she must have foreseen at least the possibility of it. It must be
that there was no other way.

"Let's go, then," I sent.

The old cat curled up on the pillow beside Rushton's head

and bade me lay my body in a comfortable position.

I climbed onto the bed beside Rushton and lay full length against him. Taking his hand in mine, I looked over at Maruman.

"Must prepare/change to travel the dreamtrails," he sent.

I closed my eyes, put myself into a light doze, and sank through the levels of my mind until I could hear the humming song of the mindstream. I locked myself in balance and visualized a tiny stream of the river flowing up toward me. This time, the response was immediate, but still it cost an enormous effort to bring it to me. When the gleaming thread was within reach, I took hold of it and gasped as the stream flowed into me. I willed myself to rise, and as the thread connecting me to the mindstream payed out, it occurred to me that what I was doing was oddly similar to diving, the silver cord as much a lifeline as the air hose.

Once I had willed myself to see through the eyes of my light form, the room was transformed into torrents of vibrating color. I concentrated until I could make out Rushton's aura beside my own. His was dim, and the cord running away from his body seemed so smoky and insubstantial that a cold fear ran through me.

"Fly with me."

The tyger of light that bore Maruman's consciousness gathered itself and leaped up. I jumped instinctively after it. The air around us was filled with flowing color, but as before, this faded first to a pure white light and then to a brilliant blue. Now I could see the tips of the mountains I had seen before and wondered whether they were real or some sort of etheric echo.

Then we were approaching the glimmering road laid impossibly through the billowing clouds. Maruman landed lightly upon it, and I, clumsily beside him. Only when I touched down did I become aware of my nakedness. I visualized trousers and a loose tunic and sandals, and immediately I was dressed.

"You learn swiftly," Maruman assayed a rare compliment. He was now fully a tyger in appearance rather than a light form, and his eyes glimmered like mismatched jewels.

"Let us go," I sent, suddenly impatient.

"Look," Maruman sent.

I did and found that the road was now crossed by the fortress wall. Black it looked to my eyes, not gray as it had been before.

"It becomes more and more solid. Soon, even Mornirdragon will not be able to cross."

I was chilled, for he was clearly saying that Dragon was on the verge of being truly lost to us. "That is why the oldOnes summoned me back. Why didn't they tell me sooner? I could have tried before. . . ."

"No," Maruman sent. "Before, all possibilities were dark. Only now, at this last moment, is there hope of success. But only hope."

Intuitively, I understand it was because Rushton was there. He was the Misfit I had needed to bring back from Sutrium so that his battered mind could be sucked into Dragon's. Somehow, he changed things.

"I will bring them back," I sent.

"Do not be overambitious," Maruman warned. "Beyond this wall lies a world real/unreal. Memory and nightmare are grown strong by brooding on themselves. We must first summon dragonbeast, but will not be easy."

I opened my mouth to ask why, then remembered that Dragon was at a passive state in her cycle of madness.

I looked at the wall. It was formed of great blocks that no man could lift. Such a wall could only be an unreal thing, no matter how solid it looked.

"Call," Maruman sent. "Call Mornirdragon."

I took a deep breath and shouted. "Dragon! Come out. I am here."

"Call with *mind*," Maruman sent with slight exasperation.

Feeling like an idiot, I focused my mind and called. There was no answer. I called again and again, to no avail.

"The wall grows ever more solid," Maruman urged. "Use all of your strength."

I meant to tell him that I was using every bit of my ability, but then I realized it was not true. But surely he could not mean for me to use the dark power coiled at the base of my mind?

He growled under his breath, and I knew that this was exactly what he intended. I took a deep breath and reached down into myself, summoning up the power that had so recently seared through me, praying I would be able to control it. It surged up, thick and potent, and I thought suddenly that it would be delicious to fly about using that power rather than to risk my life on an arduous quest.

I fought the insidious desire and managed to shape it into a probe. This done, I sent it rocketing up and over the wall, seeking Dragon.

"DRAGON! COME TO ME!"

And she came. Snarling and screaming her fury, she rose above the wall on leathery wings.

"Dragon, take me over the wall," I commanded, this time using my dark power to coerce her. She fought me, but I could sense that part of her wanted to obey.

When she had landed on the road before me, I realized I

was no longer afraid of her. I strode up to her, Maruman padding calmly beside me.

She snarled like a thousand cats as we climbed aboard her. Then she leapt into the air.

When we rose above the fortress wall, I looked beyond it expectantly. But I could see nothing but a dense roiling mist. As we descended into it, I felt its damp touch on my skin and shuddered.

And suddenly, with no sensation of movement, I was no longer flying on the dragon's back but was standing on a road. It was night, and the land about was swathed in a light mist that coiled along the ground and licked up against a few leafless trees growing on the bare hills. It looked like wintertime, and yet it was terrifically hot. Sweat was already trickling down between my shoulder blades.

I willed myself to be wearing lighter clothing, but nothing happened. Shrugging, I removed my overshirt and slung it round my shoulders. Maruman was sniffing the ground in his tyger form, but he sent that there was no sign of Dragon.

"Mornirdragon does not dwell in dragonbeast form on this side of wall," he added.

I tried to scry out Dragon's mind, but I found nothing. I guessed this must be because everything around us was a product of Dragon's mind; a probe could not locate her, because in a sense she was everywhere.

Broadening the focus of my probe, I let it run along the road, but I could not find Rushton's mind either. It was hard to ascertain anything very clearly.

"Nothing stable here," Maruman sent.

"I think I felt some sort of town or settlement ahead. We might as well go there as stay here. I don't understand why I can't feel where Rushton is."

"OldOnes said Rushtonmind will lead you to sign," the tyger sent, reminding me pointedly of the purpose of this journey.

We walked, and the mist thickened appreciably, hiding all but fleeting glimpses of the land on either side of the road. It seemed to change constantly and impossibly. One minute I would see a flat snow-covered plain, and then I would see a thick-forested cliff; two steps on, I would be looking at the shore of an ocean. But the heat was unchanging.

Eventually, I heard the sound of voices on the road ahead of us.

"I say we sell it," said a man; or maybe it was a boy, I thought, for though masculine, the voice was curiously high-pitched.

"I say we train it and make it dance for the crowds," a second man spoke. His voice was sharp and sly.

"It will never dance." This was a third voice and sounded as if it belonged to a querulous old woman. "We ought to offer it to the queen. She will reward us for our goodness."

"The best place for it is the arena. It's been cut up pretty bad." This was the first voice again, and now I was close enough for my eyes to penetrate the mist and make out the speakers. As I had thought, there were two men and an old woman, but all three were little people of the sort sometimes born to ordinary-sized Landfolk.

Just as it occurred to me that a woman with a tyger might be judged a dangerous oddity, the three turned to stare at us.

"Who are you?" the smaller of the two men demanded, seeming untroubled by Maruman. But then the man held on the end of a leash an enormous muzzled black bear with a great silvery ruff at its neck. The bear did not look up, and I wondered if the poor thing had been drugged to keep it

972

docile. Even at that distance, I could see whip scars all over its back and flank, and there was a cluster of scabs over one of its eyes, covering what looked to be a deeper wound.

"I am Elspeth, and I am a traveler on the road just as you are."

"I have never seen you before," retorted the younger of the men.

"Do you know all travelers on the road?" I asked, deciding I might as well be aggressive. The man shrugged and did not respond, but the old woman clacked her teeth irritably.

"I don't suppose you want to sell your beast," the other man called to me, goggling at Maruman.

"The tyger is not for sale," I said firmly.

Maruman gave a low, rumbling growl and eyed the three-some as if he was considering his hunger. When his tongue swept out and along his teeth, they skittered back nervously.

"You will excuse us, mistress," said the woman. "It has been pleasant speaking with you, but we have important business in the town." She glared pointedly at her companions, and all three hurried away, tugging the bear's leash to make it follow. It went meekly, and I wondered what had happened to the poor thing.

I tried to reach it, but its mind was utterly closed. "Maybe we should have made them let it go," I murmured.

"It is not a truecreature but a dreamsymbol," Maruman sent. "Everything here is part of Mornirdragon's dreamings."

We let a little gap open up between us and the strange group before continuing along the road.

Before long, we came to the town, and a strange place it was. The majority of the buildings were square and composed of reddish stone. I was irresistibly reminded of the place in my dreams where I had seen Matthew. But mixed in among these buildings were streets that reminded me of Sutrium and even of parts of Obernewtyn. Steam rose in plumes from holes in the ground, and the heat grew ever more intense. A multitude of people swarmed about, clad lightly in a bizarre assortment of clothes. I was fascinated and relieved to see that there were all manner of beasts walking about, many of them free from restraint as Maruman was. Far from appearing out of place, I realized we would have no trouble blending with the strange inhabitants of the town.

The trouble was going to be finding Dragon and Rushton in such a teaming throng, especially when they were not likely to look like themselves.

For a time, we simply went with the main flow, drawn hither and thither by our curiosity. Maruman was as fascinated as I, though he sent he could smell something bad underneath the city. "Something rotten," he corrected.

Many of the animals I saw were completely unfamiliar to me. There was a plump skittish horse with black tyger stripes and some sort of beast with an incredibly elongated neck covered in velvety, spotted fur. I tried to greet them, but most of their minds were closed to me. Finally, I was able to beast-speak a tawny-eyed elk with a magnificent rack of antlers. Thinking of the conversation I'd overheard among the little people on the road, I asked if he had met the queen of this place.

"Of course," he responded somewhat distantly. "When I first came to the town, I requested an audience with the Red Queen."

I stared after the elk, openmouthed. The *Red* Queen?

My mind reeled, until I realized that Dragon could have absorbed the Red Queen from our dreams of Matthew, incorporating the figure into her disturbed mental universe.

"I think this Red Queen might be the key," I murmured.

I stopped a plump, round-faced man with oiled curls and asked him politely how I could arrange an audience with the queen.

He gave me an incredulous look. "Go to the center palace, of course. Where else?"

Where else, indeed, I thought. And if the center of a dream is its dreamer, then Dragon would be there, too.

As we penetrated the strange town more deeply, the mist grew steadily lighter. At last we came to a cobbled road that ran along a red stone wall. I could see treetops beyond it and could hear enough birdsong to guess it was some sort of park, enclosed at the very center of the town. We followed the wall until we reached an ornate gateway with beautiful wrought-metal gates touched here and there with gold.

The gates stood open, but a very tall, bald man stood before them, clad in magnificent red robes edged in gold braid. He was smoking a long, thin pipe from which dribbled purple smoke. His eyes were slitted against it; this and a complex set of whorls and dots adorning his cheeks accentuated the hawkish cast of his features. He was enough to gawk at, but my attention shifted immediately to the people before him, for it was the trio we had met on the road.

In the real world, I would have put our arrival together at these gates down to coincidence. But this was a false reality constructed on mad dream logic. Kella had speculated that behind the walls of her mind, Dragon was reliving over and over whatever memory she had repressed, seeking to resolve it. She had been only half right. This surreal place was less a true memory than some tapestry of symbols, but whatever Dragon had repressed lay beneath it, and so there was a reason for every flourish, every strange feature of what was unfolding. This grotesque trio and their bear were part of it; of that I was sure.

The robed man was clearly some sort of elite gatekeeper, for he told them, "Your beast is badly marked and sullen-looking. Her Majesty loves beauty, and this bear lacks it. I suggest—"

A bell sounded a questioning note from somewhere within the walls, and a look of intense irritation flickered over the gatekeeper's face. He stepped to one side and indicated a path running from the gate into the trees beyond. "Her Majesty will see you. Go along the path."

The trio exchanged glances, then bowed and went past, jerking the bear's leash to make it come. The robed man watched until they had vanished from sight before turning to Maruman and me.

"You bring the beast as an offering to the Red Queen?"

"No," I said. "I do not own the beast. We are companions and wish to pay our respects to the queen."

A brilliant but humorless smile lifted the man's thin lips. "The queen will be delighted." He reached over and rang a tiny bell suspended from a chain. It rang out a clear, lovely peal, and within moments, a slender woman wearing a simple red shift hurried forward.

"My Lord Gatekeeper?" She made a graceful curtsy to the robed man.

"These travelers wish to pay their respects to Her Majesty. Escort them to her."

The girl curtsied again and gave me a shy smile before gesturing for us to follow her. I did so, wondering why we had warranted an escort.

Beyond the gate lay a truly lovely garden with ancient trees and great banks of vivid flowers. A path wound through them, bringing us to a small pavilion where a woman sat upon a golden throne, her long red hair unbound and falling to the ground about her like a veil. She was clad in a flowing white dress with sleeves slashed in red. Suspended from a white ribbon about her neck was a crimson jewel shaped as an immense droplet.

"The Red Queen," the girl murmured unnecessarily, cautioning us to wait until the previous supplicants were dismissed before approaching.

The Red Queen looked very much as Dragon might in thirty years. In fact, she looked like the sleeping princess the coercers had summoned up during the moon fair. I tried to probe her mind. Though it was shielded, I was certain this was not Dragon. Whatever she had repressed had happened when she was a very small child, and children were seldom the center of anything.

"We would offer this bear for your collection, but the gatekeeper did not see fit to approve him," the old woman was saying in a wheedling tone.

The queen's face was grave. "My gatekeeper is a dear friend and my faithful protector, but he is wrong in thinking I love only the beauty that is in perfection. There is beauty in that which is pitiable as well. Even ugliness has its own radiance." She looked at the bear. "You have been treated ill, but no one shall ever harm you again. Be welcome to my garden."

The bear only stared at the ground.

The queen rose from her throne and approached it, her eyes shining with tears. "Poor thing." She began to remove the bear's muzzle, and the old woman backed away hurriedly.

"You . . . uh, Your Majesty, perhaps the muzzle . . ."

But it was off. The bear looked at the queen for a long time, then shambled away into the trees.

"Go now," the queen said to the woman and the little men. "The girl will reward you for your troubles. Enjoy my city."

Bowing and cringing, the three left, and the queen nodded for me to approach. I had no plan whatsoever. I curtsied as best I could in trousers and introduced myself and Maruman.

"You do not come from here," the queen said in her lovely voice.

"I . . . we're travelers," I said.

"We?" Her eyes fell to Maruman.

"The beast is a free creature as I am," I said.

The queen's blue eyes widened. "From whence do you come, young woman, that you speak of free beasts?"

"I came from beyond the wall that surrounds your land," I said, deliberately referencing the fortress to see how she would react.

"I do not know of this wall," she said lightly, returning to her throne and waving her hand to a chair. "I would wish all folk would see that beasts are no less than humans. If I did not rule here, beasts would be slaves and chattels."

"You have never been beyond the wall about your land?" I persisted, but the queen's attention was now on Maruman. I was stunned to hear her mind reach out to his.

"You are very beautiful," she sent.

Maruman made no response, but he purred deep in his throat when she reached forward to stroke his head.

"Mami!" a voice cried.

I looked up to see Dragon hurtling across the grass toward the pavilion.

✦ 33 ✦

"Mami, did you see the bear?" Dragon cried.

The queen rose and turned to her with gentle reproach. "My dear, you are interrupting an audience."

"I am sorry, but, Mami, the bear. It has been whipped, and it is proof that the arena exists."

The queen sighed. "My dear child, no such thing exists outside nightmare. But you are right that the bear has been abused. It is not forbidden beyond this city, though someday it shall be. Perhaps you can reach it with food or physical kindnesses. Its mind was closed to me."

"But, Mami—"

"Go now," the queen said gently but with regal firmness.

Dragon's shoulders slumped in dejection as she walked off into the garden. How odd, I thought, that her dream self should be the daughter of some mythical, faraway queen.

The queen turned to me with a sigh. "My daughter is as headstrong as I was, and as filled with imagination. But she will grow and become wise."

"What is it that she fears?" I asked carefully.

"There is a foolish myth that within my city, where beasts are welcome and protected, is an arena where they are forced to kill one another for the pleasure of an audience. Of course, it is madness, for my gatekeeper knows every street and canal running through this place. If such a thing existed, he would know of it." She shook her head. "But I do not wish to trouble you. I am pleased to have met you, and I bid you welcome to the city."

"Uh . . . Your Majesty, I wonder if we might walk awhile in your garden? The road has been long and the city, though fair, is not so to Maruman."

The queen smiled graciously. "Why not. My gatekeeper will disapprove, but I have seen into the beast's heart, and no harm lies there." She waved us away, and as we went, I heard the bell ring out again.

"I wouldn't trust that gatekeeper as far as I could throw him," I muttered as soon as we were out of earshot. "I'll wager that arena does exist, and he knows about it. Look at the way his eyes devoured you."

"Let us seek out Mornirdragon," Maruman sent.

I sighed and tried farseeking her, but as before, I could find nothing.

"I can sniff her out," Maruman sent, and proceeded to do so.

The garden became more wild and dense as Maruman led us deeper. I realized we were walking steeply downward and thought of the wall we had followed—there had been no dip in it. I reminded myself that the physical rules of the real world did not necessarily apply here, but just the same, I felt a deep unease when Maruman brought us to the lip of a hollow where mist lay thick and heavy as soup in a bowl. The only hint of what lay beyond were the very tips of trees protruding above the mist.

I hesitated, thinking that the mist looked almost exactly like the purplish smoke that had straggled from the gatekeeper's pipe, and then I heard Dragon's voice coming from the misty depression.

"O, Bear, why can't you let my mother into your mind? I know you have escaped from the arena. If you could just show her! Her sweetness makes her blind. When I am queen, I shall not be so good nor so blind."

I took a few careful steps into the clinging mist, and then I saw them: Dragon and the bear, standing in a clearing. I had made no noise, but the bear lifted its head in my direction and sniffed.

"Who is there?" Dragon demanded. She spotted me and frowned. "My mother's visitors. But what are you doing spying on me?"

"Not spying," I said. "Your mother gave us leave to enjoy a walk about her garden."

Dragon's stiffness dissolved, and she sighed. "It does not surprise me. She cannot imagine any evil in people, and that is surely a saintly kind of stupidity." She studied me for a time. "Do I know you? Your face seems familiar."

"Perhaps you dreamed of me," I said, unable to decide what to do now. What would happen if I simply told her the truth: that everything around us was a dream and that she was the dreamer? Kella had said she would never come out of her coma sane unless she resolved whatever had been repressed. Just being told would not achieve that, or else she would never have repressed anything in the first place.

"I do dream of things," Dragon murmured. "I dreamed of the bear. I thought if he came, she would see the truth."

I tried to ignore the specifics and see the pattern underneath. Here was a mother blind to something that a loved daughter could see and fear. Was that what had happened in Dragon's past? Had she known about something, some danger, that her mother had not been able to see? And what did her real mother have in common with the Red Queen?

"Maybe we can help," I said, the words rising unbidden to my lips.

Dragon looked at me. "What do you know of the arena?"

"Only rumor," I said. "Road gossip."

Dragon shook her head. "That's not good enough. My mother does not believe gossip. I need proof."

"Why do *you* believe it if you have no proof?"

For a long moment, Dragon looked utterly confused, and I sensed that somehow I had pressed too hard upon the reality of the illusion. To my horror, the mist about us thickened appreciably, and I found it hard to breathe. "What did you dream about the bear?" I asked hurriedly.

She blinked. "I . . . I thought she would see in his mind what was happening."

"Are you so sure he is from the arena?"

Dragon looked at me, and again confusion clouded her eyes, but she said, "Nowhere would such hurts as he has suffered be inflicted except within the arena. I have seen whipped animals before, but they are not like this." As she spoke, she stroked the bear.

All at once, Dragon shot to her feet, her eyes wide with horror.

"Mami!" she screamed, and she raced back the way we had come.

"Quick, let's follow her," I sent to Maruman.

Without waiting to see if he obeyed, I ran up out of the mist and through the forest until I came to the pavilion. There the queen was struggling with the robed gatekeeper. Even as Dragon flew across the open space, I saw him lift a dagger and stab the queen. She fell to the ground with a soft moan, blood streaming from her breast.

Dragon shrieked and threw herself on her mother.

Maruman gave a growl. He launched past me, but a net flew out to cover him. At the same time, another landed over my own head, and as I struggled against it, men ran from their places of concealment. We were caught.

Instinctively, I tried to coerce my captors, but their minds were closed. I realized this was because all of their minds were really Dragon's. I could use the dangerous killing power I possessed, but I didn't trust my control over it. What damage might it do to Dragon? Better to go with the dream and see what happened next, I decided.

Dragon, held by two men, was screaming curses and struggling to get to her mother.

The gatekeeper glanced over at me. "It is a pity you were caught up in this. I should have liked that beast of yours for the arena, but there are enough like the queen to look into its mind and see too much."

At that moment, the bear burst from the trees to attack the men holding me. One man fell beneath his claws, screaming; then a bow sang, and the bear fell at my feet.

"Let's finish this," the robed man said in a bored voice. "I want no evidence of any disturbance when the queen's loss is discovered."

Dragon and I were dragged to a shed wherein stood a long, peculiar, windowless coach. It had no stocks or strapping for horses and no place for a driver to sit. Yet it was meant to go somewhere, for its wheels were grooved to sit neatly along two metal strips laid parallel on the ground and running to the entrance to a tunnel going under the ground.

Dragon and I were forced inside the carriage. I fought, not wanting to be separated from Maruman, but it did me no good, for my captors were strong. The door slammed shut, and the carriage began to jerk and vibrate. A dreadful squeal of metal upon metal rent the air, the noise increasing to the point that it seemed a physical assault. Then there was a thunderous clanging.

We were moving!

Clutching my ears and unable to brace myself, I was thrown from side to side until I managed to press myself into a corner using my knees and elbows.

An eternity of unbearable noise later, the carriage stopped. The air seemed to resound with the shrieking cacophony. I tried to ask Dragon if she was all right, but I could not hear my own voice.

The doors swung open, and I squinted against a blinding light. There was an unmistakable salty odor. It was some minutes before I could see well enough to confirm that we had reached the sea.

The silver rails upon which the metal carriage had traveled ran from an opening in the cliff behind us, across the narrow strip of rocky beach, to the end of a rickety pier. I barely had time to notice there was a ship moored before men in long, flowing robes herded us roughly along the pier. They spoke, but I could hear nothing.

The gatekeeper was standing on the deck of the ship, talking to a dark man in a blue robe. His air of authority marked him the captain of the ship. He looked us over as if we were bales of wheat, and suddenly I was sure that he was a slaver.

Just then I spotted Maruman trussed up on the deck. Relief at seeing him gave way to fear, for he was still, and a trickle of blood ran from one ear.

I probed him, and to my relief, his life force pulsed strongly. He had simply been rendered unconscious by a blow. Nearby lay the bear, also bound and muzzled. This meant it had not been killed when the arrow hit it. I could not enter its mind to discern how badly it had been wounded, but I could see the end of the arrow protruding from a sodden patch of fur, beneath which blood lay in a dark congealing puddle on the oiled deck.

I heard a cry, muffled as if through many layers of cloth, and swung my head to see Dragon again struggling against her captors. The queen lay ashen-faced before her on a pile of hessian bags, her once white gown stained crimson from neck to hem.

"Mami!" Dragon shouted. "Mother!"

"Don't worry, my dear. She is wounded but not dead," said the gatekeeper, a cruel smile twisting his lips. "I could have killed her, you understand, but it pleases me to think of her shackled and enslaved. Let her bitterly repent her refusal to take me as her consort."

"Traitor!" Dragon screamed.

His smile broadened, and for the first time, there was a glint of real humor in his eyes. "Traitor? Some might say so. I have deposed the queen, after all. It is a pity she had to go, but she was so bound up in the past and pretty legends that she could not see what could be made of this land. Rest assured, I will be an admirable and progressive replacement."

"You can't replace her," Dragon hissed. "You have the wrong blood. No one will obey you!"

"Oh, I think they will, my dear, because I will uphold the legend of the Red Queen and vow to guard the throne against all comers until she returns. All know how deeply she trusted me. I am the logical choice to watch over the land in her stead, and if I am a trifle—heavy-handed, shall we say?—well, the legend can be stretched to cover that, can't it?"

The seaman made a sign to the men holding Dragon and me. "Tie them up, and we'll cast off."

Dragon resisted, kicking and shouting, until one of the seamen lost patience and slapped her hard enough to stun her. I did not resist, and soon my hands were shackled to the rail that ran around the deck. I sat passively as the seamen set about casting off. When I was certain I was not being watched, I stretched out my foot to touch the tip of Maruman's tail. The physical contact allowed me to force his mind to wakefulness.

"I am here/awake," he responded at last in groggy ill humor.

I withdrew my foot with relief. "Dragon and I are tied up behind you," I sent.

I glanced over my shoulder to see the shore receding and thought in dismay of Rushton.

"Perhaps he lies elsewhere," Maruman sent.

"I hope so. I just wish I could make head or tail of all this. I can't figure out why Dragon would impose herself on this legend of the Red Queen. Where does the fiction end and Dragon's actual memories begin?"

"No choice but going on. We are part of Dragondreaming now. But if cycle completes itself, will start again, only we will have less freedom. Only first time has no set pattern."

I didn't like the sound of that.

Dragon's wild tears and curses had become a dry, hurt sobbing that lanced my heart, and impulsively I turned to her. Before I could even think what to say, the queen groaned softly and stirred between us.

Dragon gasped and bent as close to her mother as the rope around her wrists would allow. "Mami?"

The queen opened her eyes and chided her daughter in a frail, papery whisper. "Queens do not shed tears except when they are completely alone, my darling daughter. Now listen to me. I was a fool. I who would not see ugliness am destroyed by it. You will be wiser. But the important thing—the only thing you must think of—is returning to claim the throne. For the sake of Cassandra and the promise made to her by our ancestor."

The name Cassandra turned me to stone.

"I d-don't understand," Dragon stammered.

The queen continued. "I know you are young, but you must remember the day I showed you the grave marker of the first Red Queen. Beside that was the grave marker of her brother. I thought there would be time to impress it more indelibly on your mind. Yet you can remember if you try. You must remember, for someday one will come for what is hidden there, and it must be given lest the world fall into darkness."

"Mami, we will find a way to go home, and you—"

The queen gave a coughing laugh that ended in a moan of pain, silencing her daughter. "I will die soon. I am not afraid. All men and women die, even queens, my darling. The only good and true immortality humans have lies in their dreams and in their children."

"No!" Dragon pleaded hoarsely, but there was no answer. The queen had fainted again.

Dragon's cries echoed piteously in my ears as all I had thought I knew shattered and reformed into a new and compelling picture. The truth of Dragon's history wasn't merely symbolized in what I was witnessing.

This had actually happened to her. She had truly come from that red land where Matthew was now enslaved. And she was heir to that land's throne.

She and her mother had been betrayed and sold away to slavers. Somehow, Dragon had ended up alone in ruins on the Land's west coast, where we had found her years later.

Either she had been put overboard, or something had happened to the ship. That would certainly explain her mysterious terror of water.

It did not bode well for the Red Queen.

She had spoken of Cassandra, which was almost the same name as Kasanda. And it fit. All of it. Cassy had been a Beforetimer who had opposed Govamen with Hannah Seraphim. The flamebird had told her she was telepathic, and she had been an artist. Later, for some reason, she had become D'rekta and had led a group of people who called themselves gypsies to the land of the first Red Queen in the aftermath of the Great White. Her Tiban lover must have died, for she had bonded with the Red Queen's brother, who later perished at the hands of slavers. A vision had bade her seek out the Land, and she had done so, leaving something with the Red Queen for me. For the Seeker. Then she had come to the Land and had given birth to a child—a son to whom she had left the duty of guarding the signs she had created for the Seeker. Again slavers had taken a hand, capturing her and bringing her to New Gadfia, from which the Sadorians rescued her. Whereupon she became the seer, Kasanda.

A chill ran down my spine like a trickle of ice at the thought that I now had what Kasanda and Atthis had directed me to find: I knew the keeping place of some necessary key, knowledge that had been passed down from one Red Queen to the next for generations.

In terms of my quest, there was no reason for me to stay.

I thought of the dark power coiled deep inside my mind, and I knew that I could leave with Maruman whenever I wanted. That's why the cat had been silent when I'd asked how I was to get back. Getting back wasn't the problem. And the darkness within me seemed to ask, *Aren't one girl and a mindless man a small price to pay for saving the world?*

No, I thought savagely. *I won't leave them. All of us will go free, or none of us.*

"Can you untie my paws?" Maruman sent.

"I will try." I focused a probe to the point it could be used as a physical force, working at his bonds until he could slip free when he chose. My head was thumping, and I could feel sweat running down my spine by the time I had finished.

"Now the bear," Maruman sent, licking his paws to restore their circulation.

I rested for a time, then turned my attention to the bear. Its bindings were looser than Maruman's. Nevertheless, by the time I had finished, I was utterly drained of energy. My bindings were long enough that I was able to lie down, if uncomfortably. I closed my eyes, thinking to rest before releasing myself.

It grew considerably colder. By dusk, the mist had become mackerel clouds infused with lilac and streaks of green over a dazzling ocean of molten gold and red. I lay for a long while simply admiring it, but finally the throbbing pain in my wrists forced me to sit up.

Refreshed, it did not take long to loosen my bonds. Then I looked around. Land, if indeed it was land, was little more than a bluish shadow on the horizon.

Maruman sent, "Red Queen bids us be ready to act when the funaga-li are distracted."

"Distracted by what?" I asked.

Without warning, the ship shuddered violently and lurched sideways.

"Shoal! Shoal!" someone cried. On deck, men ran frantically back and forth, tugging on ropes and craning their necks to peer over the rail.

"Have we hit a shoal or not?" the blue-robed captain demanded of the man up in the crow's nest.

"I can't see," he bellowed. "There's something—"

The ship gave another lurch, and everyone standing was thrown to their knees.

"Whales! Whales!" screamed the man in the crow's nest. "They're attacking us!"

"Get the harpoon," the captain yelled, and I heard a note of real fear in his voice. I slid my hands free of their ropes and untied Dragon's. She bent over her mother, and I turned to look into the water. Incredibly, the waves seethed with gigantic black fish with shining, smooth skins.

"They come at the bidding of the queen," Maruman sent.

I looked to the Red Queen, who had dragged herself into a sitting position. "You must jump over the side while the men are busy," she told her daughter.

Dragon shook her head. "I will not leave without you."

The queen hesitated, a strange look on her face. Then she smiled and nodded. "I will come with you, of course. Why not?"

"But . . . Mami, you can't swim," Dragon protested.

"I have summoned friends who will help us."

"The whales?" I asked.

The Red Queen looked at me. "They will deal with the ship. My other friends are smaller and silver-gray. They are some distance away, but they come."

"Ship fish?"

A smile flickered over her face. "I have heard them named so, though they call themselves Vlar-rei."

"Children of the waves?" I said, translating from beast-speech.

Her eyes widened. "Who are you?"

"Another who understands the minds of beasts."

To my amazement, the queen spoke directly to my mind then. "Help me up. There is little time."

"You have lost too much blood," I sent.

"My daughter must not fall into the hands of the slavers," the Red Queen responded.

I nodded and bent to take the queen under her arms. The coppery smell of her blood made me feel sick.

The ship lurched again, and the queen groaned and slumped against me. I helped her to stand upright and was horrified to see fresh blood flowing from the stab wound. Her eyes, cloudy with pain, met mine. "Do not hesitate or all will be lost. More is at stake here than my life."

"Stop them!" I heard the captain cry, and there was the sound of running footsteps.

I heard the bear roar and a man scream in fright, but I dared not look back. "You must jump with her. You will have to support her until the ship fish come," I told Dragon.

"I . . . I am afraid," she whispered, her face as white as milk.

I reached out and grasped her roughly by the arm, knowing there was no time to explain or coax. "You are the daughter of a queen! Have you less courage than your mother?"

Some of the terror in her blue eyes abated, and she clenched her teeth and climbed the rail. For a second, mother and daughter were balanced there; then they were falling away from me into the churning waves.

I turned to find Maruman and the bear positioned to shield me from a phalanx of seamen, several of whom were attempting to nock arrows to bow strings on the shuddering deck.

"Go now, ElspethInnle," the old cat sent imperiously. "We will follow."

I dived over the edge, praying I would not land on one of

the whales. There was a swift rush of salty air, and then I hit the water hard enough to wind myself. It was icy cold. I fought my way back to the surface, shedding boots and outer clothes so that I could swim. All around me were the silken black whales, but if they were savage, I could not see it in their mild eyes. There was no sign of Dragon or the queen, but I sensed they were close.

I looked up in time to see a flash of black and gold, and Maruman landed in the water beside me, emanating loathing. Fortunately, although he hated being wet, he could swim quite well.

There was another splash as the bear leapt into the water.

I felt a rush of fear, because we would be easy targets for their arrows. Then I sensed the queen coldly command the whales to destroy the ship. They battered it now with terrifying force. The hull cracked and splintered, and in a remarkably short time, the ship sank, leaving nothing behind but a mess of floating timber. Not a single seaman survived, though I could not tell if they drowned or if the whales ate them. The enormous creatures vanished as mysteriously as they had appeared, and all at once, there were just the five of us, surrounded by shattered splinters of debris, with the sky darkening above and a profound silence about us.

Struggling to control my fear by reminding myself that everything that was happening was part of a dream, I paddled over to where Dragon swam, supporting her mother with obvious difficulty.

"She's so heavy . . . ," she gasped.

"Her clothes," I said breathlessly, and began ripping away the billowing cloth. Only then did I see the water around her was red with blood. I summoned a probe and found her life force was running away as rapidly as her blood. Giving up on the dress, I slid my arm around her neck to relieve Dragon.

"You are bleeding badly," I sent.

"I am dying."

"The ship fish . . ."

"Will bring my daughter to shore," she sent gently. "The important thing is that she lives and returns to sit on my throne."

I farsought until I located a solitary ship fish making its way toward us, but it was very far away. Too far for the queen.

"Mami," Dragon gasped through chattering teeth. "I can't see the shore, and I'm so tired."

"The ship fish will come soon to carry you. It will know the way," the queen murmured. She frowned a little, staring up. "It grows light. I would like to see . . . to see . . ." Her voice faded, and I felt her life force dissipate.

"Mami! Mami!" Dragon screamed. She thrashed about so wildly in her distress that she wrenched the queen's body from my grip and pushed me under the water. I almost panicked, for the draperies the queen wore wound about my arms and face, dragging me down as she began to sink.

I fought my way free and struggled to the surface, trying to drag the queen back up, but again Dragon struck me with her flailing arms and the queen slipped from my grasp. I had no breath left to gather her again, and Dragon gave a hoarse scream of anguish as her mother vanished under the dark waves.

I felt terribly weak all of a sudden, and Maruman sent, "The cords that hold us to our bodies begin to fade. If you do not break the dream, we will drown, and the cycle will begin again," he sent.

Break it? I thought dimly. I couldn't break us free without abandoning Dragon, but if I could guide her . . .

993

I felt a stab of sheer horror, for she had vanished beneath the waves. Groping about desperately, I found her and dragged her back to the surface.

"You . . . must . . . not . . . ," I gasped, holding her above the water.

"I am no queen," she whispered. "I should have died instead of her. I want to die."

I forced myself to answer. "Then she died for nothing."

"I . . . ," Dragon began, but a wave slapped her in the face, silencing her.

"You must live and remember all she taught you," I cried as the waves pulled her away from me. She sank again. This time, before I could dive for her, a silvery ship fish rose up between us.

Its voice entered my mind as fluid and lovely as a song. "The Red Queen begged my aid, but I am only one and can save only one."

"Save her daughter," I sent.

Obediently it dived, emerging with Dragon clinging to its shining fin, coughing and sobbing.

"Dragon! Remember who you are, for all our sakes!" I shouted as the ship fish bore her away.

I watched until they were lost in the dark contours of the waves.

"Help me," Maruman sent, and I found him struggling to hold the bear above the surface of the waves. "He fainted from the wound."

I wanted to say that it didn't matter, that we were all going to drown, but instead, I pulled myself wearily to his side and grasped hold of the bear.

It opened its eyes. They were a brilliant and unmistakable green.

"Rushton!" I croaked in disbelief.

The bear merely sighed and closed his eyes again. I felt him slipping from my grasp. I clung, but he was too heavy. His fur pulled from my clenched fingers, and he sank.

"No!" I dived.

Somehow, despite the inky blackness, I could see him as a dark shape slowly drifting downward. Kicking hard, I reached out, but my grasp was too short. My lungs burned, but I kicked again and grabbed, this time catching hold of his fur.

"I won't let you die," I sent grimly.

I tried to pull him back to the surface, but his weight was too great, and he drew me inexorably with him down into the dark sea's deadly embrace. I should have let go, but I would not. I could not.

"Maruman," I sent despairingly, and suddenly we were not so much sinking in the sea as drifting through the air. The darkness lightened, and the pressure on my lungs ceased. I could see the silvery cord drawing me through the clear blue sky, down through pristine whiteness to the world of swirling color visible to my spirit eyes.

I floated above my body, thinking how dull and cold it was, repelled at the thought of confining myself to it.

"You do not live only for yourself," Maruman sent urgently, and I felt his fear as a sharp blow to the face. Only then did I realize that the cord linking my light form to my body was beginning to fade. Propelled by fright, I sank down immediately, releasing the silver thread, and as it fell away from me, I rose gently to consciousness.

I opened my eyes.

Kella was looking into my face and gave a little scream of surprise. "Elspeth? Are you . . . Can you understand me?"

I made myself nod.

"It is a miracle," she breathed.

I licked my lips and summoned the energy to speak. "Dragon?"

Kella frowned at me worriedly. "I don't understand."

That meant her condition was unchanged.

"Rushton?" I croaked.

She bit her lip. "Elspeth, we moved you from his room. Let me get Roland or Dameon. . . ."

"He lives?"

"He . . . he lives, yet, but is . . . Elspeth, don't you remember Darius coming here? What he said?"

I struggled to sit up. "I want to see Rushton," I said.

Kella protested, but even though I was as weak as a newborn calf, I was determined enough that she agreed to help me into the room where he lay.

He looked exactly as he had before. I thought of my recurring vision of him swimming through dark waters always just beyond my reach.

I laid my hand on his cheek and whispered, "My love, I came looking for you and I found you, but you must swim this last stretch to me."

He did not stir. Had I failed him after all, then? I had recognized him at the last instant, but maybe that had been too late.

Yet I remembered the feel of rough, wet fur in my fingers. I had caught hold of him—I had not let him go.

I thought then of Dameon's story of the sleeping princess.

Shaking myself free of Kella's restraining hands, I leaned over and kissed him on the lips. Summoning the longing of my soul, I called his name with my mind.

His eyes opened.

I heard Kella gasp but ignored it.

"Rushton?"

"Elspeth," he sighed. A faint, sweet smile lifted the corners of his lips. Then a spasm of anguish wrenched his entire body, and I threw my arms about him and clung tightly until the fit faded. "They . . . they . . . ," he panted.

I kissed him to silence. "I know, my love. They hurt you. . . . We will talk of it later. Now you must rest and regain your strength."

"You will not leave me?"

"I will stay by your side until you wake," I promised, taking his hand in mine. "Sleep, my love. Sleep and heal."

✦ EPILOGUE ✦

"You know, the story doesn't say what happened after the prince awakened the sleeping princess," I said. "It doesn't say if the princess liked the prince, or if they were happy."

Dameon and I were seated at the window of my turret room, enjoying mugs of cold cider as the sun fell behind the mountains. Maruman was curled on the sill, sleeping soundly.

"Such stories are about events, not aftermaths," the empath said. "It will take time for Rushton to recover fully."

I sighed, realizing he would always see to the heart of things. "He will have to face what the Herders did to him sooner or later. . . ."

"Be patient," Dameon said mildly. "Has he not resumed his place as Master of Obernewtyn? Didn't he meet with Brydda and present our suggestions to the rebels admirably?"

"I know he works hard, and outwardly there is nothing wrong with him. But until he opens his memories, they will poison him."

Dameon sat up and turned his blind eyes to me. "I think you are troubled more because of his manner toward you than because he will not let anyone inside his mind."

I wanted to tell him he was talking like a fool, but all at once I was close to tears. "Shouldn't that trouble me?" I asked at last. "He avoids me."

Dameon sighed and reached out to touch my arm. "If he avoids you, Elspeth, it is because he fears to see your contempt."

"Contempt!"

Dameon shrugged. "He feels he is failing you, because he cannot yet cope with delving into what happened to him. It would not be so if you did not demand so much."

I swallowed a bitter feeling of injustice. "*Do* I demand so much?" My voice sounded flat and unhappy even to my own ears.

"Of yourself, perhaps, as well as him," the empath said gently.

Blinking back tears, I turned to look out the window. Dusk cast a reddish light over the trees and rooftops, and a warm breeze lifted the hair from my face.

Dameon set his mug down and stretched, saying he had better go. "I want to see Dragon before nightmeal." He hesitated. "Will you come with me?"

I shook my head. "I am the last person she would care to see."

"Elspeth, you take her memory loss too personally. The important thing is that her coma has broken. And although no one can get into her mind, Maryon is confident that she will remember all when she is ready."

"You really believe that?"

He smiled. "I do, and you must as well."

Dameon rose and embraced me before he left.

I had been devastated when it became clear that, although awake and sane, Dragon remembered nothing. Not only was she unable to recall her distant past, but she also had no recollection of her time at Obernewtyn. All she remembered was her feral existence in the ruins on the west coast, and upon waking, she had barricaded herself in a corner, shrieking and gibbering in fright and confusion. No one had been able to approach her except Dameon, who wooed her with empathy and his own patient gentleness.

When I had visited her, she bared her teeth at me in a snarl, cowering into the Empath guildmaster's arms. Dameon urged me to persist, but as yet, I had not been able to bring myself to it.

I wandered back to the window and sat on the sill, enjoying the breeze and watching everything vanish into shadow. I felt less melancholy than when the empath had arrived with a jug of cider, and I suspected he had been subtly empathising hope and comfort to me the whole time we had talked. I had imagined my distress over the rift between Rushton and me was unnoticeable, but of course, Dameon had sensed it.

I took a deep breath of the sweet night air and counseled myself to be patient, as Dameon had urged.

"At least they are safe here at Obernewtyn," I murmured aloud.

That was more than could be said for all the Misfits trapped on the west coast or for Domick. The coercer-knights had been unable to locate him—or Miryum, who had completely vanished with Straaka's body. Neither had Brydda managed to locate Daffyd, who needed to hear that his beloved Gilaine was alive in the same distant land as Matthew. The likelihood was that both Domick and Daffyd were on the west coast, but there was no way to be sure until the rebel ships were completed.

Brydda felt these would be ready to sail by the end of the following spring. A year away. And it would be at least that long before I could begin to search for the clues and signs left me on the west coast by Kasanda.

Unless Swallow returned for the diving suit.

I reached into my pocket and withdrew Fian's tattered translation and read it through, though by now I knew the lines by heart.

I was fairly certain that the key lay wherever Hannah was buried. Given Garth's fascination with the Beforetimer, it was only a matter of time before he learned the whereabouts of her grave. In addition, Kasanda had left something where she gave birth to her son and something else inside a monument built to acknowledge the pact between the Council and the gypsy community, and she had given yet another thing to the Red Queen before leaving her land.

I sighed and thrust the paper back into my pocket.

I had learned much since the beginning of the rebellion, yet still I had not managed to find a single sign left by Kasanda. In fact, I was still trying to come to terms with the fact that the Cassy of my dreams was the Sadorians' revered Kasanda and the gypsy D'rekta.

And that Ariel was the dreaded Destroyer.

"Have patience," Maruman sent.

"It is harder to wait than to act," I responded.

Maruman sniffed contemptuously. "Time does not care about you, ElspethInnle. Nor this barud nor any who dwell here. It cares nothing for this world nor for your quest to save it." His mindvoice had taken on a fey tone that chilled me, and he turned to stare out at the moon, newly risen above the jagged horizon.

It was fat and red. An ominous moon, almost full.

"Maruman . . ."

"The moon waits," Maruman sent distantly. "The H'rayka waits. The glarsh waits. All wait for ElspethInnle to walk the darkroad." He looked at me. "Are you so eager to walk it?"

I licked my lips and found them dry. "I don't want to leave Obernewtyn. I love . . . I love it here. But my whole life has shaped me to go."

"And go you will," Maruman sent sternly, turning his single flaring eye back to me. "When all things are as they must be. Until then, eat the days and nights that come. Do not wish them gone/away. They will succor you when all is dark and you are alone."

His words frightened me, but they also drove away the last remnants of my melancholy. Dameon was right. I had felt that Rushton was failing me, and Dragon too. That they were getting in the way of my quest. In truth, it was I who had been failing them.

I farsent a probe to Rushton and found him with Alad on the farms.

His mind reacted with a wariness that hurt me, but which I knew I deserved.

"I thought we could go for a walk after nightmeal," I sent gently. "It is so warm, and it will be light enough to swim in the high springs."

I felt his cautious pleasure. "You would like that? To walk and swim?"

I laughed and sent my laughter to him. "Why not? We have time."

✦ ACKNOWLEDGMENTS ✦

To Nan McNab, for stepping into the breach with her own particular brand of sensitive, meticulous editing; to the Australia Council, for their creative grants which allow that things sometimes grow where you least expect them; to Choice Connections in Geelong, and in particular to Adrian, who gave emergency computer counseling, on the phone and sometimes halfway round the world. And thanks to Mallory, Nick, and Whitney, for giving the stories new life in America.

Last but not least, thanks to Jan and to my darling Adelaide, for tolerating this immense cuckoo in our nest!

*Captured by an old enemy, can Elspeth stop an
ambitious plot to thwart the rebellion?*

THE DREAMTRAILS

Includes two complete novels
WAVESONG • THE STONE KEY

I LEFT THE bedchamber and found Harwood focused on
Mendi, but the others turned to look at me as I entered the
firelit audience chamber.

I gathered my wits and told them, seeing their faces reflect
the shattered dismay I felt. Harwood had ceased probing
Mendi, and he asked in disbelief, "Did you say *everyone* will
die?"

"Everyone," I said, and I seemed to hear the high mocking
sound of Ariel's laughter.